**Louisa Heaton** lives on H[...] Hampshire, with her husba[...] a small zoo. She has work[...] the health industry—most recently four years as a Community First Responder, answering 999 calls. When not writing Louisa enjoys other creative pursuits, including reading, quilting and patchwork—usually instead of the things she *ought* to be doing!

**Emily Forbes** is an award-winning author of Medical Romance for Mills & Boon. She has written over thirty-five books and has twice been a finalist in the Australian Romantic Book of the Year Award, which she won in 2013 for her novel *Sydney Harbour Hospital: Bella's Wishlist*. You can get in touch with Emily at emilyforbes@internode.on.net, or visit her website at emily-forbesauthor.com.

# SINGLE MUM'S ALASKAN ADVENTURE

LOUISA HEATON

# RESCUED BY THE AUSTRALIAN GP

EMILY FORBES

MILLS & BOON

First published in Great Britain 2024
by Mills & Boon, an imprint of HarperCollins*Publishers* Ltd,
1 London Bridge Street, London, SE1 9GF

www.harpercollins.co.uk

HarperCollins*Publishers* Macken House, 39/40 Mayor Street Upper, Dublin 1, D01 C9W8, Ireland

Single Mum's Alaskan Adventure © 2024 Louisa Heaton

Rescued by the Australian GP © 2024 Emily Forbes

ISBN: 978-0-263-32153-1

03/24

This book contains FSC™ certified paper and other controlled sources to ensure responsible forest management.

For more information visit www.harpercollins.co.uk/green.

Printed and Bound in the UK using 100% Renewable Electricity at CPI Group (UK) Ltd, Croydon, CR0 4YY

# SINGLE MUM'S ALASKAN ADVENTURE

LOUISA HEATON

MILLS & BOON

For Lorna and Bonny x

# CHAPTER ONE

CHARLIE GRIFFIN HAD been told she would need to make two flights to get to the remote town of Vasquez, Alaska, and had assumed, as anyone would, that this would mean two proper aeroplanes.

*How wrong could I be?*

The first flight had been easy enough, and her daughter, Alice, had sat and watched a cartoon movie for most of it, holding her teddy, and Charlie knew that they would be met and escorted to their second plane, which would bring them into Vasquez. She figured it would be a kind of meet-and-greet service that would whisk her through all the security checks and baggage reclaim and, to a point, it was. But the guy in cargo shorts and a sign that had her name on it led her away from the airport and out towards a car.

Charlie stopped, holding her daughter's hand. 'There's meant to be a second flight that takes us to Vasquez. Have you got the right Griffin?'

The guy, who'd introduced himself as Chuck, grinned, chewing gum, and nodded. 'That's right. Your next plane is in the bay.'

'The *bay*?'

'It's a seaplane. Ain't no airport in Vasquez...you come in and land on the water.'

'Oh.' Suddenly she wasn't sure. But wasn't this what she

wanted? Somewhere remote? Vasquez, Alaska, fitted that bill perfectly. The perfect hideaway for her and Alice. To go someplace where nobody would know her. She preferred to hide. To keep mobile and have no one know her shame and, most importantly of all, *never* become the next hot topic of conversation.

'I get it. I'm a strange guy. Look…' Chuck pulled a piece of paper from his pocket and handed it to her. 'That's the number of the clinic you'll be working at. Why don't you give them a ring and they'll confirm what I'm saying? So you know you're not just getting in a vehicle with someone you shouldn't.' Chuck went and sat in the car.

She had to be cautious. She'd learned that a lot lately. There was paperwork in her purse with the clinic's number on, too. She pulled it out and checked the number against the one Chuck had given her. It was the same. But she wouldn't take any chances. So she phoned the number, told them who she was and the receptionist confirmed that Chuck was who he said he was and that she was perfectly safe to get into his car.

The engine was idling by the time she opened the back door and got in with Alice. 'Buckle up, baby,' she said, reaching over Alice to strap her in. 'How far to the bay?'

'Twenty minutes, if traffic's okay.'

'Thank you.'

'No problem.' Chuck smiled at her in the rear-view mirror and drove them away from the airport. As the journey continued she pulled her instructions and second ticket from her purse and now understood why it looked different from the first. The instructions had said she'd be met after her first flight and escorted to the second, but they could at least have mentioned it was a car ride away.

When they pulled up alongside a big stretch of water, Alice gaped out of the window. 'Is that our plane?'

Charlie hoped not. It didn't look fit to fly! It had to be at least thirty or more years old. It looked battered. Ancient. And was that *rust* she could see? Dirt? She hoped it was dirt. 'I don't know. Chuck, is that…?'

'Sure is! Best seaplane on the Alaskan coast.'

The best? 'What does the worst look like?' she muttered under her breath, trying to put a brave face on things as she dragged her cases out of the trunk of the car.

Alice was excited. She'd never even flown before today. Now she'd experienced a jet and a raggedy old seaplane… This was all an adventure to her and Charlie wished she had the same optimism as her daughter.

Adjusting her sunglasses onto the top of her head to hold back her long hair, she dragged the cases along the pier. The wheels bumped and jolted the cases all over the place and, once or twice, Charlie thought she might lose them in the bay, which looked dark and forbidding. Her heels kept slipping into the gaps too, tripping her, and she must have looked quite ungainly.

Chuck opened the doors and loaded the cases into the back and then helped Alice, then Charlie up into the plane. 'Seat belts on, ladies.' And then he climbed through to the cockpit.

'Wait, you're our pilot, too?'

'You bet!' Chuck grinned, gave them a thumbs up and then reached for a large set of headphones, which he placed on his head, and then began flicking switches and starting up the engine.

It choked a couple of times before the engine started and Charlie began to wish that she had some sort of faith she could cling to. In the meantime, she simply smiled at her daughter, who seemed to be incredibly excited at this new adventure, and hoped that this old rust bucket would get them to Vasquez safely.

'How long?' she called to Chuck.

'Little over an hour,' he called back as the plane began to move away from the short pier.

An hour. She could do an hour, right?

Lift-off was bumpier than she expected, but Alice loved it. 'Yee-haw!' she cried out as they hit another small wave before the seaplane made it into the air.

*Just get us there in one piece, Chuck.*

Charlie gripped the edge of her seat and wished she'd had the foresight to include travel sickness tablets in her hand luggage. She'd never needed them before, but this small seaplane seemed to feel and experience every piece of turbulence that existed in the air and it dipped and bumped and rattled loudly with every disturbance.

'What made ya want to come to Vasquez? It's a little out of the way for city folks like you,' asked Chuck, looking over his shoulder.

'Oh, you know…needed a change of pace,' she said, teeth chattering.

Chuck laughed. 'You'll get that! It's a different way of life out there, you know? Probably nothing like you're used to.'

'Great.'

*That's just what I need.*

'You got the Internet out there in Vasquez?'

'Oh, yeah. All the mod cons. It ain't reliable, though. Thing goes on the fritz more often than not, so most folks have a CB radio on hand, just in case they need to call for help.'

Citizens Band radios. Wow. Charlie had thought those things were obsolete. But it made sense if you lived in the middle of nowhere, which was exactly where Vasquez was. And an unreliable Internet sounded perfect.

'What do you do in Vasquez, Chuck?'

'I mush.'

Charlie blinked. She must have heard wrong. 'I'm sorry, what?'

'I mush dogs. Train them for racing. You know, for dog sledding? I raise huskies, breed them, work them when the tourists come a calling.'

'You have dogs?' asked Alice, suddenly enraptured. Alice loved animals more than anything and had been persuaded that Vasquez would be an amazing place for her to indulge her fascination with wildlife.

'Forty-two of them and counting.'

'Mom! He's got forty-two dogs!'

'I heard, honey. Do you need that many, Chuck? I mean… how many tourists do you get?'

Chuck laughed. 'Most of those are pups. I'm just waiting for them to be old enough to go to their new homes. Racers and the like. I got champions in my line and they fetch a pretty price. But when they're gone, I'll only have like sixteen.'

*Only* sixteen dogs.

Charlie smiled, unable to imagine it. 'What can you tell me about the people?'

'Oh, they're a friendly bunch. Most people live in town, but there are a few homesteads that are isolated, so you don't get to see those folks as often.'

'And Dr Clark? What's he like?' Dr Clark was going to be her boss. He'd emailed her once or twice to let her know her responsibilities during her temporary contract covering for some doctor that had gone on maternity leave. His emails had been short. Sweet.

'Eli? Oh, he's great. Best doctor we've ever had.'

Eli. She'd known an Eli once and it hadn't been the greatest of experiences. But that was a long time ago, in a different life. She didn't have to worry about that any more. It was in the past and she'd moved on. Just as he had, most probably.

'I've had to fly him out to patients in the past, if we couldn't get there by car or dog sled.'

'You don't have ambulances?'

'I am the ambulance.' He laughed and turned back around.

Charlie raised her eyebrows.

*I wanted remote. I'm getting remote.*

Alice was open-mouthed as she gazed out of the windows of the small seaplane. They flew over some gorgeous country— snow-capped mountains, glaciers, lakes, hills of green, the occasional small town. But mostly Charlie could feel the immensity of the space they were in. The city and all its hectic complications, its computers and endless streams of invasive social media were far behind her and with every mile that passed she felt some of her stress ebbing away with it. There was something soothing about looking out at all that country. At the peace of it. The anonymity of it. Its vastness made all her worries seem insignificant. And the sky... The sky was never-ending. An eternity of blue and space. She dared hope that she could lose herself beneath it and somehow be reborn into the woman she used to be. The Charlie she'd been before meeting Glen.

'Mom, I think I can see a bear!' Alice pointed down at a brown speck that seemed to be making its way alongside a river.

Maybe it was a bear. Maybe it was a moose? Or an elk? It was hard to say. 'I can see it, baby.'

'You like bears?' asked Chuck.

'I do! They're my favourite animal in the whole wide world!' enthused Alice, squeezing her own teddy tightly.

'Well, plenty of grizzlies near Vasquez. You keep your distance. Especially from the mama bears, you hear? They're not as sweet and nice as the one you've got there.'

'I will.'

Charlie felt slightly alarmed by this piece of news, but also protective. She was her own mama bear and would do anything to protect her child from danger. 'How much further?' she asked Chuck.

'You see that lake down there to your right? With the settlement alongside it?'

'I do.'

'That's Vasquez. That's home.'

They both gazed down upon it. Vasquez seemed to have been built on a headland that jutted out from the eastern side of the lake. To the west were snow-capped mountains, but Vasquez and the land around it were verdant and green. There was a forest and within it a river that seemed to feed into the lake and, beyond the river, hills and rocks and the occasional homestead.

'Better be ready. Landings can be bumpy.'

Charlie checked Alice's belt first, then redid her own lap belt, fussing with it until it felt right and having one last moment where she hoped she was doing the right thing for both of them.

The plane banked as Chuck turned it to approach Vasquez from the south and then he slowly began to descend. The green became more defined as plants and trees and grass, the buildings along the waterfront became more apparent— a B & B, a diner, a groceries store. And they all seemed to belong to the Clarks—Clark's Diner. Clark's B & B. Clark's

General Store. And before she could think about that some more, the plane hit the water, bouncing slightly until it aquaplaned smoothly for a while, the engine dying down as the battered old bucket of a vehicle delivered them safely to another wooden pier.

Chuck got out first, mooring the plane with ropes, and then helped Alice out first, offering a steadying hand to Charlie as she disembarked. 'Boss is here,' he said, grinning and indicating behind her, with a brief nod of his head and a salute to the unseen man behind them.

Dr Clark had said he'd meet them so he could drive them straight to their residence—a two-bedroomed property owned by Dr Clark's own mother. From what Charlie understood, the Clarks owned a lot of property and businesses in Vasquez.

She wanted to make a great first impression, even though she was here only temporarily to cover a maternity contract, and so she adjusted her sunglasses onto the top of her head again, straightened and turned around, with a smile upon her face. A smile that began to fade as the large, massively muscled Dr Eli Clark came closer.

He'd filled out since she'd last seen him.

He'd never been scrawny or short before, but he'd never been this…well…*developed*. But the grin was the same. The eyes, the same.

The boy she'd known as Eli Johns, the boy who'd teased her and played jokes on her endlessly at the orphanage they'd lived in.

That boy who had somehow struck lucky and found a family.

Was now Dr Eli Clark.

Her boss.

Waiting for her with that same cheeky grin across his face, as if his next prank was already waiting...

# CHAPTER TWO

'*ELI?*'

There was so much he wanted to say. So much he could say, but, rather than answer her straight away, he knelt so he could be on the same level as her daughter. 'Hey there. What's your name?'

The daughter was the spitting image of her mother. Long, dark brown hair, same dark brown eyes. Like melted chocolate. The same bone structure.

'Alice.'

She seemed shy, but she was smiling and she had a beautiful smile, too. 'Hey, Alice. Who's that?' he asked, pointing to the teddy bear that she carried with her.

'Mr Cuddles.'

'*Mr Cuddles?*' He glanced up at Charlie and registered the shock that was still painted large across her face. 'Well, he sounds like a very friendly bear. Can I shake his paw?'

Alice giggled slightly and held out the bear.

Eli gently took a paw and shook it. 'Nice to meet you, Mr Cuddles. I'm Eli. Is it okay if I talk to your mom for a little while now?'

Alice nodded.

He stood, towering over Charlie and her little girl. He'd always been slightly taller than Charlie, but he'd clearly not finished growing before he got adopted and now he was a good head and a half taller than she. 'I hoped it was you, when I saw your name.'

'Really? You *hoped*? I've emailed you six times since accepting this posting—you didn't think to tell me who you really were?'

He grinned. 'I thought it could be a surprise.'

'Oh, it's definitely that,' she replied, not sounding the least bit happy about it and looking at anything that wasn't his face.

He got it. When they'd been kids, she'd often told him that she could have quite happily punched him in the nose every time he had grinned at her, and he couldn't help but grin now. He liked that they were being reunited. Here was someone who understood his past better than anyone else in Vasquez. And she was only here a short time. It was why he'd agreed to hire her.

'You don't seem thrilled.'

'Why would I be?' Now she looked at him. Intently so and he realised as he stared back that she'd changed too. As a young teen, she'd been scrawny and much too thin. But now, as a grown woman, she'd developed. He noted the hint of delicious curves beneath her blouse and skirt and those heels she was wearing? Well, he couldn't remember the last time he saw a woman wearing heels in Vasquez. Most people wore boots of some kind.

The heels drew his eye to parts of her anatomy that he really ought not to stare at. Little Charlie Griffin had grown from a gauche, skinny teen with angry acne into a beautiful, elegant young woman. A mother herself! And though he wondered what the story was there and why she was alone and hadn't brought a partner, he knew he would not ask. Not yet, anyway. Time would reveal all. It always did. But he envied her the fact that she had real family. That blood connection.

The Clarks might have taken him in, made him one of their own, given him their name and their love, but they weren't blood. Eli had always hoped that one day he would have a family of his own. Get married, have loads of kids, but even that had been taken away from him.

So yeah. He envied her having achieved something he never would.

'Aren't reunions meant to be happy occasions?' He grinned, holding out his arms as if suggesting she ought to step into them and give him a hug.

She smiled back. A fake smile. One that didn't touch her eyes. 'You'd think so.' And she sidestepped him, pulling her cases behind her, not realising that the pier was not as wide as she hoped. The case rumbled over the edge and, before she knew it, the weight of it caused it to slip from her fingers as it caught on the slats and tumbled with a big splash into the water.

'No!' she yelled, collapsing to her knees to try and grab for it as it floated near her, her arms not long enough to grasp it.

Eli tried his hardest not to smile, but he couldn't help it. It was kind of funny. If she'd not been in such a snoot with him, it wouldn't have happened at all. 'Want some help?'

'I don't need any help from you, thank you very much!' she snarled.

'Okay.' He stood there, arms crossed, watching her as she tried to reach her case to no avail. She stretched and grunted and even, at one point, got up to grab a thin stick from the shore to try and prod the case back towards her. Unfortunately she only succeeded in pushing her case further away from her and it began to float away into the bay.

'Damn it!'

'Mom, you swore.'

Charlie turned to look at her daughter. 'Sorry, baby.' But then she glanced up at him. Those chocolate eyes of hers angry and furious.

He knew she would not ask him again, but he also knew he couldn't leave her stranded like this, with the majority of her possessions that she'd brought with her floating away into the bay. Eli began to undo his boots.

'What are you doing?' she asked.

'Helping out.' He pulled off the boots and then his socks. He knew the water would be cold. It always was here in Vasquez, even when they had warmer days and the sun shone, as it did today. The water could be deceptive. Eli didn't bother rolling up his jeans. They were going to get wet no matter what he did and so he splashed down into the water and by the time he reached her case? It was up to his waist.

Charlie could not believe her eyes.

Eli was wading through the water to retrieve her case and by the time he got it the water was creeping up his shirt.

She couldn't think about how kind a gesture it was. She was too busy trying to stop thinking about how hot he looked doing so.

Eli was a huge man. Muscled. And…oh, yes…she could see the dark shapes of some sort of tribal tattoo on his arms and back. And with his shaggy locks and beard, the scar through his eyebrow and all of the things that made Eli *Eli*, he looked like a barbarian. The kind of barbarian that you wouldn't mind invading your village and throwing you over his shoulder.

He hefted her heavy case easily, lifting it out of the water, and began the slow wade back to shore.

His jeans were now moulded to his muscled thighs as he emerged from the water like a demigod and set her case down on the ground. He was breathing steadily and she noticed a necklace around his neck, tied with a leather loop. It looked to be a piece of turquoise and it rested on his slightly hairy chest, drawing her eye. Lust smacked into her like a tsunami.

'Thank you,' she managed.

'No problem.' He smiled at her, as if knowing the effect he was having on her, and for that she didn't like him even more. Felt her anger grow again as she watched him pull his socks onto his wet feet, and then his boots.

'I know you said you'd take us to where we're staying, but if you just give me the address, I'm sure we can find it on our own. You're soaked...' Her gaze drifted over his body once again. His broad chest. His flat, narrow waist. His toned and shapely thigh muscles. She felt heat surge into her cheeks. 'And you probably want to get changed.'

She did not want to feel this way about Eli! She'd been glad when he'd been adopted. It had meant she didn't have to put up with him any more! But this? This was too much.

'It's just water. My truck's seen worse. Come on.' He stepped ahead of her, leading her towards a flatbed truck that was parked on the side of the road near Clark's Diner.

Not knowing how else she could get out of being in his truck with him, she managed a smile at her daughter and took her hand, following him up the slight incline towards the vehicle.

If it were her, she would have wanted to be out of those wet jeans as soon as possible. She hated the feeling of wet material against her legs. She'd been caught in a sudden downpour once and been soaked. She'd not been able to get into work quick enough to put on some nice dry scrubs and feel comfortable again.

Yet he was still happy to show her around? To sit in those

wet jeans? Drive in them? The man was crazy, but then she knew that. He always had been the type to look out for odd things. Strange things. To experience life. Perhaps this meant nothing to him?

Eli hefted her case into the back of his truck and then opened the passenger-side door for her and Alice. 'My ladies.'

Alice giggled and clambered in, so that she would be sitting between them, which suited Charlie just fine. She didn't need to be squashed up against him, feeling his body and his heat against her own.

'Let's get you strapped in.' Eli leaned over her daughter, reaching for her seat belt, his face coming alarmingly close to Charlie's, so that she had to turn away for her own seat belt and stare out of the window, while she blindly tried to click it into position, her hands trembling.

Why were they trembling? Was this just shock at seeing Eli again? Or was it more to do with her body's alarming response to him? If someone had sat her down and told her that whenever the day occurred that she would meet up with Eli Johns again, she would be sexually attracted to him immediately, Charlie would have laughed with obscene amounts of hilarity in their face. Because nothing of the sort could ever be possible.

And yet here she was.

The engine rumbled into life. 'We all ready?'

She managed a smile and tried not to focus on his large, square hands on the steering wheel. He had lots of thin leather bracelets on his wrists. They were old and worn, but contrasted beautifully with his darker skin tone. Her gaze travelled up his arms, hidden by the flowing shirt he wore, and she couldn't help but wonder what his forearms would look like. She liked forearms. Found them sexy. She didn't know why.

'My mom's been in and spruced up the cottage for you. Fresh bed sheets, some flowers. She's even put some things in your fridge.'

*My mom.*

Eli had received the most amazing present any kid in an orphanage could receive—adoption. They'd both given up on the idea. Teenagers didn't often get picked by families looking to foster or adopt. They'd been told that they were the hardest to place and it was something that you just learned to accept, and yet Eli had got the best gift in the world. Charlie remembered them coming to the orphanage. Had been aware of them sitting at the back of the room, talking quietly with some of the staff. Then they'd been mucking around with an indoor archery kit and Eli had hit the gold every single time he took a shot. She'd thought he was showing off and he'd gone over to talk to Jason, one of the care workers, who'd been standing with the Clarks, and they'd all begun to laugh and joke with one another and after that day Eli had kept getting invited out for day trips, or weekends with this family and then suddenly Eli was gone. For ever.

Charlie had never wanted to be jealous of Eli ever! But she had been back then. And she'd hated herself for it. She'd tried to make herself feel better by telling herself that at least Eli was gone now and she wouldn't have to put up with his teasing any more, or his practical jokes or the way he'd keep looking at her across the room, as if he was planning his next trick. She'd spent most of her childhood being aware of where he was, just so she could keep an eye out and, with him gone, she didn't have to worry about that any more.

What she hadn't expected to feel after he'd left was how much she'd actually *missed* him. It had hit her, unexpectedly, left her feeling emotionally winded. She'd not realised just how much he'd been a part of her life. The two of them, the oldest ones, watching the younger kids arrive and then going, never to be seen again. Losing Eli had been incredibly difficult to accept. That had been quite the shocker. But time had passed. More kids had arrived. Some others had left. And then Charlie had been accepted into medical school and she'd moved out. Moved away. Begun to live on her own and make her own way in life. And Eli had been mostly forgotten.

Until now.

She had a brief, blurry memory of Mrs Clark. Back then, she'd been a tall woman, dark-haired. Quite pretty. And she'd thought nothing of squatting down to talk to and enjoy the company of some of the younger kids. Charlie had never spoken to her, though. She'd always held back to protect herself. If you didn't have hope, then you couldn't be disappointed.

'You must thank her for me.'

'No doubt you'll run into her at some point. Alice? Are you going to go to the school here in Vasquez?'

Alice looked up at her, uncertainly.

So Charlie answered for her. 'Yes. The one on Pelican Point, I think it's called.'

'Yep. That's the one Mom teaches at. She's probably going to be Alice's teacher.'

'Oh. Right.'

There was a brief uncomfortable silence where she determinedly looked out of the truck window, rather than at him, to observe the passing scenery. Vasquez was a small town. Neat, clean streets. Well-tended, older properties with great gardens. Often, people would notice the truck and give them a wave, smiling broadly, and she realised that Eli was liked here. Loved. Clearly he'd settled well into this place and she was surprised. When she'd known him as a young boy, he'd been into rap music and video games and technology. He'd loved living in the city and she would never have guessed that he would settle so well into a place that was a little more remote. Briefly, she wondered where he'd trained to become a doctor.

Beyond the streets she saw mountains, lush and green at the moment, but the tops of them were obscured by the white clouds that drifted high above. Birds soared high above in the sky, but she didn't know what kind. They looked quite large. Seabirds? Or hunting birds like ospreys or kites?

Maybe she'd learn all of that after being here a few months, and thank goodness there was an end date to her contract and she'd not moved here permanently! Because she really didn't think she'd be able to deal with working with Eli for much longer than she had to.

'Here we go.' Eli hit a left and pulled up at a small log-cabin-style cottage that had some hanging baskets full of flowers either side of the front door. It had a wrap-around porch, with a bench and what looked like a hammock and some potted plants too. 'Home, sweet home.'

'For a little while, anyway.' She felt the need to say it. To remind him that she wasn't here very long. It was what she was used to. Always moving. Never quite settling anywhere. It was why she'd never bought a house. Why she'd never bought a car. Why she always worked as a locum, or covered temporary contracts. It made her feel better to keep on moving. To get to know people for a little while and then move on. Because the past could creep up on you unexpectedly and the internet had a long memory. Something you thought was gone could return in a nanosecond, if people wanted it to.

Eli was already hefting her case out of the back of the truck and pulling it towards the front porch and squatting to the welcome mat, lifting it and retrieving a key.

*Quaint.*

But she didn't want him in their home. She didn't want to see him in there, all damp and muscly and devastatingly handsome. She wanted him gone, so that she and Alice could look around themselves. Get settled in. She'd have to see Eli at work and that would be enough as it was.

He was already unlocking the door and swinging it open, stepping back so they could pass him.

Alice ran in excitedly, but Charlie paused and took the key from his fingers, trying not to register what it felt like when her fingers brushed his. Like electricity. 'We can get settled in, thanks. I'll see you at the clinic on Monday morning?'

He got the message. Well, she hoped so, when he grinned and folded his arms, leaning against the doorjamb.

'Yes, you will. Eight o'clock sharp. You ready for a taste of Alaskan medicine? It might not be what you're used to.'

She had no idea what he meant. Surely all medicine was the same? 'Of course.'

'Great. Okay. I'll be seeing you,' he said, staring at her and smiling in that ridiculous way he'd had when they were kids. As if he'd got something up his sleeve that she simply wasn't prepared for.

'You will.'

'Mom! Come see the back yard!'

'Excuse me.' And she closed the door on him with some satisfaction.

Eli could wait.

Eli could go home.

And she was going to get settled in and hope that the next few months would fly by.

# CHAPTER THREE

THE VASQUEZ MEDICAL CLINIC AND HOSPITAL appeared to be the largest building she'd seen here yet. It was long and low, all on the same storey, but stretched out, abutting the lush green mountain that sat behind it.

Charlie was very nervous of going in. She knew she needn't be. She was a very capable doctor and she was so used to having first days at work. Getting to know everyone, finding out where everything was. One of her strongest skills was adaptation and she prided herself on settling somewhere quickly and easily, to make her working life run smoothly. All she had to do was be friends with these people. They didn't have to have any heart-to-hearts. They never needed to know her past. They just needed her to fit in and do her job and that worked for her.

But here? That was going to be a different story.

Earlier this morning, she'd dropped Alice off at the school. It was her first year in kindergarten, but Charlie had no worries about her daughter fitting in either. Alice was a confident and independent young lady, just as Charlie had taught her to be.

*Who is the only person you can rely on?*
*Me!*
*Who is the only person who can make you happy?*
*Me!*

Sentences she'd drilled into her from an early age. It was important that Alice understand that the world was a harsh place. Because it was. In the early years, of course, Alice hadn't really known they were moving so much. Last year, in pre-kindergarten, she'd kind of got a little upset at leaving her friends behind, but Charlie knew she would make new ones! And everyone always wanted to be friends with the new kid and Mrs Clark, Eli's adopted mother and Alice's new teacher, had seemed wonderful.

'Charlie! Alice! It's a pleasure to meet you, at last!' Mrs Clark had crouched to smile at Charlie's daughter and shake her hand. 'Eli's told me so much about you, already!'

Had he? What was there to tell? What did *he* even know about her?

'Are you excited, Alice? First day!'

Alice was excited. Of course she was. Charlie had raised a confident daughter, there would be no tears, no clinging to her mother's leg.

'We're going to do lots of fun things today, so I hope you're ready?'

'I'm ready!' Alice took Mrs Clark's hand.

Eli's mother stood again and looked at Charlie. 'Settled in all right? Is everything okay with the cottage?'

'It's great, thank you. And thanks again for putting some foodstuffs in the fridge for us. You didn't have to do that. You must let me know what I owe you.'

'You don't owe me anything! It's an absolute pleasure.'

'No, I insist.'

'Look, I tell you what…you can pay me back by coming over tonight and I'll cook you both a nice hot meal. I'd love for us to sit and chat and get to know one another. Six o clock be okay? My grandkids will be there, so people for Alice to play with.'

Charlie couldn't think of how to get out of it. What to say, so as not to offend this woman? 'It won't seem right you feeding us again, when we're the ones that owe you.'

'Then let's call it a potluck! You make something and bring it over—how does that sound?'

'Er…great. Sure. Thanks.' Charlie smiled, figuring she'd do this the once and then gently extract herself and Alice from Mrs Clark's home, claiming a school night. That she'd need to get Alice in the bath and then bed before school the next day.

It wasn't that she didn't like Mrs Clark. Far from it. She seemed a lovely, warm and welcoming woman. Her hair a little greyer than before, but still the same genuine smile. But this much attention made Charlie feel uncomfortable. Generally she was introverted and liked her own company. Being with someone so…open and full of life was a little…disturbing. It made her want to retreat and hide so she could breathe again.

She'd glanced at her watch and said goodbye and now she was standing outside the clinic, wondering just what awaited her inside. Had Eli told everyone in there who she was and where she was from? She hoped not, because that wasn't something she told anyone, ever. Her private life was her own and no one needed to know it. Exposure, she'd learned, came at a cost.

Mrs Clark had already superimposed herself into Charlie's life with her expectations, what would Eli do?

She pushed open the glass door and headed inside, her gaze instantly taking in all the information. A reception desk straight ahead. An empty waiting area to her right. This looked like the primary care area of the clinic. There was a corridor in the middle signposting X-Ray, Ultrasound, Day

Surgery and Inpatient Care. It was bright. Welcoming. A nurse walked up the corridor in pale green scrubs, before turning into a doorway and disappearing.

Charlie walked up to Reception. Behind it sat a lady who looked to be in her fifties. She was working on a sudoku puzzle. 'Hello. I'm Dr Charlotte Griffin. Dr Clark is expecting me?'

The woman looked up in surprise. 'Oh! Are you the new doctor taking over for Nance? My name's Dorothea. Welcome, we spoke on the phone the other day!'

Charlie smiled. 'Thanks. I can't help but notice that you don't have anyone waiting…is that normal? Or haven't you opened yet?'

'Oh, this is normal! The folks around here are quite hardy. We have to be. We don't go running to our doctor with every little twinge or headache like they do in the big city. It has to be gushing blood or about to fall off before anyone will walk in here!' Dorothea laughed. 'Except for Stewie. You'll meet him soon, no doubt.' She leaned in. 'Bit of health anxiety and keeps us on our toes with all his imagined diagnoses, which we have to check out, just in case.'

'I'll look forward to meeting him.' Charlie was used to frequent fliers. 'And where would I find Dr Clark?'

Dorothea checked her watch. 'He'll be in his office. See that corridor? Down to the end, last door on the right.'

'Thanks. Very nice to meet you, Dorothea.'

'Call me Dot.'

Dot. Okay. Charlie smiled her thanks and began to walk down the corridor, feeling the butterflies in her stomach begin their dance. Sweat began to bloom in her armpits and the small of her back, despite the antiperspirant she'd sprayed on this morning, anticipating such a thing.

It really was ridiculous. She shouldn't be feeling this way.

*What I need to do is pretend that I don't know him at all. It's just a normal first day and I want to get stuck into treating patients. Just do the job I'm here to do. Easy, right?*

She squared her shoulders and sucked in a breath as she reached his office. His door was open and as she turned the corner to enter, hand raised to rap her knuckles on the door, she expected she'd see him behind his desk, either on the phone, or at his computer completing a report or something.

What she *did not* expect was to see him doing press-ups, bare-chested, down on the ground.

She'd never goggled in her life, but she did in that moment.

He was a thing of beauty. As if he'd been carved. Each muscle apparent across his back and shoulders, his long hair loose, the waves touching the carpet each time he lowered himself down. He had a tattoo in the centre of his upper back, just beneath his neck, of the caduceus. The staff, entwined with two snakes, used to symbolise medics.

She had to lick her lips before she could speak. 'Good morning.'

He grunted one last time as he pushed himself to his feet and turned to face her, his cheeks red with effort, his smile broad. 'Good morning, Dr Griffin! Sorry about this, I usually like to start my day with some cardio exercises.'

Charlie could think of other cardio exercises that might be more fun, but she quickly pushed those thoughts to one side.

*Be professional. First day, remember. Pretend you don't know him.*

'So do I. It's called getting Alice up and ready for school.'

He smiled that charming and effortlessly cheeky smile of his that made her heart go thumpety-thump, raising her blood pressure by a few points. Which made her feel angry and raised it a little more.

Eli grabbed a towel off his chair and began to wipe himself down with it, before grabbing a loose shirt and shrugging that on, once he'd sprayed himself with some cologne he didn't need. It was unfair enough that he looked as fine as he did, did he really need to smell nice, too?

She turned away as he buttoned his shirt. She wasn't sure why. She'd just seen him half naked, why should she turn away as he put clothes *on*? But then she figured that getting dressed and undressed was something a person normally did in private and perhaps she didn't want to witness him doing private things? Or maybe it was because she would focus too much on the disappearing sight of his chest and stomach? Either way it was because of lust or etiquette.

Quite frankly Charlie was amazed that his primary care clinic wasn't filled every day with every young woman in town with drooling issues, just so they could spend time with him, being dazzled by his eyes and attention. Imagine what it would feel like to be besotted with Eli and have him sitting close to you as he listened to your chest with his stethoscope… Where would you look exactly? At those eyes? His luscious hair? The shape of his fine arms? Or would you just be so busy trying to slow and calm your breathing?

'Take a seat. Can I get you anything? Coffee? Tea? Juice?' Eli walked to the other side of his desk and got settled in.

'I'm fine, thanks.'

'Okay. Well, I thought for this first week you could shadow me in both the clinic and the hospital and, that way, you'll get to know where everything is and how we work here. I took the courtesy of making your ID card. Here you go.' He pulled a lanyard from his top desk drawer. 'This will log you into the system each time you need it. Just swipe it in the card reader.'

'Great.' She hung it around her neck.

'You'll be expected to take care of patients in the primary care setting, as well as out in the field. We occasionally do house visits. We often get called to accidents themselves.'

'Chuck told me.'

'Yeah. Great guy. He ever tell you about the time we almost had to amputate his leg?'

'No. He didn't.'

'He'll probably save that story for when you're eating. Right! Shall I show you around the place?'

She stood and nodded. 'Sounds perfect.'

She had her walls up. He sensed that immediately. Charlie was trying to show him that she was there to be professional and do the work, but he wished that she'd chill out a little. It was hard trying to be friendly when all the other person would do was give you a tight smile, or a nod.

She'd loosen up, no doubt. She'd have no choice living out here in Vasquez. This wasn't the city. She wasn't living in a place where everyone was strangers. Everyone knew each other here. The same families had lived here for decades. You couldn't walk down the street without stopping to say hello a lot, or passing the time over a garden fence, or waving at someone across the street walking their dog. Everyone relied upon each other here. There was no other way to be when you lived in such an isolated spot.

If you didn't have each other's back, then you wouldn't survive. Alaska could kill you. Easily. There were creatures here that would happily rip you to shreds. The weather could turn in an instant and give you hypothermia, or block off roads, and if you tried to stay within your own bubble here? You wouldn't survive.

She'd begin to understand this at some point, he had no doubt, and he was looking forward to watching her learn. He could tell her outright, but where would the fun in that be? He'd keep an eye on her. Make sure that she and Alice remained safe. He just wouldn't tell her, because he figured that she wouldn't be too happy about that if he got all knight in shining armour on her. But he'd keep an eye out. Help when he was needed. It was always the same with these city folks that came to town. They thought they could continue to live their lives the way they did in the urban jungle, but you just couldn't do that out here. It was a culture shock, that was for sure. Things might be fine right now, but that was because the weather was okay right now, but when it turned?

'I'll show you the primary care clinic first. That's where you'll do the majority of your work.'

'Where do you do the majority of yours?'

'The clinic, but I also do surgeries in the theatre.'

'Impressive.'

'You have to be able to multitask out here. Some patients wouldn't last if they had to wait for a medical evacuation flight out to a big hospital, so I do what I can here to keep them alive before the big guns arrive.'

'Like a first responder?'

'Pretty much, but you'd be surprised at how much more we do.'

'What was your last big case that got transported out?'

He thought for a moment. 'Cindy Kramer. Pregnant with triplets, naturally. We were all set up, knew how we'd handle it if she made it to term, but she went into labour prematurely at twenty-eight weeks and we simply didn't have the capacity to care for three premature babies of that gestation. Thirty weeks onwards, maybe, but her babies were guesstimated at less than a pound each, it would have been arrogant of us to assume we could help them the best, so we arranged for transport. Before that, it was Ken Palmer. Creutzfeldt-Jakob disease. Cruel way to go. We thought stroke initially. Something neuro definitely, maybe encephalitis or meningitis, and he was deteriorating fast. He got flown to Anchorage and they diagnosed the CJD. He died within the week.'

'It attacks fast.'

Eli nodded. 'Just two weeks prior he'd been telling me about how he'd booked flights to go and visit his grandbabies. He'd been so excited. Hadn't seen them for three months, not since they were born.' He shook his head. Even now, knowing what he knew about CJD, he still could not quite believe how fast that disease had progressed. Ken had seemed fine. Until he wasn't. And his family had felt as though they'd missed out on saying goodbye, because Ken hadn't been conscious enough to realise.

But Eli believed Ken knew. That he'd heard. Because he did believe that the hearing was one of the last senses to go and that, even though Ken couldn't respond, he heard his family say 'I love you'.

'This will be your room.' Eli stepped back, so Charlie could go in and take a look around. He watched her carefully. Observing her facial expression. The way she moved. The way she now looked. She was a couple of years younger than him, but he'd known, even back then, that she would grow up to be beautiful. He'd just not anticipated *how* beautiful. The acne had gone and now her skin was smooth and soft. Long, thick chestnut-coloured hair. Wide brown eyes, beautiful high cheekbones and full, soft lips. She was elegant. Maybe a little too thin still? But she'd always been highly strung. An anxious mess of nerves as a kid. Maybe she was still the same and living off nervous energy all the time?

Charlie trailed fingertips across her desk, then stopped and frowned, reaching to pick up the large plastic frog he'd left on top of her computer. 'Really, Eli?'

He couldn't help but chuckle. Glad she'd noticed it. Happy that she'd remembered the reference. 'Just a reminder of happy times past.'

'Happy times past? You should give me the dictionary you're using because I don't think happy times past means what you think it means.'

'Oh, come on, the frog thing was funny.'

She stared at him, no hint of humour on her face. 'For you, maybe.' She threw the plastic frog into the trash can underneath the desk.

Okay, so maybe leaving a live frog in her bed as a parting gift before he left with the Clarks wasn't the greatest thing to do, but he'd been scared! As an orphan, you always hoped the day would come in which you'd finally get a family, but then when you did, it was terrifying, because what if those people weren't what you hoped they'd be? The Clarks had seemed great and he'd got along fantastic with them, but what if it was all for show? What if they weren't who they seemed to be? Other kids kept coming back because it hadn't worked out. Some kids came back because the police had got involved. Eli was having to say goodbye to the one family he did know and he wanted everyone, including Charlie, to remember him. And as he'd joked around and pranked her before, he figured another prank was the way to go!

It was his way of saying *I'm gonna miss you, kid.*

There was a pond near to the orphanage and on the day he

knew he was going to go away with the Clarks, he sneaked out quickly after breakfast with everyone and caught the frog. It might even have been a toad. Ugly little thing it was, brown and lumpy, and he tucked it into her bed, down near the foot end, knowing she made her bed every day after breakfast. He could have put that frog in anyone's bed, but he put it in hers, because...well, he didn't know why.

He hoped to be around to see her find it. To give her a hug and say goodbye, but the Clarks made good time in the traffic and they arrived early and so he never got to see her reaction...

*I guess she didn't enjoy it.*

'Is this how it's going to be every day, while I'm here?' she asked.

'Maybe not *every* day.' He tried to say it as a joke, but it landed on deaf ears. She didn't find it funny and it left him feeling a little frustrated, but he chose not to show it.

'I'm here to do a job, Eli. Not have a replay of our childhood years, which for you might have been great fun, but for me they're not something I choose to recall with fondness. I'd appreciate it if you'd just let me do my job and not tell other people about how you know me.'

Well, it might be a little late for that. Because his family knew. He'd told them already when he'd recognised her name on the information sent over by the agency. 'All right.'

She nodded. 'Good.'

A buzzer sounded. A short, sharp sound.

She looked up. 'What's that?'

Eli smiled. Saved by the bell. 'It means we have a patient in the clinic.'

'Great.'

'Follow me.' He led the way back to his consulting room, a room he loved and adored.

His walls were covered in photographs that he'd taken. The beauty of Vasquez. The landscape. The wild animals. A grizzly catching salmon. A moose scratching its head on a tree. An osprey that had just caught a large trout. But then there were all the other photos. Eli on a parachute jump in mid-air. Eli paddle-boarding on Vasquez Lake. Another of him hand-feeding a wolf cub. Then there were the trophies that lined his cabinets. First place in that chainsaw competition he'd participated in. Second place for most fish caught in an ice-fishing competition. Fastest ascent on Rainier's Peak. Third place in the 2022 Vasquez Ironman Race. A medal for coming tenth in an extreme one hundred K race.

'Are these all yours?' she asked in surprise.

'Just a few that I keep on display.'

'There's *more*?'

'You should see my house.' He grinned, thinking of his trophy room. It was silly really, but it was something his new mom had started when they'd adopted him. Every achievement he ever had, she either made him a certificate or got him a gift. If he got a high score on an essay. When he got into college. When he learned to drive. When he got accepted into medical school. He'd thought she was just being cute, but then he'd realised he really began to value the recognition that he'd achieved something, that he was good at something, and it drove him to join clubs and societies.

At med school, everyone thought that he might fail because so much of his spare time was taken up doing sports or something. But he not only passed, he was top of his year. He had so many friends, so many dudes he knew he could rely on. So much female attention it was almost embarrassing. But he'd never been so admired or loved before and it was heady. Being active, engaging in extreme sports and testing himself became a way for him to feel good about himself. Especially after the cancer. These things, these trophies, they became proof that he was still who he wanted to be. Loved. *Able*. In every way except the one way he craved.

Eli swiped his ID card through the reader and tapped some details into the computer to bring up the patient who had arrived in clinic.

'Camille Henriksen. Injury to hand' was what it said on the screen. Could be anything.

'First patient is Camille. Fine ol' gal. Must be ninety, if she's a day. Came here with her husband over fifty years ago.'

Charlie nodded.

Eli went to call his patient and stood in the doorway waiting for her. When she came shuffling into view, he noticed that she had a dish towel wrapped around her left hand that looked bloody. 'Camille, what have you done to yourself this time?'

'Oh, I was just cleaning some fish that Marv brought back and the knife slipped. I'm sure it's just a small nick, but Marv insisted I come because I ain't had my tetanus in a while.'

'All right, well, you come on in and take a seat and we'll have a look. I got our new temporary doctor in here with me observing, Dr Charlie Griffin, is that okay with you?'

Camille looked in at Charlie and smiled and tried to wave with her bloodied towel. 'Hello, Charlie. Always nice to see a new face around here.'

'Pleasure to meet you, Mrs Henriksen.'

'Oh, call me, Camille. Everyone does.' Camille shuffled over to the patient's seating area and sat down with a heavy breath. 'Whoo! That's quite the walk. I'm getting my steps in today.'

Eli grabbed some gloves, passed a pair to Charlie and then sat opposite Camille after he'd assembled some gauze pads, a saline wash and some proper bandaging on a small trolley. 'Let's see what we've got here. You okay for me to unwrap this?'

'You do what you have to, Eli, I'm a tough ol' bird.'

'You're a sprightly young thing, Camille. Less of the old,' he said with a smile, playing the game they always played when Camille mentioned her age.

She smiled back at him, wincing slightly as he got closer to the injury.

The dish towel was soaked with blood. And he knew his patient was always dramatically reducing the description of her illnesses and injuries. Once she'd mentioned she was a little hot and she'd been running a fever of a hundred and two. Another time she'd complained about *a bit of a rash* she had and it had turned out she'd had the worst case of shingles he'd ever seen! Considering the amount of blood, he knew he wasn't about to see *a small nick*. Whatever she'd done, he expected to be putting in stitches. The question was, how many?

He unwrapped the final part of the towel and kept his face neutral, but he heard Charlie suck in a small gasp. The *small nick* was her missing the top half of her left index finger!

'Camille…'

'It ain't that bad. You just stitch me up and give me my shot and I'll be on my way.'

'Where's the fingertip, Cam?' he asked.

She grimaced slightly. 'Well, that's a bit of a story in itself.'

'Tell me.'

'It rolled off the chopping board and onto the floor and

you know Sookie, you know what she's like when I'm in the kitchen preparing food, she's always there. Watching. Waiting.'

'Who's Sookie?' Charlie asked.

'My Labrador. Been with me eight years.' Camille smiled with fondness. 'Anyway, she might have run off into the garden with it and by the time I'd wrapped my hand and got out there to take it off her, it was all mangled and chewed and so I had to throw it away.'

'It's in the garbage?' asked Eli.

''Fraid so. There'd have been no point in bringing it along here anyways, so just you stitch me up and send me on my way. I've still got that mess to clean in the kitchen and my Marv don't like to wait for his dinner.'

'Marv can make his own dinner just this once. I can't just stitch you up, Camille. I've got to clean this out and somehow join up the edges. I might need to do a small skin graft or create a skin flap.'

'Sounds expensive.'

'Sounds *necessary*,' he replied in a sterner voice, knowing he needed to let her know that they couldn't just rush this or put a sticking plaster on it.

Camille sighed. 'I'm gonna be here a while?'

'You're gonna be here a while,' he answered, this time with understanding and sympathy. He glanced at Charlie. She was listening and watching intently. 'Listen, I'll give Marv a ring, explain the situation and, if he's really put out, I'll get someone to go to your place with a sandwich or something. What do you say?'

Camille smiled and patted Eli's cheek with her good hand. 'You're a good boy to me.'

He cradled her hand with his own. 'You make it easy. Now

then. Let me clean this and bandage it up so a nurse can get you to X-Ray. Afterwards you can sit in the TV room for a while, all right?'

'All right.'

He made quick work of cleaning and dressing her wound then got up and went over to his desk. Lifted the phone and punched in a number. 'Hi, yeah, can you send Diana through to take Camille to X-Ray? Cheers.' He put down the phone. 'The nurse is going to take you to X-Ray, just to make sure you haven't chipped the bone.'

Camille nodded and then shuffled away with the nurse after she arrived.

He turned back to Charlie with a smile. 'Yes, before you ask. They're all like that here.'

'She just seemed fine with the idea that she'd lost the top of her finger.' Charlie was helping him clear away the debris left behind by him redressing Camille's wound. 'What do you think she'll prefer?'

He thought for a minute. 'Knowing Camille? Local anaesthetic and a skin flap, so she can get home quicker. If the bone isn't damaged, we can just clean it back a little, remove the rest of the nail and stitch the skin into position. Want to assist?'

'Yes, of course.'

'Ever done one of these before?'

'Yes, but it was a full finger amputation, though.'

'Great.' He went to write up his notes on Camille, his fingers racing over the keyboard. A new file popped up in the corner of his screen and when he accessed it, he saw it was Camille's X-ray. 'Tell me what you see.' He knew she was qualified. More than qualified. Charlie had had experience in many different centres, primary care clinics and emergency rooms, but he still wanted to assess her skill.

Charlie came behind him and leaned forward to look at the screen, her long brown hair brushed over his shoulder and he couldn't help but inhale her scent. It was something soft. Feminine. Meadow-like? It did delicious things to his insides and he had to silently inhale a long, slow breath.

'Looks clean to me. The bone hasn't been damaged. The distal phalanx looks complete. Some signs of arthritis, but that's to be expected in a woman her age.'

'I agree. Okay. Let's go offer Camille an upgrade.'

Eli looked different in scrubs and, with his hair tied back and a face mask on, all she could see were his eyes smiling at her from across their patient.

It was an unsettling thing being smiled at by Eli. The shared knowledge of their history beamed out from every glance, every twinkle, every crease of his eyes when he laughed or joked and tried to include her. His smile said *I Know You* and all she could feel was fear, because of it. She didn't like people knowing her. She didn't like people getting close. She preferred to be an unknown entity.

Camille was more than happy with the treatment plan and had clutched Charlie's hand intensely as Eli had injected the ring block to numb Camille's finger completely.

Ring blocks were painful, because the needle had to be inserted in sensitive areas at the base of the finger where it met the palm and also had to be inserted a couple of times, on both sides to ensure that the correct nerves were anaesthetised, so that the procedure could be completed painlessly.

'All done,' Charlie said, smiling, dabbing away at the spots of blood that had appeared.

'I think that hurt more than chopping the tip off,' said Camille.

'You just lie back now and think of something nice,' said Eli. 'Think of lying on a nice warm beach, cocktail in one hand and a damn fine book in the other.'

'Hah!' said Camille. 'I'd rather think of a handsome young man wafting me with an ostrich-feather fan. Is that okay, or am I being sexist?'

'You think of whatever you want,' said Charlie, smiling. She liked Camille. The lady was feisty and funny and brave, with a kick-ass attitude to life that Charlie wished she could have. 'You don't want to think of Marv wafting you with a fan?'

'Oh, honey, where's the fun in that? I've seen my husband without a shirt and, though I love him dearly, I'd much rather think of a strongly muscled torso, if you don't mind?'

Charlie couldn't help but remember the sight of Eli half naked doing press-ups in his office and how the sight of *him* had affected *her*.

Eli chuckled. 'Whatever works.'

Thinking of Eli's muscles certainly worked to help fire Charlie's imagination! He'd changed from a tall, lanky teen to a hunk of edible proportions who'd look more at home doing a calendar shoot.

Physically, he'd changed, that was for sure. But mentally? Emotionally? He still seemed like a prankster. A joker. Someone who always saw the lighter side of life, who was always on the lookout for laughs. And that made him dangerous, because she'd had enough of humiliation. Was too sensitive to it.

Maybe he ought to have pursued a life as a stand-up comedian? Because he'd never mentioned wanting to be a doctor. She'd have remembered that conversation. Becoming a doctor was all Charlie had ever wanted to do and she'd adored watching the medical dramas on the TV as a young kid, imagining herself doing the same kind of work. Saving lives. Making a difference.

The human body was amazing. It had a vast amount of different systems within, it had millions of different things that could go wrong with it. Diseases, conditions, bacteria, viruses, genetics, accidents. Sometimes it was a mystery, but, mostly, problems could be resolved and people walked away better. Healthier. Happier. Her entire childhood, she'd felt insignificant. As if she wasn't important and becoming a doctor would make her feel as though she did have a purpose. That what she did mattered. That she *was* important.

She'd never expected to become a mother so quickly, but it had happened, and when she'd given birth to Alice and held her in her arms? She'd known that she mattered now, more than anything. Her daughter needed her. Relied on her. Loved her. Unconditionally. And that love was such an overwhelming force! She no longer felt like a nobody.

That fascination with the human body had then terrified her, because she knew of all the horrible things that could possibly assail her daughter and there might be something that she wouldn't be able to save Alice from. That was what kept her up at night and staring at the ceiling and occasionally creeping into her daughter's room to check on her and stare at her and feel love for her ooze from every pore. And then, when Glen had done what he did…she'd realised all the other dangers that Alice might face in her future, too.

Eli worked quickly. Deftly. Chatting with Camille to keep her calm, making her laugh, making her smile. Doing the thing that Eli did best.

'You hear about Abe being knocked into the bay by a laker?' He chuckled.

'Laker?' Charlie frowned, not sure of the term.

'It's a fish. A lake trout.' Camille smiled. 'And no, I hadn't. What happened?'

'He was out fishing and got a bite. Stood up to reel it in, not realising he'd got a whopper on the other end. Damn thing fought him tooth and nail, he said, and, with all the lunging and fighting, knocked Abe off balance and he fell into the bay. Said it was a forty-pounder, at least.'

Camille laughed. 'Hah! Typical of Abe. I bet it was tiny, but he fell into the bay because of how many beers he'd been drinking.'

'Couldn't say for sure. He didn't come in here afterwards for a check-up, but his wife told me he came home soaking wet with a tall tale to tell.'

'Sounds like Abe!'

Charlie smiled, listening. Everyone seemed to know everyone here and maybe that was a good thing in such an isolated spot? Maybe it wasn't. What about having some privacy? 'Did he bring home the fish?' she asked.

Eli met her gaze and she was hit by the impact of it. It made her feel warm and gooey inside and that disturbed her greatly, so she looked away, breaking eye contact to reach for another gauze pad. 'No. Said we all needed to take his word for it. Now he's obsessed with going out there every day to catch his giant laker. Says it might be a record-breaker.'

'Maybe he's telling the truth,' she suggested.

Camille smiled at her in that way that told Charlie she was being naive. 'Once you've met Abe, then maybe you'll reassess your position on that one.'

'I do like to make my own mind up on people. Not just listen to what others say. Who's to know their reason for telling a story a certain way?'

They both looked at her.

'Fair enough,' said Eli. 'You're absolutely right.'

She smiled, glad to have made her point.

'But we're right, too.' He grinned at her and continued tying off the last stitch, snipping the stitch free with his scissors. 'All done! Gonna get this bandaged up now, then give you your tetanus shot, okay?'

'Okay.'

'We're gonna need you to keep this dry as much as you can and come back in ten days to have the stitches removed. I'll book you in an appointment now. But if you have any pain, or develop any fever or feel unwell, I want you to call immediately, okay?'

'I know, I know. This ain't my first time at a rodeo.'

When Camille had gone home, they returned to the clinic to discover there were two more people waiting patiently. One was sitting with a laptop, furiously writing away with what looked like a large sticking plaster, leaking blood, stuck to the side of her face, and the other was a guy sitting with one gloriously swollen ankle propped up on a chair.

Charlie looked at Eli and whispered, 'Is everyone accident-prone, here in Vasquez? Does anyone turn up with, say, a sore throat?'

Eli smiled at her. 'What do you think?'

# CHAPTER FOUR

WHEN CHARLIE COLLECTED her daughter from kindergarten, Alice came running out, happily clutching a painting she'd done of two figures in purples, reds and greens. 'Look what I did!' she said, showing her mom the art.

'That's amazing! Is that me and you?' Charlie asked.

'No, that's me and Mrs Clark, my teacher!'

'Oh. Lovely.' She tried not to act surprised. They'd been here in Vasquez five minutes and by all accounts the Clark family owned most things round here and already Mrs Clark, Eli's mother, had usurped Charlie's position in Alice's drawings. Was this teacher superwoman? She had to be bloody amazing to have inspired this.

Trying not to let it bother her, she walked Alice home, her daughter chatting all the way about what her first day had been like. Apparently kindergarten was *the best*.

She was happy for her. Truly. But this was the first time Charlie had spent so much time away from her daughter and she was already beginning to feel a little displaced. A part of her had hoped that Alice would have missed her and they'd spend this time walking home and making something for the potluck together, so that they could soak up being with each other again, but Alice seemed like a new child.

*I mean, it's great. I love that she's so independent. I raised her to be that way, of course.*

But was it backfiring?

*Who is the only person you can rely on?*

*Me!*

*Who is the only person who can make you happy?*

*Me!*

Had Charlie inadvertently ingrained into her daughter that she couldn't even rely on her own mother? Because that was not what she'd intended the mantras to mean. She'd meant that Alice couldn't rely on anyone else *except* her. That *she* could still make her daughter happy.

Charlie bit her lip as she unlocked the door to the cottage and let them in. 'We're going to a potluck tonight at Mrs Clark's house.'

'We are?' Alice looked thrilled and began bouncing around the house. 'That's amazing! She's so great, Mom!'

'So I keep hearing.' She gave a bit of a rictus grin and then turned to open the fridge and examine the contents. 'What do you think we should make?'

'PB and J sandwiches.'

Charlie smiled. 'You don't take sandwiches to a potluck, honey. You cook something. Take something hot.'

'Oh.'

'I could do chicken enchiladas? You fancy those?'

'Great! Can I go outside and play until then?'

'Sure, honey.' The cottage came with a small but pretty enclosed garden, with a six-foot wooden fence at the back that offered some protection from the forest and mountains that rose up behind it. Charlie felt sure that she'd be safe out there. There was no pond to worry about, no rockery for her to fall on and crack her head open—which was what the woman with the laptop had done, needing two stitches for her trouble. The cottage had simple flower beds and a lawn. That was it.

Charlie began chopping onions, peppers and chillies, while a pan gently warmed on the hob, then she set them to frying, while she cut the chicken breasts into small chunks.

She tried not to think of Eli. She tried even harder not to think of Alice's painting stuck to the fridge by magnets, of her daughter and her kindergarten teacher. One day at school and already the effusively warm Mrs Clark had taken Charlie's place in her daughter's affections.

It seemed unfair. It seemed wrong and, Charlie had to admit, she felt a little jealous about it. An ugly emotion she didn't like feeling.

Stirring the refried beans into the passata and sweetcorn, she mused on the day and what it had been like to work with Eli. Apart from the half-naked workout and the frog reminder, it hadn't gone too badly. Clearly Eli was liked by his patients, who all seemed on first-name terms with him, which seemed odd. Charlie was used to being addressed as Dr Griffin. She liked that. It helped establish a professional distance from the patient and she'd worked hard to get the Dr part before her name. Hearing patients calling her Charlie had seemed weird.

'Eli' was a talented doctor, who stitched neatly despite the size of his large hands, who was adept with a scalpel and listened to his patients and involved them with their medical choices and options. He was still as ebullient as ever. Always looking for the joke, always grinning that cheeky grin of his, which she had to admit was actually kind of hot, and so the only two issues she had to face with him were the facts that he knew too much about her and that he was insanely attractive.

But she could never get involved with someone like Eli. Absolutely no way! She had a daughter to think about for one, and her daughter's father had humiliated her to such a level that she could never think of being with anyone else, never mind Eli, who thought that looking for laughs was the way to live life. She didn't need someone like that in her and Alice's life. Men were off-limits big-time. She had no time for them any more. It was just going to be herself and Alice from now on.

*Unless Alice runs off with the amazing Mrs Clark.*

On the walkover to the Clarks' house, Charlie was giving Alice the rules. 'We're not going to stay long, okay? It's a school night for one and I don't want you out too late. And remember, this is your teacher's house, so you call her Mrs Clark at all times. Once we've been there an hour, we're going to leave, okay?'

'Only an hour, Mom?'

'Alice, please…'

'Okay.' Alice didn't sound thrilled, but agreed. Clearly she had wonderful ideas about learning all about Mrs Clark by exploring her house and holding her teacher's hand all night, without letting go, because she was her *'new, most favouritest teacher ever!'*

The Clark house was the biggest in Vasquez. Of timber construction and painted white, it looked to be only a few years old. A new build? Maybe. The lawns were neatly trimmed and the front porch had a swing seat, lanterns and pots of beautiful flowers that Charlie couldn't name. A chocolate Labrador watched them approach up the front pathway, thumping its wagging tail against the floorboards.

'Mom, look! A doggy!' Alice let go of her hand and tried to dash forward, forgetting everything Charlie had ever told her about the dangers of unknown dogs. She managed to grab Alice before she could get to it.

Of course the Clarks would have a dog. Of course it would

be the cutest, friendliest-looking dog Charlie had ever met. Because for the last year, Alice had been begging her for a dog. She'd bought Alice dog plushies and always answered with *'One day, baby, not yet...'* and Alice would pout and frown and whine.

So, of course the perfect Clarks would have a dog. Why wouldn't they?

'It might not be friendly.' She tried to warn her daughter, as she always did when they were out and about in the world. Strange dogs could never be trusted, Alice should know that.

The front door that was hung with a handmade sign, adorned with ribbons and dried flowers that said *Welcome!* on it, opened and out stepped Mrs Clark with a beaming face. 'Hey, Alice! That's okay, you can give Mitch a cuddle! He loves cuddles.'

Charlie let go and her daughter ran the last few steps to the dog, knelt and threw her arms around it as Mitch proceeded to lick her face as if she were a lamb chop.

'Alice, don't let it—'

But it was too late. Alice was giggling and chuckling as Mitch slobbered all over her.

Mrs Clark smiled. 'Hello, Charlie. Mitch's tail is kind of like an early warning system here. As soon as we hear it thumping on wood, we know someone's coming. How are you, my dear?' Mrs Clark leaned forward and dropped a surprising kiss of welcome on Charlie's cheek. She stood back and waited for a response.

'I'm good, thanks. Alice had a great first day, by all accounts.'

'And did you?' Mrs Clark slipped her arm through Charlie's. 'You must come in and tell me all about it. Eli's told me his version, but I want to hear all about it from you.'

'Eli's here?' She stopped abruptly, surprised as to why she didn't consider that Eli might be at his mother's potluck.

'Of course! Now come on in and tell me all about it. Alice, sweetheart? Why don't you bring Mitch in and I'll find you some treats to feed him?'

And before Charlie could protest or say she'd changed her mind about coming, Mrs Clark was sweeping her into the house, saying, 'And you must call me Gayle.'

The Clark house had that warm and inviting cottage look. Lots of floral prints and soft, pale stripes on cushions and rugs. Cream-coloured lamps lit pastel-painted bookcases, filled with leather-bound books. Huge, soft sofas adorned the living space, and next to one sat a wicker basket, filled with hand-wound balls of wool and what looked like a hat mid-make on a set of circular needles. Charlie knew they were called that, because a few years back she'd decided to try to knit Alice a jumper and the lady in the shop had told her that circular needles and using the magic loop method was the best way to do so, because then the jumper wouldn't have side seams. Well, Charlie had got hopelessly lost and the jumper, or what there was of it, had ended up being stuffed in a bag and donated to a craft library. A huge waste of money, but at least she had tried, hoping it would give her something to do after Alice was in bed and she had to sit alone in an apartment, pondering her life.

There were lots of people standing around that Charlie didn't know and Gayle lost no time in introducing her to everyone. A sea of names was given—mostly Clark relations—and she had no hope of remembering who was who, or who was a cousin, or an aunt or a nephew, but she saw Alice brush past her, being taken to the back garden to play with a bunch of other kids and Mitch. She wanted to tell her to be careful, but her voice got stuck in her throat, because suddenly Eli was there, holding a bottle of beer and looking ravishing in a soft off-white linen shirt and jeans.

'Hey.'

She awkwardly felt her cheeks colour. 'Hi.'

'It must be lovely to be reunited after all these years,' said Gayle. 'You two must have *so much* to talk about! Let me get you a drink, Charlie. What would you like?'

'Just an orange juice, if you have one, thanks.'

'You don't want anything stronger? We have wine?'

'I don't drink.'

'All right, orange juice it is. Let me take that, it looks wonderful!' and Gayle disappeared with her chicken enchilada dish, through the throng of people.

Charlie looked at the assembled guests, feeling awful. 'Is this a party? A birthday or an anniversary? Am I missing something? Should I have brought a gift?'

'Nope. Just a little get-together.'

'*Little?* You and I have different dictionaries.'

He laughed. 'This is just what it's like here. This is what having a family is like.'

'Is it?' She crossed her arms in front of her, feeling uncomfortable. She wasn't used to this! She'd never been part of anything this large. Even when she was married! Her husband hadn't had any close family. Even when they'd married it had just been a couple of witnesses at City Hall.

'Look, I know you're still feral and all, but try to relax. Enjoy it!'

She looked straight at him. 'I'm not feral!'

'Aren't you? I've seen more confident looks in cats backed into a corner.'

'I'm not feral. I know how to be around people.'

'But you don't know how to be comfortable around people who want to know more about you. I saw it today. You were taken aback when a patient called you Charlie, instead of Doctor. When people close the distance, your hackles go up. I can tell just by looking at you. Standing there with your arms crossed and looking for the exits with that frightened look upon your face. Relax a little. No one's going to bite you.' He took a swig from his bottle of beer.

She hated that he could tell! So she uncrossed her arms, but then she didn't know how to stand all of a sudden, without something to do with her hands, so she crossed her arms again.

Eli chuckled.

'Shut up!'

He laughed some more and she wanted to turn tail in that moment, find Alice and get the hell out of there!

But wouldn't that be proving his point?

So she wasn't great at people being close, so what? Eli had led a different life from hers. Their paths had diverted when he'd got adopted into the Clark family. Hers had continued to be hard, lonely and painful.

'I'm trying my best,' she said quietly.

And he looked at her in that moment, in this strange, intense way, so that she imagined he could somehow see all that had happened to her, every moment of hardship and humiliation, and she felt naked beneath his gaze.

'Here you go! One orange juice. Now then, Eli, don't monopolise Charlie! I want to introduce her to Gran.' Suddenly Gayle was pulling her away from the heat of Eli's gaze and through the crowds once again, into the kitchen this time to be introduced to a tiny silver-haired lady, who wore an apron and seemed to be deeply involved in the mass production of chocolate-chip cookies.

'Gran? This is Charlie, Eli's friend and new colleague at the clinic.'

Charlie extended a hand, but Gran looked at her oddly and stepped forward for a hug, instead.

'Hello, Charlie. Short for Charlotte, is it?'

Surprised by the sudden hug, she squeezed back and, when she was released, nodded, with a smile. 'Yes, that's right.'

'I always wanted to call Gayle Charlotte, but my husband—*may he rest in peace*—didn't like it and so Gayle it was. Eli never told us you were a pretty little thing.'

She wasn't sure how to respond to that. To be pleased that Gran thought she was pretty, or upset that Eli hadn't mentioned it? Not that she needed him to notice, but she worked hard to try and look good. She worked out at home often. Yoga. Pilates. Cardio twice a week. She ensured she always had her hair done every ten weeks and tried to eat healthily. But she wasn't doing it for any man. She did it for herself, for her own strive to perfection. Sometimes, she overdid it. Punishing herself with harsh exercise and high-intensity interval workouts. The last time had been after Glen had…

No. She didn't want to think about that again. It had already occupied too much of her life and decisions.

'Do you bake, Charlie?'

'Er, sometimes.'

'What's your favourite dessert? There's only one right answer, now!'

Panicked under the sudden pressure, she squeaked out an answer. 'Apple pie?'

Gran stared at her for a moment, then chuckled, slapping

Charlie on the arm. 'Perfect! You're a keeper, for sure! Now, why don't you help me with the next batch?'

The next hour or so whizzed by in a whirlwind of flour, eggs and chocolate chips. Gran shared all her secrets—a pinch of cinnamon and nutmeg—and talked non-stop while they were in the kitchen.

At first, Charlie felt a little uncomfortable, but after a while she relaxed into it and laughed and chuckled at Gran's stories of her early years romancing her soon-to-be husband, George, and how he'd sneak up the trellis at nights to knock on her bedroom window and sneak a kiss, and all the romance of their midnight escapes to take a walk beneath the moon and stars, hand in hand. Sometimes, Charlie just stood there and listened, not realising that she had been whisked away into a world of old-fashioned romance and wooing and how much she yearned for the world to be as simple as it was many decades ago. If you made a mistake relationship-wise back then, hardly anyone knew about it. Today? In this modern world? With social media being so prolific? You could be plastered across anyone's page in seconds, for the whole world to see. Until the end of days.

She didn't realise that Eli had been standing in the kitchen doorway watching her, until he spoke. 'Time to eat.'

Charlie turned, blushing, pulled back into the present, and she washed her hands, drying them on a towel. 'How can I help?' she asked.

'You've helped plenty. You're a guest. Gran? You shouldn't have worked her so hard…she's already had a long day.'

'Nonsense, Eli! This girl's got spirit. Now, Charlie, why don't you help me take these cookies through?'

She was happy to help. In fact, she liked helping and feeling a part of them. She wasn't sure how it had happened. One minute she'd been feeling trapped, the next she was revelling in the warmth of them all. This family group. And though, technically, she was an outsider, she'd been made to feel welcome. To feel an honorary member of this family. Even if it was just for this night. Gran had made her feel secure, as if she'd known that Charlie didn't want to answer personal questions, and so Gran had kept her questions light. What sports team did she follow? What was her favourite music? Had she seen last night's episode of some soap that Gran liked to watch?

At the rear of the house was a large porch that had a few long picnic tables set up, which was slowly beginning to groan with food, and, around the tables, all the gathered Clark family, her and Alice. Her daughter was at the far end, chuckling with kids her own age, and Charlie smiled to see her look so happy as she slid into a seat between Gayle and Eli. There didn't seem to be any standing on ceremony, everyone just dived into whatever food they fancied, and she couldn't help but notice that Eli loaded up his plate with her chicken enchiladas, a huge forkful of a green salad and a couple of dinner rolls. Charlie helped herself to some pasta that looked to be mixed with a spicy sausage of some kind and peppers, along with a different salad that was decorated with bacon bits and herby croutons.

'This is delicious,' she said to Gayle. 'How often do you guys get together like this?' She expected her to say that they didn't do it very often.

'All the time! Birthdays, anniversaries, graduations, days that end in the letter Y!' Gayle laughed and took a sip of her drink.

'Really? Isn't it a lot of hard work?'

'No! It's fun! Family is the most important thing in the

world and, when you have it, you need to celebrate it as often as you can. Show people that you love them and want them around. That you're there as a supportive network for anything.' Gayle leaned in. 'Life is hard, you know? We know that more than most. But no one has to walk their path in life alone. With family? You can be strong and no matter what the world throws at you, it can't bring you down.'

Charlie smiled, slightly awestruck by the difference in their lifestyles. The Clarks clearly believed that together they were a force to be reckoned with, whereas Charlie had raised Alice to believe in the fact that they stood alone in this world and they could rely only on themselves. Who was right and who was wrong?

'Having family and having love is something you want to share. It's useless on its own when we all have so much love to give. That's why we decided we'd adopt. There are so many kids in this world that just need a chance, you know?'

Charlie nodded.

'Our lives have been so enriched since we brought Eli into our fold. Even through all his trials and tribulations, we wouldn't have had it any other way.'

His trials and tribulations? Surely his life had been perfect?

'We were pulled into his orbit. I mean…how could we not be? Have you seen him? He's gorgeous! But no, seriously, when you know, you know. Eli's vitality for life is infectious. He's always smiling, or laughing, and when we spoke to him, we just gelled, you know? You must know, you knew him back then!'

Yes, she'd known him. And Gayle was right. He did have and still had a vitality for life and seeking joy, but she hadn't known how to deal with him back then and she wasn't sure she knew how to deal with him now. Sitting this close, being part of his family, being welcomed, made her feel confused. It made her question her own life and what she might have been missing in it. It made her feel sad.

'I did.'

Gayle leaned in, conspiratorially. 'He told us about the frog.' She laughed.

Charlie nodded, smiling. 'He did?'

'Took him till last week to tell us, when he knew you were coming.'

'Did he tell you he put a frog in my office today, too?'

'A real one?'

'Plastic.'

'Eli!' Gayle scolded him and he chuckled beside her. Clearly happy to have surprised his mom and made her smile.

His *mom*.

He truly had been accepted as a member of this family. He was one of them, that was clear, the adoption was just paperwork. Eli was a Clark, through and through.

Charlie had always been sceptical of what it might feel like to be adopted. Whether you would truly feel a part of someone else's family. Whether they would accept you and treat you the same as their actual blood relatives.

But it had happened here, or so it seemed. Maybe Eli was just so laid-back and chill about everything, he didn't stress about it the way she once had?

Did she need to take a leaf out of Eli's book?

She couldn't believe she was even having to consider it.

# CHAPTER FIVE

HE'D BEEN FOR his usual ten-kilometre run and was just arriving at the clinic in his running gear of sleeveless grey vest
and red shorts when he noticed Charlie arriving with Frank
Schwarz.

Charlie appeared to be trying to escort Frank into the building, but Frank was having none of it, slapping away Charlie's
efforts to get him inside.

'Now, hold your horses there, missy!'

'Sir? You need to come inside, so I can treat you!'

'Hold up! Hold up, Charlie. This is Frank, he doesn't like
going into hospitals or clinics.'

'But he's hurt!' she insisted, indicating the large fishing
hook piercing his neck.

Eli had noticed the hook already. It had quite the barb poking out of Frank's skin, blood trickling down past his collar
and staining his usual blue-checked flannel. 'I know that, but
Frank doesn't come inside.'

'Whyever not?'

'Because everyone he's ever loved has gone into this building behind us and not come out again, plus Frank has quite
the phobia about needles.'

Charlie looked at him. 'Oh. I see, but he can't go around
with that thing in his neck—it has to come out!'

'*Really?* I was thinking of leaving it in.' He smiled at her and Frank and steered him over towards the bench that was situated out front. 'How'd this happen, Frank?'

'I was prepping *Molly*, moving some fishing gear about, and I slipped on some oil or what have you and when I got up again, realised there was something catching on my collar. I wouldn't have come here at all. Was gonna clip off the barb and yank it out myself. Except this...' Frank gestured at Charlie '...this *lady* insisted. She was very forceful.'

Eli smiled. 'She can be and she was right to do so, Frank, this can't stay in and it's near to some pretty important structures in the neck.'

'You mean my jugular?'

'Or your carotid. Plus that hook's probably not the cleanest thing in the world either, so we're going to need to get you on some antibiotics.'

Frank frowned. 'I don't like taking tablets.'

'Well, you're going to have to, just this once, okay?'

'You can't just snip this thing and yank it out?'

'I'm sure we can, but I'd really like to get a scan done, first. It does look superficial, but we need to be sure. You hit your head when you fell?'

I don't think so.'

'You lose consciousness?'

'No. I don't want to go inside there, Eli. I lost my Jane in there.'

Jane had been Frank's wife. They'd been married over forty years, until she had a sudden splitting headache, that had turned out to be a burst aneurysm. She died within minutes, before the medical evacuation could be arranged.

'It'll take five minutes, I promise you. Charlie and I will know what we're dealing with and we can get that sorted and have you back to *Molly* before you know it.'

'Who's Molly?' asked Charlie.

'My boat,' answered Frank.

'Oh.'

Eli smiled at Charlie. She looked beautiful today. Mornings agreed with her. Her hair was soft and floaty as she'd not yet tied it back for work and it cascaded over her shoulders like silk. She had a small divot that formed between her eyebrows, like now, when she was concerned, and her eyes looked darker, somehow.

'What do you say, Frank? You'll come in for the scan? Get treated. I'll give you antibiotics that you must take every day for a week and I'll come round to check on the wound in a couple of days. What do you say? I'll throw in a six-pack of beers, too.'

'He shouldn't drink on antibiotics,' Charlie said.

'I'll bring them when his course is over.' Eli smiled at her and winked at Frank, conspiratorially.

Frank gazed at the building behind them, as if considering it. 'On one condition.'

'What's that?'

'That I can sit outside, while I'm waiting. I don't want to feel trapped inside.'

'I'll open up the quad. There's a small garden. A bench. Some ducks have built a nest there next to the pond. You'll have nature.'

Frank considered it and as he did so, Eli's gaze drifted to Charlie.

She looked disbelieving. As if she couldn't quite believe that he was making all of these concessions for a patient. But she had to know that they performed medicine differently up here. It was hard enough getting patients to come in, in the first place. He would make whatever adaptations necessary to ensure they still received first-class treatment.

'Okay.'

Eli grinned. 'Great. Let's get you in, then.'

They got a hesitant Frank to X-Ray and while the radiologist did her thing, Charlie pulled him to one side. 'That man needs a scan, a tetanus shot, antibiotics and surgery that may or may not be minor! You can't let him sit outside in a garden and promise him a beer!'

'Relax! He's going to get the best treatment he will allow me to give him.'

'That *he* will allow *you*?' she scoffed. 'As doctors, it is up to us to give patients the options for treatment that will keep them safe and healthy for as long as possible. I'm sorry that he's scared of hospitals and needles, but I have never heard of a doctor promising to share a six-pack of beer with a patient, as some sort of bribe!'

'No? Maybe you haven't been working in the right kind of hospitals, then?' Eli was not going to be put off by her sterile, big-city ways. It was different out here in Vasquez. Keeping his patients healthy was a journey and it often felt like bargaining, when a lot of them were stubborn as mules and didn't like to admit to weaknesses. It was a tough crowd out here and he'd learned that quickly. Especially when he'd got sick himself. The people out here braved it out. They lifted their chins, squared their shoulders and faced death head-on. Whether that was from the isolation, the extreme winter weather or the wildlife. Or, in his case? Cancer.

Death was everywhere, a constant friend. The people here acknowledged that and they fought that quietly every time they set foot outside their homes. It wasn't so bad right now, what with it being springtime, but as fall approached and winter threatened, the people here hunkered down and looked out for one another. That was what he was doing for Frank. Supporting him. Acknowledging his fear and offering him a trade. That was all. Something for something. The Vasquez way.

'The right kind of hospitals? People need to understand the risks to their health and Frank needs a proper assessment. He had a fall. What caused that? And are you going to take his word that he didn't pass out? He could be lying to get out of here quicker.'

'He could be, but I'll keep an eye on him.'

'What? He needs to be admitted for tests, as well as the procedure to remove that hook from his neck.'

'I get it, I do, and I can pass Frank's boat every day on my morning run and check in on him. It's the best we're going to get with him and you need to understand that.'

'You're too laid-back about this, Eli.'

He smiled. 'And you're too wound up. City life has got you acting all…shrill and brittle.'

'Shrill and brittle?' Her hands went to her hips and he saw an anger flare in her dark chocolate eyes that he liked and was waiting to hear what she said next when the radiologist opened the door and allowed Frank to exit.

'Where's that quad?'

Eli turned to Charlie. 'My esteemed colleague from Anchorage will show you, Frank. Charlie, why don't you stay with Frank? Sit with him in the garden for a while. Might be nice for both of you to just sit back and relax?'

He saw the frustration in her eyes, but he kept smiling, knowing she wouldn't disagree with him in front of a colleague, and watched her force a polite smile at their patient instead.

'I'll show you. Follow me.'

Eli watched her go. Felt his gaze drop to her shapely behind as she walked away from him towards the quad. She was still the fiery Charlie he remembered from many years ago, but there was something else there, too. Something he didn't remember. Something he didn't recognise. She was scared. And he wondered what of.

And whether he'd be able to protect her from it.

Or whether he was the one causing it?

# CHAPTER SIX

IT SEEMED HERE, in Vasquez, that Charlie couldn't walk more than five yards down the street without some local stopping her to say hello or wanting to chat.

It was midweek. Wednesday lunchtime and she'd been given a whole hour for lunch, which quite frankly was something she'd never experienced in the city hospitals. Mostly food was eaten on the run, or sometimes missed completely and she'd try to grab a bite of something if she passed the staff room, gulping it down as she hurried along to her next patient or emergency.

A whole hour felt like luxury and so she'd decided to go out for a walk and get some fresh air. She was greeted by a mailman who seemed to know her name, even though she didn't know him, an older lady waved hello as she wiped the outdoor tables of her diner, and a guy who looked as old as the hills surrounding Vasquez ambled towards her with his walking stick, doffed his cap and said, 'Hello, Charlie. How's everything going?'

'Oh, it's going very well, thank you.' She smiled, felt awkward. 'How are you?'

'Ooh, not bad. Carrying on, as you do.' He winced slightly. 'Are you okay?'

'Bit of heartburn. Just on my way to get some of those antacids.'

Her instincts kicked in and now she noticed other things

about this old man. He looked clammy and his colour was off. Of course, he could look like that normally, but she had noticed in the short time that she was here that Vasquez natives all seemed to look quite weathered and healthy, no matter their age. This gent looked somewhat paler.

'How long have you had the heartburn?'

'Came on about an hour ago and the damn thing won't go away.' He winced again and, with his spare hand not holding the stick, he rubbed at his chest. 'Think it's something bad?'

Was he having a heart attack? 'Let's get you in one of these seats for a moment.' She guided him over to one of the diner chairs and sat him down, then placed her fingers on his wrist to check his pulse.

'Everything okay?' The lady who had waved to her earlier came out looking concerned. 'Stewie? You all right?'

So this was Stewie. The frequent flyer. The hypochondriac she'd been warned about. But this didn't seem like anxiety.

Charlie turned around to her. 'Could you call the clinic and let them know that I need them to send someone out to assist me with this gentleman, please? Query MI.'

The woman nodded hurriedly and bustled back inside.

'Okay, Stewie, is it? I need you to look at me and I need you to take nice, steady breaths and remain calm, okay?'

'What's going on?'

'I think you're having a heart attack.'

Stewie raised his eyebrows at her and gulped. 'R-r-really?'

'Do you feel sick? Have you any pain in your jaw, neck or left arm?'

'I guess a little, but it's not bad at all. If I'm having a heart attack, why aren't I on the floor gasping, clutching at my chest?'

'They don't all present the way you see them on TV. Sometimes they're a little like this. Quieter. Less dramatic.'

'Not like me then. Oh.' He rubbed at his chest again and laid his walking stick up against the table. 'I thought it was because I'd eaten too much breakfast this morning. My wife makes excellent biscuits and gravy.'

She smiled at him.

'Guess I was lucky running into you, huh? I promise I wasn't stalking you as a doctor.'

Charlie smiled sympathetically.

'Eli told me you were coming. He's been really excited about it.'

'Yeah?' She was surprised, but also kind of pleased. 'That's nice.'

'He's a good boy. He's looked after me and my wife for years now. It was a shame that he had to go through what he did. It was a nasty business, him just a young man an' all.'

Charlie assumed he meant the orphanage. Having to live in a children's home and not find a family until he was fifteen years old and adopted by the Clarks. 'But he's landed on his feet here,' she said.

'Yeah. The Clarks...they're good people.' Stewie looked at her. 'You seem nice, too.'

'Thank you. So do you.'

At that moment a vehicle arrived and Eli jumped out, with Diana, one of the nurses from the clinic. 'Stewie? When I send my doctors out for lunch break, I expect them to rest, not find patients on the fly.' Eli was already placing an oxygen mask on Stewie's face as the old man chuckled, then he placed his stethoscope in his ears to listen to Stewie's chest.

She caught his quick nod of acknowledgement that Stewie was most definitely having a heart attack. 'Let's get you in the back of the truck and over to the hospital.'

'Will someone call my Joan?'

'I'll do it,' Charlie offered, clambering into the back of the truck with him to hold his hand as Diana got IV access and Eli placed a BP cuff around the old man's arm. He was a sweet old man and, granted, she barely knew him, but he exuded the warmth and friendship that everyone had seemed to give her since arriving here. Even now, in this moment, where his life was hanging in the balance, Stewie was being warm and charming.

'You're a good 'un,' he said, patting her hand with his. 'Don't scare her, will you?'

'I won't, I promise.'

'Your Joan is made of stern stuff. She doesn't scare easily,' Eli said.

Stewie smiled behind the oxygen mask. 'Nigh on fifty years we've been married, you know, and never a cross word between us.'

Charlie smiled at him. That was the dream, wasn't it? To find someone who suited you perfectly. To find someone who loved you deeply every day. Who enjoyed your company. Who was there for you and supported you and adored you. Someone with whom you could live out every day, happily. She'd hoped to have that with Glen, but it had all gone so horribly wrong.

It was the sort of relationship that she'd never got close to. Her own romantic history being somewhat more…fraught.

'You make sure to tell her I love her.'

'You can tell her that yourself,' Eli said.

But Stewie met her gaze and looked deeply into her eyes and wordlessly begged her to tell his wife what he wanted her to hear. And she saw it in his eyes—he knew. The end was coming.

Charlie knew they would do everything to make sure he

got through this, but if Stewie thought he was going to die, then she should also respect his last request, so she nodded and squeezed his hand and mouthed *I will.*

He smiled and then closed his eyes and the ECG monitor suddenly went crazy, beeping out an alarm.

'He's arresting!' Eli said, stepping out of his seat to stand by Stewie and begin compressions. 'How much further, Diana?'

'Less than a minute!'

'Get us there!'

They leapt into action around their patient. Now was no longer the time to hold Stewie's hand. Charlie needed to help and she'd seen enough MIs to know that even when you were right there, with all the equipment, it didn't mean success was guaranteed. Ninety per cent of cardiac arrests in the United States were fatal, which meant you had a one in ten chance of surviving. Those weren't great odds. But Charlie was not one who bet on the odds. At the end of the day they were just numbers and no one could say whether it was pointless or not.

You helped. If someone was dying, you tried to stop it. If someone was flailing, you tried to save them.

She took over compressions as the truck stopped and Eli thrust the doors open and helped manoeuvre the gurney outside, so they could rush it into the clinic. They'd shocked Stewie twice, but he still wasn't responding and as they rushed into the clinic, alarms blaring from the machines, his rhythm changed from ventricular fibrillation to asystole.

Flatline.

You couldn't shock a flatline.

She kept pushing.

Chest compressions, chest compressions, chest compressions.

*One, two, three, four...*

Eli pushed epinephrine, but nothing was happening and Stewie's walking stick that had been laid on the gurney next to him fell to the floor with a clatter. It was like a sign that it was no longer needed. Final.

Charlie checked the clock. He'd been asystole for far too long. She caught Eli's eye as Eli stepped back and went over the history of the case, rounds completed, drugs given and how long Stewie had been down for in an unshockable rhythm, with no change. 'I think we should stop. Does everyone agree?'

Charlie continued to do CPR. She would not stop unless everyone agreed and she quickly met everyone's gaze as they all agreed. Stewie would not be coming back.

She stopped. Stood back. Breathless. 'Agreed.'

Eli looked up at the clock. 'Time of death, one twenty-two p.m.' He looked at her. 'Want me to call Joan?'

'No. I said I'd do it.' She was grateful to him for offering but she wanted to be the one. She and Eli left Stewie in the capable hands of the nurses.

'Are you okay?' Eli asked.

'Of course. I've lost patients before. I'll lose them again. This isn't my first time.'

'I know, it's just that here in Vasquez everyone is so close that, when we do lose a patient, we look out for one another. It's not something that just gets forced under the rug, so that you can deal with the next patient and save your tears for when you get home.'

'I didn't know him. Not like you.' She turned to face him. 'Do *you* need to take some time away? I can cover for you, if you like?'

'I'd like to be with you when you tell Joan. I'd like to be there for her. Familiar face and all of that.'

She nodded. 'Okay. If that's what you want.' It was strange to see him so serious, but expected under the circumstances. She was used to the jovial, cheeky Eli. The one with a constant twinkle in his eye, not this.

When Joan arrived, she was taken to a family room and Eli and Charlie followed her in.

'I'm too late, aren't I? I can see it in your faces.' Joan stood staring at them.

Charlie indicated she should take a seat and when she'd sat down, she began to explain. 'I'm so sorry. Your husband suffered a cardiac arrest and despite our best efforts to revive him, I'm afraid he passed away.'

Joan paused, taking it in. 'He just went out for antacids. Said the walk might help his digestion. He had heartburn. It wasn't heartburn?'

Charlie shook her head. 'I'm afraid not.'

'Did he collapse in the street?'

'No. I met him outside the diner and we began to talk. He described his symptoms, which worried me, and I called for an ambulance. We worked hard to revive him, but we were not successful.'

Tears began to well in Joan's eyes.

This was the difficult moment. The moment where Charlie had to be strong and distance herself. Watching other people lose it and become emotional was always a difficult thing for her.

'We almost didn't get together,' Joan said.

Charlie said nothing. If Joan needed to talk to get through this, then she'd let the older woman talk.

'I didn't like him when we first met. He was so full of himself. Good-looking.' She smiled ruefully. 'But he knew it, too.

I thought he was playing with me. That he'd asked me out on a dare from his friends, so I said no at first.'

'When did you say yes?' Eli asked.

Joan looked at him, eyes shining with tears. 'Almost five years later. He'd been away, in the army, seeing the world, and when he came back under a medical discharge he came straight to see me. He'd been writing me letters while he was away, telling me that the thought of me was what kept him going, and my feelings for him changed. So I said yes. I wished I'd said yes before, because then I could have had those five extra years with him. We were good together. Never a cross word.'

Charlie smiled. 'He told me that. He also told me that I had to tell you that he loved you. It was the last thing he said. His last thought was of you.' And she envied Stewie and Joan in that moment. To have had such a strong, enduring and powerful love that had spanned decades. They'd been lucky to find such a rare thing.

Joan nodded and sniffed, dabbing at her eyes with a handkerchief. 'I don't know how to live without him. We've never been apart since he came back. How do I do this now?'

'Everyone will help you, Joan. You know that,' Eli said. 'Vasquez won't let you be alone.'

She smiled sadly at him. 'They'll try, but at the end of the day, I'll be alone in our bedroom and one side of the bed will be empty—' Her voice broke on the word 'empty' and she began to sob.

Charlie broke all her rules and draped an arm around Joan's shoulder and Eli mirrored her on the opposite side, their arms touching as they comforted the older woman. She felt his hand graze hers. It was like a lightning strike and she shifted her hand away, her cheeks flaming. She tried to concentrate hard on Joan, but then Eli met her gaze and Charlie couldn't deal with it and stood up abruptly. Not knowing what to say. What to do. What did most people do in this situation?

'I'll get you a strong cup of tea.' She gave a smile to Joan and left the room, glad to be out of such an oppressive, emotional atmosphere. She'd wanted to comfort Joan and she had, but when Eli had mirrored her and his hand had brushed hers, she'd panicked, feeling that they were somehow more and that had scared the living daylights out of her! She was here to work and keep her distance and finish this contract, so she could move on, but Eli had somehow made her feel that she was being pulled further into his orbit and if she got too close, then what? She'd never leave Vasquez? That was an impossibility! That could never happen!

Here in this town, it was as if the Clarks, and Eli, especially, were the sun, And she were Icarus. She could not get too close, or she would get burned. It was just something that she felt implicitly. And she did not want to crash and burn because of him.

In the small kitchenette, she struggled to find tea. There was coffee, but *where was the goddamned tea*? Charlie rummaged through the cupboards, finally finding a box and adding a teabag to a mug. She had no idea if Joan had milk or sugar and so she prepped a small tray. Doing this helped. Being busy helped. Being away from that small room helped. Eli was a big man and his presence in that small room had felt suffocating to her, especially as she'd listened to Joan's story and empathised with her pain over not being with the man she loved for those lost five years.

Why had that story hit Charlie so hard?

She wasn't sure she wanted to examine that too much, if she was being honest with herself. Maybe it was because of the lost chances? Joan's lost five years with Stewie. Charlie's lost chance at being with her own family. Her biological parents, whoever they might be. Her lost chance at a successful marriage. Her lost chance at a successful relationship. Her lost ability to trust anyone. Her lost chance at giving Alice the father she so desperately deserved.

Joan's life was so different from hers. She'd been with one man and lived in the same place for years and it had been all that she needed.

Charlie had never had that and, though she told herself she didn't need it, maybe she did yearn for the simplicity of that kind of life? Could that ever be hers? Or were she and Alice doomed to be nomads for ever?

She took a slow walk back to the family room and she inhaled a long, deep breath before she knocked lightly and entered.

Eli and Joan were still sitting close together, Eli listening as Joan told a story about her husband.

Charlie laid the tray down on the low coffee table and sat and listened from a chair, away from the sofa that Eli and Joan sat upon. It was strategic. Protection. By distancing herself, maybe she'd get some clarity?

'Is there anyone I can call for you, Joan? Someone who can come and sit with you? Or take you home?'

Joan thought for a moment. 'I guess you could call my neighbour, Connie.'

'I'll get Diana to come and sit with you, until Connie arrives,' said Eli.

He and Charlie left the room together and Eli looked down at her. 'You sure you're okay?'

His concern for her was touching, but it was heady and dangerous, too. 'Absolutely!' She smiled as sweetly as she could, to imply confidence. 'I'll go fetch Diana.' And she turned and walked away from him, her breathing getting easier the further she went.

Eli was out chopping wood for his woodpile when his phone rang. He answered it and heard his mom on the other end of the line.

'Oh, Eli, I'm so glad you answered! I've got a little problem and wondered if you could fix it for me.'

'Sure. What's up?'

'Well, Charlie rang and apparently there's a leaking tap in her kitchen that won't shut off. She's tried to ring Pete, but he's gone to Fairbanks this week to visit his sister.' Pete was the local plumber. 'Could you pop on over to take a look?'

Go to Charlie's? Sure, he could do that. 'No problem. Let her know I'll be over there in about ten minutes.'

'You're a star.'

He laughed. 'I try.' Eli ended the call and put away his axe, after cleaning the blade. He quickly stacked the blocks of wood he'd chopped over on his winter woodpile and then grabbed his flannel shirt and shrugged it on. It was covered in little bits of wood and he brushed them off, grabbing his car keys.

It would be good to see Charlie and Alice again. He'd not seen Charlie's daughter since his mother's potluck, but he had heard about her. His mother had sung the little girl's praises, telling him how clever she was, how good at English and arithmetic she was. How she had a wonderful imagination and was a very neat painter. The little girl excelled, but the one thing his mom had noticed was that Alice pretty much kept to herself at school, the way she had at the potluck. Yes, she'd been with the other children, but she hadn't interacted much, as if she preferred to be by herself. 'I wondered if it's because they move around a lot. Alice told me there's no point in making friends properly, because they always leave,' she'd suggested.

That was odd. 'Maybe. She'll be okay,' he'd said, because Alice's mom was Charlie and Charlie was the most self-sufficient person he'd ever known. She was a strong, capable woman and no doubt she was raising her daughter to be the same way.

He arrived outside her cottage and switched off the engine, getting out of the vehicle and raising a hand in hello at Charlie's next-door neighbour, Angus, who was up a ladder fixing some guttering by the looks of it.

'Leaves?' he called out, trying to guess the blockage.

'Bird nest.'

Eli raised an eyebrow. 'Any eggs?'

'Not yet. Think I should leave it? Or evict them?'

Eli smiled. 'Your call, my friend.' At Charlie's front door, he set down his bag of tools and knocked.

From inside the cottage he could hear music. And then the door was being opened and there stood Charlie. She looked down at the bag as he reached for it.

'You're my plumber, too?'

'Your lucky day, huh?' He liked what she was wearing. She wore a tight-fitting black tee underneath a pair of loose-fitting khaki dungarees and around her hair she had a bright red headscarf. Some of her hair had escaped, loose brown tendrils that hung in gentle waves, and he felt a pang of something that could have been lust, but was most definitely attraction.

'You can fix taps as well as people?'

'Taps are easy.'

'Then you'd better come in.' She stepped back, her cheeks

flushing, averting her eyes as he passed and he smiled, glad
to know that he was having just as much of an effect on her.
It felt good to know he had an effect, because that meant she
was just as uncomfortable with the situation as he was.

'Where's Alice?'

'In her room.'

'Has she been bad?'

'No. She just likes to spend time in her room. I think she's
drawing, if you want to go say hi.' Clearly she did not expect
him to want to say hi.

But he did.

'That'd be great.' He walked down the small corridor that
led to the bedrooms, heading to the smaller one of the two
and noting Alice's name plaque on the door. He rapped his
knuckles against it.

'Come in!'

He pushed open the door. 'Hey, squirt. How are you doing?'

'Eli!' She put down her pencil and ran over to him and he
scooped her up and hefted her onto his hip.

'I think you've grown.'

Alice chuckled. 'Want to see my drawing? I'm making a
comic.'

'Sure.' He put her down again and she ran over to her table.

Behind him, Charlie leaned on the doorjamb. 'Since when
did you two become best friends?'

'Eli showed me some of his funny drawings at that potluck, Mom.'

'Did he, now? What kind of drawings?'

Eli looked up at her. 'Just dogs and chickens and how to
sketch in some basic shapes when she wants to create things,
so instead of, say, trying to draw a dog's outline from scratch,
you think about the shapes first. A rectangle for the body,

rectangles for the legs and tail, circles for the neck and head and then how she can construct her drawing on top of those.'

'She's five, Eli.'

He turned to her. 'Your daughter has a gift. Have you seen her drawings?'

'Of course I have!'

He smiled. 'Good. Then you should know that her skill level is way above that of any other five-year-old. You should nurture this.'

He could see in her eyes that she didn't like being told about her daughter in this way. As if he were criticising her for not noticing or something. 'I'm just trying to help, is all.'

'Then come help me in the kitchen. That is what you're here for.' She disappeared from view.

Eli smiled at Alice. 'While I'm fixing that tap, what are you going to draw for me?'

Alice beamed. 'What would you like?'

'How about a dragon?'

'With flames coming out of its mouth?'

'Sounds perfect. See you in a bit.' And he left Alice in her room and made his way to the kitchen, where Charlie was bustling about with mugs.

'Want a coffee?'

'If you're having one.'

He placed his bag of tools down on the floor and examined the kitchen tap. It was indeed dripping quite a lot. 'Probably just needs a new washer fitted. I should have it fixed in no time.'

'Great.'

Eli got busy opening up the cupboard beneath the sink to find the stopcock that would turn off the water supply while he worked. Then he stood and put the plug in the sink. 'Got a spare towel?'

'What for?'

'To place in the sink so I don't scratch it with anything.'

'Oh, okay.' She passed him a red-and-white-checked cloth.

Next he began to unscrew the tap.

'Who taught you all of this?' she asked, pouring hot water into two mugs and watching him closely.

'My dad.'

She nodded. 'Is he a handy guy?'

'Oh, yeah. A man with his fingers in many pies, but also a guy that likes to be hands on. When they did up the hotel he could have got in some tradesmen to do all the work, but he liked to save some jobs for himself. Plumbing, carpentry, electrics. He's a jack of all trades and master at every one.'

'He seemed a nice guy at the potluck.'

Eli looked at her and smiled. 'He is.'

There was a pause and then she said, 'You really got lucky, huh?'

He unscrewed the valve to access the washer and nodded, thoughtfully. 'I really did. Did you miss me when I'd gone?' He meant it as a joke.

But she looked at him oddly. 'Are you kidding me? It was lovely and quiet without you there. I could sleep easily without worrying if you'd put itching powder in my socks. I could go sit in the garden and not have you drop a water balloon on me from your room.'

He smiled ruefully at the memories, having forgotten half of the stuff he used to do. It seemed like a lifetime ago and maybe it was. The kids' home belonged to a previous life, almost as if it weren't his at all. But he remembered that day with the water balloon. He'd been messing about with the guys in their dorm and he'd been half soaked himself, then Cam, his bestie, had noticed Charlie sitting outside and dared him to drop one as close to her as possible, without actually hitting her.

He'd tried to back out of it. Said it wasn't right, that she'd hate it. Get mad. But then they'd started winding him up. Saying he must fancy her or something, and he hadn't needed that rumour starting, so he'd done it. He'd forced a laugh, as if he really hadn't cared, but he had. He'd not wanted to upset her and, as he'd suspected, she'd been furious. Storming inside, soaking wet, the yellow dress she'd been wearing stuck to her, and she'd screamed at him. Called him a whole load of names he wouldn't be comfortable saying in front of Alice.

Inside, he'd felt guilty, but because of Cam and the others he'd toughed it out. Acted as if he weren't bothered.

'I'm really sorry about that. Honestly. I never wanted to make you mad.'

'Well, you did.'

He nodded. 'Want to get even?'

She laughed. 'Strangely enough, I don't have any water balloons handy.'

'You have a garden hose.'

Charlie looked at him, incredulous. 'Don't be ridiculous.'

'I'm not.' He replaced the washer. It had worn through. He quickly reassembled the tap, turned the water back on and ran the tap. It worked perfectly. The water shutting off without a singular drip. 'I mean it.'

She laughed, not quite believing him.

So he decided to make her believe. He made a *watch this* face, then walked out to the back porch door, opened it and strode through into the back garden. He located the tap by the hose and turned it on, handed it to a bewildered Charlie and then stood in the middle of the lawn. Arms wide open, smiling right at her. Daring her. 'Do your worst.'

He was kidding, right? How had trying to fix a tap turned into this? It had been a simple Saturday morning, she'd been getting things done and then she and Alice were going to go for a walk around Vasquez later, to get better acquainted with the town. Maybe pop into the diner, because a patient during the week had told her that they made the most amazing pistachio ice cream and she knew that was one of Alice's favourites.

But then Gayle had offered to send Eli round to fix the tap and, though she'd not been happy about that fact, she'd accepted it. How long would it take, after all? Not long, right? He could be in and out within the hour and her day could carry on as normal.

But now he wanted her to douse him in water?

At the end of the hose was a nozzle that allowed her to alter the water. Spray. Mist. Soak. High Pressure. Low Pressure. She could use any one and clearly he wanted her to do it. Was offering her the chance to get even, but she stood there, hesitating.

'Come on! Get your revenge!' Eli laughed.

He was fully clothed! He was going to get soaked! But she recalled their arrival on the pier and how he'd waded into the bay to fetch her floating suitcase and the way he'd driven her to her new home in soaking-wet clothes. Clearly he didn't worry about things like that.

And there was a small part of her that wanted to get her own back.

She raised the nozzle and pointed it at him.

He smiled back at her, nodded. *Do it.*

Smiling, she reached forward and twisted the nozzle to high pressure—and then let him have it full blast.

Eli gasped as the cold water hit him squarely in the chest, but he didn't try to run, or to avoid the water stream, he just started to laugh and blow water droplets away from his face as it sprayed upwards, splashing him, and before Charlie knew it she was laughing, too. Laughing so hard she almost couldn't catch her breath. So that her stomach began to hurt and, once he was thoroughly drenched, she dropped the hose to the floor and put her hands on her knees to try and catch her breath.

She became aware that he had stepped close to her and she stood up and one look at his face had her laughing again, until he ran his hands through his long hair to get the wet strands from his face and she felt a punch of lust to the gut. The water was making his jeans and tee and flannel shirt stick to every delicious, muscled inch of him and suddenly it wasn't funny any more.

'Mom, what are you doing?' Alice asked from the back door.

Her head whipped round so fast. 'Nothing, honey. We had a bit of an accident with the hose.'

Alice giggled at the state of Eli.

'You'd better come in. Dry off. I can put your clothes in the dryer.'

'It's okay.'

'No. I can't let you drive around in wet clothes again. This seems to be a theme and I know how it feels, so...' She led him back into the cottage and pointed at the bathroom. 'There are towels in there. Bring your wet clothes when you come back out.'

He left wet footprints across the dark, hardwood floors and she mopped them over with paper towel, until he came back out, bare-chested, with a pink, fluffy towel wrapped around his waist.

His chest was magnificent. Developed pecs that were glorious to look at. Beneath, a six-pack that was enviable. Tight and bristling with muscle.

*Huh. I didn't think this through. Or did I?*

She felt an eyebrow raise and she couldn't stop herself from taking in every delicious inch of skin. She licked her lips and swallowed hard, smiling as she took his wet pile of clothes from him. 'Couldn't wear the bathrobe on the back of the door, huh?'

He smiled ruefully. 'It didn't fit.'

'Ah. Won't be a minute.' She took his clothes to the dryer room and popped them into the machine, praying that the thirty-minute economy cycle would be the fastest thirty minutes in the history of time. Perhaps she could hide out in the laundry room? It needed a little tidy and there was a pile of clothes there that needed folding. But she could hear Alice's bright voice showing Eli her dragon picture that she'd drawn, and leaving her daughter out there alone with a guy who had nothing on beneath his towel seemed wrong, even though she knew that Eli was a good guy.

'That's amazing, Ally! That fire looks great!'

He was calling her Ally? No one called her Ally. Her name was Alice. 'Let's see.'

Alice showed her the picture and, Charlie had to admit, it was pretty great. There was detail there that she would never have expected a five-year-old to have added—creases around the eyes, scales along the body. There was depth to the picture, so that it wasn't completely two-dimensional. 'Alice, this is amazing! You're so good!'

Alice beamed. 'Thanks. Will you put it on the fridge?'

'Better. I'll get it framed. Hang it on the wall and when you're a rich and famous artist, I'll be able to show people your early work.'

Her daughter chuckled and headed off back to her bedroom to draw some more.

'She's a good kid.'

'She's the best.'

'You're lucky.'

She glanced at him. A quick look was all she could safely manage. Anything longer meant her gaze lingered on his finer details and she didn't want to be focusing on anything like that, thank you very much. His nipples were exposed. That low V from his hipbones was visible. She swallowed hard. 'I am?'

'To have had Alice. To have started a family.'

'Well, you have one, too.'

He nodded. 'I do. And they're great. The best, actually.'

But he sounded sad about something and she couldn't work out why. If they were the best, then what did he have to be sad about? 'Wish they'd found you sooner?'

He met her gaze. Briefly. Before she felt her cheeks flame and she had to turn away. 'Sure.'

Charlie nodded, smiling, straightening the pile of magazines on the coffee table. 'Do you, er...want another drink? We didn't get to drink the last one.'

He straightened a leg, drawing her eye as it tracked his movement. She saw a thick, darkly haired leg and swallowed hard, imagining what it led up to.

'Coffee would be great, thanks.'

Charlie scurried into the kitchen, glad of the escape. She rinsed out the old mugs, washed them, dried them and began making coffee again. It gave her something to do with her hands. Made her feel purposeful. Calmed her. At least until he spoke and she realised he was leaning against the doorjamb in his towel, watching her. 'What made you come to Vasquez?'

She turned guiltily, spilling the milk on the floor. Damn! Why was she so clumsy around him? He was making her nervous. He had no right to make her nervous! 'Oh, you know. I fancied a change. Wanted to get away from the big city.'

'You always loved the city.'

She mopped the milk with paper towels, nodding. 'I did, yes, but sometimes you have too much of a good thing.' She stood again and dropped the paper towels into the trash.

He frowned. 'Can you?'

She glanced at him. A muscled, handsome god. He was the epitome of a good *thang*.

'Oh, yes.'

'What did you have too much of in Anchorage?'

What was this? The Spanish Inquisition? Her cheeks flamed at the thought of all she'd gone through with Glen. The way he'd put their relationship online. The secret videos he'd taken of the two of them, in their bedroom. The photos he'd taken of her without her consent, sharing them with his friends. The embarrassment. The *humiliation*.

Glen had thought it hilarious. Laughing at her when she'd turned up at his door, humiliated and furious. It was why she was so sensitive to being made fun of. It brought it all back and Eli was the champion of practical jokes. He wouldn't understand and nor would she tell him about it, because what if he tried to look her up online? He'd see it all and it was bad enough that her work friends at the last hospital she'd worked at—a place where she'd considered putting down roots for the first time—had seen them, forcing her to move away again. To resist the urge to settle. To keep on running. To keep on moving. Never giving anyone time enough to witness her shame. To know that she would always have to do this, if she was to keep her anonymity.

But Eli changed all of that, because she didn't have anonymity with him. He knew parts of her. They'd lived in the same building for years together and, whether you were close or not, that still allowed someone to know you.

'I don't really want to go into all of that.' She handed him the coffee mug and stepped away, almost as if he were poison. As if he was dangerous. And in a way, he was. It should be illegal to look the way he looked. She knew he worked at it. She'd seen him on that first day and he'd told her that he liked to start the day with a bit of cardio. But he made it look effortless. Easy. And she knew it was anything but. He'd not really been into fitness as a teenager. What had changed? Had he just seen all those guys on social media with six-packs? Or all those superhero movies where the guys were ripped and wanted to look the same? Was it ego?

'Why not? Did something happen?'

'You ask a lot of questions.'

'You avoid answering them.'

'Yes, well, maybe I don't want to share with you.'

He grinned. 'Oh, come now. I'm a good listener. A problem shared is a problem halved, or so they say.'

'Well, *they* say wrong. No amount of sharing will ever solve that issue. In fact *sharing* is what caused the issue in the first place.' The kitchen felt small with his hulking form in it and so she walked past him, irritated, into the living space and sat down, cradling her mug and hoping he'd change the subject.

Eli slowly followed her in and settled down in a chair opposite her. 'You know what I think you need?'

'What?' She sounded petulant and hated it. She didn't want

to be so irritated, or snippy, but Eli was creeping very close to the big open wound that she nursed on a daily basis.

'You need to relax.'

'Is that your official diagnosis, Doctor?'

He smiled. 'It is. You seem tense. Stressed. You need to experience the Vasquez beauty and chill out for a little while.'

'And how would I achieve that, exactly?'

'Next weekend. You, me and Alice, if you want, go for a drive up to Lawton Lake. I'll take the paddle boards, we'll have fun and then afterwards the beauty of the place will bring your blood pressure down a few notches. What do you say?'

It sounded amazing. But a whole day with Eli? Having fun? Spending time together deliberately? In a beautiful, secluded spot? Could be dangerous, too. But with Alice there…nothing would happen. So… 'All right. I've never tried paddle-boarding. I've always wanted to.'

'Then it's a date.' He smiled.

# CHAPTER SEVEN

ELI WOULD DESCRIBE himself as a guy who was comfortable in his own skin. He'd got to know his body quite well over the years, especially during his cancer treatment. He'd had so many scans he was amazed he didn't glow in the dark. And afterwards, when he'd pursued health and fitness? He'd got used to focusing on muscle groups, or improving his cardio-vascular system, or taking up yoga to stretch and breathe and focus. He made sure his body was a finely tuned machine and he was proud of it. Felt comfortable in it.

Until he had to wear a solitary towel at Charlie's house and knew he would have to control his thoughts.

Alice was about, for one, even if she was mostly in her room, but as he'd chatted with Charlie in the kitchen and stood close to her a couple of times, he'd felt a definite arousal at being around her and had had to cool his jets.

When she'd sat away from him, he'd taken a little sigh of relief, thanking his lucky stars and praying that the dryer would be finished soon, so he could get dressed, because the thought kept repeating in his head that he was nearly naked with Charlie Griffin and Charlie seemed utterly oblivious to the effect she was having on him.

She was most definitely his type. It was something he'd been aware of back in the orphanage, though he'd been able to hide it in the teasing and the jokes, and it was something he was most definitely aware of now. He'd not meant to ask her out like that. To imply a date of any kind. But she seemed so tense all the time and he knew that if she just sat back for a little while and let the beauty of Vasquez in, then she would feel herself unwinding.

She was wound tight right now. Prickly and unforgiving and he was interested in seeing what she'd be like if she let loose. He always had been.

He'd seen a brief image as she'd sprayed him with that water and collapsed with laughter and it had been in that moment, as the water had gushed at him and she'd been laughing, he'd seen a glimpse of the real Charlie.

And he really liked what he'd seen and wanted more.

Her eyes had sparkled, her mouth wide and her laughter? Her real laugh and not the polite one she used at work when she was humouring him? Oh, dear Lord, that laughter was moreish. He wanted to hear it again and again. He wanted to see her face relax, that broad smile, hear that lovely sound, but more than anything he wanted to be the cause of it. Wanted her to collapse with laughter into his arms and gaze up into his eyes and…

It was the same as when they'd been kids. He'd wanted to make her smile. Wanted to make her laugh, but she'd always seemed to react differently to him joking around and hadn't laughed the way the other kids had. He'd thought maybe the practical-joke route and clowning around weren't the way to her heart, and so he'd backed off for a bit, but then the Clarks had come and he'd been about to leave, and the only way he'd known to say goodbye was to play one last trick…

But he was an adult now and though the urge to revert to type was strong every time he looked at her, he also knew he had to approach her differently.

Charlie was skittish. Someone or something had hurt her and he knew how that felt. But Charlie wore her wound out in the open, whereas he hid his, under layers and layers of smiles and confidence so that something like that would never happen again.

Because he wouldn't allow it.

If you didn't put your trust in people, then they couldn't betray you.

Everyone put their trust in him. He was their doctor. He was a Clark now, and that was fine, because he knew he was dependable and he wanted people to trust him. He just couldn't do it in return, because that was harder and so he remained out in the open, armoured by his sense of humour.

From the utility room, there was a ping and then silence.

'Your clothes are dry!' Charlie got up so fast, he felt a wry smile cross his face, glad that she'd been just as uncomfortable with the situation as he'd been.

When she passed him his clothes they were warm and soft. 'Thanks.'

'I'll leave you to get dressed.' She gave him a smile and closed the door to the utility, so he had privacy.

Eli dropped the towel and put on his jersey shorts, then jeans, then tee, then flannel shirt. She must have put a scented dryer sheet in with the clothes because now he smelled like her, which was a little disturbing and not altogether unpleasant.

He scooped up the towel, folded it and placed it on a wooden rail. When he stepped out of the room, the relief on her face made him smile.

'Well, thank you for fixing the tap, Eli, and coming over so promptly. I appreciate that and I'd hate to take up more of your Saturday.'

'It was no problem. I guess I'll see you Monday?'

She nodded. 'You will.'

He grabbed his bag of tools from the kitchen. 'Say good-bye to Alice for me.'

'Of course.' She opened the front door and stood there expectantly, hoping, clearly, that he would just walk straight out and disappear.

But the urge to mess with her mind one last time surged forth in his brain. Having intently watched her deal with his inherent nakedness and the fact that he'd asked her and Alice to go paddle-boarding with him, he knew he couldn't just walk out.

He stopped right beside her, as he went to go. Smiled and then bent forward to kiss her on the cheek.

He hoped to see her cheeks flame with colour. They did.

He hoped she'd look a little awkward and not know where to look. She did.

He thought it would make him smile.

But brushing his lips over her soft, soft skin and inhaling the scent of her did strange things to his own insides, muddling his thoughts and confusing him, and it was almost as if he couldn't get his mouth to form the word goodbye.

All he could manage was a nod and then he was stepping out into the clean Vasquez air and away towards his truck.

As he got behind the wheel, he was still mulling over how it had felt to kiss her.

But more importantly, he was disturbed by the urge he'd had to press his lips to hers and kiss her as she'd never been kissed before.

# CHAPTER EIGHT

'I CAN'T TELL you how nice it is to have a lady doc back again,' said Teresa Muller, who sat in front of Charlie in her own consultation room. Her time shadowing Eli was over and she was familiar with the layout of this place and how Eli liked things done. 'I love Eli to bits, but sometimes you just like to talk to another girl, you know?'

Charlie nodded. 'And what can I do for you today?'

Teresa sighed. 'Well, I think I'm at that age in which I might need a little something-something.'

Teresa was fifty-one. 'What exactly do you need me to help you with?'

'Hormones! That replacement stuff.' Teresa leaned in and whispered, 'I think I'm in menopause.'

'Okay. What have your symptoms been?'

'Where do I begin? I get those hot-flash things. Feel like someone's turned the heating way up high in the middle of my chest. It creeps up my neck, makes me go bright red, I begin to sweat like I'm in a sauna.' Teresa leaned in again. 'I'm no oil painting to begin with, but when one of those things begins, I look and feel awful! Don't do my marriage no favours, let me tell you, and that's the other thing.' She began to whisper again. 'It's gone funny. *Down there.*'

'You're experiencing dryness?'

'Damn straight! Makes no sense, when I've got so much

water pouring out of my head and down my back, that down there is drier than the Sahara. It hurts when we…you know! And my Greg, he's a patient, understanding man, but I've had to tell him to stop so many times, because it hurts, he's started not even trying to initiate…well…you know.'

'Have you tried lubrication?'

'I ordered some online and it does help, but it takes the romance out of it, when you have to stop to use it first, you know? I'm hoping those replacement hormones might give me back some of my go-go juice, if you'll pardon the expression.'

Charlie smiled. 'Any other symptoms?'

'Does a bear poop in the woods? I'm tired. My body aches. Sometimes I can't remember anything anyone's told me. I get headaches. Ratty. That's the other thing. My Greg says I can go from happy and smiley to grizzly bear in an instant!'

'So you've noticed a change in your mood?'

Teresa nodded. 'I have and he's right. I just want to be *myself* again, Charlie. I can't remember what it's like to just be me. To just live and not worry. It's just… I feel like I'm losing myself and that's a scary thing. Becoming someone you don't recognise.'

Charlie could understand. She'd like to just live and be the woman she was before Glen ruined her life. Since the humiliation of Glen putting all that stuff out there on the Internet and she'd practically gone into hiding, she didn't like who she'd become, either. She'd always been a little bit twitchy, but since the disaster with him, it had got worse.

She did some basic observations on Mrs Muller, checking her blood pressure, her height, her weight. She read up on her patient's history and saw there was no family history of blood clots, breast cancer or strokes. 'You'll need to check your breasts monthly and make sure you attend all your mammogram appointments. HRT is safe, but some cancers respond to the hormones, so you need to be vigilant. Keep using the lubrication, but this should kick in soon and begin to help in that direction. We'll start you on a low dose and see how you go. Come and see me again in three months and we'll reassess. See if we need to raise it, or if it's causing any problems.'

'Thanks, Charlie. You're an absolute doll. What do you think of Vasquez? Beautiful, huh?'

She nodded. 'It most certainly is.'

'You staying long, or...?'

'I'm just covering Nance's maternity leave.'

'Well, I like you. I think you're very nice and you've been very helpful, too. I hope we can make you stay. You never know!' Teresa stood, grinning, and walked to the door.

'You never know,' she agreed. Hiding in Vasquez for the rest of her life. How would that look? How would that feel? Was it even a possibility, with Eli here?' Probably not. Nance would come back eventually, right? And then she wouldn't have a job and this was such a small town, there weren't any other medical facilities she could work at.

The likelihood was she would be moving on from here at the end of her contract. Not back to Anchorage, though. She couldn't face people there. It would just be tricky. So somewhere else, then. But where? It would all depend on what job opportunities there were.

She had no more patients waiting after Teresa Muller. So she typed up her notes, cleaned down her room and decided she'd go make herself a coffee. See if anyone else had any interesting cases.

As she passed Eli's consulting room, she could hear his voice and she stopped when she heard him laugh out loud.

Her tummy was doing strange things as she lingered by

his door, remembering yesterday when he'd seemed to linger slightly after dropping that kiss on her cheek when he'd said goodbye. Her tummy had done strange things then, too. She'd not known where to look. She certainly hadn't been able to meet his eyes, but then he'd been striding away from her, down the path, towards his truck and she'd been mesmerised by the way the wind caught his long hair, the way he moved, the way his eyes briefly met hers before he got inside his vehicle.

It had been like a lightning strike.

Had he really just been practically naked in her home for half an hour?

*How on earth did I get through that?*

Charlie was so lost in her reverie, she didn't notice that the voices inside the room had changed from conversational to ones of people saying goodbye and suddenly the door to Eli's room was opening and, because she'd been leaning against it, listening, lost in her thoughts, she practically stumbled in.

'Oh! Sorry, I was…er…' Her brain scrambled for an excuse as Eli and a silver-haired old gentleman stared at her quizzically and with wry amusement, as if they knew *exactly* what she'd been doing. 'I was just about to knock.'

*There. That seems believable, right?*

'Oh? You need me for something?' Eli asked.

He came to stand by her as his patient doffed his cap at her and said, 'Good morning, miss.'

After the patient had gone, Charlie quickly realised that her mouth wasn't going to work properly, especially as her brain seemed to have stopped functioning. 'Yes, um…it's about next weekend. I don't think I'm going to be able to make it.'

'Oh.'

He looked disappointed, which made her feel…what?

'Yeah, it's just what with Alice being in school now and everything, I don't get to see her and spend time with her as often as I'd like and the weekends are usually our special time and...'

She could see that he was smiling again, almost as if he was tolerating her. That he could see she was using Alice as an excuse. Her voice trailed off. 'Why are you smiling?'

'You're freaking out because I said it's a date. I didn't mean it as a *date* date. Like romance and asking you out. I meant it as *Okay, we've agreed to go paddle-boarding.* I swear to you, I'm not going to try to seduce you.'

'Good. I'm glad, because you would have failed,' she said, feeling a little disappointed that he could so easily dismiss the idea of being on a date with her. That maybe she'd been wrong to imagine all the things she'd imagined, but she always had had a very active imagination.

'If I was going to seduce you, I would have done it yesterday, when I wasn't wearing anything but a towel,' he said seductively, moving closer to her, causing her to take a step back as her cheeks flamed.

She smiled nervously. Wanting to back further away, but the doorjamb was in the way and she collided with it awkwardly. Her brain flooded with the images of him from the weekend. Chest bare. Strong arms on show. His powerful legs and that pink, fluffy towel wrapped tightly around his waist. How his mere physical presence had felt, so close to her in her own home.

Had he meant, just now, to remind her of that moment? Knowing that she would remember how he looked, just to make her blush? Had he mentioned seduction to make her imagine how he might do it? Had he stepped closer to her to see if she would step back?

Was all this just another joke to him? A wind-up? Because that wasn't fair!

'That's good to know,' she managed to say, but her voice didn't sound like her own, it sounded strangled, as if her throat were closing up. His proximity doing alarming things to her blood pressure and pulse rate. And had it got hot in here? Had the air conditioning broken down, somehow?

And then he smiled and stepped away again, as if pleased that he'd had the reaction he'd wanted from her, pleased that she'd amused him, and she didn't like feeling as though she was a plaything. 'I'll take Alice paddle-boarding by myself, if you don't mind,' she said, trying to control the rising anger in her.

'All right.'

Oh. She'd expected him to put up more of a fight. When he didn't, she felt a little deflated.

He'd been testing a theory. Needing to know how she'd react, whether she was as affected by him as he was affected by her.

There was something between them and it wasn't just their shared history. There was something more and he could feel it. It was palpable whenever they were close, or in the same room, especially. It had been there for him when they were kids, but it hadn't been as powerful then, it had just been a crush thing that he'd felt he had to deal with and then forget about when he'd moved away to Vasquez, adopted by the Clarks.

He'd never forgotten Charlie. How could he? She'd been the first girl he'd ever wanted. She was always going to be a piece of his history and that was where he'd relegated her memory.

To history.

But now she was here and, though he knew he had nothing

to offer her in the future—she'd always mentioned wanting a large family of her own and he couldn't give her that—he was still sorely tempted by her. One moment he'd be telling himself to just leave it alone. Let her work out her contract and go. But then later, another voice would kick in and tell him to pursue something with her. Let her know in no uncertain terms that what he was offering was temporary but that they both could have some fun, until it was time to leave. Sweeten the history between them.

And so when she'd practically fallen into his office, as if she'd been eavesdropping at the door, he'd wondered why she'd been there. Was she intrigued by him, as attracted to him as he was to her? He'd just had to know, and seeing the look of embarrassment and the way her cheeks had flamed and how fast her pulse had been throbbing at her throat had told him that he was onto something for sure.

He'd kept himself restrained at the weekend, because of Alice's presence, but when they were alone...? That was different.

The only question was...would Charlie want something with no strings attached? Was she that type of person? Or was she so tightly strung, as she appeared to be, that she wouldn't be able to cut loose with him for a while?

He didn't want to use her. He wanted her to get as much out of their short time together as he would. He thought they'd be a great fit together and he knew he would treat her with respect and that somehow, at the end, they would go for a drink and clink their glasses together and toast what fun they'd had. Knew how they'd hug each other and say goodbye on the pier before she flew off with Chuck to go back to the big city.

And then he paused, thinking hard.

Saying goodbye...the thought made him still. Could he

lose her for a second time? Would he be able to watch her walk away?

He'd be able to do it. Wouldn't he? He could put whatever they had in a box and push it to one side. He'd have to.

'But it was very kind of you to offer.'

He looked up at her and smiled, nodding.

'I have another offer for you.'

She looked wary. 'Oh?'

'Come on in. Take a seat. You might want to close that door,' he said with a grin, feeling his heart race madly, knowing that if he asked and she said no, then this whole thing was going to be mighty embarrassing. But what did he have to lose?

# CHAPTER NINE

SHE WATCHED HIM walk behind his desk and sit down, so after she'd apprehensively closed the door, wondering what this was all about, she did the same, sitting opposite.

Eli gave her an appraising look, a broad smile across his face. 'I think we should get married.'

Charlie stared at him and went still. She didn't blink. She didn't breathe. But internally, her heart raced, her blood pressure went up and adrenaline and cortisol flooded her body. *'What?'*

'I think we should get married,' he said again, watching her intently with amusement.

'This is one of your jokes again, isn't it?' She laughed wryly, but without humour. 'Typical Eli. Always out for a laugh. Well, I don't need it.' She got up out of her chair, glad to see that her legs were still working after that initial shock.

'Okay, okay!' He laughed. 'That was a joke. I couldn't help it, you looked so…tense.'

'I wonder why?' she said, heart still thudding.

'I apologise. Do you forgive me?'

He looked at her with such sweet, imploring eyes, she felt her anger begin to fade. Part of her did not want to forgive him at all! But another, more logical part knew that she still had to work with him for a while longer and work would be a whole lot easier if they were getting along. 'Fine. But only if you're going to be serious.'

'Life's too short for serious. You have to have fun sometimes.'

'Do you really have something you want to talk to me about?'

He nodded. 'I do.'

'Well, get on with it, then! The clinic could be filling with patients.'

He tapped a couple of keys on his keyboard, then turned his screen so she could see. Apparently Eli could access the security cameras in the waiting room. And the waiting room itself? Was empty. There was no way she could leave by saying she had a patient waiting.

'What do you want to talk to me about, Eli?'

'I do want to talk about us, that bit is true.'

*Us.*

What did he want? Was he going to probe into their pasts? Talk some more about what it had been like together as kids? Or was he going to talk about her being here? That there didn't seem to be enough work for two people sometimes and that maybe he'd made a mistake in asking her here? And that last unexpected thought suddenly terrified her. Because, as much as she hated knowing that Eli knew about her past, the idea of leaving Vasquez was scary. Probably because Alice was settling so well into kindergarten and was loving every minute of Mrs Clark's classes. Probably because she had nothing else in the pipeline just yet. Probably it was because, despite the overfamiliarity of the residents of Vasquez, she had never felt so welcomed anywhere. Probably it was because when she lay in bed alone at night, she harboured secret thoughts of what it might be like to actually settle here.

'Us?'

'Yes. I like you, Charlie, and I think you like me, too.' He smiled, waiting for her response.

'You're not too bad, I guess.'

'I don't mean as friends.'

'You mean as…work colleagues?'

'No. I do not. I mean I think I want to talk about the fact that we're both attracted to one another.' He was searching her face, looking for clues that she agreed with him.

He was right. She was attracted to him. But she didn't normally just come straight out and tell a guy that. She usually let them buy her a drink. Take her out on dates. It was something done gradually. Incrementally. Each date either increasing or decreasing that attraction until it reached critical level and they either fell into bed with one another or split up. Or she moved away.

She never just admitted it out loud.

It felt weird.

'Well, that's the elephant in the room,' she said, not sure what else to say.

'I thought it best to acknowledge it. I'm a straightforward guy.'

'Are you saying this because you mean it? Or are you saying this because you can't actually go out with anyone in Vasquez, because, technically, they're all your patients and that would be stepping over a line?'

He got up out of his chair and came to stand by her. Looking down at her. Intensity in his eyes.

His proximity caused her heart to race again.

'Because I mean it and I think we're two responsible adults, who both have a bit of freedom, who could maybe take advantage of that attraction.'

She stood up to face him, not liking how it felt to have him tower over her like that. She wanted to feel stronger. More assured. Even though her mouth had gone dry and her palms had gone sweaty. 'I thought you said you weren't trying to seduce me,' she whispered.

'I'm not. I'm talking about us both using the time we have together to enjoy a bit of…adult fun. No strings attached. No life getting in the way and when it's over, it's over. We part as friends and with some pretty excellent memories of the time we shared together.'

'You're talking about a fling?'

He took another step closer. His gaze drifting down towards her lips as he smiled 'I'm talking about a fling. So, Charlie Griffin. What do you say to my…proposal?'

She should slap him across the face. Maybe accuse him of sexual harassment? And if she did then he would profusely apologise and make sure he scheduled their work so she didn't have to be there at the same time as him, if that would make her day and time here easier.

He was prepared for both.

But she did neither. For a while, she just stared at him and he could tell her mind was racing with possibilities. Possible actions. Possible responses.

She was fighting an internal battle and he wondered which side would win. The side that just wanted to work out her contract and get away from Vasquez as quickly as she'd arrived? Or the side that was attracted to him and wondered what it might be like if she was brave enough to take this further?

'This…fling…it would be private between us?' Her cheeks had reddened.

'It would. Unless you wanted otherwise.'

'You wouldn't worry about people finding out?'

'I have nothing to hide. Would you be worried about people finding out?'

She blinked. 'Alice. I don't want there to be a string of men in her mother's life that she has to call Uncle.'

So she was seriously contemplating this.

'And this isn't a joke?' she asked.

'Maybe I could prove it?'

'How?'

'By kissing you. And then you could tell me afterwards, if I truly meant it. If it felt real. And if you had any doubts about my intent afterwards, you could end it as quickly as it began.'

She blushed and looked away. 'A kiss?'

'One kiss.' He stepped closer, desperate to touch her. Desperate to stroke her cheek with his finger. To run his hands into her hair. To hold her against him. 'A fair test, wouldn't you say?'

'I could say a lot of things.'

'Charlie?'

'What?'

'Say yes. To a single. Solitary. Mind-blowing kiss.' His voice had grown husky as his desire for her increased.

She looked up at him, deeply into his eyes, searching for something. To see if he was still, somehow, joking? To make sure he was serious? But there was something else there.

Desire.

Charlie wanted this—he could tell. She was just trying to work out how to give herself permission.

Her hand suddenly rose and she pressed it upon his chest and he hoped she could feel how fast his heart was beating for her. Her fingers spread slightly and her hand moved over his pectoral muscle and stilled.

*Thump-thump.*

*Thump-thump.*

Her touch made him want to do a thousand things to her. To take her in his arms and push her up against the wall. To rip her blouse out of her waistband and allow his hands to explore her soft flesh. To taste her. To hear her groan with pleasure.

But he'd made a promise. Just a kiss.

One kiss.

A smile hesitantly touched her lips. 'All right. One kiss.'

Triumphant, he slowly began to lean in.

The smile broadened. 'Let's see what you can do,' she whispered.

Eli grinned. 'Challenge accepted.'

And he slowly pressed his lips to hers.

# CHAPTER TEN

IT WAS ALL just going to be pretty wrapping. Wasn't it? That was what she told herself before the kiss. That all the muscles, the tattoos, the long, dark brown, Viking-esque hair, the smile, the twinkle in the eyes, were all dressing and that maybe, once she kissed him, she would be able to relax and realise that that was all it was. Because there wouldn't be any depth. There wouldn't be any *feelings* and once it was proved, once and for all, she'd be able to put this irritating attraction that she had for Eli to bed.

But she was wrong.

So *incredibly* wrong.

It wasn't just aesthetics. It wasn't that he was just so tall, and so broad and so strong. His lips touched hers, so softly at first. Tenderly. Tentatively. A whisper of his lips against hers. A brush that promised a heat. An awakening of the senses.

And then it all changed.

Everything. Dizzying. All at once. An overwhelming feeling as his tongue passed by her lips and entered her mouth, and the knowledge that he had penetrated her somehow, that she had allowed him access because she wanted it, seemed to stir something within her as the kiss deepened.

Her hands came to rest against his chest, without her realising, as the rest of the world dropped away and all that seemed to matter was the two of them, pressed against one another as she tasted him. Feeling the brush of his light beard against her skin. Inhaling the scent of him, her senses going into overdrive, every nerve ending alive and expectant of more.

And as she sank into him, as she allowed herself to enjoy and experience his kiss, to yearn for more, to yearn to feel his flesh beneath her fingertips, he pulled back and away and stared at her, smiling. Leaving her breathless. Wanting more. Why had he stopped? Was this another joke?

No…it wasn't a joke. His eyes were dark with desire.

The attraction was real and she wanted him.

And he was offering himself to her if she wanted it.

No strings attached, he'd said.

She felt stunned by his kiss. A little wild inside as if she wanted to lock the door behind him, sweep everything off his desk and have wild and crazy sex with him, right there, in that very room.

His offer would allow her to sate her desires and then leave again, with no complications, because there'd be no way she was going to fall for Eli. This was lust, pure and simple, right? It was all it could be. But she'd allowed herself to trust a guy before and her instincts had been wrong. He'd secretly filmed her. Had hidden cameras. Had put that stuff on the Internet and Alice might grow up and one day see it. She didn't think she had the misfortune of running into two guys exactly the same. She didn't think Eli would have cameras anywhere, but…this was his office and maybe she could have what she wanted, without putting herself at risk?

'That was a good kiss.'

His smile increased. 'I'm glad.'

'But this is our workplace and we can't do anything here.'

'We just did. Look, come paddle-boarding with me. Come

up to Lawton Lake. It's quiet up there. Isolated. We could have some time alone.'

'What about Alice?'

'I can behave myself around your daughter. But I'd like to spend time with you, even if I can't touch you.'

She frowned. 'It's that easy?'

'Stopping myself from touching you? No.' He reached up to stroke her face, had another thought and pulled her close once again, more forceful this time, as if knowing his moments with her would have to be brief.

She sank into the kiss once again, amazed once again as to how the world fell away, all her cares disappearing. Moaning softly, her desire rocketing high, she reached to pull up his shirt, needing to feel his flesh beneath her fingertips, when suddenly, there was a knock at his door and someone was opening it and they broke apart so quickly. Guiltily.

Dot, the receptionist, put her head around the door.

Had she seen? Did she know what they'd been doing?

But Dot's face remained normal. 'Eli? Printer's playing up again. Can you come and give it your magic touch?'

Eli nodded. 'Of course!' He passed Charlie by and she pressed her fingertips to her lips, before smiling at Dot.

'Tech problems?'

'Always. But Eli can fix anything.' Dot looked her up and down. 'And anyone.' She smiled.

The rest of the week passed in a blur. Charlie worked hard and saw a wide variety of patients. A young child who had hurt their hand after grabbing an iron that was cooling down. A case of pneumonia. A spider bite that had become infected. She was enjoying herself immensely here in Vasquez—the range of health queries and injuries that came through their doors at the clinic was wide and varied, from the normal and everyday to the crazy, like the guy who came in after he'd actually tried to juggle a chainsaw and the even younger guy who'd climbed a tree, slipped and fallen through the branches, impaling himself on a stick. Her eyes had nearly dropped out of her head when he'd come walking in through the sliding doors, half a branch sticking out of his abdomen, smiling self-consciously. The kid had been lucky. The branch hadn't gone through any of his major organs, but rather than remove the branch themselves, in case it was blocking any major bleeders, they had stabilised him and flown him out to a major hospital.

It was strange working in the same building as Eli, passing him in the corridors, sharing a secret smile with him around the other staff. Occasionally their hands would brush as they passed each other in the corridor and every single time her body lit up like a fourth of July parade. Once, he'd even pulled her into a linen cupboard, just to kiss her, and when they'd both emerged... It was fair to say they'd both looked a little ruffled. The anticipation of their snatched moments was adrenaline-fuelled. Hiding. Trying to act normal around everyone else.

Her dreams at night filled with him and what it might be like to actually *be* with him. Physically. Her dreams had become so erotic at one point, she'd woken up so aroused that she'd had to take a very long and very cold shower before she could drop Alice off at school and then go into work.

Mrs Clark greeted her every morning that she dropped Alice off and Charlie would smile and feel awkward that her daughter's teacher had no idea about all the sinful and naughty thoughts she was having about her adopted son.

But all the stolen glances, all the thoughts, all the yearnings... they were all adding up into something quite exciting and, though

Charlie was still scared, she'd not had this much fun in ages. Because she knew it wasn't just aesthetics any more.

He looked good.

He tasted good.

His kisses and his touch were amazing.

She could only hope and imagine that the rest was just as mind-blowing.

The weekend came around quickly and the day that she would be going up to Lawton Lake with him. She woke, her body fizzing with nerves, her hands trembling with so much anticipation she dropped her tube of toothpaste in the sink and she could barely floss her teeth.

But when she went to wake up Alice, her daughter looked pale and ill.

'Mommy, I don't feel well.'

Instantly, her nerves dissipated as a new concern entered her brain and took prime position. 'What's wrong?'

'My tummy hurts.'

Lots of kids got tummy aches. This was probably nothing. But if Alice was ill, they couldn't go out today. It was her first time being in kindergarten and she was being exposed to a whole new plethora of germs and bacteria, it was no wonder she was ill.

*I should have expected this.*

'Do you feel sick?'

A nod.

'Okay, honey. Well, we won't go out today, then. Don't you worry about that.'

'I wanted to go paddle-boarding with Eli.'

'So did I. But that lake won't disappear and maybe we could do it next weekend? I'll call Eli and let him know, you just rest. Here.' She passed her daughter her tablet. 'Why don't you watch some cartoons? Take your mind off it. I'll go get you a drink and some dry toast, in case you want to try and eat.'

She felt disappointed, yet also somehow relieved. Charlie had wanted Eli, yes, but the last time she'd fallen for a guy, he'd turned out to be wholly unreliable and weird and, though Eli was nothing like the last one, there had still been that fear that she was rushing into something again, just because of an infatuation. And doubt was an insidious drug, too. Maybe starting something with, not only her work colleague, but her boss was a dangerous thing?

Maybe this was life telling her that this thing with Eli shouldn't get off the ground at all? That they'd had their fun. They'd shared spectacular kisses and fumbles in closets and that would have to be enough.

Downstairs, she picked up her phone and rang him.

He answered straight away. 'Hi.'

'Hey, Eli, listen, I'm sorry, but we won't be able to make it today.'

'Oh.' He sounded incredibly disappointed. 'Are you having second thoughts?'

'No.' She smiled, even though it was partly a lie. 'But I do have an ill Alice. She's woken up with a bad tummy and feels sick. I guess I should have expected something like this, what with her having started school, but I need to stay here and look after her.'

'Of course. Do you need anything?'

'No, no. We're fine. I'm sorry we've had to put off our weekend.'

'Well, the lake isn't going anywhere, so maybe another time?'

She smiled. She'd said the exact same thing to her daughter. 'Absolutely, unless…'

'Unless what?'

'Unless this is a sign that maybe we shouldn't be doing it at all?'

'You believe in signs?'

She shrugged. 'I don't know. Maybe?'

'Okay. Well, is it a sign that you want to follow?'

She thought of him. Of his kisses. His lips. His tongue.

*Dear God, his tongue...*

Of the way he made her feel all excited and that everything had possibilities. That she wanted to feel that way again. 'No.'

There was a silent pause. 'Good. I'm glad. Want me to come round? I could sit with you. Help you take care of her.'

'I don't know if that's a good idea.'

'I can help. And I promise to control myself in front of your daughter.'

She liked that he was offering to help. And this way? She could still see him. 'Okay.' She smiled.

# CHAPTER ELEVEN

HE CALLED IN to the shop first. Bought ice lollies, jelly and some plain dry crackers for Alice. Then he picked up some items for himself and Charlie. They might not be able to go to Lawton Lake, but he was still determined that they would have a good day together.

When he arrived at her door, she opened it with a smile and he raised his bag of shopping. 'I've brought supplies.'

'How long do you think you're staying?' she asked with a quiet laugh.

'Long enough for you to be glad I called round.'

She stepped back. 'Come on in.'

He waited for the door to be closed, then he turned to her. 'Where's Alice?'

'In her room. Sleeping.'

'She okay?'

'It's just a virus, or something.'

He smiled and stepped towards her. Bent his head towards her to let her know he was coming in for a kiss, now that he'd clarified the fact that Alice wouldn't see.

The smile on her face was enough for him to know that his kiss was welcome and he pressed his lips to hers. She let out a small groan in her throat that did all kinds of exciting things to his insides, that told him she'd been looking forward to this.

Because so had he. The thoughts of spending this Saturday

with her at Lawton Lake had been all he could think about. He'd imagined getting them both on their paddle boards, teaching them how to balance. How to get back on their board when out on the water, if they fell in. The water at the lake was notoriously calm. Flat. It was the perfect place for them to learn and the scenery around it, breathtaking. But he'd known he wouldn't need to look around to have his breath stolen away. Being with Charlie would do that and so he didn't need to be at a lake. He didn't need to be in a secluded place with her. He just needed her to be close by. And now...? With her lips pressed to his and her body sinking against his...?

When the kiss ended, she was smiling, which made him smile, too.

'Want a drink?'

'You do make me thirsty,' he said.

She laughed. 'Come through to the kitchen. You can show me what you've got.'

'I could show you right here.'

'The bag, silly! You've been to the shop?'

He growled. He'd known exactly what she'd meant, but he hadn't been able to resist. Following her through to the kitchen, he laid the bag on the counter and got out all the goodies he'd bought. Alice's supplies, a rosé wine, cheeses and meats for a charcuterie board, baguettes, fruit, chips, ice cream.

A huge teddy bear.

'Wow.'

'I thought we could have a picnic in the back yard.'

'Great idea. Coffee?'

'Sure.'

She set about making them both a drink and he watched her move about the kitchen. Now that they had a new understanding between them, he felt able to openly watch her and concentrate on her. There were no other eyes watching them. No one making assumptions. Their fling, their relationship, whatever you wanted to call it, was theirs alone. And she was beautiful to watch. His. He liked that.

While the coffee machine did its thing, he reached out for her hand, taking her fingers in his and pulling her close, up against his body. She looked up at him, mildly amused, her eyes sparkling with mischief. 'Something I can do for you?'

'Plenty of things.'

'Such as?'

He smirked. 'Don't poke the bear, Charlie. Not with your daughter just in the next room. I've woken from hibernation and I want to feed. I want to feed a lot and you just happen to be the snack I want to feast on.'

'Tell me what you want to do to me, then,' she said, teasingly, smiling, looking up at him through thick, lush lashes, her lips parted, the glimpse of her tongue, wet and slick, giving him all sorts of X-rated ideas.

He groaned softly. 'I want to know we have a space that is just our own. No interruptions. Nothing else to worry about but each other's pleasure.' He stroked her cheek with the back of his finger. 'I want to be able to slowly undress you and marvel at every inch of your skin. Touch every inch. Your beautiful neck. This collarbone.' His finger trailed down the slope of her throat, brushing aside her top to reveal her clavicle. 'I want to reveal every delicious part of you. Slowly. Admire you. Kiss you. Taste you.'

He could see her breathing was increasing. Felt her push herself against him.

'I want to take my time over you. Discover what makes you breathe hard. What makes you gasp. What makes you arch your back. What makes you move against me as you beg for more. As you beg me not to stop.' He dropped a soft kiss on her collarbone, inhaled her dreamy scent and then backed off, remembering his promise. Remembering that they weren't alone. That her daughter was in the next room and that no matter how much he wanted to take this further, he could not. He sucked in a deep breath. It wasn't easy moving away from her. Not when he wanted her so badly. It was taking an enormous amount of control, especially since he'd been waiting for this weekend so badly.

She looked disappointed that he moved away, but understanding too. And he saw that she respected him for controlling himself. Charlie cleared her throat. 'Okay. Well, I look forward to us finding a place that's just our own.'

He nodded and smiled. 'Can I go see her? Say hello?'

'Sure.'

They both needed the distraction. They both needed to remember the priority here. It was Alice. Not what they wanted physically. And he didn't want Charlie to think that he was only with her because he hungered for her body. He liked her. Really liked her. Always had. But Charlie had a daughter now and he liked Alice too. She was a great kid.

He knocked on her bedroom door.

'Come in.'

Grinning broadly and holding the huge teddy bear he'd bought, he poked his head around the door. 'Hi. How you doing? Your mum tells me you're not feeling too great.'

Alice's eyes landed on the bear and widened as she sat up in bed. 'Is that for me?'

'Sure is. A friend for Mr Cuddles.' He passed the bear over and smiled as she hugged it tight. He remembered being her age. Young and in care already, he'd always had dreams of someone turning up one day, maybe on his birthday, with a big bear and a load of gifts that were just for him, that let him know that there was someone out there who cared. That maybe his life so far had been a terrible mistake and they'd not meant to leave him at a fire station when he was a baby. That someone would come and rescue him and let him know that actually he was a prince from a far-off country.

Of course, it never happened. He never got gifts and so he started making his own fun. It was the only way to brighten his day and try to make him forget how lonely and alone he actually was.

Luckily Alice didn't have to experience any of that. She had a mom. She wasn't in a kids' home and she was loved very much. And looking around her room, he saw she had plenty of stuff. Toys, plushies, games, books. He wondered if Charlie had ever felt the same way, too.

'What's his name?' Alice asked.

'I don't know. I think maybe you ought to name him.'

Alice turned the bear to look at his face properly. 'He looks like a Sprinkles.'

Eli grinned. 'Great name! Sprinkles it is.' He looked around her room. Saw her sketch pad on the table. 'You been drawing?'

She nodded.

'Can I take a look?'

Another nod.

He picked up her pad and began to flick through the pages. There was the usual stuff. Cats. Dogs. A unicorn that had been coloured in with a multitude of bright, rainbow colours. And then he came across a drawing that made him smile even more. 'Is that *me*?'

Alice had drawn a picture that was clearly herself, her

mom, and a seaplane floating on water, with a man wading through water to reach a case. She'd drawn him big, as if he was a giant, with masses of long, wild hair, and he had a huge smile on his face. He liked it very much.

'Do you like it? You can keep it, if you want.'

He thanked her. 'All great artists *sell* their work. They don't just give it away. I tell you what—I'll give you five dollars so I can put it on my fridge.' He reached into his pocket and pulled a note from his wallet and placed it on her bedside table.

'Mom! Eli gave me five dollars for my drawing!'

Behind him, Charlie walked across the room from her position in the doorway and ruffled her daughter's hair, before laying a hand on her forehead to test her temperature. 'I heard! That's great! You should put it in your little safe and when you're better you can spend it on something nice.'

'I'm already feeling better.'

'You feel it. No temperature. Why don't you go out in the garden and get some fresh air for a bit?'

'Okay.' Alice swung her legs out of bed and grabbed her bathrobe, slid her feet into slippers shaped like bunnies and headed on out.

Charlie turned to look at him. 'That was very sweet. You didn't have to pay her for her drawing.'

'I believe in nurturing talent and she's got one.'

'She's five.'

'And already drawing like a twelve-year-old. Who knows where she'll be in a few years' time?'

He wouldn't know. Because she and Charlie would be leaving in a few months' time. It was painful to think about. Sad.

'Maybe you can call me one day and tell me? I'd like to know how she's doing.'

The idea that they wouldn't be around…that he wouldn't…
was sobering.

'You don't have to do that, you know.'

'Do what?'

'Show an interest in my kid because you're interested in
me.'

'I'm not. I like Alice and I can tell she's something special.' He frowned. 'You never drew. Who does she get that
creativity from? Her father?'

Instantly, he saw the walls come up as her hackles raised.
Clearly the father was a difficult subject.

'Glen would consider himself an artist, sure. But I didn't
like what he created. What he chose to share with the world.'

He wasn't sure what she meant. 'Was it like, abstract?
Weird stuff?'

'He experimented with film.'

'Okay. Would I have seen any of it, anywhere? Did he ex-
hibit?' He got the feeling she was trying to tell him the truth,
but felt unable to give concrete details, so she was skirting
around the edges of the confession.

'Unfortunately.' She walked past him, towards the kitchen.

He followed her from the room and went to stand beside
her as they watched Alice in the garden. Her daughter was
sitting by a flower bed, watching something crawl over the
back of her hand. A ladybug?

'Why did you break up with this… Glen?' He was curious.
He really wanted to know. The Charlie he'd known had been
keen to find and create her own family. She'd wanted loads
of kids—had said she wouldn't be happy until she had loads
of them and would surround herself with their love. That she
would create a happy home, with a white picket fence.

'I don't really want to talk about him, if you don't mind?'

'Sure. Sure.' He gazed out of the window, trying not to look at her, but he'd heard something in her voice, just then. A hurt. A pain. A deep wound that she would prefer to ignore, but Eli knew, from practice, that hiding pain only caused it to get worse and fester.

He'd hid his own. Not wanting to tell anyone. Not wanting to tell his brand-new family that he thought something was wrong with him, in case they realised they'd made a bad choice in choosing him, and when he'd got so scared that he'd finally spoken up, it had been far too late. The cancer had been well established and, though the seminoma and his left testicle had been removed, he'd still had to undergo chemotherapy and radiation, which had left him sterile. Since then, he'd thankfully had no recurrences, but he maintained his body as if it was the most precious possession he had on this earth, which of course it was, because the one thing he'd always wanted—a child—would never be within his reach.

'But I'm here for you, if you ever want to.'

He felt, rather than saw, her look over at him, then glance away, before her fingers gently entwined with his, squeezing his hand briefly, before letting go as Alice stood up and came back towards the house.

'Mom, could I have a drink?'

'Sure, though Eli brought some popsicles—want one of those instead?'

'What flavour?'

'Orange or cherry?'

'Orange, please!'

He was glad Alice was okay, though she still had a strange pallor that told him that, whatever she had, she wasn't over it yet.

Alice sat in the living area, holding Sprinkles and sucking on her popsicle and then the television was put on.

Eli leaned against the kitchen counter as Charlie put away the things he'd brought from the shop. When she'd got nothing left to fiddle with, nothing left to clear up, she looked at him awkwardly. 'I bet this is the sexiest fling you've ever had,' she said quietly, so Alice couldn't hear.

He laughed. 'You have no idea.' The truth was, he'd never had a fling with anybody. He'd only ever had serious relationships and none since Lenore. Her leaving had pained him greatly, resulting in him feeling like the best way forward was to never get involved with anyone ever again. Not seriously, anyway.

'If you want to go, you can. I'd hate for you to waste a precious day off, hanging around with us.'

'Forget it! I love hanging around with you guys. You're refreshing.'

'We're new, so we're fun?'

'You're not new to me. I know you, remember?'

'Not deeply, though. You don't know all my deep, dark secrets. You don't know who I've cried over, who I've laughed with, who my friends are, what my favourite food is. You just think you know me because we shared a childhood.'

He considered her, knowing he couldn't let her push him away. He wanted to stay. Wanted to prove to her that she wasn't just a plaything. She was important. 'I know Alice's father hurt you and that you don't want to talk about it. Probably because you're embarrassed about it or ashamed for some reason. I think you've cried over him. Or maybe, more precisely, you've cried over losing what he represented—the happy family unit you always dreamed of having. All those kids. He hurt you, took something from you and you're still healing and you're trying to decide if you can trust a man ever again.

'I think Alice makes you laugh. Alice makes you happy, because it's just you and her against the world and she is your world, because you take her with you everywhere you go. I'd like to think you have loads of friends and maybe you do, but you never stay around long enough for them to know.' He smiled, but not with triumph. 'And your favourite food is grilled cheese. Or at least it was before.'

Charlie stared at him in shock, her face a mask of surprise and fear.

He continued. 'Today, you're a great doctor and I know what it takes to become a doctor in this world, which means that you're clever and strong and determined and you've learned how to harden your heart from all the tragedy and upset in this world, but that in private you still feel it keenly and you shed tears when you're home alone. You're a professional and you want to show your daughter that working is important and that if you want success, you have to earn it. You yearn for relationships, but fear them at the same time. Am I even close?'

He knew it was a scary thing to say all of that, but he had to let her know that he could see the real her and not the shiny exterior that she revealed to their patients. But he also said it all with a grin on his face, because he needed her to know that he wasn't judging her, just trying to show that he knew her better than she realised.

She paused a long while before she answered. 'Maybe you should be a shrink, with insight like that. But are you able to turn that keen eye upon yourself?'

He didn't get a chance to answer because suddenly, from

the living area, they heard a strange sound and then Alice was being ill all over the hard wooden floors.

Charlie rushed to her daughter, whereas Eli grabbed paper towels and cleaning spray from under the sink before hurrying over.

Alice was crying. 'I'm sorry, Mom!'

'It's okay, honey. It's okay.'

They cleared her up and took her back to her bedroom, settling her beneath the covers with Sprinkles and giving her her tablet to watch some shows on, a bucket beside her, just in case.

When the drama was over and they were back in the kitchen alone, Eli stared at her. 'I can turn that eye upon myself. I don't get involved in relationships any more because I got hurt so badly in my last one, which was two years ago. I maintain my happy-go-lucky persona because it makes me happy and I like making other people smile. Everyone in Vasquez is my friend, but they are also my patients, so my friendships with them are strange ones. The last time I cried I was twenty-one years of age and I cried because I felt like my happy life I'd built was spinning out of my control. And my favourite food is cheesecake, which is a total bummer, because to look like this?' He indicated his own body with his hands. 'You don't get to eat cheesecake often enough.'

She smiled at him, shyly, clearly pleased that he'd shared something with her, after he'd so expertly psychoanalysed her. And then she laughed. 'Okay.' She picked a piece of imaginary fluff off the kitchen surface. 'What made you cry?'

His cancer diagnosis. But he didn't want her to know about that. What was the point? It was over with now. Done. He'd had no recurrences and he was too busy living in the present to keep returning to the past. 'I don't remember,' he lied. Hating himself for lying.

'I think you do. You remembered you were twenty-one when it happened, so I also think you do know what caused it, you just don't want to say.'

He crossed his arms and stepped closer to her, towering over her, smiling. 'I tell you what…if you tell me about what happened with Alice's father, I'll tell you why I cried.'

She considered it. He saw it cross her eyes. But then she looked down and away. Defeated. 'I guess we'll never know then, huh?'

Alice slept for a couple of hours and when she woke, she looked much brighter and asked if she could come out and watch a movie with them.

She and Eli had spent the time chatting in the lounge, discussing some of his weirdest cases and sharing tales of their medical training. They'd trained in different schools, but discovered that they'd both done a placement in the same emergency room, though obviously not at the same time, and had shared stories about an attending that they both knew, who'd made an impression on the pair of them with his crazy uncombed hair and the fact that he always sounded as if he was winging his way through the day. Eli had been most amused to hear that this guy had even asked Charlie out once and she'd given him the benefit of the doubt and enjoyed a drink with him, only to put up with the fact that his mother kept texting him all night long and she discovered he lived in her basement. That had been the end of that!

They put on an animated movie and Alice lay between them on the couch. Eli was at Alice's feet and Charlie let her daughter lay her head upon her lap. As the movie played,

Eli stretched out his hand across the back of the couch, as if reaching for her fingers, and, once she'd checked that Alice couldn't see, Charlie reached out too.

Their fingers entwined on the back of the couch and Eli looked at her and smiled, his eyes sparkling, and she realised that, even though she'd been worried about Alice and they'd never made it up to Lawton Lake, Eli had still somehow made the day special. He'd not shown boredom once. Had never been impatient. Had never been rude. Never selfish. He'd helped care for Alice. Been thoughtful. He'd been kind and funny and made her laugh and his presence had been reassuring and comforting. He'd made the day easier and she liked having him around. An hour ago, he'd insisted on preparing their charcuterie lunch and had pretended to be her private waiter, pulling out her chair for her to sit down, draping a serviette across her lap and calling her 'miss'.

As she played with his fingers, she wondered about what kind of a father he would make. He seemed to adore kids, so she had no doubt he would make a wonderful dad. Look at how he kept trying to nurture Alice's drawing! That had been so sweet—buying one of her pictures. She'd never seen Alice smile so broadly.

Holding his hand secretly felt good and she found herself smiling and imagining what a future with Eli in her life might look like. And when she realised that she would like it very much, she froze, feeling her heart beat faster.

*What am I even thinking?*

She risked a glance at him, to see if he'd noticed the change in her, but he hadn't. He was staring at the screen, laughing at the antics of a pack of hyenas.

He might be good with kids because, at heart, he was a kid himself, and hadn't he told her before that he hadn't been in a relationship for over two years? That he'd got hurt and wouldn't risk it again? This was not a man looking for an instant family and nor was she in the market for making one with him.

This was a *fling*.

Or at least was trying to be.

*We've only shared kisses. Heated fumbles. Perhaps I should stop this before it goes even further?*

# CHAPTER TWELVE

'CHARLIE! GREAT—YOU'RE HERE. We've had a field call. Hikers trapped down a crevasse. Mountain Rescue have also been informed, but they've asked for two doctors to attend.'

'Oh, okay. But who will man the clinic?'

'The nurses are here and our resident, has said he'll stay as long as we need him to cover.'

She got up from behind her desk, downing the last of her coffee. 'How are we getting there?'

'Driving most of the way, then I'm afraid it might be a bit of a hike. It's up in the White Mountains.'

She stepped out from behind her desk, to reveal sandal shoes. 'I don't have hiking boots.'

'I think we may have some spares to loan you. We keep a supply, just in case. What size are you?'

'Size nine.'

'Perfect. Come on—I'll talk you through it.' He turned to go, hearing her steps quickly catching up with him as he began to stride down the corridor towards the field supply room. Here they kept everything they would need for a field call. Go bags, filled with equipment they might need— oxygen, defib, masks, gloves, bandages, splints, needles, syringes, painkilling medications. There were jackets and high-vis vests, helmets, boots, torches, blankets, supplies of water, IV bags, a bit of everything and anything. All clearly labelled, so it could just be grabbed quickly.

Eli searched the boots labelled nines and passed a pair to Charlie. 'Try these on. Mountain Rescue will have sent out a team via helicopter, but they have to come in from Anchorage, so we might get there before them, depending upon how far up into the mountains the incident is. We've been given the coordinates and Chuck is readying the vehicle now.'

'Pilot Chuck?'

'The very same. The guy knows this area like the back of his hand. He'll get us to where we need to go.'

'I guess I should be glad it hasn't been snowing and we're not going by dog sled.'

He smiled. 'It's a shame you'll be gone before any snow hits the ground. A dog-sled ride is something not to be missed.'

He was hauling equipment onto his back, so almost didn't notice the look of uncertainty on Charlie's face. The way it had changed when he'd said she'd be gone. It was almost wistful. Almost sad.

'Here. Take this.' He passed her a second go bag and then began to lead her to the back of the clinic where Chuck was apparently waiting.

'What do we know about the patient's injuries?'

'We don't know, but a fall into a crevasse could be anything. Broken bones, blood loss, loss of consciousness, hypothermia depending upon how long they've been out and exposed to the wild. Maybe dehydration?'

She nodded, hefting the bag higher onto her shoulder.

At the vehicle, he swung open the trunk and hauled in their equipment. 'You ever attend a field call?'

'Only during training. I did a shift with some paramedics.'

'In the wild?'

'No. Inner city.'

He smiled at her. 'Well, this is a little bit different, but don't worry. I'll keep you safe.'

'I'm glad to hear it.'

Chuck started the engine and began to drive them away from Vasquez and up into the mountain range. There was nothing to do but wait until they arrived, so Eli looked over at Charlie to see what she made of the scenery.

Her face was a mask of awe and wonder as the urban signs began to drop away and they drove further into nature. The grey-purple mountains rose up all around them, thick with vegetation and, after one turn, the vehicle actually scared a group of three or four deer off the tarmac, sending them scattering into the trees.

'How you settling in, Doc?' Chuck asked her.

'Yeah, good, thanks. How are your dogs doing?'

'Good. Got a new litter of pups due soon.'

'Well, don't tell Alice.'

'Too late. I gave a talk at the school last week and she was there listening as I told her all about it. But don't worry, they're not the kind of dogs you'd want as a household pet. My dogs are working animals and they're made for the outside and pulling sleds and racing, not for lying on a couch and getting fat.'

Charlie nodded and glanced at Eli.

Every smile she gave him made him feel good inside. He wanted to reach out and take her hand in his, but Chuck was here and he didn't think she'd want anyone to know about how they felt about one another, or that they were in a relationship. It was crazy, really. They'd agreed to a fling with no strings, but hadn't actually done anything yet, but kiss. That goodbye kiss they'd shared after he'd spent the day with her and

Alice... It had been tropical in its heat and seriously tempting him to break his promise to be a gentleman about this. And he wasn't actually sure how many other guys would agree to a fling with a woman and just be happy to spend time with her, without touching, and help her take care of her sick kid.

Because he'd been more than happy to do that. It had felt nice. As if they were a little family together. And he should have run a mile from that, because it was a dangerous road for him to travel down, hoping like that. Allowing his imagination to run away with all those fancy ideas of settling down with someone, maybe getting married, maybe having a family he could call his own. Because he'd never have that.

He couldn't give Charlie all those babies she'd said she wanted. He couldn't give her the big family she'd once dreamed of. If she got involved with him on a serious level? Then there would be no more pregnancies. No more babies. Alice would be her one and only child and he knew he couldn't do that to her.

So, he should have shut down those thoughts.

Should have turned tail and run. But being with Charlie was just so right and so good that she was a drug at this point.

So instead, he'd found himself lingering at her door, as they'd said goodnight.

He'd so wanted to stay. Had so wanted to suggest that he stay the night and he'd leave really early in the morning, but he'd refrained from doing so, because who knew if Alice would come into Charlie's room in the middle of the night with a tummy ache? What would have happened then? And maybe it was best for them if they just took each other in little bite sizes? So it didn't become overwhelming, so they didn't start getting ideas about each other that they shouldn't?

And so, before she'd opened the door to let him out, they'd

stood there, together, staring into each other's eyes, their heartbeats feeling as though they were synced, and he'd gently cupped her face and kissed her softly. The longing he'd felt for her all day long contained in a single, gratifying, mind-blowing kiss.

'Goodnight, Eli,' she'd whispered, her voice husky and a little breathy afterwards.

'Goodnight, Charlie.' He'd swept his thumb over her bottom lip, stared at her mouth some more, imagining the wonders of those lips elsewhere, and then he'd torn himself away, every step that he took walking away from her house a torture.

He'd felt so comfortable there. So right. And maybe he was an incredible fool for letting his mind imagine the possibilities with her, but so be it. He couldn't help it. Charlie was different. Charlie was special and always would be.

It took them just under an hour before Chuck pulled over on a dirt road as a chopper circled overhead, looking for a space to land.

'Looks like we've both got here at the same time. We'll head off on foot. Chuck, you've got the co-ordinates?'

'Sure have. It's this way,' he said, pointing towards a small dirt trail that led higher into the mountains, before he reached into his flatbed truck and opened up a metal case that contained a rifle. He pocketed some ammo and hauled the rifle over his shoulder. 'Let's go.'

'What's the rifle for?' Charlie asked, looking a little shocked.

'It's preventative.'

Chuck led the way, Charlie second, so that Eli could bring up the rear and keep an eye on her and keep her safe. There could be anything out here. Mountain lion. Elk. Wolf. Grizzly. All manner of creatures. That was the reason for the gun. If the patients had shed any blood, any kind of predator would have tracked that scent over many miles and be on their way too and no one would want to fight off a grizzly, or worse, without some kind of backup to scare off the predator before they could be rescued. The rifle was protection. Chuck wouldn't actually shoot an animal unless he absolutely had to. They weren't hunting here.

The steep incline was quite the workout for his calf muscles and he was glad of all the cardio he undertook. Charlie sounded out of breath and Chuck sounded as if he might be the one to need the oxygen, when suddenly the trail evened out and the pace got easier.

Chuck checked his map, looked out across the view and continued on down the path. It was getting quite rocky underfoot and the scrubby trees were becoming sparse as they began climbing over large boulders that seemed to block their way.

'Watch your footing, guys. You don't want to turn an ankle here,' Chuck advised.

They began to make their way along a ledge that had a stony path. Clearly this was a way up for some mountaineers. The path turned in and out of view, and after they'd been ascending for about ten minutes they saw a guy, dressed in red, waving his arms furiously and calling.

'Over here! We're over here! Jackie, Adam, they're here.'

Jackie and Adam must be the patients, Eli thought.

There was the temptation to rush these last few metres, but Chuck stopped them from pressing ahead too fast and made sure that Charlie kept the same pace they'd been walking at, until they reached the guy in red.

'Thank God you're here! Jackie slipped and fell down a crevasse. She was unconscious for a while, so we think she banged her head. Adam went down to rescue her, but was afraid to move her, so he's been trying to keep her awake and warm.'

'Any medical history we should know?'

'Jackie's just got the all-clear from breast cancer. She had a double mastectomy, chemo and radiation treatments over the last year.'

'Is she on any meds right now? Any allergies?'

'I don't think so.'

'Okay. Mountain Rescue are on their way. Is there a way that one of us can abseil down to Jackie?'

'Sure. We can attach one of you to our ropes.' The guy looked them over and kept his gaze on Charlie. 'It's gonna have to be you. The gap in the crevasse isn't big enough for anyone else.'

Charlie looked at him. 'I've never done anything like that before.'

She looked apprehensive.

'Don't worry. We'll talk you through it, every step of the way.'

She nodded and took note as Gerry, the guy in red, attached her to a harness, rope and karabiners. He gave her instructions on how to hold the rope, how to break, how to feed the rope through so that she would descend.

Eli attached a go bag to her harness with an extra karabiner. 'You're all set. You can do this,' he said, smiling at her, hoping that his encouragement would give her the belief that she needed. But he understood her reticence. She was a city girl. She'd never rock climbed or abseiled in her life and now she had to because someone's life depended upon it. He wanted to have the utmost confidence in her, but knew she'd be afraid.

So would he. He wanted to keep her safe and if it could be him to make his way down to the patient, he'd prefer it.

'Okay.'

She kept her gaze on him as she backed out towards the crevasse. Gerry wasn't joking, there was only a small narrow channel through the rock, which opened out into a bigger chamber below.

Eli looked over and down through the crevasse. It was a long drop. Charlie would have to rappel freely for quite a way and even though Adam was there beneath her at the icy, rocky bottom to help her break or slow down, if she lost control, he still felt apprehensive. Having to place his trust in a guy he didn't know.

He met Charlie's gaze. Saw the fear in her eyes. Nodded. *You can do this.*

Her hands were trembling and he wanted to reach out and lay his hand on hers so much, to still them. To let her know he believed in her.

Something in his eyes must have given her the confidence, because suddenly she was moving away from him. Backwards and down, over the edge, hesitating slightly as she looked where to place her feet.

'That's it. Slow and steady.'

He watched her disappear from view and felt a lump of dread settle in his stomach. 'You okay?' he called out.

'I'm okay,' came back her voice, echoing around the rock.

He hated not being able to see her. To not view her progress, or lack thereof, and suddenly he wished they'd waited for Mountain Rescue. Surely they wouldn't have been much longer? They'd seen the helicopter hovering, knew they were close! But the fact that Jackie had lost consciousness and suffered a head injury had made them forge ahead to get a doctor down to her.

'How are you doing?' he called again, his stomach in absolute knots. He should never have let her go. She had a child! A daughter! She had someone who depended on her, he didn't. It should have been him. They could have found a way, surely?

There was no response.

'Charlie!'

A pause. Then, 'I'm okay! I'm nearly there! About ten more metres to go.'

Her voice echoed again and he'd never been so relieved to hear it. But then he heard something he didn't like.

A man's voice, calling out. 'Too fast! Watch out!'

There was the sound of a thud. Of a person hitting rock.

'Charlie!'

There was a cry of pain and he instantly felt sick. 'Charlie!' He spun around and faced Gerry. 'Hook me up. I don't care. I'll make it down there somehow.'

'You're too big.' Gerry looked sorry.

'Doc? I think the other doc has broken her leg or something!' called Adam.

*Damn it!*

He spun around, wanting to be with her. To scoop her up into his protective arms and take her someplace safe. But that was an impossibility. It wasn't just Charlie he had to worry about, but Jackie, too.

'How's Jackie?' he called.

'Conscious. Her head has stopped bleeding, but she can't remember much.'

'And she's breathing okay?'

'Yes, sir!'

'Okay, you need to get the oxygen out of the go bag and place the oxygen mask over Jackie's face,' he continued to yell.

'Already on it! Charlie here is already telling me what to do.'

He smiled with relief. That Charlie was still putting her patient first over herself was remarkable and proved just what kind of a doctor and person she was. Selfless. But then again, she always had been. Even as a kid, she'd helped out the other kids at the home. Especially the littler ones. Helping patch up their cuts and grazes and trying to cheer them up afterwards. She had to be afraid and in a great deal of pain herself, if it was true she'd broken something from her bad landing, but was still determined that Jackie would receive help first.

As he listened to what was going on at the bottom of the crevasse, he heard Chuck behind him. 'Rescue's here.'

He quickly got to his feet and summarised the situation to them.

Two of the rescue guys, small in stature, thankfully, hooked up some more ropes and began to abseil down the crevasse and Eli felt much better knowing that Charlie would also receive help.

The rescue guys had radios and had passed one to Eli before disappearing over the edge and when they got to the bottom, he was very much relieved to hear Charlie's voice. 'Hey.'

'Hey. How are you doing?' His voice softened.

'I'm all right. I got Adam to put a headcollar on Jackie and they're bringing her up now. I think she may have a broken arm or wrist, but it's the head injury that's the major concern.'

'And you? Run it down for me.'

He heard her sigh. 'Possible lower leg or ankle fractures.'

'Plural?'

'Yeah. Both hurt. My left leg has a noticeable deformity

about an inch above the ankle and the right one hurts like you wouldn't believe.'

'You did drop from a height onto rock. We'll get you X-rayed when we get you back to the clinic.'

'Take care of Jackie first.'

'I will take care of you both. Now, have you taken any of the painkillers?'

'No. I wanted to keep a clear head for Adam while I told him what to do.'

'Then do it now.'

'Yes, boss.'

He heard the slight smile in her voice and had to stop himself from cradling the radio. He couldn't hold *her*, but he could hold the item that was bringing him her voice. He hated the idea that she was hurt and lying at the bottom of the crevasse.

The mountain rescue guys ascended with Jackie, wearing a neck collar and with bandages wrapped around her head and one arm in a sling. The bandage on her head was bleeding through at the right temple and he attended to it by adding another pressure bandage to try and stop the bleeding. But they couldn't take any risks and now that Jackie was out of the crevasse, they were able to strap her to a back board. They would have to carry her back down the ravine towards where the truck was parked and then drive her to the helicopter, so she could be airlifted.

'Sending up Adam.'

Eli grabbed the radio. 'You first. You're injured.'

'I'm sending up Adam, Eli,' she replied more firmly, and before he could say anything else Adam's relieved face appeared as he was pulled back up.

'How is she?' he asked the man.

'Bloody amazing! She splinted her own legs, while telling me what to do!'

Eli stood over the crevasse and clicked the button on the radio. 'Tell me when you're ready.'

'I'm ready.'

Eli nodded to Gerry and they began to winch Charlie back up through the small gap in the crevasse. His heart was already pounding fast, but felt as if it went into tachycardia the second he spotted her rising up through the gap. She turned and her legs bumped against the rock on the edge and she winced, but Eli knelt and scooped her up into his arms and moved her away from the ledge.

'I'm fine. See to Jackie.'

'The rescue guys are already seeing to her. She's fine. Just concussed, I think. I couldn't feel any fractures. Let me look at you.'

'I'm fine and put me down!'

'I'm carrying you back to the truck.'

'That's a long way, Eli.'

'I'm a strong guy.'

As they spoke, the helicopter hovered above them, brought in by the rescue team, who hooked up Jackie's scoop to a cable and she was airlifted up off the mountain. The downward pressure from the helicopter was intense, but thankfully they were sheltered by an overpass.

One of the rescue team turned to Eli. 'We don't have another scoop for her, but we can help you carry her down.'

'What about Jackie?'

'There's a driver and EMT waiting with the truck, so they'll be able to unhook Jackie and get her loaded into the helicopter.'

'Honestly, I'm fine,' Eli said.

'Mate, let us help you.'

Fair enough. There was no point in being proud and help would be appreciated, no matter how much he wanted to wrap his arms around her and protect her. But already his mind was racing. If one of her legs was broken, then that could be a problem, depending on the severity of the break. If both legs were broken? She'd be in a wheelchair for a while. Because even though he'd advise her to rest, he couldn't imagine her accepting that.

*I can work from a wheelchair.*

He could already imagine her saying it. But it wasn't just work, was it? What about Alice? What about getting her to school and home again?

The rescue guy and Eli joined hands to make a seat beneath Charlie's rear. She draped an arm around each of their shoulders and they began to make their way back down the ravine.

He couldn't stop himself from glancing at her. Checking her colour. Her respiratory rate. Whether she looked to be in pain. She had one break for sure and was putting a brave face on it. High pain threshold?

It took them some time to make it back to Chuck's truck, as they had to move slower, to make sure their steps were steady and they didn't trip over the numerous obstacles on the path—rocks, roots that emerged from the ground and dipped back in again like sea serpents, loose gravel, divots where rabbits, or some other burrowing animal, had decided to dig.

Chuck lowered the back end and they placed her onto the back of the truck.

Eli climbed on with her and settled beside her.

'What are you doing?'

'Riding with you.'

'I'm fine! You'll get bounced around back here. No need for us both to be uncomfortable.'

'This selfless nature of yours is endearing, but could you keep your trap shut for once? I'm riding in back with you, whether you like it or not.'

Her mouth opened as if to say something, but then clamped shut again.

Eli smiled. 'That's right. Jeez, doctors really are the worst patients.' He sat next to her and draped an arm around her shoulders. He felt her freeze initially and then she sank against him.

'Thanks.'

'You're welcome. I figured you might be cold and that's what I'll say if Chuck mentions it, okay?'

'What about when we drive into Vasquez?'

'I'll repeat it.'

Again she opened her mouth and shut it again, without speaking.

Chuck started the engine, backing up and turning around, giving the rescue boys a lift back to the helicopter. He dropped them off and they watched as the helicopter rose into the air, stirring up dust and dirt in whorls, before it inclined slightly and surged forward and away from the mountains.

'Jackie's going to Anchorage?'

'It's the best place for her, especially if she has a closed head injury. I couldn't feel one, but that doesn't mean there isn't one there.'

'She was a nice lady. Confused, but nice.'

'So, tell me, what happened during your descent?'

Charlie shrugged. 'I don't know. I was feeding the rope through like I was told and then Adam panicked because Jackie got sick and I tried to speed up, but the rope just whizzed through my grip, so then I got scared and couldn't remember which hand slowed me down and which one sped me up. Next thing I knew, I went crashing onto the rocks.'

'You didn't bang your head?'

'No. I landed on my feet.'

He leaned forward to examine the splints. 'You did these yourself?'

She nodded.

Eli looked right into her eyes. 'You're amazing, you know that, right?'

She flushed and this time he really saw it, because her skin had been pale to begin with. He liked that she was affected by his compliment.

'When we get to the clinic, we'll get you into X-Ray.'

'What if it's bad? What if I need surgery? I can't go back to Anchorage.'

'I've done my fair share of orthopaedics. In fact, I worked two whole years on an orthopaedic surgery ward and I worked with the best. If you need plates and screws, then I'm your man.'

'I could make a rude comment for that, but I won't.'

'Don't hold back on my account.' He grinned.

She smiled. 'I was going to say I bet you're good for more than just a casual screw.'

He raised an eyebrow and stared right at her, a smile touching his lips. 'You bet I am.'


'Your left tib and fib are fractured at the distal end, with a rotation. We should be able to twist them back into place and get you in a cast for a while. Your right ankle has a hairline fracture, which shouldn't need anything but rest.' Eli stood by her bed in the clinic, delivering the news.

'You're joking?'

'Nope.'

'Damn it.' How was she going to cope with everything if she had to be off her feet? 'I'll get about in a wheelchair for a bit. I can still work, just you watch.'

'And Alice? How will you get her to school? Cook for her? Clean up after her?'

'She's a capable girl. I raised her right. She'll help me.'

'She's five. She shouldn't have to be her mother's nurse and she'll be tired from having been at kindergarten all day. I have another solution.'

'I'm all ears.'

'I'll help you.'

Eli? Help her? 'How?'

'I'll move in for a bit. I can take Alice to school, drive us both to work, where you can be parked behind your desk all day, and then I'll take us home, cook dinner, help you bathe and get you into bed.' He grinned.

It felt as though her brain suddenly stopped working as her jaw practically hit the floor. Eli? Move in? 'No!'

'It's the perfect solution.'

'No, it's not. What would Alice think with you sleeping over?'

'She'll know that I'm there to help you both. I can sleep on the couch, if that's what you're worried about.'

'I'm not worried about you sleeping on the couch.'

'Good, because I could always sneak back to it, before Alice wakes.'

'No. She comes in my room sometimes. Clambers into bed with me in the middle of the night and I don't know about it, until I wake up.'

He shrugged. 'Then I'll just take my sweet time putting

you to bed. Tuck you in nice and tight and stroke your brow until you fall fast asleep.'

'Eli—'

'I'm joking! I'm not going to take advantage of a woman who is incapable of standing on her own two feet.'

'Good.'

'Besides, I've heard bed baths are very entertaining these days.' He grinned.

'Eli!'

'Joke.' He looked around to make sure no one was watching, then leaned forward and kissed her on the forehead. 'It's just a joke. Unless…you *do* want me to give you a bed bath?'

'My hands work perfectly well and I will be more than capable of running a wet flannel over my body all by myself.'

His gaze travelled down her body. 'Shame.'

Honestly, he was exhausting! 'I'll let you stay and help out and I thank you for thinking of me and Alice, but in front of my daughter? In our home? My body is mine and you don't get to touch it, understood?'

He saluted her. 'Understood.'

'Good. Now go see if there's any update on Jackie.'

# CHAPTER THIRTEEN

JACKIE, LUCKILY, DID not have a closed head injury, apart from concussion and the need for eight stitches to sew up her head laceration. She did, however, have a dislocated shoulder, a fractured wrist and a proximal break on her humerus—her upper arm bone.

The doctors in Anchorage had treated her with fluids and a couple of casts, but she would need surgery in the morning to help realign and plate her humerus. 'The shoulder has been reduced and the doctors have told me that they believe Jackie's lack of memory will improve after the concussion begins to dissipate.'

'That's great news,' Charlie said as he wheeled her into place at her dinner table.

They'd already collected Alice from kindergarten. His mom had been so surprised to see them turn up to collect Alice together, with Charlie in her wheelchair, and had been amazed at their story, smiling at them both and patting Charlie's hand. Alice, on the other hand, far from being scared about seeing her mom in a wheelchair, had thought it was cool and insisted on sitting on her mom's lap, all the way back to the truck.

'Can I have a go in it, Mom?'

'Maybe later.' She'd smiled, glad that her daughter hadn't been upset to hear of her mother's injuries. In fact, most perturbingly, Alice had been thrilled that Eli would be moving in for a while to help out. 'I can sell him another one of my drawings!'

As she sat at the table, she couldn't help but notice that Eli knew where everything was in her kitchen. He picked the right cupboard when he needed a saucepan. A right, yet *different* cupboard when he was looking for the strainer. 'How do you know where everything is?'

He looked over his shoulder at her with a smile as he reached up high for the cheese grater. 'This is my mom's, remember?'

'And?'

'Who do you think does all the maintenance?'

Of course. He'd fixed her drippy tap and everyone in Vasquez seemed to multitask with their jobs. It wasn't just them in their clinic. It was Chuck who drove ambulance trucks and bred and raced working malamute dogs. It was Eli's mom, who owned, not only this lodge, but the town's hotel and the town's diner and God only knew what else, while *also* being the kindergarten teacher!

'And what are you making for dinner?'

'Pasta.'

'Oh.' Well, that was easy. 'I thought you'd be an amazing chef, too, and not just pour something out of a packet.' It was good to know he wasn't an expert on human bodies *and* house repair *and* cooking.

'I'm making my own dough. You haven't tried real pasta until you've tried my goat's cheese and spinach ravioli.'

*Huh.*

He could cook, too. 'Where did you learn to cook?'

'My mom.'

'I like that you call her Mom.'

He shrugged. 'It's what she is. From the day they drove me home, I was made to feel like one of them. Like I'd always been there and that the missing years didn't matter.'

'Do they matter?'

He seemed to think for a minute. 'They do, but in a different way now. Those early years I was just trying to find my own way, not knowing where I wanted to steer to. Becoming a Clark gave me roots. It gave me guidance. And they've been there for me through every difficulty.'

Difficulty? 'Like medical school?'

He smiled. 'Yeah.'

She felt then in the way that he looked as if maybe he was referring to something else. The girl that walked away and left him? Who broke his heart? He'd mentioned her before, but didn't speak of her much. Lenore. What had happened there?

Charlie knew she could ask him, but would he answer? She didn't speak of Glen and what had happened with him. She just couldn't get the idea out of her head that once Eli knew the real truth, he'd go racing over to a computer and look up those pictures and she couldn't bear the idea of him seeing her like that. Vulnerable.

It was bad enough he was seeing her like *this*. In a wheelchair. It was hardly sexy, was it? This man had wanted a fling with her and she had wanted one with him, but it seemed that every time they tried to be together, something stopped them. Alice getting ill. Charlie abseiling badly. Broken ankles... And tonight he would be sleeping in her home. Just yards from her bedroom. How was that going to feel?

She gazed at the slope of his arm over his triceps. The way the muscles flexed as he kneaded dough. The way his hands forced the dough this way, then that. She could imagine his fingers tracing over her skin and she shivered.

'Cold? I can get you a blanket.'

He had a splash of white flour on his black tee, near his waist. She wanted to brush it away and feel those rock-hard abs beneath her fingers. 'No, not cold. I'm okay, thanks.'

'Shame.' He looked around them both, checked that Alice was absorbed somewhere in her bedroom, the door closed. 'I would have found a fun way to warm you up.' He winked at her and smiled naughtily.

Okay. She'd play along. Maybe this would have to be a fling with words only? 'How exactly?'

He raised an eyebrow at her, wiped his hands on a clean towel and then sauntered over towards her, leaning down low so that his hands rested either side of her on the wheelchair arms. 'First I'd make you close your eyes,' he whispered. 'Then I'd gently kiss you on the neck. Once. Twice. I'd breathe hot air over your goose-pimpling skin and then brush my lips over yours and then, baby? I'd make you forget the rest of the world.'

Her breathing had become heavy as she imagined each and every delicious image. A smile crept back onto her face. 'How?' She chuckled slightly, feeling incredibly naughty.

He grinned and placed one hand on the back of her neck, beneath her hair, and pulled her in close for a long, languorous kiss.

He wasn't lying. Kissing Eli did make her forget everything. The pain in her legs. Everything that had happened that day. All she could think was...*oh, my God!*

His hand slowly traced the line of her neck, one finger trailing down her chest bone and then circling around her breast to find her taut nipple that was thrusting against the material of her top. She ached—*physically ached*—to feel his skin against hers.

*Damn this blouse! Damn this bra!*

And then, when she felt as though she couldn't contain herself any more, he released her nipple and stopped kissing her and backed away, smiling.

And with perfect timing too!

Alice's bedroom door swung open. 'Mom, when is dinner ready?'

'Not long, Alice. Twenty minutes?' Eli said, looking perfectly innocent as he spoke to her daughter, while Charlie still sat in her chair, breathless and aroused.

'Okay.' Alice disappeared back into her bedroom.

Charlie met Eli's gaze. He looked happy. Smug. Normally she would want to wipe that smile off his confident face, but her brain wasn't really working well enough to come up with a retort. 'Erm…' She cleared her throat. Swallowed. 'Is there going to be a dessert?'

He grinned. 'There just may be.'

*What is happening?*

She watched him cut his pasta into squares and spoon little hills of goat's cheese and spinach onto them, before sealing them with another thin layer of pasta. Then he began chopping up some tomatoes, which he added to a sauce in a pan, grinding black pepper over the top.

Draping a dish towel over his shoulder, he then went to the fridge and pulled out some chilled moulds.

'What are those for?'

'Chocolate soufflés.'

Soufflés. That was risky. She'd watched enough cooking shows to know that the soufflé was feared. They either came out perfect or wrong. No in between. But she liked his confidence. That was something Eli had never been short of. Something she envied.

He poured some juice into a large jug that he added ice and slices of orange to and placed it on the table with three glasses. Then he placed the pasta into boiling water gently. 'Let's get you washed up,' he said.

'I can get myself to the bathroom sink. Alice! Time to wash your hands, please!'

She was glad of the cool water. It helped diffuse some of the heat she'd felt earlier when Eli had kissed her. When she reversed out of the bathroom, Eli was waiting for her.

'I can wheel myself.'

'You've just washed your hands. Let me push you.'

She let him guide her to the table, then he held out Alice's seat and draped a serviette over her lap, like a waiter in a posh restaurant. Alice giggled.

'Can I pour the young lady a drink?' he asked, bowing low.

Again, Alice laughed. 'Yes, please.'

After he'd done Alice's drink, he held the juice over Charlie's glass. 'Madam?'

'Please.' She smiled at him, feeling a real warmth towards him. He was putting in so much effort for her, but when hadn't he? Ever since she'd arrived here, he'd been there, helping out, always with a smile or a joke. He'd helped out when Alice was poorly. He'd been incredibly concerned when she'd got hurt and now he'd moved in to help them out.

What had she given him in return?

Feeling a little guilty, she watched him go and drain the pasta, before he transferred it into their bowls, with a helping of the tomato sauce. He brought the three plates over to the table, serving Alice first, then Charlie, then himself, before he sat down.

*'Bon appetit.'*

*'Bon appetit.'*

And, of course, it tasted absolutely delicious! The rich, succulent goat's cheese, the freshness of the spinach, the soft, thin pasta, all mixed with the spiced heat of the tomatoes that had a kick of chilli when it hit the back of your throat. But not so much that Alice couldn't eat it.

'Mom...there's a sports day happening soon, will you come?'

'Oh, sure, honey! Of course, I will. I wouldn't miss it.'

Alice smiled. 'Mrs Clark said that there's going to be a parents' race for mummies and daddies. Will you still be able to race in your wheelchair?'

'Oh, sorry, honey, but I don't think so. Maybe next time?'

'I could do it,' suggested Eli.

Charlie looked at him as Alice beamed. 'Yes! Please? Can Eli do it, Mom?'

'Well, I don't know...what would people think? He's not your daddy, sweetheart. It might be cheating,' she said, with a sympathetic smile and hoping Alice wouldn't push it, because what would people think? Eli running in a parent's place at the sports day? The rest of Vasquez would be there. Would it start any gossip? Or had that horse already bolted? People would soon know that he'd moved in to help out. They might assume something anyway.

'I don't think it's cheating, Mom.'

'Nor me,' said Eli, grinning at Alice and dabbing at his mouth with his napkin.

His helpful addition did not go unnoticed. She gave him a look. 'It's a *parents'* race and you're *not* her parent. Thank you for the offer, but I don't think we should do it. You should save your strength and speed for when you have children of your own.'

A look crossed his face that she couldn't read, because it

came and went so fast and then he was taking his plate back into the kitchen.

She felt somehow that she'd upset him, but didn't understand why.

He was clattering about. Whisking the chocolate, filling the ramekins, and then wiping the rims with a clean finger, before he placed them into the oven and set a timer for ten minutes.

Charlie put her and Alice's plates onto her lap and wheeled herself into the kitchen and placed them down next to the sink, so she could position herself to open up the dishwasher. But she couldn't quite get the angle.

'Let me.'

'No, it's fine, I can do it.'

He sighed and stepped back and she could feel his eyes on her as she lowered the door, put in the plates and then lifted the door back, shoving it closed.

'Are you okay?' she asked.

'I'm fine!' he said with a smile, before checking his watch.

'You don't need to check your watch. You've set a timer.'

'I know I have.'

'I've upset you, haven't I?'

He shook his head with a smile forced onto his face. 'Nope!'

'I have. When I said you should wait to become a parent yourself. I wasn't trying to imply that you were trying to steal my child or adopt her or anything.' She checked to make sure Alice couldn't hear. 'Or imply that our relationship is anything but what it is.'

'I know that.'

'Then why are you upset?'

'I'm not.'

'I don't believe you.'

'Look, it was just a race. I thought I could be Alice's champion. She's a great kid and she's excited about sports day. Or I could be your champion. Whichever way you want to look at it, that's all I wanted to be. To step in and save the day. To let Alice have someone she could cheer for at the race. I didn't want her to feel left out. It should just be a bit of fun, that's all. I don't happen to think that anyone will read anything into it. And if they did? So what?'

'Well, that's easy for you to say,' she said quietly. 'You've not been the centre of gossip before.'

He raised an eyebrow. 'You don't know that.'

She groaned. 'Okay, so everyone probably talked about the Clarks when they adopted you. Big deal. That's positive talk, nothing horrible. And maybe they talked when you and Lenore broke up. Big deal. You don't know what nasty gossip feels like.'

'Actually, I do. But it sounds, right now, like we're not actually talking about me, but talking about you.' He glanced over at Alice, who was absorbed with the television blaring away behind her. 'You've been the subject of malicious gossip?'

She coloured, thinking of Glen and what he'd done. It hadn't been Charlie's fault. She'd thought she was in a loving relationship to begin with, but it had all turned sour.

'It was a while ago and I don't need people talking about me again.'

Eli glanced at his soufflés.

They were rising nicely, of course.

'If you want, we can talk about this later?'

She nodded. Maybe it was time? She didn't have to tell him *all* the details. It might be nice to tell someone how she felt about it all. So far, she'd kept it all hidden deep inside, where it had begun to fester. But she had been thinking about how it might feel to share her problem with him. Share the burden.

He gave her a wink.

Hesitantly she smiled back.

When the soufflés were done, Eli served the biggest to Alice. 'Be careful. That small little dish is hot.'

They were a delight! Rich and chocolatey, without being too sweet. The perfect accompaniment to his ravioli pasta parcels. Good-looking, sexy, intelligent, kind, considerate, a good cook, an excellent baker, an amazing kisser. Was there anything he was bad at? Or even moderately bad at? There had to be something. A man wasn't wrapped up in such an amazing parcel, like Eli, without there being something! She just figured she hadn't discovered it yet. The only clue she had was that he'd had a relationship sour and his girlfriend had left. Why? Was it because of something he'd done? Or *hadn't* done? Maybe it was because he was always joking around and laughing? Maybe she'd thought he couldn't take anything seriously?

Leaving Alice to watch the television after dinner, Eli wheeled Charlie out into the garden and sat down on a seat next to her. 'So…spill the beans. What happened to you?'

# CHAPTER FOURTEEN

'IT'S ALL TO do with Alice's father.'

'Glen? Okay.' He wasn't sure what the man might have done to result in Charlie being the subject of bad gossip.

'He was perfect when we met. A bit like you, actually. Handsome, charming, suave. Great to look at. What people call a real catch. We just hit it off and we married early and I was head over heels in love. Or I thought it was love. Looking back now, I think it was just infatuation that this great guy wanted to be with me.'

'You're a great catch too. He was lucky to be with you.' He meant it.

'Thanks. Things were great to begin with, but I noticed little things that, on their own, weren't too concerning, but added together threw up a few red flags.'

'Such as?'

Charlie turned to make sure the patio door was closed, so that Alice couldn't hear. 'He was a security guy. Dealt with tech and private home security. He worked for a company that installed cameras and alarms in people's property. Mansions, even. They were top notch. Glen always seemed a little on edge about people knowing our business. I felt it was just because of his job, you know? I thought he was just trying to protect me and at first, I thought it was great, you know, that he cared so much.'

'I'm sensing a *but...*'

'But it was low-level control of me. *"Are you really going to wear that dress at work?" "You look better without make-up." "I don't think you should hang around with Suzie any more, she said horrible things about me."*'

'He was isolating you.' Eli could feel ire building. He'd met a couple of controlling men in his time. There were one or two in Vasquez.

'Yes. But I've always been isolated. I have no family. I have no friends. I've never settled anywhere, until I met him, and he made me feel like he could give me everything I ever wanted in life—stability. A future. Start a family. The works. You know how much I've always wanted a big family of my own.'

He nodded, feeling a pang. Because he wanted the same thing too and couldn't have it.

'He wanted us to try for a kid straight after we married and one morning I woke up feeling sick and took a test. I was pregnant with Alice and that's when Glen changed big time.'

'How so?'

'He just seemed... I don't know...upset at the attention I got from people because of my growing bump. He tried to say it was because he didn't want people fawning over me, touching my belly, because how was I to know whether they had a knife or not? Whether they were dangerous or not? He began telling me to stay at home and I pretty much only left the house to go to work, OBGYN appointments and scans.'

'And...people at your work were noticing?'

'They told me I was beginning to look ill. Pale. Withdrawn. And I guess it was because I didn't want to attract attention, because I knew it would just send Glen into a funk. He didn't hit me or call me names or anything. He kept saying it was just concern for my well-being. But his silences were legendary and I couldn't bear the silence and I would find myself doing anything I could to make him happy again.'

'And you didn't like the talk, because people at work were concerned for you?' It didn't seem that this would be enough to have upset her as she'd seemed.

'No, that wasn't the problem. Glen became even more controlling. Wanted me to give up work, stay at home. He monitored my phone, checked all my messages, questioned me over everything. And then one night, I noticed I was spotting. I was about six months pregnant and very scared, but Glen wouldn't let me go to get checked out. He said he didn't want a man looking at me like that, or examining me. I said I'd ask for a woman, but he still wasn't happy. He locked the doors.'

'You're kidding me?'

She shook her head. 'I'd put up with his behaviours for far too long and when we left to see his mother the next day, I escaped through a bathroom window and went straight to a hospital.'

'Was everything okay?'

'Just a breakthrough bleed. But I couldn't believe he'd possibly endangered the life of our child and put me through a sleepless night, just because he was so paranoid. So I left him. I had nowhere to go. Nowhere to live. I got a cheap room at a motel and that's when everything went incredibly bad.'

'It wasn't *already* bad?'

'He shared things that he shouldn't,' she said, not feeling brave enough to say it straight out.

Eli frowned. 'I don't understand.'

'He…um…he'd had secret cameras around the house.' She glanced at him, judging how much to say. Wanting to say it straight out, afraid of his reaction. 'Ones I didn't know about…in the bedroom…and he'd made videos and taken photos of me when I was naked and…' she paused a long time '…posted them online.'

She couldn't look at him then, afraid to see the shock on his face. Afraid to see the pity. Or what if she saw something worse? Curiosity? Wonderment. A need to see these pictures for himself? They were in a relationship after all. A strange one, maybe, but perhaps he'd feel possessive, too? And she couldn't bear to see that on his face.

But then she heard him shift in his seat and suddenly he was kneeling before her, her hand in his, and he had to reach up to gently guide her face to turn to his. 'That should never have happened to you. This Glen…he should be the one to feel ashamed. Not you. Did you call the police?'

She nodded, tears forming in her eyes, burning them. 'They got him to take the stuff down, but people can make copies. Save it. They are still out there and I have to live with that and raise a daughter to believe that nothing can bring her down, and yet she lives in a world where men can do this to women and justify their actions to themselves. How do I tell her that? How do I teach her to protect herself, when we live in a world where there are cameras watching us always?'

'You teach her to always be on the alert, but that there are good men out there, too. Men who will respect her if she chooses not to consent. If she chooses to say no. You teach her to live a life well-lived and not one that resides in fear.'

'You mean like me? I live in fear, because of what Glen did. I ran away, unable to cope with the influx of harassment I got after those things went public. I moved. I kept on moving, even when I had Alice, afraid to settle anywhere, afraid to let people know me, in case they found out. And now I've told you, I'm afraid that you will look at me differently.'

He smiled at her. 'I will always look at you the same way. That before me is the most beautiful woman I have ever seen in my entire life. A clever, kind, compassionate woman. An excellent mother. A brilliant doctor. An...' he grinned '...incompetent abseiler. But!' He chuckled and stroked her face. 'Never a victim. Because you fight for everything. You may have moved around, but you stand your ground when you are right. You love your daughter and try the best for her every day. You keep her safe and, in my opinion, she has the best role model a young girl could ever have.'

Charlie made a strange noise. Somewhere between a laugh, cry and a hiccup. But then she leaned forward in her chair and kissed him on the cheek. Quickly. Briefly. Glancing back through the patio doors to make sure that Alice hadn't seen. 'You're a good man, Eli.'

He winked at her, smiling. 'I try.'

Her legs ached, from the injuries, but also from the fact that, normally, she was an active person and this forced sitting down that she was having to do was becoming frustrating. As she sat listening to a patient, she made a mental note to herself that when she saw Eli, she'd ask if she could use crutches, somehow, instead.

He'd been amazing last night, listening to what she had to say, and she had to admit to herself that even though telling him had first felt as if it were the last thing she'd ever do, now that she had? It felt amazing. As if a weight had lifted and she knew now, in her heart, that Eli would not go looking for those images of her if they still existed somewhere in some dark recesses of the web. In fact, she actually believed that even if he did come across them, he would report them and track down the owners and forcibly have them removed on her behalf.

He'd been appalled at Glen.

But he had not judged her for trusting him. Because that was what you did in relationships, wasn't it? You trusted the other person. You gave them the benefit of the doubt. And if that relationship was an important one? As hers had been? Then you forgave people for little discrepancies in their behaviour in case they were having a bad day, or were acting a little out of character, because they just might be stressed. Glen's overprotective nature had seemed cute, at first. She'd loved that he wanted to keep her safe.

She just hadn't realised to what extent he'd been monitoring her.

'...and Chuck was out feeding the dogs and so he didn't see anything. It was all over by the time he came back in.'

Her patient was Chuck's wife, Angela. She'd come in that morning, after experiencing something odd at home.

'I don't normally come to the docs. You can see from my chart, I think the last time I was here was, ooh, a good five years ago and I've always been fit and well.'

'And did you experience anything else with the dizzy spell?'

'The room spun. I felt it *and* saw it. It made me feel incredibly sick and I began to panic a bit, to be honest with you.'

'And when this happened...had you bent down, or were you in a strange position? Or just standing normally when it happened?'

'Just standing. I was doing the breakfast dishes at the sink.'

'Looking down?'

'Yes. I was scrubbing the frying pan. We'd just had eggs.'

'And did you fall, or sway? What happened?'

'I squeezed my eyes shut, so I couldn't see it spinning. I could still feel it though, for just a few seconds and then it felt like it might have stopped, so I opened my eyes and the room was still again, but my heart rate was fast, I felt incredibly sick and shaky and so I made my way over to the kitchen chair and sat down.'

'And then Chuck came back in?'

'Yes. He said I was white as a sheet.'

'And did you have a headache at all?'

'Afterwards, yes. For about a half-hour.'

'Do you normally get headaches?'

'Not really. Not unless I haven't slept much.'

'Okay. Well, it could be an inner ear infection, so I'll check your ears first, okay?'

'Okay.'

'Any history of ear problems?'

'No. I've always been as fit as a fiddle.'

Charlie got out the otoscope and looked in Angela's ears, but both were clear. No wax build-up and no sign of infection. The eardrums looked exactly as they should. 'Any colds, recently? Sore throat?'

'No.'

'Ever get Covid?'

'Didn't everybody?'

'And how were you with that?'

'Fine! Just a cough for about a week. A bit of tiredness, but nothing bad.'

'I'd like to do an Epley manoeuvre, if that's okay? Just to see if it's debris in the ear canals moving around causing you to feel dizzy.'

'Okay.'

'But I'll need to call in Eli. I can't do it myself in this chair.'

'Fine. It'll be lovely to see him, I haven't seen him in a while…probably not since he got sick when he was still a student.'

Charlie frowned. Eli was sick? It couldn't be anything serious, surely? He seemed fine right now. She dismissed it and typed an instant screen message that would send to Eli's computer. Seconds later, she got a reply. He'd be right in.

'He's coming.'

'Bless him. He's a good man.'

'He is. The best.'

Angela looked at her, head tilted to one side in question. 'You're enjoying working together?'

'I am.'

'Vasquez is such a strange place. It must have taken some getting used to?'

'It's been great, actually. Eli and the Clarks and everyone here have been most welcoming.'

'And you get on well with Eli?'

'I think everyone does,' she said, laughing.

Angela smiled. 'He makes it easy. Mind you, it certainly helps that he's so easy on the eye, wouldn't you say?'

Charlie blushed.

'I thought so!' Angela preened with her point having been made, just as Eli rapped his knuckles on her door and came in.

'Angela! How are you?' He smiled at her patient.

'Fine. Just this dizzy spell that was worrying. I think Chuck thought I might have had a TIA, or something, so best to get it checked out.' A TIA was a transient ischaemic attack. Sometimes called a mini stroke, in which effects of a stroke occurred for a short period of time and then dissipated, leaving no sign it had ever happened. Visually, anyway.

'Ears are normal, BP is spot on. I thought we could do an Epley?' Charlie said.

Eli nodded. 'No problem. Angela, would you be a darling and hop up onto the examination bed for me?'

'Of course.'

Once Angela was on the bed, Eli held her head in his hands and then turned it forty-five degrees to her left and then quickly lowered her to a prone position in which her head was lower than her body over the edge of the bed. Then he turned her head ninety degrees to the other side, watching her eyes all the time for signs of nystagmus—an involuntary movement of the eyes—then asked Angela to rotate her body so it was in alignment with her head, before sitting her up again, with her head still turned to the side. 'Feel anything?' he asked.

'No.'

'Let's do the other side.'

He repeated the procedure, but nothing happened. No nystagmus was reproduced.

'I want you to replicate the stance you were in when it happened,' Charlie suggested.

Angela did so, but again, nothing occurred.

'It might be worth doing some bloods, just a general MOT, see if that flags anything and if not, then we can put it down to being idiopathic in nature. But if you get dizzy again, Angela, I want you to call me right away, okay?'

'Okay. What will you check for in the bloods?'

'A full blood count, blood sugars, thyroid, electrolytes are considered standard in these cases.'

'All right.'

Charlie gathered together the things she would need and procured a quick sample from Angela's arm. 'You go home and take it easy for the day.'

'Are you kidding me? With all those dogs, a house and a husband to look after? Not to mention I've got the grandkids coming over. We've promised them a movie night.'

'Well, maybe let Chuck organise the grandkids?' Charlie smiled.

Angela laughed. 'We'll see.'

'Just take it easy, okay?'

Angela nodded and left the room.

Charlie turned to Eli. 'Thank you for helping out. I hope you weren't busy?'

'Not at all. How are you doing?'

'It's frustrating being in the chair. I'm not used to letting people do things for me that usually I'm capable of doing for myself.'

He nodded. 'I get that. I had it too, once.'

'You ever break your ankles?'

'Not quite. I got sick once and they brought me home from medical school. The Clarks looked after me. Fetched my shopping. Cooked my food. Mom practically never left my side for weeks.'

That had to be what Angela had mentioned. 'What were you sick with?'

'I don't really like to talk about it. It's gone now. No need to worry.' He smiled. 'Well, I'd better be off.'

And then he left her room so abruptly, she was left shocked into silence. No secret cuddle? No secret kiss? Something was most definitely off and she didn't like not knowing. The least he could do was open up to her, the way she'd opened up to him. She felt closer to him now. They were in a relationship in which they could confide their secrets. Their fears. Why wouldn't he share?

Wheeling her chair forward, she began to go after him.

There were no more patients scheduled and she was due a break anyway. She found him in his office, staring out of the window. 'What's wrong, Eli?'

He turned. Smiled. 'Nothing!'

'No, you're lying to me. Something *is* wrong and I want you to feel that you can talk to me about anything. The way I talked to you. I told you something about me last night that I swore to never tell you, but I did so because I thought that...' she sighed, unsure as to whether to admit this '...I thought that maybe we weren't actually having a fling and that instead we were in some kind of relationship. One that involved feelings, because I don't know how to explain what else we have here. I mean, we haven't even, you know, slept together yet and yet I feel closer to you than I have to anyone in a long, long time.'

He looked down at the ground, then back up at her when she began speaking again.

'Flings don't help their bit on the side care for their sick child. They don't stay with them all day just to keep them company and then say that they've had a really nice time. They don't come round and cook. They don't move in when that fling has a stupid accident at work. They don't buy their daughter's artwork and buy them teddy bears. They don't look at me the way that you look at me.'

'I know. But we share a past, you and I. We're not just strangers.'

'No, we're not. But what are we, Eli? Is this simply a thing that goes one way? Am I the fool for thinking that you might feel more for me? Am I the idiot for confiding in you my deepest, darkest, shameful secret, when you won't tell me yours? Am I *deluded*?'

'Of course not.'

'Then why won't you speak to me and tell me what's wrong? How can I feel any of the things I feel for you, if you won't let me know you?'

'You do know me.'

She shook her head. 'No, I don't. After you left? This life you've built? I hardly know anything about it. You got taken in by the Clarks, you had a seemingly mysterious illness you won't talk about and you had a relationship fail, but I don't know the ins and outs of your life. You don't share *anything*. You keep me on the edge and that's not how I want to be! If I'm going to be in someone's life, then I want to be in it. Heart and soul. I deserve that and I can't be with a man who wants to keep his secrets. Because I've been there, Eli. You know I have and look how that turned out for me.'

'I don't have cameras, Charlie. I'm not Glen.'

'But you have something you won't talk to me about,' she challenged him. Staring him down. Waiting for him to lower his gaze, but he didn't. He simply stared back at her and she realised that he was admitting that she was correct. Yes. There was something. 'I see. Then this?' She gestured between them. 'Is over. I can't stay here and look at you every day and pretend that we're close, when clearly we are not. I was a fool to stay here when I found out it was you. I should have trusted my instincts.'

'What are you saying?'

'I'm saying I'll find something else. Another job. Someplace else. The second my contract here is over, I'm gone!'

'But Alice is settled here! Are you really going to keep hauling her around the country every few months because of a few pictures? What kind of life is that?'

'It's better than what we had.'

'Is that what you want for her? Something that's a little bit better than awful? Or do you want her to have a happy life? A future? In a place where she could build it?'

'What do you mean?'

'She has skills. Way beyond those of a normal five-year-old. She can draw. And here in Vasquez there is so much she could capture.'

'So you want me to stay so my daughter can draw some grizzlies, is that it? Way to go, Eli. Way to go in giving me an astounding reason to stay!' Now she felt angry. How could she ever have believed that this man would ever be serious with her? He never had been and all she'd been was fun to him. A plaything. Someone to entertain him for a bit. 'And how dare you imply that our lives were awful before? You know nothing about us!'

He stared at her then and nodded. 'You're right. I know nothing about you. Nothing that matters.' He turned and walked away and she was so shocked by it, she just sat there, staring at the empty space where he had once been.

# CHAPTER FIFTEEN

THE DRIVE TO pick up Alice from kindergarten was tense.
Charlie had insisted on getting into the truck all by herself
and it had been quite the sight to see, seeing as the truck
was higher than the wheelchair. But she'd come armed, he'd
seen. Bringing with her some crutches to help support her
body weight as she transferred from the chair to the truck.
He'd itched to help her, but had known that if he'd tried, he
would only have been sworn at or shook off and so, instead,
he'd stood back, patiently waiting while it took her over two
minutes to finally haul herself into the front passenger seat
of his truck. She'd held the crutches tightly, so he'd taken the
wheelchair, folded it up and placed it in the back of the truck.

Driving over to the school, he could have cut the tension
in the vehicle with a chainsaw. But what could he do? Talk
about it? What was there to say? Was there even a point to
saying anything? What they'd had never even got properly
started, it sure as hell was never going to last. Charlie would
leave with Alice. In every iteration of this scenario she would
leave and be gone for ever. Maybe he'd get the occasional
email? A Christmas card at best. So it was probably best to
just let this burn on out. They'd manage somehow, tensions
would finally ease. Probably just as she was about to pack
up and go anyway.

He was used to people leaving him. He'd hardened his

heart to it. It was the only way to survive. He'd left her behind once, now it was only right and fair that she had a turn.

He left Charlie in the truck when he went to collect Alice.
Normally they would meet her together in the schoolyard and
listen to Alice natter about her day on the way back to the
truck, examining paintings or models she'd made, or hearing her chat about something they'd done, or which friends
she'd made.

Alice came running out of her class, as usual, with a broad
smile upon her face. 'Eli!' She slammed into him and he
whisked her up in the air with a broad smile and, laughing,
twirled her around, before putting her down again. God, he
would miss this kid!

'Good day?'

'The best! Mrs Clark was telling us about a school trip
that's coming up!'

'Oh, yeah? Where to?' He knew where to. His mom took
the kids up to the reindeer farm on Elk Ridge each year. They
had a small visitor and education centre there, next to a much
larger animal rescue and convalescence place.

'We're going to see some reindeer! And elk and bears and
owls and all kinds of animals, Mrs Clark says!'

He smiled, knowing how much Alice would love the place.
'It's gonna be wild, huh?'

'It's in September. Think Mom will let me go?'

September. Ah. Charlie's contract ended in August. 'I don't
know. You'll have to ask her.'

'Is she here? Why didn't she come with you?'

'Her legs were bad. She, er...wanted to wait in the truck to
rest for a little while. It's been a long day at work, so...' He
*hated* lying to her. He'd never lied to a kid, if he could help
it, because he remembered how much it had hurt when adults

had lied to him as a child. Mostly with making promises they knew they could never keep. Okay, so the lies weren't big, right now, but it could be a slippery slope.

'Oh. Okay. She must be in a lot of pain, then, because she always comes.'

He thought of the pained look he'd seen in Charlie's eyes when they'd been arguing. The hurt he'd seen, because she felt that their relationship was all one-sided.

She was wrong. But how could he tell her that?

Best to let her think that it was true. Then she could walk away at the end of all of this without guilt. If she walked away hating him, then that was better than walking away knowing he couldn't give her what she'd always wanted.

He held Alice's hand as she skipped back to the car to keep up with his longer strides. He liked this part. This part was nice. Where he could pretend he was her father.

*This must be what it feels like.*

He felt a huge pang then of longing. So close to what he wanted, but so far away.

He wanted to harden his heart. Letting go of her hand and not allowing himself to have such thoughts would be better for him when they walked out of his life for good. Pretending to be Alice's dad? Only pain waited for him in that iteration of life.

As they got to the truck, he opened up the back passenger door and lifted Alice in.

'Hey, Mom! Are you okay? Do your legs hurt?'

'I'm okay, baby, don't you worry,' Charlie answered.

He buckled her in and closed her door, then he got back behind the driver's wheel. 'Home?'

'Yay!' Alice said as he started the engine. 'Mom…there's a

trip to see reindeer and all these other animals in September with Mrs Clark and my class. Can I go? Please?'

'Sounds great, baby, but I don't think we'll still be living in Vasquez when it gets to September. You'll be in a new school.'

'But I *love* my school. I love Mrs Clark. I love living *here*. Can't we stay here?'

Charlie turned around in her seat. 'There won't be a job for me, baby. The one I have now is only temporary, remember?'

Glancing through the rear-view mirror, he could see a sulk settle onto Alice's face. 'Not fair!'

'I'm sorry, honey.'

He wanted to make it better. He wanted to fix it. He didn't like seeing Alice upset and he hated not being able to talk to Charlie about it. But she was right. There wasn't a job for her. Not unless Nance chose to stay at home and not return to her old post. She might, even though she'd always said she would come back. But Ryan was Nance's first baby and who knew how she might feel about returning to work, now that Ryan was born?

Unable to do or say anything that would help, he drove them home in silence, fetching Charlie's wheelchair when they parked outside her place and standing awkwardly, yet again, as she stubbornly alighted from his truck, down to the seat in silence.

Inside, he went straight to the kitchen, while Charlie helped Alice get changed. He knew he needed to keep busy, or he'd go insane, so he gathered all the ingredients to make a chicken pot pie and began making shortcrust pastry.

He knew the secret to a good shortcrust was to make sure the butter was cold as he proceeded to rub it into the sifted flour with his fingers, to make it a breadcrumb texture. Then he added milk, slowly, until it formed a dough. He wrapped it in cling film and placed it in the fridge, pulling out the chicken breasts so he could chop them into bite-size chunks. It helped to keep busy. It helped to form the dough. It allowed him to not think too hard about what he was having to let go of.

'You don't have to cook.'

He turned to face Charlie. 'No offence, but I don't think you'd be able to do this on your own.'

'Well, that's just it, Eli. I can do everything on my own. It's all I've ever done. Occasionally I've let someone into my life and each time it has been an unmitigated disaster. To be honest with you, I'd feel much more comfortable in my home if I didn't have to see you all the time. I'll finish whatever this is and you can go and pack your things.'

He stared at her. 'You want me to go?'

# CHAPTER SIXTEEN

'YOU WANT ME *to go?*'

Yes, she did. Because it hurt to have him around. It hurt that he wouldn't open up and share his innermost feelings with her. Because he thought if he kept his distance, he wouldn't get hurt.

*Turns out that maybe neither of us has changed our ways since we were small.*

She'd been vulnerable and though, in the moment, it had felt good to share, now it felt truly awful. There was an imbalance in their relationship and she didn't like how it left her feeling weak and exposed. Because she'd been exposed before and wouldn't be so ever again.

'I can make a pie, or whatever this is.'

'It's a pie.' He continued to stare at her, as if weighing her up. As if deciding to say something else. But then she saw the decision in his eyes that he wasn't going to and he turned away and washed his hands to rid them of the flour. 'I'll pack up now.'

'I'll find a way to get Alice to school tomorrow, you don't have to do it.'

'But—'

'And I'll find a way to work, too.'

He sighed and dried his hands on a towel. 'Fine.' He grabbed his holdall from by the front door and began moving around the place, picking up his stuff. His hoodie from the back of the chair. His toothbrush and toiletries from the bathroom. All thrown into the bag. A book he'd been reading that was on the coffee table.

She'd got used to those things. He hadn't been living with her long, but it had become surprisingly nice how much she liked seeing his things about the place. Seeing them gone felt weird. As if the place was emptying somehow, which was ridiculous.

'I'll see you at work, then.' He stood by the door.

'Yes, you will.'

'Can I say goodbye to Alice?'

Honestly? She just wanted him to be gone. So she could get to the end of this unpleasantness. But she knew how much Alice would complain if he left without saying goodbye. 'Sure.'

'Alice?' he called.

Alice came out of her room, smiling. A smile that faltered when she saw him holding his bag and standing by the door. Perhaps she could even sense the tension in the room. 'Are you leaving?'

'Yeah. Come here and give me a hug.'

'But I don't want you to leave! Mom! Tell him to stay!' she pleaded, tears welling up in her eyes.

Charlie felt awful. This was why she never let guys get close. This was why guys never met her daughter. Because of this moment right here. 'He has to go, honey.'

'But, why?' she cried, slamming her little body into Eli's as he hefted her up into his arms and squeezed her tight.

Alice wrapped her little legs around his waist and cried into his shoulder.

'You'll see him again, some time. It's not like he's leaving Vasquez.'

But Charlie wasn't sure she was heard. Alice was crying so loudly. So hard.

The look on Eli's face was pained, his eyes closed as he held her little girl. It looked painful for him too, and she hated to see that. It made the guilt worse. She'd not expected this. For him to get close to her daughter. But he had.

'Come on, baby. Let him go.'

'No!' Alice cried, squeezing ever tighter.

'Alice? Alice, I want you to listen to me. Look at me. Alice?' Eli pulled back, until Alice looked up at him with a red, tear-streaked face. 'I'm just going back to my place. That's all. You'll still see me around.'

Alice shook her head, as if she didn't believe him.

'I promise you, you will see me around. Okay? Because I need to see all those fabulous drawings you do. I want to be able to say to people, *Oh, you like Alice Griffin's art? I knew her since she was a little kid. I bought the very first piece she ever sold!*'

Alice sniffed and managed a short smile.

'Let go, Alice,' Charlie said as Eli lowered her daughter to the ground.

'Can I walk with you to your truck?' Alice asked.

Eli glanced at Charlie and she looked away. Unable to meet his gaze. She felt awful. That Alice was getting hurt because of this? Of her mistake? Of letting Eli get close?

'Sure.'

She watched from the doorway, witnessing another painful hug, whispered promises and then watching her daughter cry as Eli got in his truck and drove away.

Charlie hoped that now that he'd gone, it would be easier.

She was wrong.

Alice stomped up the path and yelled at Charlie as she passed. 'You always spoil things!' And then she slammed her bedroom door, with the ferocity of a teenager.

Charlie sat there, blinking, unsure of how she'd even got herself into this mess in the first place. But it was clear. Coming here to Vasquez, staying, once she knew Eli was here, had been a tremendous mistake.

Charlie had not arrived at work at her usual time, and he knew because for the last hour he'd stared alternately at the clock and then out of the window of the clinic, trying to work out what he would say to her when she got there.

An apology. That would be first. Clear. Profound. Touching. He'd let her know that he deeply regretted upsetting her. That he was upset that he had hurt her. And that he would understand if she wanted to be angry with him, but that he hoped that they could put it behind them while they worked together.

His cell rang in his back pocket.

Charlie? Ringing to apologise for being late? She was trying to do everything herself from that wheelchair.

But no. It was his mom.

*Odd. Isn't she in class?*

'Mom? Everything okay?'

'Well, no. I'm confused, honey. Charlie has pulled Alice from the school—she notified the office first thing and I've only just been told. Has something happened?'

She'd pulled Alice out of kindergarten? 'Oh…er…we had a bit of a falling out.'

'What kind of falling out?'

'We were…um…kind of…seeing one another. But…secretly…like a bit of fun.'

'Did she know it was just a bit of fun?'

And that was when he realised that it hadn't been *a bit of fun* for either of them.

Eli groaned. 'I did something stupid.'

There was a pause while his mom digested this. 'Is it something you can fix?'

'She wants kids, Mom. I can't give her that. Why keep her here when I can't give her the one thing she wants?'

'Honey…well, she wouldn't have been in a relationship with you, if she wanted that. Unless, of course, you didn't exactly tell her? I know you, Eli, better than you realise and you need to understand that sometimes you act like you haven't quite grown up properly.'

She always did have a polite way of telling him off. Mild chiding. Like a proper mom. He smiled briefly, glad to have found his mom in life, if he couldn't have anyone else. 'I couldn't tell her.'

'Why? Hasn't she always been special to you?'

'How do you know that?'

'Oh, honey, I heard the way you talked about her, even before she came here. I saw it in your eyes. She's something special and you'd be a fool to let her get away, without telling her everything.'

'I don't know if I'm brave enough.'

'You're the bravest guy I know. All you've been through? But tell me this…how scared are you of the idea of a future without her in it?'

He let out a breath. 'Terrified. There will always be something missing.'

She sighed. 'The piece of your heart you left behind with her, when you left the first time. When we took you from her.'

'You think she'd want me?'

'I think you should give her the option. Tell her the truth and let her decide, because if you don't, then you'll always regret it. If you tell her and she still wants to go, then at least you will know that you tried and she said no, knowing *all* the facts.'

His phone beeped. Another incoming call. This one from Chuck.

'I gotta go.'

'Good luck, honey. I love you.'

'Love you, too, Mom.'

He answered Chuck's call. 'Chuck? Sorry, my friend, but I got to run. Can I call you back later?'

'Er…sure. Just thought I'd let you know that Charlie rang me.'

He stilled. 'She did?'

'Yeah. She wants me to fly her to the airport. Her and Alice. I'm meeting her at the bay in an hour. She leaving already?'

'I hope not. Listen, I've got to rearrange a few things here, as I've got patients in the clinic, but can you do me a favour?'

'Sure.'

'Stall her?'

'Charlie?'

'Yeah. I need to see her before she goes. I mucked up, I need to apologise and I'm hoping to persuade her to stay.'

'Okay. Can do. I must say we all think you'd make a great couple.'

'We *all*? Who's *we all*?'

'Vasquez.'

'What?'

'Talk of the town, mate. You think patients and staff haven't noticed the way you two look at one another? You think you're hiding it, but when you ride through town in the back of a truck cradling her after a fall, people begin to talk.'

'Okay, okay. I get the picture. But you can stall, right?'

'Sure. I can tell her the right rotavator needs cranking.'

'Do planes have rotavators?'

'Does it matter?' He could hear Chuck's smile in his voice.

'No. I guess it doesn't.'

# CHAPTER SEVENTEEN

'WHAT'S TAKING SO LONG, Chuck?' Charlie kept glancing at her watch as she sat in her wheelchair on the small wooden pier.

The pilot had opened a flap to expose part of the plane's engine. It all looked terribly complicated inside.

'Just some final checks. You wouldn't want us to fly without me checking it's safe for you and this precious cargo, huh?' he said, ruffling a sulky Alice's hair.

'No. Of course not.' She checked her watch and looked out behind her. She didn't think Eli would come chasing after her. Not after the way they'd parted. Not after the resignation letter she'd left on the clinic desk. Had he seen it yet? He might not have. Especially if he didn't have any clinic patients yet. She'd wanted to leave it in his office, but the door had been locked and, quite frankly? She'd wanted to get out of there, the sooner the better. Especially in this damn chair.

Nothing had gone right for her since coming here and now she was flying back to what? Home? That was a joke. She didn't really have one. The only place she'd ever felt comfortable living in had been here, strangely. Was that personal growth? Or just because Alice had begun to settle in a place? She'd certainly grown attached to Mrs Clark and Eli...

But so had she.

And that was why she had to go. Because how could she allow herself to get attached to someone who wasn't prepared to get attached to her? He'd only wanted a fling anyway, so this was no biggie, right? And she was sick of making mistakes over men.

'Can't we at least get in the plane? It's chilly out here on the pier,' she complained to Chuck.

'Sorry. Aviation rules. Pre-flight checks have to be completed first.'

She had no idea if that was true, but Chuck didn't look sorry. Not one bit. In fact, he looked a little amused, if anything.

Behind her, she heard footsteps clomping towards her on the wooden pier. Then they stopped. She knew whose footsteps they were and felt her heart sink.

'Charlie?'

It was him.

'Eli!' Alice dropped her rucksack and went running towards him and, as before, he scooped her up high into the air.

'Hey, pumpkin.'

She watched as Eli kissed her daughter on the head and gave her a huge squeeze.

Chuck closed the engine flap, wiped his hands on a dirty rag and gave her a smile as he passed. 'Hey, Alice. Come and look at these geese with me. Leave your mom and Eli to talk in private.'

And that was when she realised that Chuck had been stalling intentionally. Long enough for Eli to get here.

She stared at Eli. 'You made him stall us?'

'Guilty as charged, Your Honour.'

'Why are you here, Eli? There's nothing more to be said. You've made that abundantly clear.'

'You're wrong. There's plenty to be said.'

'Like what? Enlighten me, why don't you?'

He took a few more steps towards her. 'Not here. On the

pier, it's exposed. Can we go over there and talk?' He pointed at a waterside bench.

He wore jeans, a fitted tee and a loose flannel shirt over the top. Rugged work boots on his feet made him look like a grungy rock star, rather than a doctor who had just come from a clinic. But that was Vasquez for you. It was more relaxed out here. It was why she liked it. As he settled onto the bench, he took a deep breath.

'I was wrong before. To not tell you what you wanted to hear.' He sighed. 'I was being stupid.'

'You won't hear me arguing.'

'Will I hear you be quiet, so I can say what you want me to say?' he asked with a smile.

She opened her mouth to respond, thought better of it and clamped it shut again.

'Thank you. Charlie…of course I want you to stay. You and Alice. And if not for me, then for that little girl, who loves it here and wants to stay.'

'You want me to stay?'

'Of course I do!'

'Why? Tell me why, exactly, you want me here.'

'Because…you have never been out of my mind, Charlie Griffin. I had to leave you once and I hated it and when you walked back into my life again, I couldn't believe my luck. But I didn't think you'd want to stay for me, because I can't give you what I know that you want.'

'And what do I want?' she asked breathlessly.

'You want a family. You want loads of kids. You said so, only recently.'

'And you think I want that with you?'

'Don't you?'

Now it was her turn to look uncomfortable. 'I'd be a liar if I said I hadn't thought about it.'

'I can't give you kids, Charlie. I'm sterile. I had testicular cancer in medical school and we found out then. The Clarks? They got me through the worst time in my life. A time in which I was scared. Surgery. Chemo. They kept me strong. Mom sitting by my bedside every day. Dad getting me out in the fresh air when I had the energy. Like I was their actual, biological child. They wept for my pain. Would have suffered for me in my place if they could. I couldn't have got through it without them and that was when I realised I truly was one of them.'

Cancer? Her heart ached for him! What an awful thing for him to have gone through! And she'd thought his life had been perfect since he was adopted.

*I was wrong.*

'I thought if we kept it simple between us—a fling—then it would be easy to say goodbye. But it has never been easy to say goodbye to you and I don't want to have to do so again. I may have gained a family here, but I have also lost so much.'

'I can't stay here. There's no job for me.'

'There is. Nance has informed me that she doesn't want to return full-time after her maternity leave is over. She even said she might not return ever. So there is a post for you. A job share, at least.'

'Why should I stay?'

'Because you love it here. Because Alice loves it here. Because the people here love you and I...' He took her hands in his. 'Because *I* love you.'

It was all so much! He'd gone from telling her nothing to telling her everything and it was all so overwhelming!

'I don't know what to say.'

'If you don't love me back, then say goodbye and do it quickly, because I don't think I could do another long, drawn-out goodbye. But if you feel the same way as me…then stay. We could build a life together. A great life. You, me, Alice.'

'We could adopt,' she said, the words surprising her as they came out of her mouth.

'What?'

'We could do what your mom did. Adopt a kid who needs a home. Maybe more than one, if we wanted. We could build a family that way. We're ideally situated to understand what that gift would mean to a child. What do you think?'

He smiled. Broadly. And she felt her heart lift.

'I would do anything to make you happy.'

She smiled back, felt tears of happiness pricking at her eyes. Wanted nothing more than to stand and wrap her arms around him and pull him close, but she couldn't.

'You make me happy,' she said. 'You're enough. You've always been enough.'

'I love you, Charlie Griffin.'

'And I love you, Eli Clark.'

And he reached for her, cradling her face in his hands as he gave her a long, deep kiss.

# EPILOGUE

'I'M NERVOUS!'

Eli pulled her close. One to stop her from pacing, but two… he just liked having her close and looking into her eyes. She softened when he did so. The frantic worry would leave her face and she would relax. 'Take a breath. Look at me. We're gonna do great.'

'How can you know for sure? We've never done this.'

He smiled. 'I know what it's like to be chosen and to drive off in a car with a couple you've only met a couple of times.'

'Do I look okay? Do I look like a good mom?' she asked, glancing down at her outfit. A beautiful soft blue summer dress, dotted with white daisies.

'You look perfect.'

'What about me? I'm about to be a big sister,' said Alice.

They both turned to her. She'd been so thrilled about the idea of having a sibling and she'd wanted to choose a gift to give to David. Picking out a dump truck and a football and a colouring book with a pack of felt-tip pens to go along with it.

'You look great,' Eli said. He liked that he could help re-assure and calm them down, because honestly…? He was pretty nervous himself. This had been a long time coming. A lengthy process they'd gone through to be able to go to an orphanage and choose a child with the help of the agency they were doing it through. There'd been many sets of paperwork.

Lots of background checks. Plenty of visits. And they'd finally settled on David. A little boy, three years of age, who had been abandoned at a fire station when he was six weeks old.

As orphans, both he and Charlie were in the special position of knowing the gift they were giving to a child and to each other in building their family.

He'd never known a proper home, but he and Charlie had fallen for David's cheeky smile and lively character from day one. He had a great chuckle. It was infectious! And at their last visit, he'd fallen asleep on Charlie's lap for over an hour, snuggled into her and she'd looked so beautiful, sitting there, stroking the little boy's golden hair.

How could it possibly have been anyone else?

And here they were today. Ready to take him home to Vasquez.

It had been a kind of whirlwind, the last year and a half. Charlie had gone permanently full-time at the clinic—though she was going on maternity leave once they got home with David—Alice had had a piece of art win a competition on a children's show on TV and they'd moved into a bigger home. One that would be big enough for the family they aspired to build.

He had adopted Alice officially.

The door opened and in walked Karen, the support worker they'd been working with, and standing beside her, holding her hand, was David. He beamed when he saw them and ran forward into Charlie's arms.

She scooped him up and hoisted him onto her waist. 'Hey, you!'

'Hi,' he said.

'I have a question for you.'

'Okay.'

'Do you want to come home with us?'

He nodded, smiling. 'To stay?'

'Yes. For ever and ever.'

'For ever and ever?' he repeated, his eyes lighting up.

'That's right,' Eli said.

'Yay!'

Eli scooped up Alice and moved closer so that Alice and David could hug. They'd both got on so brilliantly with each other from day one. 'Let's go home.'

They waved goodbye to Karen after she'd walked them to the truck with David's case of clothes and a couple of teddy bears he liked.

As they drove away, with their two kids chattering in the back of the truck, Charlie reached for his hand and squeezed it. 'We did it.'

He raised her hand in his and kissed it. 'We did. I love you.'

She smiled at him, quickly glancing at the two kids in the back seat—the start of their big family.

'I love you, too.'

* * * * *

# RESCUED BY THE AUSTRALIAN GP

EMILY FORBES

MILLS & BOON

For Charlotte.

Thank you!

Having an editor who makes my job easier,
my stories better, and who genuinely champions
romance authors is a wonderful thing.

Thank you for your words of wisdom, your support
and your enthusiasm. You are very much appreciated!
This is one of those times when I can honestly say,
'I couldn't do it without you.'

Here's to the next book,

Emily

# CHAPTER ONE

'HIGHER, MUMMY, HIGHER!'

Ella gave her daughter another push on the swing, sending her soaring through the air. Her little legs stuck out, brown and thin against the blue summer sky, as her blonde pigtails streamed behind her. She squealed and laughed, and her giggles were a balm to Ella's tired, tormented soul. She was exhausted, so tired that her head ached constantly and now her joints were starting to ache too.

She lifted her face to the sun. Despite the early hour, she could already feel the warmth in the air. It would be another hot day she knew as she felt the sun beat down on her. She was dressed in a long skirt and a long-sleeved shirt but, even though she couldn't see anyone else nearby, she resisted the urge to push up her sleeves. She hoped her outfit gave the impression she was being sun-smart but, in reality, her clothes hid a secret.

Her eyes followed the arc of Liv's body as she swung through the air but her thoughts drifted away. Ella had hoped to stop in Pelican's Landing for several days to give her time to catch her breath after the long drive. She'd been driving for days; she was tired and dusty.

She looked past the playground equipment and out to

the river. She'd had visions of swimming in the river, of washing away the grime and dirt on her body and in her head, but the river was in flood and, in fact, she could barely even see it over the temporary levee bank that had been built to hold back the flood waters.

She'd driven halfway across the country, over three thousand kilometres across the desert from Western Australia, but in her haste had failed to notice that the eastern states were under water. The Darling and Murray Rivers were flooded and the water had swallowed everything in its path, houses and all, as it made its way from the outback and the mountains to the sea. She was tired and dusty but hadn't even been able to enjoy a swim. All water activities, including swimming, had been banned due to the flood event.

But she had stayed in Pelican's Landing anyway. She couldn't face driving any further. Not just yet. Over a week on the road with just a four-year-old for company hadn't been a lot of fun, and navigating the desert highway alongside massive road trains, grey nomads towing caravans and backpackers in their campervans, had added to the difficulty.

She'd stopped in Pelican's Landing because she liked being near water. She could breathe then. There were plenty of towns just like this one along the river but she'd liked the name. She loved watching the majestic birds glide through the air on the thermal currents, free and easy. All the river towns were in the same predicament—flooded, struggling. If she'd realised this before she'd left Western Australia, she might have headed north, but she really needed a break from driving. And from sleeping in her car.

She could afford to stop here for a few nights. The night skies were clear. The trees were magnificent. The birdlife varied. It was what she was used to. She wasn't a big-city person; she needed space. She felt safer when she had room to move. Room to run.

If the river hadn't been flooded and the town suffering because of it, she might even have considered staying longer. She might have looked for work—just something temporary. Something to top up her income and perhaps put some money in the bank to help her and Liv start over. Cleaning houseboats or cleaning the facilities in the caravan park would have been perfect—it would need to be something she could do with Liv in tow—but jobs were scarce because of the floods.

The town survived on the tourist trade, in particular the summer holiday period, but because of the flood, which was the biggest in fifty years, all water activities on the river had been banned. There was no swimming, no fishing, no boating, no houseboats, no skiing and, therefore, all holidaymakers had made other plans. They hadn't seen any point in coming for a holiday at the river if they couldn't use it. The town was suffering from the lack of overnight tourists and the few day trippers who visited weren't enough to make a difference.

The town had been divided by a massive levee bank. What she imagined would normally be a picturesque town, with its historic old buildings, marina and paddle steamers, had been split in two by it. It even blocked the view of the river from the main street. But at least the levee bank meant the caravan park could stay open. Even if there were no tourists there had been engineers, labourers and machine operators employed to build the bank and they had needed somewhere to stay. Most of them had moved on now but the caravan park remained open.

Now it was home to dozens of people who had been forced to move out of their riverfront houses because of the floods. Most of these people were retirees and, while Ella knew her daughter would have liked some playmates, she was happy with the lack of families in the park. She wasn't obliged to make small talk with other parents at the playground and that suited her. She preferred to keep her business to herself. And she didn't want Liv to form friendships just to be dragged away again.

They'd have to move soon. She needed to find a job and somewhere to settle before Liv started school. They were sleeping in a tent; that wasn't a viable long-term option but she couldn't afford to rent a cabin and a tent was better than sleeping in the car. The little bit of money she'd managed to save wasn't going to last much longer. She got a single mother's benefit every fortnight, but she was trying to save that, knowing she'd need a deposit in order to get a roof over her head.

Her plan was still to head north, to Queensland ultimately, somewhere with good weather and maybe the chance of a job and the opportunity to finish studying. Queensland had a booming tourist sector; she was sure she'd be able to find work doing something. She was smart, and pretty, and could make herself presentable if she had a little bit of time and money for some new clothes. Something decent from the thrift shop would do. She was thin—probably too thin—but at least that meant almost anything in a thrift shop would fit her and she knew she could make almost anything look okay.

'Push me, Mummy!'

Ella had drifted off into planning mode and Liv's swing was slowing down. 'Use your legs, Liv, you can keep yourself going,' she answered, needing to give her tired arms a rest. 'Five more minutes and we'll get an ice-cream,' she added, trying to sweeten the deal.

She checked the handbag that was strung across her body, hoping she had enough money for the treat. It was another three days until her next government cheque hit her bank account and that wasn't money that she could fritter away. But Liv deserved a treat. Ella had some tins of tuna and some pasta, and the caravan park manager had given her some eggs and fresh tomatoes. She should be able to stretch that out to make dinner for three nights, which left her just enough money in her purse for two ice-creams.

She pushed her hair out of her eyes as she zipped her bag closed. The wind had picked up and was stirring the surface of the river, forming little waves, capped with white. She looked to the trees as a flock of sulphur-crested cockatoos took to the sky, screeching in protest. She wondered what had startled them.

Movement to her left caught her eye and, as she turned her head, she saw water trickling over the levee bank. Ella frowned as she tried to process what she was seeing, initially thinking the wind must be pushing the water over the barrier. But then she watched in horror as the levee bank began to collapse and a torrent of water gushed into the caravan park as the bank gave way. Within seconds, muddy water was swirling around her ankles as the river continued to force its way through the levee. Tree branches of all shapes and sizes swept through the breach, rushing towards her. The water kept coming and was up to her knees before she reacted.

She had to move. She and Liv needed to get to higher ground. The water wasn't stopping and the force as it flowed around her almost knocked her off her feet. If they didn't move, they were going to get swept away or, worse, sucked under. If she lost sight of Liv, she knew she'd never find her in the muddy water. Neither of them would stand a chance against the current.

She pulled Liv off the swing, grabbing her by one arm.

'Ow, Mummy, you're hurting me.'

There was no time to apologise. There was no time to think about the bruises she might leave on her daughter's skin. No time to worry about what anyone would think if they saw the marks. Ella looked around, frantically searching for higher ground, looking for somewhere safe to flee to before the water swallowed them.

The water frothed around them; eddies formed and brown foam swirled past. Ella felt something slice into her right leg and she staggered as pain pierced her right calf and her knee almost gave way. Liv screamed as Ella momentarily lost her balance. She barely managed to keep her feet and straightened up, only to find that the water was now up to her thighs. She was running out of time.

There was an old set of monkey bars near the swings. It was their only chance. She limped through the water as quickly as she could, the current pushing her in the direction of the monkey bars. Her leg complained with every step but she had to keep going. Stopping was not an option. Liv's weight made covering the short distance difficult but at least she was going with the flow of water. She knew she wouldn't stand a chance trying to fight against it but, even so, she was still worried about getting knocked off her feet. She reached out with her left hand and grabbed the ladder of the monkey bars, not daring to relax yet. She pushed Liv up and hoped the equipment was firmly concreted into the ground.

'Climb, Liv. Hurry. As fast as you can. You need to get to the top.'

She hoped that would be high enough. She had no way of knowing when the water would stop rising but she was out of time. She had no way of getting anywhere else. She fought the current as it tried to prise her from the ladder, holding on with two hands now. As soon as Liv was halfway up, she scrambled up the rungs of the ladder behind her daughter.

She curled her toes around the rungs as the water swirled around her legs, realising she'd lost her sandals somewhere along the way. Sharp pain stabbed her right calf with each step. Liv was perched on the monkey bars. Ella scooted along and wrapped her arm around Liv's slender body, holding onto her firmly. She couldn't lose her.

Her leg throbbed, her skirt was ripped and she could see a nasty gash in her calf. She made sure Liv was stable on the play equipment before tearing off a piece of her skirt, thinking as she did so that she had nothing else to wear, but she needed to bandage her leg. She wound dirty, wet fabric around her calf and worried it might make things worse. It might not stop the bleeding and might give her an infection to boot. But she had to try to stem the blood.

By the time she finished, her clothes were almost dry but despite the heat she was shivering. She was feeling light-headed. She wasn't sure if it was blood loss, shock, heat, dehydration or all of the above.

'What happened, Mummy?' Liv was looking around, bewildered.

'Remember how I told you the river was flooded, full of water and dangerous? It got more flooded and came over the bank.'

There was no point explaining to Liv about the burst levee. It didn't matter now. She'd warned Liv not to go near the levee bank, her daughter was afraid enough already. This event wouldn't have helped. It frightened Ella—she could only imagine how Liv felt. Ella could see fear and confusion in her daughter's eyes and she fought hard to keep her own expression neutral. She didn't want her expression to mirror Liv's. She didn't want to frighten her any more.

Ella looked around the park as the water continued to rise. She was beginning to worry that it would keep rising and swallow their precarious perch along with everything else. Her heart was racing in her chest. She had no idea what to do next.

'Ella? Are you okay?'

She looked up at the sound of a man's voice calling to her. The caravan park manager and his wife were on the veranda of their house. The house was at the entrance to the park, at the top of the small slope, but the water was lapping at the steps to their veranda. Below them camp sites and cabins stretched down the hill to the river's edge all the way to the levee bank which had been holding. Until now.

Ella had put her faith in that bank, in the engineers and labourers who had built it. It was just another example of people letting her down.

'Stay there. Someone will come for us,' Bill called out.

She didn't know where he thought they could go. His comment would have been funny if their situation wasn't so dire. She could see the other park residents, clinging to their balcony railings. The ones who had cabins closer to the river had clambered onto the outdoor furniture. Ella knew most of the current park tenants were retirees. She hoped they had all managed to scramble to safety. She knew most of these people had already been evacuated from their houses due to the flood. They would have expected to be safe here.

'I don't like it here...' Liv's voice wobbled.

Ella didn't care for the place much either at the moment. What she'd initially seen as a quiet, almost idyllic spot to stop and gather their breath had turned into a nightmare.

'We're safe now. Someone will come to rescue us.' She mentally crossed her fingers, hoping Bill was right.

A siren blasted and Ella jumped, almost losing her balance. The wind had died down, disappearing as quickly as it had blown in, and the siren was sharp and piercing in the still summer air.

'What's that noise?' Liv put her hands over her ears as Ella gripped her more firmly, terrified she'd lose hold of her over this treacherous water.

'That's to let people know we need help,' she replied, even though she had no idea. She assumed it was an emergency siren, activated to let the emergency responders know they were needed. She hoped that was what it was for, and not to alert people of another impending disaster.

The water appeared to have stopped rising. It was a foot or so below the rungs of the monkey bars and Ella hoped it wouldn't rise again. She and Liv couldn't get to anything higher. They were stranded until help arrived. The water was too deep to wade through and flowing too strongly to swim through. She could see whirlpools forming randomly, even without Liv, Ella didn't think it would be safe to try.

The caravan park and the adjacent bowling club and pub were completely surrounded by a levee bank. On Ella's left was the river and to her right, behind the other levee bank that *had* held was the town's main road. The caravan park was now a massive lake as the newly flooded area levelled out with the river. Ella hoped the levee bank to her right continued to hold otherwise the town itself would also be flooded.

She looked over to where their tent had been pitched. The tent and all their belongings had disappeared. Her car was still where she had parked it but the water was halfway up the windows. Everything they had, everything she owned, was either gone or destroyed. She hadn't had much to begin with but now she'd lost it all. She and Liv literally had the clothes on their backs and her handbag. Her heart sank as she surveyed the scene. Hadn't they suffered enough? Life could be cruel. She didn't need this.

She stifled a cry. She couldn't let Liv see her upset. She had to be brave for her. She had to stay strong. But, right now, she didn't know where she would find that strength. She'd been tested before but she'd always worried that one day something would break her.

Was this the day?

No. She shook her head. She wasn't going to be beaten. She was a fighter. She could do this. She tried to count her blessings as she clung to the play equipment. She still had Liv and they were lucky to be alive.

Although it didn't always feel like that.

# CHAPTER TWO

'MAISIE!' LUKE WHISTLED to his dog and waited for her to leap onto the boat and settle herself on the bow before he opened the throttle on his dinghy and pulled away from the mooring. He kept his speed low and scanned the river, watching out for submerged objects—logs, outdoor furniture, barbecues. All manner of things had been washed down the river with the flood and he knew that, as these things took on water, they often sank just below the surface. Colliding with one could damage the propeller, or worse, put a hole in the bottom of his small boat.

He'd grown up on this river. He and his friends had spent hours swimming and fishing and, as they'd grown older, they'd spent their teenage days skiing and their nights sitting on the bank under the stars, drinking beer and kissing girls. He knew the river well and, while he'd seen it in flood, he'd never seen a flood like this before. The last major flood had been well before he was born.

He fought the current, travelling upstream towards the caravan park. He'd heard the emergency siren and had responded to the call for help, as had plenty of other locals who had access to a boat.

He steered his dinghy through the break in the levee bank, following a couple of other small boats. He scanned the park for victims. He could see a State Emergency Services volunteer helping an elderly woman who was clinging to her veranda. The river had stopped rising, and she wasn't in immediate danger any more, but her cabin was surrounded by water and the only way out was in a boat.

He saw Bill, the park manager, with his wife on their front deck and lifted a hand in greeting. Bill and his wife were safe enough for now but he could see Bill pointing towards the river. He could see his lips moving but his words were drowned out by the sound of many engines. Luke turned his head, looking behind his dinghy back towards the levee bank and saw two figures perched above the water. He turned the rudder on the outboard engine and headed in their direction. As he got closer he could see it was a young woman and younger girl, perched on what must be some play equipment. The woman had a tight grip on the child, who was pointing at Maisie.

'...Dog on the boat!'

The noise of his outboard motor drowned out the first few words but Luke caught the end of the young girl's sentence.

'Stay, Maisie,' Luke instructed his border collie, who was now standing at the front of the boat and barking excitedly as Luke approached them. Luke didn't want her jumping in the river and trying to round them up. His dog was a strong swimmer but Luke knew she'd be no match for the current.

'Careful, Liv, don't lose your balance,' he heard the woman caution the child.

Both of them were thin and blonde with large brown eyes. Even though there appeared to be several years' age difference between them, perhaps fifteen, the similarity was obvious and he assumed they were sisters. The young woman pushed her blonde hair back, revealing a heart-shaped face and flawless skin. Her hair might be a tangled mess but she was stunning and Luke felt himself do a double-take, while hoping she hadn't noticed.

'Hi, my name is Luke. Can I give you a hand to get down from there?' he asked as he cut the engine, finally remembering he was here to get the two of them to dry land.

The woman appraised him with her large brown eyes before looking around, as if searching for a better option.

'Here.' Luke held onto the play equipment with one hand to stabilise the boat and reached down to his feet with his other hand to pick up two life jackets. 'These are for you. It's safer to put the jackets on before we move you to the boat. This one is small,' he said as he passed the first one up. 'Can you get it on?'

The woman was looking at him again. 'I think so,' she replied. She slipped the jacket over the little girl's head but then looked a little flummoxed as to how to secure it.

'Put her arms through the straps and then you can clip it together at the front,' he instructed. 'And now yours,' he said as he passed her the second jacket.

He busied himself securing the boat to the climbing frame while she got her jacket on. He attached a rope from the stern of the dinghy to a rung of the monkey bars. It wasn't perfect—he would have preferred to have had two ropes—but it would stop the current from pushing him away and it would have to do.

'What are your names?' he asked once he'd tied the

dinghy up and the young woman had had time to fasten the straps on her life jacket.

'I'm Ella,' she replied. 'And this is Olivia.'

'Okay, Olivia, let's get you into the boat.' He'd start with the little one. He reached up and lifted her off the play equipment. She weighed next to nothing and he picked her up effortlessly and sat her on the bench seat running across the middle of the dinghy.

Once she was settled, he turned back to the to help the other woman. 'Can you put your feet either side of the seat?' He indicated the seat in the centre of the boat where Olivia sat. 'That will distribute your weight evenly and keep the boat stable,' he explained. She wasn't going to be heavy but her high centre of gravity while she transferred into the dinghy could be enough to unsettle the boat.

She was staring at him but didn't move.

'Take my hand.' He reached out towards her but, rather than reassuring her, it seemed he'd spooked her. She leant back, withdrawing herself, leaning away.

Her dark-brown eyes were hard to read. Was she nervous? Scared? Was she afraid of the water? Afraid of him?

'You need to get in the boat. Hold on to me.'

'Mummy, get in!'

*Mummy?* This young woman was a mother? Luke saw her eyes dart to Olivia: her daughter. Ella looked to be in her early twenties, and Olivia looked to be about five. He wasn't judging but he had made assumptions—something his profession should have taught him not to do.

She looked nervous, frightened and vulnerable. She was very thin, and perhaps her slight build combined with her vulnerability made her look younger than she really was. Not that it mattered to him—he just needed to get her into the boat.

'It's all right. You'll be okay; you need to come with me.' He spoke slowly and calmly; he didn't want to startle her or add to her wariness. He didn't want to risk an accident.

Ella hesitated. She was reluctant to reach for him, reluctant to touch him. She didn't like being touched, unless it was by Liv. And she definitely did not like being touched by strangers—men in particular. But she knew she needed his support; she needed to be steadied. She only had one good leg and she had to make it into an unstable vessel. A very small unstable vessel.

Ella was looking into his eyes, trying to summon the courage to reach for his hand, when Liv pleaded with her to get in. He was watching her, and she saw his expression change as Liv called her 'Mummy'. Ella recognised confusion in his expression and saw the judgement in his blue eyes before he seemed to gather his thoughts and put them aside. She knew he would have made the same initial assumption that most people did—that she and Liv were siblings, not mother and daughter.

He was still watching her, waiting. 'You'll be okay,' he repeated.

He might have judged her but he was still there, waiting to help her. He had a calmness about his manner and his eyes, which were a startling blue, looked kind. She had to go with him; what choice did she have?

As she reached for his hand, the sleeve of her shirt rose

up, revealing her wrist and the bruises that encircled it. They were fading from purple to yellow but they were still visible. She quickly pulled her sleeve down, hoping he hadn't seen them.

Her heart hammered in her chest as his fingers gripped her hand. His grip was firm but not painful and she willed herself to relax. He had come to help them; he wasn't going to hurt her. But, even so, she kept her left hand wrapped around the bars of the climbing frame, not prepared to give herself over to him completely just yet. His hold was light but strong. He wasn't forcing her to move. She knew she could withdraw her hand at any time if she wanted to; he wasn't overpowering her, he was simply offering support.

His skin was warm and soft, which surprised her. She'd expected his hand to feel rough but his skin was surprisingly smooth. She relaxed slightly, preparing to accept his assistance. He couldn't hurt her—not here. She had to trust him.

She forced herself to look away from his face, focusing instead on the boat. She stretched out her left leg first, not trusting her right leg to hold her weight. She didn't want her leg to give way, upset the boat and tip them all into the river. She placed her left foot on the bottom of the boat. The metal was warm under her bare skin as she made sure she had her foot firmly planted. She tried to keep her weight on her left leg as she lowered herself into the boat but that proved impossible.

The boat wobbled and she let go of the bars as she redistributed her weight. She shifted her weight onto her right leg to counterbalance the movement of the boat and that action sent a bolt of pain through her right calf. She winced and took in a quick breath of air, fighting not to cry out. She felt herself lean more heavily on Luke's hand as she tried to take some weight off her leg.

'Are you all right?'

Her gaze flew to his and she nodded, her teeth gritted, fighting discomfort. She wasn't about to whinge; she was used to pain and she'd learned to battle through it in silence. She saw his eyes move from her face to her leg and she sat down quickly on the seat next to Liv, in a hurry to get off her feet and to hide her leg from his curious gaze.

Only then did he let go of her hand, leaving her feeling as if she'd been cast adrift. She lifted her right leg over the seat, away from Luke, getting it out of view. She pulled her skirt down as best she could, trying to hide her makeshift bandage, which she could feel was soaked with blood. Fortunately, the fabric was dark. Maybe he couldn't see the blood; maybe he hadn't noticed.

He turned away from her, pulling on the cord to fire up the engine on the outboard and, once he'd got it restarted, he untied the rope that he'd fastened to the monkey bars before pushing them off, opening the throttle and puttering towards the main street.

Ella held onto the straps of Liv's life jacket and tried to keep her gaze on the front of the boat as Luke steered it out through the gap in the collapsed levee bank and down the river. She could feel her attention being drawn to Luke. His presence seemed to fill the air around her, making him impossible to ignore.

She sneaked a glance at him under the guise of checking the contents of her handbag. His eyes scanned the water as he navigated the river. He appeared to be concentrating hard but, despite his solemn expression, there was no denying he had a very handsome face. His blue eyes were perfectly set in his face above a straight, symmetrical nose, full lips and a strong jaw covered with light stubble. His hair was thick and dark and swept back from his forehead, which was creased in concentration. There were little wrinkles at the corners of his eyes and she guessed him to be around thirty years of age. He looked fit and his limbs were long and tanned, muscular but lean.

She watched his hands on the rudder as the boat chugged down the river. He looked like a workman, but his hands were smooth and his nails were filed and clean. They weren't the hands of a labourer or a famer, despite what his breed of dog might suggest. She recalled how it had felt to hold his hand and she wondered what he did when he wasn't rescuing people.

Luke's gaze met hers and, flustered at having been caught out, she turned back towards the front of the little boat. The breeze against her face provided welcome relief from the heat of the morning and she closed her eyes as she tried not to worry. She had no idea what would happen next, but for the moment she and Liv were safe, and that might be the best she could hope for.

She opened her eyes as she heard the engine cut out and the boat bumped to a stop. Luke had pulled up around the far side of the levee bank that ran along the main street. A crowd of people stood on top of the bank, waiting to help the stranded caravan park tenants onto dry land. A man wearing a fluorescent vest emblazoned with the words *Murray Bunyip* raised a camera to his face and started snapping pictures. Ella turned her face away from the press photographer. She did not want her picture taken.

Luke tossed a rope up to a stocky man with a deep tan and a bald head who caught it easily, while a younger man looped a second rope round the front of the boat to hold it steady.

'Hey, Luke, I should have known I'd find you here.' A third person, an older man with close-cropped grey hair and wearing a police uniform, greeted Luke. 'What happened to taking the day off?'

'This is a day off.' Luke was grinning broadly; all the seriousness of his earlier expression had disappeared and, as his features relaxed, Ella thought he looked even more handsome. 'Mucking about in a boat on the river is the best sort of day.'

'Rightio, then, and who do you have to offload?'

'This is Ella and her daughter, Olivia.'

'All right, let's get you out of there, shall we?' the policeman said as he reached out and offered a hand to help them to shore. 'My name is Sam. I reckon you should go first, Olivia.'

Liv was on the side of the boat closest to the bank. Ella nodded at her daughter and waited for Liv to reach out and take Sam's hand before she forced herself to let go of the straps on Liv's life jacket. The water was dirty and flowing quickly. She didn't want to think about Liv slipping and falling. If she slid down the levee bank she could disappear into the river in an instant.

'Put one foot on the edge of the boat,' Sam instructed Liv as he took her hand. Liv did as she was told and, once one foot was on the edge of the boat, Sam didn't wait for her to step across onto the bank. He was sturdy and tall and he plucked her from the boat before putting her onto solid ground.

'Your turn, Ella.'

Ella could feel herself shaking. She stood up, temporarily forgetting about her sore leg until her calf exploded with pain, and she quickly took her weight off it.

'Can you call Penny and ask her to take a look at Ella's leg? She's hurt it,' Luke asked Sam as Ella regained her balance.

'I'm fine,' Ella replied.

Luke looked at her but said nothing. He simply looked back at Sam with an expression that said, *ignore her and listen to me.*

'It's nothing, just a scratch,' Ella said as she glared at Luke. Despite the fact that he'd rescued them, had got Liv and her safely to dry land, he wasn't a knight in shining armour. He was a good-looking guy in a slightly battered, not very shiny, aluminium dinghy but that didn't give him the right to interfere in her well-being. Ella sensed that Luke was used to getting his way—Sam certainly didn't seem to have taken offence with him issuing instructions—but he wasn't the boss of Ella. No one was. Not any more.

She took Sam's hand and stepped out of the dinghy with as much grace as she could muster, given her sore leg and her dishevelled state. She gritted her teeth and forced herself to distribute her weight equally on both legs, despite the searing discomfort. She wasn't going to give Luke the satisfaction of seeing her grimace or falter again.

Ella had expected Luke to argue with her. She was sure he would want the last word: that was usually how things went. But, once she was on the levee bank he simply raised one eyebrow, shrugged his broad shoulders and said, 'Suit yourself,' before he restarted the engine, pushed himself off the bank, turned the boat around and headed back in the direction of the caravan park.

She watched him go before belatedly remembering her manners. 'Thank you,' she called out, hoping he'd hear her over the whine of his outboard motor, the noise of the crowd gathered on the bank and the sounds of the river.

He raised one hand in reply but he didn't turn around, didn't look back, leaving Ella strangely disappointed. He'd unsettled her and she wasn't sure why. No, it wasn't him, she decided. She wasn't going to let a man, a stranger, unsettle her. She was on edge, but that was understandable, given the situation she found herself in.

'Penny is a nurse at the local medical clinic,' Sam said, interrupting Ella's thoughts. 'She'll be happy to take a look at your leg for you.'

Ella shook the disappointment from her mind and tried to formulate a reply.

'That water is filthy. There are dead animals, contents of septic tanks and who knows what else in that river at the moment,' Sam continued, before Ella had a chance to respond. 'A small scratch can easily become infected. You don't want that,' he stated, mistaking her silence for reticence and trying to convince her of the foolishness of ignoring Luke's advice.

Ella looked around. She was bewildered, suddenly overwhelmed by the situation. She had no idea what she was supposed to do next. Where were she and Liv supposed to go? They had nowhere. Nothing.

She decided the easiest course of action was to follow Sam's instructions. That would save her having to make any decisions for herself right now and would hopefully buy her time to make sense of what had just happened.

'Sit down here while I make a phone call,' he said, settling them on a pile of sandbags and wrapping a silver insulating blanket around them both before pulling out his phone. Within minutes a woman in her late fifties pulled up at the side of the road and hopped out of her car. Sam waved her over to where Ella and Liv waited and introduced her.

Penny was no-nonsense, efficient but kind. She bundled them into her car before Ella even had time to thank Sam. She drove them up the main street, keeping a steady stream of conversation going as they passed the supermarket, a pub, a bakery and a few other assorted shops on the way up the hill to the high end of town.

'Is it just your leg that needs to be looked at? No other injuries?'

Ella shook her head.

'What about Olivia?'

'She's fine.' Ella felt bad that her answers seemed abrupt but she was fatigued and uncomfortable and close to tears. She was fighting hard just to keep herself together and didn't have the head space to make polite conversation.

Penny turned into the car park at the front of a modern

building that appeared to house the medical clinic and an allied health facility. She ignored the parking spaces and pulled up directly in front of the main door. Ella slid out of her seat, wincing in pain, but determined to help Liv. Penny took one look at Ella's face and wisely didn't offer to help her get inside.

'The clinic isn't open?' Ella asked as Penny unlocked the door.

'No, it's closed on weekends. There's an after-hours number for emergencies or a hospital in the next town.'

Penny switched on lights and opened a door to a treatment room. 'Have a seat on the bed, Ella. Put your feet up,' she instructed. 'Olivia, why don't you sit here while I take a look at your mum's leg?' she said as she pulled a chair away from a desk.

'How much is this consultation going to cost?' Ella asked. She'd given up her objections now, too physically and emotionally exhausted to continue to argue, and it was probably wise to get the wound looked at. She couldn't afford to be sick but could she afford to pay for treatment? 'I have a health-care card,' she added. She hated being a welfare recipient but she'd learnt a long time ago to swallow her pride when it came to these sorts of benefits. There was no way she could afford health care without government assistance.

'Let's just see what needs to be done first,' Penny replied. 'I can't imagine there will be any charge above the government fee.'

Which meant there would be no out-of-pocket expense for Ella. 'Thank you.'

As Penny washed her hands and pulled on a pair of

latex gloves, Ella pulled her ripped skirt up above her knees and tucked it around her legs. She needed to expose her injury but she didn't want Penny to see more of her legs than she needed to.

'Just lift your leg up for me,' Penny instructed as she stood at the edge of the bed, waiting to slide a waterproof sheet under Ella's legs. As Ella lifted her leg, her skirt rode up, exposing her upper leg. She saw Penny's eyes dart to the bruise that stretched along the length of her thigh. The bruise began at her buttock but she knew her skirt hid most of it and Penny was only getting a glimpse. It was turning yellow, it was obviously old, and Ella held her breath as she wondered if Penny would ask about it.

'That looks painful,' Penny commented.

'It wasn't too bad,' she lied. It had been painful—she'd fallen heavily, landing on her right hip. 'I bruise easily,' she lied again. That lie slipped off her tongue—she'd said it plenty of times.

Penny was watching her but Ella averted her eyes, looking at Liv as an excuse to break eye contact, but then wondered if she shouldn't have done that. Did it look as if she was warning Liv not to say anything? She'd become so paranoid. She had to remember that this move was a chance to start fresh, to reinvent herself and her life. And it didn't matter what people thought of her in Pelican's Landing, she wasn't planning on being here for long.

Penny turned her attention to the cut on Ella's leg and let the topic rest. Her makeshift bandage was soaked with blood. It hadn't been able to completely stem the flow of blood and was thoroughly saturated but at least that meant it peeled off easily. The wound ran from the outside of her shin, just below her knee, sloping down and back towards the top of her calf. It looked to be about four or five inches long and Ella could see it gaping at the bottom end.

She couldn't watch—it made her feel a little queasy—but thankfully she had an empty stomach and knew she wouldn't be sick.

'You'll need stitches in that,' Penny said as she cleaned the wound. 'I'll call Dr Donato.'

'What about those butterfly things? Won't that hold it?' Ella didn't want treatment. She didn't want more help. She didn't want a doctor to look too closely.

'I think it's too deep for that. But the doctor can have a look; we can let him decide.'

Penny covered the wound with gauze and a temporary bandage. 'That should hold it for now.' Blood and saline had soaked into the protective cover. Penny bundled it up and threw it away before replacing it with a fresh sheet.

'How many doctors are there?' Ella asked.

'Just one. Why?'

Penny had said 'we can let him decide'. She didn't want a male doctor. 'I'd prefer a female doctor.'

'This isn't the city, love, we're lucky to have a doctor at all,' Penny told her. 'I'm pretty sure it's going to need stitches if you want it to heal. So, shall I call him?'

Ella hesitated but her leg was throbbing and she knew it needed to be treated. She'd be no good to Liv if she let it get infected. She nodded.

'All right, then,' Penny said. 'I'll give him a ring and then I'll make you both a sandwich while you wait.'

'You don't need to do that,' Ella protested. 'But a glass of water would be lovely.'

Penny took a paper cup from a stack on the bench and filled it with water from the tap at the sink. 'It's no trouble,' she said as she passed Ella the cup. 'Just a cheese and Vegemite sandwich. What do you think, Olivia? Would you like that?'

Liv nodded as Ella's stomach rumbled, protesting loudly, as she sipped the water.

'Sounds like you could do with a feed too,' Penny commented. 'Do either of you have any allergies?'

Ella shook her head.

'Why don't you come with me, Olivia? You can give me a hand and let your mum have a little rest.'

Ella wondered if she should resist and keep Liv with her, but she was so tired, and the thought of having a few moments to herself—even if it was while she was stuck on a treatment plinth waiting for a doctor she didn't want to see—was an opportunity she couldn't pass up. It wasn't often she had a minute to herself. She closed her eyes as Penny closed the door.

Her mind whirled, running through the events of the past hour as she wondered what it meant for them. She had planned to rest here for a few days before continuing to Queensland, but now she was without a car. How would they get there?

She had insurance, but she had no idea how long a claim would take to get processed, and had she insured for replacement value, or more? She didn't know what her car was worth but it probably wasn't much. Would the pay-out be enough to buy her something decent—

something that would make the two-thousand-kilometre trip to Queensland?

'Here you go.'

Ella woke with a fright when Penny and Liv returned. Penny was carrying two plates, each with a sandwich and half an apple on it. She put one on the desk for Liv and passed the other one to Ella. 'This one's for you; it'll do you the world of good. Dr Donato is on his way but I'll leave you two to eat while I take care of a few things.'

'Will you come back when the doctor gets here?' Ella could hear a slight note of hysteria in her voice but she didn't want to be left alone with the doctor.

Penny was in the doorway but she glanced over her shoulder, looking at Ella. Had she picked up on it too? She nodded and answered, 'Yes, I'll be back.'

Ella had washed her hands, devoured her sandwich and was just finishing the apple when Penny walked back into the room. This time she carried an armful of clothes, which she laid on the end of the treatment plinth.

Ella frowned. 'What's all this?'

'You and Olivia need to get out of your clothes. They're wet, muddy and ripped. You can have a look through this pile and see what fits.'

'Where did they come from?'

'We keep a cupboard of donated items. You'd be surprised how often we need a change of clothes. People are sick on themselves or kids come in after falling off their bikes and their clothes are torn or bloodied. I don't have any spare shoes, though. I'll have to get some for you.' She handed Ella a container of wet wipes. 'You can use these to clean some of the mud off you before you get changed.'

Ella rifled through the pile as Penny left, closing the door behind her. She found a pair of shorts and a T-shirt that would fit Liv and helped her to put them on before she looked through the pile again, searching for something for herself.

There was a sleeveless summer dress. She put that back in the pile—it was pretty but far too revealing. There was a skirt, a T-shirt, a pair of lightweight cotton trousers and a button-up shirt. Had Penny chosen those last two items deliberately? They were an unusual choice, considering the temperature. Did Penny have suspicions? Had she picked them out to give Ella on option that would provide some coverage? And would Ella be confirming those suspicions by choosing to cover up?

Ella didn't know the answer, but these items were just what she needed, and she put them to one side before she stripped off her shirt and skirt. She gave her skin a quick rub with the wet wipes to remove some of the caked-on river mud before pulling on the trousers and shirt. She couldn't worry about Penny. Whatever she surmised from Ella's choice of clothing was irrelevant—there was no way Ella was going to wear anything that revealed her arms.

She buttoned up the shirt and threw her ruined skirt into the bin next to the sink but kept her old top and Olivia's clothes. They could be washed. There was a small mirror above the sink and Ella laughed wryly as she caught sight of her reflection. Despite the clean clothes, she was a mess. Her face was still streaked with mud and her hair was tangled. She'd lost her shoes and was dressed in second-hand clothes without even a hairbrush to her name. She didn't know why she'd thought her luck might change. At this point, it seemed as though it had certainly run out.

She grabbed a wet wipe and ran it over her face, removing as much of the dirt as she could, before turning her attention to her hair. She tried to tease some of the tangles from it before giving up just as there was a knock on the door.

It opened a crack and Penny stuck her head in. 'Are you decent?'

Ella nodded and the door opened wider, admitting both Penny and a man who looked very much like Luke but, instead of wearing old shorts and a T-shirt, he was dressed in blue hospital scrubs. He must be Luke's identical twin, Ella decided.

He smiled at her as he crossed the room and Ella's heart skipped a beat.

She'd wondered what Luke would have looked like if he'd cracked a smile. She'd thought he was handsome but this version of him—this tall, smiling version—was breath-taking.

Caught unawares by her reaction, she was about to smile back when he said, 'Ella, you gave in.'

Ella frowned. He recognised her—so, not Luke's identical twin, then. Just Luke.

'What are you doing here?' she asked as her brain tried to process the turn of events. Her thought processes felt delayed. A lack of sleep, lack of food, stress, shock, adrenalin, or a combination of all of the above, was making her brain foggy.

'I'm the doctor.'

# CHAPTER THREE

HE WAS THE DOCTOR?

Ella's reasoning was taking time to catch up to her vision. The scruffy, brusque, albeit calm and attractive man who had turned up in his dinghy to rescue her was the doctor?

'You didn't say anything in the boat,' she accused.

'Would it have made any difference? I wasn't sure you were going to take my advice. But it's good to know you've got some common sense,' he continued.

'What's that supposed to mean?' Ella bristled.

'Flood water is notoriously filthy. The last thing you want is an infection. Best to get any cuts cleaned up and treated.' He had his back to her as he stood at the sink and washed his hands.

He was tall and he had to stoop over the sink. She looked at the broad expanse of his shoulders and his long legs, lean hips. When he'd arrived in his little boat she'd assumed, swayed by both his muscular build and his clothing, that he was a labourer or a farmer. A man who did a physical job. She would never have picked him as a doctor.

He reached up to pull paper towel from a dispenser on the wall. She looked at his hands. At his long fingers.

She'd noticed his soft, clean hands in the boat but hadn't paid attention. They should have been a giveaway that perhaps her first impressions had been inaccurate.

She watched him dry his hands but her attention was diverted to Penny who was having a conversation with Liv while she prepared equipment for Luke. She hoped Penny didn't get too much information out of her daughter. Pre-schoolers could, unwittingly, be a font of knowledge, divulging all sorts of secrets.

'How old are you, Olivia?'

'I'm going to be five soon. How many sleeps, Mummy?'

'Fifteen more,' Ella replied. Liv turned five on the same day Ella turned twenty-six. She had been Ella's twenty-first birthday gift.

'Wow, that's not far away. You must be getting excited,' Penny said.

*Please don't ask if she's having a party*, Ella thought.

Liv had never had a party. Ella had no family and, by the time Liv was old enough to invite friends, Ella had avoided the topic. She hadn't wanted to negotiate hosting a party, not knowing what might trigger her ex's mood. She and Liv had kept to themselves. She'd been a stay-at-home mum for two years. Liv had gone to kindergarten but Ella hadn't fostered any friendships with the other parents. She hadn't volunteered at the kindy; she hadn't been involved. It was easier that way. And now, stuck in this small town, halfway between their old life and their new one, they had no one to invite.

'You'll be starting school soon, then,' Penny continued as Liv nodded.

Ella relaxed. School was something they had talked

about. That was one reason she was making this move. She wanted a fresh start and she hadn't wanted to enrol Liv in a school where people already knew, or thought they knew, their business. Making this move was hard but it would be harder if Liv had been happy and settled in school. Ella would have felt guilty about pulling her out if she'd made friends.

'All right, Ella, let's have a look.' Luke was talking to her. She turned her attention back to him, still trying to reconcile the scruffy first impression with this current version. He was clean-shaven, but he had been before: she could recall the strong line of his jaw. But a simple change of clothes had made a huge difference to his appearance. Whereas before, in the boat, he'd appeared relaxed and capable, he now looked neat, efficient and competent. She wished a change of clothes had the same effect on her but she suspected she still looked a dishevelled mess.

His hands reached for the hem of her trousers and Ella quickly pulled the loose leg up above her knee, keeping one hand on the fabric to hold it close against her thigh. She didn't want him to lift it any higher; she didn't want to expose her bruises. They were fading slowly, changing colour from purple to yellow after a week, but they were still obvious on her pale skin.

'Let's get this bandage off.' She was tense but his hands were gentle. She recalled how he'd lifted Liv, how his quiet voice had soothed her. She couldn't imagine him yelling or hurting anyone. Doctors took an oath, didn't they, to do no harm?

He unwound the bandage from her calf and fresh blood

ran down her leg as he removed the gauze. Penny was there, ready to mop up.

'Yep, I reckon a couple of stitches will pull this together nicely. I'll give you a local anaesthetic just to numb the area.' He held a piece of clean gauze against the wound while Penny drew up the anaesthetic.

'This might sting a little.'

Ella turned her head away, not wanting to watch the injection being administered, or wanting to look at Luke. She was frightened and emotional and worried she'd burst into tears if someone showed her kindness.

'Are you up to date with a tetanus shot?' he asked as he waited for the anaesthetic to take effect.

'Yes. I had one at the same time as Liv.'

'Good. Let's get you stitched up.'

Ella closed her eyes as Penny handed Luke the needle and thread.

'All done.' She opened her eyes to find the wound covered by a dressing. 'You'll need a course of antibiotics just to be on the safe side.'

She lifted her eyes to meet his, amazed again how the colour of his scrubs made his blue eyes even more hypnotising.

'Is the pharmacy open today?' Pelican's Landing was a small country town. She didn't expect the pharmacy to be open on a Sunday.

'No, it will be closed until tomorrow. I'll give you enough tablets for a couple of days and a prescription to take to the chemist for more. A five-day course should be enough but I'll need you to come back after that for me to check the wound,' he said as he applied a waterproof dressing over the stitches. 'You can shower with the dressing on but no swimming or taking baths—you don't want to soak it.'

She swung her legs over the side of the bed and stood up. Black spots danced before her eyes and the room swayed. She closed her eyes and groped for the bed to steady herself while the dizziness eased. Her hand found fresh air as she felt her knees buckle.

But before she hit the floor she felt hands grip her elbows, stopping her fall. She tensed, her body automatically responding to the unexpected pressure of a pair of hands on her body. She waited for the pressure to increase, waited for the hands to squeeze her arms, waited for the discomfort. But, instead of the hands tightening their grip, she felt them release her and then an arm wrapped around her back, supporting her. She opened her eyes, her vision clearing, to find Luke watching her closely with his blue-eyed gaze. He had caught her and continued to hold her as she regained her equilibrium. She was leaning into him. He was solid and firm but his hands were gentle as he supported her. She let herself be held momentarily before she came to her senses and pulled away.

So much for standing on her own two feet—the first slight hiccough and she was fantasising about being able to lean on someone, about having someone to shoulder some of her worries.

She backed away, only to find herself trapped between Luke and the bed. She leant against the edge of the plinth. It was better to let the bed support her than to lean on Luke.

'I think you should lie down again.'

'I'm fine. I just stood up too quickly.'

'Let me check your blood pressure before you go, just to be on the safe side.'

'I'm fine, really.'

'Humour me,' he said as he scooped up her legs and lifted them back onto the bed, before reaching out to pick up a sphygmomanometer.

Ella was emotional, close to tears. *Get a grip*, she admonished herself.

She'd always had an active imagination and had always been able to retreat into fantasy. It was an escape, a preservation technique, but lately she hadn't been able to do that. Real life had taken over. Responsibilities and motherhood meant she couldn't afford to daydream any more. Now she had to deal with reality, and the simple reality was she had been planning to start over. Now she would have to start from scratch. And there was a difference between the two. A big difference. And she couldn't expect anyone else to help her. There was no one else. She couldn't let a moment of kindness weaken her. She had to manage on her own.

Before she had time to react he'd slid her sleeve up and his fingers were on her wrist, feeling for her pulse.

She knew he would see the bruises but she had no way of hiding them. She waited for him to say something but he kept silent as he wrapped the cuff around her arm and inflated it.

'Your blood pressure is okay. Have you eaten today?'

'Yes, Penny made us both a sandwich.'

'What brings you to Pelican's Landing? Are you visiting friends?'

Ella shook her head. 'No, just passing through.'

'You're travelling on your own? Just the two of you?'

She nodded, wondering if this was his way of getting information about her background? About her bruises?

'You don't know anyone in town?'

'No. We are on our way to Queensland—we just stopped here for a few nights to break up the trip.'

'On your way from where?'

'Western Australia.'

'Well, you won't be able to go back to the caravan park.'

She wasn't stupid, she knew that. Her situation was getting more dire by the minute. She'd taken Liv and fled Geraldton with the bare minimum, just what she could fit into her car, and now she had lost everything. She had nothing left and nowhere to go.

'You'll need somewhere to stay.'

'I've spoken to Sam,' Penny said. 'He told me the SES are setting up emergency accommodation at the community hall. I can take Ella and Olivia up there and see what's been organised.'

'I guess that's a good place to start. Is that okay, Ella?'

Ella was too tired, too emotionally spent to problem-solve, and it didn't sound as if she had any other option. There wasn't going to be a knight in shining armour coming to her rescue. This was real life, not a fairy tale, but unfortunately for her and Liv their life appeared to be one drama followed closely by another. And she didn't want to deal with any more dramas today. She *couldn't* deal with any more; she didn't have the energy.

If Penny could get them to the hall, it would be one less thing for Ella to think about.

She'd worry about tomorrow, tomorrow.

She nodded and said, 'I appreciate your help, Penny, thank you.'

Ella collapsed onto a chair in front of the general store. She was exhausted. She appreciated that the community of Pelican's Landing had organised temporary accommodation for the caravan park guests who had been so unceremoniously forced from their sites, but the accommodation was basic at best, and she'd slept fitfully. Liv had been wiped out by the events of the day and, despite sleeping on a gym mat covered by a light sheet, she'd fallen asleep quickly. Ella, on the other hand, had not. But it hadn't been physical discomfort that had kept her awake. The gym mat was thick enough, and the night was warm, but being housed in a hall full of strangers had Ella on edge.

While some of the other faces were familiar to her from the caravan park, she didn't know any of the other people. She'd nodded and said hello in passing over the previous two days, but she hadn't really spoken to them, and she was nervous. She felt as though she'd slept with one eye open, looking for threats, prepared to flee at the first sign of danger. People had been quiet, silent, frightened but they were still strangers, traumatised and upset. They'd all been through the same experience, but there was no sense of bonding, and Ella had been wary.

She had spent the morning in town, Liv trailing beside her, as she investigated their options for accommodation.

Volunteers from the State Emergency Service, the local council and a local charity had arrived early in the day to get people's details and ostensibly assist them with finding temporary accommodation. Ella had been optimistic at first but her hopes had quickly been dashed. There was a rental crisis with no vacancies in the district—never mind in Pelican's Landing—and she couldn't afford the holiday accommodation in the motel, pubs and bed and breakfast. The council was planning to contact shack owners who didn't live permanently in Pelican's Landing to see if they would offer their holiday homes for temporary accommodation but Ella couldn't pin her hopes on that. The message seemed to be that their best bet was to stay with family and friends—but Ella didn't have any.

She'd also visited the tourist information centre to enquire about other caravan parks in the region. Her car was submerged, and her tent and their meagre belongings were god knew where, so Ella's only option was to find a park on the bus route from Pelican's Landing that had a cabin to rent. The lady in the office had booked her a cabin in a town across the border in Victoria but the bus wasn't coming until Thursday.

Ella let out a sigh as she contemplated three more nights in the community hall. She'd dropped her prescription for antibiotics at the pharmacy and then bought Liv the ice-cream she'd promised her yesterday from the general store next door. She collapsed onto a chair in front of the shop. Her leg was throbbing; she knew she'd walked on it more than she should have today. It felt swollen and sore. She put her foot up on a second chair, while Liv devoured her ice-cream, and tried to ignore the ache. It would be fair to say this move was not turning out as she'd anticipated. She hadn't thought it would be smooth sailing or easy—nothing in her life was—but she had thought it might be a little less dramatic, a little less difficult.

Some people were lucky. But not her. Could you make your own luck? Ella hoped so. Maybe it was her turn. Things could hardly get worse. She was determined to make a better life for her and Liv.

By herself. No one was coming to rescue her—she was well aware of that—and she'd learned that if she wanted things to change it was up to her. She had to have faith in herself. She was on her own but she could do it.

'Ella, hello.' Ella looked up to see Penny standing in front of her, carrying a bag from the pharmacy. 'How are you today?'

Ella thought of all the words she could use to describe her current state. Tired. Overwhelmed. Dejected. Frustrated. But she didn't want to sound like a victim. Or to sound like she wasn't coping. 'We're okay,' she replied.

'You look tired.'

'I didn't sleep well. Being in a room full of strangers was a little unnerving. Hopefully tonight will be better.'

'Do you have to spend another night at the hall? I thought they were looking for something a bit more substantial than mats on the floor?'

Ella nodded. 'Apparently there's an accommodation shortage in the area. It doesn't look like there's much the authorities can do. It's impossible to conjure beds out of thin air.'

'What will you do?'

'The staff in the tourist office have found me some accommodation in a caravan park in Swan Hill, but my car is somewhere in the river and there's no bus until Thursday, so we'll stay until then.'

Penny's brow creased and Ella could see she was mulling something over. 'I might know a place that you could stay in for a few days. Why don't you meet me at the clinic at half-past five and I'll make some enquiries?'

'Are you sure?'

'Not a hundred percent, but there's no harm in asking. Bring your things with you in case it works out.'

Ella gave a half-smile. 'I'm not sure that you could call one change of clothes and a toothbrush "things", but we'll do that. Thank you.' Her spirits lifted. It might not happen but just to know someone cared enough to try to help made a world of difference. She'd accept Penny's offer of help and tomorrow she'd start again. On her own.

Penny put her bag of supplies on the café table and opened her purse. She pulled out some cash and handed it to Ella. 'There's a country Target in the shopping complex up the hill from the scout hall. Why don't you go and get yourselves some essentials?'

Ella shook her head. 'Thank you, but we'll manage.'

'Don't be silly. You can pay me back later if it makes you feel better,' Penny insisted, picking up her bags and refusing to let Ella return the money. 'I'll see you in a couple of hours.'

'I'm off to see Mrs Macdonald,' Luke said as he stuck his head into Penny's office. His elderly patient had been discharged from hospital in Adelaide following cardiac surgery and he wanted to check on her recovery. 'Call me if anything urgent comes up.'

'Before you go, I needed to ask you something.' Penny waylaid him. 'I bumped into Ella in town earlier. She needs a place to stay for a few nights.'

'What's wrong with the community hall?'

'She's a single mum with a young daughter. She doesn't feel safe there.'

'Did she tell you that?'

'Not exactly. She did say she didn't sleep well because of all the strangers sharing the space. I think she was frightened or nervous, or both.'

'You think she's had some past trauma? In addition to the flood, I mean?' Luke looked at Penny. He'd seen the bruises on Ella's arms and legs, despite her efforts to hide them from view. Should he have questioned her? 'Do you think I should have asked her if she was safe?'

He'd been thrown by his reaction to Ella. Her presence had caused colliding thoughts and conflicting emotions in him. She was stunning but young and he'd felt his reaction to her was inappropriate. She was scared and vulnerable—a patient. A mother and possibly a partner too. But being forbidden didn't stop her from being desirable. There was something special about her that had drawn him in, almost bewitched him. He knew he hadn't been thinking clearly and now he was worried he'd made a professional mistake.

'Ella is obviously wary of men, and it's possible she could be in an abusive relationship or not long out of one,' Penny replied. 'But I don't think we should be jumping to conclusions, and I'm not sure that she was in the right headspace to discuss anything like that after what happened yesterday,' she continued, letting him off the hook.

'She did say she and Olivia were travelling alone so I think, for the moment, she's out of harm's way. She told me she spent the day looking for an alternative place to stay but there's nothing suitable in Pelican's Landing— it's bursting at the seams with displaced people. And she has no means of getting anywhere else, as her car was swallowed by the flood. She's stuck here and she needs somewhere to live. Would you be willing to let her use your cottage? You've been saying for six months you plan to let the cottage to people in the community who need assistance but you haven't done it yet. Why don't you have Ella as your first tenant?'

Luke had converted an old barn on his parents' property into self-contained accommodation for his sister but it had been sitting empty and unused for many years. As Penny rightly pointed out, he had recently toyed with the idea of renting it to locals who needed assistance, but he hadn't actually taken that step yet. And he wasn't sure he wanted Ella living on his doorstep.

Besides, if Ella had suffered some trauma or abuse at the hand of a man, he couldn't imagine she'd feel comfortable staying in his cottage. The converted barn was in close proximity to his home and he was, to all intents and purposes, a stranger to Ella. 'If Ella is wary of men, strangers or otherwise, she'll hardly want to stay at my house,' he said, thinking that was a valid excuse. 'Why don't you have them?'

'I would gladly have them but we're about to start our

renovations. We can't take guests at the moment. We're going to have a portable loo and no kitchen.'

'They've been sleeping in a tent. I'm sure they'll be happy just to have proper beds.'

'Which you can offer them,' Penny insisted. 'Along with a kitchenette and bathroom.'

He recognised Penny's tone, and knew he would have difficulty convincing her that her idea was not a sound one, but he wasn't quite sure if he was ready to confront the reality of having someone living in the cottage that had been meant for Gemma. And he was even more cautious about offering it to Ella. Her vulnerability reminded him of his sister and he didn't need a daily reminder of how he'd let his sister down.

'She's not a local in need, though, is she?' he said, trying to find an argument that would hold up to Penny's persistence.

'Think of it as redemption for Gemma.'

That was the trouble with Penny. She'd known him since he'd been born, and she had worked for his father in the clinic before Luke had taken over. Penny knew everything Luke had been through and knew how guilty he felt over what had happened to Gemma. The idea of renting out the cottage had begun as a way of making sense of Gemma's death but that didn't mean Ella was the right first tenant. 'I don't think it's a good idea. I don't know her.'

'That doesn't matter. You always wished someone would help Gemma when you couldn't. You can help Ella. Offer her a kindness—she looks like she could use it.'

Penny was right, he had tried to help Gemma, but she'd

refused his efforts. She'd moved away, probably in order to escape everyone she knew, but that didn't mean someone else might not have been able to get through to her. If only someone else had tried she might still be alive today. And Luke *did* want to help Ella but that didn't necessarily extend to offering her a place to live which was quite literally in his own back yard.

'Can I at least show her the cottage and see what she thinks?' Penny asked. 'She only needs it for a few days.'

He wasn't convinced that having Ella as a neighbour would be a wise decision but he nodded reluctantly, knowing that Penny would keep hounding him until he relented. 'If she wants to see it you can take her up there when you leave here.'

He could only hope Ella wouldn't accept the offer. If she was as wary of men as he suspected, perhaps the option wouldn't appeal to her.

Ella and Liv were at the clinic on time to meet Penny. Luke was nowhere to be seen. Ella found herself partly relieved and partly disappointed.

Penny drove them west out of town but, instead of turning up the hill away from the river, she took a road that followed the curve of the river bank. Ella could see some houses overlooking the water on her left, but the area looked rather agricultural, with plantings of olive groves, fruit orchards and even a few sheep in the paddocks around the houses.

Penny turned left onto a long dirt driveway that ran down towards the river. The driveway ended at a grand two-storey stone house that faced the water. From the back Ella could see wide verandas that ran along both sides of the house, nestled under top floor balconies, and she assumed the verandas continued across the front. The house would have an amazing view over the river. Surely this wasn't the cottage Penny had been talking about? But, just as Ella was about to clarify the offer Penny turned left again, driving behind the house, and came to a stop near another stone building that sat a few hundred feet from the main dwelling.

'Here we are,' Penny said as she switched off the engine, and Ella and Liv climbed out of the car.

It was obvious this building would have once been the barn for the imposing house that sat in front. Chickens scratched in the dirt nearby, catching Liv's attention, but Ella was captivated by the old barn which had been renovated and converted into accommodation. Set back and to the left behind the main house, it still had a view down the gentle slope that stretched away to the river. A small garden had been planted in front of the cottage. Ella could smell mint and rosemary, and spied strawberry plants and cherry tomato bushes, both laden with fruit, sprouting between rose bushes. A small outdoor table and chairs sat underneath a wisteria-covered arbour. It was enchanting.

'It's so pretty,' she said as Penny opened a small metal gate set into the wire fence and Ella followed her along the brick path, through the garden, to the barn door.

Penny pushed the heavy wooden door and stepped inside as it swung wide.

'It wasn't locked?' Ella was surprised and a little worried but, as she turned to close the door behind Liv, she saw it was fitted with a deadlock.

'No,' Penny replied. 'Lots of the locals don't tend to lock up but there will be a key somewhere if you want it.'

Ella looked around the room. The old stone walls had been repointed and the floor tiled. The layout was simple, the furnishings comfortable. There was a living room at one end where a large leather couch, piled high with cushions in neutral colours, faced a pot-belly stove. A sisal rug stretched from the couch almost to the fireplace and a single arm chair was tucked under a window. Straight ahead was a small, round wooden dining table with four ladder-back chairs and beyond that a simple kitchen ran along the back wall. There was a window above the kitchen sink, which looked out onto a grove of olive trees. It was idyllic. Peaceful.

Despite the heat of the day, the room was cool. The thick stone walls of the old stable had kept the heat out, but the air had a musty smell, as if the building had been closed up for a while. Penny whizzed around, opening the few windows in the barn walls to let some fresh air in.

The high-pitched roof had exposed timber beams but at one end of the room, to Ella's right, there was a staircase leading to a mezzanine level.

'Can I go outside and see the chickens?' Liv asked as Ella followed Penny up the stairs to a mezzanine floor, which she guessed had probably been an old hayloft, and which had been converted into a bedroom.

'Yes. But stay inside the garden, don't go through the gate. And don't go near the river.' The lawn around the main house sloped away from the barn down to the river.

Ella didn't want Liv anywhere near that water. After what had happened yesterday, she didn't think Liv would be tempted to go near the river, but she was grateful that the cottage was surrounded by a fence.

She checked that the gate was closed before returning to make her way up the stairs to where a large bed, an arm chair and a chest of drawers took up most of the space.

'There's only one bed, I'm afraid,' Penny said.

'That doesn't matter.' After sleeping in her car, in a tent and on the floor of the community hall a bed, any bed, would be a luxury. 'Liv is small; I can easily share with her.'

Ella retreated down the stairs and stuck her head into the bathroom which was tucked under the mezzanine. It was compact but had everything she needed and even a small washing machine. She stepped out and had another look around the living space.

The converted barn was small but she didn't need space. Because of its history as a barn, there were few windows, which Ella saw as a positive. Large windows were a security risk, in her opinion. The only flaw in her mind was that the building only had one external door. If that was blocked, there was no other means of escape.

She tried to relax. She only needed a place to stay for a few days. No one was looking for her. No one knew where she was. She would be safe here.

'What do you think?'

'It's gorgeous. I'd love to stay for a few nights, if you're sure that's all right.'

'Mummy, Mummy, it's Maisie!' Liv's voice interrupted.

Ella wandered out into the garden to find Liv wrapped around a shaggy black-and-white dog. Standing beside the dog was Luke.

Ella frowned. 'Luke, what are you doing here?'

'I've brought you some linen for the cottage.'

Ella was confused. 'Why?'

'This is my cottage.'

'Yours?' Ella looked at Penny, who was squatting down with Liv. Was she avoiding Ella's gaze?

He thrust the pile of linen into her arms before saying, 'Hopefully, that's everything you need. Penny can help you settle in.'

'Penny, can I speak to you for a minute?' Ella asked.

Penny straightened up and said, 'Olivia, why don't you go with Luke to collect the chickens' eggs?'

Ella expected Luke to say he was too busy but he just looked at Liv, waiting for her reply. When she nodded eagerly, Luke gave a whistled command to Maisie and he and Liv wandered off.

Ella wanted to tell her to stay, her natural instinct to protect her daughter rising to the fore, but she had no reason to suspect he had any ulterior motives. He had only shown them kindness so far. But, still, trust was hard for her.

'She'll be all right,' Penny said.

Ella looked at her. How did she know what Ella was thinking? She wanted to ask but she had another, more pressing, question for Penny. She looked at her as Luke retreated. 'Are you sure he's okay with me staying here?'

Penny was staring after Luke, her expression blank. Ella couldn't get a read on what she was thinking but she replied, 'He'll be fine with it.'

That sounded to Ella as though he hadn't offered the accommodation to her but had rather been coerced. And that presented Ella with a dilemma. She didn't want to be a nuisance but she definitely didn't want to go back to the community hall. She was between a rock and a hard place. 'Why didn't you tell me this was Luke's cottage?'

'Does it matter?'

Of course it mattered. She didn't want to owe Luke, or any man, any favours.

'Is that his house too?' she asked, pointing to the large house between them and the river.

'Yes. He lives there.'

'We can't stay here.' Ella was disappointed. The cottage would be perfect for a few days—it was small but plenty big enough for the two of them, it had everything they could need and was a space of their own—but Ella didn't feel comfortable accepting the offer. It would have been an appealing offer if only it didn't belong to Luke. To any man. She wished it were Penny's.

'Why not?'

'I don't want to be reliant on anyone—especially not a man,' she said, trying not to sound ungrateful.

'It's just for a few days and he won't even notice you're here. You don't have a lot of options,' Penny said. 'And I thought you didn't want to go back to the community hall.'

'I don't.'

'He lives in the big house,' Penny said. 'But he's never home. He's a good man,' she added. ''you'll be safe here.'

Ella looked warily at Penny.

'You don't need to tell me anything,' Penny continued. 'All I'm saying is that you'll be safe here. I've known Luke all his life and, even if I hadn't, it's a small town and I'd know anything there is to know. I work with him. I can vouch for him. He's a good man. He's got some baggage but he's calm and gentle. This is a good community. You don't need to stay here for ever, just take some time to catch your breath,' she said as Liv returned.

'Luke said we could have these eggs for dinner,' she said, proudly displaying a bucket which contained half a dozen fresh eggs.

Ella looked past Liv to the door but her daughter was on her own. Luke had disappeared.

'Go on, take those sheets inside.' Penny bossed Ella while she stood there looking out the door. Ella had forgotten all about the pile of linen in her arms. 'I'll grab some things from my car and then come back and help you make up the bed. Stay here tonight and if you change your mind you can look for something else tomorrow.'

Ella knew she was unlikely to find an alternative at this point in time. She could go back to the tourist office and see if there was another option, but it was too late to do that today, and she didn't want to return to the community hall. She wanted to stand on her own two feet but she wasn't going to look a gift horse in the mouth. Even if the gift horse felt like a Trojan horse. That was between Penny and Luke.

If Luke was happy for Ella to stay, she would accept. She was tired and the cottage did have appeal.

She didn't need to cross paths with Luke. She only needed three nights.

# CHAPTER FOUR

ELLA KISSED LIV goodnight and turned off the bedside light.

'Come on, Maisie, downstairs now,' she said to the dog, who was curled up on the floor. Maisie had appeared at their door as they'd finished dinner and Liv had cajoled Ella to let her inside. Ella had seen Luke come home—she could see the driveway from the kitchen window—and she'd seen him go out again. She tried not to notice what he was doing, but it was difficult when she could hear his car, and when his dog turned up looking for company.

The dog was well-trained, so she was no trouble, and Liv was besotted with her. Ella didn't mind letting Liv spend time with her, as it was an easy way to keep Liv happy. An easy reward after a couple of trying days.

Ella flicked the kettle on and leant on the kitchen bench, waiting for it to boil. Her leg was throbbing; she and Liv had walked into town earlier to do some errands and buy some groceries and she'd carried home more than she should have. Penny had given her some basic supplies yesterday, obviously expecting Ella to take up the offer of temporary accommodation. She had bread, milk, tea, coffee and cheese in her car which, together with the fresh eggs, had provided dinner for Liv and Ella.

But she'd needed to supplement the supplies for another day. Now her calf was swollen, and she was looking forward to a hot shower before hopping into bed, but first she'd have a cup of tea and put her feet up for a minute.

As she dropped a tea bag into her mug, she heard the sound of Luke's car, the throb of the engine and the crunch of the tyres on the dirt driveway. Dusk was falling and his headlights swept across the kitchen window as he negotiated the slight bend at the start of the drive. She poured hot water into her mug and carried it outside.

It was a beautiful evening, warm, and the air was still. She sat at the outdoor table and put her feet up on a spare chair. Maisie lay down beneath the table. Ella knew she should probably open the gate to let her out but, having just sat down, she couldn't summon the effort required to get up again. She'd enjoy the sunset and drink her tea first. From the garden she could see down the sloping block to the river. The setting sun had turned the cliffs on the opposite side of the river glorious shades of orange, gold and pink. She could hear frogs croaking in the distance and a pod of pelicans flew overhead.

It was a beautiful scene, calm and peaceful to look at, serene on the surface. But Ella knew there were all sorts of dangers lurking beneath the calm water: snags, logs, eddies and strong currents. She'd warned Liv about the dangers of the river but she'd still kept a close eye on her today. She thought Liv was old enough to understand the dangers but accidents happened. She wondered if she should fashion a more secure latch for the garden gate but they only had one more day here. She'd stay vigilant.

She hoped that one day she would be able to stop being

so anxious, stop looking over her shoulder for trouble, but she knew that day was a while off yet.

*'Maisie!'* Luke's voice, followed by a whistle, cut through the still evening air before Ella saw him round the corner of his house and head towards the driveway.

Maisie's ears pricked up and she leapt to her feet, tail wagging.

'She's at the cottage,' Ella called out, belatedly realising she shouldn't have said anything, because now her words had Luke retracing his steps and heading in her direction. She should have just opened the gate and let the dog run back to her master.

'Sorry about her,' Luke said as he opened the gate to let Maisie out. 'Was she being a nuisance?'

'No,' Ella replied, looking at the dog who was now turning circles at Luke's side, looking up at him adoringly. 'Liv is her biggest fan—I was afraid she was planning on keeping Maisie captive, but she's asleep now, so you get your dog back.'

'Has Liv ever had a dog?' Luke asked.

'No. But she is an animal lover.'

'And you're not?'

'I wouldn't say that, but raising a pre-schooler is hard work some days. I don't think I need a pet to look after too, but I don't mind having Maisie around as long as she's not my responsibility.' If Ella was completely honest, she'd tell him that she found Maisie's presence reassuring. She felt more secure in an unfamiliar place with the dog there. Ella was pretty sure they were safe here but there was no harm in having Maisie around as an extra layer of protection.

'Fair enough. How was your day today, on a scale of easy to hard?' He smiled at her and the setting sun seemed to lose a bit of its shine, paling against the force of his smile. He was standing on the outside of the fence, leaning against it, separated from her by the wire but still close. The strength of his smile made her want to reach out to him, to move further into his sphere, but she resisted the feeling, dismissing it as nonsensical, and stayed on her side of the fence.

'About middle of the road,' she replied. Not because of Liv; she'd been compliant enough, bribed with the promise of no chores and something fun to do tomorrow. But there were a million unanswered questions hanging over her head that weighed heavily on her, and on top of that her leg was throbbing, which shortened her tolerance and concentration. Funny, though, that she'd forgotten about her leg since seeing Luke.

'Do you have everything you need in the cottage?'

She nodded. 'Yes. Thank you. It's rather gorgeous and so much better than the community hall.'

She sipped her tea as Luke watched. He seemed in no hurry to be on his way.

'Can I make you a cup of tea or a coffee?' Ella asked, feeling obliged to offer. She was drinking her tea, sitting in Luke's garden. If he was in no hurry to head home, she felt she needed to be hospitable.

'I'd love a black coffee, thanks.'

'I was out here watching the sunset. If you want to have a seat, I'll be back in a minute.' Even though the cottage belonged to Luke, she didn't want to ask him in. It was small and he was large and she knew she'd feel a little bit hemmed in if they were alone together in the small space. It didn't matter that Penny had vouched for him, and that Ella trusted Penny: experience had taught her to be wary.

'Do you normally rent this cottage out?' she asked, when she returned with a fresh cup of tea for herself and a coffee for Luke. She put his mug on the table and sat down opposite him, keeping some distance.

'No.'

She'd got that impression, but the cottage was so cute, it would make a perfect bed and breakfast. But maybe he didn't want to be bothered with that. Penny had said he lived alone, and Ella had seen no evidence of a girlfriend or partner or anyone else who might run the accommodation for him, but he didn't elaborate further and she didn't want to pry.

'Why did you let Penny talk you into letting us stay?' She did want to know that much.

'How do you know I didn't offer?'

'It was pretty obvious the idea was spur of the moment, and you didn't seem that keen when you brought the linen over.'

'I've got used to having the place to myself,' he said. 'But I've known Penny all my life and I've learnt from experience that it's usually easiest to do as she suggests.'

'Sam said the same thing today.'

'Sam?'

'My car was swallowed by the flood waters when the levee bank burst. I had to go to the police station to file a report for the insurance claim. Sam knew the whole story of Liv and me staying here for a few days. He said

Penny had decided that it was a good decision, and once Penny decided something it usually happened. I did think it was strange that Sam knew all about it until he told me that he is Penny's husband.'

'I'm sure the news would have spread through town anyway, especially as the cottage isn't normally for rent. Everyone knows everyone's business around here. There are no secrets.'

'None?'

'Not many.'

Ella frowned and sipped her tea. Pelican's Landing was a lot smaller than Geraldton, where she had been living in in Western Australia and she knew about small-town gossip, but she hadn't expected her news to travel so quickly, and to think that the whole town could know about her business within the space of a few days had her worried. She was right to be moving on in a couple of days.

'What's the matter?' Luke asked in response to her expression.

'I don't like people knowing my business. I guess it's just as well we'll be off to Swan Hill on Thursday.'

'Swan Hill, Victoria?'

Ella nodded.

Now he was frowning. 'You're still going on your holiday? You're not going home?'

Ella shook her head. 'We weren't on holiday. I was relocating to Queensland but I thought we'd have few days in Pelican's Landing to break up the trip. Not my best idea,' she said with a wry smile.

'But Swan Hill? Why don't you just stay here in Pelican's Landing?'

'Because there's no accommodation in town. The town is full.'

'You're welcome to stay here for a bit longer than a few days. I don't need the cottage.'

'I appreciate the offer,' she said, even if she thought he didn't really mean it, 'and I appreciate having a few nights here for now but the reason for this move is to make a life for myself and Liv. On my own. I don't want to rely on other people. I want to stand on my own two feet.'

'And how are you planning on getting to Swan Hill without a car?'

'There's a bus that goes on Thursday. The lady in the tourist information office found us a spot in the caravan park, I just had to wait a few days to get there.'

'Well, the offer is there if you change your mind. Or even if you just want to wait until you replace your car.'

'Thank you, but I have no idea how long it will take to get a new car, and Liv is supposed to start school in a couple of weeks. I need to keep moving if we're going to be settled somewhere in time for that.' It was a generous offer but Ella didn't want to be beholden to anyone. What if Luke expected something in return? She'd learnt the hard way that gifts came with strings attached and, having barely broken free of the last lot of strings, she wasn't about to get herself into that position again. It didn't matter that Penny trusted Luke, Ella wasn't going to risk repeating her previous mistakes.

Luke's phone beeped with an incoming text message as he finished his coffee. He put his mug on the table and stood up to pull his phone from his pocket.

'Thanks for the coffee, but I need to get going,' he said as he read the message.

'Are you on call?' she asked.

'You could say that. I'm always on call; I'm the only doctor in town,' he said as he slid his phone away. 'Would you like me to leave Maisie in your garden? I can collect her when I get back.'

Did he think she was in danger? She knew he'd seen her bruises but he hadn't asked anything. She wondered if she should tell him what had been going on. She had a sense she could confide in him, but then someone else would know her secrets, her shame, and she didn't want that person to be Luke.

She was making changes, moving forward. She had left her old life behind her and she didn't need to talk about her past, no matter how recent it was. She wanted a clean slate, a new beginning, a chance to be a different person. Stronger. Self-sufficient. Admitting what had happened to her would feel like admitting to being a failure. 'It's fine,' she said. 'She can go with you.' She wouldn't have minded keeping Maisie with her but she didn't want to look weak or needy. She'd go inside and lock the door instead.

Luke left the cottage and Ella in a conflicted state.

She had obviously been the subject of gossip or innuendo in the past. He should have reassured her. He could tell she was concerned about small-town conversations, and he'd had enough experience to know how bad that could be. But there was an up side to a small town and that was that people stuck together, they rallied around when needed. All you had to do was ask for help. But that wasn't something that seemed to sit comfortably with her.

He wanted her to trust him but he sensed her suspicion of people's motives, her distrust of strangers and her preservation of her own space. To gain her trust, he'd have to be careful. He felt protective of her. She was intriguing, captivating, but she was also a stranger, someone who would be gone from his life in a few days. He didn't want to cultivate a relationship—he didn't want to risk letting her down. He'd done that before; he wouldn't do it again.

Confronted with the reality of having someone living in the barn that had been converted for Gemma, even though Gemma had never lived there, had reignited his feelings of loss and guilt. And compounding that were the similarities between Ella and Gemma. Both young, thin and fragile. Was he making it more difficult for himself by having her live, not with him exactly, but in very close proximity? It had nothing to do with her being a patient or not being a local but everything to do with how he'd felt when she'd collapsed into his arms. His reaction to her had been far from familial but he wasn't ready to examine those feelings. It was easier to keep her at arm's length.

But that wouldn't be fair to Ella. She needed assistance and he could offer it. The cottage had been renovated as a refuge for his sister. It hadn't helped Gemma but maybe it could help Ella.

He stopped at the service station to pick up ice-cream before turning into the nursing-home car park, which was deserted at this hour of the night. He should be at home, like all the other sensible people. Sometimes it felt as if he had no life other than work and visiting his father. When he had spare time, he usually took his boat out and went fishing, or water skiing if he could round up a few people, but with the flood that was off the agenda. Perhaps he'd get out on the water soon. According to the reports from upstream, the river would peak in a few days and the flood waters would start to recede—unfortunately not before creating havoc with the levee bank—and a fishing trip might give him some clear head space.

'Hey, Dad, it's Luke.' He switched the radio to classical music as he greeted his dad.

'Luke! Is your mother coming in?'

'Not tonight, Dad, it's Tuesday—she has her craft group.' He'd learnt from experience that it was easier just to make an excuse for his mother's whereabouts rather than explain that she was no longer with them. When his dad was already restless or agitated, that discussion always ended badly. It would either make him more upset or argumentative and Luke didn't want to risk an argument tonight. 'I brought you an ice-cream, would you like that now?'

He unwrapped the ice-cream, which was on a stick, and handed it to his dad. He could still manage to feed himself if cutlery wasn't required.

'I saw John Collins at the pharmacy today,' Luke said. This was a complete fabrication, but his dad had known John since they had first moved to Pelican's Landing as young men—one a doctor, the other the local pharmacist. Luke knew that there would be enough long-term memory for his dad to have a coherent conversation, even if it was irrelevant.

'How did he look?' his dad asked. 'I haven't seen him

at the clinic for a while. He must be due to have his cholesterol level checked.'

'I'll get him to make an appointment. He was saying that Sally has just had another baby, so that's grandchild number six.'

John and his wife had five children and several grandchildren, and Luke knew his dad could comfortably run through the list of ailments that they'd experienced, even if they were not current. He knew, once he got his dad talking about old patients, he would talk happily without expecting anything more than a nod or an occasional comment in agreement. He was happy holding court and hearing the sound of his own voice.

Luke occasionally wondered if his dad missed company. Did he still have enough wits about him to know that, if he misbehaved for the staff, they would call Luke who would then come and sit with him and keep him company?

He finished his own ice-cream as he wondered if this was going to be his life. He loved his work, and he didn't normally mind spending time with his dad, but he realised that tonight he'd rather be talking to Ella. He'd rather be with her talking about their days But he listened as his father chatted away and eventually calmed down and allowed Luke to settle him into bed for the night.

He left the nursing home and drove home, pulling in beside his house and walking around the back he checked on the cottage. Maisie greeted him but the cottage was in darkness. He couldn't disturb Ella now. It wasn't particularly late but a knock on the door would most likely frighten her.

He opened the back door of his own house, letting Maisie inside, and flicked on a light. His house usually welcomed him home after a long day. He found the smell of the river and the sight of moonlight on the water relaxed him, and he found comfort in the familiar sounds of the creaking floorboards and rattling windows. Normally it was his sanctuary, but tonight it just felt cold, empty and lonely.

Ella had spent the best part of Wednesday morning completing paperwork for the insurance company. She was confident they would accept her claim, but they hadn't said how long it would be before she was likely to get the money to buy another car. She had no funds of her own to use so she had to wait for the claim to go through and in the meantime, they were going to have to rely on public transport. Which was non-existent in Pelican's Landing.

Maybe she shouldn't move to Swan Hill tomorrow. Even though there was accommodation available, would she be able to get to where she needed? Perhaps they'd be better off heading straight to Queensland. They could travel by bus—it was a long way, but once they arrived she might have more options for accommodation, transport and even finding a second-hand car in a bigger town. She really didn't know which was her best option and her head was pounding as she tried to work it out.

She sighed. She needed a break from decision-making—or attempted decision-making—and she'd promised Liv they would do something fun in exchange for the time Liv had spent traipsing around doing errands over the past two days and now waiting for Ella to complete all the paperwork. There was an adventure playground at the top of the hill coming into town. It was an uphill walk from Luke's cottage, but not too far, and she knew Liv would enjoy it.

Five minutes after arriving at the playground, Liv was in her element, exploring the gigantic wooden pirate ship that dominated the park. It sat on a large mound and had tunnels running up through the hill into the hold, climbing nets strung from the masts, a ladder to a crow's nest—which thankfully wasn't that high—and even a plank to walk, which ended in a fireman's pole to the ground. At the bottom of the pole there was a choice between a large slippery dip or a flying fox to traverse the rest of the mound down to the picnic area.

Ella sat at a picnic table under a shade sail and tried to let her mind go blank as she kept an eye on Liv, who had already befriended a couple of children, a boy and a girl of similar age. The boy was a little more adventurous than the girls and, after climbing to the crow's nest, he was now encouraging the girls to walk along the plank. The plank was really more of a bridge but the suggestion was there. It had hand rails, with marine-wire sides preventing children from falling off, but it was the pole at the end that made Ella nervous. She'd never liked fireman's poles. She always had visions of the pole being too far away to reach safely and children plummeting to the ground. She had left the picnic table and was halfway up the slope when Liv reached the end of the plank. Before she could remind her to be careful, Liv had grabbed the pole and was sliding down with no problems.

'Are you having fun?' Ella asked, curbing her concerns when she met Liv at the bottom of the pole.

Liv nodded, a broad grin plastered across her little face. 'Can I try that next?' she said, pointing at the flying fox, where her two new friends were now standing.

Ella watched as the little boy went first again. The flying fox was more like a flying swing. Rather than children reaching overhead and hanging on with their hands there was a small seat at the end of the rope. The little boy sat on the seat, wrapped his legs around the rope and flew down the short slope of the hill. Ella wasn't convinced the flying fox was a good idea, but Liv had been so well-behaved all day she didn't have the heart to argue.

It wasn't an overly long distance, and she reckoned Liv should be able to cling on to reach the bottom. They wandered over to the flying fox as the little boy ran back up the hill, pulling on the rope to drag the seat back up behind him.

'This is Chloe, Mum, she's five.' Liv introduced Ella to the little girl who was waiting for a turn. Ella watched as Chloe successfully managed to fly down the hill. That she was much the same age as Liv reassured her a little, and when she brought the contraption back to the top Ella held the rope steady while Liv sprang onto the seat.

Liv didn't wait for instructions—she'd obviously been watching the other kids. She wrapped her skinny legs around the rope and crossed them at the ankles. Ella gave Liv a little push—not hard, just enough to get her moving—and ran down the hill beside her, keeping one hand outstretched, prepared to grab the rope to slow it down if Liv picked up too much speed. Liv was only a lightweight so she didn't go terribly fast but Ella had forgotten about her own injury and, as she jogged down the hill, keeping pace beside Liv, she felt the wound in her calf pulling.

'Can I do it again, Mummy? That was fun!' Liv asked when they reached the bottom.

'I'm not sure that I can run down the hill again, Liv.' Ella wasn't sure her calf would withstand a second turn.

'Please, Mummy,' she begged. 'I can do it by myself.'

She was probably right—the other children had managed. Liv hadn't gone fast: the incline wasn't steep and Liv wasn't heavy. Ella hadn't needed to control the swing. There was no reason to think she couldn't have a go on her own so Ella relented and together they walked back up the hill, pulling the swing behind them. Ella held it as Liv jumped on for the second time before giving her a gentle push.

She stayed at the top of the hill as Liv swung down the ride. Liv was halfway down the slope when Ella saw her start to slip sideways. She waited for her to correct herself, but her feet had uncrossed, and Ella gasped in fear as her daughter's bottom slipped off the seat. As Ella started to run, Liv tumbled from the seat and landed heavily on her side. Ella's calf screamed in protest as she sprinted down the hill.

'Olivia!'

Liv didn't move. Ella reached her side and knelt in the patchy grass. The ground was hard under her knees, baked by the summer sun. She put her hand on Liv's face. Her eyes were closed but she was breathing—Ella could see her little chest rise and fall.

'Liv? Can you hear me? Liv!'

# CHAPTER FIVE

'LIV?' ELLA REPEATED. 'Can you hear me?'

Olivia's eyes remained closed.

'Don't move her. She hit her head when she fell.'

Ella turned round at the sound of a woman's voice. It was another mother, who Ella had seen sitting at a picnic table while her children played.

Ella turned back to her daughter. 'Olivia?' she repeated. Her heart raced as fear and panic overcame her, but she reluctantly heeded the woman's advice, resisting the urge to scoop Liv up, worried now that Liv had sustained a serious injury.

'Olivia?' she said for the third time, hearing her daughter's name catch in her throat as tears threatened to overflow. What had she been thinking, letting Liv ride the flying fox on her own? Maybe those other children had played on it a hundred times before; maybe they'd known exactly what they were doing.

Liv's eyes opened and Ella could breathe again.

'Liv, can you hear me? Are you okay?' she asked. Liv's eyes had a glazed sheen, as if she was having trouble focusing. 'I'm right here, darling. Are you hurt? Can you move your feet and your fingers?'

Liv opened and closed her fists as her eyes slowly re-gained focus.

'You should take her to the doctor to get her assessed,' the other woman advised, just as Chloe, the little girl Liv had befriended earlier, arrived at her side. This woman must be Chloe's mother. 'She hit her head pretty hard. Do you want me to help you carry your things to your car?' she offered.

'I don't have a car. We walked here.' Ella knew there was only one doctor in town and, while Luke's house was in walking distance, the clinic wasn't, even if Liv could walk on her own.

'I can give you a lift if you like,' the other woman said.

'What happened, Mummy?' Chloe asked at the same time as Ella said,

'Really?'

'Of course. It's no problem,' she said to Ella. 'Just let me round up Jack.' She turned to Chloe and said, 'Chloe, darling, can you fetch Jack? Tell him we need to go in a hurry. I'll bring you back here after we drive Olivia to the doctor.' Chloe ran off as the woman waited with Ella. 'I'm Hayley, by the way.'

'I'm Ella,' she replied with a smile. 'And a lift would be brilliant if you're sure it's no trouble.'

Ella waited for Hayley to gather her kids and their stuff and then she carried Liv to Hayley's car. Liv felt heavier than normal and Ella realised it was because she wasn't clinging onto her. She seemed lethargic and unfocused and Ella was trying hard not to freak out.

'Do you need some help to get her inside?' Hayley asked when she pulled up in front of the clinic.

'No, I'll manage. Thank you so much for the lift.'

'No problem. No doubt we'll bump into you again,' Hayley said as Ella picked Liv up and pushed the car door closed with her hip.

Hayley drove off with a wave as Ella carried Liv inside. It was getting late in the day and Ella hoped Luke was still in the clinic. What if he'd been called out to an emergency or was doing a home visit? She was momentarily relieved to see three people in the waiting room; at least that meant Luke was around. But then she realised she was at the end of a queue of patients, and Ella hoped she didn't have to wait too long. She was worried about Liv. Did this qualify as an emergency? Would Luke let her jump the queue? Liv was conscious and coherent now. She'd probably have to wait her turn.

Penny was behind the reception desk, chatting to a younger woman who was sitting at a computer.

'Ella! I didn't know you had an appointment today,' she said as Ella approached, still carrying Liv.

'We don't. But Liv had an accident at the playground. She hit her head quite hard and blacked out for a bit. I was hoping Luke could take a look at her?'

Liv had her head buried against Ella's shoulder but she stirred in her arms as Ella stood at the front desk. Ella initially thought it was being moved that made her stir until she said, 'I don't feel well, Mummy. I feel sick.'

'Come with me,' Penny said, 'I'll put you straight in a room.'

Ella followed Penny down a passage way and into an examination room. She put Liv down on the bed and stood beside her. Penny handed Ella a green plastic bowl.

'You might want to keep this handy,' she said. 'I'll let Luke know you're here.'

Penny left the door open, returning in a few minutes to check on them. She handed Ella some forms to complete while she waited and said, 'Luke won't be long.'

Ella had just started on the forms when Liv vomited. She was crying—she hated vomiting. 'My head hurts.' Ella turned on the tap and filled a paper cup with water, holding it to Liv's lips.

'Have a sip of water to rinse your mouth out,' she told her. 'And then spit it into the bowl.'

Ella was carrying the bowl back to the sink when Luke came into the room, closing the door behind him.

'Hello, Ella, hello Liv—I hear you've taken a tumble,' he said, directing his statement to Liv before turning to Ella. 'What happened?'

Ella's heart skipped a beat as Luke looked at her. Each time she saw him she was surprised again at how good-looking he was and how confident he was in himself. His confidence reassured her. 'We were at the adventure playground, the one with the pirate ship—do you know it?' Luke nodded and Ella continued, 'She was on the flying fox but she came off and hit her head on the ground. She fell hard. We think she knocked herself out.'

'We?'

'There was another mum there—she saw Liv fall too. She drove us here.'

'How long was Liv out for?' Luke wanted to know.

'I'm not really sure.' It had felt like a lifetime but in reality she knew it hadn't been too long. Ella had said her name three times, relatively quickly. 'Probably less than a minute,' she said. 'But she's just vomited and is complaining of a headache.'

'Do you remember what happened, Liv?'

'No.'

'Do you remember what you had for lunch today?'

Liv looked blankly at Ella. 'A Vegemite sandwich,' Ella answered for her.

'Do you remember my name?' Luke asked.

Liv shook her head.

'I'm Luke. Do you remember I have a dog?'

Liv smiled now and said, 'Yes! Maisie,' and Ella's worry eased slightly.

'That's right,' Luke said, before turning to Ella. His eyes were very blue but somehow still managed to convey a feeling of warmth. 'Has she had a concussion before?'

'No.' Ella had. She'd been hit in the head many times but she'd always protected Liv. She hoped Luke wasn't judging her parenting; she felt bad enough already, and she was relieved that Hayley had been there to witness Liv's accident.

She watched and listened as he checked Liv. Some of his questions seemed difficult and she didn't blame Liv for not being able to answer—what four-year-old knew what day of the week it was? Every day was the same when you were four.

'I'm going to tell you five words now, Liv.' Luke had moved on to another task. 'And then I'm going to ask you to repeat them back to me: elbow, apple, carpet, saddle, bubble,' he said, talking slowly and leaving gaps between the words, before asking her if she could tell him the days of the week, going backwards from Sunday. Liv couldn't do that but she was able to repeat some numbers in reverse order.

Ella wondered if he'd forgotten about the five words he's asked Liv to remember but, before she could ask about that test, he had moved on from what Ella assumed were comprehension tests to some more physical ones.

He checked Liv's eyes and felt her neck, which Liv said wasn't sore, before getting her to take her shoes off and stand up. He had a lovely manner with Liv and Ella found herself softening towards him even more. There were definitely some kind, gentle people in the world and it seemed as though he was one of them. Penny might have been right when she said he could be trusted.

'All right, Liv, stand with your feet together and put your hands on your hips. Like this,' he said as he stood up too and demonstrated what he meant. 'Good. Now, close your eyes. I'm going to count to see how long you can stand still, okay?'

Liv glanced at Ella, a look of concern on her face. Ella nodded, encouraging her to follow Luke's instructions. Liv closed her eyes and after twenty seconds Luke got her to open them, change her foot position to one foot in front of the other and close her eyes again. Liv completed both tests easily.

'Great, well done. Now, do you remember those five words I told you before? Can you tell me what any of them were? In any order.'

'Bubble and apple,' Liv responded. 'I can't remember the others.' She looked at Ella again, obviously wondering if she'd done something wrong.

'Good job, Liv, you did well,' Luke reassured her. 'You can put your sandals back on, if you like; we're all done.'

He had a natural rapport with Liv that pleased Ella. She was well aware that Luke lived alone but she wondered if he had children of his own. Perhaps he was divorced and any children were with his ex. He'd said he was familiar with the playground. She wanted to ask but didn't want to pry.

'I think she'll be okay,' he said as he turned to Ella. 'I'll give her some paracetamol and then you can take her home. Give her a light supper and water to drink then lots of rest for the next twenty-four hours. If you want to wait, I've just got to see the last couple of patients and then I can drop you off before my nursing home visit.'

Ella had been relying on the kindness of strangers more over the past three days than she ever had before, despite her plan to stand on her own two feet. But she didn't relish the idea of walking back to the cottage, possibly having to carry Liv as well, so she nodded gratefully.

Ella heard Luke's car returning not long after she'd put Liv to bed. Luke had dropped them back to the cottage, carried Liv inside and then left for the nursing home. Ella expected him to take the driveway directly to his house and was surprised to hear his car pull to a stop in front of the cottage. She unlocked the door and opened it as he stepped through the gate.

'Hi.'

'Hi, I'm not disturbing you, am I?' he asked as he

walked up the path through the garden. 'I just thought I'd check on Liv,' he added after she shook her head.

'She seems fine,' Ella told him. 'She's sleeping.'

'Did she eat?'

'Just some toast.'

'And how about you? How are you?' he asked.

'I'm okay.' Was he worried about her emotional state? 'I had a shock but I'm okay now that Liv seems fine.'

'What about your leg?'

Ella frowned. 'My leg? Why do you ask?'

'You were limping when you walked to my car.'

'Oh. I ran to Liv when she fell; it was a bit sore but I'm sure it's all right.'

'Would you like me to take a look at it for you?'

'It'll be fine; you've had a long day already.' Ella knew her calf hadn't fared too well in the events of the afternoon but she didn't want to be an imposition.

'All my days are long. I think being a doctor is a lot like being a parent. I can't switch off, not completely; there are always one or two patients who concern me. Much like a troublesome child, or any child, I imagine.'

'I don't want to be the troublesome child.'

He smiled at her and she could feel herself relenting. 'You're supposed to come to the clinic for a check tomorrow anyway. Wouldn't it be easier to do it now?'

'We're off to Swan Hill tomorrow; I can get it looked at there.' She tried one last time to stay firm, knowing that letting him look at her calf would mean inviting him in. She knew her resistance was more about being wary of having him at close quarters than about imposing on him.

'Even more reason for me to do it today. It will only take a minute.'

'Are you sure you don't mind?'

'I don't mind. I'll need to change the dressing, so I'll grab my bag from the car and see you inside.'

She sat at the kitchen table and put her foot up on another chair. She thought about putting something she could use as a weapon close to hand—a kitchen knife or a heavy pot—but then she thought about how that would look. What would Luke make of that if he noticed? It would look as if she didn't trust him. If she wasn't going to trust him now, after the past three days when he'd done nothing to suggest she shouldn't, when would she?

Luke returned, carrying a large medical bag, which he left by her side before going to wash his hands in the bathroom. He returned and pulled a chair over to sit near her feet. He peeled off the waterproof dressing that he'd applied over her calf. 'You've pulled some of the stitches,' he said as his fingers ran along the wound.

His hands were warm and gentle and Ella could feel her heart racing. 'But they're still holding.'

'They are, but it will take longer to heal and you'll have a bigger scar. I should be able to pull it together with some Steri-Strips.'

'I wanted those in the first place.'

'Well, now you get your wish.' He smiled at her as he replied and her heart skipped a beat.

She was about to drop her gaze, afraid he might see the effect he was having on her, afraid of how he made her feel. But he had already looked away, ducking his head to open his medical bag, remaining professional and seemingly unaware of the power of his smile.

He found Steri-Strips and another waterproof dressing. He pulled the edges of her wound together and taped the Steri-Strips across it.

'I can do this bit,' Ella said as Luke peeled open the sleeve containing another waterproof dressing. His touch was beginning to feel intimate. It was unsettling her now.

He looked at her quizzically. 'So can I,' he replied, 'And my hands are clean. Life is easier if you let people help you.'

She wasn't used to people helping her. She didn't want it, nor did she expect it. 'I don't want to rely on anyone else. I want to stand on my own two feet.'

'I'm not suggesting you can't manage, and it's not a case of relying on people—it's just accepting help. They're not necessarily the same thing.'

Either way, she was determined to manage on her own. Determined to do better for Liv.

Oh, God, Liv…! She caught her breath as a thought hit her. Was she doing better for Liv? Liv had a concussion; what if Luke thought it was her fault? Was it? Was it something that needed to be reported?

'Did I hurt you?' Luke was smoothing the edges of the dressing down on her skin but he looked up when he heard her sharp intake of breath.

'No.' She shook her head as she wondered if she should she tell him what was bothering her. What if he'd reported her already? 'You don't have to report Liv's accident, do you?' she asked, deciding she had to know one way or the other.

'To whom?'

'I don't know. Child protection?' she replied as she took her feet off the chair and pushed them under the table.

'No, accidents happen. You weren't responsible, and from what I've seen Liv is well looked-after.' Luke packed his medical kit up, keeping his eyes on his equipment as he asked, 'Have you had any involvement with child protection before? Has Liv been hurt before?'

Ella shook her head.

'But your story is different, isn't it?' He was looking at her now but his tone was gentle, much like his hands.

She dropped her gaze, unable to maintain eye contact. She didn't hear any judgement in his voice but she knew he'd seen her bruises and she couldn't deny his conclusion.

'Ella, it's not something to be ashamed of or embarrassed about. It's not your fault.'

She looked up. 'But that's exactly how I felt—that it was my fault. That I wasn't enough. That I was a failure, I was letting people down.'

'You're not a failure, Ella. I've seen the evidence of the harm that was inflicted on you. I assume it was your partner?' he continued after Ella confirmed his suspicions with a nod. 'You and Liv have been let down, Ella. Did you ever report the abuse?'

'No.' Ella shook her head. 'I was afraid of what would happen if he found out I'd gone to the police.' Trent had held all the power.

'Does your partner know where you are?'

'*Ex*-partner,' Ella stressed. 'And, no, he doesn't know where we are.'

'And where is he?'

'He's out of the country. He's on a job that means he'll be away for several weeks. It gave me a chance to leave.'

'That was a brave thing to do.'

'I didn't do it for me. I did it for Liv. I was terrified that one day Liv would be in the firing line of Trent's temper. I moved to keep her safe.'

'Do you feel safe here?'

'I'm not sure,' she said honestly. 'I don't remember what it's like to truly feel safe, and while Trent is still around I'm not sure I'll ever feel completely safe. I can't believe he won't find me.'

'Is he Liv's father? Are you going to have to tell him where you are?'

'No. Liv's father isn't part of our lives.' Ella rarely thought of Liv's father, and certainly not in those terms. He was just the man who'd got her pregnant. He was a backpacker, visiting Australia from Italy and they'd had a brief relationship. She hadn't discovered she was pregnant until he'd left the country. She'd told him about the pregnancy but he hadn't been interested in being a father. He didn't even know if Ella had given birth to a girl or a boy. She'd never heard anything more from him. 'It was just me and my mum when Liv was born. I met Trent when Liv was two.'

'Three years ago?'

'Almost.' She could hear the surprise in his voice and knew he was wondering why she'd stayed so long. Surely he must know it wasn't as simple as walking out a door? 'It wasn't always bad,' she said, hating that she was still making excuses for herself—and, by association, for Trent.

'When I met him, he seemed charming and successful and I was flattered that he would be interested in me, a single mother. I was working in the restaurant at the local marina and taking bookings for berths for visiting yachts. Trent worked as a diesel mechanic in the mines. He was a fly-in fly-out worker, and lots of the miners had boats—cruisers or yachts. They had a lot of money. He worked two weeks on, two weeks off, and I got used to him coming to the restaurant, chatting to me about my life. I started to look forward to seeing him and I admit initially his interest in me was addictive. I never thought he was looking for specific information that made me an easy target, but in hindsight I know that was what he was doing.

'Liv and I moved in to his house and that's when things began to change—all orchestrated by him—but I didn't notice at first. Things were small and gradual, and seemingly inconsequential, and he framed his requests in such a way that he made them seem reasonable.'

'What sort of requests?'

'He asked me to quit my job. He said he'd support me, and because it meant I could stay home with Liv, because it meant she didn't need to go to day care, I said yes. But his real reason, I realised later, was because he didn't want me socialising with anyone. He wanted me isolated. Dependent on him. He tracked my phone, telling me he was worried about my safety, but it was so he always knew where I was and could corroborate my story.

If I went out to meet friends, he'd turn up randomly if he was in town, or call them later to check on my story.'

'What about your family?'

She shook her head. 'I haven't seen my father since I was six. He walked out one day and never came back. My mum died when Liv was one. I don't have siblings. It's just me. And Liv. There was no one to worry about me. I've since found out that was one of the things that appealed to him. That it would be easy to manipulate me, to control me. If I'd been stronger, if I'd had a network around me, it would have made things more difficult for him but I was flattered. I had no idea there was such a thing as emotional abuse. I thought he was concerned about me. I thought he loved me.'

She'd justified it initially by telling herself he'd given them a roof over their heads and wasn't she lucky? She was able to stay at home with Liv without having to worry about going to work.

'But when the emotional abuse became physical, I knew I needed to make some changes. If not for my sake, then for Liv's. I didn't want her growing up witnessing that behaviour, or worse, being subject to violence herself.'

'Ella, I'm so sorry this has happened to you. How long was this going on for?'

He reached out a hand to her but she pulled away. She didn't want him to touch her. She couldn't let him cross her boundaries. She was afraid if he showed her sympathy she might crumble. She wasn't looking for sympathy and she didn't want pity, but she wanted him to understand what she'd been through. She knew he'd worked out she'd been a victim of abuse but she didn't want him to think of her as a victim. She wanted him to think she was strong. She realised his opinion of her mattered and she wanted him to know she was a survivor.

Luke withdrew his hand and Ella continued to explain.

'Trent lost his job eighteen months ago. He started drinking daily. When he was working, he'd have a few drinks at the marina, but once he had time on his hands he spent more and more time at the pub. He didn't go to the marina any more—he had to sell his boat and his berth because he couldn't afford to keep it and that infuriated him. He had no savings, he'd been spending everything he earned. He accused me of being a freeloader but he refused to let me get my job back. I was damned if I did and damned if I didn't.

'I said I'd leave. I said I'd never expected him to support me. That was the first time he hit me. He called me ungrateful. I should have left then, but I had nowhere to go, and he swore he was sorry. He said he'd never meant to hurt me, he told me I'd provoked him. He said he'd never hit me again.

'And then he started drinking every day—at the pub and at home. I had changed the details of the bank account that my single mother's payment went into, so that it went into his account instead. It made me feel like I was contributing. But that came back to bite me. He was spending my money on alcohol.

'I couldn't go back to work, I couldn't leave Liv with him, I was too frightened, and full-time childcare would cost more than I could earn. I was trapped. I couldn't work out how to leave him. If he wasn't at the pub, he was at home. I had no money and it wasn't just me I had to think about. It would have been easier if it was but I needed to get Liv out too.'

Luke was a good listener. It was something she imagined would be a requirement of being a good GP but she was surprised at how the words flowed from her tongue. She'd only known him for three days and it was unlike her to discuss her past with anyone. Was it dangerous to confide in him like this? How would he judge her? What would he think? But it was too late to worry about that now. Besides, she was leaving tomorrow. She'd never see him again.

'Then Trent got a call from someone he used to work with,' she continued. 'They offered him a job on an oil rig. He'd be gone for three months initially, and I realised this was my opportunity to get away. I planned to save some money and then find something to rent but I couldn't access the joint account without him noticing so I needed a job. I managed to call in a favour from someone I knew before I had Liv, and I got a job at the university hub where there was also child care.

'I thought I had it all worked out—but I didn't know that Trent had asked some of his mates to keep an eye on me and one of them told him I was "gallivanting" around town. Trent came back unexpectedly—he'd made up a family emergency—and confronted me. He accused me of cheating on him and became extremely violent. I knew that I couldn't stay in Geraldton; I knew I'd never be safe. I had to run. If I didn't, I was risking my life and Liv's. When Trent left to go back to the oil rig, I packed up my car, took Liv and a few essentials and headed east. That was two and a half weeks ago.'

'That was an incredible effort, Ella; you should be proud of yourself. He hasn't tried to contact you?'

'I assume he has by now but I had I emailed him and told him Liv dropped my phone in the bath. I said I had to get a new one but couldn't afford it so for the time being I wouldn't have a phone. Obviously, I changed my number when I got a new phone, I didn't want him to be able to trace me, but he'll be wondering why he hasn't heard from me by now. Leaving Western Australia was supposed to be our fresh start, and I was prepared for that, but losing the few things that I brought with us, and losing my car in the flood, has just made it that much harder.'

She refused to feel sorry for herself but sometimes it was hard not to get despondent. She sighed. 'I'll just have to start again.'

Luke was watching her carefully and she wished she knew what he was thinking.

'You've done an amazing thing for you and Liv, Ella,' he said. 'The hardest part is walking out the door and not going back.'

'Believe me, I have no intention of going back. I might have only just left my old life behind physically but I moved on emotionally months ago.'

'And you've made it this far all on your own. Will you let us help you now?'

'Us?'

'Me. Penny. Sam. There must be a way we can help. Finding you somewhere permanent to live? A job?'

She shook her head. 'I'm not staying.' She appreciated the offer but she would be leaving in the morning. She'd never see him again.

'Are you still planning on going to Swan Hill tomorrow?' Luke asked, and when Ella nodded he added, 'On the bus?'

'Yes.'

'At the risk of overstepping—and this comes as medical advice—can I suggest delaying your departure for a few days if possible, to give Liv time to recover from her concussion?'

'I thought you said she will be fine.'

'I did. But she still has a concussion and putting her on a bus and travelling six hours is not ideal if it can be avoided. Why don't you wait for the insurance money for your car?'

'Because I don't know how long that will be,' she said.

She should leave. She'd told him more than she needed to—far too much—based on the fact she wouldn't be staying but she didn't want to jeopardise Liv's health. 'I guess I can check the bus timetable and see when the next one goes.' Maybe she could delay just a few days but she didn't want to be an imposition.

'If we're going to stay a bit longer can I at least pay you something for rent? I've been accused of being a freeloader before.' She smiled in an attempt to relieve some of the tension she was feeling.

'No, that's not necessary. This isn't the same thing at all. This comes under the umbrella of letting someone help you.'

'Can I make you dinner, then?' She couldn't offer nothing in return for his generosity. 'Tomorrow night, as we'll still be here?'

'I wouldn't say no to that.' He smiled, and that was enough to make Ella think maybe she should stay for one more night.

# CHAPTER SIX

LUKE STEPPED OUT of his house and headed for the cottage, followed by Maisie. He wasn't doing a very good job of keeping his distance, he realised. That strategy was failing dismally. He was unable to keep away. He felt himself drowning in the depths of Ella's dark eyes whenever she looked at him, captivated by her beauty and in awe of her strength. He knew she felt vulnerable but he saw her determination, her strength, her courage.

And so, once again, he found himself on her doorstep, unable to keep away. He had a small gift in one hand, a hostess gift. He'd deliberated if he should take one and what it should be. Ella was the hostess but it was his house. But the manners his parents had instilled in him wouldn't let him turn up empty handed. He could have taken flowers but she had a garden full of flowers at the cottage and would a bunch of flowers have given the wrong message?

What was the right one? What message was he trying to impart? What was their relationship? Landlord and tenant? Friends? She wasn't paying rent. And she wasn't a friend. Not yet.

He had settled on a box of shortbread, baked by Penny. Everyone loved Pen's baking.

* * *

Ella's hands shook as she took the pasta bake out of the oven and put it on top of the stove. She was equal parts excited and nervous. She was being ridiculous, she chided herself as she closed the oven door and straightened up. Luke was coming to dinner with her and Liv. That was all. It wasn't a date. It was a convenience for him and a thank you, a return favour, from her. There was no reason for her sense of anticipation.

Meeting someone she was attracted to when she'd embarked on her new path hadn't even crossed her mind. When she'd left Trent behind, she'd been determined to forge her own path, and survival had been her only goal. She hadn't had time to think about what her future would look like besides hoping she and Liv would have somewhere safe to live and she would have a job.

Meeting Luke was unexpected but she knew she had to put her feelings to one side. She had moved on physically and emotionally from Trent but she didn't trust herself to make good decisions with relationships. She knew Luke was a good man but that didn't mean he would be good for her. She'd made mistakes in the past and she had other priorities, bigger priorities, than getting involved in another relationship—even assuming Luke was attracted to her. And why would he be? She was a single mother with nothing to her name—no qualifications, no money, not even any possessions. It was her and Liv against the world. Who would want to take them on?

She would give Luke dinner as a thank you for his help and then they'd be gone, following her own path. Just her and Liv. As much as she liked the fantasy of a different life, she knew it wasn't likely to be her reality. Her luck was already tenuous; surely it wouldn't stretch to that she thought as she put any romantic notions aside and checked the table. Bowls, cutlery, a jug of water, glasses and paper napkins had been set out.

She'd placed a vase of flowers picked from the cottage garden in the centre of the table, but she reached for it now, removing it. Flowers were unnecessary. She carried them up to the bedroom and put them on the dresser, out of sight, before checking the time—again. She'd invited Luke for six-thirty.

Liv was lying on the floor drawing and she jumped up and ran to the door when they heard a knock. She opened it to let Luke and Maisie in.

Liv wrapped her arms around Maisie, who was wagging her tail vigorously in greeting, despite having spent most of the day at the barn with Liv, while Luke handed Ella a container filled with shortbread.

'I brought you these,' he said.

The biscuits looked home-made. 'Did you make these?' she asked.

'I wish I could lay claim to them but Penny baked them.'

'Well, they look delicious, thank you.'

He looked delicious as well. He was wearing shorts and a T-shirt and smelt clean and fresh, as if he'd just stepped out of the shower.

'Can I get you a drink?' she asked, stepping away to put the shortbread on the kitchen bench, trying to put some distance between Luke and herself.

'Just water will be fine, thanks,' he replied, before turning to Liv. 'How have you been today, Liv?'

'Good,' Liv replied. 'I taught Maisie to shake hands.'

'Did you? Can you show me?'

'Sit, Maisie.' Liv waited for the dog to follow her instructions before she held out her hand and moved it up and down in the air. 'Shake.'

Maisie lifted a front paw and Liv shook it gently. 'Clever girl!'

'That's well done, Liv,' Luke said as Ella passed him a glass of water. He winked at Ella. She knew Maisie had already mastered that trick before but she appreciated that Luke was giving Liv all the credit. She smiled back at him as her nerves dissipated. He was a generous man, a kind man, and she didn't need to be so tense.

Luke sat on the couch, nursing his water, and continued his conversation with Liv while Ella dressed the salad she'd made.

'Have you had a headache today, Liv?'

'No.'

'You can see properly?'

'Yes.'

'Your eyes aren't blurry?' Liv shook her head. 'And you haven't been dizzy at all?'

'No. Can I play outside with Maisie now?' Liv asked Ella, apparently tired of Luke's questions.

'We're about to eat. Go and wash your hands now; you can play with her after dinner.'

Liv went to the bathroom and Luke turned to Ella. 'Liv didn't have any trouble following instructions or paying attention today? No nausea, no pain?'

Ella shook her head. 'No. We had a quiet day. Liv seemed fine, normal. We did some cooking—made this pasta bake and a cake. And she helped as normal.'

'That's good news.'

Liv monopolised the conversation through dinner, which relieved some of Ella's nervousness, and by the time she went outside to play with Maisie Ella had relaxed. She was getting used to Luke's company and to the cottage. She was beginning to feel safer, if still not completely safe, but she was more comfortable, less afraid and less nervous. Almost as though things might be okay.

'So, you didn't get on the bus today?' Luke asked when they were alone at the table.

'No. And there's not another bus until next Thursday.'

'Is that right?'

'You knew!'

'Does that matter? My advice still stands. Liv didn't need to be travelling today.'

'But I need to get settled somewhere before Liv starts school.'

'What's wrong with here?'

Ella pondered the question. What was wrong with here? It wasn't where she had planned to be but did that matter? The town had some appeal. It was peaceful, had plenty of country charm and the people seemed nice— present company in particular. But already people knew her business. The town was small. Too small for her.

'I had a larger town in mind,' she said. Somewhere with more opportunity. Somewhere she could have anonymity. But to say those things out loud would sound like harsh judgement to someone who had chosen to make a life here. Someone who might have always lived here. 'You said you've known Penny all your life. Did you grow up here?'

'I was born here, grew up here. I went away to university and now I'm back.'

'What brought you back?'

'My dad was the local doctor. He retired a couple of years ago now. He had early dementia, and as it progressed he couldn't continue to work, so I came back.'

'Had you always planned to come back?'

'Not really. But it got to the point where I felt I didn't really have a choice. I knew Dad's mind was failing. He'd been managing at work—it was automatic; learned behaviour over so many years—but then Sam found him wandering in the main street. Dad couldn't remember how to get home. And alarm bells started ringing about how he was coping at home on his own. Penny and I arranged for some home help but then it became clear that work was too much for him as well. Eventually he needed full-time care and he moved into the nursing home. I'm the only family he has so I felt I needed to stay in town. He was also the only doctor, so I took over the clinic. Penny had worked for my dad, so she stayed to help me.'

'So is that why you go to the nursing home so often? Your dad is there?'

'I try to visit him every day. Sometimes it's more. He can get quite agitated and, if the staff can't calm him down, they call me.'

'That's a lot to deal with on top of being the only doctor in town,' Ella said. 'Do you ever bring your dad back here?'

'I used to bring him home for a meal but it's become too confusing for him. This was my parents' property—it's where I grew up—and Dad expects to see Mum here. He's forgotten she died and there's no point explaining that to him over and over. He finds it distressing or thinks I'm lying to him and gets upset. It's better if I see him at the nursing home. That feels familiar to him now.'

'So that explains why you live in such a big house on your own. Isn't it lonely?' She knew she was fishing for information but she couldn't understand why Luke didn't appear to be in a relationship. What was wrong with him?

'I'm not home enough to get lonely. Staying here was a convenience. I didn't think it would become permanent.'

'You didn't want to take over your dad's practice?'

'It wasn't my long-term intention and it certainly wasn't my fiancée's plan.'

'Your fiancée?' Ella couldn't believe she was only hearing about a fiancée now. Where had Luke been hiding her? Did he have skeletons in his closet too? 'Where is she?'

'In Adelaide, I think. I should have said *ex*-fiancée. She was my fiancée then but not now.'

'How long ago were you engaged?'

'We broke up two years ago. I came back to look after Dad but Mikayla had just started a new job in Adelaide—she's a doctor too—so we figured we'd be able to make a long-distance relationship work for a while. We'd take it in turns to make the ninety-minute commute every weekend.'

'And then?'

'Then Mikayla started refusing to drive up on weekends. Not outright refusing, but she had plenty of reasons why she couldn't make it. To be fair, there were times where I couldn't get away either, because of the clinic or because of Dad. And, when I decided to take over the practice, I assumed Mikayla would join me but she wasn't interested. Turns out she wasn't interested in living in the country. She wasn't a fan of the house, the job, Pelican's Landing or, in the end, of me. This move was never meant to be permanent and she accused me of being selfish. She said I didn't prioritise her, and she was right. I let her down and she left because of it.'

'Couldn't you have got another doctor to take over the clinic?'

'I tried but getting doctors to move to the country is a constant battle and I couldn't in good conscience close the clinic. I couldn't let my dad or the community down. Mikayla and I possibly could have reached a compromise but, by that time, the writing was on the wall. Our differences when we were twenty-five had seemed minor, but at twenty-nine they started to multiply, so we called off the engagement.'

'You don't have any regrets?'

'Plenty. I wish I'd been more considerate. I wish I hadn't let her down but I don't regret not being married to her.'

'And is Pelican's Landing where you want to be?' She wondered if he still thought of it as a temporary move.

'For now. I'm a country boy at heart. But, if you're worried about me being lonely, you and Liv can keep me company on Saturday.'

He was smiling, he certainly didn't look unhappy with his lot.

'Doing what?' she asked.

'It's the district agricultural show. It's a big deal around here. Liv will enjoy it. You might too.'

Ella had taken care getting dressed. She wanted to create a good first impression. Luke was taking Liv and her to the local agricultural show and, even though she knew it wasn't a date, she knew Luke would know everyone there and she wanted to look nice. For her own confidence and for Luke too.

She'd picked out a floaty summer dress, loose-fitting with long sleeves and a flowing skirt, to hide her bruises. She hoped people would think that her style was bohemian. She'd tied her hair into a low ponytail, trying to counteract the heat of the day. She adjusted her ponytail to accommodate a hat and then grabbed her bag and helped Liv out of Luke's car.

It was early afternoon and streams of people were heading in and out of the show grounds. They stopped at the gate and Ella's stomach dropped when she saw the entry prices. It was going to cost her fifteen dollars just to get in. She had water bottles in her bag but she wished she'd thought to bring some snacks with her. She'd been so full of anticipation and Liv had been such a bundle of excitement that she hadn't really considered how much a day out could cost her. But there was no turning back now. She'd have to figure out how to save her pennies once they were inside.

'Two adults and a child, please.' Luke had his wallet out and was buying tickets without being asked.

'Thank you,' she said as he handed her two tickets. 'Is it okay if I pay you back later?' If she paid him back now, she'd have no money left for anything inside the show grounds, and she was also still paying Penny back the money she had lent her to go shopping.

'Don't...'

She knew Luke had been about to say 'don't worry' before he stopped himself, saying, 'Sure. I'm happy to pay for your tickets but, if you'd feel more comfortable paying me back, that's fine.'

'Thank you.' She appreciated his comment. It gave her back her independence. She didn't want to owe people favours, she wanted to stand on her own two feet, and his reply make her think she was being heard, that he was listening to her, and that was important.

'What would you like to see first?' he asked Liv as they walked through the gates. 'There's a sideshow alley, rides, food, animals, animal rides...'

'What animals?' Liv asked. 'Is it a zoo?'

'No. This is a show for the farmers and their families. The farmers win prizes for the best-looking cow and the prettiest chicken. You can look at the farm animals and you can hold baby chickens.'

'Can we do that first?' Liv asked, tugging on Ella's hand.

Ella looked at Luke.

'Of course, follow me,' he said.

Liv spent the next hour holding baby chicks—being amazed by the different types of chickens, some with feathery feet and crested heads—and bottle-feeding lambs. Luke chatted to Liv about the baby animals in the nursery, amazing Ella again with how good he was with children, with people. He didn't ignore her either. He took her hand and made her sit on a hay bale to hold chicks and, when Liv insisted he have a turn, he sat beside Ella, their thighs touching as they squeezed onto the hay bale.

Ella's instinctive reaction was to shift herself away to create more personal space, but she had no room to move, so she forced herself to relax. Luke's presence wasn't threatening; in fact, she could feel his body heat radiating through the thin cotton of her dress and she found it strangely reassuring. She felt slightly disappointed when he stood up after handing the chicks back to the attendant.

As they left the animal nursery, they walked past a pony-ride enclosure where families were lined up, waiting for rides.

'Mummy, look, it's Chloe.' Liv was pointing at a family standing at the back of the queue.

Ella was surprised. She hadn't expected to see anyone she recognised but Liv was right: it was Hayley and her children from the adventure playground, Chloe and Jack.

'You know the Perrys?' Luke asked.

'If you mean Hayley, then sort of,' Ella replied. 'Hayley drove Liv and me to your clinic after Liv's fall. I'm surprised Liv remembers Chloe. She doesn't remember falling off the flying fox or being taken to the medical clinic.'

'Concussion can affect memory in strange ways,' Luke said. 'Do you want to say hello?'

'Can I have a pony ride? Please, Mum?'

Ella let Luke and Liv take her over to the queue, where Luke introduced her to Hayley's husband, Josh. Of course, Luke knew the family. By the time the introductions had been made, Ella had thanked Hayley once again for her help and Hayley had asked after Liv's recovery, they were at the front of the queue and Ella hadn't yet made up her mind as to whether or not Liv should ride.

'Is it safe for Liv?' she asked Luke. 'What if she falls off? She's just recovering from concussion as it is.'

'Liv can run faster than these ponies are walking,' Luke reassured her with a smile. 'And the ponies are guided and the kids are wearing helmets. She'll be fine.'

Ella relented, trusting Luke's professional opinion.

'Stand next to Liv,' Luke instructed once Liv was settled on her pony. 'I'll take a photo for you.' He snapped a couple of photos of them both before taking his leave. 'I have to head off to the cake pavilion—I'm judging the scones. You can meet me there if you like or text me later and I'll catch up with you.'

'You're judging the scones?' Ella asked, but of course he was. Was there anything Luke couldn't, or didn't, do in this town?

Ella and Liv spent an hour with Hayley and her family, while Hayley tried to convince Ella of the merits of enrolling Liv in school in Pelican's Landing, before they met Luke again at the cake pavilion where Penny had won the prize for best scones.

'That seems a little bit like favouritism, if you ask me,' Ella teased.

'It's a blind tasting,' Luke argued, as he handed Ella

and Liv a plate of assorted scones. 'Here, I've saved these for you.'

'Don't tell me you don't recognise the taste or consistency of Penny's scones! You must have been eating them all your life!'

'Shh, I don't want you to get me kicked off the judging panel,' Luke laughed. 'When else do I get to eat as much as I like, all for a good cause? Now, time for sideshow alley.'

Luke took them to the row of sideshow games, where Liv played a fishing game before Luke shot basketball hoops to win a black-and-white soft toy dog for her, which she promptly named Maisie.

'What would you like, Ella?' he asked.

'I don't need anything.' She laughed.

'Of course you do. You know the old showground saying: *every player wins a prize.*'

'In that case, I've always wanted one of those sparkly dolls on a stick.'

'Really?'

'Yes, but I don't need one.'

'I can't imagine anyone would ever *need* one of those.' Luke grinned. 'But your wish is my command.'

'No, don't be silly. It's a waste of money.'

'I'll win you one.'

'You don't have to do that. Besides, you still have to pay to play a game. It comes to the same thing.'

'Well, it's my money,' he said as he promptly handed his cash over in exchange for table-tennis balls, which he proceeded to feed into the moving clown heads, calculating carefully until he did, in fact, win her the doll as promised.

good news. 'Are you going to deliver the baby here?' she asked Luke.

'I'll have to,' Luke said as he stood up. 'Jane told me her husband is meeting her at the hospital in Murray Bridge. He's called an ambulance to meet Jane on the road but unless it arrives in the next few minutes they're not going to get here in time. I'm going to need your help.'

'My help?' Ella's eyes were wide.

'Yes,' he said as he rifled through his medical bag. He passed her a packet containing surgical gloves. 'Can you open the packet so I can get the gloves out, please?' he asked as he took a bottle of hand sanitiser and liberally covered his hands before rubbing them vigorously. He pulled the gloves from the packet and slid his hands into them. 'There should be a pack with a sterile sheet in the bag too. Can you find that and slide it under Jane?'

Ella couldn't believe Luke was going to deliver a baby on the side of the road. It was not an ideal situation in anyone's imagination. The road wasn't busy but the location still felt very exposed and vulnerable. She opened a second sterile sheet and clipped it to the seat belt and the door of the car, fashioning a temporary screen in an attempt to offer Jane a little privacy.

'Ella, can you climb in behind Jane?' Luke asked. 'Help her sit up slightly and then support her. It will be easier for her to deliver in a semi-reclined position.'

Ella went round to the other side of the car and crawled in behind Jane. Over her shoulder she could see a contraction rippling under Jane's dress. 'It hurts!' Jane cried out in pain.

'So I keep hearing,' Luke said, 'But apparently you'll

forget all about it the minute you hold your baby. Isn't that right, Ella?'

'Have you got children?' Jane asked, her sentence broken into words uttered between panting breaths.

'A daughter.' Ella could tell Luke wanted her to distract Jane and she did her best to keep the woman focused on her. 'And Luke's right. You remember that it hurts but you really don't remember how much.'

'I want to push!' Jane cried out.

'Not yet,' Luke cautioned.

'You're doing great,' Ella told her. 'Just breathe in and out with me. We'll count to ten.' She hoped that was long enough for Luke to do whatever he needed to or to get Jane through the next contraction.

'Okay, Jane, well done,' Luke said. 'You can push with the next contraction.'

Jane gripped Ella's hand as she bore down. Her grip was ferocious but Ella knew she wasn't aware of it. Over Jane's shoulder she could see Luke ease the baby's head out.

'Stop pushing now, Jane. Little breaths,' he said as Ella watched him feel for the cord and ease it over the baby's head.

'All right,' he said. 'Push again with the next contraction.'

The baby, a boy, came out in a slippery rush and Luke scooped him up. He rubbed him firmly and was rewarded with a loud cry.

'Congratulations, Jane. You have a son,' he said as Ella heard the wailing of an ambulance siren in the distance. She climbed out of the car, knowing Jane wouldn't notice her absence now that she had a baby to hold, and flagged the ambulance down.

She waited while Luke handed over the care of his patient to the paramedics and they transferred Jane and her son to the ambulance. As they drove off she looked at Jane's car, abandoned on the side of the road. 'What are we going to do about that?' she asked Luke.

'Jane and her husband live in Pelican's Landing. I said I'll drop it off to their house. But only if you're okay to drive my car and follow me back?'

Ella was a little shaky; adrenalin was coursing through her system and she could only imagine how Luke was feeling. But she knew she was okay to drive. She nodded. She could do this favour.

Ella followed Luke back to town, collecting him from Jane's house and driving him back to the barn. Liv had fallen asleep and Luke carried her up to the loft while Ella put the kettle on.

'Thank you for your help,' he said to Ella as he came back downstairs.

'I'm not sure that I did much. You seemed to have it under control. Do you deliver many babies?'

'No. Luckily most mums make it to hospital. And being on the roadside was a first for me.'

'Jane was lucky you were there. Is it strange for you, knowing everyone in town socially and also treating them?'

'I don't treat all of them. I can separate one from the other. Some people choose not to use me as their doctor. There are other options—they can go to Murray Bridge—but I can be trusted not to break a confidence.'

She knew that about him already. He had many good qualities; discretion was but one.

'Can I ask your opinion on something?' she continued as she poured water from the kettle into their mugs.

'Sure.'

'Hayley invited Liv over for a play date with Chloe. She might ask me to stay for a cup of tea but, if she doesn't, do you think it would be okay to leave Liv there? It's in the afternoon but I don't know if Josh will be home. Would Liv be safe there?'

'Josh and Hayley are good people. Josh and I went to high school together. Most people are, but I'm happy to be your sounding board while you're in Pelican's Landing. But what will you do when you move to Queensland? You're going to have to trust your own instincts about people.'

Ella shook her head. 'My instincts haven't been all that great in the past; I'm not sure I can trust them. And I'm also wondering about whether I should make the next move. I'm thinking that this place is starting to grow on me. And I have a favour to ask. I know you said no when it was a short-term proposition, but I'm thinking about enrolling Liv in school here. If I did that, we'd need somewhere permanent to live. Would you reconsider renting the cottage to me?'

Luke didn't answer immediately and Ella could see from his expression that he was reluctant. 'Is there a reason you don't normally rent it out?'

'Not one that makes sense to most people.'

'But it's so charming. It seems a shame to just let it sit empty. Why was it renovated in the first place?'

'I did it up for my sister, Gemma. But she never lived in it.'

'Your sister?' He'd never mentioned a sister. She'd asked about siblings and he'd said there was no one else around. She'd assumed he meant no one else anywhere. 'I didn't know you had a sister. Where is she?'

'She died.'

'Oh, Luke, I'm sorry. Was it recently?' That would explain why the cottage had been sitting vacant but Luke was shaking his head.

Ella handed Luke his coffee and put a plate of Penny's shortbread on the kitchen table as Luke took a seat and started talking. 'She died seven years ago. I'd just turned twenty-four; I was in Adelaide, in my sixth year of medical school, when it happened. Gemma was only nineteen. She had always been rebellious, born with a wilful streak, and she and Dad had frequent personality clashes. Dad expected us to study hard, set goals and achieve them. I followed a straight road, Dad's path, because it suited me. I'm a rule follower, but that wasn't Gemma's path. Her path was meandering, definitely not straight, but Mum was her champion. She always said that if Dad gave Gemma time she'd come good, she'd find her way. But then Mum died when Gemma was in her final year of school and Gemma lost her ally and her way.

'She and Dad were hurting—we all were—but Gemma and Dad couldn't support each other. Dad didn't know how to get through to her. She scraped through her final year of school and moved out of home the moment it was over. She got mixed up with a bad crowd and moved to Murray Bridge.

'I spent a summer fixing up the barn, hoping that if I could provide her with an alternative place to live, showed her that we cared about her, wanted to help her, she'd move back here. I knew she wouldn't move back into the main house but I thought she could be safe here. But she refused to move.'

'Sometimes it's hard for people to get themselves out of a situation,' Ella said. She knew that all too well from her own experience. It was easy to make excuses, much easier than finding a way out.

'I know. That's why I was trying to help her. I wanted to take a year off uni. I thought if I was close by I'd eventually be able to persuade her to come home, but my father insisted I go back. I still regret that. I failed her. And I failed Mum. Gemma never got the time to come good.'

'People make mistakes, Luke. You can't blame yourself.'

'So I'm told, but I'm not convinced. Gemma wasn't listening to me but I wish there had been someone else who could have helped her. People said that Gemma made her own decisions, but she was being influenced by the wrong type of people, and it cost her her life.'

'What happened?'

'Her boyfriend was a heavy recreational drug user and he was driving the car high on drugs. Gemma was with him and he crashed the car. She died. He lived. And I lost my sister.'

'That must have been devastating.' Ella knew what it was like to lose people, but he'd lost his sister and his mother in a relatively short space of time. It would have been horrendous, and compounded by the fact that he felt responsible in a way for Gemma's death.

Luke gave a wry smile. 'It wasn't the easiest of times. I gave up on the cottage after that.'

'It's sat empty for seven years?'

Luke nodded. 'I ignored it for the next six years. The cottage was meant as a refuge for Gemma, and I couldn't get my head around the fact that Gemma wasn't going to use it, so I just let it sit there. I was living in Adelaide; it was easy to ignore it. People suggested I rent it out but it seemed wrong to make a profit from something that was supposed to save my sister but ultimately failed.

'But the recent floods made me think of an alternative option. I have been considering using it as a refuge for locals in need of a place to stay. I thought that letting people stay for free would perhaps be a way to make sense of everything that had happened, but I was still finding it hard to let go of the idea that this was meant to be for Gemma. It was an emotional sticking point. I knew the physical act of letting the cottage out shouldn't be that difficult and what should be, in theory, a small gesture from me could be a much bigger deal to someone else. Penny says I couldn't have saved Gemma—she says I can't save everyone—but I didn't want to stop trying. And maybe letting someone in need use the cottage would help me to let go of my guilt over Gemma.'

'Is that what you were doing when you said I could stay? Were you trying to save me?'

'I'm not sure. Maybe, initially. But then I realised you didn't really need saving, you just needed time to breathe, time to process what had happened to you. I knew you'd figure out what you wanted to do next if you just had time to stop, recover and recuperate.

'I wasn't sure how it would go, having you in the cottage. I wasn't sure how I would feel. And I wasn't sure you'd accept the offer. I actually thought you might say no, that you might feel uncomfortable about staying so close to a stranger. I decided to let you take the decision out of my hands. You reminded me of Gemma in the beginning. You seemed fragile, in need of help, but I was mistaken. You're stronger than she was. You've got yourself out of a difficult situation. But I'm glad now that you're here. I'm glad the cottage has helped you, and you're welcome to use it for as long as you like.'

'Thank you. But I'll only stay if you let me pay rent. Even if you don't need the money, or it's an insignificant amount, I will feel better. I don't need charity. I don't want it. I'm wary of offers that are presented in neat little packages tied up with string. It's not what's in the package that bothers me. It's the strings.'

Luke nodded. 'Okay. I'll come back to you with a price.'

'Thank you.'

'Who wants another marshmallow?'

Luke had taken Liv, Jack and Chloe to find the perfect sticks for toasting marshmallows. He'd made a campfire and Hayley, Josh, Penny and Sam had joined Luke, Ella and Liv for a barbeque dinner to celebrate Liv's fifth birthday. They were sitting on Luke's front lawn, surrounding a fire pit which was set back from the river near a stand of gum trees. The pit was surrounded by cut tree trunks which the girls and Jack were sitting on to toast their marshmallows.

Ella had been touched by Luke's offer to host a party for Liv and she was trying not to be too disappointed that no one knew it was her birthday as well. She hadn't said anything; she didn't want a fuss and she'd become accustomed to giving her day over to Liv. But seeing the fuss everyone was making of her daughter—when it was usually all up to her—made her a tiny bit jealous that no one was making a fuss over her too.

'I hope you're leaving room for cake,' Penny said as the children devoured yet another marshmallow and Penny emerged from Luke's house carrying a large chocolate cake which she had decorated like a farm yard with some figures from a play set: chickens, a little girl and a sheep-dog like Maisie.

'Cake! Cake!' The children jumped up, abandoning their marshmallow sticks, to gather around Penny while everyone sang *Happy Birthday* to Liv. Luke had been boiling a billy can on the camp fire and he made tea and coffee to have with the cake.

'Ella, have you had any luck finding a replacement car yet?' Sam asked as he tucked into a sizeable piece of cake.

'No.' Ella shook her head. 'There is absolutely noth-ing suitable in my price range anywhere near here and I can't look further afield as I've got no way of getting to the car yards to inspect anything.'

'My nephew in Adelaide is selling his car. It was my sister-in-law's first, so we know the history. It's a small four-wheel drive—I thought it might be a good option for you. He's happy for you to take a look at it before he advertises it.'

'Is it in Adelaide?'

Sam nodded. 'He's in the Adelaide Hills, about fifteen minutes out of the city.'

'Tell him thank you, but how would I get there? Is there a bus from here that would stop in the hills?'

'Do you think he'd be happy to hold on to it until next weekend?' Luke asked Sam. 'I've got a meeting in the city on Saturday afternoon,' he said, looking at Ella. 'You could come with me and we can look at the car on the way.'

'I hate to sound ungrateful, but what would Liv and I do while you're at your meeting?'

'You could look around the city. My meeting won't be longer than two hours.'

'Or Liv could come to us for the afternoon, if you prefer, rather than dragging her to the city,' Hayley offered. 'We'd be happy to have her.'

'I'll message my nephew and let everyone know,' Sam said. 'That sounds like a good plan.'

Ella wasn't sure what the plan was, exactly. As with most things in Pelican's Landing, the locals made swift decisions and sorted things out with little debate. She wasn't sure if she liked the idea of not having a say. But the idea of spending a day with Luke alone had its merits.

Once everyone had finished eating cake, Hayley and Josh packed up their kids and headed home. Ella took Liv to the cottage to watch her brush her teeth before she hopped into bed. She came back to the fire to find Penny and Sam preparing to leave.

'You're going?'

'I'm afraid so,' Penny said. 'Sam is working tomorrow.'

'Thank you for celebrating with us,' Ella said. 'Liv had a fabulous day.' She was feeling quite emotional as she hugged Penny and Sam goodbye. It felt strange but good to be able to do that. She would never have been able to do that a couple of weeks ago. She was beginning to feel safe and comfortable surrounded by these good people, none of whom felt like strangers any more. They felt like friends.

As Sam and Penny drove away, Luke smiled at Ella.

'What are you smiling at?' she asked.

'You. I'm just thinking about how much you've changed in the past few weeks.'

'In what way?'

'You were so prickly, defensive.' He held up his hands and laughed as she opened her mouth to explain why. 'I get it, you had good reasons—your caution was perfectly understandable—but you've slowly relaxed your boundaries, dropped your guard. You're letting people in. And that's a good thing. Could you imagine, just two weeks ago, that you'd be hugging Penny and Sam? Or that you'd let Liv go on an unsupervised play date?'

Ella shook her head, amazed that Luke's train of thought echoed hers. 'No, I couldn't. I was just thinking how lucky Liv and I were to be stranded here. I feel like we're healing. It's been good for us. You and Penny and Hayley have been good *to* us, and I don't know how I can ever repay the favours.'

'We don't expect to be repaid. We're all happy to support you. It makes people feel good to help others. Seeing you enjoying life and smiling again is reward enough.'

'I know I've found it difficult to accept help, and I've probably sounded ungrateful, but I really do appreciate everything you've done and tonight you've really gone above and beyond, so thank you.'

'It's been my pleasure. And, now that we have the camp fire to ourselves, will you stay and have another coffee with me? It's only early.'

Ella smiled. 'I'd like that.'

'Grab a seat. I'll refill the billy and be back in a minute.'

He returned a few moments later carrying the billy in one hand and a small bag in another. He put the bag on the ground and the billy on the fire and sat down on the log beside her. Their thighs were almost touching and Ella found herself wanting to move a fraction closer so they would, in fact, be in contact.

Luke picked up the bag and handed it to her. 'Happy birthday.'

Ella looked at him with a confused expression as she took the gift. 'How did you know?'

'You filled in a form at the clinic. Your details were on there. Penny pointed out to me that your birthday is the same day as Liv's but we figured, seeing as you didn't mention it, you must want to keep it low key. But a birthday has to be acknowledged.'

'You didn't need to give me something. Having the party for Liv was enough.'

'The party was for Liv. This is for you.'

'Thank you,' Ella said as opened the bag, slightly over-

whelmed that he had gone to this effort for her. Inside
the bag was a gift-wrapped parcel, which she opened to
reveal a photo frame. She turned it over. Luke had put a
picture into the frame—it was the photo of her with Liv,
the one Luke had taken at the show when Liv was on the
pony. Ella was standing beside her, smiling directly at
the camera, smiling at Luke. She barely recognised herself; she looked happy and relaxed.

'Thank you. I love it,' she said as, without thinking,
she leant over and kissed his cheek.

'I'm glad you like it,' he replied as the billy started to
boil on the fire. But Luke ignored it, choosing instead to
reach out and hold her hand. He lifted it to his lips and
kissed the back of her fingers. His lips were soft and
warm. He lowered her hand into her lap before he lifted
his hand slowly and stroked her cheek with his thumb.

Ella didn't move.

She didn't flinch.

She didn't pull back.

She knew it had become a muscle memory, an involuntary reflex, to retreat from contact but, if she'd learnt
one thing over the past few weeks, it was that she could
trust Luke not to hurt her. He'd been nothing but gentle
and compassionate. Her world was gradually becoming what she'd hoped. Safe. Happy. And she had a lot to
thank Luke for.

She knew she was safe from harm with him and it was
a wonderful feeling. She closed her eyes as his thumb
traced the line of her jaw and ran over her lips.

'Ella?' His voice was deep and soft.

She opened her eyes. The camp fire was dying down

but there was enough light to see his features clearly. His blue eyes were dark, intense. 'Yes?'

'I would really like to kiss you.'

He'd asked for her permission. Ella's heart pounded in her chest and her breath caught in her throat. Unable to speak, she simply nodded.

'It would mean you'd have to find yourself another doctor,' he clarified.

'That's a sacrifice I'm prepared to make,' she replied with a smile.

Luke moved closer and she met him halfway, closing her eyes as his lips touched hers. She parted her lips, welcoming his tongue into her mouth, letting him explore her and taste her as she tasted him.

She opened her eyes to find him watching her. His gaze was unwavering and she could see desire in the dark depths of his eyes. She felt her temperature rise as a flush stole over her cheeks and anticipation burned bright inside her. She couldn't breathe; his gaze was so intense, it felt as if the air lacked oxygen, as if it was being burnt up in his gaze. She parted her lips to take a breath. Her lips were dry so she licked them with the tip of her tongue.

Luke groaned, giving in to his desire, giving in to hers. He wrapped one arm around her back, pulled her to him and kissed her hard. He tasted of chocolate and coffee, of happiness and dreams. She waited for her nerves to raise the alarm, to ask her what she thought she was doing, but the anxiety didn't come, the alarm didn't sound. She wanted this; she needed this. There was no fear. She felt safe. She felt beautiful.

She could feel her desire building. She could feel herself falling into him. But she couldn't do it. She put a hand on his chest and Luke immediately stopped. Her lips felt cold and lonely but she had to stay strong.

'I can't do this,' she said. 'Not now. Not here.'

'But you're not saying never?'

Ella shook her head. The more time she spent with him, the more she liked him. She wished she was confident enough to tell him just how much, but she had no idea how he'd react to that.

She couldn't deny she was attracted to him—she had been since the day she'd met him, although she'd spent countless hours trying to talk herself out of it—but he was out of her league. Successful, educated, well-respected.

But, as much as she would like to, she couldn't throw caution to the wind. Her judgement had let her down before. While at this moment this felt right, it felt special and magical, if she started something she didn't know if she would be able to stop it.

Liv was in the bed in the cottage. Ella couldn't take Luke there and she couldn't go with him to the main house and leave Liv alone, unprotected. At least by the camp fire she had a clear view of the door to the cottage. She would hear if Liv needed her. She would see her if she came outside. She had to stay on guard. She couldn't get distracted by Luke. She couldn't follow her desire. She couldn't forget her priorities, and her priority was Liv.

She didn't need any complication in her life.

And men always complicated things.

# CHAPTER EIGHT

LUKE'S LITTLE BOAT was tied to the jetty in front of his house. The river had peaked a couple of weeks ago and was almost back to pre-flood levels. It wasn't safe enough to water-ski on yet but Luke had said it was safe enough for a sightseeing excursion.

He stepped into the dinghy and handed out life jackets. He had a cooler box, a picnic basket, a blanket and beach towels sitting on the edge of the jetty and he stowed them in the dinghy while Ella and Liv put their jackets on.

Maisie jumped in and stood on the bow. Luke lifted Liv into the boat and then reached out a hand for Ella. His gesture reminded her of the day he had come to their rescue, but today she didn't hesitate. She took his hand as he helped her into the boat.

'Are we going swimming?' Liv asked.

'It's not safe enough to swim in the river yet. The current is still strong and there's a lot of debris floating in the water, but there's a little lagoon not far from here which we can check out,' Luke replied.

Ella looked around. There was no breeze and the surface of the river was flat and calm. Clouds overhead were reflected in the water and it mirrored the cliff face too. It looked beautiful. It looked peaceful, safe. But she understood that things were not always as they seemed. A calm exterior could hide all sorts of disturbing things.

Luke steered the dinghy through a narrow channel into a lagoon, past tall reeds and under low hanging branches, where he pulled into a small sandy beach.

'Will this be safe?' Ella asked as Luke jumped out of the boat and secured it to a tree. The water was murky and there was no way of seeing how deep it was or what lay beneath the surface.

'The water isn't flowing so quickly through here. There are no whirlpools or strong currents, so as long as there are no submerged logs or trees it'll be safe,' Luke said. 'But I'll go in first just to check it out.'

Ella and Liv waited on the bank as Luke stripped off. He removed his life jacket and then his shirt until all he was wearing was a pair of shorts. Ella let her gaze run over him. His shoulders were broad, his stomach flat, his arms muscular. For a man who seemed to always be at work, he was in good shape—very good shape.

Luke waded into the water, followed by Maisie.

Feeling self-conscious, Ella waited until his back was turned before she stripped off. She didn't have a bathing suit but took off her shirt to reveal a cotton camisole. She put her life jacket back on, fastening it above her shorts, and waded into the water with Liv when Luke gave them the all-clear.

The mud of the riverbed squelched under her feet. The water and the mud felt soft against her skin, not abrasive like beach sand and salt water, but she was reluctant to put her face into the river. She didn't like being unable to see the bottom, a fact that wasn't bothering Liv. Her daughter was a confident swimmer, having grown up on the coast, on the beach, but the life jacket was cumbersome, making things awkward. Liv was floating on her back and kicking her legs, swimming in and out from the shore with Maisie by her side.

Ella floated in the water, kept buoyant by her life jacket. Luke stood beside her. He wasn't wearing a life jacket but he was tall enough that his feet touched the ground.

The slight current started to pull her away from his side. Luke held onto the strap at the back of her jacket and pulled her back to him. He was gentle, not rough, and she knew if she felt uncomfortable she'd be able to propel herself away and he'd let her go. But she liked being close to him. He felt dependable. He'd only shown her kindness, respect and consideration so far. He was handsome, smart and well-liked in the community—the sort of man who would make a good partner.

But that was a dangerous train of thought. Could she imagine settling down here? Despite the kiss she and Luke had shared, her intention was still to leave Pelican's Landing but, the more time that passed, the less she thought about it. Leaving was now an idea rather than a firm commitment.

Was she making a mistake? Was she letting desire turn her head, influence her decision? Was she imagining they could have something more than a platonic relationship? Despite the kiss, she wasn't sure she could even say they had a friendship—not yet. But she sensed they were on the edge of a precipice. The question was, how dangerous was the precipice—how high? If she stepped over the edge, would it all end in disaster?

She needed to keep her wits about her, she decided as she got out of the water. Getting caught up with Luke was sure to complicate things. She stripped off her life jacket, suddenly aware that her now-wet outfit was quite revealing. She stayed wrapped in her towel as she started to unpack the picnic Luke had prepared.

Luke took a rug from the boat and spread it out on the sand and Ella arranged fruit, cheese, cordial, water and ham sandwiches on the centre of the rug.

'What's it like to be five, Liv?' Luke asked.

'Good. How old is Maisie?' Liv wanted to know. She had a sandwich in one hand and was throwing a stick for Maisie with the other. The dog had endless energy and was happy to retrieve the stick from the water time after time.

'Four. But in dog years she's only a little bit older than your mum,' he teased.

'Hey!' Ella protested in mock offence. Luke winked at her and Ella melted.

He lay on his back on the rug, propped up on his elbows, keeping one eye on Liv, who had returned to the water with Maisie. Ella sat cross-legged next to him. She had ditched her towel and they sat close, almost touching.

'Ella, about next weekend, when we go to look at Sam's nephew's car—are you going to leave Liv here with Hayley for the day?'

'I think so, if she really is happy to have her. I thought if she came with us I could take her to the zoo or the beach while you're at your meeting, but if the car isn't suitable I might have to spend that time looking at other second-hand cars. That's not going to be much fun for Liv. And dragging her around car yards won't be much fun for me either.'

'In that case, I have a suggestion to make. I was thinking along the same lines. The price of the car is in your budget but there's nothing to say the car will be any good. My meeting isn't until the afternoon, but if we stay in Adelaide overnight we can look at other cars on Sunday before we come back, if we need to. Then it's just a case of whether you want to bring Liv with you or not. Hayley might be happy to have her for a sleepover. Or, if not Hayley, then Penny.'

'Where would we stay?'

'There's a hotel in the heart of the city not far from my meeting. I could book us two rooms there.'

'I appreciate the thought, but I don't think my budget would stretch to a city hotel.'

'I'm attending a board meeting. My accommodation gets paid for.'

'That's one room.'

'I'm happy to give you that room and book another one for myself.'

'Really?'

'Yes. And, just to be clear, it's a favour without strings. I remember, you're wary of strings. Think about it and let me know what you decide.'

A night in the city—just Luke and her. Was this the precipice? If she took up the offer, would the step prove to be too big for her? It felt huge, but was it really?

He wasn't asking her to make any promises. It was

just a trip to the city; it didn't have to be anything more. Maybe he didn't intend it to be anything more but she knew she wanted to find out. She didn't feel comfortable pursuing anything in this small country town where everyone knew everyone else and their business. Perhaps in the city, if it felt right, they could explore this attraction.

Perhaps.

'I think you've got a good buy with that car,' Luke said as they turned off the highway and headed to the city.

'I really appreciate your help. I wouldn't have known what to look for,' she said. The best part about it, other than giving her back her independence, was the price. It had cost less than the insurance pay-out, leaving her with some extra money in the bank.

'What time did you organise to collect it tomorrow?'

'Around midday. We can have a late breakfast before we head off.'

Luke had determined there was no need to drive two cars into the city, so they would collect the car on their way back to Pelican's Landing. Ella could see the city skyline up ahead as Luke drove through the parklands that surrounded the CBD but she was surprised to see dozens of large tents, a Ferris wheel and several amusement rides set up in the park.

'What's all this?' she asked.

'The Adelaide Fringe Festival is on. It's an arts festival, a big one. Everything from cabaret shows, burlesque, magic, comedy, acrobatics, music and dance to visual arts. There are hundreds of artists and thousands of shows—it's a month-long party, basically. I thought we could wander through the gardens after I finish today, grab something to eat and go to see a show. What do you think?'

'It sounds like fun.' She had decided she would go with the flow for the weekend. No plans, no expectations. Hayley had Liv and Ella had nothing she needed to do, no one who needed anything from her. She could do as she pleased for twenty-four hours.

Luke pulled off the street into the driveway of the hotel, a few streets from the parklands. He handed his keys to the valet as a porter came to collect their bags.

'This looks a bit smart,' Ella said, meaning 'expensive'. Her brow furrowed as she wondered how much her room had cost. How much Luke had paid on her behalf.

'Ella, it's my treat,' Luke said as they approached the reception desk. 'The board has paid for my room and I'm happy to pay for yours. I can afford it; I don't have a lot to spend my money on. No strings, remember?'

Ella nodded as they stepped into the lift. Arriving upstairs, Luke swiped the card to unlock a door and held it open for her. 'This is your room—I'm next door.'

Her room had a view to the east, over the parklands with the hills in the distance. 'There's a Fringe guide on the table, if you want to look through it for a show that appeals to you. Will you be okay by yourself for the afternoon? I should be finished around five.'

'I'll be fine.' She smiled. 'I'm looking forward to having some time to myself.'

'Ouch! I thought you enjoyed my company.'

'I've been pretending, to make sure you let me stay in the cottage,' she teased. 'I do enjoy your company but I will be quite okay on my own for a few hours. I'll window-shop on Rundle Street and then lie by the pool.'

'That sounds tempting—the lying by the pool part, not the shopping. I'll see you later, then.'

Ella switched off the hairdryer and slipped her new sundress over her head. She had window-shopped along Rundle Street before using some of the money she had saved on the car to buy herself a cotton sundress and a bikini from a discount department store at end of the mall. It felt decadent to have new clothes but she refused to feel guilty about spending the money. She'd paid the insurance premium on her car and the money was hers to spend as she wished.

She'd bought Liv a present and she planned to use some of the remaining funds to pay for Luke's dinner. She had also bought herself a novel and had sat by the pool for an hour, reading. It was the first time in five years that she had had time to sit and relax without anyone making any demands of her.

She brushed her hair and used the hotel moisturiser on her skin. Her bruises had disappeared over the past four weeks and, for the first time in months, her skin was unmarked and she was able to wear a sleeveless summer dress in public. She had a slight tan from tending to Luke's garden beds, which had helped to camouflage the bruises as they had gradually faded. She applied a light lipstick and pulled her hair back into a ponytail; the day was still too hot to leave it loose.

She adjusted the straps on her dress, wondering if the emerald-green shade was a little too bright, a little attention-seeking, but the colour had seemed cheerful and had suited her mood. She felt reinvented, and it had been a while since she had felt so optimistic. Her new car represented freedom and independence. Wandering the streets of Adelaide alone, where nobody had recognised her or knew her business, had been cathartic. In Pelican's Landing, her secrets had been exposed to Luke and Penny and, even though they'd been nothing but supportive, it was naive to feel as though her past didn't shadow every step she took.

But now that she had a car it was time to think about her next move. She was pleased to have made the purchase, and very pleased to have her independence back, but she no longer had the excuse of a lack of transport keeping her in Pelican's Landing. It was time to make a decision about her next step—whether to stay or go. There were pros and cons to both options.

As she slid her feet into her sandals, she heard a knock on her door. Luke had changed into a pair of light cotton trousers and a blue polo shirt that enhanced the colour of his eyes. He was smiling at her and she found herself grinning in return. She was surprised at how easily he could make her smile.

'Hi. How was your meeting?'

'A little tedious, to be honest. I'm looking forward to some fresh air. Are you ready?'

Ella nodded and said, 'I'll just grab my bag.'

'Is that a new dress?' he asked as she stepped away to retrieve her bag.

'Yes.'

'That colour suits you.'

'Thank you.' Ella could feel a blush darken her cheeks and she was glad her back was turned. His comment was simple, an easy compliment that sounded sincere. She didn't think Luke was the type of man to give false compliments, but she'd been wrong about men before.

'Did you have a look at the Fringe guide? Was there anything that took your fancy?' Luke asked as they waited for the lift.

'It was a bit overwhelming, to be honest. There were far too many options. Would you mind if we just went for a walk among the tents and see if something jumps out at us?' She was quite happy just to wander and soak up the atmosphere.

'Of course.' Luke replied as they negotiated the crowds.

The streets had filled up as evening approached and Rundle Street had been closed to traffic. They wandered down to the parklands, mingling with the diverse crowd. Families, young couples and groups of friends sat at pavement tables or gathered around street performers.

Luke had booked a table at a Thai restaurant and, after dinner, he suggested dessert in the Garden of Unearthly Delights, which was part of the festival. They wandered down Rundle Street and into the parklands where the Garden sprawled under the enormous Moreton Bay fig trees, illuminated by lanterns. They wandered among the performance tents, soaking up the atmosphere, listening to the sound of hundreds of conversations competing with music from various shows and amusement rides, until they reached the far end of the garden, where a Ferris wheel loomed above them. A stall selling hot cinnamon doughnuts sat near the ticket office.

'How about doughnuts for dessert?' Luke asked.

'Can we take them on the Ferris wheel?' Ella replied. She wasn't one for high-speed amusement rides but she loved Ferris wheels.

They hopped onto the wheel just as the sun was setting. They chose west-facing seats, looking over the city and out to sea, where the sky was glowing red.

'Did you speak to Liv today?' Luke asked between bites of his doughnut.

'I spoke to Hayley this afternoon. Liv was far too busy to stop for a chat, but I could hear her in the background, and she sounded perfectly happy.' Hayley had offered to have Liv for the weekend, an arrangement that suited everyone.

'And you? Are you happy?' he asked.

She nodded. Right at that moment, she was happy. She had no cares. No worries. She felt light. Renewed. Refreshed. 'I am. I feel like I have turned a page and started a new chapter. I'm feeling positive about the future.'

'What does that look like for you?'

'I guess, now that I have a car, I'll get back onto Plan A,' she said.

'Queensland?'

She nodded.

'Soon?'

'I'm not sure exactly. I'm not in a huge hurry but I need to make the move at some point.'

'Why? Liv is happy at school. She seems settled.'

'She's five—she'll settle in somewhere else.' Ella knew she spoke the truth but she also knew that the sooner they moved, the easier it would be.

'Do you still want to move?'

She'd spent so many months dreaming of the move, planning the move, that she felt obliged to follow it through. And it still seemed like the most sensible option. She was happy in Pelican's Landing but her happiness wasn't going to pay the bills.

'I need to find a job. I think that will be easier to do in Queensland,' she said just as the Ferris wheel came to a stop with a jerk, throwing her against Luke. They were at the top of the wheel and the light breeze was swinging the carriage. Luke wrapped an arm around her shoulders to steady her. The sunset bathed his face in pink and orange but his eyes remained a brilliant blue.

'Is there any way I could convince you to change your mind?' he asked.

She smiled and tilted her face up to his. 'You can try.'

He pulled her closer and bent his head. She lifted her face to him and then his lips were on hers, warm and soft. She parted her lips as his pressure increased. He tasted sweet. He tasted of cinnamon sugar.

Luke had one hand resting on her bare arm, the other cupping her face. Her skin was on fire and she melted against him as her body responded to his touch. She was aware of nothing else except the sensation of being fully alive. She wanted for nothing except Luke. All her senses came to life and a line of fire spread from her stomach to her groin. She deepened the kiss, wanting to lose herself in him.

Her eyes flew open as the Ferris wheel started to move again, surprising her. Surprising them both.

Luke was studying her face, as if committing each

of her features to memory. His fingers trailed down the side of her cheek, sending a shiver of desire through her. Her heart was racing in her chest and her breaths were shallow. That kiss might have been enough to make her consider changing her mind.

Luke took her hand as they stepped off the Ferris wheel when their carriage reached the bottom. They walked back to the hotel in silence. Ella was unsettled, her mind whirling. Jumbled thoughts rushed through her head so fast she didn't have time to formulate any words, let alone a full sentence.

The kiss had been wonderful, magical. She was attracted to Luke but she'd made mistakes with men before. She wasn't sure if she should get involved. Would she just complicate things? She wouldn't deny herself a chance to know Luke intimately if the opportunity presented itself, but she had vowed to be independent. Perhaps they could share one night; it didn't mean she had to change her plans.

'Would you like to come in?' she asked as they reached her door.

'Would you like me to?'

She nodded. She would take this as the opportunity she was after. He'd promised her the decision would be all hers—no strings. This was it.

Luke followed her into the room as she opened the door. As Ella stopped to slide her key card into the slot to turn on the lights, she was aware of how much space Luke took up in the entrance. He was broad, strong and tall and he towered over her, and she had a moment of nervousness in the semi-darkness until she flicked on the room lights.

As the room brightened her dark memories receded. If she was going to have any sort of future, in Pelican's Landing or anywhere else, she couldn't keep glancing over her shoulder looking for trouble or expecting the worst of people. Over the past few weeks, she and Luke had spent plenty of time together. They'd had many conversations. She knew she was safe with him. She had never had anyone listen to her or talk to her the way Luke did. She felt seen by him. Acknowledged.

And she couldn't deny she was attracted to him. She couldn't deny the desire he stirred in her. She didn't want to. She wanted him to make love to her. She wanted a new experience. She wanted newer, better memories to wipe out her painful past. Could she have this one night? One memory to take with her? She didn't expect anything more from him. Just one night was all she wanted.

But, now that they were in her room, she wasn't sure if she could take the lead. What did she do now? Should she reach for him? Tell him how she was feeling? She was unsure and her uncertainty made her take a step back just as he reached for her. She felt his fingers on the side of her face and she froze, waiting to see what he did next. But his touch was gentle.

Of course it was. This was Luke. She looked up and met his gaze. His eyes were a vivid blue, his expression serious. Everything about his body looked hard and intense but his touch was gentle, his fingers warm.

She put a hand on his chest. She wasn't sure if she was about to push him away or pull him closer. She waited for her nerves to raise the alarm, but the anxiety didn't come, the alarm didn't sound. Her heart was racing but not with fear or trepidation. Instead, she recognised the feeling as anticipation. It was a new sensation. She realised she wanted this, she needed this. There was no fear.

His left hand moved further down her back, cupping her bottom, pulling her hips in hard against him. She could feel his erection, separated from her only by a couple of layers of thin summer clothing. He was hard and long and now all she could think about was how he would feel inside her. She could feel the moisture between her thighs as she imagined him thrusting into her. Her knees wobbled and she clung to him.

His lips met hers, warm and soft. There was nothing hard about them, but his intentions were clear, spelt out in his touch as he pressed his lips against hers. Ella opened her mouth, desperate to taste him, to feel him, to experience him. She breathed out a sigh as he wrapped his arms around her, holding her to him. Her hands wound around the back of his neck. In another moment, there would be no turning back.

That was good—she didn't want to turn back. She felt safe in his arms. She felt beautiful. Desirable.

She reached one hand behind his head, holding him to her as she kissed him back. His tongue was warm in her mouth. His hands were warm on her skin. Every inch of her was on fire, consumed with desire. She felt his fingers on her bare arm, could feel them tracing a line up to her shoulder, across her collarbone to the sweet hollow at the base of her throat, felt his thumb dip into the little dimple. She couldn't breathe; she'd forgotten how.

She needed to breathe. She pulled away and he lifted his hands, releasing her from his touch. She almost begged him not to. She didn't want him to let her go.

'Are you okay?' he asked.

She nodded again, still unable to speak.

His dark gaze moved lower, over her chest. How could such blue eyes hold such heat, such intensity?

She held her breath, trying to stop the rise and fall of her breasts, but still her nipples peaked in response to his gaze burning through the thin fabric of her dress. She could feel the moisture between her legs as her body responded as his gaze devoured her. He wasn't laying a finger on her now and yet she felt ready to self-combust. A look, a glance, a smile was all it would take for her to melt under him.

'Do you want to stop?'

'No.' Her voice was breathless. 'I want you to make love to me.'

She didn't need to ask twice. With one arm, he scooped her up and held her against his chest, pressing her to him, and carried her to the bed.

# CHAPTER NINE

LUKE GENTLY LOWERED her onto the bed and then eased himself over her and supported his weight on his elbows. She reached up and ran her hands over his biceps, feeling his strength, marvelling at the firmness within him. His body was hard but his touch was light.

His breath was coming fast now—she could hear it and feel it as it hit the bare skin of her shoulders and neck—but he didn't move. How could he hold himself so still? He was poised to move forward, to take this to the next level, but somehow he held his position. He was in no hurry. How could he be so calm when desire threatened to consume her? The waiting was exquisite agony. A delicious sense of anticipation battled with the desire to have him take her now, right now. She arched her hips up towards him, pushing herself against his groin, and was rewarded when she felt his matching desire, hard and firm, straining against his trousers.

She breathed out on a sigh as she let her knees fall open and wrapped her legs around him, pulling him closer, pulling him down against her. She heard him groan and he lowered his body until it covered the length of her. She wanted this. She wanted to feel his weight on her; she needed to know this was real.

* * *

Luke pulled out of the show grounds and headed back towards Pelican's Landing. Ella's mind drifted as she looked out of the window and watched the crop fields and livestock paddocks give way to orchards and olive groves as they got nearer the river and the town.

Luke hit the brakes, jolting Ella back to the present. A car was parked on the dirt beside the road. The hazard lights were flashing and the driver's side door was open but Ella couldn't see anyone.

'What is it?' she asked as Luke parked behind the seemingly abandoned vehicle.

'I recognise the car. I'll just be a minute,' he said as he stepped out.

Ella saw him crouch down beside the car and she could just make out the figure of a person slumped at the wheel. Luke looked back at her and gestured towards her with a wave. She unbuckled her seat belt and opened her door.

'Ella, can you bring my medical bag from the boot?' he called to her.

She nodded, told Liv to wait in the car, grabbed the bag and ran to Luke. A heavily pregnant woman sat behind the wheel. She was covered in a sheen of sweat and her hands were wrapped tightly around the steering wheel, giving the impression she was hanging on for her life. She cried out in pain as Ella handed Luke the bag, and Ella didn't need a medical degree to recognise she was in labour.

# CHAPTER SEVEN

ELLA STEPPED BACK, uncertain about what she should do. Why was this woman on her own? Should she offer to help or stay out of the way? She stood silently as Luke spoke to the woman.

'Jane, I'm going to help you into the back seat after the next contraction. I need to see how far along your labour is.' His voice was quiet and calm. If he was concerned about the situation, he was hiding it well. He turned to Ella. 'Can you help me support Jane? She's going to need both of us to move her.'

Ella nodded and stepped closer. She waited for Luke's instructions and together they wrapped their arms around Jane's waist and half-pulled, half-lifted her out of the driver's seat and settled her as much as possible in the back seat.

'Let me have a look to see what's going on.' Ella stood in the open door, trying to afford Jane some privacy. 'The baby's head is crowning.'

'What?' Jane exclaimed, her tone equal parts fear and disbelief. Ella felt the same. 'The baby's coming now?'

'Yes,' Luke replied. 'But I can see the baby's head, which means he's up the right way. So that's good news.'

Ella wasn't sure she agreed with Luke's definition of

Every cell of her body tingled in anticipation. She could feel each cell straining, reaching out to him. Her skin was on fire and every nerve-ending quivered with anticipation, alive with the possibilities of what was to come. Her expectations were almost painful, her reaction intense.

He reached for her, ending her suspense. His lips were on her ear lobe, soft and warm, his breath in her ear. He kissed her neck and then his lips covered hers. She melted into him and let him consume her. His fingers skimmed over her nipples, which grew hard and peaked. He swept the strap of her dress from her shoulder and exposed her left breast to the cool air. His thumb brushed over her nipple, teasing, tantalising. She cried out as a wave of desire washed over her and a bolt of heat scorched through her, sweeping from her nipple to her groin in a searing flash.

His lips left a trail of hot spots from her lips to her throat and collarbone, until finally he took her breast in his mouth, rolling his tongue over the taut flesh until Ella thought she might come then and there. But she didn't want it to end—not yet, maybe never. She wanted to feel him, to touch him, to arouse him too.

She pulled his shirt from his trousers and slid her hand under the fabric, running her hands over the warm skin of his chest. His body was firm under her fingertips. He cupped her breast in his hand and ran his thumb over her nipple, making her moan. She arched her back, offering herself to him, and he took one breast in his mouth again, sucking hard. Ella almost exploded in his arms.

She ran her index finger from his sternum down along the line separating his abdominal muscle, following the line of dark hair that led to his waist band. She concentrated on him, wanting to extend the pleasure, wanting to share the pleasure. She unbuckled his belt and snapped open the button on his trousers, unzipping his fly and pushing his trousers low on his hips. His erection strained against the fabric of his boxer shorts. She ran her hand over his shaft; it was strong and thick, and she felt it rise to meet her. Luke groaned and the sound of his arousal urged her on.

His hand ran up her thigh and the soft folds of her dress fell away with his touch. His fingers met the elastic of her underwear and slid under the lace of her undies. Ella let her legs fall apart, opening herself to him, giving herself to him as his fingers slid inside her. She was slick and wet, throbbing. His thumb found her centre and she gasped as his touch took her to the edge.

But she didn't want it this way. She wanted to share the experience. She wanted all of him and she wanted him to have all of her. She let go of him and quickly pulled her dress over her head to lie naked before him. His dark eyes roamed over her body, setting her on fire with his gaze.

'You are so beautiful,' he murmured as he ran his hand over her belly and down between her thighs, seeking her warmth, sliding into her wetness.

She wanted to feel him inside her. She wanted them to be joined together. She lifted her hips and reached behind him, holding his hips, cupping his buttocks, pulling him close. Her knees were bent and she arched her back as she fitted him to her like pieces of a jigsaw. She thought she might melt on the spot as a burst of heat raced through her, flaring from her breasts to her groin. She sighed as he thrust into her, filling her, consuming her as they became one.

She gave herself to him and he claimed all of her.

'Oh, God, Luke,' she said as she clung to him, and she could hear the desire and need in her voice. Nothing else mattered.

There was nothing else.

She closed her eyes as stars burst behind her eyelids and sparks shot through her groin. She was panting now, unable to take deep breaths, as her body was focused on other sensations. She was close to a climax; she could feel it building, taking control.

Luke was drowning in Ella. He was losing control.

He felt her hand on his chest, felt it brush over one nipple and felt another surge of blood to his groin. He breathed her name and that was the last coherent thought he had. Her legs wrapped around his waist, pinning him to her. She pushed her hips against his and his resistance crumbled.

Her skin was soft, her eyes soulful, her body slim but not boyish. Her hips were rounded, her breasts full; he was completely mesmerised.

She tilted her hips and fitted him to her. He heard his own guttural moan as he thrust into her, filled her. He couldn't hold back, he couldn't resist, and when he heard her call his name it pushed him further.

There was nothing gentle in their love-making. It was fuelled by pure desire—desperate, all-consuming desire.

Everything else in his life was forgotten as Ella took

over his senses. The world ceased to exist except for Ella. There was nothing else that mattered.

He wanted to go slowly; he wanted to savour the moment; he wanted time to commit it all to memory but he couldn't resist her. He couldn't fight it. He was only a man, a powerless man, and he could feel himself being swept away.

He thrust into her again. Up and down he moved, faster and faster, harder and stronger, and she met each thrust. She arched her back and held him close with her legs, opening herself to him, offering herself to him.

He buried himself deep inside her and, when he felt her shudder and come undone, he came with her. They climaxed together and, when they were completely spent, he gathered her to him, holding her close, reluctant to let her go as he savoured this next moment.

She had blown his mind. She was bold and confident. This was the Ella who had been hiding—the one he had suspected might be in there somewhere, the one who had been swamped by trauma and stress. He was finally piecing her together. Bit by bit, he was getting to know her and he was amazed by her strength, resilience and positivity.

He felt a drop of moisture on his naked shoulder and his heart missed a beat as he saw Ella wipe away a tear.

'Ella? Are you okay? Did I hurt you?'

He was horrified to think that he had upset her or, worse, hurt her; she needed tenderness, kindness and compassion.

But she hurriedly reassured him. She smiled as she looked at him and said, 'No. Not at all. These are happy tears. Emotional but in a good way. I didn't know sex could be like that.'

'Like what?'

'Amazing. Satisfying. I've never had a partner bring me to an orgasm before.'

'Never?'

She shook her head. 'I've only achieved that on my own. I don't think sex has ever been about me before.'

'What about before your ex? With Liv's father?'

'No. We were young. I don't think he really considered me at all. It was all over in a flash. Her conception wasn't the beautiful experience I would have chosen.'

'We will have to see what we can do to change your experiences.'

'Tonight was enough.'

'Really? You don't want to do that again? I'm sure we will only improve with practice,' he said as he turned onto his side and gathered her in his arms.

'No strings, remember?' she said. 'And don't forget my Plan A.'

Her Plan A. She was moving to Queensland.

But, as he felt the weight of her in his embrace, as he looked at her face, something tugged at his heart and he felt something tug at his soul. 'What if you didn't have to go? What if you got a job in Pelican's Landing?'

What was he doing? The words were out of his mouth before he had time to think things through. They'd had great sex but that didn't have to mean anything more. It didn't have to *be* anything more. He wasn't ready for a commitment so what exactly was he proposing?

She frowned. 'What would I do?'

It was too late now. He was in over his head but he couldn't retract his suggestion. 'What were you planning on doing in Queensland?'

'Something in the hospitality sector, probably. I thought I could get a job in a hotel reception.'

'Is that what you'd like to do?'

'Not really. But it's something I have experience in.'

'What's your passion?'

'Numbers.'

'Numbers?'

Ella nodded. 'I was at university studying accountancy when I got pregnant with Liv. I was in second year but I never went back. I had a student job in a pub and I went from there to work in the yacht club.'

'Why don't you go back and finish your degree?'

'I haven't got the time or the money to go back to uni. I need to work, but I have been thinking about doing a bookkeeping course. Maybe even combining that with some work in the domestic violence space. Women almost always suffer financially as well as emotionally and physically in those situations. There must be a need for education or assistance around that.'

'If you could get a part-time job and study would you consider staying in Pelican's Landing?'

'Are you asking me to stay?'

'I'm asking you to consider it. Liv seems to be settling well; it would be a shame to move her, and it's a good community. I think you could be happy there.' He didn't want to let her go but he was afraid to ask her to stay. Afraid he'd let her down.

* * *

Ella couldn't pinpoint exactly when she'd given in and decided to stay in Pelican's Landing.

Maybe she'd given in because she saw how happy and settled Liv was. Maybe she'd given in when she'd enrolled in an online bookkeeping course, or maybe it was when she'd found part-time work at the local pharmacy, thanks to Luke's contacts.

Or maybe it was because she wasn't ready to say goodbye to Pelican's Landing or to Luke. Not that she'd admitted to herself yet that the move might be permanent, and still wary of relationships she was reluctant to acknowledge that her feelings for Luke had played a part, but she was finding him addictive.

They weren't officially dating but there was no denying their relationship was progressing. They hadn't put any labels on it—she thought they were both afraid of having that discussion—but she was enjoying his company. It felt safe, and he was gentle and considerate, both in and out of bed.

They hadn't gone public yet, and even Liv was unaware of the fledgling relationship between her mother and Luke, although Penny and Hayley knew. Luke had convinced Ella to tell them and she had to admit that, without Penny's and Hayley's assistance, she and Luke would have very little time together. Last night had been a prime example. Liv had been at a sleepover at Chloe's house, giving Ella a precious night to spend in Luke's bed.

She lay on her side in his enormous bed, watching him as he slept. He was so beautiful—beautiful, gentle, kind and generous—and she was slowly learning to trust him. Slowly learning that letting him into her life didn't mean giving up her independence or her identity. Rather, with his kindness and compassion, she felt she was beginning to blossom into the person she was supposed to be.

At moments like this she wondered if she could, just for now, let desire rule her head and heart and allow herself one tiny glimpse of how life would be if it were perfect. What woman with red blood coursing through her veins would be able to resist temptation when it was presented as beautifully as this?

But every now and then she experienced a niggle of anxiety, a strange sense of foreboding. Had she given in too easily? Had she sold out her dream of independence for a man she barely knew? A man who barely knew her? Sometimes she was afraid the answer was yes and her decision was going to turn out to be a bad one.

Luke opened his eyes and smiled when he found her watching him. The bed sheet was around her waist. She was naked, they both were, and she saw his blue eyes darken with desire as he took in her nakedness. She was amazed at how unselfconscious she felt as she returned his gaze.

He reached out and rested the palm of his hand against her ribs and she could feel the beat of her heart pulsing under his fingertips. He ran his fingers lightly over her nipple. It peaked and throbbed under his touch. She licked her lips and Luke groaned, and then his hand was on her face, cupping it with infinite gentleness and tipping her face down to his.

The moment his lips touched hers, Ella was no longer quite aware of where she was; all she knew was this moment should go on for ever. She was no longer sure where his body ended and hers started, couldn't have said whether she was standing or sitting. There was only the kiss. Nothing else. Only Luke's mouth on hers, touching, kissing, caressing, as if they'd been made for this moment. She sank deeper into his touch, his taste, all her senses trained on Luke and how he was making her feel. Every molecule was alive with his touch and her head was pounding with desire.

He ran a hand from her cheek to her shoulder and down her arm to her elbow, leaving a trail of fire in his wake. Then slowly, gently, he slid his fingers between her thighs. She parted her knees, letting her legs fall apart, granting him access to her soul. His fingers worked their magic, turning her insides into a pool of treacly deliciousness and compelling the blood to rush from her extremities to where it was really needed, leaving her toes strangely numb and her belly on fire. She arched her back as his fingers took her to the peak of ecstasy. Behind closed eyelids, all she could see were colours dancing to the thrum of her blood in her ears as she gasped and shuddered, climaxing while he watched her.

Satisfied and happy, she caught her breath and then sat up and straddled him. She put her hands on either side of his head as she let him guide himself inside her. She straightened up and traced her fingers across his chest where the morning sun touched his skin. His hands were on her hips, lifting her up and down, and she leant backwards, making sure she could take his whole length, riding him until he joined her in exquisite relief...

'Good morning.'

'It is a good morning,' she replied with a grin as she collapsed onto his chest. 'It's a beautiful morning.'

'What time do you need to collect Liv?'

'Not until ten.'

'Well, I'll let Maisie out and make us both a cup of tea, and then we might as well spend the next hour in bed. Unless you have other plans?

'I have absolutely zero plans.'

Ella lay back on the pillows as Luke got out of bed and padded naked out of the room. She watched him go with a smile on her face, enjoying this moment of complete bliss and satisfaction. This was a good moment. This life felt like a fantasy, a dream. Could it be real? She was having amazing sex with a gorgeous man, she had a job, Liv was happy in school and they were safe. It was the new start she had dreamed of but she still didn't dare to think it could be real.

Luke had told her she deserved this life. That she had been brave and strong and had made this happen. He tried to allay her fears, had told her not to over-think it, to enjoy it, but sometimes it was hard to let go of the anxiety.

Luke was smiling as he made the tea. His relationship with Ella was progressing slowly, their time together limited by Liv, but the slow pace had removed some of the pressure.

Ella was strong, resilient and determined to make her own way and his fears of letting her down were gradually dissipating in the face of her independence. She wasn't making any demands on him. She was busy, they both were, and he was just enjoying spending time with her when he got the chance. They hadn't put any labels on what they were doing and they'd made no promises, no commitments. If their relationship wasn't official it took the pressure off them both. It lifted the weight of expectation from his shoulders and removed some of Ella's doubts about her choices.

The only, somewhat ironic, concern he had was his own increasing reliance on Ella. Since his return to Pelican's Landing, he'd always had plenty to keep him occupied— his work, community events and his father—and he'd never felt lonely but now, the nights when Ella was not in his bed felt long and empty and his thoughts constantly turned to her. He had no idea if she planned to make Pelican's Landing her permanent home—they hadn't broached that subject—but as the days and nights passed he was beginning to wonder if they should have that conversation. Perhaps one day soon he'd find a way to raise the topic, he thought as he carried the tea into the bedroom.

Ella was sitting up in bed holding her phone, but his heart dropped like a stone when he saw her expression. Her face was pale, her brown eyes wide.

'What's happened? What's wrong?' he asked.

She looked up at him and her hand shook as she let her phone fall on the bed.

'My ex. He's back. He's looking for me.'

'I thought you said you had a new phone? A new number?'

'I do. This is an email.'

'You didn't change your email?'

Ella shook her head. 'I needed it for my government accounts. He can't track me through an email, can he?'

Luke wasn't sure. He didn't think so, but he'd never had to consider that question before. He crossed the room, put the tea cups on the bedside table and picked up Ella's phone. The email was still on the screen. He scanned the contents. The message was brief but the tone was menacing and threatening, promising he would find her. It was nasty and Luke could understand why Ella was shaken. If she replied, would there be any way of him tracking where it had come from?

'Don't reply,' he said. He couldn't imagine she would want to but it was better to make sure she didn't. It was better to be safe than sorry.

'What if he comes after me?'

'Does anyone know where you are?'

She shook her head.

How did people track someone down? Luke had no idea. Liv wasn't Trent's child, so he had no rights there, but joint assets would have to be disclosed, wouldn't they? 'Do you have any joint assets?' he asked. 'Did you have a joint bank account?'

'We did but I took my share of the money out and opened another one with a different bank before I left. I haven't used the joint account. Could he find me through my car?'

'The car that was swallowed by the river?'

Ella gave a half-smile. 'I can't believe I'd forgotten

about that for a minute. It's one way to get my mind off my other problems.'

'Was the car in joint names? Is he on the insurance policy?'

'No.'

'So, the insurance company doesn't need to notify him, so that's a plus. Is this the first time he's tried to find out where you are?'

She nodded. 'He has been away for six weeks for work. He would have just got back to Geraldton and realised we weren't there.'

'I don't think he'll be able to find you.'

'But you said everyone in town will know I'm staying in your cottage.'

'Ella, he sent you an email, he doesn't know where you are. He'd have to track you to South Australia first and then to Pelican's Landing. It would be like finding a needle in a haystack.

'But can I make a suggestion that might help allay your fears? Why don't you speak to Sam? He'll have a better idea of what you should do in these circumstances. I'll call him and see if he can meet us at the station later today. We can pick up Liv and I'll look after her while you speak to Sam.'

'Can you call him now? The longer I wait, the more I'll worry.'

Ella was exhausted. She'd taken Luke's advice and had come to speak to Sam but having to recount all the details of her relationship with Trent had left her shaken and distressed. Going over the abuse had been almost as traumatic as the abuse itself.

And Sam's questions kept coming. 'Have you ever called the police for assistance? Made a complaint? Pressed charges?'

No. Why hadn't she? She'd left because he'd hit her in front of Liv. She hadn't want Liv to see that and she didn't want Liv to be in danger. But she'd never pressed charges. Never called the cops.

'Have you ever been to the doctor? Would a GP have any record of any injuries you sustained from Trent?'

Ella shook her head. 'Luke is the only doctor who has seen the bruises but that was when he stitched my leg up after the flood. That was weeks after the last incident and I wasn't consulting him about the violence.'

'Do you have any dated photos of any of the bruises?'

'Yes.' She nodded. 'I do have some on my email.' She'd taken some and emailed them to herself, knowing she couldn't leave them on her phone in case Trent saw them.

'That will help. I would suggest that you put an interim intervention order on him. That will prohibit him from contacting you or coming near you or Liv.'

'What evidence do I need?'

'This statement you've given me plus some photos will suffice initially. If he disputes the order, then the matter would go to court.'

Ella paled at the thought of having to confront Trent in court.

'You wouldn't have to be there in person,' Sam reassured her.

'How long does it take to put an intervention order in place?'

'It is in place as soon as it is served—so, as soon as it is handed to Trent. All I need is his address details in Western Australia. I'll get someone there to deliver the order.'

Luke had collected Ella from the police station and taken Liv and her out for dinner. Neither of them had felt like thinking about cooking meals, and Luke had thought it would keep Ella occupied. But neither of them had counted on Sam calling with the news that the West Australian police hadn't been able to locate Trent. Sam had wanted to know if there was anywhere else Trent might be, any common haunts, but Ella had only been able to think of the local pub. She'd left dinner feeling queasy and nervous.

'Will you and Liv come and spend the night in the big house? Would you feel safer there?' Luke asked when they got home and Liv ran ahead of them to cuddle Maisie, who was waiting to greet them.

'Thanks, but I don't want to have to explain why we'd be sleeping in your house to Liv. I don't want to tell her what's happening. We'll be okay in the cottage.'

'Well, in that case, why don't you get Liv to bed and I'll come back and sleep on the couch? I'd feel better if Maisie and I stayed here. Would that be all right? I'll be gone in the morning before Liv wakes up.'

Ella was trying to be brave, trying not to rely on Luke but his offer was too generous to refuse. She knew she would sleep better knowing Luke was there. 'Thank you, that would make me feel better.'

It had been days since she'd given Sam her statement and put the interim intervention order in place, and still

Trent hadn't been served with it. Ella was on edge and she knew she would be until Sam came with good news.

She had picked Liv up from school and was preparing afternoon tea when she heard a car coming down the drive. It wasn't Luke's—she knew the sound of his car now—so she glanced out of the kitchen window to see who was approaching the property and her heart jumped as fear and disbelief gripped her.

Behind the wheel was a familiar but unwelcome face.

Trent, her ex, was heading for the cottage.

She clutched at the kitchen bench and took a deep breath, trying to slow her racing heart. What was he doing here? How had he found them?

She had no time to run.

And nowhere to run too.

Her mouth was dry as her eyes darted around the room, looking in vain for an escape. What could she possibly do to keep Liv and her safe? Did she have time to get Liv into her car? Even if she did, there was only one way out of the property, and she'd come face to face with Trent on the driveway. She knew he would park behind her car, blocking her in, and the path would lead him though the garden, directly to the cottage door.

The one door mocked her complacency from across the room. That sole exit point had bothered her from the get-go but she'd convinced herself she was safe. She'd been foolish, lulled into a false sense of security by the remoteness and slow pace of Pelican's Landing. She hadn't been able to imagine anyone looking for her here.

The wooden door was solid but would it be secure enough to keep him out? Oh, God, had she locked it? She ran to check it. She was sure she would have; it was still a force of habit, even if she'd started to feel safe.

She breathed out a sigh of relief as she saw the lock was set. Out of the corner of her eye she could see Trent's car heading towards Luke's house. He'd missed the turn-off to the cottage. How long did she have before he realised his mistake?

She quickly yanked the curtains across the windows overlooking the garden; perhaps she could pretend they weren't here. But he would eventually see her car parked out the front. He must have followed her here from town. Her car was going to give them away.

Liv was sitting at the kitchen table, pulling her lunch box and reading folder out of her school bag.

'Liv,' Ella said, fighting hard to keep her voice calm and steady as she returned to the kitchen bench. Fear made it wobble but she hoped Liv wouldn't notice. 'Can you go into the bathroom and wash your hands, please?' Her hands were trembling as she picked up Liv's cup and plate. She squeezed the cup hard, not wanting to spill the drink, and followed Liv into the bathroom. She heard the car stop and reverse. He must have gone past the fork in the driveway that led to the cottage. He would have seen her car. She heard the sound of his car reversing back before turning towards the cottage.

She needed to hurry.

'Liv, I need you to listen to me. Trent is here. He's driving up to the house now.'

Liv's eyes were wide.

'I need you to stay in here and lock the door. You can eat in there, but be very quiet, and do not come out until

I knock on the door and tell you he's gone. Okay? Can you do that for me?'

She kissed her forehead and closed the door. She heard Trent's car stop out the front and the engine cut out. 'Lock it now, Liv.'

Her heart was hammering.

She went and stood in the kitchen, putting the kitchen table between her and the front door as she heard Trent's car door slam.

The knife she'd used to cut Liv's apple was in the sink. Should she grab it? Arm herself? Protect herself? But what if he took it off her and used it against her? She was frozen in place by indecision and fear.

Her bag was on the table. She grabbed her phone from it and opened her messages. Penny had been the last person to message her. She tapped the message and quickly typed:

Call the police. My ex is here.

She hit send just as she saw the door handle turn. Her heart was in her throat, her eyes wide with fear as she watched the handle turn and prayed the lock would hold.

'Ella, what the…' His next word was drowned out by the sound of a heavy crash against the door. 'I know you're in there. Let me in.'

Ella's throat was tight with fear. There was no way she could speak, no way she could answer him. She knew she needed to defend herself but she hadn't the slightest clue how to do that.

She had to keep him out. The door vibrated as Trent either kicked it or rammed it with his shoulder again.

Should she have locked herself in with Liv?

No; she couldn't risk him getting to Liv.

Should she go outside or wait here for the police? She was trapped in here, caged. Would she have more chance of escape if she was out in the open? But she couldn't risk leaving Liv in the house unguarded. She needed to keep Trent away from her.

Ella's heart was hammering. She had to stall Trent until the police came and she was about to call out when the lock splintered under Trent's force and the door flew open. Ella darted behind the kitchen table, needing to put something between her and Trent.

His eyes blazed with anger as he advanced towards her. 'You're mine, Ella. If you think you can run off, you're a stupid woman. I told you'd I'd find you.'

'Trent, we were just taking a trip. A holiday. That's all.' She needed him to think she'd been coming back.

'Don't lie to me! You've stolen my money and changed the bank accounts.'

'That was *my* money I took. Mine!'

He stepped towards her fast, and she wasn't quick enough to get away. She was angry and frightened and she wasn't paying enough attention. He lashed out with his right hand, backhanding her across her face, and she went flying.

Her left hand hit the tiled floor, breaking her fall before she crashed into the kitchen cupboards. Her head hit the cupboard and Ella saw stars. She could feel an egg form immediately on the back of her skull.

Trent took two steps towards her and, dazed, she struggled to her feet, afraid if she stayed on the floor that he would kick her. Her left forearm was hanging at her side and as she tried to bend her elbow she cried out in pain. She squeezed her left arm against her side and tried to dash past Trent. If she could make it out of the door, she'd have more room to run and she'd be able to lead him away from Liv.

She thought she'd made it past him until she felt herself being pulled off her feet. He'd grabbed her by her hair and she felt a chunk of it being ripped out by his hands. Her knees buckled as she tried to find her footing and Trent pulled her to her feet again, but this time his hands were around her throat.

She could feel him squeezing, and she tried desperately to claw his hands off her, but her left arm was useless and she was no match for him with only one hand.

She was running out of air.

She was crying in fear, desperation and pain. She knew she was using up her last gasps of precious air but she couldn't stop.

Trent's face was contorted with rage. She could see his lips moving, and she knew he was yelling at her, but she couldn't hear anything. Her senses were fading with her breath.

Black spots danced before her eyes…and then there was nothing.

# CHAPTER TEN

LUKE TURNED INTO his drive and took the left fork to the cottage. He'd picked up some fresh peaches for Ella from a roadside stall on his way back from a home visit and thought he'd drop them off for Liv to have for an after-school snack before he returned to the clinic.

An unfamiliar car was parked behind Ella's four-wheel drive and he assumed Ella must have invited a friend of Liv's over for a play. Luckily, he'd bought a whole tray of peaches, he thought as he parked and lifted the tray from the back seat.

The door to the cottage was open but it was very quiet. He couldn't see or hear anyone. He stepped through the doorway and searched the room.

The tray of peaches hit the floor with a dull thud as he launched himself across the room. His legs propelled him forwards before his brain had properly registered what he was seeing.

A man was standing over Ella.

His hands were around her throat.

Luke's movements were a reflex, a preservation reflex. Not for his own sake, though—for Ella's.

Luke collided with the man, laying a rugby tackle on him and taking him by surprise. He let go of Ella and

Luke was vaguely aware of her collapsing to the floor before he landed heavily on the kitchen table with Ella's assailant underneath him.

The table splintered under their weight and the man came up swinging. Luke had just enough time to register that this must be Trent, Ella's ex, before he felt Trent's fist smash into his face, just above his left eye. Luke shook his head, committing to the fight. All he could think of was that he had to keep Trent engaged. He had to keep him occupied, had to keep him focused on himself and away from Ella.

He landed a fist in Trent's stomach and was pleased to see Trent double over. His satisfaction was short-lived, though, as he copped a return blow to his abdomen before he felt Trent's knee slam into his thigh.

The fight wasn't pretty, fighting wasn't his style, but he had to protect Ella. He managed to land a couple more hits while taking a couple in return until suddenly the blows stopped coming. Trent's hands were covering his face and Luke could hear him coughing.

Luke turned and saw Sam standing beside him, holding a canister of pepper spray. All the fight went out of Trent as Sam handcuffed him and led him outside.

Luke hurried to Ella's side.

She was sitting on the floor, her knees pulled up against her chest, as if trying to make herself as small as possible, as inconspicuous as possible. She was leaning against the couch, her arms at her sides. Her face was pale but Luke could see angry red marks on her neck where Trent had choked her with his hands and he knew the marks would turn into bruises.

He crouched down beside her and wrapped his arms around her. She closed her eyes and let him hold her. He could feel her shaking. 'It's okay. You're safe. Are you all right?'

'Yes. No. I don't know.' Her voice was hoarse.

'Where's Liv?' Luke was concerned.

'She's in the bathroom. I need to tell her she can come out.' Ella started to get up.

'I'll get her.'

'No.' She held onto his arm and pulled herself to her feet with her right hand, wincing in pain. 'I told her not to come out until I came for her.'

'Are you hurt?'

'My arm.'

Ella's left arm was dangling at her side. She had her right hand pressed to her left upper arm, holding it against her body, but Luke could see her left elbow was misshapen and he knew immediately that it had been dislocated. He put his arm around her waist, letting her lean against him, supporting her. She was wobbly on her feet, pain and shock combining to make her unsteady.

A drop of moisture fell from Luke's brow. He wiped it away with the back of his hand while still holding onto Ella. His hand came away streaked with blood. Trent's fist must have split the skin above his eye. He pressed his fingers against the cut, trying to stem the blood, knowing Liv would be scared and not wanting to frighten her any further.

Ella knocked on the bathroom door. 'Liv, sweetheart, it's Mummy. Trent is gone, you can open the door now.'

Luke heard the key turn in the lock but Liv didn't

emerge. Ella opened the door to reveal Liv, pressed against the wall between the basin and the toilet. She looked terrified.

Ella let go of Luke and hurried across the small room, her injuries forgotten in her haste to reach her traumatised daughter. He watched her gather Liv to her with her good arm, holding her close.

'It's okay, we're safe.'

'Where's Trent?'

'Sam has taken him away. He's putting him in the police car right now.'

Ella was talking quietly to Liv but from his position mere steps away Luke could hear every word. He wondered how often this scene had played out before Ella had found a way to escape.

Liv and Ella were both shaking, shivering, and he knew Ella must be in agony. He let her comfort Liv and then guided them to the couch. He used his body to try to block the view of the destruction—the room was littered with fragments of broken furniture and smashed crockery.

Luke took a moment to assess Ella's arm. It was definitely dislocated but, listening to her describe what had happened, he was concerned that she might have fractured it as well. Fortunately, the colour and sensation in her hand and fingers was normal, and so was her wrist pulse, so he hoped she had escaped any serious nerve damage, but she'd need an X-ray before he could safely reduce the dislocation.

Ella was quiet throughout his examination and Luke was worried about her.

Sam reappeared, carrying a first-aid kit. Luke knew that wasn't what he needed to take care of Ella. 'I need to take Ella to the clinic,' he said, one eye on the kit in Sam's hand. 'She's dislocated her elbow.'

'The kit's for you,' Sam said. 'You need a dressing over that cut on your eye to stop the bleeding.' Sam opened the case and let Luke rummage through it to select a dressing. 'Can you give me a couple of minutes before you move Ella? I need to get some pictures of the damage and I don't want them to see Trent. They've had enough trauma.'

'No.' Luke shook his head. Ella could barely speak. She was obviously in pain and her throat was probably sore as well. 'Ella can't wait. Can you move your car around the side of the big house, out of view?'

Sam nodded. 'Will you take photos of Ella's injuries? I'll need them for evidence.'

Luke photographed Ella's elbow and X-rayed her left arm. As expected, the X-ray showed a posterior dislocation of her elbow but there was no accompanying fracture which was good news. If there was such a thing as good news in this situation.

He explained the results of the X-ray, trying to quell his feelings of guilt as spoke to Ella. If he focused on the medical facts he could put aside, for now, the idea that he'd let her down. That he should have stopped this somehow. Even if that was an unrealistic expectation to put on himself.

'I can put your elbow back into place but it will be sore,' he told her, unsure how much of what he was saying made sense. She was still sucking hard on the green whistle he'd given her for pain relief but he didn't take it away from her. She would need it when he relocated the elbow. 'I'm just going to get Penny to give me a hand with your elbow. I won't be long.'

He ducked out quickly, asking Penny to get Liv to sit with the receptionists and then come to assist him.

'Lie face-down on the bed, Ella, and let your arm hang over the side,' Luke instructed on his return as he lowered the back of the bed and helped her to lie down. 'Penny, I need you to hold Ella's left hand and apply gentle traction towards the floor.' Luke placed his thumbs on the back of Ella's elbow, gently applying a downward force to the olecranon process to realign the joint.

He fitted a sling for Ella and then got Penny to help as he photographed the bruising on Ella's neck. The bruising was in the shape of a man's hands, and Luke asked Penny to hold a tape measure against the finger marks so they could be compared for size against Trent's.

'Now, you need to let me attend to your eye,' Penny said as they completed the photos.

'I have to take a second X-ray and document Ella's injuries.'

'You can do that in a minute. Let Ella rest and come with me to my exam room.'

Luke was going to argue, to say that Penny could look at his eye just as easily in this room, but he could tell by her expression that she had things on her mind that she didn't want to say in earshot of anyone else. He sighed and got off the chair.

'I've asked Janine to reschedule the rest of the afternoon's list,' Penny said as she cleaned his wound, gluing the edges together. 'There was nothing urgent; she'll fit them in over the next couple of days.'

'I'm fine.'

'You're in no state to treat patients and someone needs to look after Ella.'

'I'm not doing a very good job of that,' he said as Penny's comment reminded him that he'd failed to protect her.

'It could have been worse, a lot worse, if you hadn't got there when you did. This was her ex's doing. You're not to blame.'

Luke shook his head. He was unconvinced. 'What was I thinking, letting her stay in the barn? It wasn't nearly secure enough. Anyone could just drive onto the property, the door wasn't nearly as substantial as it looked and there was no escape exit.' In his mind, he had to accept some of the blame.

'You weren't to know that Trent would follow Ella halfway across the country,' Penny argued. 'Sam said Trent could have killed Ella if you hadn't been there. Sam will deal with him now. You need to take care of Ella. She's frightened and in pain. She needs to go home and lie down. And you look like you've gone two rounds in the boxing ring.'

'I'll look worse tomorrow,' Luke said, glancing in the mirror and touching his eyebrow. He knew the bruising would be worse in a day or two. 'Besides, Ella probably doesn't want me anywhere near her.' He wouldn't blame her if she never wanted to see him again.

'You saved her life,' Penny said in a tone that told him she thought he was being ridiculous.

But, while that might be true, he didn't expect any thanks. He had wanted her to stay in Pelican's Landing for selfish reasons and he'd put her in harm's way. If he hadn't asked her to stay, Trent wouldn't have been able to track her down. How Trent had found her was a mystery but Luke couldn't help feeling that it was somehow his fault.

Luke turned into his driveway and bypassed the cottage, taking Ella and Liv directly to the big house.

'Where are we going?' Ella asked as he missed the fork in the driveway that led to the barn.

'I'm taking you to my place. I'm not leaving you alone tonight.' As usual, Penny had been right—Ella had been more than happy to let him drive Liv and her back to the property—but there was no way he was taking her back to the barn.

'Penny said Sam will send Trent to Murray Bridge, he'll be in custody overnight. We can stay in the cottage.'

The effects of the analgesia from the green whistle had worn off and he could see Ella's discomfort increasing. She needed some ice on her elbow and some more pain relief.

'You can't manage Liv with one arm. You need to let me take care of you tonight and I'm not spending another night on your couch. It's comfortable enough to sit on but it's not long enough to sleep on.'

He helped Ella out of the car and into the house, settling her on the couch. He gave her some pain relief and put an ice pack on her elbow. He put the television on for Liv, who was quite content lying on the floor watching cartoons with Maisie by her side.

'Do you need something for your head? Is it sore?' Ella asked him as she swallowed her tablets.

'No, it's fine.' His eye was swollen now, and he was having difficulty seeing out of it, but it seemed like a small price to pay compared to Ella's injury. 'I'll go and fetch some things for you from the cottage if you tell me what you need. I'll tidy up the mess and then make us all something to eat,' he said as his phone pinged with a message.

'That's Sam,' he continued as he read the text. 'He wants to come and take a statement from you, if you're up to it.'

The pain relief was making her drowsy and Ella had to concentrate hard as she listened to Sam speak.

'We've charged Trent with "assault occasioning bodily harm" based on what we witnessed but I need you to make a statement,' Sam told her.

'But I need to warn you, I expect he'll get released on bail tomorrow, if he can post it, but I'll ask for him to be sent back to Western Australia and for the bail conditions to prohibit him from leaving the state. He'll appear in court later, and if convicted he'll have a criminal record.'

'*If* convicted?'

'I can't see him escaping a conviction, but I will warn you that it's unlikely he will go to gaol if this is his first charge. And I couldn't find any previous convictions for him. I'm assuming he's got a prior history but, unless he's been charged before, there is no record. But we have served him with the intervention order, so if he breaches those conditions then gaol time would be a very real possibility. That should be enough of a deterrent to keep him away from you.'

'Do you know how he found Ella?' Luke asked when Sam had finished recording Ella's statement.

'He had a photograph from our local paper in his pocket. Apparently, someone Trent works with is related to the photographer, so he often looks at his photos. He'd met Ella before, when you worked at the marina in Geraldton, and he thought he recognised you in the picture so he showed Trent.'

Ella remembered the photographer who'd taken her picture on the day that Luke had rescued her and Liv from the flood. The one she'd turned away from, not wanting her photo taken.

'Trent turned up here on the chance Ella was still in Pelican's Landing. He figured you would have put Liv in school, so he waited outside the primary school and followed them home. We've got footage of his car on CCTV going past the school.'

Ella felt sick. All her planning and still he'd found her so easily.

'So it was my fault,' Luke said. He looked stricken with guilt.

'How is it your fault?' she asked.

'I asked you to stay in Pelican's Landing. If you'd moved on when you wanted to, Trent wouldn't have found you.'

'This isn't your fault. This is all on Trent.' She hated

the idea that he would blame himself. 'You saved my life, Luke,' she said, knowing that was a debt she could never repay.

Ella slept fitfully in the same room as Liv. Despite knowing that Trent was spending at least one night in custody, she hadn't wanted to let Liv out of her sight. It was for Ella's peace of mind, rather than any real threat.

Luke had moved an arm chair into the room, as Ella found it more comfortable to be in a semi-reclined position, but despite this, and plenty of pain relief, her arm kept her awake for most of the night. Luke gave her more analgesia in the early hours of the morning and she finally fell into a deep sleep not long before sunrise.

She woke to the sound of cockatoos. She was briefly disoriented and, when she saw Liv's empty bed, she panicked for a moment until she saw Luke's note propped on Liv's pillow.

*We're downstairs having breakfast. Kettle is on when you wake up.*

Luke and Liv were in the kitchen. Liv was sitting at the table with a bowl of cereal and Luke was making a sandwich. He was packing Liv's lunch box and Ella realised he and Liv must have been across to the cottage while she slept.

'Good morning,' he greeted her as she kissed the top of Liv's head. 'How are you feeling?'

'Like a punching bag.'

'I'll drop Liv at school,' Luke said. 'You stay here and rest.'

But Ella shook her head. She didn't want to stay in the

house alone but, more than that, she had things she needed to do. 'Would you be able to drop me in town?' she asked. She knew she wouldn't be able to drive today, her arm was too sore but she was hoping that tomorrow would be a different story.

'I can get whatever you need at lunch time.'

'I need some bags to start packing.'

Luke's brow furrowed. 'Packing?'

She'd decided, during her restless and sleepless night, that she and Liv would have to leave Pelican's Landing, and since the flood she'd accumulated enough things that meant she would need a few bags to pack it all up in.

Liv had finished her breakfast and was sitting quietly, listening intently and obviously hoping Ella wouldn't notice. 'Liv, can you go and get dressed and clean your teeth, please?' Ella asked, wanting to get her out of the room. 'Now, please,' she added, as she could see Liv about to argue.

'We can't stay here,' Ella told Luke once Liv had headed upstairs.

'With me?'

'In Pelican's Landing,' she clarified. 'I'd hoped we could be safe here but Trent has found us once. He knows where we are. What if he comes back?' She appreciated Luke's help but she was also upset that she needed it. Upset and angry that Trent's actions had put her in this position. She knew Luke would say he didn't mind helping but she was sure one day he'd get tired of coming to her rescue. She had brought Trent into her life and now into Luke's. If she'd stuck to her plan of moving to Queensland instead of being seduced by a kind man and good sex, she wouldn't have been in this position. Trent wouldn't have found her.

'You heard what Sam said last night,' Luke replied. 'Trent will be charged with assault and sent back to Western Australia. The interim intervention order has also been served—he can't afford to come near you again.'

The decision to leave was tearing her in two. She desperately wanted to stay in Pelican's Landing but she was terrified. It felt like a huge risk, but she was worried the price of staying would be too much to pay. She was worried it could cost a life—hers, Liv's or Luke's.

Luke had saved her life once and the only way to repay the debt was to make sure Trent couldn't hurt any of them ever again.

'Do you really think he'll pay attention to a piece of paper telling him to stay away from us?'

She wasn't convinced. She'd heard too many stories of people, mostly women, being subject to continued harassment and violence by their partners despite legal restrictions. She'd expected, hoped, that Luke would say that everything was under control, so she was surprised when he shook his head and agreed with her.

'I hate the fact you feel you have to leave but I understand that you can't afford to take the chance. I'm sorry I let you down,' he said.

Ella shook her head and reached out for him with her good arm. 'You didn't,' she hastened to reassure him, hating that Trent's actions had forced her into this position. 'This is on Trent, not you. If you hadn't arrived when you did, I wouldn't be here now. He would have killed me. I can't afford to take that chance again; I have to do what's best for Liv. Our safety has to be my priority.'

Ella had called a taxi to bring her home from town with the bags she'd bought for packing. She packed their things, stripped the bed and put a load of washing into the machine, hanging the sheets on the line with difficulty as she only had one good arm, before tackling the cleaning. Luke had moved the broken table and cleaned up the smashed crockery and she wondered when he had done that. It must have been last night. It was one less thing for her to worry about, but the whole cleaning-up process took far longer than it should have because of her aching elbow. But she had to keep going.

Sam had arranged for someone to collect Trent's hire car, which had been left parked in front of the cottage, blocking her car into the driveway. Once her car was clear, she was able to fetch Liv from school. She brought her home and then began to load their things into the car. She was planning to leave today. She was in fight or flight mode and she knew if she delayed it would only make it harder to leave. She needed to get going before she lost her resolve.

But she hadn't counted on histrionics from Liv. She was inconsolable, having just been told they were leaving Pelican's Landing, her school, her new friends, Luke and Maisie, and Ella was finding it difficult to offer any comfort given that she was exhausted, in pain and also reluctant to leave. But not wanting to go was very different from having to go.

She had just packed the last bag and was trying to

convince Liv to get in the car when Luke and Penny arrived at the cottage. She had hoped to be on the road before Luke came home from work. She didn't know if she was strong enough for a face-to-face goodbye but all of a sudden that was the situation they found themselves in.

Penny took Liv outside to say goodbye to Maisie, leaving Ella and Luke alone.

'Are you sure you want to go?'

She didn't want to leave but she was scared. Scared to stay. Scared of Trent. Scared to rely on Luke. 'I want to be brave,' she said, 'but I need to be safe. I was lucky you arrived when you did yesterday, but you won't always be there, and I have to put Liv first. If something happens to me, Liv has no one. I've made plenty of mistakes in my twenty-six years and I'm trying not to make any more. This is what I have to do.'

She kissed him for the last time. Her heart ached as he held her tight but eventually he had to let her go.

'Goodbye, Luke.' She hurried outside, needing to put some distance between them before she changed her mind.

'Will you let me know when you get to Mildura?' he asked as he followed her to the car.

Ella nodded before bending down to strap Liv into her seat. She fought back tears as she drove away, leaving Luke and Penny standing in front of the barn. She couldn't let Luke see her cry. She knew her resolve would wash away if she started crying now.

She managed to hold it together until she hit the outskirts of town, before she had to pull over to give in to her distress. She and Liv cried until their tears ran dry. Liv fell asleep but Ella needed to keep driving. She looked in the mirror at Liv, to remind herself of the reason she was leaving, and started the engine again. This time she drove away without looking back, hoping her heart would recover.

With time and distance, she was certain it would.


'You couldn't convince her to stay?' Penny asked Luke as they watched Ella drive away.

Luke shook his head. 'She's convinced this is the only way. I can't tell her what to do. She wants to be in control of her own life. That's her right.'

'That didn't mean she had to leave.'

'I know that but she didn't feel safe. I couldn't protect her. Not always. She was right not to rely on me.'

But Ella's departure had left him feeling broken. He hadn't been looking for a relationship, but he'd found one. He'd offered her the cottage, thinking he was making a small sacrifice that would make a big difference to Ella, but he hadn't counted on the difference she was going to make to his life.

But he'd let her down and she was right to leave.

But, if that was true, he couldn't explain why it felt so wrong.

'Ella doesn't need someone to rely on in a physical sense,' Penny said, clearly not finished giving her opinion. 'She's been on her own on and off for years. What she needs is someone to love her.'


Ella's tears had subsided but the events of the past two days had left her exhausted. She drove into Loxton, a mere two hours from Pelican's Landing, and decided she couldn't keep driving, not today. She had wanted to get to Mildura but this would have to do. Her elbow ached and she was too fatigued and upset to drive any further.

Every mile further away from Pelican's Landing and Luke she'd driven, she'd felt more bereft, as if she was leaving a little trail of herself behind. She imagined little pieces of her broken heart littering the highway behind her and she knew she'd made a mistake. She was still letting Trent and his actions dictate how she lived her life.

She checked into a caravan park, grateful that the school holidays were over and there was a vacancy, and called Luke.

'Ella? Are you in Mildura already?'

Luke's voice calmed her mind but how she wished he was there beside her. How she wished she could step into his arms.

'No. I stopped at the caravan park in Loxton.'

'Are you okay?'

'No. Not really.' She was emotionally and physically exhausted. 'My elbow is aching; I probably shouldn't have driven and I think I've made a mistake.'

'You need to rest. Don't push yourself. You've had a tough few days.'

'I'm not talking about driving. I'm talking about Trent.'

'I don't understand.'

'I've let Trent control me. I wanted to be brave and I wanted to be safe but I've let him win. By leaving you, I've let him win. I don't want that.'

'Oh, Ella, you're not the only one who's made a mistake. I let you down and I'm sorry.'

'You haven't let me down. None of this is your fault.'

'I thought you would be better off without me. I thought you were better off sticking with your plan of building a future for you and Liv by yourself.'

'I thought that was what I had to do but I'm not so sure now. I miss you.' She hadn't intended to tell him that but her brain was too tired to think one step ahead.

'I miss you too,' Luke said before he went quiet.

Ella checked her phone, thinking she had lost reception, but the call was still connected. 'Luke? Are you still there?'

'Yes. I was just thinking.'

'About…?'

'Do you trust me?'

'Yes.'

'Okay. Stay where you are. Don't check out tomorrow. Don't do anything until I speak to you again.'

'What are you going to do?' she asked.

'What I should have done earlier. Get some sleep and don't go anywhere. I promise, everything is going to be all right.'


'Luke! Luke!' Liv flew off the jumping pillow and ran at full speed towards the gate in the playground fence as Ella turned around, her brow creasing in confusion as she saw Luke walking towards them.

'Luke!' She stood up from the bench where she'd been sitting watching Liv and went to meet him. 'What are you doing here?'

'I was worried about you.'

'I'm okay,' she said, her reply automatic, the fib rolling of her tongue. She'd become so accustomed to the lie.

'Are you really?' he asked and Ella shook her head.

Luke opened his arms and she stepped into his embrace. Her elbow protested as he hugged her to him but she didn't care. All she cared about was that he was there. 'I'm glad you're here,' she admitted. 'But I don't understand.'

'You've been brave. I needed to be as well,' he said as he released her,

'What are you talking about?'

'I wanted you to stay with me in Pelican's Landing but I thought you would be better off without me. I let Gemma and Mikayla down; I didn't want to let you down too. I should have asked you to stay, but I was scared, and I also didn't want you to think I was trying to control you. You are in charge of decisions about your life. And Liv's. But the past twenty-four hours have been the longest and loneliest of my life, and when you said you missed me I thought I had one last chance to fix things. I came to see if I can convince you to change your mind.'

'About?'

'Moving to Queensland. If you don't want Trent to win, would you consider coming back to Pelican's Landing with me? I love you, Ella, and, while I can't promise never to let you down, I can promise to try my best not to.'

'Can you say that again?'

'I promise to do my best not to let you down.'

'Not that bit, the other part.'

Luke smiled and repeated, 'I love you.'

Ella's heart leapt with delight. 'I love you too.'

He took her hands in his. 'Come back to Pelican's Landing with me,' he said. 'Make your home there with me, surrounded by people who love you. We're not going to let Trent win. Please, come back with me. Start over with me. Let's make a new life together.'

'You're not getting tired of rescuing me?'

'I'm not here to rescue you, I'm here to ask you to come home with me.'

'Home,' Ella repeated. 'I like the sound of that.'

'Is that a yes?'

She nodded and Luke smiled and picked Liv up, sitting her on his hip. 'Pack your things, Liv, we're going home!'

Liv clapped her little hands as Luke wrapped his free arm around Ella, drew her to his side and said, 'Kiss me like you've missed me…and then let's go home.'

# EPILOGUE

'ARE THE GIRLS ASLEEP?' Luke asked as Ella stepped out onto the veranda of the big house.

'No.' Ella smiled and kissed Luke's cheek before she sat on the outdoor couch beside him. 'But they are in bed, trying to decide what their favourite bit of the day was.'

'What's the answer so far?'

'I think the tube rides are winning.'

It was Liv's sixth birthday and she had spent the day on the river with three friends from school. Luke had spent most of the day towing them behind his boat on an inflatable tube before they'd had a barbecue and a bonfire with marshmallows. The girls were all staying for a sleepover and Ella was preparing herself for a late night. But she wouldn't have changed a thing. It had been a perfect day.

When Ella had decided to return to Pelican's Landing with Luke, she and Liv had moved permanently into the big house, and it was the best decision Ella had made. The past eleven months had been eventful but only in a good way. Ella and Liv were safe and happy and loved.

She nestled in against Luke's side, tucking her feet underneath her and resting her head on his chest. The moon was rising behind the cliffs and she watched in awe as the golden sphere made its way into the sky. The view on the river was constantly changing. No two days were the same: misty mornings and golden sunsets; calm water and howling wind that bowed the willow trees; thunderstorms and cloudless days; pink, blue and orange skies. But she never tired of it.

'I forgot to tell you in all the birthday excitement that I got another bookkeeping client yesterday—the newsagent. Can you believe it?' Since completing her bookkeeper's training, Ella had managed to secure several clients in town and had also had a couple of referrals to businesses in neighbouring towns as well. She was earning her own money instead of relying on government hand-outs. She was supporting Liv and herself and was contributing to the household expenses as well. She was also volunteering at a women's shelter in the next town, assisting with financial advice, and the cottage, with its improved security, was now being regularly used for women in need of temporary accommodation to escape domestic violence.

'I can believe it. Your reputation is growing and I'm not surprised at all. I'm really proud of what you've achieved.'

'Thank you,' she replied. She was proud of how far she had come in a relatively short time. Her world had become big and exciting. 'But I couldn't have done it without your support.' Luke had been amazing. Just knowing he believed in her and had her back had been enough for her to challenge herself and she'd met every challenge so far.

She shifted on her seat, trying to get comfortable, as she was reminded that another challenge was coming their way, and that she'd better make the most of any peaceful moments she might be lucky enough to have in the next few months, as her peace and quiet would be coming to an end soon—even if only temporarily.

'Are you okay?' Luke asked.

'I'm fine but the baby's restless; he's kicking me in the ribs.' Ella took Luke's hand and placed it on her belly. She was almost six months' pregnant. She felt enormous but knew she was barely showing. It had been another hot summer so she was feeling slow and laborious; tired.

'He?'

'I'm positive we're having a boy. This pregnancy is so different from Liv's. Liv was quiet in the womb.' This pregnancy was different in so many ways. Both physically and mentally. She was safe, secure. Confident in her ability to raise a child. This time with a man she loved by her side.

Luke rubbed her stomach. 'Hello, Max, this is your dad.'

'Max?' Ella queried. 'You have a name for him?'

Luke nodded. 'Max—short for Maximus. It means "strong". I have no doubt our son will be strong of character. He'll get that from you.'

'What if I'm wrong and it's a girl?'

'I have a name for her too—it's Mildred. It means "gentle strength".'

'I'm not sold on Mildred.'

'How about Millie for short?'

'I like that,' she said as Luke's phone rang.

He took it out of his pocket. 'It's Christine.'

Christine was the new doctor who was due to start work at the clinic in a week's time. Ella hoped she was ringing to confirm some arrangements, not ringing with bad news. Christine and her husband were looking for a tree change. Christine was in her early fifties, not nearing retirement age yet, but her husband hadn't been well, and Christine had decided they needed a change of scenery and a slower pace and better work-life balance. She didn't want to spend sixty hours a week at work, she wanted time with her husband.

It had been Ella's suggestion for Luke to look for someone like Christine, and Ella hoped that having someone experienced on board would give Luke time to spend with their expanding family and with his father, whose health continued to decline.

Luke finished the call and Ella relaxed. She'd been able to hear from Luke's side of the conversation that Christine was just calling with some questions; she wasn't reneging on the contract. She lifted her feet and exercised her ankles, circling her feet, which had a tendency to swell at the end of a hot day.

'I'll just make you a cup of tea and then I'll massage your feet for you,' Luke offered.

'That sounds like heaven,' she replied.

Ella closed her eyes and rested her head back on the cushion, her hands clasped across her stomach, feeling the baby turning somersaults inside her. She opened her eyes when she heard the screen door bang shut, signalling Luke's return.

'Happy birthday,' he said as he put her tea on the coffee table, before handing her a white envelope he held in one hand and a gift-wrapped parcel which he had tucked under his arm. 'Another year older.'

'I'm happy to still be here to celebrate.' She still had occasional flashbacks to the assault but Sam and Luke had been right—Trent hadn't contacted her again and she was just beginning to believe that she and Liv might live happily ever after.

'And are you happy with me?'

'You know I am. I think you are the secret to my perfect life,' she said as she pulled him down to sit on the couch with her so she could kiss him.

'Open this one first,' Luke instructed as he handed her the envelope.

She slid her finger under the flap and pulled out a tube of sunscreen and some tourist brochures for Queensland.

'I thought we could spend a few days in Queensland once Christine has started work and settled in,' Luke said.

'You're going to take a holiday?'

Luke nodded. 'I'm hoping we can go before baby Max arrives.'

'And before I get too enormous,' she said. She knew Luke was enjoying her fuller figure but sometimes she felt so ungainly. She was normally so thin and the changes to her body were taking some getting used to. She didn't remember being uncomfortable or feeling huge when she'd been pregnant with Liv. But she really didn't remember much about that pregnancy at all.

'You're not enormous—'

'Not yet.'

'You are strong and healthy and you look beautiful,' Luke continued, ignoring her interruption. 'And I thought we could invite Hayley and Josh and their kids too. Liv will love the theme parks and the beach, but she'd enjoy Chloe and Jack's company as well. What do you think?'

'It sounds fabulous. As long as we stay somewhere with an amazing pool so I can float around like a whale.'

'Okay, one amazing pool coming up. Now, your next present.'

The second present was shoe-box sized but, as she removed the wrapping paper and lifted the lid, she revealed a single piece of paper on which a large black question mark was written.

She looked up at Luke. 'What is this?'

'This gift comes with a question,' he said. 'I have given my life to my family, my father, my job and now this town. They all take a little piece of me, like a leaky tap—slow and steady so that I don't notice that I'm being drained—but you, you replenish me. Being with you restores me. You feed my soul. And when I'm with you I see a future—not just an existence but a life. You have saved me from a life half-lived and I want us to be a family, a proper family. You, me, Liv and all the babies still to come. I would like to adopt Liv, to officially make her my daughter, if you think she'd like me to be her dad.'

'She would love it. I would too.' Ella didn't doubt that Luke loved Liv, or her. He was constantly telling them as much, but she was profoundly touched to know he wanted to make it official. 'Is that the question?' she asked.

'That's a question but it's not *the* question. I know we've talked about getting married and you've said you don't need it. Perhaps my failed attempt has dissuaded you. But—' Luke got off the couch and down on one knee as Ella smiled '—I love you, Ella. I love everything about you—your beauty, your compassion, your strength—and I promise to stand by your side for the rest of our lives in any way that you would like me too. But what I would really like is to be your husband. Will you marry me?'

Tears sprang unbidden to Ella's eyes. She blamed the pregnancy hormones, which could make her cry at the most inopportune times. She brushed them aside, wanting to be able to see Luke clearly. She was nodding as she spoke.

'I thought I could stand on my own two feet. I thought I wanted to be independent, and I'm sure I could have done that and been happy, but I know I wouldn't be *this* happy. You are everything I could possibly want and I want to spend the rest of my life with you. This is my home. My happy place. My sanctuary. Right here, with you. I love you and I do want to be married to you, to make our family complete. The answer, to both your questions, is yes. Liv loves you and I love you. Let's get married.'

\* \* \* \* \*

# COMING SOON!

We really hope you enjoyed reading this book.
If you're looking for more romance
be sure to head to the shops when
new books are available on

## Thursday 25th April

# MILLS & BOON®

Coming next month

## DATING HIS IRRESISTIBLE RIVAL
### Juliette Hyland

The mood around the table was far too tight.

Leaning across, he made a silly face. 'I read one self-help book. It was all about keeping lists and staying organised. I mostly remember the raised lettering on the cover. It felt nice.' Knox shook his head, horror at the memory of trying to read it returning. It had been recommended by one of his teachers, a way to focus his tasks.

She'd meant well. One of the few adults in his young life who saw through the mad-at-the-world kid to the well of potential beneath it. *If* he turned in his assignments.

If it was surgery or medical knowledge, he kept everything locked in. If it was something else, there was a good chance that he'd forget. Thank goodness for auto bill pay and a monthly subscription for Post-it notes.

'I take it from the sour look on your face you were not a fan.' Miranda tapped his knee.

Knox looked down. Her fingers had already disappeared but part of him still felt her touch. 'I prefer fantasy. Wizards, dragons, magic.'

'Wizards and dragons?'

Her smile made his heart leap. 'Yep. The more fire magic the wizard uses, the better!' He made a few motions with his hands and she giggled.

He finished his coffee, hating the sign that their outing was nearing an end. 'I can't listen while running, though. For that, I have to have a beat. I tried listening to podcasts that I enjoy since there never seems to be enough time for all the ones I love, but I couldn't make myself actually run at a good clip.'

'Why do you have to run at a good clip?' Miranda raised her eyebrow as she used her straw to pull the last of the whipped topping from the bottom of the cup.

'I—' Knox sat there, trying to figure out the answer. 'I—'

'You already said that.' Miranda laid her hand on his knee and this time she didn't pull it away. 'Just something to think about.'

'Want to get dinner Sunday?' The question popped out, and he placed his hand over hers on his knee. He had no idea what this was, but he wanted to spend it with Miranda.

She looked at his hand then back at him. Her dark eyes holding his. 'Like a date?'

'Yeah. Exactly like a date.' He watched the wheels turn in her eyes. Saw the heat dance across her cheeks.

*Say yes.*

'All right.'

The urge to pump his fist was nearly overwhelming but he kept it in check. 'I'm looking forward to it.'

*Continue reading*
**DATING HIS IRRESISTIBLE RIVAL**
Juliette Hyland

*Available next month*
millsandboon.co.uk

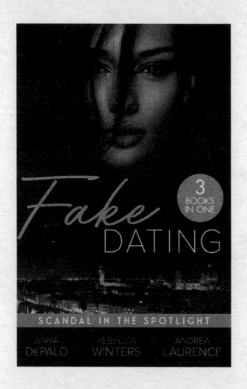

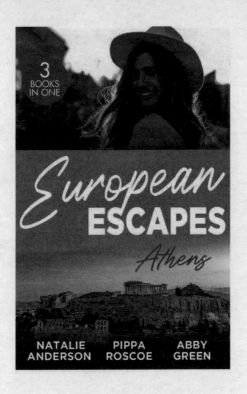

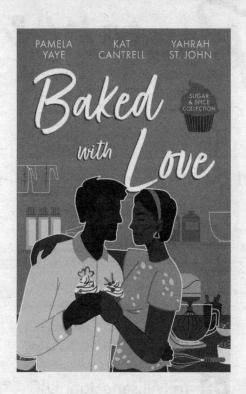

# LET'S TALK
## *Romance*

For exclusive extracts, competitions
and special offers, find us online:

**f** MillsandBoon

**X** @MillsandBoon

**⊙** @MillsandBoonUK

**♪** @MillsandBoonUK

Get in touch on 01413 063 232

# MILLS & BOON

## THE HEART OF ROMANCE

---

## A ROMANCE FOR EVERY READER

---

**MODERN** — Prepare to be swept off your feet by sophisticated, sexy and seductive heroes, in some of the world's most glamourous and romantic locations, where power and passion collide.

**HISTORICAL** — Escape with historical heroes from time gone by. Whether your passion is for wicked Regency Rakes, muscled Vikings or rugged Highlanders, awaken the romance of the past.

**MEDICAL** — Set your pulse racing with dedicated, delectable doctors in the high-pressure world of medicine, where emotions run high and passion, comfort and love are the best medicine.

*True Love* — Celebrate true love with tender stories of heartfelt romance, from the rush of falling in love to the joy a new baby can bring, and a focus on the emotional heart of a relationship.

**HEROES** — The excitement of a gripping thriller, with intense romance at its heart. Resourceful, true-to-life women and strong, fearless men face danger and desire - a killer combination!

 — From showing up to glowing up, these characters are on the path to leading their best lives and finding romance along the way – with plenty of sizzling spice!

To see which titles are coming soon, please visit

**millsandboon.co.uk/nextmonth**

# GET YOUR ROMANCE FIX!

Get the latest romance news, exclusive author interviews, story extracts and much more!

**blog.millsandboon.co.uk**

Tom Sharpe was b
College and at Pe
his National Serv
South Africa in 1
Non-European A
in Natal. He had
Pietermaritzburg from 1957 until 1961, when he was
deported. From 1963 to 1972 he was a lecturer in
History at the Cambridge College of Arts and
Technology. In 1986 he was awarded the XXXIIIème
Grand Prix d L'Humour Noir Xavier Forneret. He is
married and lives in Cambridge.

*Also by Tom Sharpe*
*in Pan Books*

Riotous Assembly
Indecent Exposure
Porterhouse Blue
Blott on the Landscape
The Great Pursuit
The Throwback
The Wilt Alternative
Ancestral Vices
Vintage Stuff

# Tom Sharpe

# WILT

### AND

# WILT ON HIGH

**PAN BOOKS**
IN ASSOCIATION WITH SECKER AND WARBURG

*Wilt* first published 1976 by Martin Secker and Warburg Ltd
and first published by Pan Books Ltd 1978 in association with
Martin Secker and Warburg Ltd

*Wilt on High* first published 1984 by Martin Secker and Warburg Ltd
and first published by Pan Books Ltd 1985 in association with
Martin Secker and Warburg Ltd

This combined edition published 1994 by Pan Books
a division of Macmillan General Books
Cavaye Place London SW10 9PG
and Basingstoke
in association with Martin Secker and Warburg Ltd

Associated companies throughout the world

ISBN 0 330 34147 2

1 3 5 7 9 8 6 4 2

A CIP catalogue record for this book is available from
the British Library

Printed and bound in Great Britain by
Cox & Wyman Ltd, Reading, Berkshire

# Wilt

for
Meat One

# 1

Whenever Henry Wilt took the dog for a walk, or, to be more accurate, when the dog took him, or, to be exact, when Mrs Wilt told them both to go and take themselves out of the house so that she could do her yoga exercises, he always took the same route. In fact the dog followed the route and Wilt followed the dog. They went down past the Post Office, across the playground, under the railway bridge and out on to the footpath by the river. A mile along the river and then under the railway line again and back through streets where the houses were bigger than Wilt's semi and where there were large trees and gardens and the cars were all Rovers and Mercedes. It was here that Clem, a pedigree Labrador, evidently feeling more at home, did his business while Wilt stood looking around rather uneasily, conscious that this was not his sort of neighbourhood and wishing it was. It was about the only time during their walk that he was at all aware of his surroundings. For the rest of the way Wilt's walk was an interior one and followed an itinerary completely at variance with his own appearance and that of his route. It was in fact a journey of wishful thinking, a pilgrimage along trails of remote possibility involving the irrevocable disappearance of Mrs Wilt, the sudden acquisition of wealth, power, what he would do if he was appointed Minister of Education or, better still, Prime Minister. It was partly concocted of a series of desperate expedients and partly in an unspoken dialogue so that anyone noticing Wilt (and most people didn't) might have seen his lips move occasionally and his mouth curl into what he fondly imagined was a sardonic smile as he dealt with questions or parried arguments with devastating repartee. It was on one of these walks taken in the rain after a particularly trying day at the Tech that Wilt first conceived the notion that he would only be able to fulfil his latent promise and call his life his own if some not entirely fortuitous disaster overtook his wife.

Like everything else in Henry Wilt's life it was not a sudden decision. He was not a decisive man. Ten years as an Assistant

Lecturer (Grade Two) at the Fenland College of Arts and Technology was proof of that. For ten years he had remained in the Liberal Studies Department teaching classes of Gasfitters, Plasterers, Bricklayers and Plumbers. Or keeping them quiet. And for ten long years he had spent his days going from classroom to classroom with two dozen copies of *Sons and Lovers* or Orwell's *Essays* or *Candide* or *The Lord of the Flies* and had done his damnedest to extend the sensibilities of Day-Release Apprentices with notable lack of success.

'Exposure to Culture', Mr Morris, the Head of Liberal Studies, called it but from Wilt's point of view it looked more like his own exposure to barbarism, and certainly the experience had undermined the ideals and illusions which had sustained him in his younger days. So had twelve years of marriage to Eva.

If Gasfitters could go through life wholly impervious to the emotional significance of the interpersonal relationships portrayed in *Sons and Lovers*, and coarsely amused by D. H. Lawrence's profound insight into the sexual nature of existence, Eva Wilt was incapable of such detachment. She hurled herself into cultural activities and self-improvement with an enthusiasm that tormented Wilt. Worse still, her notion of culture varied from week to week, sometimes embracing Barbara Cartland and Anya Seton, sometimes Ouspensky, sometimes Kenneth Clark, but more often the instructor at the Pottery Class on Tuesdays or the lecturer on Transcendental Meditation on Thursdays, so that Wilt never knew what he was coming home to except a hastily cooked supper, some forcibly expressed opinions about his lack of ambition, and a half-baked intellectual eclecticism that left him disoriented.

To escape from the memory of Gasfitters as putative human beings and of Eva in the lotus position, Wilt walked by the river thinking dark thoughts, made darker still by the knowledge that for the fifth year running his application to be promoted to Senior Lecturer was almost certain to be turned down and that unless he did something soon he would be doomed to Gasfitters Three and Plasterers Two – and to Eva – for the rest of his life. It was not a prospect to be borne. He would act decisively. Above his head a train thundered by. Wilt stood watching its dwindling lights and thought about accidents involving level crossings.

'He's in such a funny state these days,' said Eva Wilt, 'I don't know what to make of him.'

'I've given up trying with Patrick,' said Mavis Mottram studying Eva's vase critically. 'I think I'll put the lupin just a fraction of an inch to the left. Then it will help to emphasize the oratorical qualities of the rose. Now the iris over here. One must try to achieve an almost *audible* effect of contrasting colours. Contrapuntal, one might say.'

Eva nodded and sighed. 'He used to be so energetic,' she said, 'but now he just sits about the house watching telly. It's as much as I can do to get him to take the dog for a walk.'

'He probably misses the children,' said Mavis. 'I know Patrick does.'

'That's because he has some to miss,' said Eva Wilt bitterly. 'Henry can't even whip up the energy to have any.'

'I'm so sorry, Eva. I forgot,' said Mavis, adjusting the lupin so that it clashed more significantly with a geranium.

'There's no need to be sorry,' said Eva, who didn't number self-pity among her failings, 'I suppose I should be grateful. I mean, imagine having children like Henry. He's so uncreative, and besides children are so tiresome. They take up all one's creative energy.'

Mavis Mottram moved away to help someone else to achieve a contrapuntal effect, this time with nasturtiums and hollyhocks in a cerise bowl. Eva fiddled with her rose. Mavis was so lucky. She had Patrick, and Patrick Mottram was such an energetic man. Eva, in spite of her size, placed great emphasis on energy, energy and creativity, so that even quite sensible people who were not unduly impressionable found themselves exhausted after ten minutes in her company. In the lotus position at her yoga class she managed to exude energy, and her attempts at Transcendental Meditation had been likened to a pressure-cooker on simmer. And with creative energy there came enthusiasm, the febrile enthusiasms of the evidently unfulfilled woman for whom each new idea heralds the dawn of a new day and vice versa. Since the ideas she espoused were either trite or incomprehensible to her, her attachment to them was correspondingly brief and did nothing to fill the gap left in her life by Henry Wilt's lack of attainment. While he lived a violent life in his imagination, Eva, lacking any imagination at all, lived violently in fact. She threw herself into things, situations, new friends, groups and happenings with a reckless abandon that concealed the fact that she lacked the emotional stamina to stay for more than a moment. Now, as she backed away from her vase, she bumped into someone behind her.

'I beg your pardon,' she said and turned to find herself looking into a pair of dark eyes.

'No need to apologize,' said the woman in an American accent. She was slight and dressed with a simple scruffiness that was beyond Eva Wilt's moderate income.

'I'm Eva Wilt,' said Eva, who had once attended a class on Getting to Know People at the Oakrington Village College. 'My husband lectures at the Tech and we live at 34 Parkview Avenue.'

'Sally Pringsheim,' said the woman with a smile. 'We're in Rossiter Grove. We're over on a sabbatical. Gaskell's a biochemist.'

Eva Wilt accepted the distinctions and congratulated herself on her perspicacity about the blue jeans and the sweater. People who lived in Rossiter Grove were a cut above Parkview Avenue and husbands who were biochemists on sabbatical were also in the University. Eva Wilt's world was made up of such nuances.

'You know, I'm not at all that sure I could live with an oratorical rose,' said Sally Pringsheim. 'Symphonies are OK in auditoriums but I can do without them in vases.'

Eva stared at her with a mixture of astonishment and admiration. To be openly critical of Mavis Mottram's flower arrangements was to utter blasphemy in Parkview Avenue. 'You know, I've always wanted to say that,' she said with a sudden surge of warmth, 'but I've never had the courage.'

Sally Pringsheim smiled. 'I think one should always say what one thinks. Truth is so essential in any really meaningful relationship. I always tell G baby exactly what I'm thinking.'

'Gee baby?' said Eva Wilt.

'Gaskell's my husband,' said Sally. 'Not that he's really a husband. It's just that we've got this open-ended arrangement for living together. Sure, we're legal and all that, but I think it's important sexually to keep one's options open, don't you?'

By the time Eva got home her vocabulary had come to include several new words. She found Wilt in bed pretending to be asleep and woke him up and told him about Sally Pringsheim. Wilt turned over and tried to go back to sleep wishing to God she had stuck to her contrapuntal flower arrangements. Sexually open-ended freewheeling options were the last thing he wanted just now, and, coming from the wife of a biochemist who could afford to live in Rossiter Grove, didn't augur well for the future. Eva Wilt was too easily influenced by wealth, intellectual status and new acquaintances to be allowed out with a woman who believed that clitoral stimulation oralwise was a concomitant part of a fully emancipated relationship and that unisex was here to stay. Wilt had enough troubles with his own virility without having Eva demand that her conjugal rights be supplemented oralwise. He spent a restless night thinking dark thoughts about accidental deaths involving fast trains, level crossings, their Ford Escort and Eva's seat belt, and got up early and made himself breakfast. He was just going off to a nine o'clock lecture to Motor Mechanics Three when Eva came downstairs with a dreamy look on her face.

'I've just remembered something I wanted to ask you last night,' she said. 'What does "transexual diversification" mean?'

'Writing poems about queers,' said Wilt hastily and went out to the car. He drove down Parkview Avenue and got stuck in a traffic jam at the roundabout. He sat and cursed silently. He was thirty-four and his talents were being dissipated on MM 3 and a woman who was clearly educationally subnormal. Worst

11

of all, he had to recognize the truth of Eva's constant criticism that he wasn't a man. 'If you were a proper man,' she was always saying, 'you would show more initiative, You've got to assert yourself.'

Wilt asserted himself at the roundabout and got into an altercation with a man in a mini-bus. As usual, he came off second best.


'The problem with Wilt as I see it is that he lacks drive,' said the Head of English, himself a nerveless man with a tendency to see and solve problems with a degree of equivocation that made good his natural lack of authority.

The Promotions Committee nodded its joint head for the fifth year running.

'He may lack drive but he *is* committed,' said Mr Morris, fighting his annual rearguard on Wilt's behalf.

'Committed?' said the Head of Catering with a snort. 'Committed to what? Abortion, Marxism or promiscuity? It's bound to be one of the three. I've yet to come across a Liberal Studies lecturer who wasn't a crank, a pervert or a red-hot revolutionary and a good many have been all three.'

'Hear, hear,' said the Head of Mechanical Engineering, on whose lathes a demented student had once turned out several pipe bombs.

Mr Morris bristled. 'I grant you that one or two lecturers have been ... er ... a little overzealous politically but I resent the imputation that ...'

'Let's leave generalities aside and get back to Wilt,' said the Vice-Principal. 'You were saying that he is committed.'

'He needs encouragement,' said Mr Morris. 'Damn it, the man has been with us ten years and he's still only Grade Two.'

'That's precisely what I mean about his lacking drive,' said the Head of English. 'If he had been worth promoting he'd have been a Senior Lecturer by now.'

'I must say I agree,' said the Head of Geography. 'Any man who is content to spend ten years taking Gasfitters and Plumbers is clearly unfit to hold an administrative post.'

'Do we always have to promote solely for administrative

reasons?' Mr Morris asked wearily. 'Wilt happens to be a good teacher.'

'If I may just make a point,' said Dr Mayfield, the Head of Sociology, 'at this moment in time it is vital we bear in mind that, in the light of the forthcoming introduction of the Joint Honours degree in Urban Studies and Medieval Poetry, provisional approval for which degree by the Council of National Academic Awards I am happy to announce at least in principle, that we maintain a viable staff position in regard to Senior Lectureships by allocating places for candidates with specialist knowledge in particular spheres of academic achievement rather than—'

'If I may just interrupt for a moment, in or out of time,' said Dr Board, Head of Modern Languages, 'are you saying we should have Senior Lectureships for highly qualified specialists who can't teach rather than promote Assistant Lecturers without doctorates who can?'

'If Dr Board had allowed me to continue, said Dr Mayfield, 'he would have understood that I was saying . . .'

'I doubt it,' said Dr Board, 'quite apart from your syntax . . .'

And so for the fifth year running Wilt's promotion was forgotten. The Fenland College of Arts and Technology was expanding. New degree courses proliferated and more students with fewer qualifications poured in to be taught by more staff with higher qualifications until one day the Tech would cease to be a mere Tech and rise in status to become a Poly. It was the dream of every Head of Department and in the process Wilt's self-esteem and the hopes of Eva Wilt were ignored.

Wilt heard the news before lunch in the canteen.

'I'm sorry, Henry,' said Mr Morris as they lined up with their trays, 'it's this wretched economic squeeze. Even Modern Languages had to take a cut. They only got two promotions through.'

Wilt nodded. It was what he had come to expect. He was in the wrong department, in the wrong marriage and in the wrong life. He took his fish fingers across to a table in the corner and ate by himself. Around him other members of staff sat discussing A-level prospects and who was going to sit on the course board next term. They taught Maths or Economics or English, subjects that counted and where promotion was easy. Liberal Studies didn't count and promotion was out of the question. It was as simple as that. Wilt finished his lunch and went up to the reference library to look up Insulin in the Pharmacopoeia. He had an idea it was the one untraceable poison.

At five to two, none the wiser, he went down to Room 752 to extend the sensibilities of fifteen apprentice butchers, designated on the timetable as Meat One. As usual they were late and drunk.

'We've been drinking Bill's health,' they told him when they drifted in at ten past two.

'Really?' said Wilt, handing out copies of *The Lord of the Flies*. 'And how is he?'

'Bloody awful,' said a large youth with 'Stuff Off' painted across the back of his leather jacket. 'He's puking his guts out. It's his birthday and he had four Vodkas and a Babycham . . .'

'We'd got to the part where Piggy is in the forest,' said Wilt, heading them off a discussion of what Bill had drunk for his birthday. He reached for a board duster and rubbed a drawing of a Dutch Cap off the blackboard.

'That's Mr Sedgwick's trademark,' said one of the butchers, 'he's always going on about contraceptives and things. He's got a thing about them.'

'A thing about them?' said Wilt loyally.

'You know, birth control. Well, he used to be a Catholic, didn't he? And now he's not, he's making up for lost time,' said a small pale-faced youth unwrapping a Mars Bar.

'Someone should tell him about the pill,' said another youth lifting his head somnolently from the desk. 'You can't feel a thing with a Frenchie. You get more thrill with the pill.'

'I suppose you do,' said Wilt, 'but I understood there were side-effects.'

'Depends which side you want it,' said a lad with sideburns.

Wilt turned back to *The Lord of the Flies* reluctantly. He had read the thing two hundred times already.

'Now Piggy goes into the forest . . .' he began, only to be stopped by another butcher, who evidently shared his distaste for the misfortunes of Piggy.

'You only get bad effects with the pill if you use ones that are high in oestrogen.

'That's very interesting,' said Wilt. 'Oestrogen? You seem to know a lot about it.'

'Old girl down our street got a bloodclot in her leg . . .'

'Silly old clot,' said the Mars Bar.

'Listen,' said Wilt. 'Either we hear what Peter has to tell us about the effects of the pill or we get on and read about Piggy.'

'Fuck Piggy,' said the sideburns.

'Right,' said Wilt heartily, 'then keep quiet.'

'Well,' said Peter, 'this old girl, well she wasn't all that old, maybe thirty, she was on the pill and she got this bloodclot and the doctor told my auntie it was the oestrogen and she'd better take a different sort of pill just in case and the old girl down the street, her old man had to go and have a vasectomy so's she wouldn't have another bloodclot.'

'Buggered if anyone's going to get me to have a vasectomy,' said the Mars Bar, 'I want to know I'm all there.'

'We all have ambitions,' said Wilt.

'Nobody's going to hack away at my knackers with a bloody great knife,' said the sideburns.

'Nobody'd want to,' said someone else.

'What about the bloke whose missus you banged,' said the Mars Bar. 'I bet he wouldn't mind having a go.'

Wilt applied the sanction of Piggy again and got them back on to vasectomy.

'Anyway, it's not irreversible any more,' said Peter. 'They can put a tiny little gold tap in and you can turn it on when you want a nipper.'

'Go on! That's not true.'

'Well, not on the National Health you can't, but if you pay they can. I read about it in a magazine. They've been doing experiments in America.'

'What happens if the washer goes wrong?' asked the Mars Bar.

'I suppose they call a plumber in.'

Wilt sat and listened while Meat One ranged far and wide about vasectomy and the coil and Indians getting free transistors and the plane that landed at Audley End with a lot of illegal immigrants and what somebody's brother who was a policeman in Brixton said about blacks and how the Irish were just as bad and bombs and back to Catholics and birth control and who'd want to live in Ireland where you couldn't even buy French letters and so back to the Pill. And all the time his mind filled itself obsessively with ways and means of getting rid of Eva. A diet of birth-control pills high on oestrogen? If he ground them up and mixed them with the Ovaltine she took at bedtime there was a chance she'd develop bloodclots all over the place in no time at all. Wilt put the notion out of his head. Eva with bloodclots was too awful to stomach, and anyway it might not work. No, it would have to be something quick, certain and painless. Preferably an accident.

At the end of the hour Wilt collected the books and made his way back to the Staff Room. He had a free period. On the way he passed the site of the new Administration block. The ground had been cleared and the builders had moved in and were boring pile holes for the foundations. Wilt stopped and watched as the drilling machine wound slowly down into the ground. They were making wide holes. Very wide. Big enough for a body.

'How deep are you going?' he asked one of the workmen.

'Thirty feet.'

'Thirty feet?' said Wilt. 'When's the concrete going in?'

'Monday, with any luck,' said the man.

Wilt passed on. A new and quite horrible idea had just occurred to him.

# 2

It was one of Eva Wilt's better days. She had days, better days, and one of those days. Days were just days when nothing went wrong and she got the washing-up done and the front room vacuumed and the windows washed and the beds made and the bath Vimmed and the lavatory pan Harpicked and went round to the Harmony Community Centre and helped with Xeroxing or sorted old clothes for the Jumble Sale and generally made herself useful and came home for lunch and went to the library and had tea with Mavis or Susan or Jean and talked about life and how seldom Henry made love to her even perfunctorily nowadays and how she had missed her opportunity by refusing a bank clerk who was a manager now and came home and made Henry's supper and went out to Yoga or Flower Arrangement or Meditation or Pottery and finally climbed into bed with the feeling that she had got something done.

On one of those days nothing went right. The activities were exactly the same but each episode was tainted with some minor disaster like the fuse blowing on the vacuum-cleaner or the drain in the sink getting blocked with a piece of carrot so that by the time Henry came home he was either greeted by silence or subjected to a quite unwarranted exposé of all his faults and shortcomings. On one of those days Wilt usually took the dog for an extended walk via the Ferry Path Inn and spent a restless night getting up and going to the bath, thus nullifying the cleansing qualities of the Har, puffed round the pan and providing her with use to point out his faults once again in the morni

'What the hell am I supposed to do?' he had asked after one of those nights. 'If I pull the chain you grumble because I've woken you up and if I don't you say it looks nasty in the morning.'

'Well, it does, and in any case you don't have to wash all the Harpic off the sides. And don't say you don't. I've seen you. You aim it all the way round so that it all gets taken off. You do it quite deliberately.'

'If I pulled the chain it would all get flushed off anyway and you'd get woken up into the bargain,' Wilt told her, conscious that he did make a habit of aiming at the Harpic. He had a grudge against the stuff.

'Why can't you just wait until the morning? And anyway it serves you right,' she continued, forestalling his obvious answer, 'for drinking all that beer. You're supposed to be taking Clem for a walk, not swilling ale in that horrid pub.'

'To pee or not to pee, that is the question,' said Wilt helping himself to All-Bran. 'What do you expect me to do? Tie a knot in the damned thing?'

'It wouldn't make any difference to me if you did,' said Eva bitterly.

'It would make a hell of a lot of difference to me, thank you very much.'

'I was talking about our sex life and you know it.'

'Oh, that,' said Wilt.

But that was on one of those days.

On one of her better days something unexpected happened to inject the daily round with a new meaning and to awake in her those dormant expectations that somehow everything would suddenly change for the better and stay that way. It was on such expectations that her faith in life was based. They were the spiritual equivalent of the trivial activities that kept her busy and Henry subdued. On one of her better days the sun shone brighter, the floor in the hall gleamed brighter and Eva Wilt was brighter herself and hummed 'Some day my prince will come' while Hoovering the stairs. On one of her better days Eva went forth to meet the world with a disarming goodheartedness and awoke in others the very same expectations that so thrilled her in herself. And on one of her better days Henry had to get his own supper and if he was wise kept out of the house as long as possible. Eva Wilt's expectations demanded something a sight more invigorating than Henry Wilt after a day at the Tech. It was on the evenings of such days that he came nearest to genuinely deciding to murder her and to hell with the consequences.

On this particular day she was on her way to the Community Centre when she ran into Sally Pringsheim. It was one of those entirely fortuitous meetings that resulted from Eva making her way on foot instead of by bicycle and going through Rossiter Grove instead of straight down Parkview Avenue which was half a mile shorter. Sally was just driving out of the gate in a Mercedes with a P registration which meant it was brand new. Eva noted the fact and smiled accordingly.

'How funny me running into you like this,' she said brightly as Sally stopped the car and unlocked the door.

'Can I give you a lift? I'm going into town to look for something casual to wear tonight. Gaskell's got some Swedish professor coming over from Heidelberg and we're taking him to Ma Tante's.'

Eva Wilt climbed in happily, her mind computing the cost of the car and the house and the significance of wearing something casual at Ma Tante's (where she had heard that starters like Prawn Cocktails cost 95p) and the fact that Dr Pringsheim entertained Swedish professors when they came to Ipford.

'I was going to walk to town,' she lied. 'Henry's taken the car and it's such a lovely day.'

'Gaskell's bought a bicycle. He says it's quicker and it keeps him fit,' said Sally, thus condemning Henry Wilt to yet another misfortune. Eva made a note to see that he bought a bike at the police auction and cycled to work in rain or snow. 'I was thinking of trying Felicity Fashions for a shantung poncho. I don't know what they're like but I've been told they're good. Professor Grant's wife goes there and she says they have the best selection.'

'I'm sure they must have,' said Eva Wilt, whose patronage of Felicity Fashions had consisted of looking in the window and wondering who on earth could afford dresses at forty pounds. Now she knew. They drove into town and parked in the multi-storey car park. By that time Eva had stored a lot more information about the Pringsheims in her memory. They came from California. Sally had met Gaskell while hitchhiking through Arizona. She had been to Kansas State but had dropped out to live on a commune. There had been other men in her life. Gaskell loathed cats. They gave him hay fever. Women's Lib meant more than burning your bra. It meant total commitment to the programme of women's superiority over men. Lóve was great if you didn't let it get to you. Compost was in and colour TV out. Gaskell's father had owned a chain of stores which was sordid. Money was handy and Rossiter Grove was a bore. Above all, fucking had to be, just *had* to be fun whichever way you looked at it.

Eva Wilt received this information with a jolt. In her circle 'fuck' was a word husbands used when they hit their thumbs with hammers. When Eva used it she did so in the isolation of the bathroom and with a wistfulness that robbed it of its crudity and imbued it with a splendid virility so that a good fuck became the most distant and abstract of all her expectations and quite removed from Henry's occasional early morning fumblings. And if 'fuck' was reserved for the bathroom, fucking was even more remote. It suggested an almost continuous activity, a familiar occurrence that was both casual and satisfying and added a new dimension to life. Eva Wilt stumbled out of the car and followed Sally to Felicity Fashions in a state of shock.

If fucking was fun, shopping with Sally Pringsheim was a revelation. It was marked by a decisiveness that was truly breathtaking. Where Eva would have hummed and haaed, Sally selected and having selected moved on down the racks, discarded things she didn't like leaving them hanging over chairs, seized others, glanced at them and said she supposed they would do with a bored acceptance that was infectious, and left the shop with a pile of boxes containing two hundred pounds' worth of shantung ponchos, silk summer coats, scarves and blouses. Eva Wilt had spent seventy on a pair of yellow lounging pyjamas and a raincoat with lapels and a belt that Sally said was pure Gatsby.

'Now all you need is the hat and you'll be it,' she said as they loaded the boxes into the car. They bought the hat, a trilby, and then had coffee at the Mombasa Coffee House where Sally leant across the table intensely, smoking a long thin cigar, and talking about body contact in a loud voice so

20

that Eva was conscious that the women at several nearby tables had stopped talking and were listening rather disapprovingly.

'Gaskell's nipples drive me wild,' Sally said. 'They drive him wild too when I suck them.'

Eva drank her coffee and wondered what Henry would do if she took it into her head to suck his nipples. Drive him wild was hardly the word and besides she was beginning to regret having spent seventy pounds. That would drive him wild too. Henry didn't approve of credit cards. But she was enjoying herself too much to let the thought of his reaction spoil her day.

'I think teats are so important,' Sally went on. Two women at the next table paid their bill and walked out.

'I suppose they must be,' said Eva Wilt uneasily. 'I've never had much use for mine.'

'Haven't you?' said Sally. 'We'll have to do something about that.'

'I don't see that there is much anyone can do about it,' said Eva. 'Henry never takes his pyjamas off and my nightie gets in the way.'

'Don't tell me you wear things in bed. Oh you poor thing. And nighties, God, how humiliating for you! I mean it's typical of a male-dominated society, all this costume differentiation. You must be suffering from touch deprivation. Gaskell says it's as bad as vitamin deficiency.'

'Well, Henry is always tired when he gets home,' Eva told her. 'And I go out a lot.'

'I'm not surprised,' said Sally, 'Gaskell says male fatigue is a symptom of penile insecurity. Is Henry's big or small?'

'Well it depends,' said Eva hoarsely. 'Sometimes it's big and sometimes it isn't.'

'I much prefer men with small ones,' said Sally, 'they try so much harder.'

They finished their coffee and went back to the car discussing Gaskell's penis and his theory that in a sexually undifferentiated society nipple stimulation would play an increasingly important role in developing the husband's sense of his hermaphroditic nature.

'He's written an article on it,' Sally said as they drove home. 'It's called "The Man As Mother". It was published in *Suck* last year.'

'Suck?' said Eva.

'Yes, it's a journal published by the Society for Undifferentiated Sexual Studies in Kansas. G's done a lot of work for them on animal behaviour. He did his thesis on Role Play in Rats there.'

'That sounds very interesting,' said Eva uncertainly. Roll or role? Whichever it was it was impressive and certainly Henry's occasional pieces on Day Release Apprentices and Literature in the *Liberal Studies Quarterly* hardly measured up to Dr Pringsheim's monographs.

'Oh I don't know. It's all so obvious really. If you put two male rats together in a cage long enough one of them is simply bound to develop active tendencies and the other passive ones,' said Sally wearily. 'But Gaskell was absolutely furious. He thought they ought to alternate. That's G all over. I told him how silly he was being. I said, "G honey, rats are practically undifferentiated anyway. I mean how can you expect them to be able to make an existential choice?" and you know what he said? He said, "Pubic baby, rats are the paradigm. Just remember that and you won't go far wrong. Rats are the paradigm." What do you think of that?'

'I think rats are rather horrid,' said Eva without thinking. Sally laughed and put her hand on her knee.

'Oh Eva, darling,' she murmured, 'you're so adorably down to earth. No, I'm not taking you back to Parkview Avenue. You're coming home with me for a drink and lunch. I'm simply dying to see you in those lemon loungers.'

They turned into Rossiter Grove.

If rats were a paradigm for Dr Pringsheim, Printers Three were a paradigm for Henry Wilt, though of a rather different sort. They represented all that was most difficult, insensitive and downright bloodyminded about Day Release Classes and to make matters worse the sods thought they were literate because they could actually read and Voltaire was an idiot because he made everything go wrong for Candide. Coming after Nursery Nurses and during his Stand-In period, Printers Three brought out the worst in him. They had obviously brought out the worst in Cecil Williams who should have been taking them.

'It's the second week he's been off sick,' they told Wilt.

'I'm not at all surprised,' said Wilt. 'You lot are enough to make anyone sick.'

'We had one bloke went and gassed himself. Pinkerton his name was. He took us for a term and made us read this book *Jude the Obscure*. That wasn't half a depressing book. All about this twit Jude.'

'I had an idea it was,' said Wilt.

'Next term old Pinky didn't come back. He went down by the river and stuck a pipe up the exhaust and gassed himself.'

'I can't say I blame him,' said Wilt.

'Well I like that. He was supposed to set us an example.'

Wilt looked at the class grimly.

'I'm sure he had that in mind when he gassed himself,' he said. 'And now if you'll just get on and read quietly, eat quietly and smoke so that no one can see you from the Admin block, I've got work to do.'

'Work? You lot don't know what work is. All you do is sit at a desk all day and read. Call that work? Buggered if I do and they pay you to do it ...'

'Shut up,' said Wilt with startling violence. 'Shut your stupid trap.'

'Who's going to make me?' said the Printer.

Wilt tried to control his temper and for once found it impossible. There was something incredibly arrogant about Printers Three.

'I am,' he shouted.

'You and who else? You couldn't make a mouse shut its trap, not if you tried all day.'

Wilt stood up. 'You fucking little shit,' he shouted. 'You dirty snivelling ...'

'I must say, Henry, I'd have expected you to show more restraint,' said the Head of Liberal Studies an hour later when Wilt's nose had stopped bleeding and the Tech Sister had put a Band-Aid on his eyebrow.

'Well it wasn't my class and they got my goat by gloating about Pinkerton's suicide. If Williams hadn't been off sick it wouldn't have happened,' Wilt explained. 'He's always sick when he has to take Printers Three.'

Mr Morris shook his head dispiritedly. 'I don't care who they were. You simply can't go around assaulting students . . .'

'Assaulting students? I never touched . . .'

'All right, but you did use offensive language. Bob Fenwick was in the next classroom and he heard you call this Allison fellow a fucking little shit and an evil-minded moron. Now, is it any wonder he took a poke at you?'

'I suppose not,' said Wilt. 'I shouldn't have lost my temper. I'm sorry.'

'In that case we'll just forget it happened,' said Mr Morris. 'But just remember if I'm to get you a Senior Lectureship I can't have you blotting your copybook having punch-ups with students.'

'I didn't have a punch-up,' said Wilt, 'he punched me.'

'Well, let's just hope he doesn't go to the police and charge you with assault. That's the last sort of publicity we want.'

'Just take me off Printers Three,' said Wilt, 'I've had my fill of the brutes.'


He went down the corridor and collected his coat and brief-case from the Staff Room. His nose felt twice its normal size and his eyebrow hurt abominably. On his way out to the car park he passed several other members of staff but no one stopped to ask him what had happened. Henry Wilt passed unnoticed out of the Tech and got into his car. He shut the door and sat for several minutes watching the piledrivers at work on the new block. Up, down, up, down. Nails in a coffin. And one day, one inevitable day he would be in his coffin, still unnoticed, still an Assistant Lecturer (Grade Two) and quite forgotten by everyone except some lout in Printers Three who would always remember the day he had punched a

Liberal Studies lecturer on the nose and got away with it. He'd probably boast about it to his grandchildren.

Wilt started the car and drove out on to the main road filled with loathing for Printers Three, the Tech, life in general and himself in particular. He understood now why terrorists were prepared to sacrifice themselves for the good of some cause. Given a bomb and a cause he would cheerfully have blown himself and any innocent bystanders to Kingdom Come just to prove for one glorious if brief moment that he was an effective force. But he had neither bomb nor cause. Instead he drove home recklessly and parked outside 34 Parkview Avenue. Then he unlocked the front door and went inside.

There was a strange smell in the hall. Some sort of perfume. Musky and sweet. He put his brief-case down and looked into the living-room. Eva was evidently out. He went into the kitchen and put the kettle on and felt his nose. He would have a good look at it in the bathroom mirror. He was halfway upstairs and conscious that there was a positively miasmic quality about the perfume when he was brought to a halt. Eva Wilt stood in the bedroom doorway in a pair of astonishingly yellow pyjamas with enormously flared trousers. She looked quite hideous, and to make matters worse she was smoking a long thin cigarette in a long thin holder and her mouth was a brilliant red.

'Penis baby,' she murmured hoarsely and swayed. 'Come in here. I'm going to suck your nipples till you come me oral-wise.'

Wilt turned and fled downstairs. The bitch was drunk. It was one of her better days. Without waiting to turn the kettle off, Henry Wilt went out of the front door and got back into the car. He wasn't staying around to have her suck his nipples. He'd had all he could take for one day.

# 3

Eva Wilt went downstairs and looked for penis baby half-heartedly. For one thing she didn't want to find him and for another she didn't feel like sucking his nipples and for a third she knew she shouldn't have spent seventy pounds on a raincoat and a pair of beach pyjamas she could have got for thirty at Blowdens. She didn't need them and she couldn't see herself walking down Parkview Avenue looking like The Great Gatsby. Besides, she felt a bit sick.

Still, he had left the kettle on so he must be somewhere. It wasn't like Henry to go out and leave the kettle on. She looked in the lounge. It had been the sitting-room until lunchtime when Sally called her sitting-room a lounge. She looked in the dining-room, now the diner, and even in the garden but Henry had vanished, taking with him the car, and her hopes that nipple-sucking would bring new meaning to their marriage and put an end to her body contact deprivation. Finally she gave up the search and made herself a nice pot of tea and sat in the kitchen wondering what on earth had induced her to marry a male chauvinist pig like Henry Wilt who wouldn't have known a good fuck if he had been handed one on a plate and whose idea of a sophisticated evening was a boneless chicken curry at the New Delhi and a performance of *King Lear* at the Guild-hall. Why couldn't she have married someone like Gaskell Pringsheim who entertained Swedish professors at Ma Tante and who understood the importance of clitoral stimulation as a necessary con-something-or-other of a truly satisfying interpersonal penetration? Other people still found her attractive. Patrick Mottram did and so did John Frost who taught her pottery, and Sally had said she was lovely. Eva sat staring into space, the space between the washing-up rack and the Kenwood mixer Henry had given her for Christmas, and thought about Sally and how she had looked at her so strangely when she was changing into her lemon loungers. Sally had stood in the doorway of the Pringsheims' bedroom, smoking a cigar and watching her movements with a sensual calculation that had made Eva blush.

'Darling, you have such a lovely body,' she had said as Eva turned hurriedly and scrambled into the trousers to avoid revealing the hole in her panties. 'You mustn't let it go to waste.'

'Do you really think they suit me?'

But Sally had been staring at her breasts intently. 'Booby baby,' she murmured. Eva Wilt's breasts were prominent and Henry, in one of his many off moments, had once said something about the dugs of hell going dingalingaling for you but not for me. Sally was more appreciative, and had insisted that Eva remove her bra and burn it. They had gone down to the kitchen and had drunk Tequila and had put the bra on a dish with a sprig of holly on it and Sally had poured brandy over it and had set it alight. They had to carry the dish out into the garden because it smelt so horrible and smoked so much and they had lain on the grass laughing as it smouldered. Looking back on the episode Eva regretted her action. It had been a good bra with double-stretch panels designed to give confidence where a woman needs it, as the TV adverts put it. Still, Sally had said she owed it to herself as a free woman and with two drinks inside her Eva was in no mood to argue.

'You've got to feel free,' Sally had said. 'Free to be. Free to be.'

'Free to be what?' said Eva.

'Yourself, darling,' Sally whispered, 'your secret self,' and had touched her tenderly where Eva Wilt, had she been sober and less elated, would staunchly have denied having a self. They had gone back into the house and had lunch, a mixture of more Tequila, salad and Ryvita and cottage cheese which Eva, whose appetite for food was almost as omnivorous as her enthusiasm for new experiences, found unsatisfying. She had hinted as much but Sally had poohpoohed the idea of three good meals a day.

'It's not good caloriewise to have a high starch intake,' she said, 'and besides it's not how much you put into yourself but what. Sex and food, honey, are much the same. A little a lot is better than a lot a little.' She had poured Eva another Tequila, insisted she take a bite of lemon before knocking it back and had helped her upstairs to the big bedroom with the big bed and the big mirror in the ceiling.

'It's time for TT,' she said adjusting the slats of the Venetian blinds.

'Tea tea,' Eva mumbled, 'but we've just had din din.'

'Touch Therapy, darling,' said Sally and pushed her gently back on to the bed. Eva Wilt stared up at her reflection in the mirror; a large woman, two large women in yellow pyjamas lying on a large bed, a large crimson bed; two large women without yellow pyjamas on a large crimson bed; four women naked on a large crimson bed.

'Oh Sally, no Sally.'

'Darling,' said Sally and silenced her protest oralwise. It had been a startlingly new experience though only partly remembered. Eva had fallen asleep before the Touch Therapy had got well under way and had woken an hour later to find Sally fully dressed standing by the bed with a cup of black coffee.

'Oh I do feel bad,' Eva said, referring as much to her moral condition as to her physical.

'Drink this and you'll feel better.'

Eva had drunk the coffee and got dressed while Sally explained that post-contact inhibitory depression was a perfectly natural reaction to Touch Therapy at first.

'You'll find it comes naturally after the first few sessions. You'll probably break down and cry and scream and then feel tremendously liberated and relieved.'

'Do you think so? I'm sure I don't know.'

Sally had driven her home. 'You and Henry must come to our barbecue Thursday night,' she said. 'I know G baby will want to meet you. You'll like him. He's a breast baby. He'll go crazy about you.'

'I tell you she was pissed,' said Wilt as he sat in the Braintrees' kitchen while Peter Braintree opened a bottle of beer for him. 'Pissed and wearing some godawful yellow pyjamas and smoking a cigarette in a long bloody holder.'

'What did she say?'

'Well if you must know, she said, "Come here ..."' No, it's too much. I have a perfectly foul day at the Tech. Morris tells me I haven't got my senior lectureship. Williams is off sick again so I lose a free period. I get punched in the face by a great lout in Printers Three and I come home to a drunk wife who calls me penis baby.'

'She called you what?' said Peter Braintree, staring at him.

'You heard me.'

'Eva called you penis baby? I don't believe it.'

'Well you go round there and see what she calls you,' said Wilt bitterly, 'and don't blame me if she sucks your nipples off oralwise while she's about it.'

'Good Lord. Is that what she threatened to do?'

'That and more,' said Wilt.

'It doesn't sound like Eva. It really doesn't.'

'It didn't fucking look like her either, come to that. She was all dolled up in yellow beach pyjamas. You should have seen the colour. It would have made a buttercup look drab. And she'd got some ghastly scarlet lipstick smeared round her mouth and she was smoking ... She hasn't smoked for six years and then all this penis baby nipple-sucking stuff. And oralwise.'

Peter Braintree shook his head. 'That's a filthy word,' he said.

'It's a perfectly filthy act too, if you ask me,' said Wilt.

'Well, I must say it all sounds pretty peculiar,' said Braintree, 'God knows what I'd do if Susan came home and started insisting on sucking my teats.'

'Do what I did. Get out of the house,' said Wilt. 'And anyway it isn't just nipples either. Damn it, we've been married twelve long years. It's a bit late in the day to start arsing about oralwise. The thing is she's on this sexual liberation kick. She came home last night from Mavis Mottram's flower arrangement do jabbering about clitoral stimulation and openended freewheeling sexual options.'

'Freewheeling what?'

'Sexual options. Perhaps I've got it wrong. I know sexual options came into it somewhere. I was half asleep at the time.'

'Where the hell did she get all this from?' asked Braintree.

29

'Some bloody Yank called Sally Pringsheim,' said Wilt. 'You know what Eva's like. I mean she can smell intellectual clap-trap a mile off and homes in on it like a bloody dung-beetle heading for an open sewer. You've no idea how many phoney "latest ideas" I've had to put up with. Well, most of them I can manage to live with. I just let her get on with it and go my own quiet way, but when it comes to participating oralwise while she blathers on about Women's Lib, well you can count me out.'

'What I don't understand about Sexual Freedom and Women's Lib is why you have to go back to the nursery to be liberated,' said Braintree. 'There seems to be this loony idea that you have to be passionately in love all the time.'

'Apes,' said Wilt morosely.

'Apes? What about apes?'

'It's all this business about the animal model. If animals do it then humans must. Territorial Imperative and the Naked Ape. You stand everything on its head and instead of aspiring you retrogress a million years. Hitch your wagon to an orang-outang. The egalitarianism of the lowest common denominator.'

'I don't quite see what that has to do with sex,' said Braintree.

'Nor do I,' said Wilt. They went down to the Pig In A Poke and got drunk.

It was midnight before Wilt got home and Eva was asleep. Wilt climbed surreptitiously into bed and lay in the darkness thinking about high levels of oestrogen.

In Rossiter Grove the Pringsheims came back from Ma Tante's tired and bored.

'Swedes are the bottom,' said Sally as she undressed.

Gaskell sat down and took off his shoes. 'Ungstrom's all right. His wife has just left him for a low-temperature physicist at Cambridge. He's not usually so depressed.'

'You could have fooled me. And talking about wives, I've met the most unliberated woman you've ever set eyes on. Name of Eva Wilt. She's got boobs like cantaloupes.'

'Don't,' said Dr Pringsheim, 'if there's one thing I don't need right now it's unliberated wives with breasts.' He climbed into bed and took his glasses off.

'I had her round here today.'

'Had her?'

Sally smiled, 'Gaskell, honey, you've got a toadsome mind.'

Gaskell Pringsheim smiled myopically at himself in the mirror above. He was proud of his mind. 'I just know you, lover,' he said, 'I know your funny little habits. And while we're on the subject of habits what are all those boxes in the guest room? You haven't been spending money again? You know our budget this month ...'

Sally flounced into bed. 'Budget fudget,' she said, 'I'm sending them all back tomorrow.'

'All?'

'Well, not all, but most. I had to impress booby baby somehow.'

'You didn't have to buy half a shop just to ...'

'Gaskell, honey, if you would just let me finish,' said Sally, 'she's a manic, a lovely, beautiful, obsessive compulsive manic. She can't sit still for half a minute without tidying and cleaning and polishing and washing up.'

'That's all we need, a manic compulsive woman around the house all the time. Who needs two?'

'Two? I'm not manic.'

'You're manic enough for me,' said Gaskell.

'But this one's got boobs, baby, boobs. Anyway I've invited them over on Thursday for the barbecue.'

'What the hell for?'

'Well, if you won't buy me a dishwasher like I've asked you a hundred times, I'm going out to get me one. A nice manic compulsive dishwasher with boobs on.'

'Jesus,' sighed Gaskell, 'are you a bitch.'


'Henry Wilt, you are a sod,' Eva said next morning. Wilt sat up in bed. He felt terrible. His nose was even more painful than the day before, his head ached and he had spent much of the night expunging the Harpic from the bowl in the bathroom.

He was in no mood to be woken and told he was a sod. He looked at the clock. It was eight o'clock and he had Bricklayers Two at nine. He got out of bed and made for the bathroom.

'Did you hear what I said?' Eva demanded, getting out of bed herself.

'I heard,' said Wilt, and saw that she was naked. Eva Wilt naked at eight o'clock in the morning was almost as startling a sight as Eva Wilt drunk, smoking and dressed in lemon yellow pyjamas at six o'clock at night. And even less enticing. 'What the hell are you going about like that for?'

'If it comes to that, what's wrong with your nose? I suppose you got drunk and fell down. It looks all red and swollen.'

'It *is* all red and swollen. And if you must know I didn't fall down. Now for goodness sake get out of the way. I've got a lecture at nine.'

He pushed past her and went into the bathroom and looked at his nose. It looked awful. Eva followed him in. 'If you didn't fall on it what did happen?' she demanded.

Wilt squeezed foam from an aerosol and patted it gingerly on his chin.

'Well?' said Eva.

Wilt picked up his razor and put it under the hot tap. 'I had an accident,' he muttered.

'With a lamp-post, I suppose. I knew you'd been drinking.'

'With a Printer,' said Wilt indistinctly and started to shave.

'With a Printer?'

'To be precise, I got punched in the face by a particularly pugnacious apprentice printer.'

Eva stared at him in the mirror. 'You mean to say a student hit you in the classroom?'

Wilt nodded.

'I hope you hit him back.'

Wilt cut himself.

'No I bloody didn't,' he said, dabbing his chin with a finger. 'Now look what you've made me do.'

Eva ignored his complaint. 'Well you should have. You're not a man. You should have hit him back.'

Wilt put down the razor. 'And got the sack. Got hauled up in court for assaulting a student. Now that's what I call a brilliant idea.' He reached for the sponge and washed his face.

Eva retreated to the bedroom satisfied. There would be no mention of her lemon loungers now. She had taken his mind off her own little extravagance and given him a sense of grievance that would keep him occupied for the time being. By the time she had finished dressing, Wilt had eaten a bowl of All-Bran, drunk half a cup of coffee and was snarled up in a traffic jam at the roundabout. Eva went downstairs and had her own breakfast and began the daily round of washing up and Hoovering and cleaning the bath and ...

'Commitment,' said Dr Mayfield, 'to an integrated approach is an essential element in ...'

The Joint Committee for the Further Development of Liberal Studies was in session. Wilt squirmed in his chair and wished to hell it wasn't. Dr Mayfield's paper 'Cerebral Content and the Non-Academic Syllabus' held no interest for him, and besides, it was delivered in such convoluted sentences and with so much monotonous fervour that Wilt found it difficult to stay awake. He stared out of the window at the machines boring away on the site of the new Admin block. There was a reality about the work going on down there that was in marked contrast to the impractical theories Dr Mayfield was expounding. If the man really thought he could instil Cerebral Content, whatever that was, into Gasfitters Three he was out of his mind. Worse still, his blasted paper was bound to provoke an argument at question time. Wilt looked round the room. The various factions were all there, the New Left, the Left, the Old Left, the Indifferent Centre, the Cultural Right and the Reactionary Right.

Wilt classed himself with the Indifferents. In earlier years he had belonged to the Left politically and to the Right culturally. In other words he had banned the bomb, supported abortion and the abolition of private education and had been against capital punishment, thus earning himself something of a reputation as a radical while at the same time advocating a

33

return to the craft of the wheelwright, the blacksmith and the handloom weaver which had done much to undermine the efforts of the Technical staff to instil in their students an appreciation of the opportunities provided by modern technology. Time and the intransigent coarseness of Plasterers had changed all that. Wilt's ideals had vanished, to be replaced by the conviction that the man who said the pen was mightier than the sword ought to have tried reading *The Mill on the Floss* to Motor Mechanics Three before he opened his big mouth. In Wilt's view, the sword had much to recommend it.

As Dr Mayfield droned on, as question time with its ideological arguments followed, Wilt studied the pile hole on the building site. It would make an ideal depository for a body and there would be something immensely satisfying in knowing that Eva, who in her lifetime had been so unbearable, was in death supporting the weight of a multi-storey concrete building. Besides it would make her discovery an extremely remote possibility and her identification out of the question. Not even Eva, who boasted a strong constitution and a stronger will, could maintain an identity at the bottom of a pile shaft. The difficulty would be in getting her to go down the hole in the first place. Sleeping pills seemed a sensible preliminary but Eva was a sound sleeper and didn't believe in pills of any sort. 'I can't imagine why not,' Wilt thought grimly, 'she's prepared to believe in just about everything else.'

His reverie was interrupted by Mr Morris who was bringing the meeting to a close. 'Before you all go,' he said, 'there is one more subject I want to mention. We have been asked by the Head of Engineering to conduct a series of one-hour lectures to Sandwich-Course Trainee Firemen. The theme this year will be Problems of Contemporary Society. I have drawn up a list of topics and the lecturers who will give them.'

Mr Morris handed out subjects at random. Major Millfield got Media, Communications and Participatory Democracy about which he knew nothing and cared less. Peter Braintree was given The New Brutalism in Architecture, Its Origins and Social Attributes, and Wilt ended up with Violence and the Break-Up of Family Life. On the whole he thought he had done rather well. The subject fitted in with his present preoccupations. Mr Morris evidently agreed.

'I thought you might like to have a go at it after yesterday's little episode with Printers Three,' he said, as they went out. Wilt smiled wanly and went off to take Fitters and Turners Two. He gave them *Shane* to read and spent the hour jotting down notes for his lecture. In the distance he could hear the pile-boring machines grinding away. Wilt could imagine Eva lying at the bottom as they poured the concrete in. In her lemon pyjamas. It was a nice thought, and helped him with his notes. He wrote down a heading, Crime in the family, subheading (A) Murder of Spouse, decline in since divorce laws.

Yes, he should be able to talk about that to Trainee Firemen.

# 4

'I loathe parties,' said Wilt on Thursday night, 'and if there's one thing worse than parties it's university parties and bottle parties are worst of all. You take along a bottle of decent burgundy and end up drinking someone else's rotgut.'

'It isn't a party,' said Eva, 'it's a barbecue.'

'It says here "Come and Touch and Come with Sally and Gaskell 9PM Thursday. Bring your own ambrosia or take pot luck with the Pringsheim punch." If ambrosia doesn't mean Algerian bilgewater I'd like to know what it does mean.'

'I thought it was that stuff people take to get a hard-on,' said Eva.

Wilt looked at her with disgust. 'You've picked up some choice phrases since you've met these bloody people. A hard-on. I don't know what's got into you.'

'You haven't. That's for sure,' said Eva, and went through to the bathroom. Wilt sat on the bed and looked at the card. The beastly thing was shaped like a ... What the hell was it shaped like? Anyway it was pink and opened out and inside were all these ambiguous words. Come and Touch and Come.

Anyone touched him and they'd get an earful. And what about pot luck? A lot of trendy dons smoking joints and talking about set-theoretic data-manipulation systems or the significance of pre-Popper Hegelianism in the contemporary dialectical scene, or something equally unintelligible, and using fuck and cunt every now and then to show that they were still human.

'And what do you do?' they would ask him.

'Well, actually I teach at the Tech.'

'At the Tech? How frightfully interesting,' looking over his shoulder towards more stimulating horizons, and he would end the evening with some ghastly woman who felt strongly that Techs fulfilled a real function and that intellectual achievement was vastly overrated and that people should be oriented in a way that would make them community co-ordinated and that's what Techs were doing, weren't they? Wilt knew what Techs were doing. Paying people like him £3500 a year to keep Gasfitters quiet for an hour.

And Pringsheim Punch. Planters Punch. Printers Punch. He'd had enough punches recently.

'What the hell am I to wear?' he asked.

'There's that Mexican shirt you bought on the Costa del Sol last year,' Eva called from the bathroom. 'You haven't had a chance to wear it since.'

'And I don't intend to now,' muttered Wilt, rummaging through a drawer in search of something nondescript that would demonstrate his independence. In the end he put on a striped shirt with blue jeans.

'You're surely not going like that?' Eva told him emerging from the bathroom largely naked. Her face was plastered with white powder and her lips were carmine.

'Jesus wept,' said Wilt, 'Mardi Gras with pernicious anaemia.'

Eva pushed passed him. 'I'm going as The Great Gatsby,' she announced, 'and if you had any imagination you'd think of something better than a business shirt with blue jeans.'

'The Great Gatsby happened to be a man,' said Wilt.

'Bully for him,' said Eva, and put on her lemon loungers.

Wilt shut his eyes and took off his shirt. By the time they left the house he was wearing a red shirt with jeans while Eva, in spite of the hot night, insisted on putting on her new raincoat and trilby.

'We might as well walk,' said Wilt.

They took the car. Eva wasn't yet prepared to walk down Parkview Avenue in a trilby, a belted raincoat and lemon loungers. On the way they stopped at an off-licence where Wilt bought a bottle of Cyprus red.

'Don't think I'm going to touch the muck,' he said, 'and you had better take the car keys now. If it's as bad as I think it will be, I'm walking home early.'

It was. Worse. In his red shirt and blue jeans Wilt looked out of place.

'Darling Eva,' said Sally, when they finally found her talking to a man in a loincloth made out of a kitchen towel advertising Irish cheeses, 'you look great. The twenties suit you. And so this is Henry.' Henry didn't feel Henry at all. 'In period costume too. Henry meet Raphael.'

The man in the loincloth studied Wilt's jeans. 'The fifties are back,' he said languidly, 'I suppose it was bound to happen.'

Wilt looked pointedly at a Connemara Cheddar and tried to smile.

'Help yourself, Henry,' said Sally, and took Eva off to meet the freest but the most liberated woman who was simply dying to meet booby baby. Wilt went into the garden and put his bottle on the table and looked for a corkscrew. There wasn't one. In the end he looked into a large bucket with a ladle in it. Half an orange and segments of bruised peach floated in a purple liquid. He poured himself a paper cup and tried it. As he had anticipated, it tasted like cider with wood alcohol and orange squash. Wilt looked round the garden. In one corner a man in a chef's hat and a jockstrap was cooking, was *burning* sausages over a charcoal grill. In another corner a dozen people were lying in a circle listening to the Watergate tapes. There was a sprinkling of couples talking earnestly and a number of individuals standing by themselves looking supercilious and remote. Wilt recognized himself among them and selected the least attractive girl on the theory that he might just as well jump in the deep end and get it over with. He'd end up with her anyway.

'Hi,' he said, conscious that already he was slipping into the Americanese that Eva had succumbed to. The girl looked at him blankly and moved away.

'Charming,' said Wilt, and finished his drink. Ten minutes and two drinks later he was discussing Rapid Reading with a small round man who seemed deeply interested in the subject.

In the kitchen Eva was cutting up French bread while Sally stood with a drink and talked about Lévi-Strauss with an Ethiopian who had just got back from New Guinea.

'I've always felt that L-S was all wrong on the woman's front,' she said, languidly studying Eva's rear, 'I mean he disregards the essential similarity . . .' She stopped and stared out of the window. 'Excuse me a moment,' she said, and went out to rescue Dr Scheimacher from the clutches of Henry Wilt. 'Ernst is such a sweetie,' she said, when she came back, 'you'd never guess he got the Nobel prize for spermatology.'

Wilt stood in the middle of the garden and finished his third drink. He poured himself a fourth and went to listen to the Watergate tapes. He got there in time to hear the end.

'You get a much clearer insight into Tricky Dick's character quadraphonically,' someone said as the group broke up.

'With the highly gifted child one has to develop a special relationship. Roger and I find that Tonio responds best to a constructional approach.'

'It's a load of bull. Take what he says about quasars for example . . .'

'I can't honestly see what's wrong with buggery . . .'

'I don't care what Marcuse thinks about tolerance. What I'm saying is . . .'

'At minus two-fifty nitrogen . . .'

'Bach does have his moments I suppose but he has his limitations . . .'

'We've got this place at St Trop ...'

'I still think Kaldor had the answer ...'

Wilt finished his fourth drink and went to look for Eva. He'd had enough. He was halted by a yell from the man in the chef's hat.

'Burgers up. Come and get it.'

Wilt staggered off and got it. Two sausages, a burnt beefburger and a slosh of coleslaw on a paper plate. There didn't seem to be any knives or forks.

'Poor Henry's looking so forlorn,' said Sally, 'I'll go and transfuse him.'

She went out and took Wilt's arm.

'You're so lucky to have Eva. She's the babiest baby.'

'She's thirty-five,' said Wilt drunkenly, 'thirty-five if she's a day.'

'It's marvellous to meet a man who says what he means,' said Sally, and took a piece of beefburger from his plate. 'Gaskell just never says anything straightforwardly. I love down-to-earth people.' She sat down on the grass and pulled Wilt down with her. 'I think it's terribly important for two people to tell one another the truth,' she went on, breaking off another piece of beefburger and popping it into Wilt's mouth. She licked her fingers slowly and looked at him with wide eyes. Wilt chewed the bit uneasily and finally swallowed it. It tasted like burnt mincemeat with a soupçon of Lancôme. Or a bouquet.

'Why two?' he asked, rinsing his mouth out with coleslaw.

'Why two what?'

'Why two people,' said Wilt. 'Why is it so important for two people to tell the truth?'

'Well, I mean ...'

'Why not three? Or four? Or a hundred?'

'A hundred people can't have a relationship. Not an intimate one,' said Sally, 'not a meaningful one.'

'I don't know many twos who can either,' said Wilt. Sally dabbed her finger in his coleslaw.

'Oh but you do. You and Eva have this real thing going between you.'

'Not very often,' said Wilt. Sally laughed.

'Oh baby, you're a truth baby,' she said, and got up and fetched two more drinks. Wilt looked down into his paper cup doubtfully. He was getting very drunk.

'If I'm a truth baby, what sort of baby are you, baby?' he asked, endeavouring to instil the last baby with more than a soupçon of contempt. Sally snuggled up to him and whispered in his ear.

'I'm a body baby,' she said.

'I can see that,' said Wilt. 'You've got a very nice body.'

'That's the nicest thing anybody has ever said to me,' said Sally.

'In that case,' said Wilt, picking up a blackened sausage, 'you must have had a deprived childhood.'

'As a matter of fact I did,' Sally said and plucked the sausage from his fingers. 'That's why I need so much loving now.' She put most of the sausage in her mouth, drew it slowly out and nibbled the end. Wilt finished off the coleslaw and washed it down with Pringsheim Punch.

'Aren't they all awful?' said Sally, as shouts and laughter came from the corner of the garden by the grill.

Wilt looked up.

'As a matter of fact they are,' he said. 'Who's the clown in the jockstrap?'

'That's Gaskell. He's so arrested. He loves playing at things. In the States he just loves to ride footplate on a locomotive and he goes to rodeos and last Christmas he insisted on dressing up as Santa Claus and going down to Watts and giving out presents to the black kids at an orphanage. Of course they wouldn't let him.'

'If he went in a jockstrap I'm not in the least surprised,' said Wilt. Sally laughed.

'You must be an Aries,' she said, 'you don't mind what you say.' She got to her feet and pulled Wilt up. 'I'm going to show you his toy room. It's ever so droll.'

Wilt put his plate down and they went into the house. In the kitchen Eva was peeling oranges for a fruit salad and talking about circumcision rites with the Ethiopian, who was slicing bananas for her. In the lounge several couples were dancing back to back very vigorously to an LP of Beethoven's Fifth played at 78.

'Christ,' said Wilt, as Sally collected a bottle of Vodka from a cupboard. They went upstairs and down a passage to a small bedroom filled with toys. There was a model train set on the floor, a punchbag, an enormous Teddy Bear, a rocking horse, a fireman's helmet and a lifesize inflated doll that looked like a real woman.

'That's Judy,' said Sally, 'she's got a real cunt. Gaskell is a plastic freak.' Wilt winced. 'And here are Gaskell's toys. Puberty baby.'

Wilt looked round the room at the mess and shook his head. 'Looks as though he's making up for a lost childhood,' he said.

'Oh, Henry, you're so perceptive,' said Sally, and unscrewed the top of the Vodka bottle.

'I'm not. It's just bloody obvious.'

'Oh you are. You're just terribly modest, is all. Modest and shy and manly.' She swigged from the bottle and gave it to Wilt. He took a mouthful inadvisedly and had trouble swallowing it. Sally locked the door and sat down on the bed. She reached up a hand and pulled Wilt towards her.

'Screw me, Henry baby,' she said and lifted her skirt, 'fuck me, honey. Screw the pants off me.'

'That,' said Wilt, 'would be a bit difficult.'

'Oh. Why?'

'Well for one thing you don't appear to be wearing any and anyway why should I?'

'You want a reason? A reason for screwing?'

'Yes,' said Wilt. 'Yes I do.'

'Reason's treason. Feel free.' She pulled him down and kissed him. Wilt didn't feel at all free. 'Don't be shy, baby.'

'Shy?' said Wilt lurching to one side. 'Me shy?'

'Sure you're shy. OK, you're small. Eva told me . . .'

'Small? What do you mean I'm small?' shouted Wilt furiously.

Sally smiled up at him. 'It doesn't matter. It doesn't matter. Nothing matters. Just you and me and . . .'

'It bloody well does matter,' snarled Wilt. 'My wife said I was small. I'll soon show the silly bitch who's small. I'll show ...'

'Show me, Henry baby, show me. I like them small. Prick me to the quick.'

'It's not true,' Wilt mumbled.

'Prove it, lover,' said Sally squirming against him.

'I won't,' said Wilt, and stood up.

Sally stopped squirming and looked at him. 'You're just afraid,' she said. 'You're afraid to be free.'

'Free? Free?' shouted Wilt, trying to open the door. 'Locked in a room with another man's wife is freedom? You've got to be joking.'

Sally pulled down her skirt and sat up.

'You won't?'

'No,' said Wilt.

'Are you a bondage baby? You can tell me. I'm used to bondage babies. Gaskell is real ...'

'Certainly not,' said Wilt. 'I don't care what Gaskell is.'

'You want a blow job, is that it? You want for me to give you a blow job?' She got off the bed and came towards him. Wilt looked at her wildly.

'Don't you touch me,' he shouted, his mind alive with images of burning paint. 'I don't want anything from you.'

Sally stopped and stared at him. She wasn't smiling any more.

'Why not? Because you're small? Is that why?'

Wilt backed against the door.

'No, it isn't.'

'Because you haven't the courage of your instincts? Because you're a psychic virgin? Because you're not a man? Because you can't take a woman who thinks?'

'Thinks?' yelled Wilt, stung into action by the accusation that he wasn't a man. 'Thinks? You think? You know something? I'd rather have it off with that plastic mechanical doll than you. It's got more sex appeal in its little finger than you have in your whole rotten body. When I want a whore I'll buy one.'

'Why you little shit,' said Sally, and lunged at him. Wilt scuttled sideways and collided with the punchbag. The next moment he had stepped on a model engine and was hurtling across the room. As he slumped down the wall on to the floor Sally picked up the doll and leant over him.

In the kitchen Eva had finished the fruit salad and had made coffee. It was a lovely party. Mr Osewa had told her all about his job as underdevelopment officer in Cultural Affairs to UNESCO and how rewarding he found it. She had been kissed twice on the back of the neck by Dr Scheimacher in passing and the man in the Irish Cheese loincloth had pressed himself against her rather more firmly than was absolutely necessary to reach the tomato ketchup. And all around her terribly clever people were being so outspoken. It was all so sophisticated. She helped herself to another drink and looked around for Henry. He was nowhere to be seen.

'Have you seen Henry?' she asked when Sally came into the kitchen holding a bottle of Vodka and looking rather flushed.

'The last I saw of him he was sitting with some dolly bird,' said Sally, helping herself to a spoonful of fruit salad. 'Oh, Eva darling, you're absolutely Cordon Bleu baby.' Eva blushed.

'I do hope he's enjoying himself. Henry's not awfully good at parties.'

'Eva baby, be honest. Henry's not awfully good period.'

'It's just that he ...' Eva began but Sally kissed her.

'You're far too good for him,' she said, 'we've got to find you someone really beautiful.' While Eva sipped her drink, Sally found a young man with a frond of hair falling across his forehead who was lying on a couch with a girl, smoking and staring at the ceiling.

'Christopher precious,' she said, 'I'm going to steal you for a moment. I want you to do someone for me. Go into the kitchen and sweeten the woman with the boobies and the awful yellow pyjamas.'

'Oh God. Why me?'

'My sweet, you know you're utterly irresistible. But the sexiest. For me, baby, for me.'

Christopher got off the couch and went into the kitchen and Sally stretched out beside the girl.

'Christopher is a dreamboy,' she said.

'He's a gigolo,' said the girl. 'A male prostitute.'

'Darling,' said Sally, 'it's about time we women had them.'

In the kitchen Eva stopped pouring coffee. She was feeling delightfully tipsy.

'You mustn't,' she said hastily.

'Why not?'

'I'm married.'

'I like it. I like it.'

'Yes but . . .'

'No buts, lover.'

'Oh.'

Upstairs in the toy room Wilt, recovering slowly from the combined assaults on his system of Pringsheim Punch, Vodka, his nymphomaniac hostess and the corner of the cupboard against which he had fallen, had the feeling that something was terribly wrong. It wasn't simply that the room was oscillating, that he had a lump on the back of his head or that he was naked. It was rather the sensation that something with all the less attractive qualities of a mousetrap, or a vice, or a starving clam, had attached itself implacably to what he had up till now always considered to be the most private of his parts. Wilt opened his eyes and found himself staring into a smiling if slightly swollen face. He shut his eyes again, hoped against hope, opened them again, found the face still there and made an effort to sit up.

It was an unwise move. Judy, the plastic doll, inflated beyond her normal pressure, resisted. With a squawk Wilt fell back on to the floor. Judy followed. Her nose bounced on his face and her breasts on his chest. With a curse Wilt rolled on to his side and considered the problem. Sitting up was out of the question. That way led to castration. He would have to try something else. He rolled the doll over further and climbed on top only to decide that his weight on it was increasing the pressure on what remained of his penis and that if he wanted to get gangrene that was the way to go about getting it. Wilt rolled off precipitately and groped for a valve. There must be one somewhere if he could only find it. But if there was a valve it was well hidden and by the feel of things he hadn't got time to waste finding it. He felt round on the floor for something to use as a dagger, something sharp, and finally broke off a piece of railway track and plunged it into his assailant's back. There was a squeak of plastic but Judy's swollen smile remained unchanged and her unwanted attentions as implacable as ever. Again and again he stabbed her but to no avail. Wilt dropped his makeshift dagger and considered other means. He was getting frantic, conscious of a new threat. It was no longer that he was the subject of her high air pressure. His own internal pressures were mounting. The Pringsheim Punch and the Vodka were making their presence felt. With a desperate thought that if he didn't get out of her soon he would burst, Wilt seized Judy's head, bent it sideways and sank his teeth into her neck. Or would have had her pounds per square inch permitted. Instead he bounced off and spent the next two minutes trying to find his false tooth which had been dislodged in the exchange.

By the time he had got it back in place, panic had set in. He had to get out of the doll. He just had to. There would be a razor in the bathroom or a pair of scissors. But where on earth was the bathroom? Never mind about that. He'd find the damned thing. Carefully, very carefully he rolled the doll on to her back and followed her over. Then he inched his knees up until he was straddling the thing. All he needed now was something to hold on to while he got to his feet. Wilt leant over and grasped the edge of a chair with one hand while lifting Judy's head off the floor with the other. A moment later he was on his feet. Holding the doll to him he shuffled towards the door and opened it. He peered out into the passage. What if someone saw him? To hell with that. Wilt no longer cared what people thought about him. But which way was the bathroom? Wilt turned right, and peering frantically over Judy's shoulder, shuffled off down the passage.

•

Downstairs, Eva was having a wonderful time. First Christopher, then the man in the Irish Cheese loincloth and finally Dr Scheimacher, had all made advances to her and been rebuffed. It was such a change from Henry's lack of interest. It showed she was still attractive. Dr Scheimacher had said that she was an interesting example of latent steatopygia. Christopher tried to kiss her breasts and the man in the loincloth had made the most extraordinary suggestion to her. And through it all, Eva had remained entirely virtuous. Her massive skittishness, her insistence on dancing and, most effective of all, her habit of saying in a loud and not wholly cultivated voice, 'Oh, you are awful' at moments of their greatest ardour, had had a markedly deterrent effect. Now she sat on the floor in the living-room, while Sally and Gaskell and the bearded man from the Institute of Ecological Research argued about sexually interchangeable role-playing in a population-restrictive society. She felt strangely elated. Parkview Avenue and Mavis Mottram and her work at the Harmony Community Centre seemed to belong to another world. She had been accepted by people who flew to California or Tokyo to conferences and Think Tanks as casually as she took the bus to town. Dr Scheimacher had mentioned that he was flying to New Delhi in the morning, and Christopher had just come back from a photographic assignment in Trinidad. Above all, there was an aura of importance about what they were doing, a glamour that was wholly lacking in Henry's job at the Tech. If only she could get him to do something interesting and adventurous. But Henry was such a stick-in-the-mud. She had made a mistake in marrying him. She really had. All he was interested in was books, but life wasn't to be found in books. Like Sally said, life was for living. Life was people and experiences and fun. Henry would never see that.

In the bathroom Wilt could see very little. He certainly couldn't see any way of getting out of the doll. His attempt to slit the beastly thing's throat with a razor had failed, thanks largely to the fact that the razor in question was a Wilkinson bonded blade. Having failed with the razor he had tried shampoo as a lubricant but apart from working up a lather which even to his jaundiced eye looked as though he had aroused the doll to positively frenzied heights of sexual expectation the shampoo had achieved nothing. Finally he had reverted to a quest for the valve. The damned thing had one somewhere if only he could find it. In this endeavour he peered into the mirror on the door of the medicine cabinet but the mirror was too small. There was a large one over the washbasin. Wilt pulled down the lid of the toilet and climbed on to it. This way he would be able to get a clear view of the doll's back. He was just inching his way round when there were footsteps in the passage. Wilt stopped inching and stood rigid on the toilet lid. Someone tried the door and found it locked. The footsteps retreated and Wilt breathed a sigh of relief. Now then, just let him find that valve.

And at that moment disaster struck. Wilt's left foot stepped in the shampoo that had dripped on to the toilet seat, slid sideways off the edge and Wilt, the doll and the door of the medicine cabinet with which he had attempted to save himself were momentarily airborne. As they hurtled into the bath, as the shower curtain and fitting followed, as the contents of the medicine cabinet cascaded on' to the washbasin, Wilt gave a last despairing scream. There was a pop reminiscent of champagne corks and Judy, finally responding to the pressure of Wilt's eleven stone dropping from several feet into the bath, ejected him. But Wilt no longer cared. He had in every sense passed out. He was only dimly aware of shouts in the corridor, of someone breaking the door down, of faces peering at him and of hysterical laughter. When he came to he was lying on the bed in the toy room. He got up and put on his clothes and crept downstairs and out of the front door. It was 3AM.

# 5

Eva sat on the edge of the bed crying.

'How could he? How could he do a thing like that?' she said, 'in front of all these people.'

'Eva baby, men are like that. Believe me,' said Sally.

'But with a doll ....'

'That's symbolic of the male chauvinist pig attitude to women. We're just fuck artefacts to them. Objectification. So now you know how Henry feels about you.'

'It's horrible,' said Eva.

'Sure it's horrible. Male domination debases us to the level of objects.'

'But Henry's never done anything like that before,' Eva wailed.

'Well, he's done it now.'

'I'm not going back to him. I couldn't face it. I feel so ashamed.'

'Honey, you just forget about it. You don't have to go anywhere. Sally will look after you. You just lie down and get some sleep.'

Eva lay back, but sleep was impossible. The image of Henry lying naked in the bath on top of that horrible doll was fixed in her mind. They had to break the door down and Dr Scheimacher had cut his hand on a broken bottle trying to get Henry out of the bath ... Oh, it was all too awful. She would never be able to look people in the face again. The story was bound to get about and she would be known as the woman whose husband went around ... With a fresh paroxysm of embarrassment Eva buried her head in the pillow and wept.

'Well that sure made the party go with a bang,' said Gaskell. 'Guy screws a doll in the bathroom and everyone goes berserk.' He looked round the living-room at the mess. 'If anyone thinks I'm going to start clearing this lot up now they'd better think again. I'm going to bed.'

'Just don't wake Eva up. She's hysterical,' said Sally.

'Oh great. Now we've got a manic obsessive compulsive woman with hysteria in the house.'

'And tomorrow she's coming with us on the boat.'

'She's what?'

'You heard me. She's coming with us on the boat.'

'Now wait a bit . . .'

'I'm not arguing with you, G. I'm telling you. She's coming with us.'

'Why, for Chrissake?'

'Because I'm not having her go back to that creep of a husband of hers. Because you won't get me a cleaning-woman and because I like her.'

'Because I won't get you a cleaning-woman. Now I've heard it all.'

'Oh no you haven't,' said Sally, 'you haven't heard the half of it. You may not know it but you married a liberated woman. No male pig is going to put one over on me . . .'

'I'm not trying to put one over on you,' said Gaskell. 'All I'm saying is that I don't want to have to . . .'

'I'm not talking about you. I'm talking about that creep Wilt. You think he got into that doll by himself? Think again, G baby, think again.'

Gaskell sat down on the sofa and stared at her.

'You must be out of your mind. What the hell did you want to do a thing like that for?'

'Because when I liberate someone I liberate them. No mistake.'

'Liberate someone by . . .' he shook his head. 'It doesn't make sense.'

Sally poured herself a drink. 'The trouble with you, G, is that you talk big but you don't do. It's yakkity yak with you. "My wife is a liberated woman. My wife's free." Nice-sounding talk but come the time your liberated wife takes it into her head to do something, you don't want to know.'

'Yeah, and when you take it into your goddam head to do something who takes the can back? I do. Where's petticoats then? Who got you out of that mess in Omaha? Who paid the fuzz in Houston that time . . .'

'So you did. So why did you marry me? Just why?'

Gaskell polished his glasses with the edge of the chef's hat. 'I don't know,' he said, 'so help me I don't know.'

'For kicks, baby, for kicks. Without me you'd have died of boredom. With me you get excitement. With me you get kicks.'

'In the teeth.'

Gaskell got up wearily and headed for the stairs. It was at times like these that he wondered why he had married.

Wilt walked home in agony. His pain was no longer physical. It was the agony of humiliation, hatred and self-contempt. He had been made to look a fool, a pervert and an idiot in front of people he despised. The Pringsheims and their set were everything he loathed, false, phoney, pretentious, a circus of intellectual clowns whose antics had not even the merit of his own, which had at least been real. Theirs were merely a parody of enjoyment. They laughed to hear themselves laughing and paraded a sensuality that had nothing to do with feelings or even instincts but was dredged up from shallow imaginations to mimic lust. *Copulo ergo sum.* And that bitch, Sally, had taunted him with not having the courage of his instincts as if instinct consisted of ejaculating into the chemically sterilized body of a woman he had first met twenty minutes before. And Wilt had reacted instinctively, shying away from a concupiscence that had to do with power and arrogance and an intolerable contempt for him which presupposed that what he was, what little he was, was a mere extension of his penis and that the ultimate expression of his thoughts, feelings, hopes and ambitions was to be attained between the legs of a trendy slut. And *that* was being liberated.

'Feel free,' she had said and had knotted him into that fucking doll. Wilt ground his teeth underneath a streetlamp.

And what about Eva? What sort of hell was she going to make for him now? If life had been intolerable with her before this, it was going to be unadulterated misery now. She wouldn't believe that he hadn't been screwing that doll, that he hadn't got into it of his own accord, that he had been put into it by Sally. Not in a month of Sundays. And even if by some miracle she accepted his story, a fat lot of difference that would make.

'What sort of man do you think you are, letting a woman do a thing like that to you?' she would ask. There was absolutely no reply to the question. What sort of man was he? Wilt had no idea. An insignificant little man to whom things happened and for whom life was a chapter of indignities. Printers punched him in the face and he was blamed for it. His wife bullied him and other people's wives made a laughing-stock out of him. Wilt wandered on along suburban streets past semi-detached houses and little gardens with a mounting sense of determination. He had had enough of being the butt of circumstance. From now on things would happen because he wanted them to. He would change from being the recipient of misfortune. He would be the instigator. Just let Eva try anything now. He would knock the bitch down.

Wilt stopped. It was all very well to talk. The bloody woman had a weapon she wouldn't hesitate to use. Knock her down, my eye. If anyone went down it would be Wilt, and in addition she would parade his affair with the doll to everyone they knew. It wouldn't be long before the story reached the Tech. In the darkness of Parkview Avenue Wilt shuddered at the thought. It would be the end of his career. He went through the gate of Number 34 and unlocked the front door with the feeling that unless he took some drastic action in the immediate future he was doomed.

In bed an hour later he was still awake, wide awake and wrestling with the problem of Eva, his own character and how to change it into something he could respect. And what did he respect? Under the blankets Wilt clenched his fist.

'Decisiveness,' he murmured. 'The ability to act without hesitation. Courage.' A strange litany of ancient virtues. But how to acquire them now? How had they turned men like him into Commandos and professional killers during the war? By training them. Wilt lay in the darkness and considered ways in which he could train himself to become what he was clearly not. By the time he fell asleep he had determined to attempt the impossible.

At seven the alarm went. Wilt got up and went into the bathroom and stared at himself in the mirror. He was a hard man, a man without feelings. Hard, methodical, cold-blooded and logical. A man who made no mistakes. He went downstairs and ate his All-Bran and drank his cup of coffee. So Eva wasn't home. She had stayed the night at the Pringsheims. Well that was something. It made things easier for him. Except that she still had the car and the keys. He certainly wasn't going to go round and get the car. He walked down to the roundabout and caught the bus to the Tech. He had Bricklayers One in Room 456. When he arrived they were talking about grad-bashing.

'There was this student all dressed up like a waiter see. "Do you mind?" he says, "Do you mind getting out of my way." Just like that and all I was doing was looking in the window at the books . . .'

'At the books?' said Wilt sceptically. 'At eleven o'clock at night you were looking at books? I don't believe it.'

'Magazines and cowboy books,' said the bricklayer. 'They're in a junk shop in Finch Street.'

'They've got girlie mags,' someone else explained. Wilt nodded. That sounded more like it.

'So I says "Mind what?" ' continued the bricklayer, 'and he says, "Mind out of my way." His way. Like he owned the bloody street.'

'So what did you say?' asked Wilt.

'Say? I didn't say anything. I wasn't wasting words on him.'

'What did you do then?'

'Well, I put the boot in and duffed him up. Gave him a good going-over and no mistake. Then I pushed off. There's one bloody grad who won't be telling people to get out of his way for a bit.'

The class nodded approvingly.

'They're all the bloody same, students,' said another bricklayer. 'Think because they've got money and go to college they can order you about. They could all do with a going-over. Do them a power of good.'

Wilt considered the implications of mugging as part of an intellectual's education. After his experience the previous night he was inclined to think there was something to be said for it. He would have liked to have duffed up half the people at the Pringsheims' party.

'So none of you feel there's anything wrong with beating a student up if he gets in your way?' he asked.

'Wrong?' said the bricklayers in unison. 'What's wrong with a good punch-up? It's not as if a grad is an old woman or something. He can always hit back, can't he?'

They spent the rest of the hour discussing violence in the modern world. On the whole, the bricklayers seemed to think it was a good thing.

'I mean what's the point of going out on a Saturday night and getting pissed if you can't have a bit of a barney at the same time? Got to get rid of your aggression somehow,' said an unusually articulate bricklayer, 'I mean it's natural isn't it?'

'So you think man is a naturally aggressive animal,' said Wilt.

'Course he is. That's history for you, all them wars and things. It's only bloody poofters don't like violence.'

Wilt took this view of things along to the Staff Room for his free period and collected a cup of coffee from the vending machine. He was joined by Peter Braintree.

'How did the party go?' Braintree asked.

'It didn't,' said Wilt morosely.

'Eva enjoy it?'

'I wouldn't know. She hadn't come home by the time I got up this morning.'

'Hadn't come home?'

'That's what I said,' said Wilt.

'Well did you ring up and find out what had happened to her?'

'No,' said Wilt.

'Why not?'

'Because I'd look a bit of a twit ringing up and being told

53

she was shacked up with the Abyssinian ambassador, wouldn't I?'

'The Abyssinian ambassador? Was he there?'

'I don't know and I don't want to know. The last I saw of her she was being chatted up by this big black bloke from Ethiopia. Something to do with the United Nations. She was making fruit salad and he was chopping bananas for her.'

'Doesn't sound a very compromising sort of activity to me,' said Braintree.

'No, I daresay it doesn't. Only you weren't there and don't know what sort of party it was,' said Wilt rapidly coming to the conclusion that an edited version of the night's events was called for. 'A whole lot of middle-aged with-it kids doing their withered thing.'

'It sounds bloody awful. And you think Eva ...'

'I think Eva got pissed and somebody gave her a joint and she passed out,' said Wilt, 'that's what I think. She's probably sleeping it off in the downstairs loo.'

'Doesn't sound like Eva to me,' said Braintree. Wilt drank his coffee and considered his strategy. If the story of his involvement with that fucking doll was going to come out, perhaps it would be better if he told it his way first. On the other hand ...

'What were you doing while all this was going on?' Braintree asked.

'Well,' said Wilt, 'as a matter of fact ...' He hesitated. On second thoughts it might be better not to mention the doll at all. If Eva kept her trap shut ... 'I got a bit slewed myself.'

'That sounds more like it,' said Braintree, 'I suppose you made a pass at another woman too.'

'If you must know,' said Wilt, 'another woman made a pass at me. Mrs Pringsheim.'

'Mrs Pringsheim made a pass at you?'

'Well, we went upstairs to look at her husband's toys. . . .'

'His toys? I thought you told me he was a biochemist.'

'He is a biochemist. He just happens to like playing with toys. Model trains and Teddy Bears and things. She says he's a case of arrested development. She would, though. She's that sort of loyal wife.'

'What happened then?'

'Apart from her locking the door and lying on the bed with her legs wide open and asking me to screw her and threatening me with a blow job, nothing happened,' said Wilt.

Peter Braintree looked at him sceptically. 'Nothing?' he said finally. 'Nothing? I mean what did you do?'

'Equivocated,' said Wilt.

'That's a new word for it,' said Braintree. 'You go upstairs with Mrs Pringsheim and equivocate while she lies on a bed with her legs open and you want to know why Eva hasn't come home? She's probably round at some lawyer's office filing a petition for divorce right now.'

'But I tell you I didn't screw the bitch,' said Wilt, 'I told her to hawk her pearly somewhere else.'

'And you call that equivocating? Hawk her pearly? Where the hell did you get that expression from?'

'Meat One,' said Wilt and got up and fetched himself another cup of coffee.

By the time he came back to his seat he had decided on his version.

'I don't know what happened after that,' he said when Braintree insisted on hearing the next episode. 'I passed out. It must have been the vodka.'

'You just passed out in a locked room with a naked woman? Is that what happened?' said Braintree. He didn't sound as if he believed a word of the story.

'Precisely,' said Wilt.

'And when you came to?'

'I was walking home,' said Wilt. 'I've no idea what happened in between.'

'Oh well, I daresay we'll hear about that from Eva,' said Braintree. 'She's bound to know.'

He got up and went off and Wilt was left alone to consider his next move. The first thing to do was to make sure that Eva didn't say anything. He went through to the telephone in the corridor and dialled his home number. There was no reply. Wilt went along to Room 187 and spent an hour with Turners and Fitters. Several times during the day he tried to telephone Eva but there was no answer.

'She's probably spent the day round at Mavis Mottram's weeping on her shoulder and telling all and sundry what a pig I am,' he thought. 'She's bound to be waiting for me when I get home tonight.'

But she wasn't. Instead there was a note on the kitchen table and a package. Wilt opened the note.

'I'm going away with Sally and Gaskell to think things over. What you did last night was horrible. I won't ever forgive you. Don't forget to buy some dog food. Eva. P.S. Sally says next time you want a blow job get Judy to give you one.'

Wilt looked at the package. He knew without opening it what it contained. That infernal doll. In a sudden paroxysm of rage Wilt picked it up and hurled it across the kitchen at the sink. Two plates and a saucer bounced off the washing-up rack and broke on the floor.

'Bugger the bitch,' said Wilt inclusively, Eva, Judy, and Sally Pringsheim all coming within the ambit of his fury. Then he sat down at the table and looked at the note again. 'Going away to think things over.' Like hell she was. Think? The stupid cow wasn't capable of thought. She'd emote, drool over his deficiencies and work herself into an ecstasy of self-pity. Wilt could hear her now blathering on about that blasted bank manager and how she should have married him instead of saddling herself with a man who couldn't even get promotion at the Tech and who went around fucking inflatable dolls in other people's bathrooms. And there was that filthy slut, Sally Pringsheim, egging her on. Wilt looked at the post-script: 'Sally says next time you want a blow job ...' Christ. As if he'd wanted a blow job the last time. But there it was, a new myth in the making, like the business of his being in love with Betty Crabtree when all he had done was give her a lift home one night after an Evening Class. Wilt's home life was punctuated by such myths, weapons in Eva's armoury to be brought out when the occasion demanded and brandished above his head. And now Eva had the ultimate deterrent at her disposal, the doll and Sally Pringsheim and a blow job. The balance of recrimination which had been the sustaining factor in their relationship had shifted dramatically. It would take an act of desperate invention on Wilt's part to restore it.

'Don't forget to buy some dog food.' Well at least she had left him the car. It was standing in the carport. Wilt went out and drove round to the supermarket and bought three tins of dog food, a boil-in-the-bag curry and a bottle of gin. He was going to get pissed. Then he went home and sat in the kitchen watching Clem gulp his Bonzo while the bag boiled. He poured himself a stiff gin, topped it up with lime and wandered about. And all the time he was conscious of the package lying there on the draining board waiting for him to open it. And inevitably he would open it. Out of sheer curiosity. He knew it and they knew it wherever they were, and on Sunday night Eva would come home and the first thing she would do would be to ask about the doll and if he had had a nice time with it. Wilt helped himself to some more gin and considered the doll's utility. There must be some way of using the thing to turn the tables on Eva.

By the time he had finished his second gin he had begun to formulate a plan. It involved the doll, a pile hole and a nice test of his own strength of character. It was one thing to have fantasies about murdering your wife. It was quite another to put them into effect and between the two there lay an area of uncertainty. By the end of his third gin Wilt was determined to put the plan into effect. If it did nothing else it would prove he was capable of executing a murder.

Wilt got up and unwrapped the doll. In his interior dialogue Eva was telling him what would happen if Mavis Mottram got to hear about his disgusting behaviour at the Pringsheim's. 'You'd be the laughing stock of the neighbourhood,' she said, 'you'd never live it down.'

Wouldn't he though? Wilt smiled drunkenly to himself and went upstairs. For once Eva was mistaken. He might not live it down but Mrs Eva Wilt wouldn't be around to gloat. She wouldn't live at all.

Upstairs in the bedroom he closed the curtains and laid the doll on the bed and looked for the valve which had eluded him the previous night. He found it and fetched a footpump from the garage. Five minutes later Judy was in good shape. She lay on the bed and smiled up at him. Wilt half closed his eyes and squinted at her. In the half darkness he had to admit that she was hideously lifelike. Plastic Eva with the mastic boobs. All that remained was to dress it up. He rummaged around in several drawers in search of a bra and blouse, decided she didn't need a bra, and picked out an old skirt and a pair of tights. In a cardboard box in the wardrobe he found one of Eva's wigs. She had had a phase of wigs. Finally a pair of shoes. By the time he had finished, Eva Wilt's replica lay on the bed smiling fixedly at the ceiling.

'That's my girl,' said Wilt and went down to the kitchen to see how the boil-in-the-bag was coming along. It was burnt-in-the-bag. Wilt turned the stove off and went into the lavatory under the stairs and sat thinking about his next move. He would use the doll for dummy runs so that if and when it came to the day he would be accustomed to the whole process of murder and would act without feeling like an automaton. Killing by conditioned reflex. Murder by habit. Then again he would know how to time the whole affair. And Eva's going off with the Pringsheims for the weekend would help too. It would establish a pattern of sudden disappearances. He would provoke her somehow to do it again and again and again. And then the visit to the doctor.

'It's just that I can't sleep, doctor. My wife keeps on going off and leaving me and I just can't get used to sleeping on my own.' A prescription for sleeping tablets. Then on the night. 'I'll make the Ovaltine tonight, dear. You're looking tired. I'll bring it up to you in bed.' Gratitude followed by snores. Down to the car ... fairly early would be best ... around ten thirty ... over to the Tech and down the hole. Perhaps inside a plastic bag ... no, not a plastic bag. 'I understand you bought a large plastic bag recently, sir. I wonder if you would mind showing it to us.' No, better just to leave her down the hole they were going to fill with concrete next morning. And finally a bewildered Wilt. He would go round to the Pringsheims'. 'Where's Eva? Yes, you do.' 'No, we don't.' 'Don't lie to me. She's always coming round here.' 'We're not lying.

We haven't seen her.' After that he would go to the police.

Motiveless, clueless and indiscoverable. And proof that he was a man who could act. Or wasn't. What if he broke down under the strain and confessed? That would be some sort of vindication too. He would know what sort of man he was one way or another and at least he would have acted for once in his life. And fifteen years in prison would be almost identical to fifteen, more, twenty years at the Tech confronting louts who despised him and talking about Piggy and the Lord of the Flies. Besides he could always plead the book as a mitigating circumstance at his trial.

'Me lud, members of the Jury, I ask you to put yourself in the defendant's place. For twelve years he has been confronted by the appalling prospect of reading this dreadful book to classes of bored and hostile youths. He has had to endure agonies of repetition, of nausea and disgust at Mr Golding's revoltingly romantic view of human nature. Ah, but I hear you say that Mr Golding is not a romantic, that his view of human nature as expressed in his portrait of a group of young boys marooned on a desert island is the very opposite of romanticism and that the sentimentality of which I accuse him and to which my client's appearance in this court attests is to be found not in *The Lord of the Flies* but in its predecessor, *Coral Island*. But, me lud, gentlemen of the Jury, there is such a thing as inverted romanticism, the romanticism of disillusionment, of pessimism and of nihilism. Let us suppose for one moment that my client had spent twelve years reading not Mr Golding's work but *Coral Island* to groups of apprentices; is it reasonable to imagine that he would have been driven to the desperate remedy of murdering his wife? No. A hundred times no. Mr Ballantyne's book would have given him the inspiration, the self-discipline, the optimism and the belief in man's ability to rescue himself from the most desperate situation by his own ingenuity ...'

It might not be such a good idea to pursue that line of argument too far. The defendant Wilt had after all exercised a good deal of ingenuity in rescuing himself from a desperate situation. Still, it was a nice thought. Wilt finished his business in the lavatory and looked around for the toilet paper. There wasn't any. The bloody roll had run out. He reached in his pocket and found Eva's note and put it to good use. Then he flushed it down the U-bend, puffed some Harpic after it to express his opinion of it and her and went out to the kitchen and helped himself to another gin.

He spent the rest of the evening sitting in front of the TV with a piece of bread and cheese and a tin of peaches until it was time to try his first dummy run. He went out to the front door and looked up and down the street. It was almost dark now and there was no one in sight. Leaving the front door open he went upstairs and fetched the doll and put it in the back seat of the car. He had to push and squeeze a bit to get it in but finally the door shut. Wilt climbed in and backed the car out into Parkview Avenue and drove down to the round-about. By the time he reached the car park at the back of the Tech it was half past ten exactly. He stopped and sat in the car looking around. Not a soul in sight and no lights on. There wouldn't be. The Tech closed at nine.

# 6

Sally lay naked on the deck of the cabin cruiser, her tight breasts pointing to the sky and her legs apart. Beside her Eva lay on her stomach and looked downriver.

'Oh God, this is divine,' Sally murmured. 'I have this deep thing about the countryside.'

'You've got this deep thing period,' said Gaskell steering the cruiser erratically towards a lock. He was wearing a Captain's cap and sunglasses.

'Cliché baby,' said Sally.

'We're coming to a lock,' said Eva anxiously. 'There are some men there.'

'Men? Forget men, darling. There's just you and me and G and G's not a man, are you G baby?'

'I have my moments,' said Gaskell.

'But so seldom, so awfully seldom,' Sally said. 'Anyway what does it matter? We're here idyllicstyle, cruising down the river in the good old summertime.'

'Shouldn't we have cleared the house up before we left?' Eva asked.

'The secret of parties is not to clear up afterward but to clear off. We can do all that when we get back.'

Eva got up and went below. They were quite near the lock and she wasn't going to be stared at in the nude by the two old men sitting on the bench beside it.

'Jesus, Sally, can't you do something about soulmate? She's getting on my teats,' said Gaskell.

'Oh G baby, she's never. If she did you'd Cheshire cat.'

'Cheshire cat?'

'Disappear with a smile, honey chil', foetus first. She's but positively gargantuanly uterine.'

'She's but positively gargantuanly boring.'

'Time, lover, time. You've got to accentuate the liberated, eliminate the negative and not mess with Mister-in-between.'

'Not mess with Missus-in-between. Operative word missus,' said Gaskell bumping the boat into the lock.

'But that's the whole point.'

'What is?' said Gaskell.

'Messing with Missus-in-between. I mean it's all ways with Eva and us. She does the housework. Gaskell baby can play ship's captain and teatfeast on boobs and Sally sweetie can minotaur her labyrinthine mind.'

'Mind?' said Gaskell. 'Polyunsaturated hasn't got a mind. And talking of cretins, what about Mister-in-between?'

'He's got Judy to mess with. He's probably screwing her now and tomorrow night he'll sit up and watch *Kojak* with her. Who knows, he may even send her off to Mavis Contracuntal Mottram's Flower Arrangement evening. I mean they're suited. You can't say he wasn't hooked on her last night.'

'You can say that again,' said Gaskell and closed the lock gates.

As the cruiser floated downwards the two old men sitting on

the bench stared at Sally. She took off her sunglasses and glared at them.

'Don't blow your prostates, senior citizens,' she said rudely. 'Haven't you seen a fanny before?'

'You talking to me?' said one of the men.

'I wouldn't be talking to myself.'

'Then I'll tell you,' said the man, 'I've seen one like yours before. Once.'

'Once is about right,' said Sally. 'Where?'

'On an old cow as had just dropped her calf,' said the man and spat into a neat bed of geraniums.

In the cabin Eva sat and wondered what they were talking about. She listened to the lapping of the water and the throb of the engine and thought about Henry. It wasn't like him to do a thing like that. It really wasn't. And in front of all those people. He must have been drunk. It was so humiliating. Well, he could suffer. Sally said men ought to be made to suffer. It was part of the process of liberating yourself from them. You had to show them that you didn't need them and violence was the only thing the male psyche understood. That was why she was so harsh with Gaskell. Men were like animals. You had to show them who was master.

Eva went through to the galley and polished the stainless-steel sink. Henry would have to learn how important she was by missing her and doing the housework and cooking for himself and when she got back she would give him such a telling-off about that doll. I mean, it wasn't natural. Perhaps Henry ought to go and see a psychiatrist. Sally said that he had made the most horrible suggestion to her too. It only went to show that you couldn't trust anyone. And Henry of all people. She would never have imagined Henry would think of doing anything like that. But Sally had been so sweet and understanding. She knew how women felt and she hadn't even been angry with Henry.

'It's just that he's a sphincter baby,' she had said. 'It's symptomatic of a male-dominated chauvinist pig society. I've never known an MCP who didn't say "Bugger you" and mean it.'

tion to the bicycles. The bloody things were all locked. He would just have to carry one round. He put *Bleak House* in the basket, picked the bike up and carried it all the way round to the fence. Then he climbed up and over and groped around in the darkness for the doll. In the end he found it and spent five minutes trying to keep the wig on while he fastened the elastic band under her chin. It kept on jumping off. 'Well, at least that's one problem I won't have with Eva,' he muttered to himself when the wig was secured. Having satisfied himself that it wouldn't come off he moved cautiously forward skirting mounds of gravel, machines, sacks and reinforcing rods when it suddenly occurred to him that he was running a considerable risk of disappearing down one of the pile holes himself. He put the doll down and fumbled in his pocket for the torch and shone it on the ground. Some yards ahead there was a large square of thick plywood. Wilt moved forward and lifted it. Underneath was the hole, a nice big hole. Just the right size. She would fit in there perfectly. He shone the torch down. Must be thirty feet deep. He pushed the plywood to one side and went back for the doll. The wig had fallen off again.

'Fuck,' said Wilt, and reached in his pocket for another elastic band. Five minutes later Judy's wig was firmly in place with four elastic bands fastened under her chin. That should do it. Now all he had to do was to drag the replica to the hole and make sure it fitted. At this point Wilt hesitated. He was beginning to have doubts about the soundness of the scheme. Too many unexpected contingencies had arisen for his liking. On the other hand there was a sense of exhilaration about being alone on the building site in the middle of the night. Perhaps it would be better if he went home now. No, he had to see the thing through. He would put the doll into the hole to make quite sure that it fitted. Then he would deflate it and go home and repeat the process until he had trained himself to kill by proxy. He would keep the doll in the boot of the car. Eva never looked there. And in future he would only blow her up when he reached the car park. That way Eva would have no idea what was going on. Definitely not. Wilt smiled to himself at the simplicity of the scheme. Then he picked Judy up and pushed her towards the hole feet first. She slid in easily while Wilt leant forward. Perfect. And at that moment he slipped on the muddy ground. With a desperate effort which necessitated letting go of the doll he hurled himself to one side and grabbed at the plywood. He got to his feet cautiously and cursed. His trousers were covered with mud and his hands were shaking.

'Damned near went down myself,' he muttered, and looked around for Judy. But Judy had disappeared. Wilt reached for his torch and shone it down the hole. Halfway down the doll was wedged lightly against the sides and for once the wig was still on. Wilt stared desperately down at the thing and wondered what the hell to do. It – or she – must be at least twenty feet down. Fifteen. Anyway a long way down and certainly too far for him to reach. But still too near the top not to be clearly visible to the workmen in the morning. Wilt switched off the torch and pulled the plywood square so that it covered the hole. That way he wouldn't be in danger of joining the doll. Then he stood up and tried to think of ways of getting it out.

Rope with a hook on the end of it? He hadn't a rope or a hook. He might be able to find a rope but hooks were another matter. Get a rope and tie it to something and climb down it and bring the doll up? Certainly not. It would be bad enough climbing down the rope with two hands but to think of climbing back up with one hand holding the doll in the other was sheer lunacy. That way he would end up at the bottom of the hole himself and if one thing was clear in his mind it was that he didn't intend to be discovered at the bottom of a thirty-foot pile hole on Monday morning clutching a plastic fucking doll with a cunt dressed in his wife's clothes. That way lay disaster. Wilt visualized the scene in the Principal's office as he tried to explain how he came to be ... And anyway they might not find him or hear his yells. Those damned cement lorries made a hell of a din and he bloody well wasn't going to risk being buried under ... Shit. Talk about poetic justice. No, the only thing to do was to get that fucking doll down to the bottom of the hole and hope to hell that no one spotted it before they poured the concrete in. Well, at least that way he would learn if it was a sensible method of getting rid of Eva. There was that to be said for it. Every cloud had ...

Wilt left the hole and looked around for something to move Judy down to the bottom. He tried a handful of gravel but she merely wobbled a bit and stayed put. Something weightier was needed. He went across to a pile of sand and scooped some into a plastic sack and poured it down the hole, but apart from adding an extra dimension of macabre realism to Mrs Wilt's wig the sand did nothing. Perhaps if he dropped a brick on the doll it would burst. Wilt looked around for a brick and ended up with a large lump of clay. That would have to do. He dropped it down the hole. There was a thump, a rattle of gravel and another thump. Wilt shone his torch down. Judy had reached the bottom of the hole and had settled into a grotesque position with her legs crumpled up in front of her and one arm outstretched towards him as if in supplication. Wilt fetched another lump of clay and hurled it down. This time the wig slid sideways and her head lolled. Wilt gave up. There was nothing more he could do. He pulled the plywood back over the hole and went back to the fence.

Here he ran into more trouble. The bicycle was on the other side. He fetched a plank, leant it against the fence and climbed over. Now to carry the bike back to the shed. Oh bugger the bicycle. It could stay where it was. He was fed up with the whole business. He couldn't even dispose of a plastic doll properly. It was ludicrous to think that he could plan, commit and carry through a real murder with any hope of success. He must have been mad to think of it. It was all that blasted gin.

'That's right, blame the gin,' Wilt muttered to himself, as he trudged back to his car. 'You had this idea months ago.' He climbed into the car and sat there in the darkness wondering what on earth had ever possessed him to have fantasies of murdering Eva. It was insane, utterly insane, and just as mad as to imagine that he could train himself to become a cold-blooded killer. Where had the idea originated from? What was it all about? All right. Eva was a stupid cow who made his life a misery by nagging at him and by indulging a taste for Eastern mysticism with a frenetic enthusiasm calculated to derange the soberest of husbands, but why his obsession with murder? Why the need to prove his manliness by violence? Where had he got that from? In the middle of the car park, Henry Wilt, suddenly sober and clear-headed, realized the extraordinary effect that ten years of Liberal Studies had had upon him. For ten long years Plasterers Two and Meat One had been exposed to culture in the shape of Wilt and *The Lord of the Flies*, and for as many years Wilt himself had been exposed to the bar-barity, the unhesitating readiness to commit violence of Plasterers Two and Meat One. That was the genesis of it all. That and the unreality of the literature he had been forced to absorb. For ten years Wilt had been the duct along which travelled creatures of imagination, Nostromo, Jack and Piggy, Shane, creatures who acted and whose actions effected some-thing. And all the time he saw himself, mirrored in their eyes, an ineffectual passive person responding solely to the dictates of circumstance. Wilt shook his head. And out of all that and the traumas of the past two days had been born this *acte gratuit*, this semi-crime, the symbolic murder of Eva Wilt.

He started the car and drove out of the car park. He would go and see the Braintrees. They would still be up and glad to see him and besides he needed to talk to someone. Behind him on the building site his notes on Violence and the Break-Up of Family Life drifted about in the night wind and stuck in the mud.

# 7

'Nature is so libidinous,' said Sally, shining a torch through the porthole at the reeds. 'I mean take bullrushes. I mean they're positively archetypally phallus. Don't you think so, G?'

'Bullrushes?' said Gaskell, gazing helplessly at a chart. 'Bull-rushes do nothing for me.'

'Maps neither, by the look of it.'

'Charts, baby, charts.'

'What's in a name?'

'Right now, a hell of a lot. We're either in Frogwater Reach or Fen Broad. No telling which.'

'Give me Fen Broad every time. I just adore broads. Eva sweetheart, how's about another pot of coffee? I want to stay awake all night and watch the dawn come up over the bull-rushes.'

'Yes, well I don't,' said Gaskell. 'Last night was enough for me. That crazy guy with the doll in the bath and Schei cutting himself. That's enough for one day. I'm going to hit the sack.'

'The deck,' said Sally, 'hit the deck, G. Eva and I are sleeping down here. Three's a crowd.'

'Three? With boobs around it's five at the least. OK, so I sleep on deck. We've got to be up early if we're to get off this damned sandbank.'

'Has Captain Pringsheim stranded us, baby?'

'It's these charts. If only they would give an exact indication of depth.'

'If you knew where we were, you'd probably find they do. It's no use knowing it's three feet—'

'Fathoms, honey, fathoms.'

'Three fathoms in Frogwater Reach if we're really in Fen Broad.'

'Well, wherever we are, you'd better start hoping there's a tide that will rise and float us off,' said Gaskell.

'And if there isn't?'

'Then we'll have to think of something else. Maybe someone will come along and tow us off.'

'Oh God, G, you're the skilfullest,' said Sally. 'I mean why couldn't we have just stayed out in the middle? But no, you had to come steaming up this creek wham into a mudbank and all because of what? Ducks, goddamned ducks.'

'Waders, baby, waders. Not just ducks.'

'OK, so they're waders. You want to photograph them so now we're stuck where no one in their right minds would come in a boat. Who do you think is going to come up here? Jonathan Seagull?'

In the galley Eva made coffee. She was wearing the bright red plastic bikini Sally had lent her. It was rather too small for her so that she bulged round it uncomfortably and it was revealingly tight but at least it was better than going around naked even though Sally said nudity was being liberated and look at the Amazonian Indians. She should have brought her own things but Sally had insisted on hurrying and now all she had were the lemon loungers and the bikini. Honestly Sally was so authora ... authorasomething ... well, bossy then.

'Dual-purpose plastic, baby, apronwise,' she had said, 'and G has this thing about plastic, haven't you, G?'

'Bio-degradably yes.'

'Bio-degradably?' asked Eva, hoping to be initiated into some new aspect of women's liberation.

'Plastic bottles that disintegrate instead of lying around making an ecological swamp,' said Sally, opening a porthole and dropping an empty cigar packet over the side, 'that's G's lifework. That and recyclability. Infinite recyclability.'

'Right,' said Gaskell. 'We've got in-built obsolescence in the automotive field where it's outmoded. So what we need now is in-built bio-degradable deliquescence in ephemera.'

Eva listened uncomprehendingly but with the feeling that she was somehow at the centre of an intellectual world far surpassing that of Henry and his friends who talked about new degree courses and their students so boringly.

'We've got a compost heap at the bottom of the garden,' she said when she finally understood what they were talking about. 'I put the potato peelings and odds and ends on it.'

Gaskell raised his eyes to the cabin roof. Correction. Deckhead.

'Talking of odds and ends,' said Sally, running a fond hand over Eva's bottom, 'I wonder how Henry is getting along with Judy.'

Eva shuddered. The thought of Henry and the doll lying in the bath still haunted her.

'I can't think what had got into him,' she said, and looked disapprovingly at Gaskell when he sniggered. 'I mean it's not as if he has ever been unfaithful or anything like that. And lots of husbands are. Patrick Mottram is always going off and having affairs with other women but Henry's been very good in that respect. He may be quiet and not very pushing but no one could call him a gadabout.'

'Oh sure,' said Gaskell, 'so he's got a hang-up about sex. My heart bleeds for him.'

'I don't see why you should say he's got something wrong with him because he's faithful,' said Eva.

'G didn't mean that, did you, G?' said Sally. 'He meant that there has to be true freedom in a marriage. No dominance, no jealousy, no possession. Right, G?'

'Right,' said Gaskell.

'The test of true love is when you can watch your wife having it off with someone else and still love her,' Sally went on.

'I could never watch Henry . . .' said Eva. 'Never.'

'So you don't love him. You're insecure. You don't trust him.'

'Trust him?' said Eva. 'If Henry went to bed with another woman I don't see how I could trust him. I mean if that's what he wants to do why did he marry me?'

'That,' said Gaskell, 'is the sixty-four-thousand dollar question.' He picked up his sleeping bag and went out on deck. Behind him Eva had begun to cry.

'There, there,' said Sally, putting her arm round her. 'G was just kidding. He didn't mean anything.'

'It's not that,' said Eva, 'it's just that I don't understand anything any more. It's all so complicated.'

'Christ, you look bloody awful,' said Peter Braintree as Wilt stood on the doorstep.

'I feel bloody awful,' said Wilt. 'It's all this gin.'

'You mean Eva's not back?' said Braintree, leading the way down the passage to the kitchen.

'She wasn't there when I got home. Just a note saying she was going away with the Pringsheims to think things over.'

'To think things over? Eva? What things?'

'Well . . .' Wilt began and thought better of it, 'that business with Sally I suppose. She says she won't ever forgive me.'

'But you didn't do anything with Sally. That's what you told me.'

'I know I didn't. That's the whole point. If I had done what that nymphomaniac bitch wanted there wouldn't have been all this bloody trouble.'

'I don't see that, Henry. I mean if you had done what she wanted Eva would have had something to grumble about. I don't see why she should be up in the air because you didn't.'

'Sally must have told her that I did do something,' said Wilt, determined not to mention the incident in the bathroom with the doll.

'You mean the blow job?'

'I don't know what I mean. What is a blow job anyway?'

Peter Braintree looked puzzled.

'I'm not too sure,' he said, 'but it's obviously something you don't want your husband to do. If I came home and told Betty I'd done a blow job she'd think I'd been robbing a bank.'

'I wasn't going to do it anyway,' said Wilt. 'She was going to do it to me.'

'Perhaps it's a suck off,' said Braintree, putting a kettle on the stove. 'That's what it sounds like to me.'

'Well it didn't sound like that to me,' said Wilt with a shudder. 'She made it sound like a paint-peeling exercise with a blow lamp. You should have seen the look on her face.'

He sat down at the kitchen table despondently.

Braintree eyed him curiously. 'You certainly seem to have been in the wars,' he said.

Wilt looked down at his trousers. They were covered with mud and there were round patches caked to his knees. 'Yes . . . well . . . well I had a puncture on the way here,' he explained with lack of conviction. 'I had to change a tyre and I knelt down. I was a bit pissed.'

Peter Braintree grunted doubtfully. It didn't sound very convincing to him. Poor old Henry was obviously a bit under the weather. 'You can wash up in the sink,' he said.

Presently Betty Braintree came downstairs. 'I couldn't help hearing what you said about Eva,' she said. 'I'm so sorry, Henry. I wouldn't worry. She's bound to come back.'

'I wouldn't be too sure,' said Wilt, gloomily, 'and anyway I'm not so sure I want her back.'

'Oh, Eva's all right,' Betty said. 'She gets these sudden urges and enthusiasms but they don't last long. It's just the way she's made. It's easy come and easy go with Eva.'

'I think that's what's worrying Henry,' said Braintree, 'the easy come bit.'

'Oh surely not. Eva isn't that sort at all.'

Wilt sat at the kitchen table and sipped his coffee. 'I wouldn't put anything past her in the company she's keeping now,' he muttered lugubriously. 'Remember what happened when she went through that macrobiotic diet phase? Dr Mannix told me I was the nearest thing to a case of scurvy he'd seen since the Burma railway. And then there was that episode with the trampoline. She went to a Keep Fit Class at Bulham Village College and bought herself a fucking trampoline. You know she put old Mrs Portway in hospital with that contraption.'

'I knew there was some sort of accident but Eva never told me what actually happened,' said Betty.

'She wouldn't. It was a ruddy miracle we didn't get sued,' said Wilt. 'It threw Mrs Portway clean through the greenhouse roof. There was glass all over the lawn and it wasn't even as though Mrs Portway was a healthy woman at the best of times.'

'Wasn't she the woman with the rheumatoid arthritis?'

Wilt nodded dismally. 'And the duelling scars on her face,' he said. 'That was our greenhouse, that was.'

'I must say I can think of better places for trampolines than greenhouses,' said Braintree. 'It wasn't a very big greenhouse was it?'

'It wasn't a very big trampoline either, thank God,' said Wilt, 'she'd have been in orbit otherwise.'

'Well it all goes to prove one thing,' said Betty, looking on the bright side, 'Eva may do crazy things but she soon gets over them.'

'Mrs Portway didn't,' said Wilt, not to be comforted. 'She was in hospital for six weeks and the skin grafts didn't take. She hasn't been near our house since.'

'You'll see. Eva will get fed up with these Pringsheim people in a week or two. They're just another fad.'

'A fad with a lot of advantages if you ask me,' said Wilt. 'Money, status and sexual promiscuity. All the things I couldn't give her and all dressed up in a lot of intellectual claptrap about Women's Lib and violence and the intolerance of tolerance and the revolution of the sexes and you're not fully mature unless you're ambisextrous. It's enough to make you vomit and it's just the sort of crap Eva would fall for. I mean she'd buy rotten herrings if some clown up the social scale told her they were the sophisticated things to eat. Talk about being gullible!'

'The thing is that Eva's got too much energy,' said Betty. 'You should try and persuade her to get a full-time job.'

'Full-time job?' said Wilt. 'She's had more full-time jobs than I've had hot dinners. Mind you, that's not saying much these days. All I ever get is a cold supper and a note saying she's gone to Pottery or Transcendental Meditation or something equally half-baked. And anyway Eva's idea of a job is to take over the factory. Remember Potters, that engineering firm that went broke after a strike a couple of years ago? Well, if you ask me that was Eva's fault. She got this job with a consultancy firm doing time and motion study and they sent her out to the factory and the next thing anyone knew they had a strike on their hands ...'

They went on talking for another hour until the Braintrees asked him to stay the night. But Wilt wouldn't. 'I've got things to do tomorrow.'

'Such as?'

'Feed the dog for one thing.'

'You can always drive over and do that. Clem won't starve overnight.'

But Wilt was too immersed in self-pity to be persuaded and besides he was still worried about that doll. He might have another go at getting the thing out of that hole. He drove home and went to bed in a tangle of sheets and blankets. He hadn't made it in the morning.

'Poor old Henry,' said Betty as she and Peter went upstairs. 'He did look pretty awful.'

'He said he'd had a puncture and had to change the wheel.'

'I wasn't thinking of his clothes. It was the look on his face that worried me. You don't think he's on the verge of a breakdown?'

Peter Braintree shook his head. 'You'd look like that if you had Gasfitters Three and Plasterers Two every day of your life for ten years and then your wife ran away,' he told her.

'Why don't they give him something better to teach?'

'Why? Because the Tech wants to become a Poly and they keep starting new degree courses and hiring people with PhDs to teach them and then the students don't enrol and they're lumbered with specialists like Dr Fitzpatrick who knows all there is to know about child labour in four cotton mills in Manchester in 1837 and damn all about anything else. Put him in front of a class of Day Release Apprentices and all hell would break loose. As it is I have to go into his A-level classes once a week and tell them to shut up. On the other hand Henry looks meek but he can cope with rowdies. He's too good at his job. That's his trouble and besides he's not a bumsucker and that's the kiss of death at the Tech. If you don't lick arses you get nowhere.'

'You know,' said Betty, 'teaching at that place has done horrible things to your language.'

'It's done horrible things to my outlook on life, never mind my language,' said Braintree. 'It's enough to drive a man to drink.'

'It certainly seems to have done that to Henry. His breath reeked of gin.'

'He'll get over it.'

But Wilt didn't. He woke in the morning with the feeling that something was missing quite apart from Eva. That bloody doll. He lay in bed trying to think of some way of retrieving the thing before the workmen arrived on the site on Monday morning but apart from pouring a can of petrol down the hole and lighting it, which seemed on reflection the best way of drawing attention to the fact that he had stuffed a plastic doll dressed in his wife's clothes down there, he could think of nothing practical. He would just have to trust to luck.

When the Sunday papers came he got out of bed and went down to read them over his All-Bran. Then he fed the dog and mooched about the house in his pyjamas, walked down to the Ferry Path Inn for lunch, slept in the afternoon and watched the box all evening. Then he made the bed and got into it and spent a restless night wondering where Eva was, what she was doing, and why, since he had occupied so many fruitless hours speculating on ways of getting rid of her homicidally, he should be in the least concerned now that she had gone of her own accord.

'I mean if I didn't want this to happen why did I keep thinking up ways of killing her,' he thought at two o'clock. 'Sane people don't go for walks with a Labrador and devise schemes for murdering their wives when they can just as easily divorce them.' There was probably some foul psychological reason for it. Wilt could think of several himself, rather too many in fact to be able to decide which was the most likely one. In any case a psychological explanation demanded a degree of self-knowledge which Wilt, who wasn't at all sure he had a self to know, felt was denied him. Ten years of Plasterers Two and Exposure to Barbarism had at least given him the insight to know that there was an answer for every question and it didn't much matter what answer you gave so long as you gave it convincingly. In the fourteenth century they would have said the devil put such thoughts into his head, now in a post-Freudian world it had to be a complex or, to be really up-to-date, a chemical imbalance. In a hundred years they would have come up with some completely different explanation. With the comforting thought that the truths of one age were the absurdities of another and that it didn't much matter what you thought so long as you did the right thing, and in his view he did, Wilt finally fell asleep.

At seven he was woken by the alarm clock and by half past eight had parked his car in the parking lot behind the Tech.

He walked past the building site where the workmen were already at work. Then he went up to the Staff Room and looked out of the window. The square of plywood was still in place covering the hole but the pile-boring machine had been backed away. They had evidently finished with it.

At five to nine he collected twenty-five copies of *Shane* from the cupboard and took them across to Motor Mechanics Three. *Shane* was the ideal soporific. It would keep the brutes quiet while he sat and watched what happened down below. Room 593 in the Engineering block gave him a grandstand view. Wilt filled in the register and handed out copies of *Shane* and told the class to get on with it. He said it with a good deal more vigour than was usual even for a Monday morning and the class settled down to consider the plight of the home-steaders while Wilt stared out of the window, absorbed in a more immediate drama.

A lorry with a revolving drum filled with liquid concrete had arrived on the site and was backing slowly towards the plywood square. It stopped and there was an agonizing wait while the driver climbed down from the cab and lit a cigarette. Another man, evidently the foreman, came out of a wooden hut and wandered across to the lorry and presently a little group was gathered round the hole. Wilt got up from his desk and went over to the window. Why the hell didn't they get a move on? Finally the driver got back into his cab and two men removed the plywood. The foreman signalled to the driver. The chute for the concrete was swung into position. Another signal. The drum began to tilt. The concrete was coming. Wilt watched as it began to pour down the chute and just at that moment the foreman looked down the hole. So did one of the workmen. The next instant all hell had broken loose. There were frantic signals and shouts from the foreman. Through the window Wilt watched the open mouths and the gesticulations but still the concrete came. Wilt shut his eyes and shuddered. They had found that fucking doll.

Outside on the building site the air was thick with misunderstanding.

'What's that? I'm pouring as fast as I can,' shouted the

driver, misconstruing the frenzied signals of the foreman. He pulled the lever still further and the concrete flood increased. The next moment he was aware that he had made some sort of mistake. The foreman was wrenching at the door of the cab and screaming blue murder.

'Stop, for God's sake stop,' he shouted. 'There's a woman down that hole!'

'A what?' said the driver, and switched off the engine.

'A fucking woman and look what you've been and fucking done. I told you to stop. I told you to stop pouring and you went on. You've been and poured twenty tons of liquid concrete on her.'

The driver climbed down from his cab and went round to the chute where the last trickles of cement were still sliding hesitantly into the hole.

'A woman?' he said. 'What? Down that hole? What's she doing down there?'

The foreman stared at him demonically. 'Doing?' he bellowed, 'what do you think she's doing? What would you be doing if you'd just had twenty tons of liquid concrete dumped on top of you? Fucking drowning, that's what.'

The driver scratched his head. 'Well I didn't know she was down there. How was I to know? You should have told me.'

'Told you?' shrieked the foreman. 'I told you. I told you to stop. You weren't listening.'

'I thought you wanted me to pour faster. I couldn't hear what you were saying.'

'Well, every other bugger could,' yelled the foreman. Certainly Wilt in Room 593 could. He stared wild-eyed out of the window as the panic spread. Beside him Motor Mechanics Three had lost all interest in *Shane*. They clustered at the window and watched.

'Are you quite sure?' asked the driver.

'Sure? Course I'm sure,' yelled the foreman. 'Ask Barney.'

The other workman, evidently Barney, nodded. 'She was down there all right. I'll vouch for that. All crumpled up she was. She had one hand up in the air and her legs was . . .'

'Jesus,' said the driver, visibly shaken. 'What the hell are we going to do now?'

It was a question that had been bothering Wilt. Call the Police, presumably. The foreman confirmed his opinion. 'Get the cops. Get an ambulance. Get the Fire Brigade and get a pump. For God's sake get a pump.'

'Pump's no good,' said the driver, 'you'll never pump that concrete out of there, not in a month of Sundays. Anyway it wouldn't do any good. She'll be dead by now. Crushed to death. Wouldn't drown with twenty tons on her. Why didn't she say something?'

'Would it have made any difference if she had?' asked the foreman hoarsely. 'You'd have still gone on pouring.'

'Well, how did she get down there in the first place?' said the driver, to change the subject.

'How the fuck would I know. She must have fallen . . .'

'And pulled that plywood sheet over her, I suppose,' said Barney, who clearly had a practical turn of mind. 'She was bloody murdered.'

'We all know that,' squawked the foreman. 'By Chris here. I told him to stop pouring. You heard me. Everyone for half a mile must have heard me but not Chris. Oh, no, he has to go on—'

'She was murdered before she was put down the hole,' said Barney. 'That wooden cover wouldn't have been there if she had fallen down herself.'

The foreman wiped his face with a handkerchief and looked at the square of plywood. 'There is that to it,' he muttered. 'No one can say we didn't take proper safety precautions. You're right. She must have been murdered. Oh, my God!'

'Sex crime, like as not,' said Barney. 'Raped and strangled her. That or someone's missus. You mark my words. She was all crumpled up and that hand . . . I'll never forget that hand, not if I live to be a hundred.'

The foreman stared at him lividly. He seemed incapable of expressing his feelings. So was Wilt. He went back to his desk and sat with his head in his hands while the class gaped out of the window and tried to catch what was being said. Presently sirens sounded in the distance and grew louder. A police car arrived, four fire engines hurtled into the car park and an ambulance followed. As more and more uniformed men gathered around what had once been a hole in the ground it became apparent that getting the doll down there had been a damned sight easier than getting it out.

'That concrete starts setting in twenty minutes,' the driver explained when a pump was suggested for the umpteenth time. An Inspector of Police and the Fire Chief stared down at the hole.

'Are you sure you saw a woman's body down there?' the Inspector asked. 'You're positive about it?'

'Positive?' squeaked the foreman. 'Course I'm positive. You don't think ... Tell them, Barney. He saw her too.'

Barney told the Inspector even more graphically than before. 'She had this hair see and her hand was reaching up like it was asking for help and there were these fingers ... I tell you it was horrible. It didn't look natural.'

'No, well, it wouldn't,' said the Inspector sympathetically. 'And you say there was a board on top of the hole when you arrived this morning.'

The foreman gesticulated silently and Barney showed them the board. 'I was standing on it at one time,' he said. 'It was here all right so help me God.'

'The thing is, how are we to get her out?' said the Fire Chief. It was a point that was put to the manager of the construction company when he finally arrived on the scene. 'God alone knows,' he said. 'There's no easy way of getting that concrete out now. We'd have to use drills to get down thirty feet.'

At the end of the hour they were no nearer a solution to the problem. As the Motor Mechanics dragged themselves away from this fascinating situation to go to Technical Drawing, Wilt collected the unread copies of *Shane* and walked across to the Staff Room in a state of shock. The only consolation he could think of was that it would take them at least two or three days to dig down and discover that what had all the appearances of being the body of a murdered woman was in fact an inflatable doll. Or had been once. Wilt rather doubted if it would be inflated now. There had been something horribly intractable about that liquid concrete.

# 8

There was something horribly intractable about the mud-bank on which the cabin cruiser had grounded. To add to their troubles the engine had gone wrong. Gaskell said it was a broken con rod.

'Is that serious?' asked Sally.

'It just means we'll have to be towed to a boatyard.'

'By what?'

'By a passing cruiser I guess,' said Gaskell.

Sally looked over the side at the bullrushes.

'Passing?' she said. 'We've been here all night and half the morning and nothing has passed so far and if it did we wouldn't be able to see it for all these fucking bullrushes.'

'I thought bullrushes did something for you.'

'That was yesterday,' snapped Sally. 'Today they just mean we're invisible to anyone more than fifty feet away. And now you've screwed the motor. I told you not to rev it like that.'

'So how was I to know it would bust a con rod,' said Gaskell. 'I was just trying to get us off this mudbank. You just tell me how I'm supposed to do it without revving the goddam motor.'

'You could get out and push.'

Gaskell peered over the side. 'I could get out and drown,' he said.

'So the boat would be lighter,' said Sally. 'We've all got to make sacrifices and you said the tide would float us off.'

'Well I was mistaken. That's fresh water down there and means the tide doesn't reach this far.'

'Now he tells me. First we're in Frogwater Beach . . .'

'Reach,' said Gaskell.

'Frogwater wherever. Then we're in Fen Broad. Now where are we for God's sake?'

'On a mudbank,' said Gaskell.

In the cabin Eva bustled about. There wasn't much space for

bustling but what there was she put to good use. She made the bunks and put the bedding away in the lockers underneath and she plumped the cushions and emptied the ashtrays. She swept the floor and polished the table and wiped the windows and dusted the shelves and generally made everything as neat and tidy as it was possible to make it. And all the time her thoughts got untidier and more muddled so that by the time she was finished and every object in sight was in its right place and the whole cabin properly arranged she was quite confused and in two minds about nearly everything.

The Pringsheims were ever so sophisticated and rich and intellectual and said clever things all the time but they were always quarrelling and getting at one another about something and to be honest they were quite impractical and didn't know the first thing about hygiene. Gaskell went to the lavatory and didn't wash his hands afterwards and goodness only knew when he had last had a shave. And look at the way they had walked out of the house in Rossiter Grove without clearing up after the party and the living-room all over cups and things. Eva had been quite shocked. She would never have left her house in that sort of mess. She had said as much to Sally but Sally had said how nonspontaneous could you get and anyway they were only renting the house for the summer and that it was typical of a male-oriented social system to expect a woman to enter a contractual relationship based upon female domestic servitude. Eva tried to follow her and was left feeling guilty because she couldn't and because it was evidently infra dig to be houseproud and she was.

And then there was what Henry had been doing with that doll. It was so unlike Henry to do anything like that and the more she thought about it the more unlike Henry it became. He must have been drunk but even so . . . without his clothes on? And where had he found the doll? She had asked Sally and had been horrified to learn that Gaskell was mad about plastic and just adored playing games with Judy and men were like that and so to the only meaningful relationships being between women because women didn't need to prove their virility by any overt act of extrasexual violence did they? By which time Eva was lost in a maze of words she didn't understand but which sounded important and they had had another session of Touch Therapy.

And that was another thing she was in two minds about. Touch Therapy. Sally had said she was still inhibited and being inhibited was a sign of emotional and sensational immaturity. Eva battled with her mixed feelings about the matter. On the one hand she didn't want to be emotionally and sensationally immature and if the revulsion she felt lying naked in the arms of another woman was anything to go by and in Eva's view the nastier a medicine tasted the more likely it was to do you good, then she was certainly improving her psycho-sexual behaviour pattern by leaps and bounds. On the other hand she wasn't altogether convinced that Touch Therapy was quite nice. It was only by the application of considerable will-power that she overcame her objections to it and even so there was an undertow of doubt about the propriety of being touched quite so sensationally. It was all very puzzling and to cap it all she was on the Pill. Eva had objected very strongly and had pointed out that Henry and she had always wanted babies and she'd never had any but Sally had insisted.

'Eva baby,' she had said, 'with Gaskell one just never knows. Sometimes he goes for months without so much as a twitch and then, bam, he comes all over the place. He's totally undiscriminating.'

'But I thought you said you had this big thing between you,' Eva said.

'Oh, sure. In a blue moon. Scientists sublimate and G just lives for plastic. And we wouldn't want you to go back to Henry with G's genes in your ovum, now would we?'

'Certainly not,' said Eva horrified at the thought and had taken the pill after breakfast before going through to the tiny galley to wash up. It was all so different from Trascendental Meditation and Pottery.

On deck Sally and Gaskell were still wrangling.

'What the hell are you giving brainless boobs?' Gaskell asked.

'TT, Body Contact, Tactile Liberation,' said Sally. 'She's sensually deprived.'

'She's mentally deprived too. I've met some dummies in my time but this one is the dimwittiest. Anyway, I meant those pills she takes at breakfast.'

Sally smiled. 'Oh those,' she said.

'Yes those. You blowing what little mind she's got or something?' said Gaskell. 'We've got enough troubles without Moby Dick taking a trip.'

'Oral contraceptives, baby, just the plain old Pill.'

'Oral contraceptives? What the hell for? I wouldn't touch her with a sterilized stirring rod.'

'Gaskell, honey, you're so naïve. For authenticity, pure authenticity. It makes my relationship with her so much more real, don't you think. Like wearing a rubber on a dildo.'

Gaskell gaped at her. 'Jesus, you don't mean you've . . .'

'Not yet. Long John Silver is still in his bag but one of these days when she's a little more emancipated. . . .' She smiled wistfully over the bullrushes. 'Perhaps it doesn't matter all that much us being stuck here. It gives us time, so much lovely time and you can look at your ducks . . .'

'Waders,' said Gaskell, 'and we're going to run up one hell of a bill at the Marina if we don't get this boat back in time.'

'Bill?' said Sally. 'You're crazy. You don't think we're paying for this hulk?'

'But you hired her from the boatyard. I mean you're not going to tell me you just took the boat,' said Gaskell. 'For Chrissake, that's theft!'

Sally laughed. 'Honestly, G, you're so moral. I mean you're inconsistent. You steal books from the library and chemicals from the lab but when it comes to boats you're all up in the air.'

'Books are different,' said Gaskell hotly.

'Yes,' said Sally, 'books you don't go to jail for. That's what's different. So you want to think I stole the boat, you go on thinking that.'

Gaskell took out a handkerchief and wiped his glasses. 'Are you telling me you didn't?' he asked finally.

'I borrowed it.'

'Borrowed it? Who from?'

'Schei.'

'Scheimacher?'

'That's right. He said we could have it whenever we wanted it so we've got it.'

'Does he know we've got it?'

Sally sighed. 'Look, he's in India isn't he, currying sperm? So what does it matter what he knows? By the time he gets back we'll be in the Land of the Free.'

'Shit,' said Gaskell wearily, 'one of these days you're going to land us in it up to the eyeballs.'

'Gaskell honey, sometimes you bore me with your worrying so.'

'Let me tell you something. You worry me with your goddam attitude to other people's property.'

'Property is theft.'

'Oh sure. You just get the cops to see it that way when they catch up with you. The fuzz don't go a ball on stealing in this country.'

The fuzz weren't going much of a ball on the well-nourished body of a woman apparently murdered and buried under thirty feet and twenty tons of rapidly setting concrete. Barney had supplied the well-nourished bit. 'She had big breasts too,' he explained, in the seventh version of what he had seen. 'And this hand reaching up—'

'Yes, well we know all about the hand,' said Inspector Flint. 'We've been into all that before but this is the first time you've mentioned breasts.'

'It was the hand that got me.' said Barney. 'I mean you don't think of breasts in a situation like that.'

The Inspector turned to the foreman. 'Did you notice the deceased's breasts?' he enquired. But the foreman just shook his head. He was past speech.

'So we've got a well-nourished woman ... What age would you say?'

Barney scratched his chin reflectively. 'Not old,' he said finally. 'Definitely not old.'

'In her twenties?'

'Could have been.'

'In her thirties?'

Barney shrugged. There was something he was trying to recall. Something that had seemed odd at the time.

'But definitely not in her forties?'

'No,' said Barney. 'Younger than that.' He said it rather hesitantly.

'You're not being very specific,' said Inspector Flint.

'I can't help it,' said Barney plaintively. 'You see a woman down a dirty great hole with concrete sloshing down on top of her you don't ask her her age.'

'Quite. I realize that but if you could just think. Was there anything peculiar about her ...'

'Peculiar? Well, there was this hand see ...'

Inspector Flint sighed. 'I mean anything out of the ordinary about her appearance. Her hair for instance. What colour was it?'

Barney got it. 'I knew there was something,' he said, triumphantly. 'Her hair. It was crooked.'

'Well, it would be, wouldn't it. You don't dump a woman down a thirty-foot pile shaft without mussing up her hair in the process.'

'No, it wasn't like that. It was on sideways and flattened. Like she'd been hit.'

'She probably had been hit. If what you say about the wooden cover being in place is true, she didn't go down there of her own volition. But you still can't give any precise indication of her age?'

'Well,' said Barney, 'bits of her looked young and bits didn't. That's all I know.'

'Which bits?' asked the Inspector, hoping to hell Barney wasn't going to start on that hand again.

'Well, her legs didn't look right for her teats if you see what I mean.' Inspector Flint didn't. 'They were all thin and crumpled-up like.'

'Which were? Her legs or her teats?'

'Her legs, of course,' said Barney. 'I've told you she had these lovely great ...'

'We're treating this as a case of murder,' Inspector Flint told the Principal ten minutes later. The Principal sat behind his desk and thought despairingly about adverse publicity.

'You're quite convinced it couldn't have been an accident?'

'The evidence to date certainly doesn't suggest accidental death,' said the Inspector. 'However, we'll only be absolutely certain on that point when we manage to reach the body and I'm afraid that is going to take some time.'

'Time?' said the Principal. 'Do you mean to say you can't get her out this morning?'

Inspector Flint shook his head. 'Out of the question, sir,' he said. 'We are considering two methods of reaching the body and they'll both take several days. One is to drill down through the concrete and the other is to sink another shaft next to the original hole and try and get at her from the side.'

'Good Lord,' said the Principal, looking at his calendar, 'but that means you're going to be digging away out there for several days.'

'I'm afraid it can't be helped. Whoever put her down there make a good job of it. Still, we'll try to be as unobtrusive as possible.'

Out of the window the Principal could see four police cars, a fire engine and a big blue van. 'This is really most unfortunate,' he murmured.

'Murder always is,' said the Inspector, and got to his feet. 'It's in the nature of the thing. In the meantime we are sealing off the site and we'd be grateful for your cooperation.'

'Anything you require,' said the Principal, with a sigh.

In the Staff Room the presence of so many uniformed men peering down a pile hole provoked mixed reactions. So did the dozen policemen scouring the building site, stopping now and then to put things carefully into envelopes, but it was the arrival of the dark blue caravan that finally clinched matters.

'That's a Mobile Murder Headquarters,' Peter Fenwick explained. 'Apparently some maniac has buried a woman at the bottom of one of the piles.'

The New Left, who had been clustered in a corner discussing the likely implications of so many paramilitary Fascist pigs, heaved a sigh of unmartyred regret but continued to express doubts.

'No, seriously,' said Fenwick, 'I asked one of them what they were doing. I thought it was some sort of bomb scare.'

Dr Cox, Head of Science, confirmed it. His office looked directly on to the hole. 'It's too dreadful to contemplate,' he murmured. 'Every time I look up I think what she must have suffered.'

'What do you suppose they are putting into those envelopes?' asked Dr Mayfield.

'Clues,' said Dr Board, with evident satisfaction. 'Hairs. Bits of skin and bloodstains. The usual trivial detritus of violent crime.'

Dr Cox hurried from the room and Dr Mayfield looked disgusted. 'How revolting,' he said. 'Isn't it possible that there has been some mistake? I mean why should anyone want to murder a woman here?'

Dr Board sipped his coffee and looked wistfully at him. 'I can think of any number of reasons,' he said happily. 'There are at least a dozen women in my Evening Class whom I would cheerfully beat to death and drop down holes. Sylvia Swansbeck for one.'

'Whoever did it must have known they were going to pour concrete down today,' said Fenwick. 'It looks like an inside job to me.'

'One of our less community-conscious students perhaps,' suggested Dr Board, 'I don't suppose they've had time to check if any of the staff are missing.'

'You'll probably find it had nothing to do with the Tech,' said Dr Mayfield. 'Some maniac . . .'

'Come now, give credit where credit is due,' interrupted Dr Board. 'There was obviously an element of premeditation involved. Whoever the murderer was . . . is, he planned it pretty carefully. What puzzles me is why he didn't shovel earth down on top of the wretched woman so that she couldn't be seen. Probably intended to but was disturbed before he could get around to it. One of those little accidents of fate.'

In the corner of the Staff Room Wilt sat and drank his

coffee, conscious that he was the only person not staring out of the window. What the hell was he to do? The sensible thing would be to go to the police and explain that he had been trying to get rid of an inflatable doll that someone had given him. But would they believe him? If that was all that had happened why had he dressed it up in a wig and clothes? And why had he left it inflated? Why hadn't he just thrown the thing away? He was just rehearsing the pros and cons of the argument when the Head of Engineering came in and announced that the police intended boring another hole next to the first one instead of digging down through the concrete.

'They'll probably be able to see bits of her sticking out the side,' he explained. 'Apparently she had one arm up in the air and with all that concrete coming down on top of her there's a chance that arm will have been pressed against the side of the hole. Much quicker that way.'

'I must say I can't see the need for haste,' said Dr Board. 'I should have thought she'd be pretty well preserved in all that concrete. Mummified I daresay.'

In his corner Wilt rather doubted it. With twenty tons of concrete on top of her even Judy who had been an extremely resilient doll was hardly likely to have withstood the pressure. She would have burst as sure as eggs were eggs in which case all the police would find was the empty plastic arm of a doll. They would hardly bother to dig a burst plastic doll out.

'And another thing,' continued the Head of Engineering, 'if the arm is sticking out they'll be able to take fingerprints straight away.'

Wilt smiled to himself. That was one thing they weren't going to find on Judy, fingerprints. He finished his coffee more cheerfully and went off to a class of Senior Secretaries. He found them agog with news of the murder.

'Do you think it was a sex killing?' a small blonde girl in the front row asked as Wilt handed out copies of *This Island Now*. He had always found the chapter on the Vicissitudes of Adolescence appealed to Senior Secs. It dealt with sex and violence and was twelve years out of date but then so were the Senior Secretaries. Today there was no need for the book.

'I don't think it was any sort of killing,' said Wilt taking his place behind the desk.

'Oh but it was. They saw a woman's body down there,' the small blonde insisted.

'They thought they saw something down there that looked like a body,' said Wilt. 'That doesn't mean it was one. People's imaginations play tricks with them.'

'The police don't think so,' said a large girl whose father was something in the City. 'They must be certain to go to all that trouble. We had a murder on our golf course and all they found were bits of body cut up and put in the water hazard on the fifteenth. They'd been there six months. Someone sliced a ball on the dogleg twelfth and it went into the pond. They fished out a foot first. It was all puffy and green ...' A pale girl from Wilstanton fainted in the third row. By the time Wilt had revived her and taken her to the Sick Room, the class had got on to Crippen, Haigh and Christie. Wilt returned to find them discussing acid baths.

'... and all they found were her false teeth and gallstones.'

'You seem to know a lot about murder,' Wilt said to the large girl.

'Daddy plays bridge with the Chief Constable,' she explained. 'He comes to dinner and tells super stories. He says they ought to bring back hanging.'

'I'm sure he does,' said Wilt grimly. It was typical of Senior Secs that they knew Chief Constables who wanted to bring back hanging. It was all mummy and daddy and horses with Senior Secretaries.

'Anyway, hanging doesn't hurt,' said the large girl. 'Sir Frank says a good hangman can have a man out of the condemned cell and on to the trap with a noose around his neck and pull the lever in twenty seconds.'

'Why confine the privilege to men?' asked Wilt bitterly. The class looked at him wth reproachful eyes.

'The last woman they hanged was Ruth Ellis,' said the blonde in the front row.

'Anyway with women it's different,' said the large girl.

'Why?' said Wilt inadvisedly.

'Well it's slower.'

'Slower?'

'They had to tie Mrs Thomson to a chair,' volunteered the blonde. 'She behaved disgracefully.'

'I must say I find your judgements peculiar,' said Wilt. 'A woman murdering her husband is doubtless disgraceful. The fact that she puts up a fight when they come to execute her doesn't strike me as disgraceful at all. I find that . . .'

'It's not just that,' interrupted the large girl, who wasn't to be diverted.

'What isn't?' said Wilt.

'It's being slower with women. They have to make them wear waterproof pants.'

Wilt gaped at her in disgust. 'Waterproof what?' he asked without thinking.

'Waterproof pants,' said the large girl.

'Dear God,' said Wilt.

'You see, when they get to the bottom of the rope their insides drop out,' continued the large girl, administering the *coup de grâce*. Wilt stared at her wildly and stumbled from the room.

'What's the matter with him?' said the girl. 'Anyone would think I had said something beastly.'

In the corridor Wilt leant against the wall and felt sick. Those fucking girls were worse than Gasfitters. At least Gasfitters didn't go in for such disgusting anatomical details and besides Senior Secs all came from so-called respectable families. By the time he felt strong enough to face them again the hour had ended. Wilt went back into the classroom sheepishly and collected the books.

'Name of Wilt mean anything to you? Henry Wilt?' asked the Inspector.

'Wilt?' said the Vice-Principal, who had been left to cope with the police while the Principal spent his time more profitably trying to offset the adverse publicity caused by the whole appalling business. 'Well, yes it does. He's one of our Liberal Studies lecturers. Why? Is there . . .'

'If you don't mind, sir, I'd just like a word with him. In private.'

'But Wilt's a most inoffensive man,' said the Vice-Principal. 'I'm sure he couldn't help you at all.'

'Possibly not but all the same ...'

'You're not suggesting for one moment that Henry Wilt had anything to do with ...' the Vice-Principal stopped and studied the expression on the Inspector's face. It was ominously neutral.

'I'd rather not go into details,' said Inspector Flint, 'and it's best if we don't jump to conclusions.'

The Vice-Principal picked up the phone. 'Do you want him to come across to that ... er ... caravan?' he asked.

Inspector Flint shook his head. 'We like to be as inconspicuous as possible. If I could just have the use of an empty office.'

'There's an office next door. You can use that.'

Wilt was in the canteen having lunch with Peter Braintree when the Vice-Principal's secretary came down with a message.

'Can't it wait?' asked Wilt.

'He said it was most urgent.'

'It's probably your Senior Lectureship come through at last,' said Braintree brightly. Wilt swallowed the rest of his Scotch egg and got up.

'I doubt that,' he said and went wanly out of the canteen and up the stairs. He had a horrid suspicion that promotion was the last thing the Vice-Principal wanted to see him about.

'Now, sir,' said the Inspector when they were seated in the office, 'my name is Flint, Inspector Flint, CID, and you're Mr Wilt? Mr Henry Wilt?'

'Yes,' said Wilt.

'Now, Mr Wilt, as you may have gathered we are investigating the suspected murder of a woman whose body is believed to have been deposited at the bottom of one of the foundation holes for the new building. I daresay you know about it.' Wilt nodded. 'And naturally we are interested in anything that might be of assistance. I wonder if you would mind having a look at these notes.'

He handed Wilt a piece of paper. It was headed 'Notes on Violence and the Break-Up of Family Life', and underneath were a number of sub-headings.

1 Increasing use of violence in public life to attain political ends.

a Bombing b Hijacking c Kidnapping d Assassination

2 Ineffectuality of Police Methods in combating Violence.

a Negative approach. Police able only to react to crime after it has taken place.

b Use of violence by police themselves.

c Low level of intelligence of average policeman.

d Increasing use of sophisticated methods such as diversionary tactics by criminals.

3 Influence of media. TV brings crime techniques into the home.

There was more. Much more. Wilt looked down the list with a sense of doom.

'You recognize the handwriting?' asked the Inspector.

'I do,' said Wilt, adopting rather prematurely the elliptical language of the witness box.

'You admit that you wrote those notes?' The Inspector reached out a hand and took the notes back.

'Yes.'

'They express your opinion of police methods?'

Wilt pulled himself together. 'They were jottings I was making for a lecture to Sandwich-Course Trainee Firemen,' he explained. 'They were simply rough ideas. They need amplifying of course . . .'

'But you don't deny you wrote them?'

'Of course I don't. I've just said I did, haven't I?'

The Inspector nodded and picked up a book. 'And this is yours too?'

Wilt looked at *Bleak House*. 'It says so, doesn't it?'

Inspector Flint opened the cover. 'So it does,' he said with a show of astonishment, 'so it does.'

Wilt stared at him. There was no point in maintaining the pretence any longer. The best thing to do was to get it over quickly. They had found that bloody book in the basket of the bicycle and the notes must have fallen out of his pocket on the building site.

'Look, Inspector,' he said, 'I can explain everything. It's really quite simple. I did go into that building site ...'

The Inspector stood up. 'Mr Wilt, if you're prepared to make a statement I think I should warn you ...'

Wilt went down to the Murder Headquarters and made a statement in the presence of a police stenographer. His progress to the blue caravan and his failure to come out again were noted with interest by members of the staff teaching in the Science block, by students in the canteen and by twenty-five fellow lecturers gaping through the windows of the Staff Room.

# 9

'Goddam the thing,' said Gaskell as he knelt greasily beside the engine of the cruiser, 'you'd think that even in this pre-technological monarchy they'd fit a decent motor. This contraption must have been made for the Ark.'

'Ark Ark the Lark,' said Sally, 'and cut the crowned heads foolery. Eva's a reginaphile.'

'A what?'

'Reginaphile. Monarchist. Get it. She's the Queen's Bee so don't be anti-British. We don't want her to stop working as well as the motor. Maybe it isn't the con rod.'

'If I could only get the head off I could tell,' said Gaskell.

'And what good would that do? Buy you another?' said Sally and went into the cabin where Eva was wondering what they were going to have for supper. 'Tarbaby is still tinkering with the motor. He says it's the con rod.'

'Con rod?' said Eva.

'Only connect, baby, only connect.'

'With what?'

'The thigh bone's connected to the knee bone. The con rod's connected to the piston and as everyone knows pistons are penis symbols. The mechanized male's substitute for sex. The Outboard Motor Syndrome. Only this happens to be inboard like his balls never dropped. Honestly, Gaskell is so regressive.'

'I'm sure I don't know,' said Eva.

Sally lay back on the bunk and lit a cigar. 'That's what I love about you, Eva. You don't know. Ignorance is blissful, baby. I lost mine when I was fourteen.'

Eva shook her head. 'Men,' she said disapprovingly.

'He was old enough to be my grandfather,' said Sally. 'He *was* my grandfather.'

'Oh no. How awful.'

'Not really,' said Sally laughing, 'he was an artist. With a beard. And the smell of paint on his smock and there was this studio and he wanted to paint me in the nude. I was so pure in those days. He made me lie on this couch and he arranged my legs. He was always arranging my legs and then standing back to look at me and painting. And then one day when I was lying there he came over and bent my legs back and kissed me and then he was on top of me and his smock was up and . . .'

Eva sat and listened, fascinated. She could visualize it all so clearly, even the smell of paint in the studio and the brushes. Sally had had such an exciting life, so full of incident and so romantic in a dreadful sort of way. Eva tried to remember what she had been like at fourteen and not even going out with boys and there was Sally lying on a couch with a famous artist in his studio.

'But he raped you,' she said finally. 'Why didn't you tell the police?'

'The police? You don't understand. I was at this terribly exclusive school. They would have sent me home. It was progressive and all that but I shouldn't have been out being painted by this artist and my parents would never have forgiven me. They were so strict.' Sally sighed, overcome by the rigours of her wholly fictitious childhood. 'And now you can see why I'm so afraid of being hurt by men. When you've been raped you know what penile aggression means.'

'I suppose you do,' said Eva, in some doubt as to what penile aggression was.

'You see the world differently too. Like G says, nothing's good and nothing's bad. It just is.'

'I went to a lecture on Buddhism once,' said Eva, 'and that's what Mr Podgett said. He said—'

'Zen's all wrong. Like you just sit around waiting. That's passive. You've got to make things happen. You sit around waiting long enough, you're dead. Someone's trampled all over you. You've got to see things happen your way and no one else's.'

'That doesn't sound very sociable,' said Eva. 'I mean if we all did just what we wanted all the time it wouldn't be very nice for other people.'

'Other people are hell,' said Sally. 'That's Sartre and he should know. You do what you want is good and no moral kickback. Like G says, rats are the paradigm. You think rats go around thinking what's good for other people?'

'Well no, I don't suppose they do,' said Eva.

'Right. Rats aren't ethical. No way. They just do. They don't get screwed up thinking.'

'Do you think rats can think?' asked Eva, now thoroughly engaged in the problems of rodent psychology.

'Of course they can't. Rats just are. No *Schadenfreude* with rats.'

'What's *Schadenfreude*?'

'Second cousin to *Weltschmerz*,' said Sally, stubbing her cigar out in the ashtray. 'So we can all do what we want whenever we want to. That's the message. It's only people like G who've got the know bug who get balled up.'

'No bug?' said Eva.

'They've got to know how everything works. Scientists. Lawrence was right. It's all head and no body with G.'

'Henry's a bit like that,' said Eva. 'He's always reading or talking about books. I've told him he doesn't know what the real world is like.'

In the Mobile Murder Headquarters Wilt was learning. He

sat opposite Inspector Flint whose face was registering increasing incredulity.

'Now, we'll just go over that again,' said the Inspector. 'You say that what those men saw down that hole was in actual fact an inflatable plastic doll with a vagina.'

'The vagina is incidental,' said Wilt, calling forth reserves of inconsequence.

'That's as maybe,' said the Inspector. 'Most dolls don't have them but ... all right, we'll let that pass. The point I'm trying to get at is that you're quite positive there isn't a real live human being down there.'

'Positive,' said Wilt, 'and if there were it is doubtful if it would still be alive now.'

The Inspector studied him unpleasantly. 'I don't need you to point that out to me,' he said. 'If there was the faintest possibility of whatever it is down there being alive I wouldn't be sitting here, would I?'

'No,' said Wilt.

'Right. So now we come to the next point. How is it that what those men saw, they say a woman and you say a doll ... that this thing was wearing clothes, had hair and even more remarkably had its head bashed in and one hand stretched up in the air?'

'That was the way it fell,' said Wilt. 'I suppose the arm got caught up on the side and lifted up.'

'And its head was bashed in?'

'Well, I did drop a lump of mud on it,' Wilt admitted, 'that would account for that.'

'You dropped a lump of mud on its head?'

'That's what I said,' Wilt agreed.

'I know that's what you said. What I want to know is why you felt obliged to drop a lump of mud on the head of an inflatable doll that had, as far as I can gather, never done you any harm.'

Wilt hesitated. That damned doll had done him a great deal of harm one way and another but this didn't seem an opportune moment to go into that. 'I don't know really,' he said finally, 'I just thought it might help.'

'Help what?'

'Help . . . I don't know. I just did it, that's all. I was drunk at the time.'

'All right, we'll come back to that in a minute. There's still one question you haven't answered. If it was a doll, why was it wearing clothes?'

Wilt looked desperately round the caravan and met the eyes of the police stenographer. There was a look in them that didn't inspire confidence. Talk about lack of suspension of disbelief.

'You're not going to believe this,' Wilt said. The Inspector looked at him and lit a cigarette.

'Well?'

'As a matter of fact I had dressed it up,' Wilt said, squirming with embarrassment.

'You had dressed it up?'

'Yes,' said Wilt.

'And may one enquire what purpose you had in mind when you dressed it up?'

'I don't know exactly.'

The Inspector sighed significantly. 'Right. We go back to the beginning. We have a doll with a vagina which you dress up and bring down here in the dead of night and deposit at the bottom of a thirty-foot hole and drop lumps of mud on its head. Is that what you're saying?'

'Yes,' said Wilt.

'You wouldn't prefer to save everyone concerned a lot of time and bother by admitting here and now that what is at present resting, hopefully at peace, under twenty tons of concrete at the bottom of that pile is the body of a murdered woman?'

'No,' said Wilt. 'I most definitely wouldn't.'

Inspector Flint sighed again. 'You know, we're going to get to the bottom of this thing,' he said. 'It may take time and it may take expense and God knows it's taking patience but when we do get down there—'

'You're going to find an inflatable doll,' said Wilt.

'With a vagina?'

'With a vagina.'

In the Staff Room Peter Braintree staunchly defended Wilt's innocence. 'I tell you I've known Henry well for the past seven years and whatever has happened he had nothing to do with it.'

Mr Morris, the Head of Liberal Studies, looked out of the window sceptically. 'They've had him in there since ten past two. That's four hours,' he said. 'They wouldn't do that unless they thought he had some connection with the dead woman.'

'They can think what they like. I know Henry and even if the poor sod wanted to he's incapable of murdering anyone.'

'He did punch that Printer on Tuesday. That shows he's capable of irrational violence.'

'Wrong again. The Printer punched him,' said Braintree.

'Only after Wilt had called him a snivelling fucking moron,' Mr Morris pointed out. 'Anyone who goes into Printers Three and calls one of them that needs his head examined. They killed poor old Pinkerton, you know. He gassed himself in his car.'

'They had a damned good try at killing old Henry come to that.'

'Of course, that blow might have affected his brain,' said Mr Morris, with morose satisfaction. 'Concussion can do funny things to a man's character. Change him overnight from a nice quiet inoffensive little fellow like Wilt into a homicidal maniac who suddenly goes berserk. Stranger things have happened.'

'I daresay Henry would be the first to agree with you,' said Braintree. 'It can't be very pleasant sitting in that caravan being questioned by detectives. I wonder what they're doing to him.'

'Just asking questions. Things like "How have you been getting on with your wife?" and "Can you account for your movements on Saturday night?" They start off gently and then work up to the heavy stuff later on.'

Peter Braintree sat in silent horror. Eva. He'd forgotten all about her and as for Saturday night he knew exactly what Henry had said he had been doing before he turned up on the doorstep covered with mud and looking like death ...

'All I'm saying,' said Mr Morris, 'is that it seems very strange to me that they find a dead body at the bottom of a shaft filled with concrete and the next thing you know they've got Wilt in that Murder HQ for questioning. Very strange indeed. I wouldn't like to be in his shoes.' He got up and left the room and Peter Braintree sat on wondering if there was anything he should do like phone a lawyer and ask him to come round and speak to Henry. It seemed a bit premature and presumably Henry could ask to see a lawyer himself if he wanted one.

Inspector Flint lit another cigarette with an air of insouciant menace. 'How well do you get on with your wife?' he asked.

Wilt hesitated. 'Well enough,' he said.

'Just well enough? No more than that?'

'We get along just fine,' said Wilt, conscious that he had made an error.

'I see. And I suppose she can substantiate your story about this inflatable doll.'

'Substantiate it?'

'The fact that you made a habit of dressing it up and carrying on with it.'

'I didn't make a habit of anything of the sort,' said Wilt indignantly.

'I'm only asking. You were the one who first raised the fact that it had a vagina. I didn't. You volunteered the information and naturally I assumed ...'

'What did you assume?' said Wilt. 'You've got no right ...'

'Mr Wilt,' said the Inspector, 'put yourself in my position. I am investigating a case of suspected murder and a man comes along and tells me that what two eye-witnesses describe as the body of a well-nourished woman in her early thirties ...'

'In her early thirties? Dolls don't have ages. If that bloody doll was more than six months old ...'

'Please, Mr Wilt, if you'll just let me continue. As I was saying we have a prima facie case of murder and you admit yourself to having put a doll with a vagina down that hole. Now if you were in my shoes what sort of inference would you draw from that?'

100

Wilt tried to think of some totally innocent interpretation and couldn't.

'Wouldn't you be the first to agree that it does look a bit peculiar?'

Wilt nodded. It looked horribly peculiar.

'Right,' continued the Inspector. 'Now if we put the nicest possible interpretation on your actions and particularly on your emphasis that this doll had a vagina—'

'I didn't emphasize it. I only mentioned the damned thing to indicate that it was extremely lifelike. I wasn't suggesting I made a habit of . . .' He stopped and looked miserably at the floor.

'Go on, Mr Wilt, don't stop now. It often helps to talk.'

Wilt stared at him frantically. Talking to Inspector Flint wasn't helping him one iota. 'If you're implying that my sex life was confined to copulating with an inflatable fucking doll dressed in my wife's clothes . . .'

'Hold it there,' said the Inspector, stubbing out his cigarette significantly. 'Ah, so we've taken another step forward. You admit then that whatever is down that hole is dressed in your wife's clothes? Yes or no.'

'Yes,' said Wilt miserably.

Inspector Flint stood up. 'I think it's about time we all went and had a little chat with Mrs Wilt,' he said. 'I want to hear what she has to say about your funny little habits.'

'I'm afraid that's going to be a little difficult,' said Wilt.

'Difficult?'

'Well you see the thing is she's gone away.'

'Gone away?' said the Inspector. 'Did I hear you say that Mrs Wilt has gone away?'

'Yes.'

'And where has Mrs Wilt gone to?'

'That's the trouble. I don't know.'

'You don't know?'

'No, I honestly don't know,' said Wilt.

'She didn't tell you where she was going?'

'No. She just wasn't there when I got home.'

'She didn't leave a note or anything like that?'

'Yes,' said Wilt, 'as a matter of fact she did.'

'Right, well let's just go up to your house and have a look at that note.'

'I'm afraid that's not possible,' said Wilt. 'I got rid of it.'

'You got rid of it?' said the Inspector. 'You got rid of it? How?'

Wilt looked pathetically across at the police stenographer. 'To tell the truth I wiped my bottom with it,' he said.

Inspector Flint gazed at him demonically. 'You did what?'

'Well, there was no toilet paper in the lavatory so I ...' he stopped. The Inspector was lighting yet another cigarette. His hands were shaking and he had a distant look in his eyes that suggested he had just peered over some appalling abyss. 'Mr Wilt,' he said when he had managed to compose himself, 'I trust I am a reasonably tolerant man, a patient man and a humane man, but if you seriously expect me to believe one word of your utterly preposterous story you must be insane. First you tell me you put a doll down that hole. Then you admit that it was dressed in your wife's clothes. Now you say that she went away without telling you where she was going and finally to cap it all you have the temerity to sit there and tell me that you wiped your arse with the one piece of solid evidence that could substantiate your statement.'

'But I did,' said Wilt.

'Balls,' shouted the Inspector. 'You and I both know where Mrs Wilt has gone and there's no use pretending we don't. She's down at the bottom of that fucking hole and you put her there.'

'Are you arresting me?' Wilt asked as they walked in a tight group across the road to the police car.

'No,' said Inspector Flint, 'you're just helping the police with their enquiries. It will be on the news tonight.'

'My dear Braintree, of course we'll do all we can,' said the Vice-Principal. 'Wilt has always been a loyal member of staff and there has obviously been some dreadful mistake. I'm sure you needn't worry. The whole thing will right itself before long.'

'I hope you're right,' said Braintree, 'but there are complicating factors. For one thing there's Eva ...'

'Eva? Mrs Wilt? You're not suggesting ...'

'I'm not suggesting anything. All I'm saying is ... well, she's missing from home. She walked out on Henry last Friday.'

'Mrs Wilt walked ... well I hardly knew her, except by reputation of course. Wasn't she the woman who broke Mr Lockyer's collar-bone during a part-time Evening Class in Judo some years back?'

'That was Eva,' said Braintree.

'She hardly sounds the sort of woman who would allow Wilt to put her down ...'

'She isn't,' said Braintree hastily. 'If anyone was liable to be murdered in the Wilt household it was Henry. I think the police should be informed of that.'

They were interrupted by the Principal who came in with a copy of the evening paper. 'You've seen this I suppose,' he said, waving it distraughtly. 'It's absolutely appalling.' He put the paper down on the desk and indicated the headlines. MURDERED WOMAN BURIED IN CONCRETE AT TECH. LECTURER HELPING POLICE.

'Oh dear,' said the Vice-Principal. 'Oh dear. How very unfortunate. It couldn't have come at a worse moment.'

'It shouldn't have come at all,' snapped the Principal. 'And that's not all. I've already had half a dozen phone calls from parents wanting to know if we make a habit of employing murderers on the full-time staff. Who is this fellow Wilt anyway?'

'He's in Liberal Studies,' said the Vice-Principal. 'He's been with us ten years.'

'Liberal Studies. I might have guessed it. If they're not poets manqués they're Maoists or ... I don't know where the hell Morris gets them from. And now we've got a blasted murderer. God knows what I'm going to tell the Education Committee tonight. They've called an emergency meeting for eight.'

'I must say I resent Wilt being called a murderer,' said Braintree loyally. 'There is nothing to suggest that he has murdered anyone.'

The Principal studied him for a moment and then looked back at the headlines. 'Mr Braintree, when someone is helping the police with their enquiries into a murder it may not be proven that he is a murderer but the suggestion is there.'

'This certainly isn't going to help us get the new CNAA degree off the ground,' intervened the Vice-Principal tactfully. 'We've got a visit from the Inspection Committee scheduled for Friday.'

'From what the police tell me it isn't going to help get the new Administration block off the ground either,' said the Principal. 'They say it's going to take at least three days to bore down to the bottom of that pile and then they'll have to drill through the concrete to get the body out. That means they'll have to put a new pile down and we're already well behind schedule and our building budget has been halved. Why on earth couldn't he have chosen somewhere else to dispose of his damned wife?'

'I don't think . . .' Braintree began.

'I don't care what you think,' said the Principal, 'I'm merely telling you what the police think.'

Braintree left them still wrangling and trying to figure out ways and means of counteracting the adverse publicity the case had already brought the Tech. He went down to the Liberal Studies office and found Mr Morris in a state of despair. He was trying to arrange stand-in lecturers for all Wilt's classes.

'But he'll probably be back in the morning,' Braintree said.

'Like hell he will,' said Mr Morris. 'When they take them in like that they keep them. Mark my words. The police may make mistakes, I'm not saying they don't, but when they act this swiftly they're on to a sure thing. Mind you, I always thought Wilt was a bit odd.'

'Odd? I've just come from the VP's office. You want to hear what the Principal's got to say about Liberal Studies staff.'

'Christ,' said Mr Morris, 'don't tell me.'

'Anyway what's so odd about Henry?'

'Too meek and mild for my liking. Look at the way he accepted remaining a Lecturer Grade Two all these years.'

'That was hardly his fault.'

'Of course it was his fault. All he had to do was threaten to resign and go somewhere else and he'd have got promotion like a shot. That's the only way to get on in this place. Make your presence felt.'

'He seems to have done that now,' said Braintree. 'The Principal is already blaming him for throwing the building programme off schedule and if we don't get the Joint Honours degree past the CNAA, Henry's going to be made the scapegoat. It's too bad. Eva should have had more sense than to walk out on him like that.'

Mr Morris took a more sombre view. 'She'd have shown a damned sight more sense if she'd walked out on him before the sod took it into his head to beat her to death and dump her down that bloody shaft. Now who the hell can I get to take Gasfitters One tomorrow?'

# 10

At 34 Parkview Avenue Wilt sat in the kitchen with Clem while the detectives ransacked the house. 'You're not going to find anything incriminating here,' he told Inspector Flint.

'Never you mind what we're going to find. We're just having a look.'

He sent one detective upstairs to examine Mrs Wilt's clothes or what remained of them.

'If she went away she'd have taken half her wardrobe,' he said. 'I know women. On the other hand if she's pushing up twenty tons of premix she wouldn't need more than what she's got on.'

Eva's wardrobe was found to be well stocked. Even Wilt had to admit that she hadn't taken much with her.

'What was she wearing when you last saw her?' the Inspector asked.

'Lemon loungers,' said Wilt.

'Lemon what?'

'Pyjamas,' said Wilt, adding to the list of incriminating evidence against him. The Inspector made a note of the fact in his pocketbook.

'In bed, was she?'

'No,' said Wilt. 'Round at the Pringsheims.'

'The Pringsheims? And who might they be?'

'The Americans I told you about who live in Rossiter Grove.'

'You haven't mentioned any Americans to me,' said the Inspector.

'I'm sorry. I thought I had. I'm getting muddled. She went away with them.'

'Oh did she? And I suppose we'll find they're missing too?'

'Almost certainly,' said Wilt. 'I mean if she was going away with them they must have gone too and if she isn't with them I can't imagine where she has got to.'

'I can,' said the Inspector looking with distasteful interest at a stain on a sheet one of the detectives had found in the dirty linen basket. By the time they left the house the incriminating evidence consisted of the sheet, an old dressing-gown cord that had found its way mysteriously into the attic, a chopper that Wilt had once used to open a tin of red lead, and a hypodermic syringe which Eva had got from the vet for watering cacti very precisely during her Indoor Plant phase. There was also a bottle of tablets with no label on it.

'How the hell would I know what they are?' Wilt asked when confronted with the bottle. 'Probably aspirins. And anyway it's full.'

'Put it with the other exhibits,' said the Inspector. Wilt looked at the box.

'For God's sake, what do you think I did with her? Poisoned her, strangled her, hacked her to bits with a chopper and injected her with Biofood?'

'What's Biofood?' asked Inspector Flint with sudden interest.

'It's stuff you feed plants with,' said Wilt. 'The bottle's on the windowsill.'

The Inspector added the bottle of Biofood to the box. 'We

know what you did with her, Mr Wilt,' he said. 'It's how that interests us now.'

They went out to the police car and drove round to the Pringsheims' house in Rossiter Grove. 'You just sit in the car with the constable here while I go and see if they're in,' said Inspector Flint and went to the front door. Wilt sat and watched while he rang the bell. He rang again. He hammered on the doorknocker and finally he walked round through the gate marked Tradesman's Entrance to the kitchen door. A minute later he was back and fumbling with the car radio.

'You've hit the nail on the head all right, Wilt,' he snapped. 'They've gone away. The place is a bloody shambles. Looks like they've had an orgy. Take him out.'

The two detectives bundled Wilt, no longer Mr Wilt but plain Wilt and conscious of the fact, out of the car while the Inspector called Fenland Constabulary and spoke with sinister urgency about warrants and sending something that sounded like the D brigade up. Wilt stood in the driveway of 12 Rossiter Grove and wondered what the hell was happening to him. The order of things on which he had come to depend was disintegrating around him.

'We're going in the back way,' said the Inspector. 'This doesn't look good.'

They went down the path to the kitchen door and round to the back garden. Wilt could see what the Inspector had meant by a shambles. The garden didn't look at all good. Paper plates lay about the lawn or, blown by the wind, had wheeled across the garden into honeysuckle or climbing rose while paper cups, some squashed and some still filled with Pringsheim punch and rainwater, littered the ground. But it was the beefburgers that gave the place its air of macabre filth. They were all over the lawn, stained with coleslaw so that Wilt was put in mind of Clem.

'The dog returns to his vomit,' said Inspector Flint evidently reading his mind. They crossed the terrace to the lounge windows and peered through. If the garden was bad the interior was awful.

'Smash a pane in the kitchen window and let us in,' said the

Inspector to the taller of the two detectives. A moment later the lounge window slid back and they went inside.

'No need for forcible entry,' said the detective. 'The back door was unlocked and so was this window. They must have cleared out in a hell of a hurry.'

The Inspector looked round the room and wrinkled his nose. The smell of stale pot, sour punch and candle smoke still hung heavily in the house.

'If they went away,' he said ominously and glanced at Wilt.

'They must have gone away,' said Wilt who felt called upon to make some comment on the scene, 'no one would live in all this mess for a whole weekend without ...'

'Live? You did say "live" didn't you?' said Flint stepping on a piece of burnt beefburger.

'What I meant ...'

'Never mind what you meant, Wilt. Let's see what's happened here.'

They went into the kitchen where the same chaos reigned and then into another room. Everywhere it was the same. Dead cigarette ends doused in cups of coffee or ground out on the carpet. Pieces of broken record behind the sofa marked the end of Beethoven's Fifth. Cushions lay crumpled against the wall. Burnt-out candles hung limply post-coital from bottles. To add a final touch to the squalor someone had drawn a portrait of Princess Anne on the wall with a red felt pen. She was surrounded by helmeted policemen and underneath was written, THE FUZZ AROUND OUR ANNY THE ROYAL FAMLYS FANNY THE PRICK IS DEAD LONG LIVE THE CUNT. Sentiments that were doubtless perfectly acceptable in Women's Lib circles but were hardly calculated to establish the Pringsheims very highly in Inspector Flint's regard.

'You've got some nice friends, Wilt,' he said.

'No friends of mine,' said Wilt, with feeling. 'The sods can't even spell.'

They went upstairs and looked in the big bedroom. The bed was unmade, clothes, mostly underclothes, were all over the floor or hung out of drawers and an unstopped bottle of Joy lay on its side on the dressing-table. The room stank of perfume.

'Jesus wept,' said the Inspector, eyeing a pair of jockstraps belligerently. 'All that's missing is some blood.'

They found it in the bathroom. Dr Scheimacher's cut hand had rained bloodstains in the bath and splattered the tiles with dark blotches. The bathroom door with its broken frame was hanging from the bottom hinge and there were spots of blood on the paintwork.

'I knew it,' said the Inspector, studying their message and that written in lipstick on the mirror above the washbasin. Wilt looked at it too. It seemed unduly personal.

WHERE WILT FAGGED AND EVA RAN WHO WAS THEN THE MALE CHAUVINIST PIG?

'Charming,' said Inspector Flint. He turned to look at Wilt whose face was now the colour of the tiles. 'I don't suppose you'd know anything about that. Not your handiwork?'

'Certainly not,' said Wilt.

'Nor this?' said the Inspector, pointing to the bloodstains in the bath. Wilt shook his head. 'And I suppose this has nothing to do with you either?' He indicated a diaphragm that had been nailed to the wall above the lavatory seat. WHERE THE B SUCKS THERE SUCK I UNDERNEATH A DUTCH CAP NICE AND DRY. Wilt stared at the thing in utter disgust.

'I don't know what to say,' he muttered. 'It's all so awful.'

'You can say that again,' the Inspector agreed, and turned to more practical matters. 'Well, she didn't die in here.'

'How can you tell?' asked the younger of the two detectives.

'Not enough blood.' The Inspector looked round uncertainly. 'On the other hand one hard bash ...' They followed the bloodstains down the passage to the room where Wilt had been dollknotted.

'For God's sake don't touch anything,' said the Inspector, easing the door open with his sleeve, 'the fingerprint boys are going to have a field day here.' He looked inside at the toys.

'I suppose you butchered the children too,' he said grimly.

'Children?' said Wilt, 'I didn't know they had any.'

'Well if you didn't,' said the Inspector, who was a family man, 'the poor little buggers have got something to be thankful for. Not much by the look of things but something.'

Wilt poked his head round the door and looked at the

Teddy Bear and the rocking horse. 'Those are Gaskell's,' he said, 'he likes to play with them.'

'I thought you said you didn't know they had any children?'

'They haven't. Gaskell is Dr Pringsheim. He's a biochemist and a case of arrested development according to his wife.' The Inspector studied him thoughtfully. The question of arrest had become one that needed careful consideration.

'I don't suppose you're prepared to make a full confession now?' he asked without much hope.

'No I am not,' said Wilt.

'I didn't think you would be, Wilt,' said the Inspector. 'All right, take him down to the Station. I'll be along later.'

The detectives took Wilt by the arms. It was the last straw.

'Leave me alone,' he yelled. 'You've got no right to do this. You've got—'

'Wilt,' shouted Inspector Flint, 'I'm going to give you one last chance. If you don't go quietly I'm going to charge you here and now with the murder of your wife.'

Wilt went quietly. There was nothing else to do.


'The screw?' said Sally. 'But you said it was the con rod.'

'So I was wrong,' said Gaskell. 'She cranks over.'

'It, G, it. It cranks over.'

'OK. It cranks over so it can't be a con rod. It could be something that got tangled with the propshaft.'

'Like what?'

'Like weeds.'

'Why don't you go down and have a look yourself?'

'With these glasses?' said Gaskell. 'I wouldn't be able to see anything.'

'You know I can't swim,' said Sally. 'I have this leg.'

'I can swim,' said Eva.

'We'll tie a rope round you. That way you won't drown,' said Gaskell, 'all you've got to do is go under and feel if there's anything down there.'

'We know what's down there,' said Sally. 'Mud is.'

'Round the propshaft,' said Gaskell. 'Then if there is you can take it off.'

Eva went into the cabin and put on the bikini.

'Honestly, Gaskell, sometimes I think you're doing this on purpose. First it's the con rod and now it's the screw.'

'Well, we've got to try everything. We can't just sit here,' said Gaskell, 'I'm supposed to be back in the lab tomorrow.'

'You should have thought of that before,' said Sally. 'Now all we need is a goddam Albatross.'

'If you ask me we've got one,' said Gaskell, as Eva came out of the cabin and put on a bathing cap.

'Now where's the rope?' she asked. Gaskell looked in a locker and found some. He tied it round her waist and Eva clambered over the side into the water.

'It's ever so cold,' she giggled.

'That's because of the Gulf Stream,' said Gaskell, 'it doesn't come this far round.'

Eva swam out and put her feet down.

'It's terribly shallow and full of mud.'

She waded round hanging on to the rope and groped under the stern of the cruiser.

'I can't feel anything,' she called.

'It will be further under,' said Gaskell, peering down at her. Eva put her head under the water and felt the rudder.

'That's the rudder,' said Gaskell.

'Of course it is,' said Eva, 'I know that, silly. I'm not stupid.'

She disappeared under the boat. This time she found the propeller but there was nothing wrapped round it.

'It's just muddy, that's all,' she said, when she resurfaced. 'There's mud all along the bottom.'

'Well there would be wouldn't there,' said Gaskell. Eva waded round to the side. 'We just happen to be stuck on a mudbank.'

Eva went down again but the propshaft was clear too. 'I told you so,' said Sally, as they hauled Eva back on board. 'You just made her do it so you could see her in her plastic kini all covered with mud. Come, Botticelli baby, let Sally wash you off.'

'Oh Jesus,' said Gaskell. 'Penis arising from the waves.' He went back to the engine and looked at it uncertainly. Perhaps there was a blockage in the fuel line. It didn't seem very likely but he had to try something. They couldn't stay stuck on the mudbank forever.

On the foredeck Sally was sponging Eva down.

'Now the bottom half, darling,' she said untying the string.

'Oh, Sally. No, Sally.'

'Labia babia.'

'Oh, Sally, you are awful.'

Gaskell struggled with the adjustable wrench. All this Touch Therapy was getting to him. And the plastic.

At the County Hall the Principal was doing his best to pacify the members of the Education Committee who were demanding a full enquiry into the recruitment policy of the Liberal Studies Department.

'Let me explain,' he said patiently, looking round at the Committee, which was a nice balance of business interests and social commitment. 'The 1944 Education Act laid down that all apprentices should be released from their places of employment to attend Day Release Classes at Technical Colleges ...'

'We know all that,' said a building contractor, 'and we all know it's a bloody waste of time and public money. This country would be a sight better off if they were left to get on with their jobs.'

'The courses they attend,' continued the Principal before anyone with a social conscience could intervene, 'are craft-oriented with the exception of one hour, one obligatory hour of Liberal Studies. Now the difficulty with Liberal Studies is that no one knows what it means.'

'Liberal Studies means,' said Mrs Chatterway, who prided herself on being an advocate of progressive education, in which role she had made a substantial contribution to the illiteracy rate in several previously good primary schools, 'providing socially deprived adolescents with a firm grounding in liberal attitudes and culturally extending topics ...'

'It means teaching them to read and write,' said a company director. 'It's no good having workers who can't read instructions.'

'It means whatever anyone chooses it to mean,' said the Principal hastily. 'Now if you are faced with the problem of having to find lecturers who are prepared to spend their lives going into classrooms filled with Gasfitters or Plasterers or Printers who see no good reason for being there, and keeping them occupied with a subject that does not, strictly speaking, exist, you cannot afford to pick and choose the sort of staff you employ. That is the crux of the problem.'

The Committee looked at him doubtfully.

'Am I to understand that you are suggesting that Liberal Studies teachers are not devoted and truly creative individuals imbued with a strong sense of vocation?' asked Mrs Chatterway belligerently.

'No,' said the Principal, 'I am not saying that at all. I am merely trying to make the point that Liberal Studies lecturers are not as other men are. They either start out odd or they end up odd. It's in the nature of their occupation.'

'But they are all highly qualified,' said Mrs Chatterway, 'they all have degrees.'

'Quite. As you say they all hold degrees. They are all qualified teachers but the stresses to which they are subject leave their mark. Let me put it this way. If you were to take a heart transplant surgeon and ask him to spend his working life docking dogs' tails you would hardly expect him to emerge unscathed after ten years' work. The analogy is exact, believe me, exact.'

'Well, all I can say,' protested the building contractor, 'is that not all Liberal Studies lecturers end up burying their murdered wives at the bottom of pile shafts.'

'And all I can say,' said the Principal, 'is that I am extremely surprised more don't.'

The meeting broke up undecided.

# 11

As dawn broke glaucously over East Anglia Wilt sat in the Interview Room at the central Police Station isolated from the natural world and in a wholly artificial environment that included a table, four chairs, a detective sergeant and a fluorescent light on the ceiling that buzzed slightly. There were no windows, just pale green walls and a door through which people came and went occasionally and Wilt went twice to relieve himself in the company of a constable. Inspector Flint had gone to bed at midnight and his place had been taken by Detective Sergeant Yates who had started again at the beginning.

'What beginning?' said Wilt.

'At the very beginning.'

'God made heaven and earth and all . . .'

'Forget the wisecracks,' said Sergeant Yates.

'Now that,' said Wilt, appreciatively, 'is a more orthodox use of wise.'

'What is?'

'Wisecrack. It's slang but it's good slang wisewise if you get my meaning.'

Detective Sergeant Yates studied him closely. 'This is a soundproof room,' he said finally.

'So I've noticed,' said Wilt.

'A man could scream his guts out in here and no one outside would be any the wiser.'

'Wiser?' said Wilt doubtfully. 'Wisdom and knowledge are not the same thing. Someone outside might not be aware that . . .'

'Shut up,' said Sergeant Yates.

Wilt sighed. 'If you would just let me get some sleep . . .'

'You'll get some sleep when you tell us why you murdered your wife, where you murdered her and how you murdered her.'

'I don't suppose it will do any good if I tell you I didn't murder her.'

Sergeant Yates shook his head.

'No,' he said. 'We know you did. You know you did. We know where she is. We're going to get her out. We know you put her there. You've at least admitted that much.'

'I keep telling you I put an inflatable . . .'

'Was Mrs Wilt inflatable?'

'Was she fuck,' said Wilt.

'Right, so we'll forget the inflatable doll crap . . .'

'I wish to God I could,' said Wilt. 'I'll be only too glad when you get down there and dig it out. It will have burst of course with all that concrete on it but it will still be recognizably an inflatable plastic doll.'

Sergeant Yates leant across the table. 'Let me tell you something. When we do get Mrs Wilt out of there, don't imagine she'll be unrecognizable.' He stopped and stared intently at Wilt. 'Not unless you've disfigured her.'

'Disfigured her?' said Wilt with a hollow laugh. 'She didn't need disfiguring the last time I saw her. She was looking bloody awful. She had on these lemon pyjamas and her face was all covered with . . .' He hesitated. There was a curious expression on the Sergeant's face.

'Blood?' he suggested. 'Were you going to say "blood"?'

'No,' said Wilt, 'I most certainly wasn't. I was going to say powder. White powder and scarlet lipstick. I told her she looked fucking awful.'

'You must have had a very happy relationship with her,' said the Sergeant. 'I don't make a habit of telling my wife she looks fucking awful.'

'You probably don't have a fucking awful-looking wife,' said Wilt making an attempt to conciliate the man.

'What I have or don't have by way of a wife is my business. She lies outside the domain of this discussion.'

'Lucky old her,' said Wilt, 'I wish to God mine did.' By two o'clock they had left Mrs Wilt's appearance and got on to teeth and the question of identifying dead bodies by dental chart.

'Look,' said Wilt wearily, 'I daresay teeth fascinate you but at this time of night I can do without them.'

'You wear dentures or something?'

'No. No, I don't,' said Wilt, rejecting the plural.

'Did Mrs Wilt?'

'No,' said Wilt, 'she was always very ...'

'I thank you,' said Sergeant Yates, 'I knew it would come out in the end.'

'What would?' said Wilt, his mind still on teeth.

'That "was". The past tense. That's the giveaway. Right, so you admit she's dead. Let's go on from there.'

'I didn't say anything of the sort. You said "Did she wear dentures?" and I said she didn't ...'

'You said "she was". It's that "was" that interests me. If you had said "is" it would have been different.'

'It might have sounded different,' said Wilt, rallying his defences, 'but it wouldn't have made the slightest difference to the facts.'

'Which are?'

'That my wife is probably still around somewhere alive and kicking ...'

'You don't half give yourself away, Wilt,' said the Sergeant. 'Now it's "probably" and as for "kicking" I just hope for your sake we don't find she was still alive when they poured that concrete down on top of her. The Court wouldn't take kindly to that.'

'I doubt if anyone would,' said Wilt. 'Now when I said "probably" what I meant was that if you had been held in custody for a day and half the night being questioned on the trot by detectives you'd begin to wonder what had happened to your wife. It might even cross your mind that, all evidence to the contrary, she might not be alive. You want to try sitting on this side of the table before you start criticizing me for using terms like "probable". Anything more improbable than being accused of murdering your wife when you know for a fact that you haven't you can't imagine.'

'Listen, Wilt,' said the Sergeant, 'I'm not criticizing you for your language. Believe me I'm not. I'm merely trying as patiently as I can to establish the facts.'

'The facts are these,' said Wilt. 'Like a complete idiot I

made the mistake of dumping an inflatable doll down the bottom of a pile shaft and someone poured concrete in and my wife is away from home and ...'

'I'll tell you one thing,' Sergeant Yates told Inspector Flint when he came on duty at seven in the morning. 'This one is a hard nut to crack. If you hadn't told me he hadn't a record I'd have sworn he was an old hand and a good one at that. Are you sure Central Records have got nothing on him?' Inspector Flint shook his head.

'He hasn't started squealing for a lawyer yet?'

'Not a whimper. I tell you he's either as nutty as a fruit cake or he's been through this lot before.'

And Wilt had. Day after day, year in year out. With Gasfitters One and Printers Three, with Day Release Motor Mechanics and Meat Two. For ten years he had sat in front of classes answering irrelevant questions, discussing why Piggy's rational approach to life was preferable to Jack's brutishness, why Pangloss' optimism was so unsatisfactory, why Orwell hadn't wanted to shoot that blasted elephant or hang that man, and all the time fending off verbal attempts to rattle him and reduce him to the state poor old Pinkerton was in when he gassed himself. By comparison with Bricklayers Four, Sergeant Yates and Inspector Flint were child's play. If only they would let him get some sleep he would go on running inconsequential rings round them.

'I thought I had him once,' the Sergeant told Flint as they conferred in the corridor. 'I had got him on to teeth.'

'Teeth?' said the Inspector.

'I was just explaining we can always identify bodies from their dental charts and he almost admitted she was dead. Then he got away again.'

'Teeth, eh? That's interesting. I'll have to pursue that line of questioning. It may be his weak link.'

'Good luck on you,' said the Sergeant. 'I'm off to bed.'

'Teeth?' said Wilt. 'We're not going through that again are we? I thought we'd exhausted that topic. The last bloke wanted to know if Eva had them in the past tense. I told him she did and ...'

'Wilt,' said Inspector Flint, 'I am not interested in whether or not Mrs Wilt had teeth. I presume she must have done. What I want to know is if she still has them. Present tense.'

'I imagine she must have,' said Wilt patiently. 'You'd better ask her when you find her.'

'And when we find her will she be in a position to tell us?'

'How the hell should I know? All I can say is that if for some quite inexplicable reason she's lost all her teeth there'll be the devil to pay. I'll never hear the end of it. She's got a mania for cleaning the things and sticking bits of dental floss down the loo. You've got no idea the number of times I've thought I'd got worms.'

Inspector Flint sighed. Whatever success Sergeant Yates had had with teeth, it was certainly eluding him. He switched to other matters.

'Let's go over what happened at the Pringsheims' party again,' he said.

'Let's not,' said Wilt who had so far managed to avoid mentioning his contretemps with the doll in the bathroom. 'I've told you five times already and it's wearing a bit thin. Besides it was a filthy party. A lot of trendy intellectuals boosting their paltry egos.'

'Would you say you were an introverted sort of man, Wilt? A solitary type of person?'

Wilt considered the question seriously. It was certainly more to the point than teeth.

'I wouldn't go that far,' he said finally. 'I'm fairly quiet but I'm gregarious too. You have to be to cope with the classes I teach.'

'But you don't like parties?'

'I don't like parties like the Pringsheims', no.'

'Their sexual behaviour outrages you? Fills you with disgust?'

'Their sexual behaviour? I don't know why you pick on that. Everything about them disgusts me. All that crap about Women's Lib for one thing when all it means to someone like

Mrs Pringsheim is that she can go around behaving like a bitch on heat while her husband spends the day slaving over a hot test tube and comes home to cook supper, wash up and is lucky if he's got enough energy to wank himself off before going to sleep. Now if we're talking about real Women's Lib that's another matter. I've got nothing against . . .'

'Let's just hold it there,' said the Inspector. 'Now two things you said interest me. One, wives behaving like bitches on heat. Two, this business of you wanking yourself off.'

'Me?' said Wilt indignantly. 'I wasn't talking about myself.'

'Weren't you?'

'No, I wasn't.'

'So you don't masturbate?'

'Now look here, Inspector. You're prying into areas of my private life which don't concern you. If you want to know about masturbation read the Kinsey Report. Don't ask me.'

Inspector Flint restrained himself with difficulty. He tried another tack. 'So when Mrs Pringsheim lay on the bed and asked you to have intercourse with her . . .'

'Fuck is what she said,' Wilt corrected him.

'You said no?'

'Precisely,' said Wilt.

'Isn't that a bit odd?'

'What, her lying there or me saying no?'

'You saying no.'

Wilt looked at him incredulously.

'Odd?' he said. 'Odd? A woman comes in here and throws herself flat on her back on this table, pulls up her skirt and says "Fuck me, honey, prick me to the quick." Are you going to leap on to her with a "Whoopee, let's roll baby"? Is that what you mean by not odd?'

'Jesus wept, Wilt,' snarled the Inspector, 'you're walking a fucking tightrope with my patience.'

'You could have fooled me,' said Wilt. 'All I do know is that your notion of what is odd behaviour and what isn't doesn't begin to make sense with me.'

Inspector Flint got up and left the room. 'I'll murder the bastard, so help me God I'll murder him,' he shouted at the

Duty Sergeant. Behind him in the Interview Room Wilt put his head on the table and fell asleep.

At the Tech Wilt's absence was making itself felt in more ways than one. Mr Morris had had to take Gasfitters One at nine o'clock and had come out an hour later feeling that he had gained fresh insight into Wilt's sudden excursion into homicide. The Vice-Principal was fighting off waves of crime reporters anxious to find out more about the man who was helping the police with their enquiries into a particularly macabre and newsworthy crime. And the Principal had begun to regret his criticisms of Liberal Studies to the Education Committee. Mrs Chatterway had phoned to say that she had found his remarks in the worst of taste and had hinted that she might well ask for an enquiry into the running of the Liberal Studies Department. But it was at the meeting of the Course Board that there was most alarm.

'The visitation of the Council for National Academic Awards takes place on Friday,' Dr Mayfield, Head of Sociology, told the committee. 'They are hardly likely to approve the Joint Honours degree in the present circumstances.'

'If they had any sense they wouldn't approve it in any circumstances,' said Dr Board. 'Urban Studies and Medieval Poetry indeed. I know academic eclecticism is the vogue these days but Helen Waddell and Lewis Mumford aren't even remotely natural bedfellows. Besides the degree lacks academic content.'

Dr Mayfield bristled. Academic content was his strong point. 'I don't see how you can say that,' he said. 'The course has been structured to meet the needs of students looking for a thematic approach.'

'The poor benighted creatures we manage to lure away from universities to take this course wouldn't know a thematic approach if they saw one,' said Dr Board. 'Come to think of it I wouldn't either.'

'We all have our limitations,' said Dr Mayfield suavely.

'Precisely,' said Dr Board, 'and in the circumstances we should recognize them instead of concocting Joint Honours degrees which don't make sense for students who, if their

A-level results are anything to go by, haven't any in the first place. Heaven knows I'm all for educational opportunity but—'

'The point is,' interjected Dr Cox, Head of Science, 'that it is not the degree course as such that is the purpose of the visitation. As I understand it they have given their approval to the degree in principle. They are coming to look at the facilities the College provides and they are hardly likely to be impressed by the presence of so many murder squad detectives. That blue caravan is most off-putting.'

'In any case with the late Mrs Wilt structured into the foundations . . .' began Dr Board.

'I am doing my best to get the police to remove her from . . .'

'The syllabus?' asked Dr Board.

'The premises,' said Dr Mayfield. 'Unfortunately they seem to have hit a snag.'

'A snag?'

'They have hit bedrock at eleven feet.'

Dr Board smiled. 'One wonders why there was any need for thirty-foot piles in the first instance if there is bedrock at eleven,' he murmured.

'I can only tell you what the police have told me,' said Dr Mayfield. 'However they have promised to do all they can to be off the site by Friday. Now I would just like to run over the arrangements again with you. The Visitation will start at eleven with an inspection of the library. We will then break up into groups to discuss Faculty libraries and teaching facilities with particular reference to our ability to provide individual tuition . . .'

'I shouldn't have thought that was a point that needed emphasizing,' said Dr Board. 'With the few students we're likely to get we're almost certain to have the highest teacher to student radio in the country.'

'If we adopt that approach the Committee will gain the impression that we are not committed to the degree. We must provide a united front,' said Dr Mayfield, 'we can't afford at this stage to have divisions among ourselves. This degree could mean our getting Polytechnic status.'

•

There were divisions too among the men boring down on the building site. The foreman was still at home under sedation suffering nervous exhaustion brought on by his part in the cementation of a murdered woman and it was left to Barney to superintend operations. 'There was this hand, see . . .' he told the Sergeant in charge.

'On which side?'

'On the right,' said Barney.

'Then we'll go down on the left. That way if the hand is sticking out we won't cut it off.'

They went down on the left and cut off the main electricity cable to the canteen.

'Forget that bleeding hand,' said the Sergeant, 'we go down on the right and trust to luck. Just so long as we don't cut the bitch in half.'

They went down on the right and hit bedrock at eleven feet.

'This is going to slow us up no end,' said Barney. 'Who would have thought there'd be rock down there.'

'Who would have thought some nut would incorporate his missus in the foundation of a college of further education where he worked,' said the Sergeant.

'Gruesome,' said Barney.

In the meantime the staff had as usual divided into factions. Peter Braintree led those who thought Wilt was innocent and was joined by the New Left on the grounds that anyone in conflict with the fuzz must be in the right. Major Millfield reacted accordingly and led the Right against Wilt on the automatic assumption that anyone who incurred the support of the Left must be in the wrong and that anyway the police knew what they were doing. The issue was raised at the meeting of the Union called to discuss the annual pay demand. Major Millfield proposed a motion calling on the union to support the campaign for the reintroduction of capital punishment. Bill Trent countered with a motion expressing solidarity with Brother Wilt. Peter Braintree proposed that a fund be set up to help Wilt with his legal fees. Dr Lomax, Head of Commerce, argued against this and pointed out that Wilt had, by dismembering his wife, brought the profession into disrepute. Braintree said Wilt hadn't dismembered anyone and that even the police hadn't suggested he had, and there was such a thing as a law against slander. Dr Lomax withdrew his remark. Major Millfield insisted that there were good grounds for thinking Wilt had murdered his wife and that anyway Habeas Corpus didn't exist in Russia. Bill Trent said that capital punishment didn't either. Major Millfield said, 'Bosh.' In the end, after prolonged argument, Major Millfield's motion on hanging was passed by a block vote of the Catering Department while Braintree's proposal and the motion of the New Left were defeated, and the meeting went on to discuss a pay increase of forty-five per cent to keep Teachers in Technical Institutes in line with comparably qualified professions. Afterwards Peter Braintree went down to the Police Station to see if there was anything Henry wanted.

'I wonder if I might see him,' he asked the Sergeant at the desk.

'I'm afraid not, sir,' said the Sergeant, 'Mr Wilt is still helping us with our enquiries.'

'But isn't there anything I can get him? Doesn't he need anything?'

'Mr Wilt is well provided for,' said the Sergeant, with the private reservation that what Wilt needed was his head read.

'But shouldn't he have a solicitor?'

'When Mr Wilt asks for a solicitor he will be allowed to see one,' said the Sergeant. 'I can assure you that so far he hasn't asked.'


And Wilt hadn't. Having finally been allowed three hours sleep he had emerged from his cell at twelve o'clock and had eaten a hearty breakfast in the police canteen. He returned to the Interview Room, haggard and unshaven, and with his sense of the improbable markedly increased.

'Now then, Henry,' said Inspector Flint, dropping an official octave nomenclaturewise in the hope that Wilt would respond, 'about this blood.'

'What blood?' said Wilt, looking round the aseptic room.

123

'The blood on the walls of the bathroom at the Pringsheims' house. The blood on the landing. Have you any idea how it got there? Any idea at all?'

'None,' said Wilt, 'I can only assume that someone was bleeding.'

'Right,' said the Inspector, 'who?'

'Search me,' said Wilt.

'Quite, and you know what we've found?'

Wilt shook his head.

'No idea?'

'None,' said Wilt.

'Bloodspots on a pair of grey trousers in your wardrobe,' said the Inspector. 'Bloodspots, Henry, bloodspots.'

'Hardly surprising,' said Wilt. 'I mean if you looked hard enough you'd be bound to find some bloodspots in anyone's wardrobe. The thing is I wasn't wearing grey trousers at that party. I was wearing blue jeans.'

'You were wearing blue jeans? You're quite sure about that?'

'Yes.'

'So the bloodspots on the bathroom wall and the bloodspots on your grey trousers have nothing to do with one another?'

'Inspector,' said Wilt, 'far be it from me to teach you your own business but you have a technical branch that specializes in matching bloodstains. Now may I suggest that you make use of their skills to establish ...'

'Wilt,' said the Inspector, 'Wilt, when I need your advice on how to conduct a murder investigation I'll not only ask for it but I'll resign from the force.'

'Well?' said Wilt.

'Well what?'

'Do they match? Do the bloodstains match?'

The Inspector studied him grimly. 'If I told you they did?' he asked.

Wilt shrugged. 'I'm not in any position to argue,' he said. 'If you say they do, I take it they do.'

'They don't,' said Inspector Flint, 'but that proves nothing,' he continued before Wilt could savour his satisfaction. 'Nothing at all. We've got three people missing. There's Mrs Wilt at the bottom of that shaft ... No, don't say it, Wilt, don't say it. There's Dr Pringsheim and there's Mrs Fucking Pringsheim.'

'I like it,' said Wilt appreciatively, 'I definitely like it.'

'Like what?'

'Mrs Fucking Pringsheim. It's apposite.'

'One of these days, Wilt,' said the Inspector softly, 'you'll go too far.'

'Patiencewise? To use a filthy expression,' asked Wilt.

The Inspector nodded and lit a cigarette.

'You know something, Inspector,' said Wilt, beginning to feel on top of the situation, 'you smoke too much. Those things are bad for you. You should try ...'

'Wilt,' said the Inspector, 'in twenty-five years in the service I have never once resorted to physical violence while interrogating a suspect but there comes a time, a time and a place and a suspect when with the best will in the world ...' He got up and went out. Wilt sat back in his chair and looked up at the fluorescent light. He wished it would stop buzzing. It was getting on his nerves.

# 12

On Eel Stretch – Gaskell's map-reading had misled him and they were nowhere near Frogwater Reach or Fen Broad – the situation was getting on everyone's nerves. Gaskell's attempts to mend the engine had had the opposite effect. The cockpit was flooded with fuel oil and it was difficult to walk on deck without slipping.

'Jesus, G, anyone would think to look at you that this was a goddam oil rig,' said Sally.

'It was that fucking fuel line,' said Gaskell, 'I couldn't get it back on.'

'So why try starting the motor with it off?'

'To see if it was blocked.'

'So now you know. What you going to do about it? Sit here

till the food runs out? You've gotta think of something.'

'Why me? Why don't you come up with something?'

'If you were any sort of a man . . .'

'Shit,' said Gaskell. 'The voice of the liberated woman. Comes the crunch and all of a sudden I've got to be a man. What's up with you, man-woman? You want us off here, you do it. Don't ask me to be a man, uppercase M, in an emergency. I've forgotten how.'

'There must be some way of getting help,' said Sally.

'Oh sure. You just go up top and take a crowsnest at the scenery. All you'll get is a beanfeast of bullrushes.' Sally climbed on top of the cabin and scanned the horizon. It was thirty feet away and consisted of an expanse of reeds.

'There's something over there looks like a church tower,' she said. Gaskell climbed up beside her.

'It is a church tower. So what?'

'So if we flashed a light or something someone might see it.'

'Brilliant. A highly populated place like the top of a church tower there's bound to be people just waiting for us to flash a light.'

'Couldn't we burn something?' said Sally. 'Somebody would see the smoke and . . .'

'You crazy? You start burning anything with all that fuel oil floating around they'll see something all right. Like an exploding cruiser with bodies.'

'We could fill a can with oil and put it over the side and float it away before lighting it.'

'And set the reedbeds on fire? What the hell do you want? A fucking holocaust?'

'G baby, you're just being unhelpful.'

'I'm using my brains is all,' said Gaskell. 'You keep coming up with bright ideas like that you're going to land us in a worse mess than we're in already.'

'I don't see why,' said Sally.

'I'll tell you why,' said Gaskell, 'because you went and stole this fucking *Hesperus*. That's why.'

'I didn't steal it. I . . .'

126

'You tell the fuzz that. Just tell them. You start setting fire to reedbeds and they'll be all over us asking questions. Like whose boat this is and how come you're sailing someone else's cruiser . . . So we got to get out of here without publicity.'

It started to rain.

'That's all we need. Rain,' said Gaskell. Sally went down into the cabin where Eva was tidying up after lunch. 'God, G's hopeless. First he lands us on a mudbank in the middle of nowhere, then he gefucks the motor but good and now he says he doesn't know what to do.'

'Why doesn't he go and get help?' asked Eva.

'How? Swimming? G couldn't swim that far to save his life.'

'He could take the airbed and paddle down to the open water,' said Eva. 'He wouldn't have to swim.'

'Airbed? Did I hear you say airbed? What airbed?'

'The one in the locker with the lifejackets. All you've got to do is blow it up and . . .'

'Honey you're the practicallest,' said Sally, and rushed outside. 'G, Eva's found a way for you to go and get help. There's an airbed in the locker with the lifejackets.' She rummaged in the locker and took out the airbed.

'You think I'm going anywhere on that damned thing you've got another think coming,' said Gaskell.

'What's wrong with it?'

'In this weather? You ever tried to steer one of those things? It's bad enough on a sunny day with no wind. Right now I'd end up in the reeds and anyhow the rain's getting on my glasses.'

'All right, so we wait till the storm blows over. At least we know how to get off here.'

She went back into the cabin and shut the door. Outside Gaskell squatted by the engine and toyed with the wrench. If only he could get the thing to go again.

'Men,' said Sally contemptuously, 'claim to be the stronger sex but when the chips are down it's us women who have to bail them out.'

'Henry's impractical too,' said Eva. 'It's all he can do to mend a fuse. I do hope he isn't worried about me.'

'He's having himself a ball,' said Sally.

'Not Henry. He wouldn't know how.'

'He's probably having it off with Judy.'

Eva shook her head. 'He was just drunk, that's all. He's never done anything like that before.'

'How would you know?'

'Well he is my husband.'

'Husband hell. He just uses you to wash the dishes and cook and clean up for him. What does he give you? Just tell me that.'

Eva struggled with her thoughts inarticulately. Henry didn't give her anything very much. Not anything she could put into words. 'He needs me,' she said finally.

'So he needs you. Who needs needing? That's the rhetoric of female feudalism. So you save someone's life, you've got to be grateful to them for letting you? Forget Henry. He's a jerk.'

Eva bristled. Henry might not be very much but she didn't like him insulted.

'Gaskell's nothing much to write home about,' she said and went into the kitchen. Behind her Sally lay back on the bunk and opened the centre spread of *Playboy*. 'Gaskell's got bread,' she said.

'Bread?'

'Money, honey. Greenstuff. The stuff that makes the world go round Cabaretwise. You think I married him for his looks? Oh no. I can smell a cool million when it comes by me and I do mean buy me.'

'I could never marry a man for his money,' said Eva primly. 'I'd have to be in love with him. I really would.'

'So you've seen too many movies. Do you really think Gaskell was in love with me?'

'I don't know. I suppose he must have been.'

Sally laughed. 'Eva baby you are naïve. Let me tell you about G. G's a plastic freak. He'd fuck a goddam chimpanzee if you dressed it up in plastic.'

'Oh honestly. He wouldn't,' said Eva. 'I don't believe it.'

'You think I put you on the Pill for nothing? You go around

in that bikini and Gaskell's drooling over you all the time --
if I wasn't here he'd have raped you.'

'He'd have a hard time,' said Eva, 'I took Judo classes.'

'Well he'd try. Anything in plastic drives him crazy. Why do
you think he had that doll?'

'I wondered about that.'

'Right. You can stop wondering,' said Sally.

'I still don't see what that has to do with you marrying him,'
said Eva.

'Then let me tell you a little secret. Gaskell was referred to
me . . .'

'Referred?'

'By Dr Freeborn. Gaskell had this little problem and he
consulted Dr Freeborn and Dr Freeborn sent him to me.'

Eva looked puzzled. 'But what were you supposed to do?'

'I was a surrogate,' said Sally.

'A surrogate?'

'Like a sex counsellor,' said Sally. 'Dr Freeborn used to
send me clients and I would help them.'

'I wouldn't like that sort of job,' said Eva, 'I couldn't bear
to talk to men about sex. Weren't you embarrassed?'

'You get used to it and there are worse ways of earning a
living. So G comes along with his little problem and I
straightened him out but literally and we got married. A
business arrangement. Cash on the tail.'

'You mean you . . .'

'I mean I have Gaskell and Gaskell has plastic. It's an elastic
relationship. The marriage with the two-way stretch.'

Eva digested this information with difficulty. It didn't seem
right somehow. 'Didn't his parents have anything to say about
it?' she asked. 'I mean did he tell them about you helping him
and all that?'

'Say? What could they say? G told them he'd met me at
summer school and Pringsy's greedy little eyes popped out of
his greasy little head. Baby, did that fat little man have penis
projection. Sell? He could sell anything. The Rockefeller
Centre to Rockefeller. So he accepted me. Old Ma Pringsheim
didn't. She huffed and she puffed and she blew but this little

piggy stayed right where the bank was. G and me went back to California and G graduated in plastic and we've been biodegradable ever since.'

'I'm glad Henry isn't like that,' said Eva. 'I couldn't live with a man who was queer.'

'G's not queer, honey. Like I said he's a plastic freak.'

'If that's not queer I don't know what is,' said Eva.

Sally lit a cigarillo.

'All men get turned on by something,' she said. 'They're manipulable. All you've got to do is find the kink. I should know.'

'Henry's not like that. I'd know if he was.'

'So he makes with the doll. That's how much you know about Henry. You telling me he's the great lover?'

'We've been married twelve years. It's only natural we don't do it as often as we used to. We're so busy.'

'Busy lizzie. And while you're housebound what's Henry doing?'

'He's taking classes at the Tech. He's there all day and he comes home tired.'

'Takes classes takes asses. You'll be telling me next he's not a sidewinder.'

'I don't know what you mean,' said Eva.

'He has his piece on the side. His secretary knees up on the desk.'

'He doesn't have a secretary.'

'Then students prudence. Screws their grades up. I know. I've seen it. I've been around colleges too long to be fooled.'

'I'm sure Henry would never . . .'

'That's what they all say and then bingo, it's divorce and bobbysex and all you're left to look forward to is menopause and peeking through the blinds at the man next door and waiting for the Fuller Brush man.'

'You make it all sound so awful,' said Eva. 'You really do.'

'It is, Eva teats. It is. You've got to do something about it before it's too late. You've got to liberate yourself from Henry. Make the break and share the cake. Otherwise it's male domination doomside.'

Eve sat on the bunk and thought about the future. It didn't seem to hold much for her. They would never have any children now and they wouldn't ever have much money. They would go on living in Parkview Avenue and paying off the mortgage and maybe Henry would find someone else and then what would she do? And even if he didn't, life was passing her by.

'I wish I knew what to do,' she said presently. Sally sat up and put her arm round her.

'Why don't you come to the States with us in November?' she said. 'We could have such fun.'

'Oh I couldn't do that,' said Eva. 'It wouldn't be fair to Henry.'

No such qualms bothered Inspector Flint. Wilt's intransigence under intense questioning merely indicated that he was harder than he looked.

'We've had him under interrogation for thirty-six hours now,' he told the conference of the Murder Squad in the briefing room at the Police Station, 'and we've got nothing out of him. So this is going to be a long hard job and quite frankly I have my doubts about breaking him.'

'I told you he was going to be a hard nut to crack,' said Sergeant Yates.

'Nut being the operative word,' said Flint. 'So it's got to be concrete evidence.'

There was a snigger which died away quickly. Inspector Flint was not in a humorous mood.

'Evidence, hard evidence is the only thing that is going to break him. Evidence is the only thing that is going to bring him to trial.'

'But we've got that,' said Yates. 'It's at the bott ...'

'I know exactly where it is, thank you Sergeant. What I am talking about is evidence of multiple murder. Mrs Wilt is accounted for. Dr and Mrs Pringsheim aren't. Now my guess is that he murdered all three and that the other two bodies are ...' He stopped and opened the file in front of him and hunted through it for Notes on Violence and the Break-Up of

Family Life. He studied them for a moment and shook his head. 'No,' he muttered, 'it's not possible.'

'What isn't, sir?' asked Sergeant Yates. 'Anything is possible with this bastard.'

But Inspector Flint was not to be drawn. The notion was too awful.

'As I was saying,' he continued, 'what we need now is hard evidence. What we have got is purely circumstantial. I want more evidence on the Pringsheims. I want to know what happened at that party, who was there and why it happened and at the rate we're going with Wilt we aren't going to get anything out of him. Snell, you go down to the Department of Biochemistry at the University and get what you can on Dr Pringsheim. Find out if any of his colleagues were at that party. Interview them. Get a list of his friends, his hobbies, his girl friends if he had any. Find out if there is any link between him and Mrs Wilt that would suggest a motive. Jackson, you go up to Rossiter Grove and see what you can get on Mrs Pringsheim...'

By the time the conference broke up detectives had been despatched all over town to build up a dossier on the Pringsheims. Even the American Embassy had been contacted to find out what was known about the couple in the States. The murder investigation had begun in earnest.

Inspector Flint walked back to his office with Sergeant Yates and shut the door. 'Yates,' he said, 'this is confidential. I wasn't going to mention it in there but I've a nasty feeling I know why that sod is so bloody cocky. Have you ever known a murderer sit through thirty-six hours of questioning as cool as a cucumber when he knows we've got the body of his victim pinpointed to the nearest inch?'

Sergeant Yates shook his head. 'I've known some pretty cool customers in my time and particularly since they stopped hanging but this one takes the biscuit. If you ask me he's a raving psychopath.'

Flint dismissed the idea. 'Psychopaths crack easy,' he said. 'They confess to murders they haven't committed or they confess to murders they have committed, but they confess.

This Wilt doesn't. He sits there and tells me how to run the investigation. Now take a look at this.' He opened the file and took out Wilt's notes. 'Notice anything peculiar?'

Sergeant Yates read the notes through twice.

'Well, he doesn't seem to think much of our methods,' he said finally. 'And I don't much like this bit about low level of intelligence of average policeman.'

'What about Point Two D?' said the Inspector. 'Increasing use of sophisticated methods such as diversionary tactics by criminals. Diversionary tactics. Doesn't that suggest anything to you?'

'You mean he's trying to divert our attention away from the real crime to something else?'

Inspector Flint nodded. 'What I mean is this. I wouldn't mind betting that when we do get down to the bottom of that fucking pile we're going to find an inflatable doll dressed up in Mrs Wilt's clothes and with a vagina. That's what I think.'

'But that's insane.'

'Insane? It's fucking diabolical,' said the Inspector. 'He's sitting in there like a goddam dummy giving as good as he gets because he knows he's got us chasing a red herring.'

Sergeant Yates sat down mystified. 'But why? Why draw attention to the murder in the first place? Why didn't he just lie low and act normally?'

'What, and report Mrs Wilt missing? You're forgetting the Pringsheims. A wife goes missing, so what? Two of her friends go missing and leave their house in a hell of a mess and covered with bloodstains. That needs explaining, that does. So he puts out a false trail . . .'

'But that still doesn't help him,' objected the Sergeant. 'We dig up a plastic doll. Doesn't mean we're going to halt the investigation.'

'Maybe not but it gives him a week while the other bodies disintegrate.'

'You think he used an acid bath like Haigh?' asked the Sergeant. 'That's horrible.'

'Of course it's horrible. You think murder's nice or something? Anyway the only reason they got Haigh was that stupid bugger told them where to look for the sludge. If he'd kept his trap shut for another week they wouldn't have found anything. The whole lot would have been washed away. Besides I don't know what Wilt's used. All I do know is he's an intellectual, a clever sod and he thinks he's got it wrapped up. First we take him in for questioning, maybe even get him remanded and when we've done that, we go and dig up a plastic inflatable doll. We're going to look right Charlies going into court with a plastic doll as evidence of murder. We'll be the laughing stock of the world. So the case gets thrown out of court and what happens when we pick him up a second time for questioning on the real murders? We'd have the Civil Liberties brigade sinking their teeth into our throats like bleeding vampire bats.'

'I suppose that explains why he doesn't start shouting for a lawyer,' said Yates.

'Of course it does. What does he want with a lawyer now? But pull him in a second time and he'll have lawyers falling over themselves to help him. They'll be squawking about police brutality and victimization. You won't be able to hear yourself speak. His bloody lawyers will have a field day. First plastic dolls and then no bodies at all. He'll get clean away.'

'Anyone who can think that little lot up must be a madman,' said the Sergeant.

'Or a fucking genius,' said Flint bitterly. 'Christ what a case.' He stubbed out a cigarette resentfully.

'What do you want me to do? Have another go at him?'

'No, I'll do that. You go up to the Tech and chivvy his boss there into saying what he really thinks of Wilt. Get any little bit of dirt on the blighter you can. There's got to be something in his past we can use.'

He went down the corridor and into the Interview Room. Wilt was sitting at the table making notes on the back of a statement form. Now that he was beginning to feel, if not at home in the Police Station, at least more at ease with his surroundings, his mind had turned to the problem of Eva's disappearance. He had to admit that he had been worried by the bloodstains in the Pringsheims' bathroom. To while away the time he had tried to formulate his thoughts on paper and he was still at it when Inspector Flint came into the room and banged the door.

'Right, so you're a clever fellow, Wilt,' he said, sitting down and pulling the paper towards him. 'You can read and write and you've got a nice logical and inventive mind so let's just see what you've written here. Who's Ethel?'

'Eva's sister,' said Wilt. 'She's married to a market gardener in Luton. Eva sometimes goes over there for a week.'

'And "Blood in the bath"?'

'Just wondering how it got there.'

'And "Evidence of hurried departure"?'

'I was simply putting down my thoughts about the state of the Pringsheims' house,' said Wilt.

'You're trying to be helpful?'

'I'm here helping you with your enquiries. That's the official term isn't it?'

'It may be the official term, Wilt, but in this case it doesn't correspond with the facts.'

'I don't suppose it does very often,' said Wilt. 'It's one of those expressions that covers a multitude of sins.'

'And crimes.'

'It also happens to ruin a man's reputation,' said Wilt. 'I hope you realize what you're doing to mine by holding me here like this. It's bad enough knowing I'm going to spend the rest of my life being pointed out as the man who dressed a plastic doll with a cunt up in his wife's clothes and dropped it down a pile hole without everyone thinking I'm a bloody murderer as well.'

'Where you're going to spend the rest of your life nobody is going to care what you did with that plastic doll,' said the Inspector.

Wilt seized on the admission.

'Ah, so you've found it at last,' he said eagerly. 'That's fine. So now I'm free to go.'

'Sit down and shut up,' snarled the Inspector. 'You're not going anywhere and when you do it will be in a large black van. I haven't finished with you yet. In fact I'm only just beginning.'

'Here we go again,' said Wilt. 'I just knew you'd want to

start at the beginning again. You fellows have primary causes on the brain. Cause and effect, cause and effect. Which came first, the chicken or the egg, protoplasm or demiurge? I suppose this time it's going to be what Eva said when we were dressing to go to the party.'

'This time,' said the Inspector, 'I want you to tell me precisely why you stuck that damned doll down that hole.'

'Now that is an interesting question,' said Wilt, and stopped. It didn't seem a good idea to try to explain to Inspector Flint in the present circumstances just what he had had in mind when he dropped the doll down the shaft. The Inspector didn't look the sort of person who would understand at all readily that a husband could have fantasies of murdering his wife without actually putting them into effect. It would be better to wait for Eva to put in an appearance in the flesh before venturing into that uncharted territory of the wholly irrational. With Eva present Flint might sympathize with him. Without her he most certainly wouldn't.

'Let's just say I wanted to get rid of the beastly thing,' he said.

'Let's not say anything of the sort,' said Flint. 'Let's just say you had an ulterior motive for putting it there.'

Wilt nodded. 'I'll go along with that,' he said.

Inspector Flint nodded encouragingly. 'I thought you might. Well, what was it?'

Wilt considered his words carefully. He was getting into deep waters.

'Let's just say it was by way of being a rehearsal.'

'A rehearsal? What sort of rehearsal?'

Wilt thought for a moment.

'Interesting word "rehearsal",' he said. 'It comes from the old French, *rehercer*, meaning . . .'

'To hell with where it comes from,' said the Inspector, 'I want to know where it ends up.'

'Sounds a bit like a funeral too when you come to think of it,' said Wilt, continuing his campaign of semantic attrition.

Inspector Flint hurled himself into the trap. 'Funeral? Whose funeral?'

'Anyone's,' said Wilt blithely. 'Hearse, rehearse. You could say that's what happens when you exhume a body. You rehearse it though I don't suppose you fellows use hearses.'

'For God's sake,' shouted the Inspector. 'Can't you ever stick to the point? You said you were rehearsing something and I want to know what that something was.'

'An idea, a mere idea,' said Wilt, 'one of those ephemera of mental fancy that flit like butterflies across the summer landscape of the mind blown by the breezes of association that come like sudden showers ... I rather like that.'

'I don't,' said the Inspector, looking at him bitterly. 'What I want to know is what you were rehearsing. That's what I'd like to know.'

'I've told you. An idea.'

'What sort of idea?'

'Just an idea,' said Wilt. 'A mere ...'

'So help me God, Wilt,' shouted the Inspector, 'if you start on these fucking butterflies again I'll break the unbroken habit of a lifetime and wring your bloody neck.'

'I wasn't going to mention butterflies this time,' said Wilt reproachfully, 'I was going to say that I had this idea for a book ...'

'A book?' snarled Inspector Flint. 'What sort of book? A book of poetry or a crime story?'

'A crime story,' said Wilt, grateful for the suggestion.

'I see,' said the Inspector. 'So you were going to write a thriller. Well now, just let me guess the outline of the plot. There's this lecturer at the Tech and he has this wife he hates and he decides to murder her ...'

'Go on,' said Wilt, 'you're doing very well so far.'

'I thought I might be,' said Flint delightedly. 'Well, this lecturerer thinks he's a clever fellow who can hoodwink the police. He doesn't think much of the police. So he dumps a plastic doll down a hole that's going to be filled with concrete in the hope that the police will waste their time digging it out and in the meantime he's buried his wife somewhere else. By the way, where did you bury Mrs Wilt, Henry? Let's get this over once and for all. Where did you put her? Just tell me that. You'll feel better when it's out.'

'I didn't put her anywhere. If I've told you that once I've

told you a thousand times. How many more times have I got to tell you I don't know where she is.'

'I'll say this for you, Wilt,' said the Inspector, when he could bring himself to speak. 'I've known some cool customers in my time but I have to take my hat off to you. You're the coolest bastard it's ever been my unfortunate experience to come across.'

Wilt shook his head. 'You know,' he said, 'I feel sorry for you, Inspector, I really do. You can't recognize the truth when it's staring you in the face.'

Inspector Flint got up and left the room. 'You there,' he said to the first detective he could find. 'Go into that Interview Room and ask that bastard questions and don't stop till I tell you.'

'What sort of questions?'

'Any sort. Just any. Keep asking him why he stuffed an inflatable plastic doll down a pile hole. That's all. Just ask it over and over again. I'm going to break that sod.'

He went down to his office and slumped into his chair and tried to think.

# 13

At the Tech Sergeant Yates sat in Mr Morris's office. 'I'm sorry to disturb you again,' he said, 'but we need some more details on this fellow Wilt.'

The Head of Liberal Studies looked up with a haggard expression from the timetable. He had been having a desperate struggle trying to find someone to take Bricklayers Four. Price wouldn't do because he had Mechanics Two and Williams wouldn't anyway. He had already gone home the day before with a nervous stomach and was threatening to repeat the performance if anyone so much as mentioned Bricklayers Four to him again. That left Mr Morris himself and he was prepared to be disturbed by Sergeant Yates for as long as he liked if it meant he didn't have to take those bloody brick-layers.

'Anything to help,' he said, with an affability that was in curious contrast to the haunted look in his eyes. 'What details would you like to know?'

'Just a general impression of the man, sir,' said the Sergeant. 'Was there anything unusual about him?'

'Unusual?' Mr Morris thought for a moment. Apart from a preparedness to teach the most awful Day Release Classes year' in and year out without complaint he could think of nothing unusual about Wilt. 'I suppose you could call what amounted to a phobic reaction to *The Lord of the Flies* a bit unusual but then I've never much cared for . . .'

'If you'd just wait a moment, sir,' said the Sergeant busying himself with his notebook. 'You did say "phobic reaction" didn't you?'

'Well what I meant was . . .'

'To flies, sir?'

'To *The Lord of the Flies*. It's a book,' said Mr Morris, now uncertain that he had been wise to mention the fact. Police-men were not noticeably sensitive to those niceties of literary taste that constituted his own definition of intelligence. 'I do hope I haven't said the wrong thing.'

'Not at all, sir. It's these little details that help us to build up a picture of the criminal's mind.'

Mr Morris sighed. 'I'm sure I never thought when Mr Wilt came to us from the University that he would turn out like this.'

'Quite so, sir. Now did Mr Wilt ever say anything disparaging about his wife?'

'Disparaging? Dear me no. Mind you he didn't have to. Eva spoke for herself.' He looked miserably out of the window at the pile-boring machine.

'Then in your opinion Mrs Wilt was not a very likeable woman?'

Mr Morris shook his head. 'She was a ghastly woman,' he said.

Sergeant Yates licked the end of his ballpen.

'You did say "ghastly" sir?'

'I'm afraid so. I once had her in an Evening Class for Elementary Drama.'

'Elementary?' said the Sergeant, and wrote it down.

'Yes, though elemental would have been more appropriate in Mrs Wilt's case. She threw herself into the parts rather too vigorously to be wholly convincing. Her Desdemona to my Othello is something I am never likely to forget.'

'An impetuous woman, would you say?'

'Let me put it this way,' said Mr Morris, 'had Shakespeare written the play as Mrs Wilt interpreted it, Othello would have been the one to be strangled.'

'I see, sir,' said the Sergeant. 'Then I take it she didn't like black men.'

'I have no idea what she thought about the racial issue,' said Mr Morris, 'I am talking of her physical strength.'

'A powerful woman, sir?'

'Very,' said Mr Morris with feelings.

Sergeant Yates looked puzzled. 'It seems strange a woman like that allowing herself to be murdered by Mr Wilt without putting up more of a struggle,' he said thoughtfully.

'It seems incredible to me,' Mr Morris agreed, 'and what is more it indicates a degree of fanatical courage in Henry that his behaviour in this department never led me to suspect. I can only suppose he was insane at the time.'

Sergeant Yates seized on the point. 'Then it is your considered opinion that he was not in his right mind when he killed his wife?'

'Right mind? I can think of nothing rightminded about killing your wife and dumping her body . . .'

'I meant sir,' said the Sergeant, 'that you think Mr Wilt is a lunatic.'

Mr Morris hesitated. There were a good many members of his department whom he would have classified as mentally unbalanced but he hardly liked to advertise the fact. On the other hand it might help poor Wilt.

'Yes, I suppose so,' he said finally for at heart he was a kindly man. 'Quite mad. Between ourselves, Sergeant, anyone who is prepared to teach the sort of bloodyminded young thugs we get can't be entirely sane. And only last week Wilt got into an altercation with one of the Printers and was punched in the face. I think that may have had something to do with his subsequent behaviour. I trust you will treat what I say in the strictest confidence. I wouldn't want ...'

'Quite so, sir,' said Sergeant Yates. 'Well, I needn't detain you any longer.'

He returned to the Police Station and reported his findings to Inspector Flint.

'Nutty as a fruitcake,' he announced. 'That's his opinion. He's quite positive about it.'

'In that case he had no right to employ the sod,' said Flint. 'He should have sacked the brute.'

'Sacked him? From the Tech? You know they can't sack teachers. You've got to do something really drastic before they give you the boot.'

'Like murdering three people, I suppose. Well as far as I'm concerned they can have the little bastard back.'

'You mean he's still holding out?'

'Holding out? He's counterattacking. He's reduced me to a nervous wreck and now Bolton says he wants to be relieved. Can't stand the strain any longer.'

Sergeant Yates scratched his head. 'Beats me how he does it,' he said. 'Anyone would think he was innocent. I wonder when he'll start asking for a lawyer.'

'Never,' said Flint. 'What does he need a lawyer for? If I had a lawyer in there handing out advice I'd have got the truth out of Wilt hours ago.'

As night fell over Eel Creek the wind increased to Gale Force Eight. Rain hammered on the cabin roof, waves slapped against the hull and the cabin cruiser, listing to starboard, settled more firmly into the mud. Inside the cabin the air was thick with smoke and bad feelings. Gaskell had opened a bottle of vodka and was getting drunk. To pass the time they played Scrabble.

'My idea of hell,' said Gaskell, 'is to be huis closed with a couple of dykes.'

'What's a dyke?' said Eva.

Gaskell stared at her. 'You don't know?'

'I know the sort they have in Holland . . .'

'Yoga bear,' said Gaskell, 'you are the naïvest. A dyke is——'

'Forget it, G,' said Sally. 'Whose turn to play?'

'It's mine,' said Eva. 'I . . . M . . . P spells Imp.'

'O . . . T . . . E . . . N . . . T spells Gaskell,' said Sally.

Gaskell drank some more vodka. 'What the hell sort of game we supposed to be playing? Scrabble or some sort of Truth group?'

'Your turn,' said Sally.

Gaskell put D . . . I . . . L . . . D on the O. 'Try that for size.'

Eva looked at it critically.

'You can't use proper names,' she said. 'You wouldn't let me use Squezy.'

'Eva teats, dildo is not a proper name. It's an improper thing. A surrogate penis.'

'A what?'

'Never mind what it is,' said Sally. 'Your turn to play.' Eva studied her letters. She didn't like being told what to do so often and besides she still wanted to know what a dyke was. And a surrogate penis. In the end she put L . . . O . . . V on the E.

'Is a many-splendoured thing,' said Gaskell and put D . . . I . . . D on the L and O.

'You can't have two of them,' said Eva. 'You've got one Dildo already.'

'This one's different,' said Gaskell, 'it's got whiskers.'

'What difference does that make?'

'Ask Sally. She's the one with penis envy.'

'You asshole,' said Sally and put F . . . A . . . G . . . G . . . O on the T. 'Meaning you.'

'Like I said. Truth Scrabble,' said Gaskell. 'Trubble for short. So why don't we have an encounter group instead. Let the truth hang out like it is.'

Eva used the F to make Faithful. Gaskell followed with Hooker and Sally went Insane.

'Great,' said Gaskell, 'Alphabetical I Ching.'

'Wunderkind, you slay me,' said Sally.

'Go Zelda yourself,' said Gaskell and slid his hand up Eva's thigh.

'Keep your hands to yourself,' said Eva and pushed him away. She put S and N on the I. Gaskell made Butch with the B.

'And don't tell me it's a proper name.'

'Well it's certainly not a word I've heard,' said Eva.

Gaskell stared at her and then roared with laughter.

'Now I've heard it all,' he said. 'Like cunnilingus is a cough medicine. How dumb can you get?'

'Go look in the mirror,' said Sally.

'Oh sure. So I married a goddam lesbian whore who goes round stealing other people's wives and boats and things. I'm dumb. But boobs here beats me. She's so fucking hypocritical she pretends she's not a dyke . . .'

'I don't know what a dyke is,' said Eva.

'Well let me inform you, fatso. A dyke is a lesbian.'

'Are you calling me a lesbian?' said Eva.

'Yes,' said Gaskell.

Eva slapped him across the face hard. Gaskell's glasses came off and he sat down on the floor.

'Now G . . .' Sally began but Gaskell had scrambled to his feet.

'Right you fat bitch,' he said. 'You want the truth you're going to get it. First off, you think husband Henry got into that doll off his own bat, well let me tell you . . .'

'Gaskell, you just shut up,' shouted Sally.

'Like hell I will. I've had about enough of you and your rotten little ways. I picked you out of a cathouse . . .'

'That's not true. It was a clinic,' screamed Sally, 'a clinic for sick perverts like you.'

Eva wasn't listening. She was staring at Gaskell. He had called her a lesbian and had said Henry hadn't got into that doll of his own accord.

'Tell me about Henry,' she shouted. 'How did he get into that doll?'

Gaskell pointed at Sally. 'She put him there. That poor goof wouldn't know . . .'

'You put him there?' Eva said to Sally. 'You did?'

'He tried to make me, Eva. He tried to—'

'I don't believe it,' Eva shouted. 'Henry isn't like that.'

'I tell you he did. He . . .'

'And you put him in that doll?' Eva screamed and launched herself across the table at Sally. There was a splintering sound and the table collapsed. Gaskell scudded sideways on to the bunk and Sally shot out of the cabin. Eva got to her feet and moved forward towards the door. She had been tricked, cheated and lied to. And Henry had been humiliated. She was going to kill that bitch Sally. She stepped out into the cockpit. On the far side Sally was a dark shadow. Eva went round the engine and lunged at her. The next moment she had slipped on the oily deck and Sally had darted across the cockpit and through the door into the cabin. She slammed the door behind her and locked it. Eva Wilt got to her feet and stood with the rain running down her face and as she stood there the illusions that had sustained her through the week disappeared. She saw herself as a fat, silly woman who had left her husband in pursuit of a glamour that was false and shoddy and founded on brittle talk and money. And Gaskell had said she was a lesbian. The full nausea of knowing what Touch Therapy had meant dawned on Eva. She staggered to the side of the boat and sat down on a locker.

And slowly her self-disgust turned back to anger, and a cold hatred of the Pringsheims. She would get her own back on them. They would be sorry they had ever met her. She got up and opened the locker and took out the lifejackets and threw them over the side. Then she blew up the airbed, dropped it into the water and climbed over herself. She let herself down into the water and lay on the airbed. It rocked alarmingly but Eva was not afraid. She was getting her revenge on the Pringsheims and she no longer cared what happened to her. She paddled off through the little waves pushing the lifejackets in front of her. The wind was behind her and the airbed moved easily. In five minutes she had turned the corner of the reeds and was out of sight of the cruiser. Somewhere in the darkness ahead there was the open water where they had seen the dinghies and beyond it land.

Presently she found herself being blown sideways into the reeds. The rain stopped and Eva lay panting on the airbed. It would be easier if she got rid of the lifejackets. She was far enough from the boat for them to be well hidden. She pushed them into the reeds and then hesitated. Perhaps she should keep one for herself. She disentangled a jacket from the bunch and managed to put it on. Then she lay face down on the airbed again and paddled forward down the widening channel.

Sally leant against the cabin door and looked at Gaskell with loathing.

'You stupid jerk,' she said. 'You had to open your big mouth. So what the hell are you going to do now?'

'Divorce you for a start,' said Gaskell.

'I'll alimony you for all the money you've got.'

'Fat chance. You won't get a red cent,' Gaskell said and drank some more vodka.

'I'll see you dead first,' said Sally.

Gaskell grinned. 'Me dead? Anyone's going to die round here, it's you. Booby baby is out for blood.'

'She'll cool off.'

'You think so? Try opening that door if you're so sure. Go on, unlock it.'

Sally moved away from the door and sat down.

'This time you've really bought yourself some trouble,' said Gaskell. 'You had to pick a goddam prizefighter.'

'You go out and pacify her,' said Sally.

'No way. I'd as soon play blind man's buff with a fucking rhinoceros.' He lay on the bunk and smiled happily. 'You know there's something really ironical about all this. You had to go and liberate a Neanderthal. Women's Lib for paleolithics. She Tarzan, you Jane. You've bought yourself a piece of zoo.'

'Very funny,' said Sally. 'And what's your role?'

'Me Noah. Just be thankful she hasn't got a gun.' He pulled a pillow up under his head and went to sleep.

Sally sat on staring at his back venomously. She was frightened. Eva's reaction had been so violent that it had destroyed her confidence in herself. Gaskell was right. There had been something primeval in Eva Wilt's behaviour. She shuddered at the thought of that dark shape moving towards her in the cockpit. Sally got up and went into the galley and found a long sharp knife. Then she went back into the cabin and checked the lock on the door and lay down on her bunk and tried to sleep. But sleep wouldn't come. There were noises outside. Waves lapped against the side of the boat. The wind blew. God, what a mess it all was! Sally clutched her knife and thought about Gaskell and what he had said about divorce.

Peter Braintree sat in the office of Mr Gosdyke, Solicitor, and discussed the problem. 'He's been in there since Monday and it's Thursday now. Surely they've no right to keep him there so long without his seeing a solicitor.'

'If he doesn't ask for one and if the police want to question him and he is prepared to answer their questions and refuses to demand his legal rights I don't really see that there is anything I can do about it,' said Mr Gosdyke.

'But are you sure that that is the situation?' asked Braintree.

'As far as I can ascertain that is indeed the situation. Mr Wilt has not asked to see me. I spoke to the Inspector in charge, you heard me, and it seems quite clear that Mr Wilt appears, for some extraordinary reason, to be prepared to help the police with their enquiries just as long as they feel his presence at the Police Station is necessary. Now if a man refuses to assert his own legal rights then he has only himself to blame for his predicament.'

'But are you absolutely certain that Henry has refused to see you? I mean the police could be lying to you.'

Mr Gosdyke shook his head. 'I have known Inspector Flint for many years,' he said, 'and he is not the sort of man to deny a suspect his rights. No, I'm sorry, Mr Braintree. I would like to be of more assistance but frankly, in the circumstances, I can do nothing. Mr Wilt's predilection for the company of police officers is quite incomprehensible to me, but it disqualifies me from interfering.'

'You don't think they're giving him third degree or anything of that sort?'

'My dear fellow, third degree? You've been watching too

many old movies on the TV. The police don't use strong-arm methods in this country.'

'They've been pretty brutal with some of our students who have been on demos,' Braintree pointed out.

'Ah, but students are quite another matter and demonstrating students get what they deserve. Political provocation is one thing but domestic murders of the sort your friend Mr Wilt seems to have indulged in come into a different category altogether. I can honestly say that in all my years in the legal profession I have yet to come across a case in which the police did not treat a domestic murderer with great care and not a little sympathy. After all, they are nearly all married men themselves, and in any case Mr Wilt has a degree and that always helps. If you are a professional man, and in spite of what some people may say lecturers in Technical Colleges are members of a profession if only marginally, then you can rest assured that the police will do nothing in the least untoward. Mr Wilt is perfectly safe.'

And Wilt felt safe. He sat in the Interview Room and contemplated Inspector Flint with interest.

'Motivation? Now there's an interesting question,' he said. 'If you had asked me why I married Eva in the first place I'd have some trouble trying to explain myself. I was young at the time and ...'

'Wilt,' said the Inspector, 'I didn't ask you why you married your wife. I asked you why you decided to murder her.'

'I didn't decide to murder her,' said Wilt.

'It was a spontaneous action? A momentary impulse you couldn't resist? An act of madness you now regret?'

'It was none of those things. In the first place it was not an act. It was mere fantasy.'

'But you do admit that the thought crossed your mind?'

'Inspector,' said Wilt, 'if I acted upon every impulse that crossed my mind I would have been convicted of child rape, buggery, burglary, assault with intent to commit grievous bodily harm and mass murder long ago.'

'All those impulses crossed your mind?'

'At some time or other, yes,' said Wilt.

'You've got a bloody odd mind.'

'Which is something I share with the vast majority of mankind. I daresay that even you in your odd contemplative moments have ...'

'Wilt,' said the Inspector, 'I don't have odd contemplative moments. Not until I met you anyhow. Now then, you admit you thought of killing your wife ...'

'I said the notion had crossed my mind, particularly when I have to take the dog for a walk. It is a game I play with myself. No more than that.'

'A game? You take the dog for a walk and think of ways and means of killing Mrs Wilt? I don't call that a game. I call it premeditation.'

'Not badly put,' said Wilt with a smile, 'the meditation bit. Eva curls up in the lotus position on the living-room rug and thinks beautiful thoughts. I take the bloody dog for a walk and think dreadful ones while Clem defecates on the grass verge in Grenville Gardens. And in each case the end result is just the same. Eva gets up and cooks supper and washes up and I come home and watch the box or read and go to bed. Nothing has altered one way or another.'

'It has now,' said the Inspector. 'Your wife has disappeared off the face of the earth together with a brilliant young scientist and his wife, and you are sitting here waiting to be charged with their murder.'

'Which I don't happen to have committed,' said Wilt. 'Ah well, these things happen. The moving finger writes and having writ ...'

'Fuck the moving finger. Where are they? Where did you put them? You're going to tell me.'

Wilt sighed. 'I wish I could,' he said, 'I really do. Now you've got that plastic doll ...'

'No we haven't. Not by a long chalk. We're still going down through solid rock. We won't get whatever is down there until tomorrow at the earliest.'

'Something to look forward to,' said Wilt. 'Then I suppose you'll let me go.'

'Like hell I will. I'll have you up for remand on Monday.'

'Without any evidence of murder? Without a body? You can't do that.'

Inspector Flint smiled. 'Wilt,' he said, 'I've got news for you. We don't need a body. We can hold you on suspicion, we can bring you up for trial and we can find you guilty without a body. You may be clever but you don't know your law.'

'Well I must say you fellows have an easy job of it. You mean you can go out in the street and pick up some perfectly innocent passer-by and lug him in here and charge him with murder without any evidence at all?'

'Evidence? We've got evidence all right. We've got a blood-spattered bathroom with a busted-down door. We've got an empty house in a filthy mess and we've got some bloody thing or other down that pile hole and you think we haven't got evidence. You've got it wrong.'

'Makes two of us,' said Wilt.

'And I'll tell you another thing, Wilt. The trouble with bastards like you is that you're too clever by half. You overdo things and you give yourselves away. Now if I'd been in your shoes, I'd have done two things. Know what they are?'

'No,' said Wilt, 'I don't.'

'I'd have washed that bathroom down, number one, and number two I'd have stayed away from that hole. I wouldn't have tried to lay a false trail with notes and making sure the caretaker saw you and turning up at Mr Braintree's house at midnight covered in mud. I'd have sat tight and said nothing.'

'But I didn't know about those bloodstains in the bathroom and if it hadn't been for that filthy doll I wouldn't have dumped the thing down the hole. I'd have gone to bed. Instead of which I got pissed and acted like an idiot.'

'Let me tell you something else, Wilt,' said the Inspector. 'You *are* an idiot, a fucking cunning idiot but an idiot all the same. You need your head read.'

'It would make a change from this lot,' said Wilt.

'What would?'

'Having my head read instead of sitting here and being insulted.'

Inspector Flint studied him thoughtfully. 'You mean that?' he asked.

'Mean what?'

'About having your head read? Would you be prepared to undergo an examination by a qualified psychiatrist?'

'Why not?' said Wilt. 'Anything to help pass the time.'

'Quite voluntarily, you understand. Nobody is forcing you to, but if you want . . .'

'Listen, Inspector, if seeing a psychiatrist will help to convince you that I have not murdered my wife I'll be only too happy to. You can put me on a lie detector. You can pump me full of truth drugs. You can . . .'

'There's no need for any of that other stuff,' said Flint, and stood up. 'A good shrink will do very nicely. And if you think you can get away with guilty but insane, forget it. These blokes know when you're malingering madness.' He went to the door and paused. Then he came back and leant across the table.

'Tell me, Wilt,' he said. 'Tell me just one thing. How come you sit there so coolly? Your wife is missing, we have evidence of murder, we have a replica of her, if you are to be believed, under thirty feet of concrete and you don't turn a hair. How do you do it?'

'Inspector,' said Wilt. 'If you had taught Gasfitters for ten years and been asked as many damnfool questions in that time as I have, you'd know. Besides you haven't met Eva. When you do you'll see why I'm not worried. Eva is perfectly capable of taking care of herself. She may not be bright but she's got a built-in survival kit.'

'Jesus, Wilt, with you around for twelve years she must have had something.'

'Oh she has. You'll like Eva when you meet her. You'll get along like a house on fire. You've both got literal minds and an obsession with trivia. You can take a wormcast and turn it into Mount Everest.'

'Wormcast? Wilt, you sicken me,' said the Inspector, and left the room.

Wilt got up and walked up and down. He was tired of sitting down. On the other hand he was well satisfied with his performance. He had surpassed himself and he took pride in the fact that he was reacting so well to what most people would consider an appalling predicament. But to Wilt it was something else, a challenge, the first real challenge he had had to meet for a long time. Gasfitters and Plasterers had challenged him once but he had learnt to cope with them. You jollied them along. Let them talk, ask questions, divert them, get them going, accept their red herrings and hand out a few of your own, but above all you had to refuse to accept their preconceptions. Whenever they asserted something with absolute conviction as a self-evident truth like all wogs began at Calais, all you had to do was agree and then point out that half the great men in English history had been foreigners like Marconi or Lord Beaverbrook and that even Churchill's mother had been a Yank or talk about the Welsh being the original Englishmen and the Vikings and the Danes and from that lead them off through Indian doctors to the National Health Service and birth control and any other topic under the sun that would keep them quiet and puzzled and desperately trying to think of some ultimate argument that would prove you wrong.

Inspector Flint was no different. He was more obsessive but his tactics were just the same. And besides he had got hold of the wrong end of the stick with a vengeance and it amused Wilt to watch him trying to pin a crime on him he hadn't committed. It made him feel almost important and certainly more of a man than he had done for a long, long time. He was innocent and there was no question about it. In a world where everything else was doubtful and uncertain and open to scepticism the fact of his innocence was sure. For the first time in his adult life Wilt knew himself to be absolutely right, and the knowledge gave him a strength he had never supposed he possessed. And besides there was no question in his mind that Eva would turn up eventually, safe and sound, and more than a little subdued when she realized what her impulsiveness had led to. Serve her right for giving him that disgusting doll. She'd regret that to the end of her days. Yes, if anybody was going to come off badly in this affair it was dear old Eva with her bossiness and her busyness. She'd have a job explaining it to Mavis Mottram and the neighbours. Wilt smiled to himself at the thought. And even the Tech would have to treat him differently in future and with a new respect. Wilt knew the liberal conscience too well not to suppose that he would appear anything less than a martyr when he went back. And a hero. They would bend over backwards to convince themselves that they hadn't thought him as guilty as hell. He'd get promotion too, not for being a good teacher but because they would need to salve their fragile consciences. Talk about killing the fatted calf.

# 14

At the Tech there was no question of killing the fatted calf, at least not for Henry Wilt. The imminence of the CNAA visitation on Friday, coinciding as it apparently would with the resurrection of the late Mrs Wilt, was causing something approaching panic. The Course Board met in almost continuous session and memoranda circulated so furiously that it was impossible to read one before the next arrived.

'Can't we postpone the visit?' Dr Cox asked. 'I can't have them in my office discussing bibliographies with bits of Mrs Wilt being dug out of the ground outside the window.'

'I have asked the police to make themselves as inconspicuous as possible,' said Dr Mayfield.

'With conspicuous lack of success so far,' said Dr Board. 'They couldn't be more in evidence. There are ten of them peering down that hole at this very moment.'

The Vice-Principal struck a brighter note. 'You'll be glad to hear that we've managed to restore power to the canteen,' he told the meeting, 'so we should be able to lay on a good lunch.'

'I just hope I feel up to eating,' said Dr Cox. 'The shocks of the last few days have done nothing to improve my appetite and when I think of poor Mrs Wilt . . .'

'Try not to think of her,' said the Vice-Principal, but Dr Cox shook his head.

'You try not to think of her with a damned great boring machine grinding away outside your office window all day.'

'Talking about shocks,' said Dr Board, 'I still can't understand how the driver of that mechanical corkscrew managed to escape electrocution when they cut through the power cable.'

'Considering the problems we are faced with, I hardly think that's a relevant point just at present,' said Dr Mayfield. 'What we have got to stress to the members of the CNAA committee is that this degree is an integrated course with a fundamental substructure grounded thematically on a concomitance of cultural and sociological factors in no way unsuperficially disparate and with a solid quota of academic content to give students an intellectual and cerebral . . .'

'Haemorrhage?' suggested Dr Board.

Dr Mayfield regarded him balefully. 'I really do think this is no time for flippancy,' he said angrily. 'Either we are committed to the Joint Honours degree or we are not. Furthermore we have only until tomorrow to structure our tactical approach to the visitation committee. Now, which is it to be?'

'Which is what to be?' asked Dr Board. 'What has our commitment or lack of it to do with structuring, for want of several far better words, our so-called tactical approach to a committee which, since it is coming all the way from London to us and not vice versa, is presumably approaching us?'

'Vice-Principal,' said Dr Mayfield, 'I really must protest. Dr Board's attitude at this late stage in the game is quite incomprehensible. If Dr Board . . .'

'Could even begin to understand one tenth of the jargon Dr Mayfield seems to suppose is English he might be in a better position to express his opinion,' interrupted Dr Board. 'As it is, "incomprehensible" applies to Dr Mayfield's syntax, not to my attitude. I have always maintained . . .'

'Gentlemen,' said the Vice-Principal, 'I think it would be best if we avoided inter-departmental wrangles at this point in time and got down to business.'

There was a silence broken finally by Dr Cox. 'Do you think the police could be persuaded to erect a screen round that hole?' he asked.

'I shall certainly suggest that to them,' said Dr Mayfield. They passed on to the matter of entertainment.

'I have arranged for there to be plenty of drinks before lunch,' said the Vice-Principal, 'and in any case lunch will be judiciously delayed to allow them to get into the right mood so the afternoon sessions should be cut short and proceed, hopefully, more smoothly.'

'Just so long as the Catering Department doesn't serve Toad in the Hole,' said Dr Board.

The meeting broke up acrimoniously.

So did Mr Morris's encounter with the Crime Reporter of the *Sunday Post*.

'Of course I didn't tell the police that I employed homicidal maniacs as a matter of policy,' he shouted at the reporter. 'And in any case what I said was, as I understood it, to be treated in the strictest confidence.'

'But you did say you thought Wilt was insane and that quite a number of Liberal Studies lecturers were off their heads?'

Mr Morris looked at the man with loathing. 'To put the record straight, what I said was that some of them were ...'

'Off their rockers?' suggested the reporter.

'No, not off their rockers,' shouted Mr Morris. 'Merely, well, shall we say, slightly unbalanced.'

'That's not what the police say you said. They say quote ...'

'I don't care what the police say I said. I know what I said and what I didn't and if you're implying ...'

'I'm not implying anything. You made a statement that half your staff are nuts and I'm trying to verify it.'

'Verify it?' snarled Mr Morris. 'You put words into my mouth I never said and you call that verifying it?'

'Did you say it or not? That's all I'm asking. I mean if you express an opinion about your staff ...'

'Mr MacArthur, what I think about my staff is my own affair. It has absolutely nothing to do with you or the rag you represent.'

'Three million people will be interested to read your opinion on Sunday morning,' said Mr MacArthur, 'and I wouldn't be at all surprised if this Wilt character didn't sue you if he ever gets out of the copshop.'

'Sue me? What the hell could he sue me for?'

'Calling him a homicidal maniac for a start. Banner headlines HEAD OF LIBERAL STUDIES CALLS LECTURER HOMICIDAL MANIAC should be good for fifty thousand. I'd be surprised if he got less.'

Mr Morris contemplated destitution. 'Even your paper would never print that,' he muttered. 'I mean Wilt would sue you too.'

'Oh we're used to libel actions. They're run-of-the-mill for us. We pay for them out of petty cash. Now if you'd be a bit more cooperative . . .' He left the suggestion in mid-air for Mr Morris to digest.

'What do you want to know?' he asked miserably.

'Got any juicy drug scene stories for us?' asked Mr MacArthur. 'You know the sort of thing. LOVE ORGIES IN LECTURES. That always gets the public. Teenyboppers having it off and all that. Give us a good one and we'll let you off the hook about Wilt.'

'Get out of my office!' yelled Mr Morris.

Mr MacArthur got up. 'You're going to regret this,' he said and went downstairs to the students' canteen to dig up some dirt on Mr Morris.


'Not tests,' said Wilt adamantly. 'They're deceptive.'

'You think so?' said Dr Pittman, consultant psychiatrist at the Fenland Hospital and professor of Criminal Psychology at the University. Being plagiocephalic didn't help either.

'I should have thought it was obvious,' said Wilt. 'You show me an ink-blot and I think it looks like my grandmother lying in a pool of blood, do you honestly think I'm going to be fool enough to say so? I'd be daft to do that. So I say a butterfly sitting on a geranium. And every time it's the same. I think what it does look like and then say something completely different. Where does that get you?'

'It is still possible to infer something from that,' said Dr Pittman.

'Well, you don't need a bloody ink-blot to infer, do you?'

said Wilt. Dr Pittman made a note of Wilt's interest in blood. 'You can infer things from just looking at the shape of people's heads.'

Dr Pittman polished his glasses grimly. Heads were not things he liked inferences to be drawn from. 'Mr Wilt,' he said, 'I am here at your request to ascertain your sanity and in particular to give an opinion as to whether or not I consider you capable of murdering your wife and disposing of her body in a singularly revolting and callous fashion. I shall not allow anything you may say to influence my ultimate and objective findings.'

Wilt looked perplexed. 'I must say you're not giving yourself much room for manoeuvre. Since we've dispensed with mechanical aids like tests I should have thought what I had to say would be the only thing you could go on. Unless of course you're going to read the bumps on my head. Isn't that a bit old-fashioned?'

'Mr Wilt,' said Dr Pittman, 'the fact that you clearly have a sadistic streak and take pleasure in drawing attention to other people's physical infirmities in no way disposes me to conclude you are capable of murder ...'

'Very decent of you,' said Wilt, 'though frankly I'd have thought anyone was capable of murder given the right, or to be precise the wrong, circumstances.'

Dr Pittman stifled the impulse to say how right he was. Instead he smiled prognathously. 'Would you say you were a rational man, Henry?' he asked.

Wilt frowned. 'Just stick to Mr Wilt if you don't mind. This may not be a paid consultation but I prefer a little formality.'

Dr Pittman's smile vanished. 'You haven't answered my question.'

'No, I wouldn't say I was a rational man,' said Wilt.

'An irrational one perhaps?'

'Neither the one wholly nor the other wholly. Just a man.'

'And a man is neither one thing nor the other?'

'Dr Pittman, this is your province not mine but in my opinion man is capable of reasoning but not of acting within wholly rational limits. Man is an animal, a developed animal, though come to think of it all animals are developed if we are to believe Darwin. Let's just say man is a domesticated animal with elements of wildness about him . . .'

'And what sort of animal are you, Mr Wilt?' said Dr Pittman. 'A domesticated animal or a wild one?'

'Here we go again. These splendidly simple dual categories that seem to obsess the modern mind. Either/Or Kierkegaard as that bitch Sally Pringsheim would say. No, I am not wholly domesticated. Ask my wife. She'll express an opinion on the matter.'

'In what respect are you undomesticated?'

'I fart in bed, Dr Pittman. I like to fart in bed. It is the trumpet call of the anthropoid ape in me asserting its territorial imperative in the only way possible.'

'In the only way possible?'

'You haven't met Eva,' said Wilt. 'When you do you'll see that assertion is her forte not mine.'

'You feel dominated by Mrs Wilt?'

'I *am* dominated by Mrs Wilt.'

'She bullies you? She assumes the dominant role?'

'Eva is, Dr Pittman. She doesn't have to assume anything. She just is.'

'Is what?'

'Now there's the rub,' said Wilt. 'What's today? You lose track of time in this place.'

'Thursday.'

'Well, today being Thursday, Eva is Bernard Leach.'

'Bernard Leach?'

'The potter, Dr Pittman, the famous potter,' said Wilt. 'Now tomorrow she'll be Margot Fonteyn and on Saturday we play bridge with the Mottrams so she'll be Omar Sharif. On Sunday she's Elizabeth Taylor or Edna O'Brien depending on what the Colour Supplements have in store for me and in the afternoon we go for a drive and she's Eva Wilt. It's about the only time in the week I meet her and that's because I'm driving and she's got nothing to do but sit still and nag the pants off me.'

'I begin to see the pattern,' said Dr Pittman. 'Mrs Wilt was . . . is given to role-playing. This made for an unstable relationship in which you couldn't establish a distinctive and assertive role as a husband . . .'

'Dr Pittman,' said Wilt, 'a gyroscope may, indeed must, spin but in doing so it achieves a stability that is virtually unequalled. Now if you understand the principle of the gyroscope you may begin to understand that our marriage does not lack stability. It may be damned uncomfortable coming home to a centrifugal force but it bloody well isn't unstable.'

'But just now you told me that Mrs Wilt did not assume a dominant role. Now you tell me she is a forceful character.'

'Eva is not forceful. She is a force. There's a difference. And as for character, she has so many and they're so varied it's difficult to keep up with them all. Let's just say she throws herself into whoever she is with an urgency and compulsiveness that is not always appropriate. You remember that series of Garbo pictures they showed on TV some years back? Well, Eva was La Dame Aux Camélias for three days after that and she made dying of TB look like St Vitus' dance. Talk about galloping consumption.'

'I begin to get the picture,' said Dr Pittman making a note that Wilt was a pathological liar with sado-masochistic tendencies.

'I'm glad somebody does,' said Wilt. 'Inspector Flint thinks I murdered her and the Pringsheims in some sort of bloodlust and disposed of their bodies in some extraordinary fashion. He mentioned acid. I mean it's crazy. Where on earth does one get nitric acid in the quantities necessary to dissolve three dead bodies, and one of them overweight at that? I mean it doesn't bear thinking about.'

'It certainly doesn't,' said Dr Pittman.

'In any case do I look like a murderer?' continued Wilt cheerfully. 'Of course I don't. Now if he'd said Eva had slaughtered the brutes, and in my opinion someone should have done years ago, I'd have taken him seriously. God help the poor sods who happen to be around when Eva takes it into her head she's Lizzie Borden.'

Dr Pittman studied him predaciously.

'Are you suggesting that Dr and Mrs Pringsheim were murdered by your wife?' he asked. 'Is that what you're saying?"

'No,' said Wilt, 'I am not. All I'm saying is that when Eva does things she does them wholeheartedly. When she cleans the house she cleans it. Let me tell you about the Harpic. She's got this thing about germs . . .'

'Mr Wilt,' said Dr Pittman hastily, 'I am not interested in what Mrs Wilt does with the Harpic. I have come here to understand you. Now then, do you make a habit of copulating with a plastic doll? Is this a regular occurrence?'

'Regular?' said Wilt. 'Do you mean a normal occurrence or a recurring one? Now your notion of what constitutes a normal occurrence may differ from mine . . .'

'I mean, do you do it often?' interrupted Dr Pittman.

'Do it?' said Wilt. 'I don't do it at all.'

'But I understood you to have placed particular emphasis on the fact that this doll had a vagina?'

'Emphasis? I didn't have to emphasize the fact. The beastly thing was plainly visible.'

'You find vaginas beastly?' said Dr Pittman stalking his prey into the more familiar territory of sexual aberration.

'Taken out of context, yes,' said Wilt sidestepping, 'and with plastic ones you can leave them in context and I still find them nauseating.'

By the time Dr Pittman had finished the interview he was uncertain what to think. He got up wearily and made for the door.

'You've forgotten your hat, doctor,' said Wilt holding it out to him. 'Pardon my asking but do you have them specially made for you?'

'Well?' said Inspector Flint when Dr Pittman came into his office. 'What's the verdict?'

'Verdict? That man should be put away for life."

'You mean he's a homicidal maniac?'

'I mean that no matter how he killed her Mrs Wilt must have been thankful to go. Twelve years married to that man . . . Good God, it doesn't bear thinking about.'

'Well, that doesn't get us much forrader,' said the Inspector, when the psychiatrist had left having expressed the opinion that while Wilt had the mind of an intellectual jackrabbit he couldn't in all honesty say that he was criminally insane. 'We'll just have to see what turns up tomorrow.'

# 15

What turned up on Friday was seen not only by Inspector Flint, Sergeant Yates, twelve other policemen, Barney and half a dozen construction workers, but several hundred Tech students standing on the steps of the Science block, most of the staff and by all eight members of the CNAA visitation committee who had a particularly good view from the windows of the mock hotel lounge used by the Catering Department to train waiters and to entertain distinguished guests. Dr Mayfield did his best to distract their attention.

'We have structured the foundation course to maximize student interest,' he told Professor Baxendale, who headed the committee, but the professor was not to be diverted. His interest was maximized by what was being unstructured from the foundations of the new Admin block.

'How absolutely appalling,' he muttered as Judy protruded from the hole. Contrary to Wilt's hopes and expectations she had not burst. The liquid concrete had sealed her in too well for that and if in life she had resembled in many particulars a real live woman, in death she had all the attributes of a real dead one. As the corpse of a murdered woman she was entirely convincing. Her wig was matted and secured to her head at an awful angle by the concrete. Her clothes clung to her and cement to them while her legs had evidently been contorted to the point of mutilation and her outstretched arm had, as Barney had foretold, a desperate appeal about it that was most affecting. It also made it exceedingly difficult to extricate her from the hole. The legs didn't help, added to which the concrete had given her a substance and stature approximate to that of Eva Wilt.

'I suppose that's what they mean by rigor mortice,' said Dr Board, as Dr Mayfield desperately tried to steer the conversation back to the Joint Honours degree.

'Dear Lord,' muttered Professor Baxendale. Judy had eluded the efforts of Barney and his men and had slumped back down the hole. 'To think what she must have suffered. Did you see that damned hand?'

Dr Mayfield had. He shuddered. Behind him Dr Board sniggered. 'There's a divinity that shapes our ends, rough-hew them how we will,' he said gaily. 'At least Wilt has saved himself the cost of a gravestone. All they'll have to do is prop her up with Here Stands Eva Wilt, Born So and So, Murdered last Saturday carved across her chest. In life monumental, in death a monument.'

'I must say, Board,' said Dr Mayfield, 'I find your sense of humour singularly ill-timed.'

'Well they'll never be able to cremate her, that's for certain,' continued Dr Board. 'And the undertaker who can fit that little lot into a coffin will be nothing short of a genius. I suppose they could always take a sledgehammer to her.'

In the corner Dr Cox fainted.

'I think I'll have another whisky if you don't mind,' said Professor Baxendale weakly. Dr Mayfield poured him a double. When he turned back to the window Judy was protruding once more from the hole.

'The thing about embalming,' said Dr Board, 'is that it costs so much. Now I'm not saying that thing out there is a perfect likeness of Eva Wilt as I remember her ...'

'For heaven's sake, do you have to go on about it?' snarled Dr Mayfield, but Dr Board was not to be stopped. 'Quite apart from the legs there seems to be something odd about the breasts. I know Mrs Wilt's were large but they do seem to have inflated. Probably due to the gases. They putrefy, you know, which would account for it.'

By the time the committee went into lunch they had lost all appetite for food and most of them were drunk.

Inspector Flint was less fortunate. He didn't like being present at exhumations at the best of times and particularly when the corpse on whose behalf he was acting showed such a marked inclination to go back where she came from. Besides he was in two minds whether it was a corpse or not. It looked like a corpse and it certainly behaved like a corpse, albeit a very heavy one, but there was something about the knees that suggested that all was not anatomically as it should have been with whatever it was they had dug up. There was a double jointedness and a certain lack of substance where the legs stuck forwards at right angles that seemed to indicate that Mrs Wilt had lost not only her life but both kneecaps as well. It was this mangled quality that made Barney's job so difficult and exceedingly distasteful. After the body had dropped down the hole for the fourth time Barney went down himself to assist from below.

'If you sods drop her,' he shouted from the depths, 'you'll have two dead bodies down here so hang on to that rope whatever happens. I'm going to tie it round her neck.'

Inspector Flint peered down the shaft. 'You'll do no such thing,' he shouted, 'we don't want her decapitated. We need her all in one piece.'

'She is all in one bloody piece,' came Barney's muffled reply, 'that's one thing you don't have to worry about.'

'Can't you tie the rope around something else?'

'Well I could,' Barney conceded, 'but I'm not going to. A leg is more likely to come off than her head and I'm not going to be underneath her when it goes.'

'All right,' said the Inspector, 'I just hope you know what you're doing, that's all.'

'I'll tell you one thing. The sod who put her down here knew what he was doing and no mistake.'

But this fifth attempt failed, like the previous four, and Judy was lowered into the depths where she rested heavily on Barney's foot.

'Go and get that bloody crane,' he shouted. 'I can't stand much more of this.'

'Nor can I,' muttered the Inspector, who still couldn't make up his mind what it was he was supposed to be disinterring; a doll dressed up to look like Mrs Wilt or Mrs Wilt dressed up to look like something some demented sculptor forgot to finish. What few doubts he had had about Wilt's sanity had been entirely dispelled by what he was presently witnessing. Any man who could go to the awful lengths Wilt had gone to render, and the word was entirely apposite whichever way you took it, either his wife or a plastic doll with a vagina, both inaccessible and horribly mutilated, must be insane.

Sergeant Yates put his thoughts into words. 'You're not going to tell me now that the bastard isn't off his rocker,' he said, as the crane was moved into position and the rope lowered and attached to Judy's neck.

'All right, now take her away,' shouted Barney.

In the dining-room only Dr Board was enjoying his lunch. The eight members of the CNAA committee weren't. Their eyes were glued to the scene below.

'I suppose it could be said she was *in statue pupillari*,' said Dr Board, helping himself to some more Lemon Meringue, 'in which case we stand *in loco parentis*. Not a pleasant thought, gentlemen. Not that she was ever a very bright student. I once had her for an Evening Class in French literature. I don't know what she got out of *Fleurs du Mal* but I do remember thinking that Baudelaire ...'

'Dr Board,' said Dr Mayfield drunkenly, 'for a so-called cultured man you are entirely without feeling.'

'Something I share with the late Mrs Wilt, by the look of things,' said Dr Board, glancing out of the window, 'and while we are still on the subject, things seem to be coming to a head. They do indeed.'

Even Dr Cox, recently revived and coaxed into having some mutton, looked out of the window. As the crane slowly winched Judy into view the Course Board and the Committee rose and went to watch. It was an unedifying sight. Near the top of the shaft Judy's left leg caught in a crevice while her outstretched arm embedded itself in the clay.

'Hold it,' shouted Barney indistinctly, but it was too late.

Unnerved by the nature of his load or in the mistaken belief that he had been told to lift harder, the crane driver hoisted away. There was a ghastly cracking sound as the noose tightened and the next moment Judy's concrete head, capped by Eva Wilt's wig, looked as if it was about to fulfil Inspector Flint's prediction that she would be decapitated. In the event he need not have worried. Judy was made of sterner stuff than might have been expected. As the head continued to rise and the body to remain firmly embedded in the shaft Judy's neck rose to the occasion. It stretched.

'Dear God,' said Professor Baxendale frantically, 'will it never end?'

Dr Board studied the phenomenon with increasing interest. 'It doesn't look like it,' he said. 'Mind you we do make a point of stretching our students, eh Mayfield?'

But Dr Mayfield made no response. As Judy took on the configuration of an ostrich that had absentmindedly buried its head in a pail of cement he knew that the Joint Honours degree was doomed.

'I'll say this for Mrs Wilt,' said Dr Board, 'she do hold on. No one could call her stiff-necked. Attenuated possibly. One begins to see what Modigliani was getting at.'

'For God's sake stop,' yelled Dr Cox hysterically, 'I think I'm going off my head.'

'Which is more than can be said for Mrs Wilt,' said Dr Board callously.

He was interrupted by another awful crack as Judy's body finally gave up the struggle with the shaft. With a shower of clay it careered upwards to resume a closer relationship with the head and hung naked, pink and, now that the clothes and the concrete had been removed, remarkably lifelike at the end of the rope some twenty feet above the ground.

'I must say,' said Dr Board, studying the vulva with relish, 'I've never had much sympathy with necrophilia before but I do begin to see its attractions now. Of course it's only of historical interest but in Elizabethan times it was one of the perks of an executioner . . .'

'Board,' screamed Dr Mayfield, 'I've known some fucking swine in my time . . .'

Dr Board helped himself to some more coffee. 'I believe the slang term for it is liking your meat cold.'

Underneath the crane Inspector Flint wiped the mud from his face and peered up at the awful object swinging above him. He could see now that it was only a doll. He could also see why Wilt had wanted to bury the beastly thing.

'Get it down. For God's sake get it down,' he bawled, as the press photographers circled round him. But the crane driver had lost his nerve. He shut his eyes, pulled the wrong lever and Judy began a further ascent.

'Stop it, stop it, that's fucking evidence,' screamed the Inspector, but it was already too late. As the rope wound through the final pulley Judy followed. The concrete cap disintegrated, her head slid between the rollers and her body began to swell. Her legs were the first to be affected.

'I've often wondered what elephantiasis looked like,' said Dr Board. 'Shelley had a phobia about it, I believe.'

Dr Cox certainly had. He was gibbering in a corner and the Vice-Principal was urging him to pull himself together.

'An apt expression,' observed Dr Board, above the gasps of horror as Judy, now clearly twelve months pregnant, continued her transformation. 'Early Minoan, wouldn't you say, Mayfield?'

But Dr Mayfield was past speech. He was staring dementedly at a rapidly expanding vagina some fourteen inches long and eight wide. There was a pop and the thing became a penis, an enormous penis that swelled and swelled. He was going mad. He knew he was.

'Now that,' said Dr Board, 'takes some beating. I've heard about sex-change operations for men but ...'

'Beating?' screamed Dr Mayfield, 'Beating? You can stand there cold-bloodedly and talk about ...'

There was a loud bang. Judy had come to the end of her tether. So had Dr Mayfield. The penis was the first thing to go. Dr Mayfield the second. As Judy deflated he hurled himself at Dr Board only to sink to the ground gibbering.

Dr Board ignored his colleague. 'Who would have thought the old bag had so much wind in her?' he murmured, and finished his coffee. As Dr Mayfield was led out by the Vice-Principal, Dr Board turned to Professor Baxendale.

'I must apologize for Mayfield,' he said, 'I'm afraid this Joint Honours degree has been too much for him and to tell the truth I have always found him to be fundamentally unsound. A case of dementia post Cox I daresay.'

Inspector Flint drove back to the Police Station in a state bordering on lunacy.

'We've been made to look idiots,' he snarled at Sergeant Yates. 'You saw them laughing. You heard the bastards.' He was particularly incensed by the press photographers who had asked him to pose with the limp remnants of the plastic doll. 'We've been held up to public ridicule. Well, my God, somebody's going to pay.'

He hurled himself out of the car and lunged down the passage to the Interview Room. 'Right, Wilt,' he shouted, 'you've had your little joke and a bloody nasty one it was too. So now we're going to forget the niceties and get to the bottom of this business.'

Wilt studied the torn piece of plastic. 'Looks better like that if you ask me,' he said. 'More natural if you know what I mean.'

'You'll look bloody natural if you don't answer my questions,' yelled the Inspector. 'Where is she?'

'Where is who?' said Wilt.

'Mrs Fucking Wilt. Where did you put her?'

'I've told you. I didn't put her anywhere.'

'And I'm telling you you did. Now either you're going to tell me where she is or I'm going to beat it out of you.'

'You can beat me up if you like,' said Wilt, 'but it won't do you any good.'

'Oh yes it will,' said the Inspector and took off his coat.

'I demand to see a solicitor,' said Wilt hastily.

Inspector Flint put his jacket on again. 'I've been waiting to hear you say that. Henry Wilt, I hereby charge you with . . .'

# 16

In the reeds Eva greeted the dawn of another day by blowing up the airbed for the tenth time. It had either sprung a leak or developed a fault in the valve. Whichever it was it had made her progress exceedingly slow and had finally forced her to take refuge in the reeds away from the channel. Here, wedged between the stems, she had spent a muddy night getting off the airbed to blow it up and getting back on to try and wash off the sludge and weeds that had adhered to her when she got off. In the process she had lost the bottom half of her lemon loungers and had torn the top half so that by dawn she resembled less the obsessive housewife of 34 Parkview Avenue than a finalist in the heavyweight division of the Ladies Mud-wrestling Championship. In addition she was exceedingly cold and was glad when the sun came up bringing with it the promise of a hot summer day. All she had to do now was to find her way to land or open water and get someone to ... At this point Eva became aware that her appearance was likely to cause some embarrassment. The lemon loungers had been sufficiently outré to make her avoid walking down the street when she had had them on; with them largely off she certainly didn't want to be seen in public. On the other hand she couldn't stay in the reeds all day. She plunged on, dragging the airbed behind her, half swimming but for the most part trudging through mud and water. At last she came out of the reeds into open water and found herself looking across a stretch to a house, a garden that sloped down to the water's edge, and a church. It seemed a long way across but there was no boat in sight. She would have to swim across and just hope that the woman who lived there was sympathetic and better still large enough to lend her some clothes until she got home. It was at this point that Eva discovered that she had left her handbag somewhere in the reeds. She remembered having it during the night but it must have fallen off the airbed when she was blowing it up. Well she couldn't go back and look for it now. She would just have to go on without it and ring Henry up and tell him to come out in the car and get her. He could bring some clothes too. Yes, that was it. Eva Wilt climbed on to the airbed and began to paddle across. Halfway over the airbed went down for the eleventh time. Eva abandoned it and struggled on in the lifejacket. But that too impeded her progress and she finally decided to take it off. She trod water and tried to undo it and after a struggle managed to get it off. In the process the rest of the lemon loungers disintegrated so that by the time she reached the bank Eva Wilt was exhausted and quite naked. She crawled into the cover of a willow tree and lay panting on the ground. When she had recovered she stood up and looked around. She was at the bottom of the garden and the house was a hundred yards away up the hill. It was a very large house by Eva's standards, and not the sort she would feel at home in at the best of times. For one thing it appeared to have a courtyard with stables at the back and to Eva, whose knowledge of large country houses was confined to what she had seen on TV, there was the suggestion of servants, gentility and a social formality that would make her arrival in the nude rather heavy going. On the other hand the whole place looked decidedly run down. The garden was overgrown and unkempt; ornamental bushes which might once have been trimmed to look like birds and animals had reverted to strange and vaguely monstrous shapes; rusted hoops leant half-hidden in the grass of an untended croquet lawn; a tennis net sagged between posts and an abandoned greenhouse boasted a few panes of lichened glass. Finally there was a dilapidated boathouse and a rowing boat. All in all the domain had a sinister and imposing air to it which wasn't helped by the presence of a small church hidden among trees to the left and a neglected graveyard beyond an old iron fence. Eva peered out from the weeping willow and was about to leave its cover when the French windows opened and a man came out on to the terrace with a pair of binoculars and peered through them in the direction of Eel Stretch. He was wearing a black cassock and a dog collar. Eva went back behind the tree and considered the awkwardness of her situation and lack of attire. It was all extremely embarrassing. Nothing on earth would make her go up to the house, the Vicarage, with nothing on. Parkview Avenue hadn't prepared her for situations of this sort.

Rossiter Grove hadn't prepared Gaskell for the situation he found when Sally woke him with 'Noah baby, it's drywise topside. Time to fly the coop.'

He opened the cabin door and stepped outside to discover that Eva had already flown and had taken the airbed and the lifejackets with her.

'You mean you left her outside all night?' he said. 'Now we're really up Shit Creek. No paddle, no airbed, no goddam lifejackets, no nothing.'

'I didn't know she'd do something crazy like take off with everything,' said Sally.

'You leave her outside in the pouring rain all night she's got to do something. She's probably frozen to death by now. Or drowned.'

'She tried to kill me. You think I was going to let her in when she's tried to do that. Anyhow it's all your fault for shooting your mouth off about that doll.'

'You tell that to the law when they find her body floating downstream. You just explain how come she goes off in the middle of a storm.'

'You're just trying to scare me,' said Sally. 'I didn't make her go or anything.'

'It's going to look peculiar if something has happened to her is all I'm saying. And you tell me how we're going to get off here now. You think I'm going swimming without a lifejacket you're mistaken. I'm no Spitz.'

'My hero,' said Sally.

Gaskell went into the cabin and looked in the cupboard by the stove. 'And another thing. We've got a food problem. And water. There's not much left.'

'You got us into this mess. You think of a way out,' said Sally.

Gaskell sat down on the bunk and tried to think. There had to be some way of letting people know they were there and in trouble. They couldn't be far from land. For all he knew dry land was just the other side of the reeds. He went out and climbed on top of the cabin but apart from the church spire in the distance he could see nothing beyond the reeds. Perhaps if they got a piece of cloth and waved it someone would spot it. He went down and fetched a pillow case and spent twenty minutes waving it above his head and shouting. Then he returned to the cabin and got out the chart and pored over it in a vain attempt to discover where they were. He was just folding the map up when he spotted the pieces of Scrabble still lying on the table. Letters. Individual letters. Now if they had something that would float up in the air with letters on it. Like a kite. Gaskell considered ways of making a kite and gave it up. Perhaps the best thing after all was to make smoke signals. He fetched an empty can from the kitchen and filled it with fuel oil from beside the engine and soaked a handkerchief in it and clambered up on the cabin roof. He lit the handkerchief and tried to get the oil to burn but when it did there was very little smoke and the tin got too hot to hold. Gaskell kicked it into the water where it fizzled out.

'Genius baby,' said Sally, 'you're the greatest.'

'Yea, well if you can think of something practical let me know.'

'Try swimming.'

'Try drowning,' said Gaskell.

'You could make a raft or something.'

'I could hack this boat of Scheimacher's up. That's all we need.'

'I saw a movie once where there were these gauchos or Romans or something and they came to a river and wanted to cross and they used pigs' bladders,' said Sally.

'Right now all we don't have is a pig,' said Gaskell.

'You could use the garbage bags in the kitchen,' said Sally. Gaskell fetched a plastic bag and blew it up and tied the end with string. Then he squeezed it. The bag went down.

Gaskell sat down despondently. There had to be some simple way of attracting attention and he certainly didn't want to swim out across that dark water clutching an inflated garbage bag. He fiddled with the pieces of Scrabble and thought once again about kites. Or balloons. Balloons.

'You got those rubbers you use?' he asked suddenly.

'Jesus, at a time like this you get a hard on,' said Sally. 'Forget sex. Think of some way of getting us off here.'

'I have,' said Gaskell, 'I want those skins.'

'You going to float downriver on a pontoon of condoms?'

'Balloons,' said Gaskell. 'We blow them up and paint letters on them and float them in the wind.'

'Genius baby,' said Sally and went into the toilet. She came out with a sponge bag. 'Here they are. For a moment there I thought you wanted me.'

'Days of wine and roses,' said Gaskell, 'are over. Remind me to divorce you.' He tore a packet open and blew a contraceptive up and tied a knot in its end.

'On what grounds?'

'Like you're a lesbian,' said Gaskell and held up the dildo. 'This and kleptomania and the habit you have of putting other men in dolls and knotting them. You name it, I'll use it. Like you're a nymphomaniac.'

'You wouldn't dare. Your family would love it, the scandal.'

'Try me,' said Gaskell and blew up another condom.

'Plastic freak.'

'Bull dyke.'

Sally's eyes narrowed. She was beginning to think he meant what he said about divorce and if Gaskell divorced her in England what sort of alimony would she get? Very little. There were no children and she had the idea that British courts were mean in matters of money. So was Gaskell and there was his family too. Rich and mean. She sat and eyed him.

'Where's your nail varnish?' Gaskell asked when he had finished and twelve contraceptives cluttered the cabin.

'Drop dead,' said Sally and went out on deck to think. She stared down at the dark water and thought about rats and death and being poor again and liberated. The rat paradigm. The world was a rotten place. People were objects to be used and discarded. It was Gaskell's own philosophy and now he was discarding her. And one slip on this oily deck could solve her problems. All that had to happen was for Gaskell to slip and drown and she would be free and rich and no one would ever know. An accident. Natural death. But Gaskell could swim and there had to be no mistakes. Try it once and fail and she wouldn't be able to try again. He would be on his guard. It had to be certain and it had to be natural.

Gaskell came out on deck with the contraceptives. He had tied them together and painted on each one a single letter with nail varnish so that the whole read HELP SOS HELP. He climbed up on the cabin roof and launched them into the air. They floated up for a moment, were caught in the light breeze and sagged sideways down on to the water. Gaskell pulled them in on the string and tried again. Once again they floated down on to the water.

'I'll wait until there's some more wind,' he said, and tied the string to the rail where they bobbed gently. Then he went into the cabin and lay on the bunk.

'What are you going to do now?' Sally asked.

'Sleep. Wake me when there's a wind.'

He took off his glasses and pulled a blanket over him.

Outside Sally sat on a locker and thought about drowning. In bed.

'Mr Gosdyke,' said Inspector Flint, 'you and I have had dealings for a good many years now and I'm prepared to be frank with you. I don't know.'

'But you've charged him with murder,' said Mr Gosdyke.

'He'll come up for remand on Monday. In the meantime I am going on questioning him.'

'But surely the fact that he admits burying a lifesize doll . . .'

'Dressed in his wife's clothes, Gosdyke. In his wife's clothes. Don't forget that.'

'It still seems insufficient to me. Can you be absolutely sure that a murder has been committed?'

'Three people disappear off the face of the earth without a trace. They leave behind them two cars, a house littered with unwashed glasses and the leftovers of a party . . . you should see that house . . . a bathroom and landing covered with blood . . .'

'They could have gone in someone else's car.'

'They could have but they didn't. Dr Pringsheim didn't like

172

being driven by anyone else. We know that from his colleagues at the Department of Biochemistry. He had a rooted objection to British drivers. Don't ask me why but he had.'

'Trains? Buses? Planes?'

'Checked, rechecked and checked again. No one answering to their description used any form of public or private transport out of town. And if you think they went on a bicycle ride, you're wrong again. Dr Pringsheim's bicycle is in the garage. No, you can forget their going anywhere. They died and Mr Smart Alec Wilt knows it.'

'I still don't see how you can be so sure,' said Mr Gosdyke.

Inspector Flint lit a cigarette. 'Let's just look at his actions, his admitted actions and see what they add up to,' he said. 'He gets a lifesize doll . . .'

'Where from?'

'He says he was given it by his wife. Where he got it from doesn't matter.'

'He says he first saw the thing at the Pringsheims' house.'

'Perhaps he did. I'm prepared to believe that. Wherever he got it, the fact remains that he dressed it up to look like Mrs Wilt. He puts it down that hole at the Tech, a hole he knows is going to be filled with concrete. He makes certain he is seen by the caretaker when he knows that the Tech is closed. He leaves a bicycle covered with his fingerprints and with a book of his in the basket. He leaves a trail of notes to the hole. He turns up at Mrs Braintree's house at midnight covered with mud and says he's had a puncture when he hasn't. Now you're not going to tell me that he hadn't got something in mind.'

'He says he was merely trying to dispose of that doll.'

'And he tells me he was rehearsing his wife's murder. He's admitted that.'

'Yes, but only in fantasy. His story to me is that he wanted to get rid of that doll,' Mr Gosdyke persisted.

'Then why the clothes, why blow the thing up and why leave it in such a position it was bound to be spotted when the concrete was poured down? Why didn't he cover it with earth if he didn't want it to be found? Why didn't he just burn the bloody thing or leave it by the roadside? It just doesn't make sense unless you see it as a deliberate plan to draw our attention away from the real crime.' The Inspector paused. 'Well now, the way I see it is that something happened at that party we don't know anything about. Perhaps Wilt found his wife in bed with Dr Pringsheim. He killed them both. Mrs Pringsheim puts in an appearance and he kills her too.'

'How?' said Mr Gosdyke. 'You didn't find that much blood.'

'He strangled her. He strangled his own wife. He battered Pringsheim to death. Then he hides the bodies somewhere, goes home and lays the doll trail. On Sunday he disposes of the real bodies ...'

'Where?'

'God alone knows, but I'm going to find out. All I know is that a man who can think up a scheme like this one is bound to have thought of somewhere diabolical to put the real victims. It wouldn't surprise me to learn that he spent Sunday making illegal use of the crematorium. Whatever he did you can be sure he did it thoroughly.'

But Mr Gosdyke remained unconvinced. 'I wish I knew how you could be so certain,' he said.

'Mr Gosdyke,' said the Inspector wearily, 'you have spent two hours with your client. I have spent the best part of the week and if I've learnt one thing from the experience it is this, that sod in there knows what he is doing. Any normal man in his position would have been worried and alarmed and downright frightened. Any innocent man faced with a missing wife and the evidence we've got of murder would have had a nervous breakdown. Not Wilt. Oh no, he sits in there as bold as you please and tells me how to conduct the investigation. Now if anything convinces me that that bastard is as guilty as hell that does. He did it and I know it. And what is more, I'm going to prove it.'

'He seems a bit worried now,' said Mr Gosdyke.

'He's got reason to be,' said the Inspector, 'because by Monday morning I'm going to get the truth out of him even if it kills him and me both.'

'Inspector,' said Mr Gosdyke getting to his feet, 'I must warn you that I have advised my client not to say another word and if he appears in Court with a mark on him ...'

'Mr Gosdyke, you should know me better than that. I'm not a complete fool and if your client has any marks on him on Monday morning they will not have been made by me or any of my men. You have my assurance on that.'

Mr Gosdyke left the Police Station a puzzled man. He had to admit that Wilt's story hadn't been a very convincing one. Mr Gosdyke's experience of murderers was not extensive but he had a shrewd suspicion that men who confessed openly that they had entertained fantasies of murdering their wives ended by admitting that they had done so in fact. Besides his attempt to get Wilt to agree that he'd put the doll down the hole as a practical joke on his colleagues at the Tech had failed hopelessly. Wilt had refused to lie and Mr Gosdyke was not used to clients who insisted on telling the truth.

Inspector Flint went back into the Interview Room and looked at Wilt. Then he pulled up a chair and sat down.

'Henry,' he said with an affability he didn't feel, 'you and I are going to have a little chat.'

'What, another one?' said Wilt. 'Mr Gosdyke has advised me to say nothing.'

'He always does,' said the Inspector sweetly, 'to clients he knows are guilty. Now are you going to talk?'

'I can't see why not. I'm not guilty and it helps to pass the time.'

# 17

It was Friday and as on every other day in the week the little church at Waterswick was empty. And as on every other day of the week the Vicar, the Reverend St John Froude, was drunk. The two things went together, the lack of a congregation and the Vicar's insobriety. It was an old tradition dating back to the days of smuggling when Brandy for the Parson had been about the only reason the isolated hamlet had a vicar at all. And like so many English traditions it died hard. The Church authorities saw to it that Waterswick got idiosyncratic parsons whose awkward enthusiasms tended to make them unsuitable for more respectable parishes and they, to console themselves for its remoteness and lack of interest in things spiritual, got alcoholic. The Rev St John Froude maintained the tradition. He attended to his duties with the same Anglo-Catholic Fundamentalist fervour that had made him so unpopular in Esher and turned an alcoholic eye on the activities of his few parishioners who, now that brandy was not so much in demand, contented themselves with the occasional boatload of illegal Indian immigrants.

Now as he finished a breakfast of eggnog and Irish coffee and considered the iniquities of his more egregious colleagues as related in the previous Sunday's paper he was startled to see something wobbling above the reeds on Eel Stretch. It looked like balloons, white sausage-shaped balloons that rose briefly and then disappeared. The Rev St John Froude shuddered, shut his eyes, opened them again and thought about the virtues of abstinence. If he was right and he didn't know whether he wanted to be or not, the morning was being profaned by a cluster of contraceptives, inflated contraceptives, wobbling erratically where by the nature of things no contraceptive had ever wobbled before. At least he hoped it was a cluster. He was so used to seeing things in twos when they were in fact ones that he couldn't be sure if what looked like a cluster of inflated contraceptives wasn't just one or better still none at all.

He reeled off to his study to get his binoculars and stepped out on to the terrace to focus them. By that time the manifestation had disappeared. The Rev St John Froude shook his head mournfully. Things and in particular his liver had reached a pretty pickle for him to have hallucinations so early in the morning. He went back into the house and tried to concentrate his attention on a case involving an Archdeacon in Ongar who had undergone a sex-change operation before eloping with his verger. There was matter there for a sermon if only he could think of a suitable text.

•

At the bottom of the garden Eva Wilt watched his retreat and wondered what to do. She had no intention of going up to the house and introducing herself in her present condition. She needed clothes, or at least some sort of covering. She looked around for something temporary and finally decided on some ivy climbing up the graveyard fence. With one eye on the Vicarage she emerged from the willow tree and scampered across to the fence and through the gate into the churchyard. There she ripped some ivy off the trunk of a tree and, carrying it in front of her rather awkwardly, made her way surreptitiously up the overgrown path towards the church. For the most part her progress was masked from the house by the trees but once or twice she had to crouch low and scamper from tombstone to tombstone in full view of the Vicarage. By the time she reached the church porch she was panting and her sense of impropriety had been increased tenfold. If the prospect of presenting herself at the house in the nude offended her on grounds of social decorum, going into a church in the raw was positively sacrilegious. She stood in the porch and tried frantically to steel herself to go in. There were bound to be surplices for the choir in the vestry and dressed in a surplice she could go up to the house. Or could she? Eva wasn't sure about the significance of surplices and the Vicar might be angry. Oh dear it was all so awkward. In the end she opened the church door and went inside. It was cold and damp and empty. Clutching the ivy to her she crossed to the vestry door and tried it. It was locked. Eva stood shivering and tried to think. Finally she went outside and stood in the sunshine trying to get warm.

In the Staff Room at the Tech, Dr Board was holding court. 'All things considered I think we came out of the whole business rather creditably,' he said. 'The Principal has always said he wanted to put the college on the map and with the help of friend Wilt it must be said he has succeeded. The newspaper coverage has been positively prodigious. I shouldn't be surprised if our student intake jumped astonishingly.'

'The committee didn't approve our facilities,' said Mr Morris, 'so you can hardly claim their visit was an unqualified success.'

'Personally I think they got their money's worth,' said Dr Board. 'It's not every day you get the chance to see an exhumation and an execution at the same time. The one usually precedes the other and certainly the experience of seeing what to all intents and purposes was a woman turn in a matter of seconds into a man, an instantaneous sex change, was, to use a modern idiom, a mind-blowing one.'

'Talking of poor Mayfield,' said the Head of Geography, 'I understand he's still at the Mental Hospital.'

'Committed?' asked Dr Board hopefully.

'Depressed. And suffering from exhaustion.'

'Hardly surprising. Anyone who can use language ... abuse language like that is asking for trouble. Structure as a verb, for example.'

'He had set great store by the Joint Honours degree and the fact that it has been turned down ...'

'Quite right too,' said Dr Board. 'The educative value of stuffing second-rate students with fifth-rate ideas on subjects as diverse as Medieval Poetry and Urban Studies escapes me. Far better that they should spend their time watching the police dig up the supposed body of a woman coated in concrete, stretch her neck, rip all her clothes off her, hang her and finally blow her up until she explodes. Now that is what I call a truly educational experience. It combines archaeology with criminology, zoology with physics, anatomy with economic theory, while maintaining the students' undivided attention all the time. If we must have Joint Honours degrees let them be of that vitality. Practical too. I'm thinking of sending away for one of those dolls.'

'It still leaves unresolved the question of Mrs Wilt's disappearance,' said Mr Morris.

'Ah, dear Eva,' said Dr Board wistfully. 'Having seen so much of what I imagined to be her I shall, if I ever have the pleasure of meeting her again, treat her with the utmost courtesy. An amazingly versatile woman and interestingly proportioned. I think I shall christen my doll Eva.'

'But the police still seem to think she is dead.'

'A woman like that can never die,' said Dr Board. 'She may explode but her memory lingers on indelibly.'

In his study the Rev St John Froude shared Dr Board's opinion. The memory of the large and apparently naked lady he had glimpsed emerging from the willow tree at the bottom of his garden like some disgustingly oversized nymph and scuttling through the churchyard was not something he was ever likely to forget. Coming so shortly after the apparition of the inflated contraceptives it lent weight to the suspicion that he had been overdoing things on the alcohol side. Abandoning the sermon he had been preparing on the apostate Archdeacon of Ongar – he had had 'By their fruits ye shall know them' in mind as a text – he got up and peered out of the window in the direction of the church and was wondering if he shouldn't go down and see if there wasn't a large fat naked lady there when his attention was drawn to the reeds across the water. They were there again, those infernal things. This time there could be no doubt about it. He grabbed his binoculars and stared furiously through them. He could see them much more clearly than the first time and much more ominously. The sun was high in the sky and a mist rose over Eel Stretch so that the contraceptives had a luminescent sheen about them, an insubstantiality that was almost spiritual in its implications. Worse still, there appeared to be something written on them. The message was clear if incomprehensible. It read PEESOP. The Rev St John Froude lowered his binoculars and reached for the whisky bottle and considered the significance of PEESOP etched ectoplasmically against the sky. By the time he had finished his third hurried glass and had decided that spiritualism might after all have something to be said for it though why you almost always found yourself in touch with a Red Indian who was acting by proxy for an aunt which might account for the misspelling of Peasoup while removing some of the less attractive ingredients from the stuff, the wind had changed the letters round. This time when he looked the message read EELPOPS. The Vicar shuddered. What eel was popping and how?

'The sins of the spirit,' he said reproachfully to his fourth glass of whisky before consulting the oracle once more. POSH-ELLS was followed by HEPOLP to be succeeded by SHHLPSPO which was even worse. The Rev St John Froude thrust his binoculars and the bottle of whisky aside and went down on his knees to pray for deliverance, or at least for some guidance in interpreting the message. But every time he got up to see if his wish had been granted the combination of letters was as meaningless as ever or downright threatening. What, for instance, did HELLSPO signify? Or SLOSHHEEL? Finally, determined to discover for himself the true nature of the occurrence, he put on his cassock and wove off down the garden path to the boathouse.

'They shall rue the day,' he muttered as he climbed into the rowing boat and took the oars. The Rev St John Froude held firm views on contraception. It was one of the tenets of his Anglo-Catholicism.

In the cabin cruiser Gaskell slept soundly. Around him Sally made her preparations. She undressed and changed into the plastic bikini. She took a silk square from her bag and put it on the table and she fetched a jug from the kitchen and leaning over the side filled it with water. Finally she went into the toilet and made her face up in the mirror. When she emerged she was wearing false eyelashes, her lips were heavily red and pancake make-up obscured her pale complexion. She was carrying a bathing-cap. She crossed the door of the galley and put an arm up and stuck her hip out.

'Gaskell baby,' she called.

Gaskell opened his eyes and looked at her. 'What the hell gives?'

'Like it, baby?'

Gaskell put on his glasses. In spite of himself he did like it. 'You think you're going to wheedle round me, you're wrong ...'

Sally smiled. 'Conserve the verbiage. You turn me on, bio-degradable baby.' She moved forward and sat on the bunk beside him.

'What are you trying to do?'

'Make it up, babykink. You deserve a curve.' She fondled him gently. 'Like the old days. Remember?'

Gaskell remembered and felt weak. Sally leant forward and pressed him down on to the bunk.

'Surrogate Sally,' she said and unbuttoned his shirt.

Gaskell squirmed. 'If you think ...'

'Don't think, kink,' said Sally and undid his jeans. 'Only erect.'

'Oh God,' said Gaskell. The perfume, the plastic, the mask of a face and her hands were awakening ancient fantasies. He lay supine on the bunk staring at her while Sally undressed him. Even when she rolled him over on his face and pulled his hands behind his back he made no resistance.

'Bondage baby,' she said softly and reached for the silk square.

'No, Sally, no,' he said weakly. Sally smiled grimly and tied his hands together, winding the silk between his wrists carefully before tightening it. When she had finished Gaskell whimpered. 'You're hurting me.'

Sally rolled him over. 'You love it,' she said and kissed him. She sat back and stroked him gently. 'Harder, baby, real hard. Lift me lover sky high.'

'Oh Sally.'

'That's my baby and now the waterproof.'

'There's no need. I like it better without.'

'But I do, G. I need it to prove you loved me till death did us part.' She bent over and rolled it down.

Gaskell stared up at her. Something was wrong.

'And now the cap.' She reached over and picked up the bathing-cap.

'The cap?' said Gaskell. 'Why the cap? I don't want that thing on.'

'Oh but you do, sweetheart. It makes you look girlwise.' She fitted the cap over his head. 'Now into Sallia inter alia.' She undid the bikini and lowered herself on to him. Gaskell moaned and stared up at her. She was lovely. It was a long time since she had been so good. But he was still frightened. There was a look in her eyes he hadn't seen before. 'Untie me,' he pleaded, 'you're hurting my arm.'

But Sally merely smiled and gyrated. 'When you've come and gone, G baby. When you've been.' She moved her hips. 'Come, bum, come quick.'

Gaskell shuddered.

'Finished?'

He nodded. 'Finished,' he sighed.

'For good, baby, for good,' said Sally. 'That was it. You're past the last.'

'Past the last?'

'You've come and gone, come and gone. It's Styxside for you now.'

'Stickside?'

'S for Sally, T for Terminal, Y for You and X for Exit. All that's left is this.' She reached over and picked up the jug of muddy water. Gaskell turned his head and looked at it.

'What's that for?'

'For you, baby. Mudders milk.' She moved up his body and sat on his chest. 'Open your mouth.'

Gaskell Pringsheim stared up at her frantically. He began to writhe. 'You're mad. You're crazy.'

'Now just lie quietly and it won't hurt. It will soon be over, lover. Natural death by drowning. In bed. You're making history.'

'You bitch, you murderous bitch . . .'

'Cerberuswise,' said Sally, and poured the water into his mouth. She put the jug down and pulled the cap down over his face.

The Rev St John Froude rowed surprisingly steadily for a man with half a bottle of whisky inside him and a wrath in his heart, and the nearer he got to the contraceptives the greater his wrath became. It wasn't simply that he had been given a quite unnecessary fright about the state of his liver by the sight of the things (he could see now that he was close to them that they were real), it was rather that he adhered to the doctrine of sexual non-intervention. God, in his view, had created a perfect world if the book of Genesis was to be believed and it had been going downhill ever since. And the book of Genesis *was* to be believed or the rest of the Bible made no sense at all. Starting from this fundamentalist premise the Rev St John Froude had progressed erratically by way of Blake, Hawker, Leavis and a number of obscurantist theologians to the conviction that the miracles of modern science were the works of the devil, that salvation lay in eschewing every material advance since the Renaissance, and one or two before, and that nature was infinitely less red in tooth and claw than modern mechanized man. In short he was convinced that the end of the world was at hand in the shape of a nuclear holocaust and that it was his duty as a Christian to announce the fact. His sermons on the subject had been of such a vividly horrendous fervour as to lead to his exile in Waterswick. Now as he rowed up the channel into Eel Stretch he fulminated silently against contraception, abortion and the evils of sexual promiscuity. They were all symptoms and causes and causative symptoms of the moral chaos which life on earth had become. And finally there were trippers. The Rev St John Froude loathed trippers. They fouled the little Eden of his parish with their boats, their transistors, and their unabashed enjoyment of the present. And trippers who desecrated the prospect from his study window with inflated contraceptives and meaningless messages were an abomination. By the time he came in sight of the cabin cruiser he was in no mood to be trifled with. He rowed furiously across to the boat, tied up to the rail and, lifting his cassock over his knees, stepped aboard.

In the cabin Sally stared down at the bathing-cap. It deflated and inflated, expanded and was sucked in against Gaskell's face and Sally squirmed with pleasure. She was the liberatedest woman in the world, but the liberatedest. Gaskell was dying and she would be free to be with a million dollars in the kitty. And no one would ever know. When he was dead she would take the cap off and untie him and push his body over the side into the water. Gaskell Pringsheim would have died a natural death by drowning. And at that moment the cabin door opened and she looked up at the silhouette of the Rev St John Froude in the cabin doorway.

'What the hell . . .' she muttered and leapt off Gaskell.

The Rev St John Froude hesitated. He had come to say his piece and say it he would but he had clearly intruded on a very naked woman with a horribly made-up face in the act of making love to a man who as far as a quick glance enabled him to tell had no face at all.

'I . . .' he began and stopped. The man on the bunk had rolled on to the floor and was writhing there in the most extraordinary fashion. The Rev St John Froude stared down at him aghast. The man was not only faceless but his hands were tied behind his back.

'My dear fellow,' said the Vicar, appalled at the scene and looked up at the naked woman for some sort of explanation. She was staring at him demonically and holding a large kitchen knife. The Rev St John Froude stumbled back into the cockpit as the woman advanced towards him holding the knife in front of her with both hands. She was clearly quite demented. So was the man on the floor. He rolled about and dragged his head from side to side. The bathing-cap came off but the Rev St John Froude was too busy scrambling over the side into his rowing boat to notice. He cast off as the ghastly woman lunged towards him and began to row away, his original mission entirely forgotten. In the cockpit Sally stood screaming abuse at him and behind her a shape had appeared in the cabin door. The Vicar was grateful to see that the man had a face now, not a nice face, a positively horrible face but a face for all that, and he was coming up behind the woman with some hideous intention. The next moment the intention was carried out. The man hurled himself at her, the knife dropped on to the deck, the woman scrabbled at the side of the boat and then slid forward into the water. The Rev St John Froude waited no longer. He rowed vigorously away. Whatever appalling orgy of sexual perversion he had interrupted he wanted none of it and painted women with knives who called him a motherfucking son of a cuntsucker among other things didn't elicit his sympathy when the object of their obscene passions pushed them into the water. And in any case they were Americans. The Rev St John Froude had no time for Americans. They epitomized everything he found offensive about the modern world. Imbued with a new disgust for the present and an urge to hit the whisky he rowed home and tied up at the bottom of the garden.

Behind him in the cabin cruiser Gaskell ceased shouting. The priest who had saved his life had ignored his hoarse pleas for further help and Sally was standing waist-deep in water beside the boat. Well she could stay there. He went back into the cabin, turned so that he could lock the door with his tied hands and then looked around for something to cut the silk scarf with. He was still very frightened.

'Right,' said Inspector Flint, 'so what did you do then?'
'Got up and read the Sunday papers.'
'After that?'
'I ate a plate of All-Bran and drank some tea.'
'Tea? You sure it was tea? Last time you said coffee.'
'Which time?'
'The last time you told it.'
'I drank tea.'
'What then?'
'I gave Clem his breakfast.'
'What sort?'
'Chappie.'
'Last time you said Bonzo.'
'This time I say Chappie.'
'Make up your mind. Which sort was it?'
'What the fuck does it matter which sort it was?'
'It matters to me.'
'Chappie.'
'And when you had fed the dog.'
'I shaved.'
'Last time you said you had a bath.'
'I had a bath and then I shaved. I was trying to save time.'

'Forget the time, Wilt, we've got all the time in the world.'

'What time is it?'

'Shut up. What did you do then?'

'Oh for God's sake, what does it matter. What's the point of going over and over the same things?'

'Shut up.'

'Right,' said Wilt, 'I will.'

'When you had shaved what did you do?'

Wilt stared at him and said nothing.

'When you had shaved?'

But Wilt remained silent. Finally Inspector Flint left the room and sent for Sergeant Yates.

'He's clammed up,' he said wearily. 'So what do we do now?'

'Try a little physical persuasion?'

Flint shook his head. 'Gosdyke's seen him. If he turns up in Court on Monday with so much as a hair out of place, he'll be all over us for brutality. There's got to be some other way. He must have a weak spot somewhere but I'm damned if I can find it. How does he do it?'

'Do what?'

'Keep talking and saying nothing. Not one bloody useful thing. That sod's got more opinions on every topic under the flaming sun than I've got hair on my head.'

'If we keep him awake for another forty-eight hours he's bound to crack up.'

'He'll take me with him,' said Flint.' We'll both go into court in straitjackets.'

In the Interview Room Wilt put his head on the table. They would be back in a minute with more questions but a moment's sleep was better than none. Sleep. If only they would let him sleep. What had Flint said? 'The moment you sign a confession, you can have all the sleep you want.' Wilt considered the remark and its possibilities. A confession. But it would have to be plausible enough to keep them occupied while he got some rest and at the same time so impossible that it would be rejected by the court. A delaying tactic to give Eva time to come back and prove his innocence. It would be like giving

Gasfitters Two *Shane* to read while he sat and thought about putting Eva down the pile shaft. He should be able to think up something complicated that would keep them frantically active. How he had killed them? Beat them to death in the bathroom? Not enough blood. Even Flint had admitted that much. So how? What was a nice gentle way to go? Poor old Pinkerton had chosen a peaceful death when he stuck a tube up the exhaust pipe of his car ... That was it. But why? There had to be a motive. Eva was having it off with Dr Pringsheim? With that twit? Not in a month of Sundays. Eva wouldn't have looked twice at Gaskell. But Flint wasn't to know that. And what about that bitch Sally? All three having it off together? Well at least it would explain why he killed them all and it would provide the sort of motive Flint would understand. And besides it was right for that kind of party. So he got this pipe ... What pipe? There was no need for a pipe. They were in the garage to get away from everyone else. No, that wouldn't do. It had to be the bathroom. How about Eva and Gaskell doing it in the bath? That was better. He had bust the door down in a fit of jealousy. Much better. Then he had drowned them. And then Sally had come upstairs and he had had to kill her too. That explained the blood. There had been a struggle. He hadn't meant to kill her but she had fallen in the bath. So far so good. But where had he put them? It had to be something good. Flint wasn't going to believe anything like the river. Somewhere that made sense of the doll down the hole. Flint had it firmly fixed in his head that the doll had been a diversionary tactic. That meant that time entered into their disposal.

Wilt got up and asked to go to the toilet. As usual the constable came with him and stood outside the door.

'Do you have to?' said Wilt. 'I'm not going to hang myself with the chain.'

'To see you don't beat your meat,' said the constable coarsely.

Wilt sat down. Beat your meat. What a hell of an expression. It called to mind Meat One. Meat One? It was a moment of inspiration. Wilt got up and flushed the toilet. Meat One would keep them busy for a long time. He went back to the pale green room where the light buzzed. Flint was waiting for him.

'You going to talk now?' he asked.

Wilt shook his head. They would have to drag it out of him if his confession was to be at all convincing. He would have to hesitate, start to say something, stop, start again, appeal to Flint to stop torturing him, plead and start again. This trout needed tickling. Oh well, it would help to keep him awake.

'Are you going to start again at the beginning?' he asked.

Inspector Flint smiled horribly. 'Right at the beginning.'

'All right,' said Wilt, 'have it your own way. Just don't keep asking me if I gave the dog Chappie or Bonzo. I can't stand all that talk about dog food.'

Inspector Flint rose to the bait. 'Why not?'

'It gets on my nerves,' said Wilt, with a shudder.

The Inspector leant forward. 'Dog food gets on your nerves?' he said.

Wilt hesitated pathetically. 'Don't go on about it,' he said. 'Please don't go on.'

'Now then which was it, Bonzo or Chappie?' said the Inspector, scenting blood.

Wilt put his head in his hands. 'I won't say anything. I won't. Why must you keep asking me about food? Leave me alone.' His voice rose hysterically and with it Inspector Flint's hopes. He knew when he had touched the nerve. He was on to a good thing.

# 18

'Dear God,' said Sergeant Yates, 'but we had pork pies for lunch yesterday. It's too awful.'

Inspector Flint rinsed his mouth out with black coffee and spat into the washbasin. He had vomited twice and felt like vomiting again.

'I knew it would be something like that,' he said with a shudder, 'I just knew it. A man who could pull that doll trick had to have something really filthy up his sleeve.'

'But they may all have been eaten by now,' said the Sergeant. Flint looked at him balefully.

'Why the hell do you think he laid that phoney trail?' he asked. 'To give them plenty of time to be consumed. His expression "consumed", not mine. You know what the shelf life of a pork pie is?'

Yates shook his head.

'Five days. Five days. So they went out on Tuesday which leaves us one day to find them or what remains of them. I want every pork pie in East Anglia picked up. I want every fucking sausage and steak and kidney pie that went out of Sweetbreads Meat Factory this week found and brought in. And every tin of dog food.'

'Dog food?'

'You heard me,' said Inspector Flint staggering out of the washroom. 'And while you're about it you'd better make it cat food too. You never know with Wilt. He's capable of leading us up the garden path in one important detail.'

'But if they went into pork pies what's all this about dog food?'

'Where the hell do you think he put the odds and ends and I do mean ends?' Inspector Flint asked savagely. 'You don't imagine he was going to have people coming in and complaining they'd found a tooth or a toenail in the Sweetbreads pie they had bought that morning. Not Wilt. That swine thinks of everything. He drowns them in their own bath. He puts them in plastic garbage bags and locks the bags in the garage while he goes home and sticks the doll down that fucking hole. Then on Sunday he goes back and picks them up and spends the day at the meat factory all by himself ... Well if you want to know what he did on Sunday you can read all about it in his statement. It's more than my stomach can stand.'

The Inspector went back hurriedly into the washroom. He'd been living off pork pies since Monday. The statistical chances of his having partaken of Mrs Wilt were extremely high.

When Sweetbreads Meat and Canning Factory opened at eight,

Inspector Flint was waiting at the gate. He stormed into the manager's office and demanded to speak to him.

'He's not here yet,' said the secretary. 'Is there anything I can do for you?'

'I want a list of every establishment you supply with pork pies, steak and kidney pies, sausages and dog food,' said the Inspector.

'I couldn't possibly give you that information,' said the secretary. 'It's extremely confidential.'

'Confidential? What the hell do you mean confidential?'

'Well I don't know really. It's just that I couldn't take it on myself to provide you with inside information ...' She stopped. Inspector Flint was staring at her with a quite horrible expression on his face.

'Well, miss,' he said finally, 'while we're on the topic of inside information, it may interest you to know that what has been inside your pork pies is by way of being inside information. Vital information.'

'Vital information? I don't know what you mean. Our pies contain perfectly wholesome ingredients.'

'Wholesome?' shouted the Inspector. 'You call three human bodies wholesome? You call the boiled, bleached, minced and cooked remains of three murdered bodies wholesome?'

'But we only use ...' the secretary began and fell sideways off her chair in a dead faint.

'Oh for God's sake,' shouted the Inspector, 'you'd think a silly bitch who can work in an abattoir wouldn't be squeamish. Find out who the manager is and where he lives and tell him to come down here at the double.'

He sat down in a chair while Sergeant Yates rummaged in the desk. 'Wakey, wakey,' he said, prodding the secretary with his foot. 'If anyone has got a right to lie down on the job, it's me. I've been on my feet for three days and nights and I've been an accessory after the fact of murder.'

'An accessory?' said Yates. 'I don't see how you can say that.'

'Can't you? Well what would you call helping to dispose of parts of a murder victim? Concealing evidence of a crime?'

'I never thought of it that way,' said Yates.

'I did,' said the Inspector, 'I can't think of anything else.'

In his cell Wilt stared up at the ceiling peacefully. He was astonished that it had been so easy. All you had to do was tell people what they wanted to hear and they would believe you no matter how implausible your story might be. And three days and nights without sleep had suspended Inspector Flint's disbelief with a vengeance. Then again Wilt's hesitations had been timed perfectly and his final confession a nice mixture of conceit and matter-of-factness. On the details of the murder he had been coldly precise and in describing their disposal he had been a craftsman taking pride in his work. Every now and then when he got to a difficult spot he would veer away into a manic arrogance at once boastful and cowardly with 'You'll never be able to prove it. They'll have disappeared without trace now.' And the Harpic had come in useful once again, adding a macabre touch of realism about evidence being flushed down thousands of U-bends with Harpic being poured after it like salt from a salt cellar. Eva would enjoy that when he told her about it, which was more than could be said for Inspector Flint. He hadn't even seen the irony of Wilt's remark that while he had been looking for the Pringsheims they had been under his nose all the time. He had been particularly upset by the crack about gut reactions and the advice to stick to health foods in future. Yes, in spite of his tiredness Wilt had enjoyed himself watching the Inspector's bloodshot eyes turn from glee and gloating self-satisfaction to open amazement and finally undisguised nausea. And when finally Wilt had boasted that they would never be able to bring him to trial without the evidence, Flint had responded magnificently.

'Oh yes, we will,' he had shouted hoarsely. 'If there is one single pie left from that batch we'll get it and when we do the Lab boys will . . .'

'Find nothing but pork in it,' said Wilt before being dragged off to his cell. At least that was the truth and if Flint didn't believe it that was his own fault. He had asked for a confession and he had got one by courtesy of Meat One, the apprentice butchers who had spent so many hours of Liberal Studies explaining the workings of Sweetbreads Meat Factory to him and had actually taken him down there one afternoon to show him how it all worked. Dear lads. And how he had loathed them at the time. Which only went to show how wrong you could be about people. Wilt was just wondering if he had been wrong about Eva and perhaps she was dead when he fell asleep.

In the churchyard Eva watched the Rev St John Froude walk down to the boathouse and start rowing towards the reeds. As soon as he had disappeared she made her way up the path towards the house. With the Vicar out of the way she was prepared to take the risk of meeting his wife. She stole through the doorway into the courtyard and looked about her. The place had a dilapidated air about it and a pile of empty bottles in one corner, whisky and gin bottles, seemed to indicate that he might well be unmarried. Still clutching her ivy, she went across to the door, evidently the kitchen door, and knocked. There was no answer. She crossed to the window and looked inside. The kitchen was large, distinctly untidy and had all the hallmarks of a bachelor existence about it. She went back to the door and knocked again and she was just wondering what to do now when there was the sound of a vehicle coming down the drive.

Eva hesitated for a second and then tried the door. It was unlocked. She stepped inside and shut the door as a milk van drove into the courtyard. Eva listened while the milkman put down several bottles and then drove away. Then she turned and went down the passage to the front hall. If she could find the phone she could ring Henry and he could come out in the car and fetch her. She would go back to the church and wait for him there. But the hall was empty. She poked her head into several rooms with a good deal of care and found them largely bare of furniture or with dustcovers over chairs and sofas. The place was incredibly untidy too. Definitely the Vicar was a bachelor. Finally she found his study. There was a phone on the desk. Eva went over and lifted the receiver and dialled Ipford 66066. There was no reply. Henry would be at the Tech. She dialled the Tech number and asked for Mr Wilt.

'Wilt?' said the girl on the switchboard. 'Mr Wilt?'

'Yes,' said Eva in a low voice.

'I'm afraid he's not here,' said the girl.

'Not there? But he's got to be there.'

'Well he isn't.'

'But he's got to be. It's desperately important I get in touch with him.'

'I'm sorry, but I can't help you,' said the girl.

'But . . .' Eva began and glanced out of the window. The Vicar had returned and was walking up the garden path towards her. 'Oh God,' she muttered and put the phone down hurriedly. She turned and rushed out of the room in a state of panic. Only when she had made her way back along the passage to the kitchen did it occur to her that she had left her ivy behind in the study. There were footsteps in the passage. Eva looked frantically around, decided against the courtyard and went up a flight of stone steps to the first floor. There she stood and listened. Her heart was palpitating. She was naked and alone in a strange house with a clergyman and Henry wasn't at the Tech when he should have been and the girl on the switchboard had sounded most peculiar, almost as though there was something wrong with wanting to speak to Henry. She had no idea what to do.

In the kitchen the Rev St John Froude had a very good idea what he wanted to do: expunge for ever the vision of the inferno to which he had been lured by those vile things with their meaningless messages floating across the water. He dug a fresh bottle of Teachers out of the cupboard and took it back to his study. What he had witnessed had been so grotesque, so evidently evil, so awful, so prescient of hell itself that he was in two minds whether it had been real or simply a waking nightmare. A man without a face, whose hands were tied behind his back, a woman with a painted face and a knife, the language . . . The Rev St John Froude opened the bottle and was about to pour a glass when his eye fell on the ivy Eva had left on the chair. He put the bottle down hastily and stared at the leaves.

Here was another mystery to perplex him. How had a clump of ivy got on to the chair in his study? It certainly hadn't been there when he had left the house. He picked it up gingerly and put it on his desk. Then he sat down and contemplated it with a growing sense of unease. Something was happening in his world that he could not understand. And what about the strange figure he had seen flitting about between the tombstones? He had quite forgotten her. The Rev St John Froude got up and went out on to the terrace and down the path to the church.

'On a Sunday?' shouted the manager of Sweetbreads. 'On a Sunday? But we don't work on a Sunday. There's nobody here The place is shut.'

'It wasn't last Sunday and there was someone here, Mr Kidney,' said the Inspector.

'Kidley, please,' said the manager, 'Kidley with an L.'

The Inspector nodded. 'OK Mr Kidley, now what I'm telling you is that this man Wilt was here last Sunday and he . . .'

'How did he get in?'

'He used a ladder against the back wall from the car park.'

'In broad daylight? He'd have been seen.'

'At two o'clock in the morning, Mr Kidney.'

'Kidley, Inspector, Kidley.'

'Look Mr Kidley, if you work in a place like this with a name like that you're asking for it.'

Mr Kidley looked at him belligerently. 'And if you're telling me that some bloody maniac came in here with three dead bodies last Sunday and spent the day using our equipment to convert them into cooked meat edible for human consumption under the Food Regulations Act I'm telling you that that comes under the head of . . . Head? What did he do with the heads? Tell me that?'

'What do you do with heads, Mr Kidley?' asked the Inspector.

'That rather depends. Some of them go with the offal into the animal food bins . . .'

'Right. So that's what Wilt said he did with them. And you keep those in the No. 2 cold storage room. Am I right?'

Mr Kidley nodded miserably, 'Yes,' he said, 'we do.' He paused and gaped at the Inspector. 'But there's a world of difference between a pig's head and a ...'

'Quite,' said the Inspector hastily, 'and I daresay you think someone was bound to spot the difference.'

'Of course they would.'

'Now I understand from Mr Wilt that you have an extremely efficient mincing machine ...'

'No,' shouted Mr Kidley desperately. 'No, I don't believe it. It's not possible. It's ...'

'Are you saying he couldn't possibly have ...'

'I'm not saying that. I'm saying he shouldn't have. It's monstrous. It's horrible.'

'Of course it's horrible,' said the Inspector. 'The fact remains that he used that machine.'

'But we keep our equipment meticulously clean.'

'So Wilt says. He was definite on that point. He says he cleaned up carefully afterwards.'

'He must have done,' said Mr Kidley. 'There wasn't a thing out of place on Monday morning. You heard the foreman say so.'

'And I also heard this swine Wilt say that he made a list of where everything came from before he used it so that he could put it back exactly where he'd found it. He thought of everything.'

'And what about our reputation for hygiene? He didn't think of that, did he? For twenty-five years we've been known for the excellence of our products and now this has to happen. We've been at the head of ...' Mr Kidley stopped suddenly and sat down.

'Now then,' said the Inspector, 'what I have to know is who you supply to. We're going to call in every pork pie and sausage ...'

'Call them in? You can't call them in,' screamed Mr Kidley, 'they've all gone.'

'Gone? What do you mean they've gone?'

'What I say. They've gone. They've either been eaten or destroyed by now.'

'Destroyed? You're not going to tell me that there aren't

195

any left. It's only five days since they went out.'

Mr Kidley drew himself up. 'Inspector, this is an old-fashioned firm and we use traditional methods and a Sweet-breads pork pie is a genuine pork pie. It's not one of your ersatz pies with preservatives that . . .'

It was Inspector Flint's turn to slump into a chair. 'Am I to understand that your fucking pies don't keep?' he asked.

Mr Kidley nodded. 'They are for immediate consumption,' he said proudly. 'Here today, gone tomorrow. That's our motto. You've seen our advertisements of course.'

Inspector Flint hadn't.

'Today's pie with yesterday's flavour, the traditional pie with the family filling.'

'You can say that again,' said Inspector Flint.

Mr Gosdyke regarded Wilt sceptically and shook his head. 'You should have listened to me,' he said, 'I told you not to talk.'

'I had to say something,' said Wilt. 'They wouldn't let me sleep and they kept asking me the same stupid questions over and over again. You've no idea what that does to you. It drives you potty.'

'Frankly, Mr Wilt, in the light of the confession you have made I find it hard to believe there was any need to. A man who can, of his own free will make a statement like this to the police is clearly insane.'

'But it's not true,' said Wilt, 'it's all pure invention.'

'With a wealth of such revolting detail? I must say I find that hard to believe. I do indeed. The bit about hip and thighs . . . It makes my stomach turn over.'

'But that's from the Bible,' said Wilt, 'and besides I had to put in the gory bits or they wouldn't have believed me. Take the part where I say I sawed their . . .'

'Mr Wilt, for God's sake . . .'

'Well, all I can say is you've never taught Meat One. I got it all from them and once you've taught them life can hold few surprises.'

Mr Gosdyke raised an eyebrow. 'Can't it? Well I think I can

disabuse you of that notion,' he said solemnly. 'In the light of this confession you have made against my most earnest advice, and as a result of my firm belief that every word in it is true, I am no longer prepared to act on your behalf.' He collected his papers and stood up. 'You will have to get someone else.'

'But, Mr Gosdyke, you don't really believe all that nonsense about putting Eva in a pork pie, do you?' Wilt asked.

'Believe it? A man who can conceive of such a disgusting thing is capable of anything. Yes I do and what is more so do the police. They are this moment scouring the shops, the pubs and the supermarkets and dustbins of the entire county in search of pork pies.'

'But if they find any it won't do any good.'

'It may also interest you to know that they have impounded five thousand cans of Dogfill, an equal number of Catkin and have begun to dissect a quarter of a ton of Sweetbreads Best Bangers. Somewhere in that little lot they are bound to find some trace of Mrs Wilt, not to mention Dr and Mrs Pringsheim.'

'Well, all I can say is that I wish them luck,' said Wilt.

'And so do I,' said Mr Gosdyke disgustedly and left the room. Behind him Wilt sighed. If only Eva would turn up. Where the hell could she have got to?

At the Police Laboratories Inspector Flint was getting restive. 'Can't you speed things up a bit?' he asked.

The Head of the Forensic Department shook his head. 'It's like looking for a needle in a haystack,' he said, glancing significantly at another batch of sausages that had just been brought in. 'So far not a trace. This could take weeks.'

'I haven't got weeks,' said the Inspector, 'he's due in Court on Monday.'

'Only for remand and in any case you've got his statement.'

But Inspector Flint had his doubts about that. He had been looking at that statement and had noticed a number of discrepancies about it which fatigue, disgust and an overwhelming desire to get the filthy account over and done with before he was sick had tended to obscure at the time. For one thing

Wilt's scrawled signature looked suspiciously like Little Tommy Tucker when examined closely and there was a QNED beside it, which Flint had a shrewd idea meant Quod Non Erat Demonstrandum, and in any case there were rather too many references to pigs for his policeman's fancy and fuzzy pigs at that. Finally the information that Wilt had made a special request for two pork pies for lunch and had specified Sweetbreads in particular suggested an insane cannibalism that might fit in with what he had said he had done but seemed to be carrying things too far. The word 'provocation' sprang to mind and since the episode of the doll Flint had been rather conscious of bad publicity. He read through the statement again and couldn't make up his mind about it. One thing was quite certain. Wilt knew exactly how Sweetbreads factory worked. The wealth of detail he had supplied proved that. On the other hand Mr Kidley's incredulity about the heads and the mincing machine had seemed, on inspection, to be justified. Flint had looked gingerly at the beastly contraption and had found it difficult to believe that even Wilt in a fit of homicidal mania could have ... Flint put the thought out of his mind. He decided to have another little chat with Henry Wilt. Feeling like death warmed up he went back to the Interview Room and sent for Wilt.

'How's it going?' said Wilt when he arrived. 'Had any luck with the frankfurters yet? Of course you could always try your hand at black puddings ...'

'Wilt,' interrupted the Inspector, 'why did you sign that statement Little Tommy Tucker?'

Wilt sat down. 'So you've noticed that at last, have you? Very observant of you I must say.'

'I asked you a question.'

'So you did,' said Wilt. 'Let's just say I thought it was appropriate.'

'Appropriate?'

'I was singing, I think that's the slang term for it isn't it, for my sleep, so naturally ...'

'Are you telling me you made all that up?'

'What the hell do you think I did? You don't seriously think

I would inflict the Pringsheims and Eva on an unsuspecting public in the form of pork pies, do you? I mean there must be some limits to your credulity.'

Inspector Flint glared at him. 'My God, Wilt,' he said, 'if I find you've deliberately fabricated a story . . .'

'You can't do very much more,' said Wilt. 'You've already charged me with murder. What more do you want? You drag me in here, you humiliate me, you shout at me, you keep me awake for days and nights bombarding me with questions about dog food, you announce to the world that I am helping you in your enquiries into a multiple murder thus leading every citizen in the country to suppose that I have slaughtered my wife and a beastly biochemist and . . .'

'Shut up,' shouted Flint, 'I don't care what you think. It's what you've done and what you've said you've done that worries me. You've gone out of your way to mislead me . . .'

'I've done nothing of the sort,' said Wilt. 'Until last night I had told you nothing but the truth and you wouldn't accept it. Last night I handed you, in the absurd shape of a pork pie, a lie you wanted to believe. If you crave crap and use illegal methods like sleep deprivation to get it you can't blame me for serving it up. Don't come in here and bluster. If you're stupid that's your problem. Go and find my wife.'

'Someone stop me from killing the bastard,' yelled Flint, as he hurled himself from the room. He went to his office and sent for Sergeant Yates. 'Cancel the pie hunt. It's a load of bull,' he told him.

'Bull?' said the Sergeant uncertainly.

'Shit,' said Flint. 'He's done it again.'

'You mean . . .'

'I mean that that little turd in there has led us up the garden path again.'

'But how did he know about the factory and all that?'

Flint looked up at him pathetically. 'If you want to know why he's a walking encyclopedia, you go and ask him yourself.'

Sergeant Yates went out and returned five minutes later. 'Meat One,' he announced enigmatically.

'Meet won?'

'A class of butchers he used to teach. They took him round the factory.'

'Jesus,' said Flint, 'is there anybody that little swine hasn't taught?'

'He says they were most instructive.'

'Yates, do me a favour. Just go back and find out all the names of the classes he's taught. That way we'll know what to expect next.'

'Well I have heard him mention Plasterers Two and Gas-fitters One ...'

'All of them, Yates, all of them. I don't want to be caught out with some tale about Mrs Wilt being got rid of in the Sewage Works because he once taught Shit Two.' He picked up the evening paper and glanced at the headlines. POLICE PROBE PIES FOR MISSING WIFE.

'Oh my God,' he groaned. 'This is going to do our public image no end of good.'


At the Tech the Principal was expressing the same opinion at a meeting of the Heads of Departments.

'We've been held up to public ridicule,' he said. 'First it is popularly supposed that we make a habit of employing lec-turers who bury their unwanted wives in the foundations of the new block. Secondly we have lost all chance of attaining Polytechnic status by having the Joint Honours degree turned down by the CNAA on the grounds that those facilities we do provide are not such as befit an institution of higher learn-ing. Professor Baxendale expressed himself very forcibly on that point and particularly on a remark he heard from one of the senior staff about necrophilia ...'

'I merely said ...' Dr Board began.

'We all know what you said, Dr Board. And it may interest you to know that Dr Cox in his lucid moments is still refusing cold meat. Dr Mayfield has already tendered his resignation. And now to cap it all we have this.'

He held up a newspaper, across the top of whose second page there read SEX LECTURES STUN STUDENTS.

'I hope you have all taken good note of the photograph,' said the Principal bitterly, indicating a large and unfortunately angled picture of Judy hanging from the crane. 'The article goes on ... well never mind. You can read it for yourselves. I would merely like answers to the following questions. Who authorized the purchase of thirty copies of *Last Exit From Brooklyn* for use with Fitters and Turners?'

Mr Morris tried to think who had taken FTs. 'I think that must have been Watkins,' he said. 'He left us last term. He was only a part-time lecturer.'

'Thank God we were spared him full-time,' said the Principal. 'Secondly which lecturer makes a habit of advocating to Nursery Nurses that they wear ... er ... Dutch Caps all the time?'

'Well Mr Sedgwick is very keen on them,' said Mr Morris.

'Nursery Nurses or Dutch Caps?' enquired the Principal.

'Possibly both together?' suggested Dr Board sotto voce.

'He's got this thing against the Pill,' said Mr Morris.

'Well please ask Mr Sedgwick to see me in my office on Monday at ten. I want to explain the terms under which he is employed here. And finally, how many lecturers do you know of who make use of Audio Visual Aid equipment to show blue movies to the Senior Secs?'

Mr Morris shook his head emphatically. 'No one in my department,' he said.

'It says here that blue movies have been shown,' said the Principal, 'in periods properly allocated to Current Affairs.'

'Wentworth did show them *Women in Love*,' said the Head of English.

'Well never mind. There's just one more point I want to mention. We are not going to conduct an Evening Class in First Aid with particular reference to the Treatment of Abdominal Hernia for which it was proposed to purchase an inflatable doll. From now on we are going to have to cut our coats to suit our cloth.'

'On the grounds of inflation?' asked Dr Board.

'On the grounds that the Education Committee has been waiting for years for an opportunity to cut back our budget,' said the Principal. 'That opportunity has now been given them. The fact that we have been providing a public service by keeping, to quote Mr Morris, "a large number of mentally unbalanced and potentially dangerous psychopaths off the streets" unquote seems to have escaped their notice.'

'I presume he was referring to the Day Release Apprentices,' said Dr Board charitably.

'He was not,' said the Principal. 'Correct me if I am wrong, Morris, but hadn't you in mind the members of the Liberal Studies Department?'

The meeting broke up. Later that day Mr Morris sat down to compose his letter of resignation.

# 19

From the window of an empty bedroom on the first floor of the Vicarage, Eva Wilt watched the Rev St John Froude walk pensively down the path to the church. As soon as he had passed out of sight she went downstairs and into the study. She would phone Henry again. If he wasn't at the Tech he must be at home. She crossed to the desk and was about to pick up the phone when she saw the ivy. Oh dear, she had forgotten all about the ivy and she had left it where he was bound to have seen it. It was all so terribly embarrassing. She dialled 34 Parkview Avenue and waited. There was no reply. She put the phone down and dialled the Tech. And all the time she watched the gate into the churchyard in case the Vicar should return.

'Fenland College of Arts and Technology,' said the girl on the switchboard.

'It's me again,' said Eva, 'I want to speak to Mr Wilt.'

'I'm very sorry but Mr Wilt isn't here.'

'But where is he? I've dialled home and ...'

'He's at the Police Station.'

'He's what?' Eva said.

'He's at the Police Station helping the police with their enquiries ...'

202

'Enquiries? What enquiries?' Eva shrieked.

'Didn't you know?' said the girl. 'It's been in all the papers. He's been and murdered his wife ...'

Eva took the phone from her ear and stared at it in horror. The girl was still speaking but she was no longer listening. Henry had murdered his wife. But she was his wife. It wasn't possible. She couldn't have been murdered. For one horrible moment Eva Wilt felt sanity slipping from her. Then she put the receiver to her ear again.

'Are you there?' said the girl.

'But I am his wife,' Eva shouted. There was a long silence at the other end and she heard the girl telling someone that there was a crazy woman on the line who said she was Mrs Wilt and what ought she to do.

'I tell you I am Mrs Wilt. Mrs Eva Wilt,' she shouted but the line had gone dead. Eva put the phone down weakly. Henry at the Police Station ... Henry had murdered her ... Oh God. The whole world had gone mad. And here she was naked in a vicarage at ... Eva had no idea where she was. She dialled 999.

'Emergency Services. Which department do you require?' said the operator.

'Police,' said Eva. There was a click and a man's voice came on.

'Police here.'

'This is Mrs Wilt,' said Eva.

'Mrs Wilt?'

'Mrs Eva Wilt. Is it true that my husband has murdered ... I mean has my husband ... oh dear I don't know what to say.'

'You say you're Mrs Wilt, Mrs Eva Wilt?' said the man.

Eva nodded and then said, 'Yes.'

'I see,' said the man dubiously. 'You're quite sure you're Mrs Wilt?'

'Of course I'm sure. That's what I'm ringing about.'

'Might I enquire where you're calling from?'

'I don't know,' said Eva. 'You see I'm in this house and I've got no clothes and ... oh dear.' The Vicar was coming up the path on to the terrace.

'If you could just give us the address.'

'I can't stop now,' said Eva and put the phone down. For a moment she hesitated and then grabbing the ivy from the desk she rushed out of the room.

'I tell you I don't know where she is,' said Wilt. 'I expect you'll find her under missing persons. She has passed from the realm of substantiality into that of abstraction.'

'What the hell do you mean by that?' asked the Inspector, reaching for his cup of coffee. It was eleven o'clock on Saturday morning but he persisted. He had twenty-eight hours to get to the truth.

'I always warned her that Transcendental Meditation carried potential dangers,' said Wilt, himself in a no-man's-land between sleeping and walking. 'But she would do it.'

'Do what?'

'Meditate transcendentally. In the lotus position. Perhaps she has gone too far this time. Possibly she has transmogrified herself.'

'Trans what?' said Inspector Flint suspiciously.

'Changed herself in some magical fashion into something else.'

'Jesus, Wilt, if you start on those pork pies again ...'

'I was thinking of something more spiritual, Inspector, something beautiful.'

'I doubt it.'

'Ah, but think. Here am I sitting in this room with you as a direct result of going for walks with the dog and thinking dark thoughts about murdering my wife. From those hours of idle fancy I have gained the reputation of being a murderer without committing a murder. Who is to say but that Eva whose thoughts were monotonously beautiful has not earned herself a commensurately beautiful reward? To put it in your terms, Inspector, we get what we ask for.'

'I fervently hope so, Wilt,' said the Inspector.

'Ah,' said Wilt, 'but then where is she? Tell me that. Mere speculation will not do ...'

'Me tell you?' shouted the Inspector upsetting his cup of

coffee. 'You know which hole in the ground you put her in or which cement mixer or incinerator you used.'

'I was speaking metaphorically . . . I mean rhetorically,' said Wilt. 'I was trying to imagine what Eva would be if her thoughts such as they are took on the substance of reality. My secret dream was to become a ruthless man of action, decisive, unhindered by moral doubts or considerations of conscience, a Hamlet transformed into Henry the Fifth without the patriotic fervour that inclines one to think that he would not have approved of the Common Market, a Caesar . . .'

Inspector Flint had heard enough. 'Wilt,' he snarled, 'I don't give a damn what you wanted to become. What I want to know is what has become of your wife.'

'I was just coming to that,' said Wilt. 'What we've got to establish first is what I am.'

'I know what you are, Wilt. A bloody word merchant, a verbal contortionist, a fucking logic-chopper, a linguistic Houdini, an encyclopedia of unwanted information . . .' Inspector Flint ran out of metaphors.

'Brilliant, Inspector, brilliant. I couldn't have put it better myself. A logic-chopper, but alas not a wife one. If we follow the same line of reasoning Eva in spite of all her beautiful thoughts and meditations has remained as unchanged as I. The ethereal eludes her. Nirvana slips ever from her grasp. Beauty and truth evade her. She pursues the absolute with a fly-swatter and pours Harpic down the drains of Hell itself . . .'

'That's the tenth time you have mentioned Harpic,' said the Inspector, suddenly alive to a new dreadful possibility. 'You didn't . . .'

Wilt shook his head. 'There you go again. So like poor Eva. The literal mind that seeks to seize the evanescent and clutches fancy by its non-existent throat. That's Eva for you. She will never dance Swan Lake. No management would allow her to fill the stage with water or install a double bed and Eva would insist.'

Inspector Flint got up. 'This is getting us nowhere fast.'

'Precisely,' said Wilt, 'nowhere at all. We are what we are and nothing we can do will alter the fact. The mould that forms our natures remains unbroken. Call it heredity, call it chance ...'

'Call it a load of codswallop,' said Flint and left the room. He needed his sleep and he intended to get it.

In the passage he met Sergeant Yates.

'There's been an emergency call from a woman claiming to be Mrs Wilt,' the Sergeant said.

'Where from?'

'She wouldn't say where she was,' said Yates. 'She just said she didn't know and that she had no clothes on ...'

'Oh one of those,' said the Inspector. 'A bloody nutter. What the hell are you wasting my time for? As if we didn't have enough on our hands without that.'

'I just thought you'd want to know. If she calls again we'll try and get a fix on the number.'

'As if I cared,' said Flint and hurried off in search of his lost sleep.

The Rev St John Froude spent an uneasy day. His investigation of the church had revealed nothing untoward and there was no sign that an obscene ritual (a Black Mass had crossed his mind) had been performed there. As he walked back to the Vicarage he was glad to note that the sky over Eel Stretch was empty and that the contraceptives had disappeared. So had the ivy on his desk. He regarded the space where it had been with apprehension and helped himself to whisky. He could have sworn there had been a sprig of ivy there when he had left. By the time he had finished what remained in the bottle his mind was filled with weird fancies. The Vicarage was strangely noisy. There were odd creaks from the staircase and inexplicable sounds from the upper floor as if someone or something was moving stealthily about but when the Vicar went to investigate the noises ceased abruptly. He went up-stairs and poked his head into several empty bedrooms. He came down again and stood in the hall listening. Then he returned to his study and tried to concentrate on his sermon, but the feeling that he was not alone persisted. The Rev St John Froude sat at his desk and considered the possibility of ghosts. Something very odd was going on. At one o'clock he went down the hall to the kitchen for lunch and discovered that a pint of milk had disappeared from the pantry and that the remains of an apple pie that Mrs Snape who did his cleaning twice weekly had brought him had also vanished. He made do with baked beans on toast and tottered upstairs for his afternoon nap. It was while he was there that he first heard the voices. Or rather one voice. It seemed to come from his study. The Rev St John Froude sat up in bed. If his ears weren't betraying him and in view of the morning's weird events he was inclined to believe that they were he could have sworn someone had been using his telephone. He got up and put on his shoes. Someone was crying. He went out on to the landing and listened. The sobbing had stopped. He went downstairs and looked in all the rooms on the ground floor but, apart from the fact that a dust cover had been removed from one of the armchairs in the unused sitting-room, there was no sign of anyone. He was just about to go upstairs again when the telephone rang. He went into the study and answered it.

'Waterswick Vicarage,' he mumbled.

'This is Fenland Constabulary,' said a man. 'We've just had a call from your number purporting to come from a Mrs Wilt.'

'Mrs Wilt?' said the Rev St John Froude. 'Mrs Wilt? I'm afraid there must be some mistake. I don't know any Mrs Wilt.'

'The call definitely came from your phone, sir.'

The Rev St John Froude considered the matter. 'This is all very peculiar,' he said, 'I live alone.'

'You are the Vicar?'

'Of course I'm the Vicar. This is the Vicarage and I am the Vicar.'

'I see, sir. And your name is?'

'The Reverend St John Froude. F . . . R . . . O . . . U . . . D . . . E.'

'Quite sir, and you definitely don't have a woman in the house.'

'Of course I don't have a woman in the house. I find the suggestion distinctly improper. I am a . . .'

'I'm sorry, sir, but we just have to check these things out.

We've had a call from Mrs Wilt, at least a woman claiming to be Mrs Wilt, and it came from your phone ...'

'Who is this Mrs Wilt? I've never heard of a Mrs Wilt.'

'Well sir, Mrs Wilt ... it's a bit difficult really. She's supposed to have been murdered.'

'Murdered?' said the Rev St John Froude. 'Did you say "murdered"?'

'Let's just say she is missing from home in suspicious circumstances. We're holding her husband for questioning.'

The Rev St John Froude shook his head. 'How very unfortunate,' he murmured.

'Thank you for your help, sir,' said the Sergeant. 'Sorry to have disturbed you.'

The Rev St John Froude put the phone down thoughtfully. The notion that he was sharing the house with a disembodied and recently murdered woman was not one that he had wanted to put to his caller. His reputation for eccentricity was already sufficiently widespread without adding to it. On the other hand what he had seen on the boat in Eel Stretch bore, now that he came to think of it, all the hallmarks of murder. Perhaps in some extraordinary way he had been a witness to a tragedy that had already occurred, a sort of post-mortem déja vu if that was the right way of putting it. Certainly if the husband were being held for questioning the murder must have taken place before.... In which case ... The Rev St John Froude stumbled through a series of suppositions in which Time with a capital T, and appeals for help from beyond the grave figured largely. Perhaps it was his duty to inform the police of what he had seen. He was just hesitating and wondering what to do when he heard those sobs again and this time quite distinctly. They came from the next room. He got up, braced himself with another shot of whisky and went next door. Standing in the middle of the room was a large woman whose hair straggled down over her shoulders and whose face was ravaged. She was wearing what appeared to be a shroud. The Rev St John Froude stared at her with a growing sense of horror. Then he sank to his knees.

'Let us pray,' he muttered hoarsely.

The ghastly apparition slumped heavily forward clutching the shroud to its bosom. Together they kneeled in prayer.

'Check it out? What the hell do you mean "check it out"?' said Inspector Flint who objected strongly to being woken in the middle of the afternoon when he had had no sleep for thirty-six hours and was trying to get some. 'You wake me with some damned tomfoolery about a vicar called Sigmund Freud . . .'

'St John Froude,' said Yates.

'I don't care what he's called. It's still improbable. If the bloody man says she isn't there, she isn't there. What am I supposed to do about it?'

'I just thought we ought to get a patrol car to check, that's all.'

'What makes you think . . .'

'There was definitely a call from a woman claiming to be Mrs Wilt and it came from that number. She's called twice now. We've got a tape of the second call. She gave details of herself and they sound authentic. Date of birth, address, Wilt's occupation, even the right name of their dog and the fact that they have yellow curtains in the lounge.'

'Well, any fool can tell that. All they've got to do is walk past the house.'

'And the name of the dog. It's called Clem. I've checked that and she's right.'

'She didn't happen to say what she'd been doing for the past week did she?'

'She said she'd been on a boat,' said Yates. 'Then she rang off.'

Inspector Flint sat up in bed. 'A boat? What boat?'

'She rang off. Oh and another thing, she said she takes a size ten shoe. She does.'

'Oh shit,' said Flint. 'All right, I'll come down.' He got out of bed and began to dress.

In his cell Wilt stared at the ceiling. After so many hours of interrogation his mind still reverberated with questions. 'How did you kill her? Where did you put her? What did you do with the weapon?' Meaningless questions continually reiterated in the hope they would finally break him. But Wilt hadn't broken. He had triumphed. For once in his life he knew himself to be invincibly right and everyone else totally wrong. Always before he had had doubts. Plasterers Two might after all have been right about there being too many wogs in the country. Perhaps hanging was a deterrent. Wilt didn't think so but he couldn't be absolutely certain. Only time would tell. But in the case of Regina *versus* Wilt *re* the murder of Mrs Wilt there could be no question of his guilt. He could be tried, found guilty and sentenced, it would make no difference. He was innocent of the charge and if he was sentenced to life imprisonment the very enormity of the injustice done to him would compound his knowledge of his own innocence. For the very first time in his life Wilt knew himself to be free. It was as though the original sin of being Henry Wilt, of 34 Parkview Avenue, Ipford, lecturer in Liberal Studies at the Fenland College of Arts and Technology, husband of Eva Wilt and father of none, had been lifted from him. All the encumbrances of possessions, habits, salary and status, all the social conformities, the niceties of estimation of himself and other people which he and Eva had acquired, all these had gone. Locked in his cell Wilt was free to be. And whatever happened he would never again succumb to the siren calls of self-effacement. After the flagrant contempt and fury of Inspector Flint, the abuse and the opprobrium heaped on him for a week, who needed approbation? They could stuff their opinions of him. Wilt would pursue his independent course and put to good use his evident gifts of inconsequence. Give him a life sentence and a progressive prison governor and Wilt would drive the man mad within a month by the sweet reasonableness of his refusal to obey the prison rules. Solitary confinement and a regime of bread and water, if such punishments still existed, would not deter him. Give him his freedom and he would apply his new-found talents at the Tech. He would sit happily on committees and reduce them to dissensions by his untiring adoption of whatever argument was most contrary to the consensus opinion. The race was not to the swift after all, it was to the indefatigably inconsequential and life was random, anarchic and chaotic. Rules were made to be broken and the man with the grasshopper mind was one jump ahead of all the others. Having established this new rule, Wilt turned on his side and tried to sleep but sleep wouldn't come. He tried his other side with equal lack of success. Thoughts, questions, irrelevant answers and imaginary dialogues filled his mind. He tried counting sheep but found himself thinking of Eva. Dear Eva, damnable Eva, ebullient Eva and Eva irrepressibly enthusiastic. Like him she had sought the Absolute, the Eternal Truth which would save her the bother of ever having to think for herself again. She had sought it in Pottery, in Transcendental Meditation, in Judo, on trampolines and most incongruously of all in Oriental Dance. Finally she had tried to find it in sexual emancipation, Women's Lib and the Sacrament of the Orgasm in which she could forever lose herself. Which, come to think of it, was what she appeared to have done. And taken the bloody Pringsheims with her. Well she would certainly have some explaining to do when and if she ever returned. Wilt smiled to himself at the thought of what she would say when she discovered what her latest infatuation with the Infinite had led to. He'd see to it that she had cause to regret it to her dying day.

On the floor of the sitting-room at the Vicarage Eva Wilt struggled with the growing conviction that her dying day was already over and done with. Certainly everyone she came into contact with seemed to think she was dead. The policeman she had spoken to on the phone had seemed disinclined to believe her assertion that she was alive and at least relatively well and had demanded proofs of her identity in the most disconcerting fashion. Eva had retreated stricken from the encounter with her confidence in her own continuing existence seriously undermined and it had only needed the reaction of the Rev St John Froude to her appearance in his house to complete her misery. His frantic appeals to the Almighty to rescue the soul of our dear departed, one Eva Wilt, deceased, from its present shape and unendurable form had affected Eva profoundly. She knelt on the carpet and sobbed while the Vicar stared at her over his glasses, shut his eyes, lifted up a shaky voice in prayer, opened his eyes, shuddered and generally behaved in a manner calculated to cause gloom and despondency in the putative corpse and when, in a last desperate attempt to get Eva Wilt, deceased, to take her proper place in the heavenly choir he cut short a prayer about 'Man that is born of Woman hath but a short time to live and is full of misery' and struck up 'Abide with me' with many a semi-quaver, Eva abandoned all attempt at self-control and wailed 'Fast falls the eventide' most affectingly. By the time they had got to 'I need thy presence every passing hour' the Rev St John Froude was of an entirely contrary opinion. He staggered from the room and took sanctuary in his study. Behind him Eva Wilt, espousing her new role as deceased with all the enthusiasm she had formerly bestowed on trampolines, judo and pottery, demanded to know where death's sting was and where, grave, thy victory. 'As if I bloody knew,' muttered the Vicar and reached for the whisky bottle only to find that it too was empty. He sat down and put his hands over his ears to shut out the dreadful noise. On the whole 'Abide with me' was the last hymn he should have chosen. He'd have been better off with 'There is a green hill far away'. It was less open to misinterpretation.

When at last the hymn ended he sat relishing the silence and was about to investigate the possibility that there was another bottle in the larder when there was a knock on the door and Eva entered.

'Oh Father I have sinned,' she shrieked, doing her level best to wail and gnash her teeth at the same time. The Rev St John Froude gripped the arms of his chair and tried to swallow. It was not easy. Then overcoming the reasonable fear that delirium tremens had come all too suddenly he managed to speak. 'Rise, my child,' he gasped as Eva writhed on the rug before him, 'I will hear your confession.'

212

# 20

Inspector Flint switched the tape recorder off and looked at Wilt.

'Well?'

'Well what?' said Wilt.

'Is that her? Is that Mrs Wilt?'

Wilt nodded. 'I'm afraid so.'

'What do you mean you're afraid so? The damned woman is alive. You should be fucking grateful. Instead of that you sit there saying you're afraid so.'

Wilt sighed. 'I was just thinking what an abyss there is between the person as we remember and imagine them and the reality of what they are. I was beginning to have fond memories of her and now ...'

'You ever been to Waterswick?'

Wilt shook his head. 'Never.'

'Know the Vicar there?'

'Didn't even know there was a vicar there.'

'And you wouldn't know how she got there?'

'You heard her,' said Wilt. 'She said she'd been on a boat.'

'And you wouldn't know anyone with a boat, would you?'

'People in my circle don't have boats, Inspector. Maybe the Pringsheims have a boat.'

Inspector Flint considered the possibility and rejected it. They had checked the boatyards out and the Pringsheims didn't have a boat and hadn't hired one either.

On the other hand the possibility that he had been the victim of some gigantic hoax, a deliberate and involved scheme to make him look an idiot, was beginning to take shape in his mind. At the instigation of this infernal Wilt he had ordered the exhumation of an inflatable doll and had been photographed staring lividly at it at the very moment it changed sex. He had instituted a round-up of pork pies unprecedented in the history of the country. He wouldn't be at all surprised if Sweetbreads instituted legal proceedings for the damage done to their previously unspotted reputation. And finally he had held an apparently innocent man for questioning for a week and would doubtless be held responsible for the delay and additional cost in building the new Administration block at the Tech. There were, in all probability, other appalling consequences to be considered, but that was enough to be going on with. And he had nobody to blame but himself. Or Wilt. He looked at Wilt venomously.

Wilt smiled. 'I know what you're thinking,' he said.

'You don't,' said the Inspector. 'You've no idea.'

'That we are all the creatures of circumstance, that things are never what they seem, that there's more to this than meets . . .'

'We'll see about that,' said the Inspector.

Wilt got up. 'I don't suppose you'll want me for anything else,' he said. 'I'll be getting along home.'

'You'll be doing no such thing. You're coming with us to pick up Mrs Wilt.'

They went out into the courtyard and got into a police car. As they drove through the suburbs, past the filling stations and factories and out across the fens Wilt shrank into the back seat of the car and felt the sense of freedom he had enjoyed in the Police Station evaporate. And with every mile it dwindled further and the harsh reality of choice, of having to earn a living, of boredom and the endless petty arguments with Eva, of bridge on Saturday nights with the Mottrams and drives on Sundays with Eva, reasserted itself. Beside him, sunk in sullen silence, Inspector Flint lost his symbolic appeal. No longer the mentor of Wilt's self-confidence, the foil to his inconsequentiality, he had become a fellow sufferer in the business of living, almost a mirror-image of Wilt's own nonentity. And ahead, across this flat bleak landscape with its black earth and cumulus skies, lay Eva and a lifetime of attempted explanations and counter-accusations. For a moment Wilt considered shouting 'Stop the car. I want to get out', but the moment passed. Whatever the future held he would learn to live with it. He had not discovered the paradoxical nature of freedom only to succumb once more to the servitude of Parkview Avenue, the

Tech and Eva's trivial enthusiasms. He was Wilt, the man with the grasshopper mind.

Eva was drunk. The Rev St John Froude's automatic reaction to her appalling confession had been to turn from whisky to 150% Polish spirit which he kept for emergencies and Eva, in between agonies of repentance and the outpourings of lurid sins, had wet her whistle with the stuff. Encouraged by its effect, by the petrified benevolence of the Vicar's smile and by the growing conviction that if she was dead eternal life demanded an act of absolute contrition while if she wasn't it allowed her to avoid the embarrassment of explaining what precisely she was doing naked in someone else's house, Eva confessed her sins with an enthusiasm that matched her deepest needs. This was what she had sought in judo and pottery and Oriental dance, an orgiastic expiation of her guilt. She confessed sins she had committed and sins she hadn't, sins that had occurred to her and sins she had forgotten. She had betrayed Henry, she had wished him dead, she had lusted after other men, she was an adulterated woman, she was a lesbian, she was a nymphomaniac. And interspersed with these sins of the flesh there were sins of omission. Eva left nothing out. Henry's cold suppers, his lonely walks with the dog, her lack of appreciation for all he had done for her, her failure to be a good wife, her obsession with Harpic ... everything poured out. In his chair the Rev St John Froude sat nodding incessantly like a toy dog in the back window of a car, raising his head to stare at her when she confessed to being a nymphomaniac and dropping it abruptly at the mention of Harpic, and all the time desperately trying to understand what had brought a fat naked – the shroud kept falling off her – lady, no definitely not lady, woman to his house with all the symptoms of religious mania upon her.

'My child, is that all?' he muttered when Eva finally exhausted her repertoire.

'Yes, Father,' sobbed Eva.

'Thank God,' said the Rev St John Froude fervently and wondered what to do next. If half the things he had heard were true he was in the presence of a sinner so depraved as to make the ex-Archdeacon of Ongar a positive saint. On the other hand there were incongruities about her sins that made him hesitate before granting absolution. A confession full of false-hoods was no sign of true repentance.

'I take it that you are married,' he said doubtfully, 'and that Henry is your lawful wedded husband?'

'Yes,' said Eva. 'Dear Henry.'

Poor sod, thought the Vicar but he was too tactful to say so. 'And you have left him?'

'Yes.'

'For another man?'

Eva shook her head. 'To teach him a lesson,' she said with sudden belligerence.

'A lesson?' said the Vicar, trying frantically to imagine what sort of lesson the wretched Mr Wilt had learnt from her absence. 'You did say a lesson?'

'Yes,' said Eva, 'I wanted him to learn that he couldn't get along without me.'

The Rev St John Froude sipped his drink thoughtfully. If even a quarter of her confession was to be believed her husband must be finding getting along without her quite delightful. 'And now you want to go back to him?'

'Yes,' said Eva.

'But he won't have you?'

'He can't. The police have got him.'

'The police?' said the Vicar. 'And may one ask what the police have got him for?'

'They say he's murdered me,' said Eva.

The Rev St John Froude eyed her with new alarm. He knew now that Mrs Wilt was out of her mind. He glanced round for something to use as a weapon should the need arise and finding nothing better to choose from than a plaster bust of the poet Dante and the bottle of Polish spirit, picked up the latter by its neck. Eva held her glass out.

'Oh you are awful,' she said. 'You're getting me tiddly.'

'Quite,' said the Vicar and put the bottle down again hastily. It was bad enough being alone in the house with a large, drunk, semi-naked woman who imagined that her husband had murdered her and who confessed to sins he had previously only read about without her jumping to the conclusion that he was deliberately trying to make her drunk. The Rev St John Froude had no desire to figure prominently in next Sunday's *News of the World*.

'You were saying that your husband murdered ...' He stopped. That seemed an unprofitable subject to pursue.

'How could he have murdered me?' asked Eva. 'I'm here in the flesh, aren't I?'

'Definitely,' said the Vicar. 'Most definitely.'

'Well then,' said Eva. 'And anyway Henry couldn't murder anyone. He wouldn't know how. He can't even change a fuse in a plug. I have to do everything like that in the house.' She stared at the Vicar balefully. 'Are you married?'

'No,' said the Rev St John Froude, wishing to hell that he was.

'What do you know about life if you aren't married?' asked Eva truculently. The Polish spirit was getting to her now and with it there came a terrible sense of grievance. 'Men. What good are men? They can't even keep a house tidy. Look at this room. I ask you.' She waved her arms to emphasize the point and the dustcover dropped. 'Just look at it.' But the Rev St John Froude had no eyes for the room. What he could see of Eva was enough to convince him that his life was in danger. He bounded from the chair, trod heavily on an occasional table, overturned the wastepaper basket and threw himself through the door into the hall. As he stumbled away in search of sanctuary the front door bell rang. The Rev St John Froude opened it and stared into Inspector Flint's face.

'Thank God, you've come,' he gasped, 'she's in there.'

The Inspector and two uniformed constables went across the hall. Wilt followed uneasily. This was the moment he had been dreading. In the event it was better than he had expected. Not so for Inspector Flint. He entered the study and found himself confronted by a large naked woman.

'Mrs Wilt ...' he began but Eva was staring at the two uniformed constables.

'Where's my Henry?' Eva shouted. 'You've got my Henry.'
She hurled herself forward. Unwisely the Inspector attempted
to restrain her.

'Mrs Wilt, if you'll just ...' A blow on the side of his head
ended the sentence.

'Keep your hands off me,' yelled Eva, and putting her
knowledge of Judo to good use hurled him to the floor. She
was about to repeat the performance with the constables when
Wilt thrust himself forward.

'Here I am, dear,' he said. Eva stopped in her tracks. For a
moment she quivered and, seen from Inspector Flint's view-
point, appeared to be about to melt. 'Oh Henry,' she said,
'what have they been doing to you?'

'Nothing at all, dear,' said Wilt. 'Now get your clothes on.
We're going home.' Eva looked down at herself, shuddered
and allowed him to lead her out of the room.

Slowly and wearily Inspector Flint got to his feet. He knew
now why Wilt had put that bloody doll down the hole and why
he had sat so confidently through days and nights of interrogation. After twelve years of marriage to Eva Wilt the urge to
commit homicide if only by proxy would be overwhelming. And
as for Wilt's ability to stand up to cross-examination ... it
was self-evident. But the Inspector knew too that he would
never be able to explain it to anyone else. There were mysteries
of human relationships that defied analysis. And Wilt had
stood there calmly and told her to get her clothes on. With a
grudging sense of admiration Flint went out into the hall. The
little sod had guts, whatever else you could say about him.

They drove back to Parkview Avenue in silence. In the back
seat Eva, wrapped in a blanket, slept with her head lolling on
Wilt's shoulder. Beside her Henry Wilt sat proudly. A woman
who could silence Inspector Flint with one swift blow to the
head was worth her weight in gold and besides that scene in
the study had given him the weapon he needed. Naked and
drunk in a vicar's study ... There would be no questions now
about why he had put that doll down the hole. No accusations,
no recriminations. The entire episode would be relegated to

the best forgotten. And with it would go all doubts about his virility or his ability to get on in the world. It was checkmate. For a moment Wilt almost lapsed into sentimentality and thought of love before recalling just how dangerous a topic that was. He would be better off sticking to indifference and undisclosed affection. 'Let sleeping dogs lie,' he muttered.

It was an opinion shared by the Pringsheims. As they were helped from the cruiser to a police launch, as they climbed ashore, as they explained to a sceptical Inspector Flint how they had come to be marooned for a week in Eel Stretch in a boat that belonged to someone else, they were strangely uncommunicative. No they didn't know how the door of the bathroom had been bust down. Well maybe there had been an accident. They had been too drunk to remember. A doll? What doll? Grass? You mean marijuana? They had no idea. In their house?

Inspector Flint let them go finally. 'I'll be seeing you again when the charges have been properly formulated,' he said grimly. The Pringsheims left for Rossiter Grove to pack. They flew out of Heathrow next morning.

# 21

The Principal sat behind his desk and regarded Wilt incredulously. 'Promotion?' he said. 'Did I hear you mention the word "promotion"?'

'You did,' said Wilt. 'And what is more you also heard "Head of Liberal Studies" too.'

'After all you've done? You mean to say you have the nerve to come in here and demand to be made Head of Liberal Studies?'

'Yes,' said Wilt.

The Principal struggled to find words to match his feelings. It wasn't easy. In front of him sat the man who was responsible for the series of disasters that had put an end to his fondest hopes. The Tech would never be a Poly now. The Joint Honours degree's rejection had seen to that. And then there was the adverse publicity, the cut in the budget, his battles with the Education Committee, the humiliation of being heralded as the Principal of Dollfuckers Hall ...

'You're fired!' he shouted.

Wilt smiled. 'I think not,' he said. 'Here are my terms ...'

'Your what?'

'Terms,' said Wilt. 'In return for my appointment as Head of Liberal Studies, I shall not institute proceedings against you for unfair dismissal with all the attendant publicity that would entail. I shall withdraw my case against the police for unlawful arrest. The contract I have here with the *Sunday Post* for a series of articles on the true nature of Liberal Studies – I intend to call them Exposure to Barbarism – will remain unsigned. I will cancel the lectures I had promised to give for the Sex Education Centre. I will not appear on *Panorama* next Monday. In short I will abjure the pleasures and rewards of public exposure ...'

The Principal raised a shaky hand. 'Enough,' he said, 'I'll see what I can do.'

Wilt got to his feet. 'Let me know your answer by lunchtime,' he said. 'I'll be in my office.'

'Your office?' said the Principal.

'It used to belong to Mr Morris,' said Wilt and closed the door. Behind him the Principal picked up the phone. There had been no mistaking the seriousness of Wilt's threats. He would have to hurry.

Wilt strolled down the corridor to the Liberal Studies Department and stood looking at the books on the shelves. There were changes he had in mind. *The Lord of the Flies* would go and with it *Shane, Women in Love*, Orwell's *Essays* and *Catcher in the Rye*, all those symptoms of intellectual condescension, those dangled worms of sensibility. In future Gasfitters One and Meat Two would learn the how of things not why. How to read and write. How to make beer. How to fiddle their income tax returns. How to cope with the police when arrested. How to make an incompatible marriage work. Wilt would give the last two lessons himself. There would be objections from the staff, even threats of resignation, but it would make no difference. He might well accept several resignations from those who persisted in opposing his ideas. After all you didn't require a degree in English literature to teach Gasfitters the how of anything. Come to think of it, they had taught him more than they had learnt from him. Much more. He went into Mr Morris's empty office and sat down at the desk and composed a memorandum to Liberal Studies Staff. It was headed Notes on a System of Self-Teaching for Day Release Classes. He had just written 'non-hierarchical' for the fifth time when the phone rang. It was the Principal.

'Thank you,' said the new Head of Liberal Studies.

Eva Wilt walked gaily up Parkview Avenue from the doctor's office. She had made breakfast for Henry and Hoovered the front room and polished the hall and cleaned the windows and Harpicked the loo and been round to the Harmony Community Centre and helped with Xeroxing an appeal for a new play group and done the shopping and paid the milkman and been to the doctor to ask if there was any point in taking a course of fertility drugs and there was. 'Of course we'll have to do tests,' the doctor had told her, 'but there's no reason to think they'd prove negative. The only danger is that you might have sextuplets.' It wasn't a danger to Eva. It was what she had always wanted, a house full of children. And all at once. Henry would be pleased. And so the sun shone brighter, the sky was bluer, the flowers in the gardens were rosier and even Parkview Avenue itself seemed to have taken on a new and brighter aspect. It was one of Eva Wilt's better days.

# Wilt on High

# Chapter one

'Days of wine and roses,' said Wilt to himself. It was an inconsequential remark but sitting on the Finance and General Purposes Committee at the Tech needed some relief and for the fifth year running Dr Mayfield had risen to his feet and announced, 'We must put the Fenland College of Arts and Technology on the map.'

'I should have thought it was there already,' said Dr Board, resorting as usual to the literal to preserve his sanity. 'In fact to the best of my knowledge it's been there since 1895 when—'

'You know perfectly well what I mean,' interrupted Dr Mayfield. 'The fact of the matter is that the College has reached the point of no return.'

'From what?' asked Dr Board.

Dr Mayfield turned to the Principal. 'The point I am trying to make—' he began, but Dr Board hadn't finished. 'Is apparently that we are either an aircraft halfway to its destination or a cartographical feature. Or possibly both.'

The Principal sighed and thought about early retirement. 'Dr Board,' he said, 'we are here to discuss ways and means of maintaining our present course structure and staffing levels in the face of the Local Education Authority and Central Government pressure to reduce the College to an adjunct of the Department of Unemployment.'

Dr Board raised an eyebrow. 'Really? I thought we were here to teach. Of course, I may be mistaken but when I first entered the profession, that's what I was led to believe. Now I learn that we're here to maintain course structures, whatever they may be, and staffing levels. In plain English, jobs for the boys.'

'And girls,' said the Head of Catering, who hadn't been listening too carefully. Dr Board eyed her critically.

'And doubtless one or two creatures of indeterminate gender,' he murmured. 'Now, if Dr Mayfield—'

5

'Is allowed to continue,' interrupted the Principal, 'we may arrive at a decision by lunchtime.'

Dr Mayfield continued. Wilt stared out of the window at the new Electronics Building and wondered for the umpteenth time what it was about committees that turned educated and relatively intelligent men and women, all of them graduates of universities, into bitter and boring and argumentative people whose sole purpose seemed to be to hear themselves speak and prove everyone else wrong. And committees had come to dominate the Tech. In the old days, he had been able to come to work and spend his mornings and afternoons trying to teach or at least to awaken some intellectual curiosity in classes of Turners and Fitters or even Plasterers and Printers, and if they hadn't learnt much from him, he had been able to go home in the evening with the knowledge that he had gained something from them.

Now everything was different. Even his title, Head of Liberal Studies, had been changed to that of Communication Skills and Expressive Attainment, and he spent his time on committees or drawing up memoranda and so-called consultative documents or reading similarly meaningless documents from other departments. It was the same throughout the Tech. The Head of Building, whose literacy had always been in some doubt, had been forced to justify classes in Bricklaying and Plastering in a 45-page discussion paper on 'Modular Construction and Internal Surface Application', a work of such monumental boredom and bad grammar, that Dr Board had suggested forwarding it to the RIBA with the recommendation that he be given a Fellowship in Architectural Semanticism – or alternatively Cementicism. There had been a similar row over the monograph submitted by the Head of Catering on 'Dietetic Advances In Multi-Phased Institutional Provisioning', to which Dr Mayfield had taken exception on the grounds that the emphasis on faggots and Queen's Pudding might lead to a misunderstanding in certain quarters. Dr Cox, Head of Science, had demanded to know what a Multi-Phased

6

Institution was, and what the hell was wrong with faggots, he'd been brought up on them. Dr Mayfield had explained he was referring to gays and the Head of Catering had confused the issue still further by denying she was a feminist. Wilt had sat through the controversy in silent wondering, as he did now, at the curious modern assumption that you could alter acts by using words in a different way. A cook was a cook no matter that you call him a Culinary Scientist. And calling a gasfitter a Gaseous and Liquefaction Engineer didn't alter the fact that he had taken a course in Gasfitting.

He was just considering how long it would be before they called him an Educational Scientist or even a Mental Processing Officer, when he was drawn from this reverie by a question of 'contact hours'.

'If I could have a breakdown of departmental timetabling on a real-time contact hour basis,' said Dr Mayfield, 'we could computerize those areas of overlap which under present circumstances render our staffing levels unviable on a cost-effective analysis.'

There was a silence while the Heads of Departments tried to figure this out. Dr Board snorted and the Principal rose to the bait. 'Well, Board?' he asked.

'Not particularly,' said the Head of Modern Languages, 'but thank you for enquiring all the same.'

'You know very well what Dr Mayfield wants.'

'Only on the basis of past experience and linguistic guesswork,' said Dr Board. 'What puzzles me in the present instance is his use of the phrase "real-time contact hours". Now according to my vocabulary . . .'

'Dr Board,' said the Principal, wishing to God he could sack the man, 'what we want to know is quite simply the number of contact hours the members of your department do per week.'

Dr Board made a show of consulting a small notebook. 'None,' he said finally.

'None?'

'That's what I said.'

'Are you trying to say your staff do no teaching at all? That's a downright lie. If it isn't . . .'

'I didn't say anything about teaching and no one asked me to. Dr Mayfield quite specifically asked for "real-time"—'

'I don't give a damn about real-time. He means actual.'

'So do I,' said Dr Board, 'and if any of my lecturers have been touching their students even for a minute, let alone an hour, I'd—'

'Board,' snarled the Principal, 'you're trying my patience too far. Answer the question.'

'I have. Contact means touching, and a contact hour must therefore mean a touching hour. Nothing more and nothing less. Consult any dictionary you choose, and you'll find it derives directly from the Latin, *contactus*. The infinitive is *contigere* and the past participle *contactum*, and whichever way you look at it, it still means touch. It cannot mean to teach.'

'Dear God,' said the Principal, through clenched teeth, but Dr Board hadn't finished.

'Now I don't know what Dr Mayfield encourages in Sociology and for all I know he may go in for touch teaching, or, what I believe is called in the vernacular "group groping", but in my department . . .'

'Shut up,' shouted the Principal, now well beyond the end of his tether. 'You will all submit in writing the number of teaching hours, the actual teaching hours, each member of your department does . . .'

As the meeting broke up, Dr Board walked down the corridor with Wilt. 'It's not often one can strike a blow for linguistic accuracy,' he said, 'but at least I've thrown a spanner in Mayfield's clockwork mind. The man's mad.'

It was a theme Wilt took up with Peter Braintree in the public bar of The Pig In A Poke half an hour later.

'The whole system is loony,' he said over a second pint, 'Mayfield's given up empire-building with degree courses and he's on a cost-effectiveness kick now.'

'Don't tell me,' said Braintree. 'We've already lost half

our textbook allocation this year, and Foster and Carston have been bullied into early retirement. At this rate I'll end up teaching *King Lear* to a class of sixty with eight copies of the play to go round.'

'At least you're teaching something. You want to try Expressive Attainment with Motor Mechanics Three. Expressive Attainment! The sods know all there is to be known about cars in the first place, and I haven't a clue what Expressive Attainment means. Talk about wasting the taxpayers' money. And anyway, I spend more of my time on committees than I do supposedly teaching. That's what galls me.'

'How's Eva?' asked Braintree, recognizing Wilt's mood and trying to change the subject.

'*Plus ça change, plus c'est la même chose*. Mind you, that's not entirely true. At least she's off Suffrage for Little Children and Votes at Eleven Plus. After those two blokes from PIE came round soliciting and went away with thick ears.'

'Pie?'

'Paedophile Information Exchange. Used to be called child molesters. These two sods made the mistake of trying to get Eva's support for lowering the age of consent to four. I could have told them four was an unlucky number round our way, considering what the quads get up to. By the time Eva had finished with them, they must have thought 45 Oakhurst Avenue was part of some bloody zoo, and they'd broached the topic with a tigress in cub.'

'Serve the swine right.'

'Didn't serve Mr Birkenshaw right though. Samantha promptly organized the other three into CAR, otherwise known as Children Against Rape, and set up a target in the garden. Luckily the neighbours put their communal feet down before one of the little boys in the street got himself castrated. The quads were just warming up with penknives. Well, actually, they were Sabatier knives from the kitchen, and they'd got quite good with them. Emmeline could hit the damned thing's scrotum at eighteen feet, and Penelope punctured it at ten.'

'It?' said Braintree faintly.

'Mind you, it was a bit oversize. They made it out of an old football bladder and two tennis balls. But it was the penis that got the neighbours up in arms. And Mr Birkenshaw. I didn't know he had a foreskin like that. Come to think of it, I doubt if anyone else in the street did either. Not until Emmeline wrote his name on the damned French letter and fixed wrapping paper from the Christmas cake round the end and the wind carried it ten gardens at peak viewing time on Saturday afternoon. It ended up hanging from the cherry tree in Mrs Lorrimer's on the corner. That way you could see BIRKENSHAW down all four streets quite clearly.'

'Good Lord,' said Braintree. 'What on earth did Mr Birkenshaw have to say about it?'

'Not much yet,' said Wilt, 'he's still in shock. Spent most of Saturday night at the cop shop trying to convince them he isn't the Phantom Flasher. They've been trying to catch that lunatic for years and this time they thought they'd got him.'

'What? Birkenshaw? They're out of their tinies, the man's a Town Councillor.'

'Was,' said Wilt. 'I doubt if he'll stand again. Not after what Emmeline told the policewoman. Said she knew his prick looked like that because he'd lured her into his back garden and waggled the thing at her.'

'Lured her?' said Braintree dubiously. 'With all due respect to your daughters, Henry, I wouldn't have said they were exactly lurable. Ingenious, perhaps, and . . .'

'Diabolical,' said Wilt. 'Don't think I mind what you say about them. I have to live with the hell-cats. Of course she wasn't lured. She's had a vendetta with his little pussy for months because it comes and knocks the stuffing out of ours. She was probably trying to poison the brute. Anyway, she was in his garden and according to her he waggled it. Not his version of course. Claimed he always pees on the compost heap and if little girls choose to lurk . . . Anyway, that didn't go down with the policewoman very well either. Said it was unhygienic.'

'Where was Eva while this was going on?'

'Oh, here and there,' said Wilt airily. 'Apart from practically accusing Mr Birkenshaw of being related to the Yorkshire Ripper ... I managed to stop that one going down in the police report by saying she was hysterical. Talk about drawing fire. At least I had the policewoman there to protect me and as far as I know the law of slander doesn't apply to ten-year-olds. If it does, we'll have to emigrate. As it is, I'm having to work nights to keep them at that blasted school for so-called gifted children. The cost is astronomic.'

'I thought Eva was getting something off by helping out there.'

'Helped out is more accurate. In fact, ordered off the premises,' said Wilt and asked for two more pints.

'What on earth for? I'd have thought they'd have been only too glad to have someone as energetic as Eva as an unpaid ancillary cleaning up and doing the cooking.'

'Not when the said ancillary takes it into her head to brighten up their micro-computers with metal polish. Anyway, she screwed the lot and it was a miracle we didn't have to replace them. Mind you, I wouldn't have minded handing over the ones we've got in the house. The place is a deathtrap of I triple E cables and floppy discs, and I can never get near the TV. And when I do, something called a dot matrix printer goes off somewhere and sounds like a hornets' nest in a hurry. And all for what? So that four girls of average if fiendish intelligence can steal a march on snotty-nosed small boys in the scholastic rat-race.'

'We're just old-fashioned,' said Braintree with a sigh. 'The fact is the computer's here to stay and children know how to use them and we don't. Even the language.'

'Don't talk to me about that gobbledygook. I used to think a poke was a crude form of sex. Instead it's something numerical in a programme and a programme's not what it was. Nothing is. Even bugs and bytes. And to pay for this electronic extravaganza, I spend Tuesday night at the prison teaching a bloody gangster what I don't know about E. M. Forster and Fridays at Baconheath Airbase giving lectures on British Culture and Institutions to a load of Yanks with time on their hands till Armageddon.'

'I shouldn't let the news of that leak out to Mavis Mottram,' said Braintree as they finished their beer and left the pub. 'She's taken up Banning the Bomb with a vengeance. She's been on to Betty about it and I'm surprised she hasn't roped Eva in.'

'She tried but it didn't work, for a change. Eva's too busy worrying about the quads to get involved in demonstrations.'

'All the same, I'd keep quiet about the airbase job. You don't want Mavis picketing your house.'

But Wilt wasn't sure. 'Oh, I don't know. It might make us slightly more popular with the neighbours. At the moment they've got it into their thick heads that I'm either a potential mass-murderer or a left-wing revolutionary because I teach at the Tech. Being picketed by Mavis on the wholly false grounds that I'm in favour of the Bomb might improve my image.' They walked back to the Tech by way of the cemetery.

At 45 Oakhurst Avenue, it was one of Eva Wilt's better days. There were days, better days and one of those days. Days were just days when nothing went wrong and she drove the quads to school without too much quarrelling, and came home to do the housework and went shopping and had a tuna-fish salad for lunch and did some mending afterwards and planted something in the garden and picked the children up from school and nothing particularly nasty happened. On one of those days everything went wrong. The quads quarrelled before, during and after breakfast, Henry lost his temper with them and she found herself having to defend them when she knew all the time he was right, the toast got stuck in the toaster and she was late getting the girls to school and something went wrong with the Hoover or the loo wouldn't flush and nothing seemed to be right with the world, so that she was tempted to have a glass of sherry before lunch and that was no good because then she'd want a nap afterwards and the rest of the day would be spent trying to catch up with what she had to do. But on one of her better days she did all the things she did on days and was somehow uplifted by the thought that the quads were doing wonderfully well at The School for The Mentally Gifted and would definitely get scholarships and go on to become doctors or scientists or something really creative, and that it was lovely to be alive in an age when all this was possible and not like it had been when she was a girl and had to do what she was told. It was on such days that she even considered having her mother to live with them instead of being in the old people's home in Luton and wasting all that money. Only considered it, of course, because Henry couldn't stand the old lady and had threatened to walk out and find himself digs if she ever stayed more than three days in the house.

'I'm not having that old bag polluting the atmosphere with her fags and her filthy habits,' he had shouted so loudly that even Mrs Hoggart, who had been in the bathroom at the time, didn't need her hearing aid to get the gist of the message. 'And another thing. The next time I come down to breakfast and find she's been lacing the teapot with brandy, and my brandy at that, I'll strangle the old bitch.'

'You've got no right to talk like that. After all, she is family—'

'Family?' yelled Wilt, 'I'll say she's family. Your fucking family, not mine. I don't foist my father on you—'

'Your father smells like an old badger,' Eva had retaliated, 'he's unhygienic. At least Mother washes.'

'And doesn't she need to, considering all the muck she smears on her beastly mug. Webster wasn't the only one to see the skull beneath the skin. I was trying to shave the other morning . . .'

'Who's Webster?' demanded Eva before Wilt could repeat the disgusting account of Mrs Hoggart's emergence from behind the shower curtain in the altogether.

'Nobody. It's from a poem, and talking about uncorseted breasts the old hag . . .'

'Don't you dare call her that. She's my mother and one day you'll be old and helpless and need—'

'Yes, well maybe, but I'm not helpless now and the last thing I need is that old Dracula in drag haunting the house and smoking in bed. It's a wonder she didn't burn the place down with that flaming duvet.'

It was the memory of that terrible outburst and the smouldering duvet that had prevented Eva from giving in to her better-day intentions. Besides, there had been truth in what Henry had said, even if he had put it quite horribly. Eva's feelings for her mother had always been ambiguous and part of her wish to have her in the house sprang from the desire for revenge. She'd show her what a really good mother was. And so on one of her better days, she telephoned her and told the old lady how wonderfully the quads were getting on and what a happy atmosphere there was in the home and how even Henry related to the children – Mrs Hoggart invariably broke into a hacking cough at this point – and on the best of days, invited her over for the weekend only to regret it almost as soon as she'd put the phone down. By then it had become one of those days.

But today she resisted the temptation and went round to Mavis Mottram's to have a heart-to-heart with her before lunch. She just hoped Mavis wouldn't try recruiting her for the Ban the Bomb demo.

Mavis did. 'It's no use your saying you have your hands full with the quads, Eva,' she said, when Eva had pointed out that she couldn't possibly leave the children with Henry, and what would happen if she were sent to prison. 'If there's a nuclear war you won't have any children. They'll all be dead in the first second. I mean Baconheath puts us in a first-strike situation. The Russians would be forced to take it out to protect themselves and we'd all go with it.'

Eva tried to puzzle this out. 'I don't see why we'd be a first-strike target if the Russians were being attacked,' she said finally, 'wouldn't it be a second strike?'

Mavis sighed. It was always so difficult to get things across to Eva. It always had been, and with the barrier of the quads behind which to retreat, it was practically impossible nowadays. 'Wars don't start like that. They start over trivial little things like the Archduke Ferdinand being assassinated at Sarajevo in 1914,' she said, putting it as simply as her work with the Open University allowed. But Eva was not impressed.

'I don't call assassinating people trivial,' she said. 'It's wicked and stupid.'

Mavis cursed herself. She ought to have remembered that Eva's experience with terrorists had prejudiced her against political murders. 'Of course it is. I'm not saying it isn't. What I'm—'

'It must have been terrible for his wife,' said Eva, pursuing her line of domestic consequences.

'Since she happened to be killed with him, I don't suppose she cared all that much,' said Mavis bitterly. There was something quite horribly anti-social about the whole Wilt family but she ploughed on. 'The whole point I'm trying to make is that the most terrible war in the history of mankind, up till then, happened because of an accident. A man and his wife were shot by a fanatic, and the result was that millions of ordinary people died. That sort of accident could happen again, and this time there'd be no one left. The human race would be extinct. You don't want that to happen, do you?'

Eva looked unhappily at a china figurine on the mantleshelf. She knew it had been a mistake to come anywhere near Mavis on one of her better days. 'It's just that I don't see what I can do to stop it,' she said and threw Wilt into the fray. 'And anyway, Henry says the Russians won't stop making the bomb and they've got nerve gas too, and Hitler had as well, and he'd have used it if he'd known we hadn't during the war.' Mavis took the bait.

'That's because he's got a vested interest in things staying the way they are,' she said. 'All men have. That's why they're against the women's peace movement. They feel threatened because we're taking the initiative and in a sense the bomb is symbolic of the male orgasm. It's potency on a mass destruction level.'

'I hadn't thought of it like that,' said Eva, who wasn't quite sure how a thing that killed everyone could be a symbol of an orgasm. 'And after all, he used to be a member of CND.'

' "Used to",' sniffed Mavis, 'but not any longer. Men just want us to be passive and stay in a subordinate sex role.'

'I'm sure Henry doesn't. I mean he's not very active sexually,' said Eva, still preoccupied with exploding bombs and orgasms.

'That's because you're a normal person,' said Mavis. 'If you hated sex he'd be pawing you all the time. Instead, he maintains his power by refusing you your rights.'

'I wouldn't say that.'

'Well, I would, and it's no use your claiming anything different.'

It was Eva's turn to look sceptical. Mavis had complained too often in the past about her husband's numerous affairs. 'But you're always saying Patrick's too sex-oriented.'

'Was,' said Mavis with rather sinister emphasis. 'His days of gadding about are over. He's learning what the male menopause is like. Prematurely.'

'Prematurely? I should think it must be. He's only forty-one, isn't he?'

'Forty,' said Mavis, 'but he's aged lately, thanks to Dr Kores.'

'Dr Kores? You don't mean to say Patrick went to her after that dreadful article she wrote in the *News*? Henry burnt the paper before the girls could read it.'

'Henry would. That's typical. He's anti freedom of information.'

'Well, it wasn't a very nice article, was it? I mean it's all very well to say that men are . . . well . . . only biological sperm banks but I don't think it's right to want them all

16

neutered after they've had two children. Our cat sleeps all day and he's—'

'Honestly, Eva, you're so naïve. She didn't say anything about neutering them. She was simply pointing . out that women have to suffer all the agonies of childbirth, not to mention the curse, and with the population explosion the world will face mass starvation unless something's done.'

'I can't see Henry being done. Not that way,' said Eva. 'He won't even let anyone talk about vasectomy. Says it has unwanted side-effects.'

Mavis snorted. 'As if the Pill didn't too, and far more dangerous ones. But the multi-national pharmaceutical corporations couldn't care less. All they are interested in is profits and they're controlled by men too.'

'I suppose so,' said Eva, who'd got used to hearing about multi-national companies though she still didn't know exactly what they were, and was completely at a loss with 'pharmaceutical'. 'All the same, I'm surprised Patrick agreed.'

'Agreed?'

'To have a vasectomy.'

'Who said anything about him having a vasectomy?'

'But you said he went to Dr Kores.'

'*I* went,' said Mavis grimly. 'I thought to myself, "I've had just about enough of you gallivanting about with other women, my boy, and Dr Kores may be able to help." And I was right. She gave me something to reduce his sex drive.'

'And he took it?' said Eva, genuinely astounded now.

'Oh, he takes it all right. He's always been keen on vitamins, especially Vitamin E. So I just swapped the capsules in the bottle. They're some sort of hormone or steroid and he takes one in the morning and two at night. Of course, they're still in the experimental stage but she told me they'd worked very well with pigs and they can't do any harm. I mean he's put on some weight and he's complained about his teats being a bit swollen, but he's certainly quietened down a lot. He never goes

17

out in the evening. Just sits in front of the telly and dozes off. It's made quite a change.'

'I should think it has,' said Eva, remembering how randy Patrick Mottram had always been. 'But are you really sure it's safe?'

'Absolutely. Dr Kores assured me they're going to use it on gays and transvestites who are frightened of a sex-change operation. It shrinks the testicles or something.'

'That doesn't sound very nice. I wouldn't want Henry's shrinking.'

'I daresay not,' said Mavis, who had once made a pass at Wilt at a party, and still resented the fact that he hadn't responded. 'In his case she could probably give you something to stimulate him.'

'Do you really think so?'

'You can always try,' said Mavis. 'Dr Kores does understand women's problems and that's more than you can say for most doctors.'

'But I didn't think she was a proper doctor like Dr Buchman. Isn't she something in the University?'

Mavis Mottram stifled an impulse to say that, yes, she was a consultant in animal husbandry at that, which should suit Henry Wilt's needs even better than Patrick's.

'The two aren't mutually incompatible, Eva. I mean there is a medical school at the University, you know. Anyway, the point is, she's set up a clinic for women with problems, and I do think you'd find her very sympathetic and helpful.'

By the time Eva left and returned to 45 Oakhurst Avenue and a lunch of celery soup with bran magi-mixed into it, she was convinced. She would phone Dr Kores and go and see her about Henry. She was also rather pleased with herself. She had managed to divert Mavis from the depressing topic of the Bomb and on to alternative medicine and the need for women to determine the future because men had made such a mess of the past. Eva was all for that, and when she drove down

18

to fetch the quads it was definitely one of her better days. New possibilities were burgeoning all over the place.

## Chapter two

They were burgeoning all over the place for Wilt as well, but he wouldn't have put the day into the category of one of his better ones. He had returned to his office smelling of The Pig In A Poke's best bitter and hoping he could do some work on his lecture at the airbase without being disturbed, only to find the County Advisor on Communication Skills waiting for him with another man in a dark suit. 'This is Mr Scudd from the Ministry of Education,' said the Advisor. 'He's making a series of random visits to Colleges of Further Education on behalf of the Minister, to ascertain the degree of relevance of certain curricula.'

'How do you do,' said Wilt, and retreated behind his desk. He didn't like the County Advisor very much, but it was as nothing to his terror of men in dark grey suits, and three-piece ones at that, who acted on behalf of the Minister of Education. 'Do take a seat.'

Mr Scudd stood his ground. 'I don't think there's anything to be gained from sitting in your office discussing theoretical assumptions,' he said. 'My particular mandate is to report my observations, my personal observations, of what is acutally taking place on the classroom floor.'

'Quite,' said Wilt, hoping to hell nothing was actually taking place on any of his classroom floors. There had been a singularly nasty incident some years before when he'd had to stop what had the makings of a multiple rape of a rather too attractive student teacher by Tyres Two, who'd been inflamed by a passage in *By Love Possessed* which had been recommended by the Head of English.

'Then if you'll lead the way,' said Mr Scudd and opened the door. Behind him, even the County Advisor had assumed a hangdog look. Wilt led the way into the corridor.

'I wonder if you'd mind commenting on the ideological bias of your staff,' said Mr Scudd, promptly disrupting Wilt's desperate attempt to decide which class it would be safest to take the man into. 'I noticed you had a number of books on Marxism–Leninism in your office.'

'As a matter of fact, I do,' said Wilt and bided his time. If the sod had come on some sort of political witch-hunt, the emollient response seemed best. That way the bastard would land with his bum in the butter, but fast.

'And you consider them suitable reading matter for the working-class apprentices?'

'I can think of worse,' said Wilt.

'Really? So you admit to a left-wing tendency in your teaching.'

'Admit? I didn't admit to anything. You said I had books on Marxism–Leninism in my office. I don't see what that's got to do with what I teach.'

'But you also said you could think of worse reading material for your students,' said Mr Scudd.

'Yes,' said Wilt, 'that's exactly what I said.' The bloke was really getting on his wick now.

'Would you mind amplifying that statement?'

'Glad to. How about *Naked Lunch* for starters?'

'*Naked Lunch?*'

'Or *Last Exit From Brooklyn*. Nice healthy reading stuff for young minds, don't you think?'

'Dear God,' muttered the County Advisor, who had gone quite ashen.

Mr Scudd didn't look any too good either, though he inclined to puce rather than grey. 'Are you seriously telling me that you regard those two revolting books . . . that you encourage the reading of books like that?'

Wilt stopped outside a lecture room in which Mr Ridgeway was fighting a losing battle with a class of first-year A-level students who didn't want to hear what he thought about Bismark. 'Who said anything about encouraging students to read any particular books?' he asked above the din.

Mr Scudd's eyes narrowed. 'I don't think you quite understand the tenor of my questions,' he said, 'I am here . . .' He stopped. The noise coming from Ridgeway's class made conversation inaudible.

'So I've noticed,' shouted Wilt.

The County Advisor staggered to intervene. 'I really think, Mr Wilt,' he began, but Mr Scudd was staring maniacally through the glass pane at the class. At the back, a youth had just passed what looked suspiciously like a joint to a girl with yellow hair in Mohawk style who could have done with a bra.

'Would you say this was a typical class?' he demanded and turned back to Wilt to make himself heard.

'Typical of what?' said Wilt, who was beginning to enjoy the situation. Ridgeway's inability to interest or control supposedly high motivated A-level students would prepare Scudd nicely for the docility of Cake Two and Major Millfield.

'Typical of the way your students are allowed to behave.'

'My students? Nothing to do with me. That's History, not Communication Skills.' And before Mr Scudd could ask what the hell they were doing standing outside a classroom with bedlam going on inside, Wilt had walked on down the corridor. 'You still haven't answered my question,' said Mr Scudd when he had caught up.

'Which one?'

Mr Scudd tried to remember. The sight of that bloody girl had thrown his concentration. 'The one about the pornographic and revoltingly violent reading matter,' he said finally.

'Interesting,' said Wilt. 'Very interesting.'

'What's interesting?'

'That you read that sort of stuff. I certainly don't.'

They went up a staircase and Mr Scudd made use of the handkerchief he kept folded for decoration in his breast pocket. 'I don't read that filth,' he said breathlessly when they reached the top landing.

'Glad to hear it,' said Wilt.

'And I'd be glad to hear why you raised the issue.' Mr Scudd's patience was on a short leash.

'I didn't,' said Wilt, who, having reached the classroom in which Major Millfield was taking Cake Two, had reassured himself that the class was as orderly as he'd hoped. 'You raised it in connection with some historical literature you found in my office.'

'You call Lenin's *State and Revolution* historical literature? I most certainly don't. It's communist propaganda of a particularly virulent kind, and I find the notion that it's being fed to young minds in your department extremely sinister.'

Wilt permitted himself a smile. 'Do go on,' he said. 'There's nothing I enjoy more than listening to a highly trained intelligence leapfrogging common sense and coming to the wrong conclusions. It gives me renewed faith in parliamentary democracy.'

Mr Scudd took a deep breath. In a career spanning some thirty years of uninterrupted authority and bolstered by an inflation-linked pension in the near future, he had come to have a high regard for his own intelligence and he had no intention of having it disparaged now. 'Mr Wilt,' he said, 'I would be grateful to know what conclusions I am supposed to draw from the observations that the Head of Communication Skills at this College has a shelf full of works of Lenin in his office.'

'Personally, I'd be inclined not to draw any,' said Wilt, 'but if you press me . . .'

'I most certainly do,' said Mr Scudd.

'Well, one thing's for certain. I wouldn't suppose that the bloke was a raving Marxist.'

'Not a very positive answer.'

'Not a very positive question, come to that,' said Wilt. 'You asked me what conclusions I'd arrive at and when I tell you I wouldn't arrive at any, you're still not satisfied. I don't see what more I can do.'

But before Mr Scudd could reply, the County Advisor forced himself to intervene. 'I think Mr Scudd simply wants to know if there's any political bias in the teaching in your department.'

'Masses,' said Wilt.

'Masses?' said Mr Scudd.

'Masses?' echoed the County Advisor.

'Absolutely stuffed with it. In fact, if you were to ask me . . .'

'I am,' said Mr Scudd. 'That's precisely what I'm doing.'

'What?' said Wilt.

'Asking you how much political bias there is,' said Mr Scudd, having recourse to his handkerchief again.

'In the first place, I've told you, and in the second, I thought you said you didn't think there was anything to be gained from discussing theoretical assumptions and you'd come to see for yourself what went on on the classroom floor. Right?' Mr Scudd swallowed and looked desperately at the County Advisor, but Wilt went on. 'Right. Well you just take a shuftie in there where Major Millfield is having a class with Fulltime Caterers brackets Confectionery and Bakery close brackets Year Two, affectionately known as Cake Two, and then come and tell me how much political bias you've managed to squeeze out of the visit.' And without waiting for any further questions, Wilt went back down the stairs to his office.

'Squeeze out?' said the Principal two hours later. 'You have to ask the Minister of Education's Personal Private Secretary how much political bias he can squeeze out of Cake Two?'

'Oh, is that who he was, the Minister of Education's own Personal Private Secretary?' said Wilt. 'Well, what do you known about that? Now if he'd been an HMI . . .'

'Wilt,' said the Principal with some difficulty, 'if you think that bastard isn't going to lumber us with one of Her Majesty's Inspectors – in fact I shouldn't be surprised if the entire Inspectorate doesn't descend upon us – and all thanks to you, you'd better think again.'

Wilt looked round at the ad hoc committee that had been set up to deal with the crisis. It consisted of the Principal, the V-P, the County Advisor and, for no apparent reason, the Bursar. 'It's no skin off my nose how many Inspectors he rustles up. Only too glad to have them.'

'You may be but I rather doubt . . .' The Principal hesitated. The County Advisor's presence didn't make for a free flow of opinion on the deficiencies of other departments. 'I take it that any remarks I make will be treated as off the record and entirely confidential,' he said finally.

'Absolutely,' said the County Advisor, 'I'm only interested in Liberal Studies and . . .'

'How nice to hear that term used again. That's the second time this afternoon,' said Wilt.

'And you might have added the bloody studies,' snarled the Advisor, 'instead of leaving the wretched man with the impression that that other idiot lecturer was a fee-paying member of the Young Liberals and a personal friend of Péter Tatchell.'

'Mr Tatchell isn't a Young Liberal,' said Wilt. 'To the best of my knowledge he's a member of the Labour Party, left of centre of course, but . . .'

'And a fucking homosexual.'

'I've no idea. Anyway, I thought the compassionate word was "gay".'

'Shit,' muttered the Principal.

'Or that if you prefer,' said Wilt, 'though I'd hardly describe the term as compassionate. Anyway, as I was saying . . .'

'I am not interested in what you are saying. It's what you said in front of Mr Scudd that matters. You deliberately led him to believe that this College, instead of being devoted to Further Education . . .'

'I like that "devoted". I really do,' interrupted Wilt.

'Yes, devoted to Further Education, Wilt, and you led

him to think we employ nobody but paid-up members of the Communist Party and at the other extreme a bunch of lunatics from the National Front.'

'Major Millfield isn't a member of any party to the best of my knowledge,' said Wilt. 'The fact that he was discussing the social implications of immigration policies—'

'Immigration policies!' exploded the County Advisor. 'He was doing no such thing. He was talking about cannibalism among wogs in Africa and some swine who keeps heads in his fridge.'

'Idi Amin,' said Wilt.

'Never mind who. The fact remains that he was demonstrating a degree of racial bias that could get him prosecuted by the Race Relations Board and you had to tell Mr Scudd to go in and listen.'

'How the hell was I to know what the Major was on about? The class was quiet and I had to warn the other lecturers that the sod was on his way. I mean if you choose to pitch up out of the blue with a bloke who's got no official status . . .'

'Official status?' said the Principal. 'I've already told you Mr Scudd just happens to be—'

'Oh, I know all that and it still doesn't add up. The point is he walks into my office with Mr Reading here, noses his way through the books on the shelf, and promptly accuses me of being an agent of the bleeding Comintern.'

'And that's another thing,' said the Principal. 'You deliberately left him with the impression that you use Lenin's whatever it was called . . .'

'*The State and Revolution,*' said Wilt.

'As teaching material with day-release apprentices. Am I right, Mr Reading?'

The County Advisor nodded weakly. He still hadn't recovered from those heads in the fridge or the subsequent visit to Nursery Nurses who had been deep in a discussion on the impossible and utterly horrifying topic of post-natal abortion for the physically handicapped. The bloody woman had been in favour of it.

'And that's just the beginning,' continued the Principal, but Wilt had had enough.

'The end,' he said. 'If he'd bothered to be polite, it might have been different but he wasn't. And he wasn't even observant enough to see that those Lenin books belong to the History Department, were stamped to that effect, and were covered with dust. To the best of my knowledge, they've been on that shelf ever since my office was changed and they used to use them for the A-level special subject on the Russian Revolution.'

'Then why didn't you tell him that?'

'Because he didn't ask. I don't see why I should volunteer information to total strangers.'

'What about *Naked Lunch*? You volunteered that all right,' said the County Advisor.

'Only because he asked for worse reading material and I couldn't think of anything more foul.'

'Thank the Lord for small mercies,' murmured the Principal.

'But you definitely stated that the teaching in your department is stuffed – yes, you definitely used the word "stuffed" – with political bias. I heard you myself,' continued the County Advisor.

'Quite right too,' said Wilt. 'Considering I'm lumbered with forty-nine members of staff, including part-timers, and all the teaching they ever do is to natter away to classes and keep them quiet for an hour, I should think their political opinions must cover the entire spectrum, wouldn't you?'

'That isn't the impression you gave him.'

'I'm not here to give impressions,' said Wilt, 'I'm a teacher as a matter of unquestionable fact, not a damned public-relations expert. All right, now I've got to take a class of Electronics Engineers for Mr Stott who's away ill.'

'What's the matter with him?' asked the Principal inadvertently.

'Having another nervous breakdown. Understandably,' said Wilt and left the room.

Behind him the members of the Committee looked

wanly at the door. 'Do you really imagine this man Scudd will get the Minister to call for an enquiry?' asked the Vice-Principal.

'That's what he told me,' said the Advisor.'There are certain to be questions in the House after what he saw and heard. It wasn't simply the sex that got his goat, though that was bad enough in all conscience. The man's a Catholic and the emphasis on contraception—'

'Don't,' whispered the Principal.

'No, the thing that really upset him was being told to go and fuck himself by a drunken lout in Motor Mechanics Three. And Wilt, of course.'

'Isn't there something we can do about Wilt?' the Principal asked despairingly as he and the Vice-Principal returned to their offices.

'I don't see what,' said the V-P. 'He inherited half his staff and since he can't get rid of them, he has to do what he can.'

'What Wilt can do is land us with questions in Parliament, the total mobilization of Her Majesty's Inspectorate and a public enquiry into the way this place is run.'

'I shouldn't have thought they'd go to the lengths of a public enquiry. This man Scudd may have influence but I very much doubt . . .'

'I wouldn't. I saw the swine before he left and he was practically demented. What in God's name is post-natal abortion anyway?'

'Sounds rather like murder . . .' the Vice-Principal began, but the Principal was way ahead of him on a thought process that would lead to his forced retirement. 'Infanticide. That's it. Wanted to know if I was aware that we were running a course on Infanticide for future Nannies and asked if we had an evening class for Senior Citizens on Euthanasia or Do-It-Yourself Suicide. We haven't, have we?'

'Not to my knowledge.'

'If we had I'd ask Wilt to run it. That bloody man will be the end of me.'

*

At the Ipford Police Station, Inspector Flint shared his feelings. Wilt had already screwed his chances of becoming a Superintendent and Flint's misery had been compounded by the career of one of his sons, Ian, who had left school and home before taking his A-levels, and after graduating on marijuana and a suspended prison sentence had gone on to be seized by Customs and Excise loaded with cocaine at Dover. 'Bang goes any hope of promotion,' Flint had said morosely when his son was sent down for five years, and had brought down on his own head the wrath of Mrs Flint who blamed him for her son's delinquency. 'If you hadn't been so interested in your own blooming work and getting on and all, and had taken a proper father's interest in him, he wouldn't be where he is now,' she had shouted at him, 'but no, it had to be Yes Sir, No Sir, Oh certainly Sir, and any rotten night work you could get. And week-ends. And what did Ian ever see of his own father? Nothing. And when he did it was always this crime or that villain and how blooming clever you'd been to nick him. That's what your career's done for your family. B. all.'

And for once in his life, Flint wasn't sure she wasn't right. He couldn't bring himself to put it more positively than that. He'd always been right. Or in the right. You had to be to be a good copper, and he certainly hadn't been a bent one. And his career had had to come first.

'You can talk,' he'd said somewhat gratuitously, since it was about the only thing he'd ever allowed her to do apart from the shopping and washing up and cleaning the house and whining on about Ian, feeding the cat and the dog and generally skivvying for him. 'If I hadn't worked my backside off, we wouldn't have the house or the car and you wouldn't have been able to take the little bastard to the Costa . . .'

'Don't you dare call him that!' Mrs Flint had shouted, putting the hot iron on his shirt and scorching it in her anger.

'I'll call him what I bloody well like. He's a rotten villain like all the rest of them.'

'And you're a rotten father. About the only thing you ever did as a father was screw me, and I mean screw, because it wasn't anything else as far as I was concerned.' Flint had taken himself out of the house and back to the police station thinking dark thoughts about women and how their place was in the home, or ought to be, and he was going to be the laughing-stock of the Fenland Constabulary with cracks about him visiting the nick over in Bedford to see his own homegrown convict and a drug pusher at that, and what he'd do to the first sod who called him Snowy and harrying . . . And all the time there was, on the very edge of his mind, a sense of grievance against Henry fucking Wilt. It had always been there, but now it came back stronger than ever: Wilt had buggered his career with that doll of his and then the siege. Oh, yes, he'd almost admired Wilt at one stage but that was a long time ago, a very long time indeed. The little sod was sitting pretty in his house at Oakhurst Avenue and a good salary at the ruddy Tech, and one day he'd probably be the Principal of the stinking place. Whereas any hope Flint had ever had of rising to Super, and being posted to some place Wilt wasn't, had gone up in smoke. He was stuck with being Inspector Flint for the rest of his natural, and stuck with Ipford. As if to emphasize his lack of any hope, they'd brought Inspector Hodge in as Head of the Drug Squad and a right smart-arse he was too. Oh, they'd tried to butter over the crack, but the Super had called Flint in to tell him personally, and that had to mean something. That he was a dead-beat and they couldn't trust him in the drugs game, because his son was inside. Which had brought on another of his headaches which he'd always thought were migraines, only this time the police doctor had diagnosed hypertension and put him on pills.

'Of course I'm hypertense,' Flint had told the quack. 'With the number of brainy bastards round here who ought to be behind bars, any decent police officer's got to be tense. He wouldn't be any good at nailing the shits if he weren't. It's an occupational hazard.'

'It's whatever you like to call it, but I'm telling you you've got high blood pressure and . . .'

'That's not what you said a moment ago,' Flint had flashed back. 'You stated I had tension. Now then, which is it, hypertension or high blood pressure?'

'Inspector,' the doctor had said, 'you're not interrogating a suspect now.' (Flint had his reservations about that.) 'And I'm telling you as simply as I can that hypertension and high blood pressure are one and the same thing. I'm putting you on one diuretic a day—'

'One what?'

'It helps you pass water.'

'As if I needed anything to make me do that. I'm up twice in the blasted night as it is.'

'Then you'd better cut down on your drinking. That'll help your blood pressure, too.'

'How? You tell me not to be tense and the one thing that helps is a beer or two in the local.'

'Or eight,' said the doctor, who'd seen Flint in the pub. 'Anyway, it'll bring your weight down.'

'And make me piss less. So you give me a pill to make me piss more and tell me to drink less. Doesn't make sense.'

By the time Inspector Flint left the surgery, he still didn't know what the pills he had to take did for him. Even the doctor hadn't been able to explain how beta-blockers worked. Just said they did and Flint would have to stay on them until he died.

A month later the Inspector could tell the doctor how they worked. 'Can't even type any more,' he said, displaying a pair of large hands with white fingers. 'Look at them. Like bloody celery sticks that have been blanched.'

'Bound to have some side-effects. I'll give you something to relieve those symptoms.'

'I don't want any more of the piss pills,' said Flint. 'Those bleeding things are dehydrating me. I'm on the bloody trot all the time and it's obvious there's not enough blood left in me to get to my fingers. And that's not all. You want to try working some villain over and being taken short just when he's coming up with a confession. I tell you, it's affecting my work.'

The doctor looked at him suspiciously and thought wistfully of the days when his patients didn't answer back and police officers were of a different calibre to Flint. Besides, he didn't like the expression 'working some villain over'. 'We'll just have to try you out on some other medications,' he said, and was startled by the Inspector's reaction.

'Try me out on some other medicines?' he said belligerently. 'Who are you supposed to be treating, me or the bloody medicines? I'm the one with blood pressure, not them. And I don't like being experimented with. I'm not some bleeding dog, you know.'

'I suppose not,' said the doctor, and had doubled the Inspector's dose of beta-blockers but under a different trade name, added some pills to counter the effect on his fingers, and changed the name of the diuretics. Flint had gone back to his office from the chemist feeling like a walking medicine cabinet.

A week later, he was hard put to it to say what he felt like. 'Fucking awful is all I know,' he told Sergeant Yates who'd been unwise enough to enquire. 'I must have passed more bleeding water in the last six weeks than the Aswan Dam. And I've learnt one thing, this bloody town doesn't have enough public lavatories.'

'I should have thought there were enough to be going on with,' said Yates, who'd once had the unhappy experience of being arrested by a uniformed constable while loitering in the public toilets near the cinema in plain clothes trying to apprehend a genuine loo-lounger.

'Well, you can think again,' snapped Flint. 'I was caught short in Canton Street yesterday, and do you think I could find one? Not on your nelly. Had to use a lane between two houses and nearly got nabbed by a woman hanging her washing on the line. One of these days I'll be done for flashing.'

'Talking about flashing, we've had another report of a

31

case down by the river. Tried it out on a woman of fifty this time.'

'Makes a change from those Wilt bitches and Councillor Birkenshaw. Get a good look at the brute?'

'She said she couldn't see it very well because he was on the other side but she had the impression it wasn't very big.'

'It? It?' shouted Flint. 'I'm not interested in it. I'm talking about the bugger's mug. How the hell do you think we're going to identify the maniac. Have a prick parade and ask the victims to go along studying cocks? The next thing you'll be doing is issuing identikits of penises.'

'She couldn't see his face. He was looking down.'

'And peeing, I daresay. Probably on the same fucking tablets I'm doomed to. Anyway, I wouldn't take the evidence of a fifty-year-old blasted woman. They're all sex-mad at that age. I should know. My old woman's practically off her rocker about it and I keep telling her that the ruddy quack's lowered my blood pressure so much I couldn't get the fucking thing up even if I wanted to. Know what she said?'

'No,' said Sergeant Yates, who found the subject rather distasteful, and anyway it was obvious he didn't know what Mrs Flint had said and he didn't want to hear. The whole notion of anyone wanting the Inspector was beyond him. 'She had the gall to tell me to do it the other way.'

'The other way?' said Yates in spite of himself.

'The old soixante-neuf. Disgusting. And probably illegal. And if anyone thinks I'm going to go down at my age, and on my ruddy missus at that, they're clean off their fucking rockers.'

'I should think they'd have to be,' said the Sergeant almost pitifully. He'd always been relatively fond of old Flint, but there were limits. In a frantic attempt to change the topic to something less revolting, he mentioned the Head of the Drug Squad. He was just in time. The Inspector had just begun a repulsive description of Mrs Flint's attempts to stimulate him. 'Hodge? What's that bloody cock-sucker want now?' Flint bawled, still managing to combine the two subjects.

'Phone-tapping facilities,' said Yates. 'Reckons he's on to a heroin syndicate. And a big one.'

'Where?'

'Won't say, not to me any road.'

'What's he want my permission for? Got to ask the Super or the Chief Constable and I don't come into it. Or do I?' It had dawned on Flint that this might be a subtle dig at him about his son. 'If that bastard thinks he's going to take the piss out of me . . .' he muttered and stopped.

'I shouldn't think he could,' said Yates, getting his own back, 'not with those tablets you're on.'

But Flint hadn't heard. His mind had veered off along lines determined more than he knew by beta-blockers, vasodilators and all the other drugs he was on, but which combined with his natural hatred for Hodge and the accumulated worries of his job and his family to turn him into an exceedingly nasty man. If the Head of the Drug Squad thought he was going to put one over on him he'd got another think coming. 'There are more ways of stuffing a cat than filling it with cream,' he said with a gruesome smile.

Sergeant Yates looked at him doubtfully. 'Shouldn't it be the other way round?' he asked, and immediately regretted any reference to other way round. He'd had enough of Mrs Flint's thwarted sex life, and stuffing cats was definitely out. The old man must be off his rocker.

'Quite right,' said the Inspector. 'We'll fill the bugger with cream all right. Got any idea who he wants to tap?'

'He's not telling me that sort of thing. He reckons the uniform branch aren't to be trusted and he doesn't want any leaks.' The word was too much for Inspector Flint. He shot out of his chair and was presently finding temporary relief in the toilet.

By the time he returned to his office, his mood had changed to the almost dementedly cheerful. 'Tell him we'll give him all the co-operation he needs,' he told the Sergeant, 'only too pleased to help.'

'Are you sure?'

'Of course I'm sure. He's only got to come and see me. Tell him that.'

'If you say so,' said Yates and left the room a puzzled man. Flint sat on in a state of drug-induced bemusement. There was only one bright spot on his limited horizon. If that bastard Hodge wanted to foul up his career by making unauthorized phone taps, Flint would do all he could to encourage him. Fortified by this sudden surge of optimism, he absent-mindedly helped himself to another beta-blocker.

## Chapter three

But already things were moving in a direction the Inspector would have found even more encouraging. Wilt had emerged from the meeting of the crisis committee rather too pleased with his performance. If Mr Scudd really had the influence with the Minister of Education he had claimed to, there might well be a full-scale inspection by the HMIs. Wilt welcomed the prospect. He had frequently thought about the advantages of such a confrontation. For one thing, he'd be able to demand an explicit statement on what the Ministry really thought Liberal Studies were about. Communication Skills and Expressive Attainment they weren't. Since the day some twenty years before when he'd joined the Tech staff, he'd never had a clear knowledge and nobody had been able to tell him. He'd started off with the peculiar dictum enunciated by Mr Morris, the then Head of Department, that what he was supposed to be doing was 'Exposing Day-Release

Apprentices to Culture', which had meant getting the poor devils to read *Lord Of The Flies* and *Candide*, and then discuss what they thought the books were about, and countering their opinions with his own. As far as Wilt could see, the whole thing had been counter-productive and as he had expressed it, if anyone was being exposed to anything, the lecturers were being exposed to the collective barbarism of the apprentices which accounted for the number who had nervous breakdowns or became milkmen with degrees. And his own attempt to change the curriculum to more practical matters, like how to fill in Income Tax forms, claim Unemployment Benefit, and generally move with some confidence through the maze of bureaucratic complications that had turned the Welfare State into a piggy-bank for the middle classes and literate skivers, and an incomprehensible and humiliating nightmare of forms and jargon for the provident poor, had been thwarted by the lunatic theories of so-called educationalists of the sixties like Dr Mayfield, and the equally irrational spending policies of the seventies. Wilt had persisted in his protestations that Liberal Studies didn't need video cameras and audio-visual aids galore, but could do with a clear statement from somebody about the purpose of Liberal Studies.

It had been an unwise request. Dr Mayfield and the County Advisor had both produced memoranda nobody could understand, there had been a dozen committee meetings at which nothing had been decided, except that since all the video cameras were available they might as well be used, and that Communication Skills and Expressive Attainment were more suited to the spirit of the times than Liberal Studies. In the event the education cuts had stymied the audio-visual aids and the fact that useless lecturers in more academic departments couldn't be sacked had meant that Wilt had been lumbered with even more deadbeats. If Her Majesty's Inspectors did descend, they might be able to clear the log jam and make some sense; Wilt would be only too pleased. Besides, he rather prided himself on his ability to hold his own in confrontations.

His optimism was premature. Having spent fifty minutes listening to Electronic Engineers explaining the meaning of cable television to him, he returned to his office to find his secretary, Mrs Bristol, in a flap. 'Oh, Mr Wilt,' she said as he came down the corridor. 'You've got to come quickly. She's there again and it's not the first time.'

'What isn't?' asked Wilt from behind a pile of *Shane* he had never used.

'That I've seen her there.'

'Seen whom where?'

'Her. In the loo.'

'Her in the loo?' said Wilt, hoping to hell Mrs Bristol wasn't having another of her 'turns'. She'd once gone all funny-peculiar when one of the girls in Cake Three had announced in all innocence, that she had five buns in the oven. 'I don't know what you're talking about.'

Nor, it appeared, did Mrs Bristol. 'She's got this needle thing and . . .' she petered out.

'Needle thing?'

'Syringe,' said Mrs Bristol, 'and it's in her arm and full of blood and . . .'

'Oh my God,' said Wilt, and headed past her to the door. 'Which loo?'

'The Ladies' staff one.'

Wilt halted in his tracks. 'Are you telling me one of the members of staff is shooting herself full of heroin in the Ladies' staff lavatory?'

Mrs Bristol *had* gone all funny now. 'I'd have recognized her if she'd been staff. It was a girl. Oh, do something Mr Wilt. She may do herself an injury.'

'You can say that again,' said Wilt, and bolted down the corridor and the flight of stairs to the toilet on the landing and went in. He was confronted by six cubicles, a row of washbasins, a long mirror and a paper-towel dispenser. There was no sign of any girl. On the other hand, the door of the third cubicle was shut and someone was making unpleasant sounds inside. Wilt hesitated. In less desperate circumstances, he might have supposed Mr Rusker, whose wife was a fibre freak, was having one of his problem days again. But Mr Rusker didn't use the Ladies' lavatory. Perhaps if he knelt down he might get a glimpse. Wilt decided against it. (A) He didn't want glimpses and (B) it had begun to dawn on him that he was, to put it mildly, in a delicate situation and bending down and peeping under doors in ladies' lavatories was open to misinterpretation. Better to wait outside. The girl, if there was a girl and not some peculiar figment of Mrs Bristol's imagination, would have to come out sometime.

With one last glance in the trash can for a hypodermic, Wilt tiptoed towards the door. He didn't reach it. Behind him a cubicle door opened. 'I thought so,' a voice shouted, 'a filthy Peeping Tom!' Wilt knew that voice. It belonged to Miss Hare, a senior lecturer in Physical Education, whom he had once likened rather too audibly in the staff-room to Myra Hindley in drag. A moment later, his arm had been wrenched up to the back of his neck and his face was in contact with the tiled wall.

'You little pervert,' Miss Hare continued, jumping to the nastiest, and, from Wilt's point of view, the least desirable conclusion. The last person he'd want to peep at was Miss Hare. Only a pervert would. It didn't seem the time to say so.

'I was just looking—' he began, but Miss Hare quite evidently had not forgotten the crack about Myra Hindley.

'You can keep your explanation for the police,' she screamed, and reinforced the remark by banging his face against the tiles. She was still enjoying the process, and Wilt wasn't, when the door opened and Mrs Stoley from Geography came in.

'Caught the voyeur in the act,' said Miss Hare. 'Call the police.' Against the wall, Wilt tried to offer his point of view and failed. Having Miss Hare's ample knee in the small of his back didn't help and his false tooth had come out.

'But that's Mr Wilt,' said Mrs Stoley uncertainly.

'Of course it's Wilt. It's just the sort of thing you'd expect from him.'

'Well . . .' began Mrs Stoley, who evidently hadn't.

'Oh for goodness' sake get a move on. I don't want the little runt to escape.'

'Am I trying to?' Wilt mumbled and had his nose rammed against the wall for his pains.

'If you say so,' said Mrs Stoley and left the room only to return five minutes later with the Principal and the V-P. By then, Miss Hare had transferred Wilt to the floor and was kneeling on him.

'What on earth's going on?' demanded the Principal. Miss Hare got up.

'Caught in the act of peeping at my private parts,' she said. 'He was trying to escape when I grabbed him.'

'Wasn't,' said Wilt groping for his false tooth and inadvisedly putting it back in his mouth. It tasted of some extremely strong disinfectant which hadn't been form-ulated as a mouthwash, and was doing things to his tongue. As he scrambled to his feet, and made a dash for the washbasins, Miss Hare applied a half-nelson.

'For God's sake let go,' yelled Wilt, by now convinced he was about to die of carbolic poisoning. 'This is all a terrible mistake.'

'Yours,' said Miss Hare and cut off his air supply.

The Principal looked dubiously at them. While he might have enjoyed Wilt's discomfiture in other circum-stances, the sight of him being strangled by an athletically built woman like Miss Hare whose skirt had come down was more than he could stomach.

'I think it would be best if you let him go,' he said as Wilt's face darkened and his tongue stuck out. 'He seems to be bleeding rather badly.'

'Serves him right,' said Miss Hare, reluctantly letting Wilt breathe again. He stumbled to a basin and turned the tap on.

'Wilt,' said the Principal, 'what is the meaning of this?' But Wilt had his false tooth out again and was trying desperately to wash his mouth out under the tap.

'Hadn't we better wait for the police before he makes a statement?' asked Miss Hare.

'The police?' squawked the Principal and the V-P simultaneously. 'You're not seriously suggesting the police should be called in to deal with this . . . er. . . affair.'

'I am,' Wilt mumbled from the basin. Even Miss Hare looked startled.

'You are?' she said. 'You have the nerve to come in here and peer at . . .'

'Balls,' said Wilt, whose tongue seemed to be resuming its normal size, though it still tasted like a recently sterilized toilet bend.

'How dare you,' shouted Miss Hare, and was on the point of getting to grips with him again when the V-P intervened. 'I think we should hear Wilt's version before we do anything hasty, don't you?' Miss Hare obviously didn't, but she stopped in her tracks. 'I've already told you precisely what he was doing,' she said.

'Yes, well let me tell you what . . .'

'He was bending over and looking under the door,' continued Miss Hare remorselessly.

'Wasn't,' said Wilt.

'Don't you dare lie. I always knew you were a pervert. Remember that revolting incident with the doll?' she said, appealing to the Principal. The Principal didn't need reminding but it was Wilt who answered.

'Mrs Bristol,' he mumbled, dabbing his nose with a paper towel, 'Mrs Bristol's the one who started this.'

'Mrs Bristol?'

'Wilt's secretary,' explained the V-P.

'Are you suggesting you were looking for your secretary in here?' asked the Principal. 'Is that what you're saying?'

'No, I'm not. I'm saying Mrs Bristol will tell you why I was here and I want you to hear it from her before that damned bulldozer on anabolic steroids starts knocking hell out of me again.'

'I'm not standing here being insulted by a . . .'

'Then you'd better pull your skirt up,' said the V-P, whose sympathies were entirely with Wilt.

The little group made their way up the stairs, past a class of English A-level students who'd just ended an hour with Mr Gallen on The Pastoral Element in Wordsworth's *Prelude*, and were consequently unprepared for the urban element of Wilt's bleeding nose. Nor was Mrs Bristol. 'Oh dear, Mr Wilt, what have you done to yourself?' she asked. 'She didn't attack you?'

'Tell them,' said Wilt. 'You tell them.'

'Tell them what?'

'What you told me,' snapped Wilt, but Mrs Bristol was too concerned about his condition and the Principal and the V-P's presence had unnerved her. 'You mean about—'

'I mean . . . Never mind what I mean,' said Wilt lividly, 'just tell them what I was doing in the Ladies' lavatory, that's all.'

Mrs Bristol's face registered even more confusion. 'But I don't know,' she said, 'I wasn't there.'

'I know you weren't there, dammit. What they want to know is why I was.'

'Well . . .' Mrs Bristol began, and lost her nerve again, 'Haven't you told them?'

'Caesar's ghost,' said Wilt, 'can't you just spit it out. Here I am accused of being a Peeping Tom by Miss Burke and Hare over there . . .'

'You call me that again and your own mother wouldn't recognize you,' said Miss Hare.

'Since she's been dead for ten years, I don't suppose she would now,' said Wilt, retreating behind his desk. By the time the PE teacher had been restrained, the Principal was trying to make some sense out of an increasingly confused situation. 'Can someone please shed some light on this sordid business?' he asked.

'If anyone can, she can,' said Wilt, indicating his secretary. 'After all, she set me up.'

'Set you up, Mr Wilt? I never did anything of the sort. All I said was there was a girl in the staff toilet with a

hypodermic and I didn't know who she was and . . .'
Intimidated by the look of horror on the Principal's face,
she ground to a halt. 'Have I said something wrong?'

'You saw a girl with a hypodermic in the staff toilet?
And told Mr Wilt about it?'

Mrs Bristol nodded dumbly.

'When you say "girl" I presume you don't mean a
member of the staff?'

'I'm sure it wasn't. I didn't see her face but I'd have
known surely. And she had this awful syringe filled with
blood and . . .' She looked at Wilt for assistance.

'You said she was taking drugs.'

'There was no one in that toilet while I was there,' said
Miss Hare, 'I'd have heard them.'

'I suppose it could have been someone with diabetes,'
said the V-P, 'some adult student who wouldn't want to
use the student's toilet for obvious reasons.'

'Oh quite,' said Wilt, 'I mean we all know diabetics go
round with hypodermics full of blood. She was obviously
flushing back to get the maximum dose.'

'Flushing back?' said the Principal weakly.

'That's what the junkies do,' said the V-P. 'They inject
themselves and then—'

'I don't want to know,' said the Principal.

'Well, if she was taking heroin—'

'Heroin! That's all we need,' said the Principal, and sat
down miserably.

'If you ask me,' said Miss Hare, 'the whole thing's a
fabrication. I was in there ten minutes . . . '

'Doing what?' asked Wilt. 'Apart from attacking me.'

'Something feminine, if you must know.'

'Like taking steroids. Well, let me tell you that when I
went down there and I wasn't there more than . . .'

It was Mrs Bristol's turn to intervene. 'Down, did you
say down?'

'Of course I said down. What did you expect me to say?
Up?'

'But the toilet's on the fourth floor, not the second.
That's where she was.'

'Now you tell us. And where the hell do you think I went?'

'But I always go upstairs,' said Mrs Bristol. 'It keeps me in trim. You know that. I mean one's got to get some exercise and . . .'

'Oh, belt up,' said Wilt, and dabbed his nose with a bloodstained handkerchief.

'Right, let's get this straight,' said the Principal, deciding it was time to exercise some authority. 'Mrs Bristol tells Wilt here there is a girl upstairs injecting herself with something or other and instead of going upstairs, Wilt goes down to the toilet on the second floor and . . .'

'Gets beaten to a pulp by Ms Blackbelt Burke here,' said Wilt who was beginning to regain the initiative. 'And I don't suppose it's occurred to anyone to go up and see if that junkie's still there.'

But the Vice-Principal had already left.

'If that little turd calls me Burke again . . .' said Miss Hare menacingly. 'Anyway, I still think we should call the police. I mean, why did Wilt go downstairs instead of up? I find that peculiar.'

'Because I don't use the Ladies' or, in your case, the Bisexual Toilets, that's why.'

'Oh for God's sake,' said the Principal, 'there's obviously been some mistake and if we all keep calm . . .'

The Vice-Principal returned. 'No sign of her,' he said.

The Principal got to his feet. 'Well, that's that. Evidently there's been some mistake. Mrs Bristol may have imagined . . .' But any aspersions on Mrs Bristol's imagination he was about to make were stopped by the V-P's next words.

'But I did find this in the trash can,' he said, and produced a blood-stained lump of paper towel, which looked like Wilt's handkerchief.

The Principal regarded it with disgust. 'That hardly proves anything. Women do bleed occasionally.'

'Call it a jamrag and be done with it,' said Wilt

viciously. He was getting fed up with bleeding himself. Miss Hare turned on him.

'That's typical, you foulmouthed sexist,' she snapped.

'I was merely interpreting what the Principal was . . .'

'And more conclusively, this,' interrupted the V-P, this time producing a hypodermic needle.

It was Mrs Bristol's turn to bridle. 'There, what did I tell you. I wasn't imagining anything. There was a girl up there injecting herself and I did see her. Now what are you going to do?'

'Now we mustn't jump to conclusions just because . . .' the Principal began.

'Call the police. I demand that you call the police,' said Miss Hare, determined to take this opportunity for airing her opinions about Wilt and Peeping Toms as widely as possible.

'Miss Burke,' said the Principal, flustered into sharing Wilt's feelings about the PE lecturer, 'this is a matter that needs cool heads.'

'Miss Hare's my name and if you haven't the decency . . . And where do you think you're going?'

Wilt had taken the opportunity to sidle to the door. 'To the men's toilet to assess the damage you did, then the Blood Transfusion Unit for a refill and after that, if I can make it, to my doctor and the most litigious lawyer I can find to sue you for assault and battery.' And before Miss Hare could reach him, Wilt was off down the corridor and had closeted himself in the Men's toilet.

Behind him Miss Hare vented her fury on the Principal. 'Right, that does it,' she shouted. 'If you don't call the police, I will. I want the facts of this case spelt out loud and clear so that if that little sex-maniac goes anywhere near a lawyer, the public are going to learn the sort of people who teach here. I want this whole disgusting matter dealt with openly.'

It was the last thing the Principal wanted. 'I really don't think that's wise,' he said. 'After all, Wilt could have made a natural mistake.'

Miss Hare wasn't to be mollified. 'The mistake Wilt

made wasn't natural. And besides, Mrs Bristol did see a girl taking heroin.'

'We don't know that. There could be some quite ordinary explanation.'

'The police will find out soon enough once they've got that syringe,' said Miss Hare adamantly. 'Now then, are you going to phone them or am I?'

'If you put it like that, I suppose we'll have to,' said the Principal, eyeing her with loathing. He picked up the phone.

## Chapter four

In the Men's toilet, Wilt surveyed his face in the mirror. It looked as unpleasant as it felt. His nose was swollen, there were streaks of blood on his chin and Miss Hare had managed to open an old cut above his right eye. Wilt washed his face in a basin and thought dismally about tetanus. Then he took his false tooth out and studied his tongue. It was not, as he had expected, twice its normal size, but it still tasted of disinfectant. He rinsed his mouth out under the tap with the slightly cheering thought that if his taste buds were anything to go by a tetanus germ wouldn't stand an earthly of surviving. After that, he put his tooth back and wondered yet again what it was about him that invited misunderstanding and catastrophe.

The face in the mirror told him nothing. It was a very ordinary face and Wilt had no illusions about it being handsome. And yet for all it ordinariness, it had to be the façade behind which lurked an extraordinary mind. In the past he had liked to think it was an original mind or, at the very least, an individual one. Not that that helped much. Every mind had to be individual and that didn't

44

make everyone accident-prone, to put it mildly. No, the fact of the matter was that he lacked a sense of his own authority.

'You just let things happen to you,' he told the face in the mirror. 'It's about time you made them happen for you.' But as he said it, he knew it would never be like that. He would never be a dominating person, a man of power whose orders were obeyed without question. It wasn't his nature. To be more accurate, he lacked the stamina and drive to deal in details, to quibble over procedure and win allies and out-manoeuvre opponents, in short, to concentrate his attention on the means of gaining power. Worse still, he despised the people who had that drive. Invariably, they limited themselves to a view of the world in which they alone were important and to hell with what other people wanted. And they were everywhere, these committee Hitlers, especially at the Tech. It was about time they were challenged. Perhaps one day he would . . .

He was interrupted in this daydream by the entrance of the Vice-Principal. 'Ah, there you are, Henry,' he said, 'I thought I'd better let you know that we've had to call in the police.'

'About what?' asked Wilt, suddenly alarmed at the thought of Eva's reaction if Miss Hare accused him of being a voyeur.

'Drugs in the college.'

'Oh, that. A bit late in the day, isn't it? Been going on ever since I can remember.'

'You mean you knew about it?'

'I thought everyone did. It's common knowledge. Anyway, it's obvious we're bound to have a few junkies with all the students we've got,' said Wilt, and made good his escape while the Vice-Principal was still busy at the urinal. Five minutes later, he had left the Tech and was immersed once more in those speculative thoughts that seemed to occupy so much of his time when he was alone. Why was it, for instance, that he was so concerned with power when he wasn't really prepared to do anything about it? After all, he was earning a comfortable salary – it would have been a really good one if Eva hadn't spent so much of it on the quads' education – and objectively he had nothing to complain about. Objectively. And a fat lot that meant. What mattered was how one felt. On that score, Wilt came bottom even on days when he hadn't had his face mashed by Ms Hare.

Take Peter Braintree for example. He didn't have any sense of futility or lack of power. He had even refused promotion because it would have meant giving up teaching and taking on administrative duties. Instead, he was content to give his lectures on English literature and go home to Betty and the children and spend his evenings playing trains or making model aeroplanes when he'd finished marking essays. And at the weekends, he'd go off to watch a football match or play cricket. It was the same during the holidays. The Braintrees always went off camping and walking and came back cheerful, with none of the rows and catastrophes that seemed an inevitable part of the Wilt family excursions. In his own way, Wilt envied him, while having to admit that his envy was muted by a contempt he knew to be wholly unjustified. In the modern world, in any world, it wasn't enough just to be content and hope that everything would turn out for the best in the end. In Wilt's experience, they turned out for the worst, e.g. Miss Hare. On the other hand, when he did try to do something the result was catastrophic. There didn't seem to be any middle way.

He was still puzzling over the problem when he crossed Bilton Street and walked up Hillbrow Avenue. Here too, the signs told him that almost everyone was content with his lot. The cherry trees were in bloom, and pink and white petals littered the pavement like confetti. Wilt noted each front garden, most of them neat and bright with wallflowers, but some, where academics from the University lived, unkempt and overgrown with weeds. On the corner of Pritchard Street, Mr Sands was busy among his heathers and azaleas, proving to an uninterested world that it was possible for a retired bank manager to find satisfaction by growing acid-loving plants on an alkaline soil. Mr Sands had explained the difficulties to Wilt one day, and the need to replace all the topsoil with peat to lower the pH. Since Wilt had no idea what pH stood for, he hadn't a clue what Mr Sands had been talking about, and in any case, he had been more interested in Mr Sands' character and the enigma of his contentment. The man had spent forty years presumably fascinated by the movement of money from one account to the other, fluctuations in the interest rate and the granting of loans and overdrafts, and now all he seemed prepared to talk about were the needs of his camellias and miniature conifers. It didn't make sense and was just as unfathomable as the character of Mrs Cranley who had once figured so spectacularly in a trial to do with a brothel in Mayfair, but who now sang in the choir at St Stephens and wrote children's stories filled with remorseless whimsy and an appalling innocence. It was beyond him. He could only deduce one fact from his observations. People could and did change their lives from one moment to the next, and quite fundamentally at that. And if they could, there was no reason why he shouldn't. Fortified with the knowledge, he strode on more confidently and with the determination not to put up with any nonsense from the quads tonight.

As usual he was proved wrong. He had no sooner opened the front door, than he was under siege. 'Ooh, Daddy, what have you done to your face?' demanded Josephine.

'Nothing,' said Wilt, and tried to escape upstairs before the real inquisition could begin. He needed a bath and his clothes stank of disinfectant. He was stopped by Emmeline who was playing with her hamster halfway up.

'Don't step on Percival,' she said, 'she's pregnant.'

'Pregnant?' said Wilt, momentarily nonplussed. 'He can't be. It's impossible.'

'Percival's a she, so it is.'

'A she? But the man at the petshop guaranteed the thing was a male. I asked him specifically.'

'And she's not a thing,' said Emmeline. 'She's an expectant mummy.'

'Better not be,' said Wilt. 'I'm not having the house overrun by an exploding population of hamsters. Anyway, how do you know?'

'Because we put her in with Julian's to see if they'd fight to the death like the book said, and Pervical went into a trance and didn't do anything.'

'Sensible fellow,' said Wilt, immediately identifying with Pervical in such horrid circumstances.

'She's not a fellow. Mummy hamsters always go into a trance when they want to be done.'

'Done?' said Wilt inadvisedly.

'What you do to Mummy on Sunday mornings and Mummy goes all funny afterwards.'

'Christ,' said Wilt, cursing Eva for not shutting the bedroom door. Besides, the mixture of accuracy and baby-talk was getting to him. 'Anyway, never mind what we do. I want to . . .'

'Does Mummy go into a trance, too?' asked Penelope, who was coming down the stairs with a doll in a pram.

'It's not something I'm prepared to discuss,' said Wilt. 'I need a bath and I'm going to have one. And now.'

'Can't,' said Josephine. 'Sammy's having her hair washed. She's got nits. You smell funny too. What's that on your collar?'

'And all down the front of your shirt.' This from Penelope.

'Blood,' said Wilt, endowing the word with as much threat as he could. He pushed past the pram and went into the bedroom, wondering what it was about the quads that gave them some awful sort of collective authority. Four separate daughters wouldn't have had the same degree of assertiveness and the quads had definitely inherited Eva's capacity for making the worst of things. As he undressed, he could hear Penelope bearing the glad tidings of his misfortune to Eva through the bathroom door.

'Daddy's come home smelling of disinfectant and he's cut his face.'

'He's taking off his trousers and there's blood all down his shirt,' Josephine chimed in.

'Oh, great,' said Wilt. 'That ought to bring her out like a scalded cat.'

But it was Emmeline's announcement that Daddy had said Mummy went into a trance when she wanted a fuck that caused the trouble.

'Don't use that word,' yelled Wilt. 'If I've told you once I've told you a thousand times and I never said anything about your bleeding mother going into a trance. I said—'

'What did you call me?' Eva shouted, storming out of the bathroom. Wilt pulled up his Y-fronts again and sighed. On the landing, Emmeline was describing with clinical accuracy the mating habits of female hamsters, and attributing the description to Wilt.

'I didn't call you a bloody hamster. That's a downright lie. I don't know the first thing about the fucking things and I certainly never wanted them in—'

'There you go,' shouted Eva. 'One moment you're telling the children not to use filthy language and the next you're using it youself. You can't expect them to—'

'I don't expect them to lie. That's far worse than the sort of language they use and anyway Penelope used it first. I—'

'And you've absolutely no right to discuss our sex life with them.'

'I don't and I wasn't,' said Wilt. 'All I said was I didn't want the house overrun by blasted hamsters. The man in the shop sold me that mentally deficient rat as a male, not a bloody breeding machine.'

'Now you're being disgustingly sexist as well,' yelled Eva.

Wilt stared wildly round the bedroom. 'I am not being sexist,' he said finally. 'It just happens to be a well-known fact that hamsters—'

But Eva had seized on his inconsistency. 'Oh yes you are. The way you talk anyone would think women were

49

the only ones who wanted you-know-what.'

'You-know-what my foot. Those four little bints out there know what without you-know-whating—'

'How dare you call your own daughters bints? That's a disgusting word.'

'Fits,' said Wilt, 'and as for their being my own daughters, I can tell you it's—'

'I shouldn't,' said Eva.

Wilt didn't. Push Eva too far and there was no knowing what would happen. Besides, he'd enough of women's power in action for one day. 'All right, I apologize,' he said. 'It was a stupid thing to say.'

'I should think it was,' said Eva, coming off the boil and picking his shirt off the floor. 'How on earth did you get all this blood on your new shirt?'

'Slipped and fell in the gents,' said Wilt, deciding the time was hardly appropriate for a more accurate account. 'That's why it smells like that.'

'In the gents?' said Eva suspiciously. 'You fell over in the gents?'

Wilt gritted his teeth. He could see any number of awful consequences developing if the truth leaked out but he'd already committed himself.

'On a bar of soap,' he said. 'Some idiot had left it on the floor.'

'And another idiot stepped on it,' said Eva, scooping up Wilt's jacket and trousers and depositing them in a plastic basket. 'You can take these to the dry-cleaners on the way to work tomorrow.'

'Right,' said Wilt, and headed for the bathroom.

'You can't go in there yet. I'm still washing Samantha's hair and I'm not having you prancing around in the altogether . . .'

'Then I'll wear my pants in the shower,' said Wilt and was presently hidden behind the shower curtain listening to Penelope telling the world that female hamsters frequently bit the male's testicles after copulating.

'I wonder they bother to wait. Talk about having your

50

cake and eating it,' muttered Wilt, and absentmindedly soaped his Y-fronts.

'I heard that,' said Eva and promptly turned the hot tap on in the bath. Behind the shower curtain Wilt juddered under a stream of cold water. With a grunt of despair, he wrenched at the cold tap and stepped from the shower.

'Daddy's foaming at his panties,' squealed the quads delightedly.

Wilt lurched at them rabidly. 'Not the only fucking place he'll be foaming if you don't get the hell out of here,' he shouted.

Eva turned the hot tap in the bath off. 'That's no way to set an example,' she said, 'talking like that. You should be ashamed of yourself.'

'Like hell I should. I've had a bloody awful day at the Tech and I've got to go out to the prison to teach that ghastly creature McCullum, and I no sooner step into the bosom of my menagerie than I—'

The front doorbell rang loudly downstairs. 'That's bound to be Mr Leach next door come to complain again,' said Eva.

'Sod Mr Leach,' said Wilt and stepped back under the shower.

This time he learnt what it felt like to be scalded.


# Chapter five


Things were hotting up for other people in Ipford as well. The Principal for one. He had just arrived home and was opening the drinks cabinet in the hope of dulling his memory of a disastrous day, when the phone rang. It was the Vice-Principal. 'I'm afraid I've got some rather disturbing news,' he said with a lugubrious satisfaction the Principal recognized. He connected it with funerals.

'It's about that girl we were looking for . . .' The Principal reached for the gin bottle and missed the rest of the sentence. He got back in time to hear something about the boiler-room. 'Say that again,' he said, holding the bottle between his knees and trying to open it with one hand.

'I said the caretaker found her in the boiler-room.'

'In the boiler-room? What on earth was she doing there?'

'Dying,' said the Vice-Principal, affecting an even more sombre tone.

'Dying?' The Principal had the bottle open now and poured himself a large gin. This was even more awful than he expected.

'I'm afraid so.'

'Where is she now?' asked the Principal, trying to stave off the worst.

'Still in the boiler-room.'

'Still in the . . . But good God man, if she's in that condition, why the devil haven't you got her to hospital?'

'She isn't in that condition,' said the Vice-Principal and paused. He too had had a hard day. 'What I said was that she was dying. The fact of the matter is that she's dead.'

'Oh, my God,' said the Principal and swigged neat gin. It was better than nothing. 'You mean she died of an overdose?'

'Presumably. I suppose the police will find out.'

The Principal finished the rest of the gin. 'When did this happen?'

'About an hour ago.'

'An hour ago? I was still in my office an hour ago. Why the hell wasn't I told?'

'The caretaker thought she was drunk first of all and fetched Mrs Ruckner. She was taking an ethnic needle-work class with Home Economics in the Morris block and—'

'Never mind about that now,' snapped the Principal. 'A girl's dead on the premises and you have to go on about Mrs Ruckner and ethnic needlework.'

'I'm not going on about Mrs Ruckner,' said the Vice-Principal, driven to some defiance, 'I'm merely trying to explain.'

'Oh, all right, I've heard you. So what have you done with her?'

'Who? Mrs Ruckner?'

'No, the damned girl, for God's sake. There's no need to be flippant.'

'If you're going to adopt that tone of voice, you'd better come here and see for yourself,' said the Vice-Principal and put the phone down.

'You bloody shit,' said the Principal, unintentionally addressing his wife who had just entered the room.

At Ipford Police Station the atmosphere was fairly acrimonious too. 'Don't give me that,' said Flint who had returned from a fruitless visit to the Mental Hospital to interview a patient who had confessed (quite falsely) to being the Phantom Flasher. 'Give it to Hodge. He's drugs and I've had my fill of the bloody Tech.'

'Inspector Hodge is out,' said the Sergeant, 'and they specially asked for you. Personally.'

'Pull the other one,' said Flint. 'Someone's hoaxing you. The last person they want to see is me. And it's mutual.'

'No hoax, sir. It was the Vice-Principal himself. Name of Avon. My lad goes there so I know.'

Flint stared at him incredulously. 'Your son goes to that hell-hole? And you let him? You must be out of your mind. I wouldn't let a son of mine within a mile of the place.'

'Possibly not,' said the Sergeant, tactfully avoiding the observation that since Flint's son was doing a five-year stretch, he wasn't likely to be going any place. 'All the same, he's an apprentice plumber. Got day-release classes and he can't opt out of them. There's a law about it.'

'You want my opinion, there ought to be a law stopping youngsters having anything to do with the sods who teach there. When I think of Wilt . . .' He shook his head in despair.

'Mr Avon said something about your discreet approach being needed,' the Sergeant went on, 'and anyway, they don't know how she died. I mean, it doesn't have to be an overdose.'

Flint perked up. 'Discreet approach my arse,' he muttered. 'Still, a genuine murder there makes a change.' He lumbered to his feet and went down to the car pool and drove down to Nott Road and the Tech. A patrol car was parked outside the gates. Flint swept past it and parked deliberately in the space reserved for the Bursar. Then with the diminished confidence he always felt when returning to the Tech, he entered the building. The Vice-Principal was waiting for him by the Enquiries Desk. 'Ah, Inspector, I'm so glad you could come.'

Flint regarded him suspiciously. His previous visits hadn't been welcomed. 'All right, where's the body?' he said abruptly and was pleased to see the Vice-Principal wince.

'Er . . . in the boiler-room,' he said. 'But first there's the question of discretion. If we can avoid a great deal of publicity it would really be most helpful.'

Inspector Flint cheered up. When the sods started squealing about publicity and the need for discretion, things had got to be bad. On the other hand, he'd had enough lousy publicity from the Tech himself. 'If it's anything to do with Wilt . . .' he began, but the Vice-Principal shook his head.

'Nothing like that, I assure you,' he said. 'At least, not directly.'

'What's that mean, not directly?' said Flint warily. With Wilt, nothing was ever direct.

'Well, he was the first to be told that Miss Lynchknowle had taken an overdose but he went to the wrong loo.'

'Went to the wrong loo?' said Flint and bared his teeth in a mock smile. A second later the smile had gone. He'd smelt trouble. 'Miss who?'

'Lynchknowle. That's what I mean about . . . well, the need for discretion. I mean . . .'

'You don't have to tell me. I know, don't I just,' said

54

Flint rather more coarsely than the Vice-Principal liked. 'The Lord Lieutenant's daughter gets knocked off here and you don't want him to . . .' He stopped and looked hard at the V-P. 'How come she was here in the first place? Don't tell me she was shacked up with one of your so-called students.'

'She was one of our students,' said the Vice-Principal, trying to maintain some dignity in the face of Flint's patent scepticism. 'She was Senior Secs Three and . . .'

'Senior Sex Three? What sort of course is that, for hell's sake? Meat One was sick enough considering they were a load of butcher's boys, but if you're telling me you've been running a class for prostitutes and one of them's Lord Lynchknowle's ruddy daughter . . .'

'Senior Secretaries,' spluttered the Vice-Principal, 'a very respectable course. We've always had excellent results.'

'Like deaths,' said Flint. 'All right, let's have a look at your latest victim.'

With the certainty now that he'd done the wrong thing in asking for Flint, the Vice-Principal led the way across the quad.

But the Inspector hadn't finished. 'I hear you've been putting it out as a self-administered OD. Right?'

'OD?'

'Overdose.'

'Of course. You're not seriously suggesting it could have been anything else?'

Inspector Flint fingered his moustache. 'I'm not in a position to suggest anything. Yet. I'm asking why you say she died of drugs.'

'Well, Mrs Bristol saw a girl injecting herself in the staff toilet and went to fetch Wilt . . .'

'Why Wilt of all people? Last person I'd fetch.'

'Mrs Bristol is Wilt's secretary,' said the V-P and went on to explain the confused course of events. Flint listened grimly. The only part he enjoyed was hearing how Wilt had been dealt with by Miss Hare. She sounded like a woman after his own heart. The rest fitted in with his preconceptions of the Tech.

'One thing's certain,' he said when the Vice-Principal had finished, 'I'm not drawing any conclusions until I've made a thorough examination. And I do mean thorough. The way you've told it doesn't make sense. One unidentified girl takes a fix in a toilet and the next thing you know Miss Lynchknowle is found dead in the boiler-room. How come you assume it's the same girl?'

The Vice-Principal said it just seemed logical. 'Not to me it doesn't,' said Flint. 'And what was she doing in the boiler-room?'

The Vice-Principal looked miserably down the steps at the door and resisted the temptation to say she'd been dying. That might work with the Principal but Inspector Flint's manner didn't suggest he'd respond kindly to statements of the obvious. 'I've no idea. Perhaps she just felt like going somewhere dark and warm.'

'And perhaps she didn't,' said Flint. 'Anyway, I'll soon find out.'

'I just hope you will be discreet,' said the V-P, 'I mean it's a very sensitive . . .'

'Bugger discretion,' said Flint, 'all I'm interested in is the truth.'

Twenty minutes later, when the Principal arrived, it was all too obvious that the Inspector's search for the truth had assumed quite alarming dimensions. The fact was that Mrs Ruckner, more accustomed to the niceties of ethnic needlework than resuscitation, had allowed the body to slip behind the boiler: that the boiler hadn't been turned off added a macabre element to the scene. Flint had refused to allow it to be moved until it had been photographed from every possible angle, and he had summoned fingerprint and forensic experts from the Murder Squad along with the police surgeon. The Tech car park was lined with squad cars and an ambulance and the buildings themselves seemed to be infested with policemen. And all this in full view of students arriving for evening classes. To the Principal, it appeared as if the

56

Inspector was intent on attracting the maximum adverse publicity.

'Is the man mad?' he demanded of the Vice-Principal, stepping over a white tape that had been laid on the ground outside the steps to the boiler-room.

'He says he's treating it as a murder case until he's proved it isn't,' said the Vice-Principal weakly, 'and I wouldn't go down there if I were you.'

'Why the hell not?'

'Well, for one thing there's a dead body and . . .'

'Of course there's a dead body,' said the Principal, who had been in the War and frequently mentioned the fact. 'Nothing to be squeamish about.'

'If you say so. All the same . . .'

But the principal had already gone down the steps into the boiler-room. He was escorted out a moment later looking decidedly unwell. 'Jesus wept! You could have told me they were holding an autopsy on the spot,' he muttered. 'How the hell did she get in that state?'

'I rather think Mrs Ruckner . . .'

'Mrs Ruckner? Mrs Ruckner?' gurgled the Principal, trying to equate what he had just seen in some way with the tenuous figure of the part-time lecturer in ethnic needlework and finding it impossible. 'What the hell has Mrs Ruckner got to do with that . . . that . . .'

But before he could express himself at all clearly, they were joined by Inspector Flint. 'Well, at least we've got a real dead corpse this time,' he said, timing his cheerfulness nicely. 'Makes a change for the Tech, doesn't it?'

The Principal eyed him with loathing. Whatever Flint might feel about the desirability of real dead corpses littering the Tech he didn't share Flint's opinions. 'Now look here, Inspector . . .' he began in an attempt to assert some authority.

But Flint had opened a cardboard box. 'I think you had better look in here first,' he said. 'Is this the sort of printed matter you encourage your students to read?'

The Principal stared down into the box with a horrid fascination. If the cover of the top magazine was anything to go by – it depicted two women, a rack and a revoltingly androgynous man clad in chains and a . . . the Principal preferred not to think what it looked like – the entire box was filled with printed matter he wouldn't have wanted his students to know about, let alone read.

'Certainly not,' he said, 'that's downright pornography.'

'Hard core,' said Flint, 'and there's more where this little lot came from. Puts a new complexion on things, doesn't it?'

'Dear God,' muttered the Principal, as Flint trotted off across the quad, 'are we to be spared nothing? That bloody man seems to find the whole horrible business positively enjoyable.'

'It's probably because of that terrible incident with Wilt some years back,' said the V-P. 'I don't think he's ever forgotten it.'

'Nor have I,' said the Principal, looking gloomily round at the buildings in which he had once hoped to make a name for himself. And in a sense it seemed he had. Thanks to so many things that were connected, in his mind, with Wilt. It was the one topic on which he would have agreed with the Inspector. The little bastard ought to be locked up.

And in a sense Wilt was. To prevent Eva from learning that he spent Friday evenings at Baconheath Airbase he devoted himself on Mondays to tutoring a Mr McCullum at Ipford Prison and then led her to suppose he had another tutorial with him four evenings later. He felt rather guilty about this subterfuge but excused himself with the thought that if Eva wanted to buy an expensive education plus computers for four daughters, she couldn't seriously expect his salary, however augmented by HM Prison Service, to pay for it. The airbase lectures did that and anyway Mr McCullum's company constituted a form of penance. It also had the effect of assuaging Wilt's sense of guilt. Not that his pupil didn't do his damnedest to instil one. A sociology lecturer from the Open University had given him a solid grounding in that subject and Wilt's attempts to further Mr McCullum's interest in E. M. Foster and *Howards End* were constantly interrupted by the convict's comments on the socio-economically disadvantaged environment which had led him to end up where and what he was. He was also fairly fluent on the class war, the need for a preferably bloody revolution and the total redistribution of wealth. Since he had spent his entire life pursuing riches by highly illegal and unpleasant means, ones which involved the deaths of four people and the use of a blowtorch as a persuader on several gentlemen in his debt, thus earning himself the soubriquet 'Fireworks Harry' and 25 years from a socially prejudiced judge, Wilt found the argument somewhat suspect.

He didn't much like Mr McCullum's changes of mood either. They varied from whining self-pity, and the claim that he was deliberately being turned into a cabbage, through bouts of religious fervour during which the name Longford came up rather too often, and finally to a bloody-minded belligerence when he threatened to roast the fucking narks who'd shopped him. On the whole, Wilt preferred McCullum the cabbage and was glad that the tutorials were conducted through a grill of substantial wire mesh and in the presence of an even more substantial warder. After Miss Hare and the verbal battering he'd had from Eva, he could do with some protection and this evening Mr McCullum's mood had nothing to do with vegetables. 'Listen,' he told Wilt thickly, 'you don't have a clue, do you? Think you know everything but you haven't done time. Same with this E. M. Forster. He was a middle-class scrubber too.'

'Possibly,' said Wilt, recognizing that this was not one of the nights on which to press Mr McCullum too frankly on the need to stick to the subject. 'He was certainly middle-class. On the other hand, this may have endowed him with the sensitivity needed to—'

'Fuck sensitivity. Lived with a pig, that's how sensitive he was, dirty sod.'

Wilt considered this estimation of the private life of the great author dubious. So, evidently, did the warder. 'Pig?' said Wilt, 'I don't think he did you know. Are you sure?'

'Course I'm sure. Fucking pig by the name of Buckingham.'

'Oh, him,' said Wilt, cursing himself for having encouraged the beastly man to read Forster's biography as background material to the novels. He should have realized that any mention of policemen was calculated to put 'Fireworks Harry' in a foul mood. 'Anyway, if we look at his work as a writer, as an observer of the social scene and . . .'

McCullum wasn't having any of that. 'The social scene my eye and Betty Martin. Spent more time looking up his own arsehole.'

'Well, metaphorically I suppose you could . . .'

'Literally,' snarled McCullum, and turned the pages of the book. 'How about this? January second ". . . have the illusion I am charming and beautiful . . . blah, blah . . . but would powder my nose if I wasn't found out . . . blah, blah . . . The anus is clotted with hairs . . ." And that's in your blooming Forster's diary. A self-confessed narcissistic fairy.'

'Must have used a mirror, I suppose,' said Wilt, temporarily thrown by this revelation. 'All the same his novels reflect . . .'

'I know what you're going to say,' interrupted McCullum. 'They have social relevance for their time. Balls. He could have got nicked for what he did, slumming it with one of the State's sodding hatchet men. His books have got about as much social relevance as Barbara bloody Cartland's. And we all know what they are, don't we? Literary asparagus.'

'Literary asparagus?'

'Chambermaid's delight,' said Mr McCullum with peculiar relish.

'It's an interesting theory,' said Wilt, who had no idea what the beastly man was talking about, 'though personally I'd have thought Barbara Cartland's work was pure escapism whereas . . .'

'That's enough of that,' interrupted the warder, 'I don't want to hear that word again. You're supposed to be talking about books.'

'Listen to Wilberforce,' said McCullum, still looking fixedly at Wilt, 'bloody marvellous vocabulary he's got, hasn't he?'

Behind him the warder bridled. 'My name's not Wilberforce and you know it,' he snapped.

'Well then, I wasn't talking about you, was I?' said McCullum. 'I mean everyone knows you're Mr Gerard, not some fucking idiot who has to get someone literate to read the racing results for him. Now as Mr Wilt here was saying . . .'

Wilt tried to remember. 'About Barbara Cartland being moron fodder,' prompted McCullum.

'Oh yes, well according to your theories, reading romantic novels is even more detrimental to working-class consciousness than . . . What's the matter?'

Mr McCullum was smiling horribly at him through the mesh. 'Screw's pissed off,' he hissed. 'Knew he would. Got him on my payroll and his wife reads Barbara Cartland so he couldn't stand to listen. Here, take this.'

Wilt looked at the rolled-up piece of paper McCullum was thrusting through the wire. 'What is it?'

'My weekly essay.'

'But you write that in your notebook.'

'Think of it like that,' said McCullum, 'and stash it fast.'

'I'll do no . . .'

Mr McCullum's ferocious expression had returned. 'You will,' he said.

Wilt put the roll in his pocket and 'Fireworks' relaxed. 'Don't make much of a living, do you?' he asked. 'Live in a semi and drive an Escort. No big house with a Jag on the forecourt, eh?'

'Not exactly,' said Wilt, whose taste had never been drawn to Jaguars. Eva was dangerous enough in a small car.

'Right. Well now's your chance to earn 50K.'

'50K?'

'Grand. Cash,' said McCullum and glanced at the door behind him. So did Wilt, hopefully, but there was no sign of the warder. 'Cash?'

'Old notes. Small denominations and no traceability. Right?'

'Wrong,' said Wilt firmly. 'If you think you can bribe me into . . .'

'Gob it,' said McCullum with a nasty grunt. 'You've got a wife and four daughters and you live in a brick and mortar, address 45 Oakhurst Avenue. You drive an Escort, pale dog-turd, number-plate HPR 791 N. Bank at Lloyds, account number 0737 . . . want me to go on?' Wilt didn't. He got to his feet but Mr McCullum hadn't finished. 'Sit down while you've still got knees,' he hissed. 'And daughters.'

Wilt sat down. He was suddenly feeling rather weak. 'What do you want?' he asked.

Mr McCullum smiled. 'Nothing. Nothing at all. You just go off home and check that piece of paper and everything's going to be just jake.'

'And if I don't?' asked Wilt feeling weaker still.

'Sudden bereavement is a sad affair,' said McCullum, 'very sad. Specially for cripples.'

Wilt gazed through the wire mesh and wondered, not for the first time in his life, though by the sound of things it might be the last, what it was about him that attracted the horrible. And McCullum was horrible, horrible and evilly efficient. And why should the evil be so efficient? 'I still want to know what's on that paper,' he said.

'Nothing,' said McCullum, 'it's just a sign. Now as I see it Forster was the typical product of a middle-class background. Lots of lolly and lived with his old Ma . . .'

'Bugger E. M. Forster's mother,' said Wilt. 'What I want to know is why you think I'm going to . . .'

But any hope he had of discussing his future was ended by the return of the warder. 'You can cut the lecture, we're shutting up shop.'

'See you next week, Mr Wilt,' said McCullum with a leer as he was led back to his cell. Wilt doubted it. If there was one thing on which he was determined, it was that he would never see the swine again. Twenty-five years was far too short a sentence for a murdering gangster. Life should mean life and nothing less. He wandered miserably down the passage towards the main gates, conscious of the paper in his pocket and the awful alternatives before him. The obvious thing to do was to report McCullum's threats to the warder on the gate. But the bastard had said he had one warder on his payroll and if one, why not more? In fact, looking back over the months, Wilt could remember several occasions when McCullum had indicated that he had a great deal of influence in the prison. And outside too, because he'd even known the number of Wilt's bank account. No, he'd have to report to someone in authority, not an ordinary screw.

'Had a nice little session with "Fireworks"?' enquired the warder at the end of the corridor with what Wilt considered to be sinister emphasis. Yes, definitely he'd have to speak to someone in authority.

At the main gate it was even worse. 'Anything to declare, Mr Wilt?' said the warder there with a grin, 'I mean we can't tempt you to stay inside, can we?'

'Certainly not,' said Wilt hurriedly.

'You could do worse than join us, you know. All mod cons and telly and the grub's not at all bad nowadays. A nice little cell with a couple of friendly mates. And they do say it's a healthy life. None of the stress you get outside . . .'

But Wilt didn't wait to hear any more. He stepped out into what he had previously regarded as freedom. It didn't seem so free now. Even the houses across the road, bathed in the evening sunshine, had lost their moderate attraction; instead, their windows were empty and menacing. He got into his car and drove a mile along Gill Road before pulling into a side street and stopping. Then making sure no one was watching him, he took the piece of paper out of his pocket and unrolled it. The paper was blank. Blank? That didn't make sense. He held it up to the light and stared at it but the paper was unlined and as far as he could see, had absolutely nothing written on it. Even when he held it horizontally and squinted along it he could make out no indentations on the surface to suggest that a message had been written on it with a matchstick or the blunt end of a pencil. A man was coming towards him along the pavement. With a sense of guilt, Wilt put the paper on the floor and took a road map from the dashboard and pretended to be looking at it until the man had passed. Even then he checked in the rear-view mirror before picking up the paper again. It remained what it had been before, a blank piece of notepaper with a ragged edge as though it had been torn very roughly from a pad. Perhaps the swine had used invisible ink. Invisible ink? How the hell would he get invisible ink in prison? He couldn't unless . . . Something in Wilt's literary memories stirred. Hadn't Graham Greene or Muggeridge mentioned using bird-shit as ink when he was a spy in the Second World War? Or was it lemon juice? Not that it mattered much. Invisible ink was meant to be invisible and if that bastard had intended him to read it, he'd have told him how. Unless, of course, the swine was clear round the bend and in Wilt's opinion, anyone who'd murdered four people and tortured others with a blowtorch as part of the process of earning a living had to be bloody well demented. Not that that let McCullum off the hook in the least. The bugger was a murderer whether he was sane or not, and the sooner he fulfilled his own predictions and became a cabbage the better. Pity he hadn't been born one.

With a fresh sense of desperation, Wilt drove on to The Glassblowers' Arms to think things out over a drink.

# Chapter six

'All right, call it off,' said Inspector Flint, helping himself to a plastic cup of coffee from the dispenser and stumping into his office.

'Call it off?' said Sergeant Yates, following him in.

'That's what I said. I knew it was an OD from the start. Obvious. Gave those old windbags a nasty turn all the same, and they could do with a bit of reality. Live in a bloody dream world where everything's nice and hygienic because it's been put into words. That way they don't happen, do they?'

'I hadn't thought of it like that,' said Yates.

The Inspector took a magazine out of the cardboard box and studied a photograph of a threesome grotesquely intertwined. 'Bloody disgusting,' he said.

Sergeant Yates peered over his shoulder. 'You wouldn't think anyone would have the nerve to be shot doing that, would you?'

'Anyone who does that ought to be shot, if you ask me,' said Flint. 'Though mind you they're not really doing it. Can't be. You'd get ruptured or something. Found this little lot in that boiler-room and it didn't do that murky Principal a bit of good. Turned a very queer colour, he did.'

'Not his, are they?' asked Yates.

Flint shut the magazine and dumped it back in the box. 'You never know, my son, you never know. Not with so-called educated people you don't. It's all hidden behind words with them. They look all right from the outside, but it's what goes on in here that's really weird.' Flint tapped his forehead significantly. 'And that's something else again.'

'I suppose it must be,' said Yates. 'Specially when it's hygienic into the bargain.'

Flint looked at him suspiciously. He never knew if Sergeant Yates was as stupid as he made out. 'You trying to be funny or something?'

'Of course not. Only first you said they lived in a hygienic dream world of words; and then you say they're kinky in the head. I was just putting the two together.'

'Well, don't,' said Flint. 'Don't even try. Just get me Hodge. The Drug Squad can take this mess over, and good luck to them.' The Sergeant went out, leaving Flint studying his pale fingers and thinking weird thoughts of his own about Hodge, the Tech and the possibilities that might result from bringing the Head of the Drug Squad and that infernal institution together. And Wilt. It was an interesting prospect, particularly when he remembered Hodge's request for phone-tapping facilities and his generally conspiratorial air. Kept his cards close to his chest, did Inspector Hodge, and a fat lot of good it had done him so far. Well, two could play at that game, and if ever there was a quicksand of misinformation and inconsequentiality, it had to be the Tech and Wilt. Flint reversed the order. Wilt and the Tech. And Wilt had been vaguely connected with the dead girl, if only by going to the wrong toilet. The word alerted Flint to his own immediate needs. Those bloody pills had struck again.

He hurried down the passage for a pee and as he stood there, standing and staring at the tiled wall and a notice which said, 'Don't drop your cigarette ends in the urinal. It makes them soggy and difficult to light', his disgust changed to inspiration. There was a lesson to be learned from that notice if he could only see it. It had to do with the connection between a reasonable request and an utterly revolting supposition. The word 'inconsequential' came to mind again. Sticking Inspector Bloody Hodge onto Wilt would be like tying two cats together by their tails and seeing which one came out on top. And if Wilt didn't, Flint had sorely misjudged the little shit. And behind Wilt there was Eva and those foul quads and if that frightful combination didn't foul Hodge's career up as effectively as it had wrecked Flint's, the Inspector deserved promotion. With the delightful thought that he'd be getting his own back on Wilt too, he returned to his office and was presently doodling figures of infinite confusion which was exactly what he hoped to initiate.

He was still happily immersed in this daydream of revenge when Yates returned. 'Hodge is out,' he reported. 'Left a message he'd be back shortly.'

'Typical,' said Flint. 'The sod's probably lurking in some coffee bar trying to make up his mind which dolly bird he's going to nail.'

Yates sighed. Ever since Flint had been on those ruddy penis-blockers or whatever they were called, he'd had girls on his mind. 'Why shouldn't he be doing that?' he asked.

'Because that's the way the sod works. A right shoddy copper. Pulls some babe in arms in for smoking pot and then tries to turn her into a supergrass. Been watching too much TV.'

He was interrupted by the preliminary report from the Lab. 'Massive heroin dose,' the technician told him, 'that's for starters. She'd used something else we haven't identified yet. Could be a new product. It's certainly not the usual. Might be "Embalming Fluid" though.'

'Embalming Fluid? What the hell would she be doing with that?' said Flint with a genuine and justified revulsion.

'It's a name for another of these hallucinogens like LSD only worse. Anyway, we'll let you know.'

'Don't,' said Flint. 'Deal direct with Hodge. It's his pigeon now.'

He put the phone down and shook his head sorrowfully. 'Says she fixed herself with heroin and some filth called Embalming Fluid,' he told Yates. 'You wouldn't credit it, would you? Embalming Fluid! I don't know what the world's coming to.'

Fifty miles away, Lord Lynchknowle's dinner had been interrupted by the arrival of a police car and the news of his daughter's death. The fact that it had come between the mackerel pâté and the game pie, and on the wine side, an excellent Montrachet and a Chateau Lafite 1962, several bottles of which he'd opened to impress the Home

Secretary and two old friends from the Foreign Office, particularly annoyed him. Not that he intended to let the news spoil his meal by announcing it before he'd finished, but he could foresee an ugly episode with his wife afterwards for no better reason than that he had come back to the table with the rather unfortunate remark that it was nothing important. Of course, he could always excuse himself on the grounds that hospitality came first, and old Freddie was the Home Secretary after all, and he wasn't going to let that Lafite '62 go to waste, but somehow he knew Hilary was going to kick up the devil of a fuss about it afterwards. He sat on over the Stilton in a pensive mood wishing to God he'd never married her. Looking back over the years, he could see that his mother had been right when she'd warned him that there was bad blood in 'that family', the Puckertons.

'You can't breed bad blood out, you know,' she'd said, and as a breeder of bull terriers, she'd known what she was talking about. 'It'll come out in the end, mark my words.'

And it had, in that damned girl Penny. Silly bitch should have stuck to showjumping instead of getting it into her head she was going to be some sort of intellectual and skiving off to that rotten Tech in Ipford and mixing with the scum there. All Hilary's fault, too, for encouraging the girl. Not that she'd see it that way. All the blame would be on his side. Oh well, he'd have to do something to pacify her. Phone the Chief Constable perhaps and get Charles to put the boot in. His eyes wandered round the table and rested moodily on the Home Secretary. That was it, have a word with Freddie before he left and see that the police got their marching orders from the top.

By the time he was able to get the Home Secretary alone, a process that required him to lurk in the darkness outside the cloakroom and listen to some frank observations about himself by the hired waitresses in the kitchen, Lord Lynchknowle had worked himself up into a state of indignation that was positively public-spirited. 'It's not simply a personal matter, Freddie,' he told the Home

Secretary, when the latter was finally convinced Lynch-knowle's daughter was dead and that he wasn't indulging that curious taste for which he'd been renowned at school. 'There she was at this bloody awful Tech at the mercy of all these drug pedlars. You've got to put a stop to it.'

'Of course, of course,' said the Home Secretary, backing into a hatstand and a collection of shooting sticks and umbrellas. 'I'm deeply sorry—'

'It's no use you damned politicians being sorry,' continued Lynchknowle, forcing him back against a clutter of raincoats, 'I begin to understand the man-in-the-street's disenchantment with the parliamentary process.' (The Home Secretary doubted it.) 'What's more, words'll mend no fences' (the Home Secretary didn't doubt that) 'and I want action.'

'And you'll have it, Percy,' the Home Secretary assured him, 'I guarantee that. I'll get the top men at Scotland Yard onto it tomorrow first thing and no mistake.' He reached for the little notebook he used to appease influential supporters. 'What did you say the name of the place was?'

'Ipford,' said Lord Lynchknowle, still glowering at him.

'And she was at the University there?'

'At the Tech.'

'Really?' said the Home Secretary, with just enough inflexion in his voice to lower Lord Lynchknowle's resolve.

'All her mother's fault,' he said defensively.

'Quite. All the same, if you will allow your daughters to go to Technical Colleges, not that I'm against them you understand, but a man in your position can't be too careful . . .'

In the hall, Lady Lynchknowle caught the phrase.

'What are you two men doing down there?' she asked shrilly.

'Nothing, dear, nothing,' said Lord Lynchknowle. It was a remark he was to regret an hour later when the guests had gone.

'Nothing?' shrieked Lady Lynchknowle, who had by then recovered from the condolences the Home Secretary had offered so unexpectedly. 'You dare to stand there and call Penny's death nothing?'

'I am nòt actually standing, my dear,' said Lynchknowle from the depths of an armchair. But his wife was not to be deflected so easily.

'And you sat through dinner knowing she was lying there on a marble slab? I knew you were a callous swine but . . .'

'What the hell else was I supposed to do?' yelled Lynchknowle, before she could get into her stride. 'Come back to the table and announce that your daughter was a damned junkie? You'd have loved that, wouldn't you? I can just hear you now . . .'

'You can't,' shrieked his wife, making her fury heard in the servants' quarters. Lynchknowle lumbered to his feet and slammed the door. 'And don't think you're going to—'

'Shut up,' he bawled. 'I've spoken to Freddie and he's putting Scotland Yard onto the case and now I'm going to call Charles. As Chief Constable he can—'

'And what good is that going to do? He can't bring her back to me!'

'Nobody can, dammit. And if you hadn't put the idea into her empty head that she was capable of earning her own living when it was as clear as daylight she was as thick as two short planks, none of this would have happened.' Lord Lynchknowle picked up the phone and dialled the Chief Constable.

At The Glassblowers' Arms, Wilt was on the phone too. He had spent the time trying to think of some way to circumvent whatever ghastly plans McCullum had in mind for him without revealing his own identity to the prison authorities. It wasn't easy.

After two large whiskies, Wilt had plucked up enough courage to phone the prison, had refused to give his name and had asked for the Governor's home number. It wasn't in the phone book. 'It's ex-directory,' said the warder in the office.

'Quite,' said Wilt. 'That's why I'm asking.'

'And that's why I can't give it to you. If the Governor wanted every criminal in the district to know where he could be subjected to threats, he'd put it there wouldn't he?'

'Yes,' said Wilt. 'On the other hand, when a member of the public is being threatened by some of your inmates, how on earth is he supposed to inform the Governor that there's going to be a mass breakout?'

'Mass breakout? What do you know about plans for a mass breakout?'

'Enough to want to speak to the Governor.' There was a pause while the warder considered this and Wilt fed the phone with another coin.

'Why can't you tell me?' the warder asked finally.

Wilt ignored the question. 'Listen,' he said with a desperate earnestness that sprang from the knowledge that having come so far he couldn't back down, and that if he didn't convince the man that this was a genuine crisis, McCullum's accomplices would shortly be doing something ghastly to his knees, 'I assure you that this is a deeply serious matter. I wish to speak to the Governor privately. I will call back in ten minutes. All right?'

'It may not be possible to reach him in that time, sir,' said the warder, recognizing the voice of genuine desperation. 'If you can give me your number, I'll get him to call you.'

'It's Ipford 23194,' he said, 'and I'm not joking.'

'No, sir,' said the warder. 'I'll be back to you as soon as I can.'

Wilt put the phone down and wandered back to his whisky at the bar uncomfortably aware that he was now committed to a course of action that could have horrendous consequences. He finished his whisky and ordered another to dull the thought that he'd given the warder the phone number of the pub where he was well-known. 'At least it proved to him that I was being serious,' he thought and wondered what it was about the bureaucratic mentality that made communication so difficult. The main thing was to get in touch with the Governor as soon as possible and explain the situation to him. Once McCullum had been transferred to another prison, he'd be off the hook.

At HM Prison Ipford, the information that a mass escape was imminent was already causing repercussions. The Chief Warder, summoned from his bed, had tried to telephone the Governor. 'The blasted man must be out to dinner somewhere,' he said when the phone had rung for several minutes without being answered. 'Are you certain it wasn't a hoax call?'

The warder on duty shook his head. 'Sounded genuine to me,' he said. 'Educated voice and obviously frightened. In fact, I have an idea I recognized it.'

'Recognized it?'

'Couldn't put a name to it but he sounded familiar somehow. Anyway, if it wasn't genuine, why did he give me his phone number so quick?' The Chief Warder looked at the number and dialled it. The line was engaged. A girl at The Glassblowers' Arms was talking to her boyfriend. 'Why didn't he give his name?'

'Sounded frightened to death like I told you. Said something about being threatened. And with some of the swine we've got in here . . .'

The Chief Warder didn't need telling. 'Right. We're not taking any chances. Put the emergency plan into action pronto. And keep trying to contact the bloody Governor.'

Half an hour later, the Governor returned home to find the phone in his study ringing. 'Yes, what is it?'

'Mass breakout threatened,' the warder told him, 'a man . . . ' But the Governor wasn't waiting. He'd been living in terror for years that something of this sort was going to happen. 'I'll be right over,' he shouted and dashed for his car. By the time he reached the prison his fears had been turned to panic by the wail of police sirens and the presence on the road of several fire engines travelling at high speed in front of him. As he ran towards the gate, he was stopped by three policemen.

'Where do you think you're going?' a sergeant demanded. The Governor looked at him lividly.

'Since I happen to be the Governor,' he said, 'the Governor of this prison, you understand, I'm going inside. Now if you'll kindly stand aside.'

'Any means of identification, sir?' asked the Sergeant. 'My orders require me to prevent anyone leaving or entering.'

The Governor rummaged through the pockets of his suit and produced a five-pound note and a comb. 'Now look here, officer . . .' he began, but the Sergeant was already looking. At the five-pound note. He ignored the comb.

'I shouldn't try that one if I were you,' he said.

'Try what one! I don't seem to have anything else on me.' 'You heard that one, Constable,' said the sergeant, 'Attempting to offer a bribe to—'

'A bribe . . . offer a bribe? Who said anything about offering a bribe?' exploded the Governor. 'You asked me for means of identification and when I try to produce some, you start talking about bribes. Ask the warder on the gate to identify me, dammit.' It took another five minutes of protest to get inside the prison and by then his nerves were in no state to deal at all adequately with the situation. 'You've done what?' he screamed at the Chief Warder.

'Moved all the men from the top floors to the cells below, sir. Thought it better in case they got onto the roof. Of course, they're a bit cramped but . . .'

'Cramped? They were four to a one-man cell already. You mean to say they're eight now? It's a wonder they haven't started rioting already.' He was interrupted by the sound of screams from C Block. As Prison Officer Blaggs hurried away, the Governor tried to find out what was happening. It was almost as difficult as getting into the prison had been. A battle was apparently raging on the third floor of A Wing. 'That'll be due to putting Fidley and Gosling in with Stanforth and Haydow,' the warder in the office said.

'Fidley and ... Put two child murderers in with a couple of decent honest-to-God armed bank robbers? Blaggs must be mad. How long did it take them to die?'

'I don't think they're dead yet,' said the warder with rather more disappointment in his voice than the Governor approved. 'Last I heard, they'd managed to stop Haydow from castrating Fidley. That was when Mr Blaggs decided to intervene.'

'You mean the lunatic waited?' asked the Governor.

'Not exactly, sir. You see, there was this fire in D Block—'

'Fire in D Block? What fire in D Block?'

'Moore set fire to his mattress, sir, and by the time—' But the Governor was no longer listening. He knew now that his career was at stake. All it needed to finish him was for that lunatic Blaggs to have acted as an accessory to murder by packing all the swine in the Top Security Block into one cell. He was just on his way to make quite certain when Chief Warder Blaggs returned. 'Everything's under control, sir,' he said cheerfully.

'Under control?' spluttered the Governor. 'Under control? If you think the Home Secretary's going to think "under control" means having child killers castrated by other prisoners, I can assure you you're not up-to-date with contemporary regulations. Now then, about Top Security.'

'Nothing to worry about there, sir. They're all sleeping like babes.'

'Odd,' said the Governor. 'If there was going to be an attempted breakout you'd think they were bound to be involved. You're sure they're not shamming?'

'Positive, sir,' said Blaggs proudly. 'The first thing I did, sir, by way of a precaution, was to lace their cocoa with that double-strength sleeping stuff.'

'Sweet Jesus,' moaned the Governor, trying to imagine the consequences of the Chief Warder's experiment in preventive sedation if news leaked out to the Howard League for Penal Reform. 'Did you say "double strength"?'

The Chief Warder nodded. 'Same stuff we had to use on Fidley that time he saw the Shirley Temple film and went bananas. Mind you, he's not going to get a hard-on after tonight, not if he's wise.'

'But that was double-strength phenobarb,' squawked the Governor.

'That's right, sir. So I gave them double strength like it said. Went out like lights they did.'

The Governor could well believe it. 'You've gone and given four times the proper dose to those men,' he moaned, 'probably killed the brutes. That stuff's lethal. I never told you to do that.'

Chief Warder Blaggs looked crestfallen. 'I was only doing what I thought best, sir. I mean those swine are a menace to society. Half of them are psychopathic killers.'

'Not the only psychopaths round here,' muttered the Governor. He was about to order a medical team into the prison to stomach-pump the villains Blaggs had sedated, when the warder by the phone intervened. 'We could always say Wilson poisoned them,' he said, 'I mean, that's what they're terrified of. Remember that time they went on dirty strike and Mr Blaggs here let Wilson do some washing up in the kitchen?'

The Governor did, and would have preferred to forget it. Putting a mass poisoner anywhere near a kitchen had always struck him as insane.

'Did the trick, sir. They came off dirtying their cells double quick.'

'And went on hunger strike instead,' said the Governor.

'And Wilson didn't like it much either, come to that,' said the warder, for whom the incident evidently had pleasant memories. 'Said we'd no right making him wash up in boxing gloves. Proper peeved he was—'

'Shut up,' yelled the Governor, trying to get back to a world of comparative sanity, but he was interrupted by the phone.

'It's for you, sir,' said the Chief Warder significantly.

The Governor grabbed it. 'I understand you have some information to give me about an escape plan,' he said, and realized he was talking to the buzz of a pay phone. But before he could ask the Chief Warder how he knew it was for him, the coin dropped. The Governor repeated his statement.

'That's what I'm phoning about,' said the caller. 'Is there any truth in the rumour?'

'Any truth in the . . .' said the Governor. 'How the devil would I know? You were the one to bring the matter up.'

'News to me,' said the man. 'That is Ipford Prison, isn't it?'

'Of course it's Ipford Prison and what's more, I'm the Governor. Who the hell did you think I was?'

'Nobody,' said the man, now sounding decidely perplexed, 'nobody at all. Well, not nobody exactly but . . . well . . . you don't sound like a Prison Governor. Anyway, all I'm trying to find out is if there's been an escape or not.'

'Listen,' said the Governor, beginning to share the caller's doubts about his own identity, 'you phoned earlier in the evening with information about an escape plot and—'

'I did? You off your rocker or something? I've been out covering a burst bloody bulkloader on Bliston Road for the last three bloody hours and if you think I've had time to call you, you're bleeding barmy.'

The Governor struggled with the alliteration before realizing something else was wrong. 'And who am I speaking to?' he asked, mustering what little patience he still retained.

'The name's Nailtes,' said the man, 'and I'm from the *Ipford Evening News* and—'

The Governor slammed the phone down and turned on Blaggs. 'A bloody fine mess you've landed us in,' he shouted. 'That was the *Evening News* wanting to know if there's been an escape.'

Chief Warder Blaggs looked dutifully abashed. 'I'm

76

sorry if there's been some mistake . . .' he began and brought a fresh torrent of abuse on his head.

'Mistake? Mistake?' yelled the Governor.'Some maniac rings up with some fucking cock-and-bull story about an escape and you have to poison . . .' But further discussion was interrupted by news of a fresh crisis. Three safe-breakers, who had been transferred from a cell designed to hold one Victorian convict to another occupied by four Grievous Bodily Harm merchants from Glasgow, known as the Gay Gorbals, had begun to fulfil Wilt's prophesy by escaping and demanding to be closeted with some het-erosexual murderers for protection.

The Governor found them arguing their case with warders in B Block. 'We're not going in with a load of arse-bandits and that's a fact,' said the spokesman.

'It's only a temporary move,' said the Governor, him-self temporizing. 'In the morning—'

'We'll be suffering from AIDS,' said the safebreaker.

'Aids?'

'Acquired Immune Deficiency Syndrome. We want some good, clean murderer, not those filthy swine with anal herpes. A stretch is one thing and so's a bang to rights but not the sort of stretch those Scotch sods would give us and we're fucked if we're going to be banged to wrong. This is supposed to be a prison, not Dotheboys Hall.'

By the time the Governor had pacified them and sent them back to their own cell, he was beginning to have his doubts about the place himself. In his opinion, the prison felt more like a mad-house. His next visit, this time to Top Security, made an even worse impression. A sepulchral silence hung over the floodlit building and, as the Gover-nor passed from cell to cell, he had the illusion of being in a charnel-house. Wherever he looked, men who in other circumstances he would happily have seen dead, looked as though they were. Only the occasional ghastly snore suggested otherwise. For the rest, the inmates hung over the sides of their beds or lay grotesquely supine on the floor in attitudes that seemed to indicate that rigor mortis had already set in.

'Just let me find the swine who started this little lot,' he muttered. 'I'll . . . I'll . . . I'll . . .' He gave up. There was nothing in the book of legal punishments that would fit the crime.

## Chapter seven

By the time Wilt left The Glassblowers' Arms, his desperation had been alleviated by beer and his inability to get anywhere near the phone. He'd moved onto beer after three whiskies, and the change had made it difficult for him to be in two places at the same time, a prerequisite, it seemed, for finding the phone unoccupied. For the first half hour, a girl had been engaged in an intense conversation on reversed charges, and when Wilt had returned from the toilet, her place had been taken by an aggressive youth who had told him to bugger off. After that, there seemed to be some conspiracy to keep him away from the phone. A succession of people had used it and Wilt had ended up sitting at the bar and drinking, and generally arriving at the conclusion that things weren't so bad after all, even if he did have to walk home instead of driving.

'The bastard's in prison,' he told himself as he left the pub. 'And what's more, he's not coming out for twenty years, so what have I got to worry about? Can't hurt me, can he?'

All the same, as he made his way along the narrow streets towards the river, he kept glancing over his shoulder and wondering if he was being followed. But apart from a man with a small dog and a couple who passed him on bicycles, he was alone and could find no evidence of menace. Doubtless that would come later. Wilt tried to figure out a scenario. Presumably, McCullum had given him the piece of paper as a token message, an indication that he was to be some sort of link-man. Well, there was an easy way out of that one; he wouldn't go near the bloody prison again. Might make things awkward as far as Eva was concerned though. He'd just have to make himself scarce on Monday nights and pretend he was still teaching the loathsome McCullum. Shouldn't be too difficult and anyway, Eva was so engrossed in the quads and their so-called development, she hardly noticed what he was doing. The main thing was that he still had the airbase job and that brought the real money in.

But in the meantime, he had more immediate problems to deal with. Like what to tell Eva when he got home. He looked at his watch and saw that it was midnight. After midnight and without the car. Eva would certainly demand an explanation. What a bloody world it was, where he spent his days dealing with idiotic bureaucrats who interfered at the Tech, and was threatened by maniacs in prison, and after all that, came home to be bullied into lying by a wife who didn't believe he'd done a stroke of work all day. And in a bloody world, only the bloody-minded made any mark. The bloody-minded and the cunning. People with drive and determination. Wilt stopped under a street light and looked at the heathers and azaleas in Mr Sands' garden for the second time that day, but this time with a resurgence of those dangerous drives and determinations which beer and the world's irrationality induced in him. He would assert himself. He would do something to distinguish himself from the mass of dull, stupid people who accepted what life handed out to him and then passed on probably into oblivion (Wilt was never sure about that) without leaving more than the fallacious memories of their children and the fading snapshots in the family album. Wilt would be . . . well, anyway, Wilt would be Wilt, whatever that was. He'd have to give the matter some thought in the morning.

In the meantime, he'd deal with Eva. He wasn't going to stand any nonsense about where have you been? or what have you been up to this time? He'd tell her to mind her own ... No, that wouldn't do. It was the sort of challenge the damned woman was waiting for and would only provoke her into keeping him awake half the night discussing what was wrong with their marriage. Wilt knew what was wrong with their marriage; it had been going on for twenty years and Eva had had quads instead of having one at a time. Which was typical of her. Talk about never doing things by halves. But that was beside the point. Or was it? Perhaps she'd had quads to compensate in some ghastly deterministic and genetical way for marrying only half a man. Wilt's mind shot off on a tangent once again as he considered the fact, if it was one, that after wars the birthrate of males shot up as if nature with a capital N was automatically compensating for their shortage. If Nature was that intelligent, it ought to have known better than to make him attractive to Eva, and vice versa. He was driven from this line of thought by another attribute of Nature. This time its call. Well, he wasn't peeing in a rose bush again. Once was enough.

He hurried up the street and was presently letting himself surreptitiously into 45 Oakhurst Avenue with the resolve that if Eva was awake he would say the car had broken down and he'd taken it to a garage. It was better to be cunning than bloody-minded after all. In the event, there was no need to be anything more than quiet. Eva, who had spent the evening mending the quads' clothes and who had discovered that they had cut imitation flies in their knickers as a blow for sexual equality, was fast asleep. Wilt climbed carefully into bed beside her and lay in the darkness thinking about drive and determination.

Drive and determination were very much in the air at the police station. Lord Lynchknowle's phone call to the Chief Constable, and the news that the Home Secretary had promised Scotland Yard's assistance, had put the skids under the Superintendent and had jerked him from his chair in front of the telly and back to the station for an urgent conference.

'I want results and I don't care how you get them,' he

told the meeting of senior officers inadvisedly. 'I'm not having us known as the Fenland equivalent of Soho or Piccadilly Circus or wherever they push this muck. Is that clear? I want action.'

Flint smirked. For once he was glad of Inspector Hodge's presence. Besides, he could honestly claim that he had gone straight to the Tech and had made a very thorough investigation of the cause of death. 'I think you'll find all the preliminary details in my report, sir,' he said. 'Death was due to a massive overdose of heroin and something called Embalming Fluid. Hodge might know.'

'It's Phencyclidine or PCP,' he said. 'Comes under a whole series of names like Super Grass, Hog, Angel Dust and Killer Weed.'

The Superintendent didn't want a catalogue of names. 'What's the filth do, apart from kill kids, of course?'

'It's like LSD only a hell of a sight worse,' said Hodge. 'Puts them into psychosis if they smoke the stuff too much and generally blows their minds. It's bloody murder.'

'So we've gathered,' said the Superintendent. 'Where'd she get it is what I want to know. Me and the Chief Constable *and* the Home Secretary.'

'Hard to say,' said Hodge. 'It's a Yankee habit. Haven't seen it over here before.'

'So she went to the States and bought it there on holiday? Is that what you're saying?'

'She wouldn't have fixed herself with the stuff if she had,' said Hodge, 'she'd have known better. Could have got it from someone in the University, I suppose.'

'Well, wherever she got it,' said the Superintendent grimly, 'I want that source traced, and fast. In fact, I want this town clean of heroin and every other drug before we have Scotland Yard descending on us like a ton of bricks and proving we're nothing but a bunch of country hicks. Those aren't my words, they're the Chief Constable's. Now then, we're quite certain she took this stuff herself? She could have been . . . well, given it against her will?'

'Not according to my information,' said Flint, recognizing the attempt to shift the investigation in his direction and clear Lord Lynchknowle's name from any connection with the drug scene. 'She was seen shooting herself with it in one of the Staff toilets at the Tech. If shooting's the right word,' said Flint, and looked across at Hodge, hoping to shift onto him the burden of keeping Scotland Yard at bay while screening the Lynchknowles.

The Superintendent wasn't interested. 'Whatever,' he said. 'So there's no question of foul play?'

Flint shook his head. The whole beastly business of drugs was foul play but now didn't seem the time to discuss the question. What was important from Flint's point of view was to land Hodge with the problem up to his eyebrows. Let him foul this case up and his head really would be on the chopping-block. 'Mind you,' he said, 'I did find it suspicious she was using the Staff toilet. Could be that's the connection.'

'What is?' demanded the Superintendent.

'Well, I'm not saying they are and I'm not saying they're not,' said Flint, with what he liked to think was subtle equivocation. 'All I'm saying is some of the staff could be.'

'Could be what, for Christ's sake?'

'Involved in pushing,' said Flint. 'I mean, that's why it's been so difficult to get a lead on where the stuff's coming from. Nobody'd suspect lecturers to be pushing the muck, would they?' He paused before putting the boot in. 'Take Wilt for example, Mr Henry Wilt. Now there's a bloke I wouldn't trust further than I could throw him and even then I wouldn't turn my back. This isn't the first time we've had trouble over there, you know. I've got a file on that sod as thick as a telephone directory and then some. And he's Head of the Liberal Studies Department at that. You should see some of the drop-outs he's got working for him. Beats me why Lord Lynchknowle let his daughter go to the Tech in the first place.' He paused again. Out of the corner of his eye he could see Inspector Hodge making notes. The bastard was taking the bait. So was the Superintendent.

'You may have something there, Inspector,' he said. 'A

lot of teachers are hangovers from the sixties and seventies and that rotten scene. And the fact that she was spotted in the Staff toilet . . .' It was this that did it. By the time the meeting broke up, Hodge was committed to a thorough investigation of the Tech and had been given permission to send in undercover agents.

'Let me have a list of the names and I'll forward it to the Chief Constable,' said the Superintendent. 'With the Home Secretary involved, there shouldn't be any difficulty, but for God's sake, get some results.'

'Yes, sir,' said Inspector Hodge, and went off to his office a happy man.

So did Flint. Before leaving the station, he called in on the Head of the Drug Squad with Wilt's file. 'If this is any use . . .' he said and dropped it on the desk with apparent reluctance. 'And any other help I can give you, you've only to ask.'

'I will,' said Inspector Hodge, with the opposite intention. If one thing was certain, it was that Flint would get no credit for breaking the case. And so, while Flint drove home and unwisely helped himself to a brown ale before going to bed, Hodge sat on in his office planning the campaign that would lead to his promotion.

He was still there two hours later. Outside, the street lamps had gone off and Ipford slept, but Hodge sat on, his mind already infected with the virus of ambition and hope. He had gone carefully through Flint's report on the discovery of the body and for once he could find no fault with the Inspector's conclusions. They were confirmed by the preliminary report from Forensic. The victim had died from an overdose of heroin mixed with Embalming Fluid. It was this last which interested Hodge.

'American,' he muttered yet again, and checked with the Police National Computer on the incidence of its use. Negligible, as he had thought. All the same, the drug was extremely dangerous and its spread in the States had been so rapid that it had been described as the syphilis of drug abuse. Crack this case and Hodge's name would be known, not simply in Ipford, but through the Lord Lieutenant to the Home Secretary and . . . Hodge's dreams pursued his name before returning to the present. He picked up Wilt's file doubtfully. He hadn't been in Ipford at the time of the Great Doll Case and its ghastly effects on Flint's career, but he'd heard about it in the canteen, where it was generally acknowledged that Mr Henry Wilt had outfoxed Inspector Flint. Made him look a damned fool was the usual verdict, but it had never been clear what Wilt had really been up to. No one in his right mind went round burying inflatable dolls dressed in his wife's clothes at the bottom of piling-holes with twenty tons of concrete on top of them. And Wilt had. It followed that either Wilt hadn't been in his right mind, or that he'd been covering some other crime. Diverting suspicion. Anyway, the sod had got away with whatever he'd been up to and had screwed Flint into the bargain. So Flint had a grudge against the bastard. That was generally acknowledged too.

It was therefore with justified suspicion that Hodge turned to Wilt's file and began to read in detail the transcript of his interrogation. And as he read, a certain grim respect for Wilt grew in his mind. The sod hadn't budged from his story, in spite of being kept awake and deluged with questions. And he had made Flint look the idiot he was. Hodge could see that, just as he could see why Flint had a grudge against him. But above all his own intuition told him that Wilt had to have been guilty of something. Just had to be. And he'd been too clever for the old bugger. Which explained why Flint had been prepared to hand the file over to him. He wanted this Wilt nailed. Only natural. All the same, knowing Flint's attitude to him, Hodge was amazed he had given him the file. Not with all that stuff showing what a moron he was. Must be something else there. Like the old man knew when he was beaten? And certainly he looked it lately. Sounded it too, so maybe giving him the file was tacitly acknowledging the fact. Hodge smiled to himself. He'd always known he was the better man and that his chance to prove it would come. Well, now it bloody well had.

He turned to Flint's report on Miss Lynchknowle again and read it through carefully. There was nothing wrong with Flint's methods and it was only when he came to the bit about Wilt having gone to the wrong toilet that Inspector Hodge saw where the old man had made a mistake. He read through it again.

'Principal reported Wilt went to toilet on the second floor when he should have gone to the one on the fourth floor.' And later 'Wilt's secretary, Mrs Bristol, said she told Wilt to go to Ladies' staff toilet on the fourth floor. Claimed she'd seen girl there before.' It fitted. Another of clever Mr Wilt's little moves, to go to the wrong toilet. But Flint hadn't spotted that or he'd have interviewed the sod. Hodge made a mental note to check Mr Wilt's movements. But surreptitiously. There was no point in putting him on his guard. Hodge made more notes. 'Tech laboratory facilities provide means of making Embalming Fluid. Check', was one. 'Source heroin', another. And all the time while he concentrated, part of his mind ran on different lines, involving romantic-sounding places like the 'Golden Triangle' and the 'Golden Crescent', those jungle areas of Thailand and Burma and Laos, or in the case of the 'Golden Crescent', the laboratories of Pakistan from which heroin came into Europe. In Hodge's mind, small dark men, Pakis, Turks, Iranians and Arabs, converged on Britain by donkey or container truck or the occasional ship: always at night, a black and sinister movement of the deadly opiates financed by men who lived in large houses and belonged to country clubs and had yachts. And then there was the Sicilian Connection with Mafia murders almost daily on the streets of Palermo. And finally the 'pushers' in England, little runts like Flint's son doing his time in Bedford. That again could be an explanation for Flint's change of attitude, his ruddy son. But the romantic picture of distant lands and evil men was the dominant one, and Hodge himself the dominant figure in it, a lone ranger in the war against the most insidious of all crimes.

Reality was different of course, and converged with Hodge's mental geography only in the fact that heroin did come from Asia and Sicily and that an epidemic of terrible addiction had come to Europe, and only the most determined and intelligent police action and international co-operation would bring it to a halt. Which, since the Inspector in spite of his rank was neither intelligent nor possessed of more than a vivid imagination, was where he came unstuck. In place of intelligence, there was only determination, the determination of a man without a family and with few friends, but with a mission. And so Inspector Hodge worked on through the night planning the action he intended to take. It was four in the morning when he finally left the station and walked round the corner to his flat for a few hours' sleep. Even then, he lay in the darkness gloating over Flint's discomfiture. 'The sod's getting his comeuppance,' he thought before falling asleep.

On the other side of Ipford, in a small house with a neat garden distinguished by a nicely symmetrical goldfish pond with a stone cherub in the middle, Inspector Flint would have agreed, though the cause of his problem had rather more to do with brown ale and those bloody piss pills than with Hodge's future. On the latter score, he was quietly confident. He went back to bed wondering if it wouldn't be a wise move to take some leave. He had a fortnight due to him, and anyway he could justifiably claim his doctor had told him to take it easy. A trip to the Costa Brava, or maybe Malta? The only trouble there was that Mrs Flint tended to get randy in the heat. It was about the only time she did these days, thank God. Perhaps Cornwall would be a better bet. On the other hand, it would be a pity to miss watching Hodge come unstuck and if Wilt didn't run rings round the shit, Flint wasn't the man he thought he was. Talk about tying two cats together by their tails!

And so the night wore on. At the Prison, the activities Wilt had initiated went on. At two, another prisoner in D Block set fire to his mattress, only to have it extinguished by an enterprising burglar using the slop bucket. But it was in Top Security that matters were more serious. The Governor had been disconcerted to find two prisoners wide awake in McCullum's cell, and because it was McCullum's cell, he had been wary of entering without at least six warders to ensure his safety, and six warders were hard to find, partly because they shared the Governor's apprehension and partly because they were busy elsewhere. Lacking their support, the Governor was forced to conduct a dialogue with McCullum's companions through the cell door. Known as the Bull and the Bear, they acted as McCullum's bodyguards.

'Why aren't you men asleep?' demanded the Governor.

'Might be if you hadn't turned the ruddy light on,' said the Bull, who had once made the mistake of falling madly in love with a bank manager's wife, only to be betrayed when he had fulfilled her hopes by murdering her husband and robbing the bank of fifty thousand pounds. She had gone on to marry a stockbroker.

'That's no way to speak to me,' said the Governor, peering suspiciously through the peep-hole. Unlike the other two prisoners, McCullum appeared to be fast asleep. One hand hung limply over the side of his bunk, and his face was unnaturally pallid. Considering that the swine was usually a nasty ruddy colour, the Governor was perturbed. If anyone was likely to be involved in an escape plot, he'd have sworn McCullum was. In which case, he'd have been . . . The Governor wasn't sure what he'd have been, but he certainly wouldn't have been fast asleep, with his face that ghastly grey colour, while the Bull and the Bear were wide awake. There was something distinctly fishy about his being asleep.

'McCullum,' shouted the Governor, 'McCullum, wake up.'

McCullum didn't move. 'Blimey,' said the Bear, sitting up. 'What the fuck's going on?'

'McCullum,' yelled the Governor, 'I am ordering you to wake up.'

'What the fuck's up with you?' yelled the Bull. 'Middle

of the bleeding night and some screw has to go off his nut and go round fucking waking people up. We got fucking rights, you know, even if we are in nick, and Mac isn't going to like this.'

The Governor clenched his teeth and counted to ten. Being called a screw wasn't what he liked either. 'I am simply trying to ascertain that Mr McCullum is all right,' he said. 'Now will you kindly wake him up.'

'All right? All right? Why shouldn't he be all right?' asked the Bear.

The Governor didn't say. 'It's merely a precautionary measure,' he answered. McCullum's refusal to show any sign of life – and in fact his attitude and complexion to show just the opposite – was getting to him. If it had been anyone else, he'd have opened the cell door and gone in. But the swine could well be shamming, and with the Bull and the Bear to help him, might be planning to overpower a warder going in to see what was wrong. With a silent curse on the Chief Warder for making his life so difficult, the Governor hurried off to get assistance. Behind him, the Bull and the Bear expressed their feelings about fucking screws who left the fucking light on all fucking night, when it occurred to them that there might be something to be said for checking McCullum after all. The next moment, Top Security was made hellish by their shouts.

'He's fucking dead,' screamed the Bear, while the Bull made a rudimentary attempt to resuscitate McCullum by applying what he thought was artificial respiration, and which in fact meant hurling himself on the body and expelling what remained of breath from his victim's lungs.

'Give him the fucking kiss of life,' ordered the Bear, but the Bull had reservations. If McCullum wasn't dead, he had no intention of bringing him back to consciousness to find he was being kissed, and if he had coughed it, he didn't fancy kissing a corpse.

'Squeamish sod,' yelled the Bear, when the Bull stated his views on the question. 'Here, let me get at him.' But even then he was put off by McCullum's coldness. 'You bloody murderers,' he shouted through the cell door.

'You've done it this time,' said the Governor. He had found the Chief Warder in the office enjoying a cup of coffee. 'You and your infernal sedatives.'

'Me?' said the Chief Warder.

The Governor took a deep breath. 'Either McCullum's dead or he's shamming very convincingly. Get me ten warders and the doctor. If we hurry, we may be in time to save him.'

They rushed down the passage, but the Chief Warder had yet to be convinced. 'I gave him the same dose as everyone else. He's having you on.'

Even when they had secured the ten warders and were outside the cell door, he delayed matters. 'I suggest you leave this to us, sir,' he said. 'If they take hostages, you ought to be on the outside to conduct negotiations. We're dealing with three extremely dangerous men, you know.' The Governor doubted it. Two seemed more probable.

Chief Warder Blaggs peered into the cell. 'Could have painted his face with chalk or something,' he said. 'He's a right crafty devil.'

'And pissed himself into the bargain?'

'Never does things by halves, does our Mac,' said the Chief Warder. 'All right, stand clear of the door in there. We're coming in.' A moment later the cell was filled with prison officers and in the mêlée that followed, the late McCullum received some post mortem injuries which did nothing to improve his appearance. But there was no doubt he was dead. It hardly needed the prison doctor to diagnose death as due to acute barbiturate poisoning.

'Well, how was I to know that the Bull and the Bear were going to give him their cups of cocoa?' said the Chief Warder plaintively, at a meeting held in the Governor's office to discuss the crisis.

'That's something you're going to have to explain to the Home Office enquiry,' said the Governor.

They were interrupted by a prison officer who

announced that a cache of drugs had been found in McCullum's sodden mattress. The Governor looked out at the dawn sky and groaned.

'Oh, and one other thing, sir,' said the warder. 'Mr Coven in the office has remembered where he heard that voice on the telephone. He thought he recognized it at the time. Says it was Mr Wilt.'

'Mr Wilt?' said the Governor. 'Who the hell's Mr Wilt?'

'A lecturer from the Tech or something who's been teaching McCullum English. Comes every Monday.'

'McCullum? Teaching McCullum English? And Coven's certain he was the one who phoned?' In spite of his fatigue, the Governor was wide awake now.

'Definitely, sir. Says he thought it was familiar and naturally when he heard "Fireworks" Harry'd snuffed it, he made the connection.'

So had the Governor. With his career in jeopardy he was prepared to act decisively. 'Right,' he said, casting discretion to the draught that blew under the door. 'McCullum died of food poisoning. That's the official line. Next . . .'

'What do you mean, "food poisoning"?' asked the prison doctor. 'Death was due to an overdose of pheno-barbitone and I'm not going on record as saying—'

'And where was the poison? In his cocoa, of course,' snapped the Governor. 'And if cocoa isn't food, I don't know what is. So we put it out as food poisoning.' He paused and looked at the doctor. 'Unless you want to go down as the doctor who nearly poisoned thirty-six prisoners.'

'Me? I didn't have anything to do with it. That goon went and dosed the sods.' He pointed at Chief Warder Blaggs, but the Chief Warder had spotted the out.

'On your instructions,' he said with a meaningful glance at the Governor. 'I mean I couldn't have laid my hands on that stuff if you hadn't authorized it, could I now? You always keep the drugs cupboard in the dispensary locked, don't you? Be irresponsible not to, I'd have thought.'

'But I never did . . .' the doctor began, but the Governor stopped him.

'I'm afraid Mr Blaggs has a point there,' he said. 'Of course if you want to dispute the facts with the Board of Enquiry, that is your privilege. And doubtless the Press would make something of it. PRISON DOCTOR INVOLVED IN POISONING CONVICT would look well in the *Sun*, don't you think?'

'If he had drugs in his cell, I suppose we could say he died of an overdose,' said the doctor.

## Chapter eight

'There's no use in saying you didn't come home late last night because you did,' said Eva. It was breakfast, and, as usual, Wilt was being cross-examined by his nearest and dearest. On her other days, Eva left it to the quads to make the meal a misery for him by asking questions about computers or biochemistry about which he knew absolutely nothing. But this morning the absence of the car had given her the opportunity to get her own questions in.

'I didn't say I didn't come in late,' said Wilt through a mouthful of muesli. Eva was still into organic foods and her home-made muesli, designed to guarantee an adequate supply of roughage, did just that and more.

'That's a double negative,' said Emmeline.

Wilt looked at her balefully. 'I know it is,' he said, and spat out the husk of a sunflower seed.

'Then you weren't telling the truth,' Emmeline continued. 'Two negatives make a positive and you didn't say you had come in late.'

'And I didn't say I hadn't,' said Wilt, struggling with his daughter's logic and trying to use his tongue to get the bran off the top of his dentures. The damned stuff seemed to get everywhere.

'There's no need to mumble,' said Eva. 'What I want to know is where the car is.'

'I've already told you. I left it in a car park. I'll get a mechanic to go round and see what's wrong with the thing.'

'You could have done that last night. How do you expect me to take the girls to school?'

'I suppose they could always walk,' said Wilt, extracting a raisin from his mouth with his fingers and examining it offensively. 'It's an organic form of transportation, you know. Unlike this junior prune which would appear to have led a sedentary life and a sedimentary death. I wonder why it is that health foods so frequently contain objects calculated to kill. Now take this—'

'I am not interested in your comments,' said Eva. 'You're just trying to wriggle out of it and if you expect me to . . .'

'Walk?' interrupted Wilt. 'God forbid. The adipose tissue with which you—'

'Don't you adipose me, Henry Wilt,' Eva began, only to be interrupted by Penelope.

'What's adipose?'

'Mummy is,' said Wilt. 'As to the meaning, it means fat, fatty deposits and appertaining to fat.'

'I am not fat,' said Eva firmly, 'and if you think I'm spending my precious time walking three miles there and three miles back twice a day you're wrong.'

'As usual,' said Wilt. 'Of course. I was forgetting that the gender arrangements of this household leave me in a minority of one.'

'What are gender arrangements?' demanded Samantha.

'Sex,' said Wilt bitterly and got up from the table.

Behind him Eva snorted. She was never prepared to discuss sex in front of the quads. 'It's all very well for you,' she said, reverting to the question of the car which provided a genuine grievance. 'All you have to do is—'

'Catch a bus,' said Wilt, and hurried out of the house before Eva could think of a suitable reply. In fact there was no need. He caught a lift with Chesterton from the Electronics Department and listened to his gripes about financial cuts and why they didn't make them in Communication Skills and get rid of some of those Liberal Studies deadbeats.

'Oh well, you know how it is,' said Wilt as he got out of the car at the Tech. 'We have to make good the inexactitudes of science.'

'I didn't know there were any,' said Chesterton.

'The human element,' said Wilt enigmatically, and went through the library to the lift and his office. The human element was waiting for him.

'You're late, Henry,' said the Vice-Principal.

Wilt looked at him closely. He usually got on rather well with the V-P. 'You're looking pretty late youself,' he said. 'In fact, if I hadn't heard you speak, I'd say you were a standing corpse. Been whooping it up with the wife?'

The Vice-Principal shuddered. He still hadn't got over the horror of seeing his first dead body in the flesh, rather than on the box, and trying to drown the memory in brandy hadn't helped. 'Where the hell did you get to last night?'

'Oh, here and there, don't you know,' said Wilt. He had no intention of telling the V-P he did extra-mural teaching.

'No, I don't,' said the V-P. 'I tried calling your house and all I got was some infernal answering service.'

'That'd be one of the computers,' said Wilt. 'The quads have this programme. It runs on tape, I think. Quite useful really. Did it tell you to fuck off?'

'Several times,' said the Vice-Principal.

'The wonders of science. I've just been listening to Chesterton praising—'

'And I've just been listening to the Police Inspector,' cut in the V-P, 'on the subject of Miss Lynchknowle. He wants to see you.'

Wilt swallowed. Miss Lynchknowle hadn't anything to

do with the prison. It didn't make sense. In any case, they couldn't have got on to him so quickly. Or could they? 'Miss Lynchknowle? What about her?'

'You mean you haven't heard?'

'Heard what?' said Wilt.

'She's the girl who was in the toilet,' said the V-P. 'She was found dead in the boiler-room last night.'

'Oh God,' said Wilt. 'How awful.'

'Quite. Anyway, we had the police swarming all over the place last night and this morning there's a new man here. He wants a word with you.'

They walked down the corridor to the Principal's office. Inspector Hodge was waiting there with another policeman. 'Just a matter of routine, Mr Wilt,' he said when the Vice-Principal had shut the door. 'We've already interviewed Mrs Bristol and several other members of the staff. Now I understand you taught the late Miss Lynchknowle?'

Wilt nodded. His previous experience with the police didn't dispose him to say more than he had to. The sods always chose the most damning interpretation.

'You taught her English?' continued the Inspector.

'I teach Senior Secretaries Three English, yes,' said Wilt.

'On Thursday afternoons at 2.15 p.m.?'

Wilt nodded again.

'And did you notice anything odd about her?'

'Odd?'

'Anything to suggest that she might be an addict, sir.'

Wilt tried to think. Senior Secretaries were all odd as far as he was concerned. Certainly in the context of the Tech. For one thing, they came from 'better families' than most of his other students and seemed to have stepped out of the fifties with their perms and their talk about Mummies and Daddies who were all wealthy farmers or something in the Army. 'I suppose she was a bit different from the other girls in the class,' he said finally. 'There was this duck, for instance.'

'Duck?' said Hodge.

'Yes, she used to bring a duck she called Humphrey with her to class. Bloody nuisance having a duck in a lesson but I suppose it was a comfort to her having a furry thing like that.'

'Furry?' said Hodge. 'Ducks aren't furry. They have feathers.'

'Not this one,' said Wilt. 'Like a teddy bear. You know, stuffed. You don't think I'd have a live duck shitting all over the place in my class, do you?'

Inspector Hodge said nothing. He was beginning to dislike Wilt.

'Apart from that particular addiction, I can't think of anything else remarkable about her. I mean, she didn't twitch or seem unduly pale or even go in for those sudden changes of mood you tend to find with junkies.'

'I see,' said Hodge, holding back the comment that Mr Wilt seemed exceedingly well-informed on the matter of symptoms. 'And would you say there was much drug-taking at the College?'

'Not to my knowledge,' said Wilt. 'Though, come to think of it, I suppose there must be some with the numbers we've got. I wouldn't know. Not my scene.'

'Quite, sir,' said the Inspector, simulating respect.

'And now, if you don't mind,' said Wilt, 'I have work to do.' The Inspector didn't mind.

'Not much there,' said the Sergeant when he'd left.

'Never is with the really clever sods,' said Hodge.

'I still don't understand why you didn't ask him about going to the wrong toilet and what the secretary said.'

Hodge smiled. 'If you really want to know, it's because I don't intend to raise his suspicions one little iota. That's why. I've been checking on Mr Wilt and he's a canny fellow, he is. Scuppered old Flint, didn't he? And why? I'll tell you. Because Flint was fool enough to do what Wilt wanted. He pulled him in and put him through the wringer and Mr Wilt got away with bloody murder. I'm not getting caught the same way.'

'But he never did commit any murder. It was only a fucking inflatable doll he'd buried,' said the Sergeant.

'Oh, come off it. You don't think the bugger did that without he had a reason? That's a load of bull. No, he was pulling some other job and he wanted a cover, him and his missus, so they fly a kite and Flint falls for it. That old fart wouldn't know a decoy if it was shoved under his bloody snout. He was so busy grilling Wilt about that doll he couldn't see the wood for the trees.'

Sergeant Runk fought his way through the mixed metaphors and came out none the wiser. 'All the same,' he said finally, 'I can't see a lecturer here being into drugs, not pushing anyway. Where's the lifestyle? No big house and car. No country-club set. He doesn't fit the bill.'

'And no big salary here either,' said Hodge. 'So maybe he's saving up for his old age. Anyway, we'll check him out and he won't ever know.'

'I should have thought there were more likely prospects round about,' said the Sergeant. 'What about that Greek restaurant bloke Macropolis or something you've been bugging? We know he's been into heroin. And there's that fly boy down the Siltown Road with the garage we had for GBH. He was on the needle himself.'

'Yeah, well he's inside, isn't he? And Mr Macropolis is out of the country right now. Anyway, I'm not saying it is Wilt. She could have been down in London getting it for all we know. In which case, it's off our patch. All I'm saying is, I'm keeping an open mind and Mr Wilt interests me, that's all.'

And Wilt was to interest him still further when they returned to the police station an hour later. 'Super wants to see you,' said the Duty Sergeant. 'He's got the Prison Governor with him.'

'Prison Governor?' said Hodge. 'What's he want?'

'You,' said the Sergeant, 'hopefully.'

Inspector Hodge ignored the crack and went down the passage to the Superintendent's office. When he came out half an hour later, his mind was alive with circumstantial evidence, all of which pointed most peculiarly to Wilt. Wilt had been teaching one of the most notorious gangsters in Britain, now thankfully dead of an overdose of one of his own drugs. (The prison authorities had decided to use the presence of so much heroin in McCullum's mattress as the cause of death, rather than the phenobarb one, much to Chief Warder Blaggs' relief.) Wilt had been closeted with McCullum at the very time Miss Lynchknowle's body had been discovered. And, most significantly of all, Wilt, within an hour of leaving the prison and presumably on learning that the police were busy at the Tech, had rung the prison anonymously with a phoney message about a mass breakout and McCullum had promptly taken an overdose.

If that little lot didn't add up to something approaching a certainty that Wilt was involved, Hodge didn't know one. Anyway, add it to what he already knew of Wilt's past and it was certain. On the other hand, there was still the awkward little matter of proof. It was one of the disadvantages of the English legal system, and one Hodge would happily have dispensed with in his crusade against the underworld, that you had first to persuade the Director of Public Prosecutions that there was a case to be answered, and then go on to present evidence that would convince a senile judge and a jury of do-gooders, half of whom had already been nobbled, that an obvious villain was guilty. And Wilt wasn't an obvious villain. The bastard was as subtle as hell and to send the sod down would require evidence that was as hard as ferroconcrete.

'Listen,' Hodge said to Sergeant Runk and the small team of plain-clothes policemen who constituted his private crime squad, 'I don't want any balls-ups so this has got to be strictly covert and I mean covert. No one, not even the Super, is to know it's going on, so we'll codename it Flint. That way, no one will suspect. Anyone can say Flint round this station and it doesn't register. That's one. Two is, I want Mr Wilt tailed twenty-four hours continuous. And another tail on his missus. No messing. I want to know what those people do every moment of the day and night from now on in.'

'Isn't that going to be a bit difficult?' asked Sergeant

Runk. 'Day *and* night. There's no way we can put a tail in the house and . . .'

'Bug it is what we'll do,' said Hodge. 'Later. First off we're going to patternize their lives on a time-schedule basis. Right?'

'Right,' echoed the team. In their time, they had patternized the lives of a fish-and-chip merchant and his family who Hodge had suspected were into hard-core porn; a retired choirmaster – this time for boys; and a Mr and Mrs Pateli for nothing better than their name. In each case the patternizing had failed to confirm the Inspector's suspicions, which were in fact wholly groundless, but had established as incontrovertible facts that the fish-and-chip merchant opened his shop at 6 p.m. except Sundays, that the choirmaster was having a happy and vigorous love affair with a wrestler's wife, and in any case had an aversion amounting almost to an allergy for small boys, and that the Patelis went to the Public Library every Tuesday, that Mr Pateli did full-time unpaid work with the Mentally Handicapped, while Mrs Pateli did Meals on Wheels. Hodge had justified the time and expense by arguing that these were training sessions in preparation for the real thing.

'And this is it,' continued Hodge. 'If we can nail this one down before Scotland Yard takes over we'll be quids in. We're also going into a surveillance mode at the Tech. I'm going over to see the Principal about it now. In the meantime, Pete and Reg can move into the canteen and the Student's Common Room and make out they're mature students chucked out for dope at Essex or some other University.'

Within an hour, Operation Flint was underway. Pete and Reg, suitably dressed in leather garments that would have alarmed the most hardened Hell's Angels, had already emptied the Students' Common Room at the Tech by their language and their ready assumption that everyone there was on heroin. In the Principal's office, Inspector Hodge was having more or less the same effect on the Principal and the V-P, who found the notion that the Tech was the centre for drug distribution in Fenland particularly horrifying. They didn't much like the idea of being lumbered with fifteen educationally subnormal coppers as mature students.

'At this time of year?' said the Principal. 'Dammit, it's April. We don't enrol mature students this term. We don't enrol any, come to that. They come in September. And anyway, where the hell would we put them?'

'I suppose we could always call them "Student Teachers",' said the V-P. 'That way they could sit in on any classes they wanted to without having to say very much.'

'Still going to look bloody peculiar,' said the Principal. 'And frankly, I don't like it at all.'

But it was the Inspector's assertion that the Lord Lieutenant, the Chief Constable and, worst of all, the Home Secretary didn't like what had been going on at the Tech that turned the scales.

'God, what a ghastly man,' said the Principal, when Hodge had left. 'I thought Flint was foul enough, but this one's even bloodier. What is it about policemen that is so unpleasant? When I was a boy, they were quite different.'

'I suppose the criminals were, too,' said the V-P. 'I mean, it can't be much fun with sawn-off shotguns and hooligans hurling Molotov cocktails at you. Enough to turn any man bloody.'

'Odd,' said the Principal, and left it at that.

Meanwhile Hodge had put the Wilts under surveillance. 'What's been happening?' he asked Sergeant Runk.

'Wilt's still at the Tech so we haven't been able to pick him up yet, and his missus hasn't done anything much except the shopping.'

But even as he spoke, Eva was already acting in a manner calculated to heighten suspicion. She had been inspired to phone Dr Kores for an appointment. Where the inspiration came from she couldn't have said, but it had partly to do with an article she had read in her

supermarket magazine on sex and the menopause entitled 'No Pause In The Pause, The Importance of Foreplay
In The Forties', and partly with the glimpse she'd had of
Patrick Mottram at the check-out counter where he
usually chatted up the prettiest girl. On this occasion, he
had ogled the chocolate bars instead and had ambled off
with the glazed eyes of a man for whom the secret
consumption of half a pound of Cadbury's Fruit and Nut
was the height of sensual experience. If Dr Kores could
reduce the randiest man in Ipford to such an awful
condition, there was every possibility she could produce
the opposite effect in Henry.

Over lunch, Eva had read the article again and, as
always on the subject of sex, she was puzzled. All her
friends seemed to have so much of it, either with their
husbands or with someone, and obviously it was important, otherwise people wouldn't write and talk so much
about it. All the same, Eva still had difficulty reconciling it
with the way she'd been brought up. Mind you, her
mother had been quite wrong going on about remaining
a virgin until she was married. Eva could see that now.
She certainly wasn't going to do the same with the quads.
Not that she'd have them turn into little tarts like the
Hatten girls, wearing make-up at fourteen and going
around with rough boys on motorbikes. But later on,
when they were eighteen and at university, then it would
be all right. They'd need experience before they got
married instead of getting married to get . . . Eva stopped
herself. That wasn't true, she hadn't married Henry just
for sex. They'd been genuinely in love. Of course, Henry
had groped and fiddled but never nastily like some of the
boys she'd gone out with. If anything, he'd been rather
shy and embarrassed and she'd had to encourage him.
Mavis was right to call her a full-blooded woman. She did
like sex but only with Henry. She wasn't going to have
affairs, especially not with the quads in the house. You
had to set an example and broken homes were bad. On
the other hand, so were homes where both parents were
always quarrelling and hated one another. So divorce was

a good thing too. Not that anything like that threatened her marriage. It was just that she had a right to a more fulfilling love life and if Henry was too shy to ask for help, and he certainly was, she'd have to do it for him. So she had phoned Dr Kores and had been surprised to learn that she could come at half-past two.

Eva had set off with an unnoticed escort of two cars and four policemen and had caught the bus at the bottom of Perry Road to Silton and Dr Kores' shambolic herb farm. 'I don't suppose she has time to keep it tidy,' Eva thought as she made her way past a number of old frames and a rusty cultivator to the house. All the same, she was slightly dismayed by the lack of organization. If it had been her garden, it wouldn't have looked like that. But then anything organic tended to go its own way, and Dr Kores did have a reputation as an eccentric. In fact, she had prepared herself to be confronted by some wizened old creature with a plaid shawl when the door opened and a severe woman in a white coat stood looking at her through strangely tinted dark glasses.

'Ms Wilt?' she said. Was there just the hint of a V for the W? But before Eva could consider this question, she was being ushered down the hallway and into a consulting-room. Eva looked round apprehensively as the doctor took a seat behind the desk. 'You are having problems?' she asked.

Eva sat down. 'Yes,' she said, fiddling with the clasp of her handbag and wishing she hadn't made the appointment.

'With your husband I think you said, yes?'

'Well, not with him exactly,' said Eva, coming to Henry's defence. After all, it wasn't his fault he wasn't as energetic as some other men. 'It's just that he's . . . well . . . not as active as he might be.'

'Sexually active?' Eva nodded.

'How old?' continued Dr Kores.

'You mean Henry? Forty-three. He'll be forty-four next March. He's a—'

But Dr Kores was clearly uninterested in Wilt's

astrological sign. 'And the sexual gradient has been steep?'

'I suppose so,' said Eva, wondering what a sexual gradient was.

'Maximum weekly activity please.'

Eva looked anxiously at an Anglepoise lamp and tried to think. 'Well, when we were first married . . .' she paused.

'Go on,' Dr Kores ordered.

'Well, Henry did it three times one night I remember,' said Eva, blurting the statement out. 'He only did it once of course.'

The doctor's ballpen stopped. 'Please explain,' she said. 'First you said he was sexually active three times in one night. And second you said he was only once. Are you saying there was seminal ejaculation only on the first occasion?'

'I don't really know,' said Eva. 'It's not easy to tell, is it?'

Dr Kores eyed her doubtfully. 'Let me put it another way. Was there a penile spasm at the climax of each episode?'

'I suppose so,' said Eva. 'It's so long ago now and all I remember is that he was ever so tired next day.'

'In which year did this take place?' asked the doctor, having written down 'Penile spasm uncertain.'

'1963. In July,' said Eva. 'I remember that because we were on a walking holiday in the Peak District and Henry said he's peaked out.'

'Very amusing,' said Dr Kores dryly. 'And that is his maximum sexual attainment?'

'He did it twice in 1970 on his birthday . . .'

'And the plateau was how many times a week?' asked Dr Kores, evidently determined to prevent Eva from intruding anything remotely human into the discussion.

'The plateau? Oh, well it used to be once or twice but now I'm lucky if it's once a month and sometimes we go even longer.'

Dr Kores licked her thin lips and put the pen down. 'Mrs Wilt,' she said, leaning on the desk and forming a triangle with her fingertips and thumbs. 'I deal exclusively with the problems of the female in a male-dominated social context, and to speak frankly, I find your attitude to your relationship with your husband unduly submissive.'

'Do you really?' said Eva, beginning to perk up. 'Henry always says I'm too bossy.'

'Please,' said the doctor with something approaching a shudder, 'I'm not in the least interested in your husband's opinions or in his person. If you choose to be, that is your business. Mine is to help you as an entirely independent being and, to be truthful, I find your self-objectivization highly distasteful.'

'I'm sorry,' said Eva, wondering what on earth self-objectivization was.

'For instance, you have repeatedly stated that and I quote "He did it three times" and again "He did it twice . . ." '

'But he did,' Eva protested.

'And who was the "It"? You?' said the doctor vehemently.

'I didn't mean it that way . . .' Eva began but Dr Kores was not to be stopped. 'And the very word "did" or "done" is a tacit acceptance of marital rape. What would your husband say if you were to do him?'

'Oh, I don't think Henry'd like that,' said Eva, 'I mean, he's not very big and . . .'

'If you don't mind,' said the doctor, 'size does not come into it. The question of attitude is predominant. I am only prepared to help you if you make a determined effort to see yourself as the leader in the relationship.' Behind the blue tinted spectacles her eyes narrowed.

'I'll certainly try,' said Eva.

'You will succeed,' said the doctor sibilantly. 'It is of the essence. Repeat after me "I will succeed." '

'I will succeed,' said Eva.

'I am superior,' said Dr Kores.

'Yes,' said Eva.

'Not "Yes",' hissed the doctor, gazing even more

peculiarly into Eva's eyes, 'but "I am superior".'

'I am superior,' said Eva obediently.

'Now both.'

'Both,' said Eva.

'Not that. I want you to repeat both remarks. First . . .'

'I will succeed,' said Eva, finally getting the message, 'I am superior.'

'Again.'

'I will succeed. I am superior.'

'Good,' said the doctor. 'It is vital that you establish the correct psychic attitude if I am to help you. You will repeat those auto-instructs three hundred times a day. Do you understand?'

'Yes,' said Eva. 'I am superior. I will succeed.'

'Again,' said the doctor.

For the next five minutes Eva sat fixed in her chair and repeated the assertions while Dr Kores stared unblinking into her eyes. 'Enough,' she said finally. 'You understand what this means, of course?'

'Sort of,' said Eva. 'It's to do with what Mavis Mottram says about women taking the leading rôle in the world, isn't it?'

Dr Kores sat back in her chair with a thin smile. 'Ms Wilt,' she said, 'for thirty-five years I have made a continuous study of the sexual superiority of the feminine in the mammalian world. Even as a child I was inspired by the mating habits of arachnida – my mother was something of an expert in the field before so unfortunately marrying my father, you understand.'

Eva nodded. Fortunately for her she had missed the reference to spiders but she was too fascinated not to understand that whatever Dr Kores was saying was somehow important. She had the future of the quads in mind.

'But,' continued the doctor, 'my own work has been concentrated upon the higher forms of life and, in particular, the infinitely superior talents of the feminine in the sphere of survival. At every level of development, the rôle of the male is subordinate and the female demonstrates an adaptability which preserves the species. Only in the human world, and then solely in the social context rather than the purely biological, has this process been reversed. This reversal has been achieved by the competitive and militaristic nature of society in which the brute force of the masculine has found justification for the suppression of the feminine. Would you agree?'

'Yes, I suppose so,' said Eva, who had found the argument difficult to follow but could see that it made some sort of sense.

'Good,' said Dr Kores. 'And now we have arrived at a world crisis in which the extermination of life on earth has been made probable by the masculine distortion of scientific development for military purposes. Only we women can save the future.' She paused and let Eva savour the prospect. 'Fortunately, science has also put into our hands the means of so doing. The purely physical strength of the male has lost its advantage in the automated society of the present. Man is redundant and with the age of the computer, it is women who will have power. You have, of course, read of the work done at St Andrew's. It is proven that women have the larger corpus collossum than men.'

'Corpus collossum?' said Eva.

'One hundred million brain cells, neural fibre connecting the hemispheres of the brain and essential in the transfer of information. In working with the computer, this interchange has the highest significance. It could well be to the electronic age what the muscle was to the age of the physical . . .'

For another twenty minutes, Dr Kores talked on, swinging between an almost demented fervour for the feminine, rational argument and the statement of fact. To Eva, ever prone to accept enthusiasm uncritically, the doctor seemed to embody all that was most admirable about the intellectual world to which she had never belonged. It was only when the doctor seemed to sag in her chair that Eva remembered the reason she had come. 'About Henry . . .' she said hesitantly.

For a moment, Dr Kores continued to focus on a future in which there were probably no men, before dragging herself back to the present. 'Oh yes, your husband,' she said almost absently. 'You wish for something to stimulate him sexually, yes?'

'If it's possible,' said Eva. 'He's never been . . .'

But Dr Kores interrupted her with a harsh laugh.

'Ms Wilt,' she said, 'have you considered the possibility that your husband's lack of sexual activity may be only apparent?'

'I don't quite understand.'

'Another woman perhaps?'

'Oh, no,' said Eva. 'Henry isn't like that. He really isn't.'

'Or latent homosexuality?'

'He wouldn't have married me if he'd been like that, would he?' said Eva, now genuinely shocked.

Dr Kores looked at her critically. It was at moments like this that her faith in the innate superiority of the feminine was put to the test. 'It has been known,' she said through clenched teeth and was about to enter into a discussion of the family life of Oscar Wilde when the bell rang in the hall.

'Excuse me a moment,' she said and hurried out. When she returned it was through another door. 'My dispensary,' she explained. 'I have there a tincture which may prove beneficial. The dose is, however, critical. Like many medications, it contains elements that taken in excess will produce definite contraindication. I must warn you not to exceed the stated dose by as much as five millilitres. I have supplied a syringe for the utmost accuracy in measurement. Within those limits, the tincture will produce the desired result. Beyond them, I cannot be held responsible. You will naturally treat the matter with the utmost confidentiality. As a scientist, I cannot be held responsible for the misapplication of proven formulae.'

Eva put the plastic bottle in her bag and went down the hall. As she passed the rusty cultivator and the broken frames, her mind was in a maelstrom of contradictory impressions. There had been something weird about Dr Kores. It wasn't what she said that was wrong, Eva could see her words made good sense. It was rather in the way she said them and how she behaved. She'd have to discuss it with Mavis. All the same, as she stood at the bus stop she found herself repeating 'I am superior. I will succeed' almost involuntarily.

A hundred yards away, two of Inspector Hodge's plain-clothes men watched her and made notes of the time and place. The patternizing of the Wilts' lives had begun in earnest.

## Chapter nine

And it continued. For two days, teams of detectives kept watch on the Wilts and reported back to Inspector Hodge who found the signals unambiguous. Eva's visit to Dr Kores was particularly damning.

'Herb farm? She went to a herb farm in Silton?' said the Inspector incredulously. After forty-eight almost sleepless hours and as many cups of black coffee, he could have done with some alternative medicine himself. 'And she came out with a large plastic bottle?'

'Apparently,' said the detective. Trying to keep up with Eva had taken its toll. So had the quads. 'For all I know, she went in with one. All we saw was her taking the bottle out of her bag when she was waiting for the bus.'

Hodge ignored the logic. As far as he was concerned, suspects who visited herb farms, and had bottles in their bags afterwards, were definitely guilty.

But it was Mavis Mottram's arrival at 45 Oakhurst Avenue later that afternoon that interested him most. 'Subject collects children from school at 3.30,' he read from the written report. 'gets home and a woman drives up in a mini.'

'Correct.'

'What's she look like?'

'Forty, if she's a day  Dark hair. Five foot four. Blue anorak and khaki trousers with leg-warmers. Goes in at 3.55, leaving at 4.20.'

'So she could have collected the bottle?'

'Could have, I suppose, but she hadn't got a bag and there was no sign of it.'

'Then what?'

'Nothing till the nextdoor neighbour comes home at 5.30. Look, it's all there in my report.'

'I know it is,' said Hodge, 'I'm just trying to get the picture. How did you know his name was Gamer?'

'Blimey, I'd have to be stone deaf not to, the way she gave it to him, not to mention his wife carrying on something chronic.'

'So what happened?'

'This bloke Gamer goes in the door of 43,' said the detective, 'and five minutes later he's out again like a scalded cat with his wife trying to stop him. Dashes round to the Wilts' and tries to go in the side gate round the back of the house. Grabs the latch on the gate and the next moment he's flat on his back in the flower bed, twitching like he's got St Vitus' dance and his missus is yelling like they've killed him.'

'So what you're saying is the back gate was electrified?' said Hodge.

'I'm not saying it. He did. As soon as he could speak, that is, and had stopped twitching. Mrs Wilt comes out and wants to know what he's doing in her wallflowers. By that time he's got to his feet, just, and is yelling that her fucking hellcats – his words, not mine – have tried to murder him by stealing some statuette he's got in his back garden, and they've put it in theirs, and wired up the back gate to the fucking mains. And Mrs Wilt tells him not to be so silly and kindly not to use filthy language in front of her daughters. After that, things got a bit confusing with him wanting his statue and her saying she hadn't got it, and wouldn't have it if he gave it to her because it's dirty.'

'Dirty?' muttered Hodge. 'What's dirty about it?'

'It's one of those ones of a small boy peeing. Got it on his pond. She practically called him a pervert. And all the time his wife is pleading with him to come on home and never mind the ruddy statue, they can always get another one when they've sold the house. That got to him. "Sell the house?" he yells, "Who to? Even a raving lunatic wouldn't buy a house next to the bloody Wilts." Probably right at that.'

'And what happened in the end?' asked Hodge, making a mental note that he'd have an ally in Mr Gamer.

'She insists he come through the house and see if his statue's there, because she's not going to have her girls called thieves.'

'And he went?' said Hodge incredulously.

'Hesitantly,' said the detective. 'Came out shaken and swearing he'd definitely seen it there and if she didn't believe those kids had tried to kill him, why were all the lights in the house on the blink. That had her, and he pointed out there was a piece of wire still tied to the bootscraper outside the back gate.'

'Interesting,' said Hodge. 'And was there?'

'Must have been, because she got all flustered then, especially when he said it was evidence to show the police.'

'Naturally, with that bottle of dope still in the house,' said Hodge. 'No wonder they'd fixed the back door.' A new theory had been formulated in his mind. 'I tell you we're on to something, this time.'

Even the Superintendent, who shared Flint's view that Inspector Hodge was a greater menace to the public than half the petty crooks he arrested and would gladly have put the sod on traffic duty, had to admit that for once the Inspector seemed to be on the right track. 'This fellow Wilt's got to be guilty of something,' he muttered as he studied the report of Wilt's extraordinary movements during his lunch break.

In fact, Wilt had been on the look-out for McCullum's associates and had almost immediately spotted the two detectives in an unmarked car when he'd walked out of the Tech to pick up the Escort at the back of The Glassblowers' Arms, and had promptly taken evasive action with an expertise he'd learnt from watching old thrillers on TV. As a result, he'd doubled back down side roads, had disappeared up alleyways, had bought a number of wholly unnecessary items in crowded shops and had even bolted in the front doors of Boots and out the back before heading for the pub.

'Returned to the Tech car park at 2.15,' said the Superintendent. 'Where'd he been?'

'I'm afraid we lost him,' said Hodge. 'The man's an expert. All we know is he came back driving fast and practically ran for the building.'

Nor had Wilt's behaviour on leaving the Tech that evening been calculated to inspire confidence in his innocence. Anyone who walked out of the front gate wearing dark glasses, a coat with the collar turned up and a wig (Wilt had borrowed one from the Drama Department) and spent half an hour sitting on a bench by the bowling green on Midway Park, scrutinizing the passing traffic before sneaking back to the Tech car park, had definitely put himself into the category of a prime suspect.

'Think he was waiting for someone?' the Superintendent asked.

'More likely trying to warn them off,' said Hodge. 'They've probably got a system of signalling. His accomplices drive past and see him sitting there and get the message.'

'I suppose so,' said the Superintendent, who couldn't think of anything else that made sense. 'So we can expect an early arrest. I'll tell the Chief Constable.'

'I wouldn't say that, sir,' said Hodge, 'just that we've got a definite lead. If I'm right, this is obviously a highly organized syndicate. I don't want to rush into an early arrest when this man could lead us to the main source.'

'There is that,' said the Superintendent gloomily. He

had been hoping that Hodge's handling of the case would prove so inept that he could call in the Regional Crime Squad. Instead the confounded man seemed to be making a success of it. And after that he'd doubtless apply for promotion and get it. Hopefully somewhere else. If not, the Superintendent would apply for a transfer himself. And there was still a chance Hodge would foul things up.

At the Tech, Hodge had. His insistence on putting plain-clothes detectives in, masquerading as apprentices or even more unsatisfactorily as Trainee Teachers, was playing havoc with staff morale.

'I can't stand it,' Dr Cox, Head of Science, told the Principal. 'It's bad enough trying to teach some of the students we get, without having a man poking about who doesn't know the difference between a Bunsen burner and a flamethrower. He practically burnt down the lab. on the third floor. And as for being any sort of teacher . . .'

'He doesn't have to say anything. After all, they're only here to observe.'

'In theory,' said Dr Cox. 'In practice, he keeps taking my students into corners and asking them if they can get him some Embalming Fluid. Anyone would think I was running a funeral home.'

The Principal explained the term. 'God Almighty, no wonder the wretched fellow asked to stay behind last night to check the chemical inventory.'

It was the same in botany. 'How was I to know she was a policewoman?' Miss Ryfield complained. 'And anyway I had no idea students were growing marijuana as pot plants in the greenhouses. She seems to hold me responsible.' Only Dr Board viewed the situation at all philosophically. Thanks to the fact that none of the policemen spoke French, his department had been spared intrusion.

'After all, it is 1984,' he announced to an ad hoc committee in the staff room, 'and as far as I can tell, discipline has improved enormously.'

'Not in my department,' said Mr Spirey of Building. 'I've had five punch-ups in Plasterers and Bricklayers and Mr Gilders is in hospital with bicycle-chain wounds.'

'Bicycle-chain wounds?'

'Someone called the young thug from the police station a fucking pig and Mr Gilders tried to intervene.'

'And I suppose the apprentices were arrested for carrying offensive weapons?' said Dr Mayfield.

The Head of Building shook his head. 'No, it was the policeman who had the bicycle chain. Mind you, they made a right mess of him afterwards,' he added with some satisfaction.

But it was among Senior Secretaries that Hodge's investigations had been carried out most vigorously. 'If this goes on much longer, our exam results will be appalling,' said Miss Dill. 'You have no idea the effect of having girls taken out of class and interrogated is having on their typing performance. The impression seems to be that the College is a hotbed of vice.'

'Would that it were,' said Dr Board. 'But, as usual, the papers have got it all wrong. Still, page 3 is something.' And he produced a copy of the *Sun* and a photograph of Miss Lynchknowle in the nude, taken in Barbados the previous summer. The caption read DRUG HEIRESS DEAD AT TECH.

'Of course I've seen the papers and the publicity is disgraceful,' said the Principal to the members of the Education Committee. Originally called to discuss the impending visitation of HMIs, it was now more concerned with the new crisis. 'The point I am trying to make is that this is an isolated incident and . . .'

'It isn't,' said Councillor Blighte-Smythe. 'I have here a list of catastrophes which have bedevilled the College since your appointment. First there was that awful business with the Liberal Studies lecturer who . . .'

Mrs Chatterway, whose views were indefatigably progressive, intervened. 'I hardly think there's anything to be gained by dwelling on the past,' she said.

'Why not?' demanded Mr Squidley. 'It's time someone

112

was held accountable for what goes on there. As tax- and rate-payers, we have a right to a decent practical education for our children and . . .'

'How many children do you have at the Tech?' snapped Mrs Chatterway.

Mr Squidley looked at her in disgust. 'None, thank God,' he said. 'I wouldn't let one of my kids anywhere near the place.'

'If we could just keep to the point,' said the Chief Education Officer.

'I am,' said Mr Squidley, 'very much to the point, and the point is that as an employer, I'm not paying good money to have apprentices turned into junkies by a lot of fifth-rate academic drop-outs.'

'I resent that,' said the Principal. 'In the first place, Miss Lynchknowle wasn't an apprentice, and in the second we have some extremely dedicated—'

'Dangerous nutters,' said Councillor Blighte-Smythe.

'I was going to say "dedicated teachers".'

'Which doubtless accounts for the fact that the Minister of Education's secretary is pushing for the appointment of a board of enquiry to investigate the teaching of Marxism-Leninism in the Liberal Studies Department. If that isn't a clear indication something's wrong, I don't know what is.'

'I object. I object most strongly,' said Mrs Chatterway. 'The real cause of the problem lies in spending cuts. If we are to give our young people a proper sense of social responsibility and care and concern—'

'Oh God, not that again,' muttered Mr Squidley. 'If half the louts I have to employ could even read and bloody write . . .'

The Principal glanced significantly at the Chief Education Officer and felt more comfortable. The Education Committee would come to no sensible conclusions. It never did.

At 45 Oakhurst Avenue, Wilt glanced nervously out of the window. Ever since his lunch break and the discovery that he was being followed, he'd been on edge. In fact, he had driven home with his eyes so firmly fixed on the rear-view mirror that he had failed to notice the traffic lights on Nott Road and had banged into the back of the police car which had taken the precaution of tailing him from the front. The resulting exchange with the two plain-clothes men who were fortunately unarmed had done a lot to confirm his view that his life was in danger.

And Eva had hardly been sympathetic. 'You never do look where you're going,' she said, when he explained why the car had a crumpled bumper and radiator. 'You're just hopeless.'

'You'd feel fairly hopeless if you'd had the sort of day I've had,' said Wilt and helped himself to a bottle of homebrew. He took a swig of the stuff and looked at his glass dubiously.

'Must have left the bloody sugar out, or something,' he muttered, but Eva quickly switched the conversation to the incident with Mr Gamer. Wilt listened half-heartedly. His beer didn't usually taste like that and anyway it wasn't always quite so flat.

'As if girls their age could lift a horrid statue like that over the fence,' said Eva, concluding a singularly biased account of the incident.

Wilt dragged his attention away from his beer. 'Oh, I don't know. That probably explains what they were doing with Mr Boykins' block and tackle the other day. I wondered why they'd become so interested in physics.'

'But to say they'd tried to electrocute him,' said Eva indignantly.

'You tell me why the whole damned house was out,' said Wilt. 'The main fuse was blown, that's why. Don't tell me a mouse got into the toaster again either, because I checked. Anyway, that mouse didn't blow all the fuses and if I hadn't objected to having putrefying mouse savoury for breakfast instead of toast and marmalade, you'd never have noticed.'

'That was quite different,' said Eva. 'The poor thing got in there looking for crumbs. That's why it died.'

'And Mr Gamer damn near died because he was

looking for his ruddy garden ornament,' said Wilt. 'And I can tell you who gave your brood that idea, the blooming mouse, that's who. One of these days they'll get the hang of the electric chair and I'll come home and find the Radleys' boy with a saucepan on his head and a damned great cable running to the cooker plug, as dead as a dodo.'

'They'd never do anything like that,' said Eva. 'They know better. You always look on the worst side of things.'

'Reality,' said Wilt, 'that's what I look at and what I see is four lethal girls who make Myra Hindley seem like a suitable candidate for a kindergarten teacher.'

'You're just being horrid,' said Eva.

'So's this bloody beer,' said Wilt as he opened another bottle. He took a mouthful and swore, but his words were drowned by the Magimix which Eva had switched on, in part to make an apple and carrot slaw because it was so good for the quads, but also to express her irritation. Henry could never admit the girls were bright and intelligent and good. They were always bad to him.

So was the beer. Eva's addition of five millilitres of Dr Kores' sexual stimulant to each bottle of Wilt's Best Bitter had given the stuff a new edge to it and, besides, it was flat. 'Must have left the screw top loose on this batch.' Wilt muttered as the Magimix came to a halt.

'What did you say?' Eva asked unpleasantly. She always suspected Wilt of using the cover of the Magimix, or the coffee-grinder to express his true thoughts.

'Nothing at all,' said Wilt, preferring to keep off the topic of beer. Eva was always going on about what it did to his liver and for once he believed her. On the other hand, if McCullum's thugs were going to duff him up, he intended to be drunk when they started, even if the muck did taste peculiar. It was better than nothing.

On the other side of Ipford, Inspector Flint sat in front of the telly and gazed abstractedly at a film on the life-cycle of the giant turtle. He didn't give a damn about turtles or their sex life. About the only thing he found in their favour was that they had the sense not to worry about their offspring and left the little buggers to hatch out on a distant beach or, better still, to get eaten by predators. Anyway, the sods lived two hundred years and presumably didn't have high blood pressure.

Instead, his thoughts reverted to Hodge and the Lynchknowle girl. Having pointed the Head of the Drug Squad towards the morass of inconsequentiality that was Wilt's particular forte, it had begun to dawn on him that he might gain some kudos by solving the case himself. For one thing, Wilt wasn't into drugs. Flint was certain of that. He knew Wilt was up to something – stood to reason – but his copper's instinct told him that drugs didn't fit.

So someone else had supplied the girl with the muck that had killed her. With all the slow persistence of a giant turtle swimming in the depths of the Pacific, Flint went over the facts. The girl dead on heroin and PCP: a definite fact. Wilt teaching that bastard McCullum (also dead from drugs): another fact. Wilt making a phone call to the prison: not a fact, merely a probability. An interesting probability for all that, and if you subtracted Wilt from the case there was absolutely nothing to go on. Flint picked up the paper and looked at the dead girl's photo. Taken in Barbados. Smart set and half of them on drugs. If she'd got the stuff in that circle Hodge hadn't got a hope in hell. They kept their secrets. Anyway, it might be worth checking up on his findings so far. Flint switched off the TV and went into the hall. 'I'm just going out to stretch my legs,' he called out to his wife and was answered by a grim silence. Mrs Flint didn't give a damn what he did with his legs.

Twenty minutes later, he was in his office with the report on the interview with Lord and Lady Lynchknowle in front of him. Naturally, it had never dawned on them that Linda was on drugs. Flint recognized the symptoms and the desire to clear themselves of all blame. 'About as much parental care as those bloody turtles,' he muttered and turned to the interview with the girl who'd shared a flat with Miss Lynchknowle. This time there

116

was something more positive. No, Penny hadn't been to London for ages. Never went anywhere, in fact, not even home at weekends. Discos occasionally, but generally a loner and had given up her boyfriend at the University before Christmas etcetera. No recent visitors either. Occasionally, she'd go out of an evening to a coffee bar or just wander along by the river. She'd seen her down there twice on her way back from the cinema. Whereabouts exactly? Near the marina. Flint made a note of that, and also of the fact that the Sergeant who'd visited her had asked the right questions. Flint noted the names of some of the coffee bars. There was no point in visiting them, they'd be covered by Hodge and, besides, Flint had no intention of being seen to be interested in the case. Above all, though, he knew he was acting on intuition, the 'smell' of the case which came from his long experience and his knowledge that whatever else Wilt was – and the Inspector had his own views on the matter – he wasn't pushing drugs. All the same, it would be interesting to know if he had made that phone call to the prison on the night McCullum took an overdose. There was something strangely coincidental about that incident, too. It was easy enough to hear the story from Mr Blaggs. Flint had known the Chief Warder for years and had frequently had the pleasure of consigning prisoners to his dubious care.

And so presently he was standing in the pub near the prison discussing Wilt with the Chief Warder with a frankness Wilt would have found only partly reassuring. 'If you want my opinion,' said Mr Blaggs, 'educating villains is anti-social. Only gives them more brains than they need. Makes your job more difficult when they come out, doesn't it?'

Flint had to agree that it didn't make it any easier. 'But you don't reckon Wilt had anything to do with Mac's having a cache of junk in his cell?' he asked.

'Wilt? Never. A bloody do-gooder, that's what he is. Mind you, I'm not saying they're not daft enough, because I know for a fact they are. What I'm saying is, a nick ought to be a prison, not a fucking finishing-school for turning half-witted petty thieves into first-rate bank robbers with degrees in law.'

'That's not what Mac was studying for, is it?' asked Flint.

Mr Blaggs laughed. 'Didn't need to,' he said. 'He had enough cash on the outside, he had a fistful of legal beavers on his payroll.'

'So how come Wilt's supposed to have made this phone call?' asked Flint.

'Just what Bill Coven thought, he took the call,' said Blaggs, and looked significantly at his glass. Flint ordered two more pints. 'He just thought he recognized Wilt's voice,' Blaggs continued, satisfied that he was getting his money's worth for information. 'Could have been anyone.'

Flint paid for the beer and tried to think what to ask next. 'And you've got no idea how Mac got his dope then?' he asked finally.

'Know exactly,' said Blaggs proudly. 'Another bloody do-gooder only this time a fucking prison visitor. If you ask me, they should ban all vi—'

'A prison visitor?' interrupted Flint, before the Chief Warder could express his views on a proper prison regime, which involved perpetual solitary confinement for all convicts and mandatory hanging for murderers, rapists and anyone insulting a prison officer. 'You mean a visitor to the prison?'

'I don't. I mean an authorized prison visitor, a bloody licensed busybody. They come in and treat us officers like we've committed the ruddy crimes and the villains are all bloody orphans who didn't get enough teat when they were toddlers. Right, well, this bitch of a PV, name of Jardin, was the one McCullum got to bring his stuff in.'

'Christ,' said Flint. 'What did she do that for?'

'Scared,' said Blaggs. 'Some of Mac's nastier mates on the outside paid her a visit with razors and a bottle of nitric acid and threatened to leave her looking like a

cross between a dog's dinner and a leper with acne unless
. . . You get the message?'

'Yes,' said Flint, who'd begun to sympathize with the
prison visitor, though for the life of him he couldn't
visualize what a leper with acne looked like. 'And you
mean she walked in and announced the fact?'

'Oh dear me, no,' said Blaggs. 'Starts off we've done for
Mr – I ask you, *Mister*? – fucking McCullum ourselves.
Practically said I'd hanged the sod myself, not that I'd
have minded. So we took her down the morgue – of
course it just happened the prison quack was doing an
autopsy at the time and didn't much like the look of
things by the sound of it, using a saw he was, too – and he
wasn't having any crap about anyone doing anything to
the bugger. Right, well when she'd come to, like, and he's
saying the swine died of drug overdose and anyone who
said different'd end up in court for slander, she cracked.
Tears all over the place and practically down on her
knees in front of the Governor. And it all comes out how
she's been running heroin into the prison for months.
Ever so bleeding sorry and all.'

'I should bloody well think so,' said Flint. 'When's she
going to be charged?'

Mr Blaggs drank his beer mournfully. 'Never,' he
grunted.

'Never? But smuggling anything, let alone drugs, into a
prison is an indictable offence.'

'Don't tell me,' said Blaggs. 'On the other hand, the
Governor don't want no scandal, can't afford one with his
job up for grabs and anyway, she'd done a social service in
a way by shoving the bugger where he belongs.'

'There is that,' said Flint. 'Does Hodge know this?'

The Chief Warder shook his head. 'Like I said, the
Governor don't want no publicity. Anyway, she claimed
she thought the stuff was talcum powder. Like hell, but
you know what a Rumpole would do with a defence like
that. Prison authorities entirely to blame, and so on.
Negligence, the lot.'

'Did she say where she got the heroin?' asked Flint.

'Picked it up back of a telephone box on the London Road at night. Never saw the blokes who delivered it.'

'And it won't have been any of the lot who'd threatened her either.'

By the time the Inspector left the pub, he was a happy man. Hodge was way off line, and Flint had a conscience-stricken prison visitor to question. He wasn't even worried about the effect of four pints of the best bitter being flushed through his system by those bloody piss-pills. He'd already charted his route home by way of three relatively clean public lavatories.

## Chapter ten

But if Flint's mood had changed for the better, Inspector Hodge's hadn't. His interpretation of Wilt's behaviour had been coloured by the accident at the end of Nott Road. 'The bastard's got to know we're onto him, ramming a police car like that,' he told Sergeant Runk, 'so what's he do?'

'Buggered if I know,' said the Sergeant, who preferred early nights and couldn't think at all clearly at one in the morning.

'He goes for an early arrest, knowing we've got no hard evidence and will have to let him go.'

'What's he want us to do that for?'

'Because if we pull him in again he can start squealing about harassment and civil bloody liberties,' said Hodge.

'Seems an odd way of going about things,' said Runk.

'And what about sending your wife out to a herb farm to pick up a load of drugs on the very day after a girl dies of the filth? Isn't that a bit odd too?' Hodge demanded.

'Definitely,' said Runk. 'In fact, I can't think of anything odder. Any normal criminal would lie bloody low.'

Inspector Hodge smiled unpleasantly. 'Exactly. But we're not dealing with any ordinary criminal. That's the point I'm trying to make. We've got one of the cleverest monkeys I've ever had to catch on our hands.'

Sergeant Runk couldn't see it. 'Not if he sends his missus out to get a bottle of the stuff when we're watching her, he's not clever. Downright stupid.'

Hodge shook his head sadly. It was always difficult to get the Sergeant to understand the complexities of the criminal mind. 'Suppose there was nothing remotely like drugs in that bottle she was seen carrying?' he asked.

Sergeant Runk dragged his thoughts back from beds and tried to concentrate. 'Seem a bit of a wasted journey,' was all he could find to say.

'It's also intended to lead us up the garden path,' said Hodge. 'And that's his tactics. You've only to look at Wilt's record to see that. Take that doll caper for instance. He had old Flint by the short and curlies there, and why? Because the stupid fool pulled him in for questioning when all the evidence he had to go on was a blown-up doll of Mrs Wilt down a piling-hole with twenty tons of concrete on top of her. And where was the real Mrs Wilt all that week? Out on a boat with a couple of hippie Yanks who were into drugs up to their eyeballs and Flint lets them flee the country without grilling them about what they'd really been doing down the coast. Sticks out a mile they were smuggling and Wilt had set himself up for a decoy and kept Flint busy digging up a plastic doll. That's how cunning Wilt is.'

'I suppose when you put it like that it makes sense,' said Runk. 'And you reckon he's using the same tactics now.'

'Leopards,' said Hodge.

'Leopards?'

'Don't change their bleeding spots.'

'Oh, them,' said the Sergeant, who could have done without ellipses at that time of night.

'Only this time he's not dealing with some old-fashioned dead-beat copper like Flint,' said Hodge, now thoroughly convinced by the persuasiveness of his argument. 'He's dealing with me.'

'Makes a change. And talking about changes, I'd like to go . . .'

'To 45 Oakhurst Avenue,' said Hodge decisively, 'that's where you're going. I want Mr Smart-Arse Wilt's car wired for sound and we're calling off the physical observation. This time it's going to be electronic all the way.'

'Not if I have anything to do with it,' said Runk defiantly, 'I've enough sense to know better than start tinkering with a sod like Wilt's car. Besides, I've got a wife and three kids to—'

'What the hell's your family got to do with it?' said Hodge. 'All I'm saying is, we'll go round there while they're asleep—'

'Asleep? A bloke who electrifies his back gate, you think he takes chances with his bloody car? You can do what you like, but I'm buggered if I'm going to meet my Maker charred to a fucking cinder by a maniac who's linked his car to the national grid. Not for you or anyone else.'

But Hodge was not to be stopped. 'We can check it's safe,' he insisted.

'How?' asked Runk, who was wide awake now. 'Let a police dog pee against the thing and see if he gets 32,000 volts up his prick? You've got to be joking.'

'I'm not,' said Hodge. 'I'm telling. Go and get the equipment.'

Half an hour later, a desperately nervous Sergeant wearing gum boots and electrically safe rubber gloves eased the door of Wilt's car open. He'd already been round it four times to check there were no wires running from the house and had earthed it with a copper rod. Even so, he was taking no chances and was a trifle surprised that the thing didn't explode.

'All right, now where do you want the tape recorder?' he asked when the Inspector finally joined him.

'Somewhere where we can get at the tape easily,' Hodge whispered.

Runk groped under the dash and tried to find a space.

'Too bloody obvious,' said Hodge. 'Stick it under his seat.'

'Anything you say,' said Runk and stuffed the recorder into the springs. The sooner he was out of the damned car, the better. 'And what about the transmitter?'

'One in the boot and the other . . .'

'Other?' said Runk. 'You're going to get him picked up by the TV licence-detector vans at this rate. One of these sets has a radius of five miles.'

'I'm not taking chances,' said Hodge. 'If he finds one, he won't look for the other.'

'Not unless he has his car serviced.'

'Put it where no one looks.'

In the end, and then only after a lot of disagreement, the Sergeant attached one radio magnetically in a corner of the boot and was lying under the car searching for a hiding-place for the second when the lights came on in the Wilts' bedroom. 'I told you the swine wouldn't take any chances,' he whispered frantically as the Inspector fought his way in beside him. 'Now we're for it.'

Hodge said nothing. With his face pressed against an oily patch of tarmac and something that smelt disgustingly of cats, he was incapable of speech.

So was Wilt. The effect of Dr Kores' sexual stimulant added to his homebrew – Wilt had surreptitiously finished six bottles in an effort to find one that didn't taste peculiar – had been to leave him mentally befuddled and with the distinct impression that something like a battalion of army ants had taken possession of his penis and were busily digging in. Either that, or one of the quads had dementedly shoved the electric toothbrush up it while he was asleep. It didn't seem likely. But then again the sensation he was experiencing didn't seem in the least likely either. As he switched on the bedside lamp and hurled the sheet back to see what on earth was wrong, he glimpsed an expanse of red panties beside him. Eva in red panties? Or was she on fire too?

Wilt stumbled out of bed and fought a losing battle with his pyjama cord for dragging the damned things down without bothering to undo them and pointed the Anglepoise at the offending organ in an effort to identify the cause of his agony. The beastly creature (Wilt had always granted his penis a certain degree of autonomy or, more accurately, had never wholly associated himself with its activities) looked normal enough but it certainly didn't feel normal, not by a long chalk. Perhaps if he put some cold cream on it . . .

He hobbled across to Eva's dressing-table and searched among the jars. Where the hell did she keep the cold cream? In the end, he chose one that called itself a moisturizer. That'd do. It didn't. By the time he'd smeared half the jar on himself and a good deal on the pillow, the burning sensation seemed to have got worse. And whatever was going on was taking place *inside*. The army ants weren't digging in, the sods were digging out. For one insane moment he considered using an aerosol of Flykil to flush them out, but decided against it. God alone knew what a load of pressurized insecticide would do to his bladder and anyway the bloody thing was full enough already. Perhaps if he had a pee . . . Still clutching the moisturizer, he hobbled through to the bathroom. 'Must have been a fucking lunatic who first called it relieving oneself,' he thought when he'd finished. About the only relief he'd found was that he hadn't peed blood and there didn't appear to be any ants in the pan afterwards. And peeing hadn't helped. If anything, it had made things even worse. 'The bloody thing'll ignite in a minute,' Wilt muttered, and was considering using the shower hose as a fire extinguisher when a better idea occurred to him. There was no point in smearing moisturizer on the outside. The stuff was needed internally. But how the hell to get it there? A tube of toothpaste caught his eye. That was what he needed. Oh no, it wasn't. Not with toothpaste. With moisturizer. Why didn't they pack the muck in tubes?

Wilt opened the medicine cupboard and groped among the old razors, the bottles of aspirin and cough mixture for a tube of something vaguely suitable for squeezing up his penis but apart from Eva's hair remover . . . 'Sod that for a lark,' said Wilt, who had once accidentally brushed his teeth with the stuff, 'I'm not shoving that defoliant up any place.' It would have to be the moisturizing cream or nothing. And it wasn't going to be nothing. With a fresh and frenzied sense of desperation, he lurched from the bathroom clutching the jar and stumbled downstairs to the kitchen and was presently scrabbling in the drawer by the sink. A moment later he had found what he was looking for.

Upstairs, Eva turned over. For some time she had been vaguely aware that her back was cold but too vaguely to do anything about it. Now she was also aware that the light was on and that the bed beside her was empty and the bedclothes had been flung back. Which explained why she'd been freezing. Henry had evidently gone to the lavatory. Eva pulled the blankets back and lay awake waiting for him to return. Perhaps he'd be in the mood to make love. After all, he'd had two bottles of his beer and Dr Kores' aphrodisiac and she'd put on her red panties and it was much nicer to make love in the middle of the night when the quads were fast asleep than on Sunday mornings when they weren't, and she had to get up and shut the door in case they came in. Even that wasn't guaranteed to work. Eva would always remember one awful occasion when Henry had almost made it and she had suddenly smelt smoke and there'd been a series of screams from the quads. 'Fire! Fire!' they'd yelled, and she and Henry had hurled themselves from the bed and onto the landing in the altogether only to find the quads there with her jam-making pan filled with burning newspaper. It had been one of those rare occasions when she'd had to agree with Henry about the need for a thorough thrashing. Not that the quads had had one. They'd been down the stairs and out of the front door before Wilt could catch them and he'd been unable to pursue them down the street without a stitch of clothing on. No, it was much nicer at night and she was just wondering if she ought to take her panties off now and not wait, when a crash from downstairs put the thought out of her mind.

Eva climbed out of bed and putting a dressing-gown on, went down to investigate. The next moment all thoughts of making love had gone. Wilt was standing in the middle of the kitchen with her cake-icing syringe in one hand and his penis in the other. In fact, the two seemed to be joined together.

Eva groped for words. 'And what do you think you're doing?' she demanded when she could speak.

Wilt turned a crimson face towards her. 'Doing?' he asked, conscious that the situation was one that was open to any number of interpretations and none of them nice.

'That's what I said, doing,' said Eva.

Wilt looked down at the syringe. 'As a matter of fact . . .' he began, but Eva was ahead of him.

'That's my icing syringe.'

'I know it is. And this is my John Thomas,' said Wilt. Eva regarded the two objects with equal disgust. She would never be able to ice a cake with the syringe again and how she could ever have found anything faintly attractive about Wilt's John Thomas was beyond her. 'And for your information,' he continued, 'that is your moisturizing cream on the floor.'

Eva stared down at the jar. Even by the peculiar standards of 45 Oakhurst Avenue there was something disorientating about the conjunction – and conjunction was the right word – of Wilt's thingamajig and the icing syringe and the presence on the kitchen floor of a jar of her moisturizing cream. She sat down on a stool.

'And for your further information,' Wilt went on, but Eva stopped him. 'I don't want to hear,' she said.

Wilt glared at her lividly. 'And I don't want to feel,' he snarled. 'If you think I find any satisfaction in squirting whatever's in that emulsifier you use for your face up my whatsit at three o'clock in the morning, I can assure you I don't.'

'I don't see why you're doing it then,' said Eva, beginning to have an awful feeling herself.

'Because, if I didn't know better, I'd think some

126

bloody sadist had larded my waterworks with pepper, that's why.'

'With pepper?'

'Or ground glass and curry powder,' said Wilt. 'Add a soupçon of mustard gas and you'll have the general picture. Or sensation. Something ghastly anyway. And now if you don't mind . . .'

But before he could get to work with the icing syringe again Eva had stopped him. 'There must be an antidote,' she said. 'I'll phone Dr Kores.'

Wilt's eyes bulged in his head. 'You'll do what?' he demanded.

'I said I'll—'

'I heard you,' shouted Wilt. 'You said you'd ring that bloody herbal homothrope Dr Kores and I want to know why.'

Eva looked desperately round the kitchen but there was no comfort now to be found in the Magimix or the le Creuset saucepans hanging by the stove and certainly none in the herb chart on the wall. That beastly woman had poisoned Henry and it was all her own fault for having listened to Mavis. But Wilt was staring at her dangerously and she had to do something immediately. 'I just think you ought to see a doctor,' she said. 'I mean, it could be serious.'

'Could be?' yelled Wilt, now thoroughly alarmed. 'It fucking well is and you still haven't told me—'

'Well, if you must know,' interrupted Eva, fighting back, 'you shouldn't have had so much beer.'

'Beer? My God, you bitch, I knew there was something wrong with the muck,' shouted Wilt and hurled himself at her across the kitchen.

'I only meant—' Eva began, and then dodged round the pine table to avoid the syringe. She was saved by the quads.

'What's Daddy doing with cream all over his genitals?' asked Emmeline. Wilt stopped in his tracks and stared at the four faces in the doorway. As usual, the quads were employing tactics that always nonplussed him. To combine the whimsy of 'Daddy', particularly with the inflection Emmeline gave the word, with the anatomically exact was calculated to disconcert him. And why not ask him instead of referring to him so objectively? For a moment he hesitated and Eva seized her opportunity.

'That's nothing to do with you,' she said and ostentatiously shielded them from the sight. 'It's just that your father isn't very well and—'

'That's right,' shouted Wilt, who could see what was coming, 'slap all the blame on me.'

'I'm not blaming you,' said Eva over her shoulder. 'It's—'

'That you lace my beer with some infernal irritant and bloody well poison me, and then you have the gall to tell them I'm not very well. I'll say I'm not well. I'm—'

A hammering sound from the Gamers' wall diverted his attention. As Wilt hurled the syringe at the Laughing Cavalier his mother-in-law had given them when she'd sold her house and which Eva claimed reminded her of her happy childhood there, Eva hustled the quads upstairs. When she came down again, Wilt had resorted to ice-cubes.

'I do think you ought to see a doctor,' she said.

'I should have seen one before I married you,' said Wilt. 'I suppose you realize I might be dead by now. What the hell did you put in my beer?'

Eva looked miserable. 'I only wanted to help our marriage,' she said, 'and Mavis Mottram said—'

'I'll strangle the bitch!'

'She said Dr Kores had helped Patrick and—'

'Helped Patrick?' said Wilt, momentarily distracted from his ice-packed penis. 'The last time I saw him he looked as if he could do with a bra. Said something about not having to shave so much either.'

'That's what I mean. Dr Kores gave Mavis something to cool his sexual ardour and I thought . . .' She paused. Wilt was looking at her dangerously again.

'Go on, though I'd question the use of "thought".'

'Well, that she might have something that would pep . . .'

'Pep?' said Wilt. 'Why not say ginger and have done with it? And why the hell should I need pepping up anyway? I'm a working man . . . or was, with four damned daughters, not some demented sex pistol of seventeen.'

'I just thought . . . I mean it occurred to me if she could do so much for Patrick . . .' (here Wilt snorted) '. . . she might be able to help us to have a . . . well, a more fulfilling sex life.'

'By poisoning me with Spanish Fly? Some fulfilment that is,' said Wilt. 'Well, let me tell you something now. For your information, I am not some fucking sex processor like that Magimix, and if you want the sort of sex life those idiotic women's magazines you read seem to suggest is your due, like fifteen times a week, you'd better find another husband because I'm buggered if I'm up to it. And the way I feel now, you'll be lucky if I'm ever up to it again.'

'Oh Henry!'

'Sod off,' said Wilt, and hobbled through to the downstairs loo with his mixing bowl of ice cubes. At least they seemed to help and the pain was easing off now.

As the sound of discord inside the house died down, Inspector Hodge and the Sergeant made their way back down Oakhurst Avenue to their car. They hadn't been able to hear what was being said, but the fact that there had been some sort of terrible row had heightened Hodge's opinion that the Wilts were no ordinary criminals. 'The pressure's beginning to tell,' he told Sergeant Runk. 'If we don't find him calling on his friends within a day or two, I'm not the man I think I am.'

'If I don't get some sleep, I won't be either,' said Runk, 'and I'm not surprised that bloke next door wants to sell his house. Must be hell living next to people like that.'

'Won't have to much longer,' said Hodge, but the mention of Mr Gamer had put a new idea in his mind. With a bit of collaboration from the Gamers, he'd be in a position to hear everything that went on in the Wilts' house. On the other hand, with their car transformed into a mobile radio station, he was expecting an early arrest.

# Chapter eleven

All the following day, while Wilt lay in bed with a hot-water bottle he'd converted into an ice-pack by putting it into the freezer compartment of the fridge and Inspector Hodge monitored Eva's movements about Ipford, Flint followed his own line of investigation. He checked with Forensic and learnt that the high-grade heroin found in McCullum's cell corresponded in every way to that discovered in Miss Lynchknowle's flat and almost certainly came from the same source. He spent an hour with Mrs Jardin, the prison visitor, wondering at the remarkable capacity for self-deception that had already allowed her to put the blame on everyone else for McCullum's death. Society was to blame for creating the villain, the education authorities for his wholly inadequate schooling, commerce and industry for failing to provide him with a responsible job, the judge for sentencing him . . .

'He was a victim of circumstances,' said Mrs Jardin.

'You might say that about everybody,' said Flint, looking at a corner cupboard containing pieces of silver that suggested Mrs Jardin's circumstances allowed her the wherewithal to be the victim of her own sentimentality. 'For instance, the three men who threatened to carve you up with—'

'Don't,' said Mrs Jardin, shuddering at the memory.

'Well, they were victims too, weren't they? So's a rabid dog, but that's no great comfort when you're bitten by one, and I put drug pushers in that category.' Mrs Jardin

130

had to agree. 'So you wouldn't recognize them again,' asked Flint, 'not if they were wearing stockings over their heads like you said?'

'They were. And gloves.'

'And they took you down the London Road and showed you where the drop was going to be made.'

'Behind the telephone box opposite the turn-off to Brindlay. I was to stop and go into the phone box and pretend to make a call, and then, if no one was about, I had to come out and pick up the package and go straight home. They said they'd be watching me.'

'And I don't suppose it ever occurred to you to go straight to the police and report the matter?' asked Flint.

'Naturally it did. That was my first thought, but they said they had more than one officer on their payroll.'

Flint sighed. It was an old tactic, and for all he knew the sods had been telling the truth. There were bent coppers, a lot more than when he'd joined the force, but then there hadn't been the big gangs and the money to bribe, and if bribery failed, to pay for a contract killing. The good old days when someone was always hanged if a policeman was murdered, even if it was the wrong man. Now, thanks to the do-gooders like Mrs Jardin, and Christie lying in the witness box and getting that mentally subnormal Evans topped for murders Christie himself had committed, the deterrent was no longer there. The world Flint had known had gone by the board, so he couldn't really blame her for giving in to threats. All the same, he was going to remain what he had always been, an honest and hardworking policeman.

'Even so we could have given you protection,' he said, 'and they wouldn't have been bothered with you once you'd stopped visiting McCullum.'

'I know that now,' said Mrs Jardin, 'but at the time I was too frightened to think clearly.'

Or at all, thought Flint, but he didn't say it. Instead, he concentrated on the method of delivery. No one dropped a consignment of heroin behind a telephone kiosk without ensuring it was going to be picked up. Then again, they didn't hang around after the drop. So there had to be some way of communicating. 'What would have happened if you'd been ill?' he asked. 'Just supposing you couldn't have collected the package, what then?'

Mrs Jardin looked at him with a mixture of contempt and bewilderment she evidently felt when faced with someone who concentrated so insistently on practical matters and neglected moral issues. Besides, he was a policeman and ill-educated. Policemen didn't find absolution as victims. 'I don't know,' she said.

But Flint was getting angry. 'Come off the high horse,' he said, 'you can squeal you were forced into being a runner, but we can still charge you with pushing drugs and into a prison at that. Who did you have to phone?'

Mrs Jardin crumbled. 'I don't know his name. I had to call a number and . . .'

'What number?'

'Just a number. I can't—'

'Get it,' said Flint. Mrs Jardin went out of the room and Flint sat looking at the titles in the bookshelves. They meant very little to him and told him only that she'd read or at least bought a great many books on sociology, economics, the Third World and penal reform. It didn't impress Flint. If the woman had really wanted to do something about the conditions of prisoners, she'd have got a job as a wardress and lived on low wages, instead of dabbling in prison visits and talking about the poor calibre of the staff who had to do society's dirty work. Stick up her taxes to build better prisons and she'd soon start squealing. Talk about hypocrisy.

Mrs Jardin came back with a piece of paper.'That's the number,' she said, handing it to him. Flint looked at it. A London phone box.

'When did you have to call?'

'They said between 9.30 and 9.40 at night the day before I had to collect the packet.'

Flint changed direction. 'How many times did you collect?'

'Only three.'

He got to his feet. It was no use. They'd know Mac was dead, even if it hadn't been announced in the papers, so there was no point in supposing they'd make another drop, but at least they were operating out of London. Hodge was on the wrong track. On the other hand, Flint himself couldn't be said to be on the right one. The trail stopped at Mrs Jardin and a public telephone in London. If McCullum had still been alive . . .

Flint left the house and drove over to the prison. 'I'd like to take a look at Mac's list of visitors,' he told Chief Warder Blaggs, and spent half an hour writing names in his notebook, together with addresses.

'Someone in that little lot had to be running messages,' he said when he finished. 'Not that I expect to get anywhere, but it's worth trying.'

Afterwards, back at the Station, he had checked them on the Central Records Computer and cross-referenced for drug dealing, but the one link he was looking for, some petty criminal living in Ipford or nearby, was missing. And he wasn't going to waste his time trying to tackle London. In fact, if he were truthful, he had to admit he was wasting his time even in Ipford except . . . except that something told him he wasn't. It nagged at his mind. Sitting in his office, he followed that instinct. The girl had been seen by her flat-mate down by the marina. Several times. But the marina was just another place like the telephone kiosk on the London Road. It had to be something more definite, something he could check out.

Flint picked up the phone and called the Drug Addiction Study Unit at the Ipford Hospital.

By lunchtime, Wilt was up and about. To be exact, he'd been up and about several times during the morning, in part to get another hot-water bottle from the freezer, but more often in a determined effort not to masturbate himself to death. It was all very well Eva supposing she'd benefit from the effects of whatever diabolical irritant she'd added to his homebrew, but to Wilt's way of thinking, a wife who'd damned near poisoned her husband didn't deserve what few sexual benefits he had to offer. Give her an inkling of satisfaction from this experiment and next time he'd land up in hospital with internal bleeding and a permanent erection. As it was, he had a hard time with his penis.

'I'll freeze the damn thing down,' had been Wilt's first thought and for a while it had worked, though painfully. But after a time he had drifted off to sleep and had woken an hour later with the awful impression that he'd taken it into his head to have an affair with a freshly caught Dover Sole. Wilt hurled himself off the thing and had then taken the bottle downstairs to put it back in the fridge before realizing that this wouldn't be particularly hygienic. He was in the process of washing it when the front doorbell rang. Wilt dropped the bottle on the draining-board, retrieved it from the sink when it slithered off and finally tried wedging it between the up-turned teapot and a casserole dish in the drying rack, before going to answer the call.

It was not the postman as he expected, but Mavis Mottram. 'What are you doing at home?' she asked.

Wilt sheltered behind the door and pulled his dressing-gown tightly round him. 'Well, as a matter of fact . . .' he began.

Mavis pushed past him and went through to the kitchen. 'I just came round to see if Eva could organize the food side of things.'

'What things?' asked Wilt, looking at her with loathing. It was thanks to this woman that Eva had consulted Dr Kores. Mavis ignored the question. In her dual rôle as militant feminist and secretary to Mothers Against The Bomb, she evidently considered Wilt to be part of the male sub-species. 'Is she going to be back soon?' she went on.

Wilt smiled unpleasantly and shut the kitchen door behind him. If Mavis Mottram was going to treat him like a moron, he felt inclined to behave like one. 'How do you know she's not here?' he asked, testing the blade of a rather blunt breadknife against his thumb.

'The car's not outside and I thought ... well, you usually take it ...' She stopped.

Wilt put the breadknife on the magnetic holder next to the Sabatier ones. It looked out of place. 'Phallic,' he said. 'Interesting.'

'What is?'

'Lawrentian,' said Wilt, and retrieved the icing syringe from a plastic bucket where Eva had been soaking it in Dettol in an attempt to persuade herself she would be able to use the thing again.

'Lawrentian?' said Mavis, beginning to sound genuinely alarmed.

Wilt put the syringe on the counter and wiped his hands. Eva's washing-up gloves caught his eye. 'I agree,' he said and began putting the gloves on.

'What on earth are you talking about?' asked Mavis, suddenly remembering Wilt and the inflated doll. She moved round the kitchen table towards the door and then thought better of it. Wilt in a dressing-gown and no pyjama trousers, and now wearing a pair of rubber gloves and holding a cake-icing syringe, was an extremely disturbing sight. 'Anyway, if you'll ask her to call me, I'll explain about the food side of ...' Her voice trailed off.

Wilt was smiling again. He was also squirting a yellowish liquid into the air from the syringe. Images of some demented doctor in an early horror movie flickered in her mind. 'You were saying something about her not being here,' said Wilt and stepped back in front of the door. 'Do go on.'

'Go on about what?' said Mavis with a distinct quaver.

'About her not being here. I find your interest curious, don't you?'

'Curious?' mumbled Mavis, desperately trying to find some thread of sanity in his inconsequential remarks. 'What's curious about it? She's obviously out shopping and—'

'Obviously?' asked Wilt, and gazed vacantly past her out of the window and down the garden. 'I wouldn't have said anything was obvious.'

Mavis involuntarily followed his gaze and found the back garden almost as sinister as Wilt with washing-up gloves and that bloody syringe. With a fresh effort, she forced herself to turn back and speak normally. 'I'll be off now,' she said and moved forward.

Wilt's fixed smile crumbled. 'Oh, not so soon,' he said. 'Why not put the kettle on and have some coffee? After all, that's what you'd do if Eva was here. You'd sit down and have a nice talk. And you and Eva had so much in common.'

'Had?' said Mavis and wished to God she'd kept her mouth shut. Wilt's awful smile was back again. 'Well, if you'd like a cup yourself, I suppose I've got time.' She crossed to the electric kettle and took it to the sink. The hot-water bottle was lying on the bottom. Mavis lifted it out and experienced another ghastly frisson. The hot-water bottle wasn't simply not hot, it was icy cold. And behind her Wilt had begun to grunt alarmingly. For a moment Mavis hesitated before swinging round. This time there was no mistaking the threat she was facing. It was staring at her from between the folds of Wilt's dressing-gown. With a squeal, she hurled herself at the back door, dragged it open, shot out and with a clatter of dustbin lids, was through the gate and heading for the car.

Behind her Wilt dropped the syringe back into the bucket and tried to get his hands out of the washing-up gloves by pulling on the fingers. It wasn't the best method and it was some time before he'd rid himself of the wretched things and had grabbed the second bottle from the freezer. 'Bugger the woman,' he muttered as he clutched the bottle to his penis and tried to think of what to do next. If she went to the police . . . No, she wasn't likely to do that but all the same, it would be as well to take precautions. Regardless of hygiene, he flung the bottle from the sink into the freezer and hobbled upstairs. 'At least we've seen the last of Mavis M,' he thought as he got back into bed. That was some consolation for the reputation he was already doubtless acquiring. As usual, he was entirely wrong.

*

136

Twenty minutes later, Eva, who had been intercepted by Mavis on her way home, drove up to the house.

'Henry,' she shouted as soon as she was inside the front door. 'You come straight down here and explain what you were doing with Mavis.'

'Sod off,' said Wilt.

'What did you say?'

'Nothing. I was just groaning.'

'No, you weren't. I distinctly heard you say something,' said Eva on her way upstairs.

Wilt got out of bed and girded his loins with the water bottle. 'Now you just listen to me,' he said before Eva could get a word in. 'I've had all I can stand from everybody, you, Mavis-moron-Mottram, that poisoner Kores, the quads and the bloody thugs who've been following me. In fact the whole fucking modern world with its emphasis on me being nice and docile and passive and everyone else doing their own thing and to hell with the consequences. (*A*) I am not a thing, and (*B*) I'm not going to be done any more. Not by you, or Mavis, or, for that matter, the damned quads. And I don't give a tuppenny stuff what received opinions you suck up like some dehydrated sponge from the hacks who write articles on progressive education and sex for geriatrics and health through fucking hemlock—'

'Hemlock's a poison. No one . . .' Eva began, trying to divert his fury.

'And so's the ideological codswallop you fill your head with,' shouted Wilt. 'Permissive cyanide, page three nudes for the so-called intelligentsia or video nasties for the unemployed, all fucking placebos for them that can't think or feel. And if you don't know what a placebo is, try looking it up in a dictionary.'

He paused for breath and Eva grabbed her opportunity. 'You know very well what I think about video nasties,' she said, 'I wouldn't dream of letting the girls see anything like that.'

'Right,' yelled Wilt, 'so how about letting me and Mr bleeding Gamer off the hook. Has it ever occurred to you that you've got genuine non-video actual nasties, pre-pubescent horrors, in those four daughters? Oh no, not them. They're special, they're unique, they're flipping geniuses. We mustn't do anything to retard their intellectual development, like teaching them some manners or how to behave in a civilized fashion. Oh no, we're your modern model parents holding the ring while those four ignoble little savages turn themselves into computer-addicted technocrats with about as much moral sense as Ilse Koch on a bad day.'

'Who's Ilse Koch?' asked Eva.

'Just a mass murderess in a concentration camp,' said Wilt, 'and don't get the idea I'm on a right-wing, flog 'em and hang 'em reactionary high because I'm not, and those idiots don't think either. I'm just mister stick-in-the-middle who doesn't know which way to jump. But my God I do think! Or try to. Now leave me in peace and discomfort and go and tell your mate Mavis that the next time she doesn't want to see an involuntary erection, not to advise you to go anywhere near Castrator Kores.'

Eva went downstairs feeling strangely invigorated. It was a long time since she'd heard Henry state his feelings so strongly and, while she didn't understand everything he'd said, and she certainly didn't think he'd been fair about the quads, it was somehow reassuring to have him assert his authority in the house. It made her feel better about having been to that awful Dr Kores with all her silly talk about . . . what was it? . . . 'the sexual superiority of the female in the mammalian world'. Eva didn't want to be superior in everything and anyway, she wasn't just a mammal. She was a human being. That wasn't the same thing at all.

# Chapter twelve

By the following evening, it would have been difficult to say what Inspector Hodge was. Since Wilt hadn't emerged from the house, the Inspector had spent the best part of two days tracing Eva's progress to and from the school and round Ipford in the bugged Escort.

'It's good practice,' he told Sergeant Runk, as they followed her in a van Hodge had converted to a listening-post.

'For what?' asked the Sergeant, pinning a mark on the town map to indicate that Eva had now parked behind Sainsbury's. She'd already been to Tesco's and Fine Fare. 'So we learn where to get the best discount on washing powder?'

'For when he decides to move.'

'When,' said Runk. 'So far he hasn't been out of the house all day.'

'He's sent her out to check she hasn't got a tail on her,' said Hodge. 'In the meantime, he's lying low.'

'Which you said was just the thing he wasn't doing,' said Runk. 'I said he was and you said . . .'

'I know what I said. But that was when he knew he was being followed. It's different now.'

'I'll say,' said Runk. 'So the sod sends us on a tour of shopping centres and we haven't got a clue what's going on.'

They had that night. Runk, who had insisted on having the afternoon off for some shut-eye if he was to work at night, retrieved the tape from under the seat and replaced it with a new one. It was one o'clock in the morning. Half an hour later, Hodge, whose childhood had been spent in a house where sex was never mentioned, was listening to the quads discussing Wilt's condition with a frankness that appalled him. If anything was needed to convince him that Mr and Mrs Wilt were dyed-in-the-wool criminals, it was Emmeline's repeated

139

demand to know why Daddy had been up in the night putting cake icing on his penis. Eva's explanation didn't help either. 'He wasn't feeling very well, dear. He'd had too much beer and he couldn't sleep, so he went down to the kitchen to see if he could ice cake and . . .'

'I wouldn't like the sort of cake he was icing,' interrupted Samantha. 'And anyway, it was face-cream.'

'I know, dear, but he was practising and he spilt it.'

'Up his cock?' demanded Penelope, which gave Eva the opportunity to tell her never to use that word. 'It's not nice,' she said, 'it's not nice to say things like that and you're not going to tell anyone at school.'

'It wasn't very nice of Daddy to use the icing syringe to pump face-cream up his penis,' said Emmeline.

By the time the discussion was over, and Eva had dropped the quads off at the school, Hodge was ashen. Sergeant Runk wasn't feeling very well either.

'I don't believe it, I don't believe a bloody word of it,' muttered the Inspector.

'I wish to God I didn't,' said Runk. 'I've heard some revolting things in my time but that lot takes the cake.'

'Don't mention that word,' Hodge said. 'I still don't believe it. No man in his right mind would do a thing like that. They're having us on.'

'Oh, I don't know. I knew a bloke once who used to butter his wick with strawberry jam and have his missus—'

'Shut up,' shouted Hodge, 'if there's one thing I can't stand it's filth and I've had my fill of that for one night.'

'So's Wilt, by the sound of it,' said Runk, 'walking about with his prick in a jug of ice cubes like that. Can't have been just face-cream or icing-sugar he had in that syringe.'

'Dear God,' said Hodge. 'You're not suggesting he was fixing himself with a cake-icing syringe, are you? He'd be bloody dead by now, and anyhow the fucking thing would leak.'

'Not if he mixed the junk with cold cream. That'd explain it, wouldn't it?'

'It might do,' Hodge admitted. 'I suppose if people can sniff the filthy muck, there's no knowing what they can do with it. Not that it helps us much what he does.'

'Of course it does,' said the Sergeant, who had suddenly seen a way of ending the tedium of sitting through the night in the van. 'It means he's got the stuff in the house.'

'Or up his pipe,' said Hodge.

'Wherever. Anyway, there's bound to be enough around to haul him in and give him a good going over.'

But the Inspector has his sights set on more ambitious targets. 'A fat lot of good that's going to do us,' he said, 'even if he did crack, and if you'd read what he did to old Flint you'd know better—'

'But this'd be different,' Runk interrupted. 'First off, he'd be cold turkey. Don't have to question him. Leave him in a cell for three days without a fix and he'd be bleating like a fucking baa-lamb.'

'Yes, and I know who for,' said the Inspector. 'His ruddy mouthpiece.'

'Yes, but we'd have his missus too, remember. And anyway this time we'd have hard evidence and it would just be a matter of charging him. He wouldn't get bail on a heroin charge.'

'True,' said Hodge grudgingly, 'if we had hard evidence. "If." '

'Well, there's bound to be with him getting the stuff all over his pyjamas like those kids said. Forensic would have an easy time. Take that cake-icing syringe for a starter. And then there are towels and drying-up cloths. Blimey, the place must be alive with the stuff. Even the fleas on the cat must be addicts the way he's been splashing it round.'

'That's what worries me,' said Hodge. 'Whoever heard of a pusher splashing it round? No way. They're too bloody careful. Especially when the heat's on like it is now. You know what I think?' Sergeant Runk shook his head. In his opinion the Inspector was incapable of thought. 'I think the bastard's trying the old come-on.

Wants us to arrest him. He's trying to trap us into it. That explains the whole thing.'

'Doesn't explain anything to me,' said Runk despairingly.

'Listen,' said Hodge, 'what we've heard on that tape just now is too bizarre to be credible, right? Right. You've never heard of a junkie fixing his cock and I haven't either. But apparently, this Wilt does. Not only that, but he makes a fucking mess, does it in the middle of the night and with a cake-icing syringe and makes sure his kids find him in the kitchen doing it. For why? Because he wants the little bitches to shoot their mouths off about it in public and for us to hear about it. That's why. Well, I'm not falling for it. I'm going to take my time and wait for Mr Clever Wilt to lead me to his source. I'm not interested in single pushers, this time I'm going to pull in the whole ruddy network.'

And having satisfied himself with this interpretation of Wilt's extraordinary behaviour, the Inspector sat on, savouring his eventual triumph. In his mind's eye, he could see Wilt in the dock with a dozen big-time criminals, none of whom the likes of Flint had ever suspected. They'd be moneyed men with large houses who played golf and belonged to the best clubs, and after sentencing him, the Judge would compliment Inspector Hodge on his brilliant handling of the case. No one would ever call him inefficient again. He'd be famous and his photograph would be in all the papers.

Wilt's thoughts followed rather similar lines, though with a different emphasis. The effects of Eva's enthusiasm for aphrodisiacs were still making themselves felt and, more disastrously, had given him what appeared to be a permanent erection. 'Of course I'm confined to the bloody house,' he said when Eva complained that she didn't want him wandering about in his dressing-gown on her weekly coffee morning. 'You don't expect me to go back to the Tech with the thing sticking out like a ramrod.'

'Well, I don't want you making an exhibition of yourself in front of Betty and the others like you did with Mavis.'

'Mavis got what she deserved,' said Wilt. 'I didn't ask the woman into the house, she just marched in, and anyway if she hadn't put you on to poisoner Kores I wouldn't be wandering around with a coat-hanger strapped to my waist, would I?'

'What's the coat-hanger for?'

'To keep the flipping dressing-gown off the inflamed thing,' said Wilt. 'If you knew what it felt like to have stuff like a heavy blanket rubbing against the end of a pressurized and highly sensitive—'

'I don't want to hear,' said Eva.

'And I don't want to feel,' Wilt retorted. 'Hence the coat-hanger. And what's more, you want to try bending your knees and leaning forward at the same time every time you have to pee. It's bloody agony. As it is I've banged my head on the wall twice and I haven't had a crap in two days. I can't even sit down to read. It's either flat on my back in bed with the wastepaper basket for protection or up and about with the coat-hanger. And up and about it is. At this rate, they'll have to build a special coffin with a periscope when I cough it.'

Eva looked at him doubtfully. 'Perhaps you ought to go and see a doctor if it's that serious.'

'How?' snapped Wilt. 'If you think I'm going to walk down the road looking like a pregnant sex-change artist, forget it. I'd be arrested before I was half-way there and the local rag would have a field day. TECH TEACHER ON PERMANENT HIGH. And you'd really love it if I got called Pumpkin Penis Percy. So you have your Tupperware Party and I'll stick around upstairs.'

Wilt went carefully up to the bedroom and took refuge under the wastepaper basket. Presently, he heard voices from below. Eva's Community Care Committee had begun to arrive. Wilt wondered how many of them had already heard Mavis' version of the episode in the kitchen and were secretly delighted that Eva was married to a

143

homicidal flasher. Not that they would ever admit as much. No, it would be 'Did you hear about poor Eva's awful husband?' or 'I can't think how she can bring herself to stay in the same house with that frightful Henry,' but in fact the target for their malice would be Eva herself. Which was just as it should be, considering that she'd doctored his beer with whatever poison Dr Kores had given her. Wilt lay back and wondered about the doctor and presently fell into a daydream in which he sued her for some enormous sum on the grounds of . . . What sort of grounds were there? Invasion of Penisy? Or Deprivation of Scrotal Rights? Or just plain Poisoning. That wouldn't work because Eva had administered the stuff and presumably if you took it in the correct doses it wouldn't have such awful effects. And, of course, the Kores bitch wasn't to know that Eva never did things by halves. In her book, if a little of something was good for you, twice as much was better. Even Charlie, the cat, knew that, and had developed an uncanny knack of disappearing for several days the moment Eva put down a saucer of cream laced with worm powder. But then Charlie was no fool and evidently still remembered the experience of having his innards scoured out by twice the recommended dosage. The poor brute had come limping back into the house after a week in the bushes at the bottom of the garden looking like a tapeworm with fur and had promptly been put on a high-pilchard diet to build him up.

Well, if a cat could learn from experience, there was no excuse for Wilt. On the other hand, Charlie didn't exactly have to live with Eva, but could shove off at the first sign of trouble. 'Lucky blighter,' Wilt muttered and wondered what would happen if he rang up one night and said he wasn't coming home for a week. He could just imagine the explosion on the other end of the line, and if he put the phone down without coming up with a really plausible explanation, he'd never hear the end of it when he did come home. And why? Because the truth was always too insane or incredible. Just about as incredible as the events of the week which had started with that idiot from the Ministry of Education and had gone on through Miss Hare's use of karate in the Ladies' lavatory to McCullum's threats and the men in the car who'd followed him. Add that little lot together with an overdose of Spanish Fly, and you had a truth no one would believe. Anyway, there was no point in lying there speculating about things he couldn't alter.

'Emulate the cat,' said Wilt to himself and went through to the bathroom to check in the mirror how his penis was getting on. It certainly felt better, and when he removed the wastepaper basket, he was delighted to find it had begun to droop. He had a shower and shaved and by the time Eva's little group had broken up, he was able to go downstairs wearing his trousers. 'How did the hen party go?' he asked.

Eva rose to the provocation. 'I see you're back to your normal sexist self. Anyway, it wasn't any sort of party. We're having that next Friday. Here.'

'Here?'

'That's right. It's going to be a fancy-dress party with prizes for the best costume and a raffle to raise money for the Harmony Community Play-Group.'

'Yes, and I'm sending a bill to all the people you're inviting to pay for the insurance in advance. Remember what happened to the Vurkells when Polly Merton sued them for falling downstairs blind drunk.'

'That was quite different,' said Eva. 'It was all Mary's fault for having a loose stair carpet. She never did look after the house properly. It was always a mess.'

'So was Polly Merton when she hit the hall floor. It was a wonder she wasn't killed,' said Wilt. 'Anyway, that's not the point. The Vurkells' house was wrecked and the insurance company wouldn't pay up because he'd been breaking the by-laws by running an illegal casino with that roulette wheel of his.'

'There you are,' said Eva. 'We're not breaking the law by holding a raffle for charity.'

'I'd check it out if I were you, and you can check me out

too,' said Wilt. 'I've had enough trouble with my private parts these last two days without wearing that Francis Drake outfit you rigged me out in last Christmas.'

'You looked very nice in it. Even Mr Persner said you deserved a prize.'

'For wearing your grandmother's camiknickers stuffed with straw, I daresay I did, but I certainly didn't feel nice. In any case, I've got my prisoner to teach that night.'

'You could cancel that for once,' said Eva.

'What, just before the exams? Certainly not,' said Wilt. 'You invite a mob of costumed fools to invade the house for the good of charity without consulting me, you mustn't expect me to stop my charitable work.'

'In that case, you'll be going out tonight then?' said Eva. 'Today's Friday and you've got to keep up the good work, haven't you?'

'Good Lord,' said Wilt, who'd lost track of the days. It *was* Friday and he had forgotten to prepare anything for the lecture to his class at Baconheath. Spurred on by Eva's sarcasm and the knowledge that he'd end up the following Friday in straw-filled camiknickers or even as Puss in Boots in a black leotard which fitted far too tightly, Wilt spent the afternoon working over some old notes on British Culture and Institutions. They were entitled 'The Need For Deference, Paternalism and The Class Structure' and were designed to be provocative.

By six o'clock he had finished his supper, and half an hour later was driving out along the fen roads towards the airbase rather faster than usual. His penis was playing up again and it had only been by strapping it to his lower stomach with a long bandage and a cricket box that he'd been able to make himself comfortable and not provocatively indecent.

Behind him, the two monitoring vans followed his progress and Inspector Hodge was jubilant. 'I knew it. I knew he'd have to move,' he told Sergeant Runk as they listened to the signals coming from the Escort. 'Now we're getting somewhere.'

'If he's as smart as you say he is, it could be up the garden path,' said Runk.

But Hodge was consulting the map. The coast lay ahead. Apart from that, there were only a few villages, the bleak flatness of the fens and ... 'Any moment he'll switch west,' he predicted. His hopes had turned to certainty. Wilt was heading for the US Airbase at Baconheath and the American connection was complete.

In Ipford prison, Inspector Flint stared into the Bull's face. 'How many years have you still to do?' he asked. 'Twelve?'

'Not with remission,' said the Bull. 'Only eight. I've got good behaviour.'

'Had,' said Flint. 'You lost that when you knocked Mac off.'

'Knocked Mac off? I never did. That's a bloody lie. I never touched him. He—'

'That's not what the Bear says,' interrupted Flint, and opened a file. 'He says you'd been saving up those sleeping pills so you could murder Mac and take over from him. Want to read his statement? It's all down in black and white and nicely signed. Here, take a dekko.'

He pushed the paper across the table but the Bull was on his feet. 'You can't pull that fucking one on me,' he shouted and was promptly pushed back into his chair by the Chief Warder.

'Can,' said Flint, leaning forward and staring into the Bull's frightened eyes. 'You wanted to take over from McCullum, didn't you? Jealous of him, weren't you? Got greedy. Thought you'd grab a nice little operation run from inside and you'd come out in eight years with a pension as long as your arm all safely stashed away by your widow.'

'Widow?' The Bull's face was ashen now. 'What you mean, widow?'

Flint smiled. 'Just as I say. Widow. Because you aren't ever going to get out now. Eight years back to twelve and a life stretch for murdering Mac adds up to twenty-seven by my reckoning, and for all those twenty-seven years, you're going to be doing solitary for your own protection. I can't see you making it, can you?'

The Bull stared at him pathetically. 'You're setting me up.'

'I don't want to hear your defence,' said Flint, and got to his feet. 'Save the blarney for the court. Maybe you'll get some nice judge to believe you. Especially with your record. Oh, and I shouldn't count on the missus to help. She's been shacked up with Joe Slavey for six months, or didn't you know?'

He moved towards the door, but the Bull had broken. 'I didn't do it, I swear to God I didn't, Mr Flint. Mac was like a brother to me. I'd never . . .'

Flint put the boot in again. 'Plead insanity is my advice,' he said. 'You'll be better off in Broadmoor. Buggered if I'd want Brady or the Ripper as a neighbour for the rest of my natural.' For a moment he paused by the door. 'Let me know if he wants to make a statement,' he said to the Chief Warder. 'I mean, I suppose he could help . . .'

There was no need to go on. Even the Bull had got the message. 'What do you want to know?'

It was Flint's turn to think. Take the pressure off too quickly and all he'd get would be garbage. On the other hand, strike while the iron was hot. 'The lot,' he said. 'How the operations work. Who does what. What the links are. You name it, I want it. Every fucking thing!'

The Bull swallowed. 'I don't know everything,' he said, looking unhappily at the Chief Warder.

'Don't mind me,' said Mr Blaggs. 'I'm not here. Just part of the furniture.'

'Start with how Mac got himself junk,' said Flint. It was best to begin with something he already knew. The Bull told him and Flint wrote it all down with a growing sense of satisfaction. He hadn't known about Prison Officer Lane being bent.

'You'll get me slit for this,' said the Bull when he'd finished with Mrs Jardin, the Prison Visitor.

'I don't know why,' said Flint. 'Mr Blaggs here isn't

going to say who told him and it doesn't necessarily have to come out at your trial.'

'Christ,' said the Bull. 'You're not still going on with that, are you?'

'You tell me,' said Flint, maintaining the pressure. By the time he left the prison three hours later, Inspector Flint was almost a happy man. True, the Bull hadn't told him everything, but then he hadn't expected him too. In all likelihood, the fool didn't know much more, but he'd given Flint enough names to be going on with. Best of all, he'd grassed too far to back out, even if the threat of a murder charge lost its effect. The Bull would indeed get himself sliced by some other prisoner if the news ever got out. And the Bear was going to be Flint's next target.

'Being a copper's a dirty business sometimes,' he thought as he drove back to the police station. But drugs and violence were dirtier still. Flint went up to his office and began to check out some names.

Ted Lingon's name rang a bell – two bells, when he put his lists together. And Lingon ran a garage. Promising. But who was Annie Mosgrave?

## Chapter thirteen

'Who?' said Major Glaushof.

'Some guy who teaches English or something evenings. Name of Wilt,' said the Duty Lieutenant. 'H. Wilt.'

'I'll be right over,' said Glaushof. He put the phone down and went through to his wife.

'Don't wait up, honey,' he said, 'I've got a problem.'

'Me too,' said Mrs Glaushof, and settled back to watch Dallas on BBC. It was kind of reassuring to know Texas was still there and it wasn't damp and raining all the time and goddam cold like Baconheath, and people still thought big and did big things. So she shouldn't have married an Airbase Security Officer with a thing going for German Shepherds. And to think he'd seemed so romantic when she'd met him back from Iran. Some security there. She should have known.

Outside, Glaushof climbed into his jeep with the three dogs and drove off between the houses towards the gates to Civilian Quarters. A group of men were standing well back from Wilt's Escort in the parking lot. Glaushof deliberately skidded the jeep to a stop and got out.

'What is it?' he asked. 'A bomb?'

'Jesus, I don't know,' said the Lieutenant, who was listening to a receiver. 'Could be anything.'

'Like he's left his CB on,' a Corporal explained, 'only there's two of them and they're bleeping.'

'Know any Brit who has two CBs running continuously the same time?' asked the Lieutenant. 'No way, and the frequency's wrong. Way too high.'

'So it could be a bomb,' said Glaushof. 'Why the fuck did you let it in?'

In the darkness and under threat of being blown to bits by whatever diabolical device the car concealed, Glaushof edged away. The little group followed him.

'Guy comes every Friday, gives his lecture, has coffee and goes on home no problem,' said the Lieutenant.

'So you let him drive right through with that lot buzzing and you don't stop him,' said Glaushof. 'We could have a Beirut bomb blast on our hands.'

'We didn't pick up the bleep till later.'

'Too later,' said Glaushof, 'I'm not taking any chances. I want the sand trucks brought up but fast. We're going to seal that car. Move.'

'It ain't no bomb,' said the Corporal, 'not sending like that. With a bomb the signals would be coming in.'

'Whatever,' said Glaushof, 'it's a breach of security and it's going to be sealed.'

'If you say so, Major,' said the Corporal and disappeared across the parking lot. For a moment, Glaushof hesitated and considered what other action he should take. At least he'd acted promptly to protect the base and his own career. As Base Security Officer, he'd always been against these foreign lecturers coming in with their subversive talks. He'd already discovered a geographer who'd sneaked a whole lot of shit about the dangers to bird-life from noise pollution and kerosene into his lectures on the development of the English landscape. Glaushof had had him busted as a member of Greenpeace. A car with radios transmitting continuously suggested something much more serious. And something much more serious could be just what he needed.

Glaushof ran through a mental checklist of enemies of the Free World: terrorists, Russian spies, subversives, women from Greenham Common . . . whatever. It didn't matter. The key thing was that Base Intelligence had fouled things up and it was up to him to rub their faces in the shit. Glaushof smiled to himself at the prospect. If there was one man he detested, it was the Intelligence Officer. Nobody heard of Glaushof, but Colonel Urwin with his line to the Pentagon and his wife in with the Base Commander's so they were invited to play Bridge Saturday nights, oh sure, he was a big noise. And a Yale man. Screw him. Glaushof intended to. 'This guy . . . what did you say his name is?' he asked the Lieutenant.

'Wilt,' said the Lieutenant.

'Where are you holding him?'

'Not holding him anyplace,' said the Lieutenant. 'Called you first thing we picked up the signals.'

'So where is he?'

'I guess he's over lecturing someplace,' said the Lieutenant. 'His details are in the guardhouse. Schedule and all.'

They hurried across the parking lot to the gates to the civilian quarters and Glaushof studied the entry in Wilt's file. It was brief and uninformative. 'Lecture Hall 9,' said the Lieutenant. 'You want me to have him picked up?'

'No,' said Glaushof, 'not yet. Just see no one gets out, is all.'

'No way he can except over the new fence,' said the

Lieutenant, 'and I don't see him getting far. I've switched the current on.'

'Fine,' said Glaushof. 'So he comes out you stop him.'

'Yes, sir,' said the Lieutenant, and went out to check the guards, while Glaushof picked up the phone and called the Security Patrol. 'I want Lecture Hall 9 surrounded,' he said, 'but nobody to move till I come.'

He sat on staring distractedly at the centrepage of *Playgirl* featuring a male nude which had been pinned to the wall. If this bastard Wilt could be persuaded to talk, Glaushof's career would be made. So how to get him in the right frame of mind? First of all, he had to know what was in that car. He was still puzzling over tactics when the Lieutenant coughed discreetly behind him. Glaushof reacted violently. He didn't like the implications of that cough. 'Did you pin this up?' he shouted at the Lieutenant.

'Negative,' said the Lieutenant, who disliked the question almost as much as Glaushof had hated the cough. 'No, sir, I did not. That's Captain Clodiak.'

'That's Captain Clodiak?' said Glaushof, turning back to examine the picture again. 'I knew she ... he ... You've got to be kidding, Lieutenant. That's not the Captain Clodiak I know.'

'She put it there, sir. She likes that sort of thing.'

'Yes, well I guess she's a pretty feisty woman,' said Glaushof to avoid the accusation that he was discriminatory. In career prospect terms, it was almost as dangerous as being called a faggot. Not almost; it was worse.

'I happen to be Church of God,' said the Lieutenant, 'and that is irreligious according to my denomination.'

But Glaushof wasn't to be drawn into a discussion. 'Could be,' he said. 'Some other time, huh?' He went out and back to the parking lot where the Corporal, now accompanied by a Major and several men from the Demolition and Excavation section, had surrounded Wilt's car with four gigantic dumpers filled with sand, sweeping aside a dozen other vehicles in the process. As he approached, Glaushof was blinded by two searchlights

152

which had suddenly been switched on. 'Douse those mothers,' he shouted, stumbling about in the glare. 'You want them to know in Moscow what we're doing?' In the darkness that followed this pronouncement, Glaushof banged into the wheelhub of one of the dumptrucks.

'Okay, so I go in without lights,' said the Corporal. 'No problem. You think it's a bomb, I don't. Bombs don't transmit CB.' And before Glaushof could remind him to call him 'Sir' in future, the Corporal had walked across to the car.

'Mr Wilt,' said Mrs Ofrey, 'would you like to elucidate on the question of the rôle of women in British society with particular regard to the part played in professional life by the Right Honorable Prime Minister Mrs Thatcher and . . .'

Wilt stared at her and wondered why Mrs Ofrey always read her questions from a card and why they seldom had anything to do with what he had been talking about. She must spend the rest of the week thinking them up. And the questions always had to do with the Queen and Mrs Thatcher, presumably because Mrs Ofrey had once dined at Woburn Abbey with the Duke and Duchess of Bedford and their hospitality had affected her deeply. But at least this evening he was giving her his undivided attention.

From the moment he'd entered the lecture room, he'd been having problems. The bandage he had wound round his loins had come undone on the drive over, and before he could do anything about it one end had begun to worm its way down his right trouser leg. To make matters worse, Captain Clodiak had come late and had seated herself in front of him with her legs crossed, and had promptly forced Wilt to press himself against the lectern to quell yet another erection or, at least, hide the event from his audience. And by concentrating on Mrs Ofrey, he had so far managed to avoid a second glance at Captain Clodiak.

But there were disadvantages in concentrating so

intently on Mrs Ofrey too. Even though she wore enough curiously patterned knitwear to have subsidized several crofters in Western Scotland, and her few charms were sufficiently muted by wool to make some sort of antidote to the terrifying chic of Captain Clodiak – Wilt had already noted the Captain's blouse and what he took to be a combat skirt in shantung silk – Mrs Ofrey was still a woman. In any case, she evidently liked to be socially exclusive and sat by herself to the left of the rest of the class, and by the time he'd got halfway through his lecture, he'd become positively wry-necked in his regard for her. Wilt had switched his attention to an acned clerk from the PX stores whose other courses were karate and aerobics and whose interest in British Culture was limited to unravelling the mysteries of cricket. That hadn't worked too well either, and after ten minutes of almost constant eye-contact and Wilt's deprecating observations on the effect of women's suffrage on the voting patterns in elections since 1928, the man had begun to shift awkwardly in his chair and Wilt had suddenly realized the fellow thought he was being propositioned. Not wanting to be beaten to pulp by a karate expert, he had tried alternating between Mrs Ofrey and the wall behind the rest of the class, but each time it seemed that Captain Clodiak was smiling more significantly. Wilt had clung to the lectern in the hope that he'd manage to get through the hour without ejaculating into his trousers. He was so worried about this that he hardly noticed that Mrs Ofrey had finished her question. 'Would you say that view was correct?' she said by way of a prompt.

'Well ... er ... yes,' said Wilt, who couldn't recall what the question was anyway. Something to do with the Monarchy being a matriarchy. 'Yes, I suppose in a general way I'd go along with you,' he said, wedging himself more firmly against the lectern. 'On the other hand, just because a country has a female ruler, I don't think we can assume it's not male-dominated. After all, we had Queen Boadicea in Pre-Roman Britain and I

154

wouldn't have thought there was an awful lot of Women's Lib about then, would you?'

'I wasn't asking about the feminist movement,' said Mrs Ofrey, with a nasty inflection that suggested she was a pre-Eisenhower American, 'my question was directed to the matriarchal nature of the Monarchy.'

'Quite,' said Wilt, fighting for time. Something desperate seemed to have happened to the cricket box. He'd lost touch with the thing. 'Though just because we've had a number of queens . . . well, I suppose we've had almost as many as we've had kings . . . must have had more, come to think of it? Is that right? I mean, each king had to have a queen . . .'

'Henry VIII had a whole heap of them,' said an astro-navigational expert, whose reading tastes seemed to suggest she would have preferred life in some sort of aircon-ditioned and deodorized Middle Ages. 'He must have been some man.'

'Definitely,' said Wilt, grateful for her intervention. At this rate, the discussion might spread and leave him free to find that damned box again. 'In fact he had five. There was Katherine of . . .'

'Excuse me asking, Mr Wilt,' interrupted an engineer, 'but do old queens count as queens? Like they're widows. Is a king's widow still a queen?'

'She's a queen mother,' said Wilt, who by this time had his hand in his pocket and was searching for the box. 'It's purely titular of course. She—'

'Did you say "titular"?' asked Captain Clodiak, endowing the word with qualities Wilt had never intended and certainly didn't need now. And her voice suited her face. Captain Clodiak came from the South. 'Would you care to amplify what titular means?'

'Amplify?' said Wilt weakly. But before he could answer, the engineer had interrupted again.

'Pardon me breaking in, Mr Wilt,' he said, 'but you've got kind of something hanging out of your leg.'

'I have?' said Wilt, clutching the lectern even more closely. The attention of the entire class was now focused on his right leg. Wilt tried to hide it behind his left.

'And by the look of it I'd say it was something important to you.'

Wilt knew damned well what it was. With a lurch, he let go of the lectern and grabbed his trouser leg in a vain attempt to stop the box but the beastly thing had already evaded him. It hung for a moment almost coyly half out of the trouser cuff and then slid onto his shoe. Wilt's hand shot out and smothered the brute and the next moment he was trying to get it into his pocket. The box didn't budge. Still attached to the bandage by the plaster he had used, it refused to come without the bandage. As Wilt tried to drag it away it became obvious he was in danger of splitting the seam of his trousers. It was also fairly obvious that the other end of the bandage was still round his waist and had no intention of coming off. At this rate, he'd end up half-naked in front of the class and suffering from a strangulated hernia into the bargain. On the other hand, he could hardly stay half-crouching there and any attempt to drag the bloody thing up the inside of his trousers from the top was bound to be misinterpreted. In fact, by the sound of things, his predicament already had been. Even from his peculiar position, Wilt was aware that Captain Clodiak had got to her feet, a bleeper was sounding and the astro-navigator was saying something about codpieces.

Only the engineer was being at all constructive. 'Is that a medical problem you got there?' he asked and missed Wilt's contorted reply that it wasn't. 'I mean, we've got the best facilities for the treatment of infections of the urino-genital tract this side of Frankfurt and I can call up a medic . . .'

Wilt relinquished his hold on the box and stood up. It might be embarrassing to have a cricket box hanging out of his trousers but it was infinitely preferable to being examined in his present state by an airbase doctor. God knows what the man would make of a runaway erection. 'I don't need any doctor,' he squawked. 'It's just . . . well, I was playing cricket before I came here and in a hurry not to be late I forgot . . . Well, I'm sure you understand.'

Mrs Ofrey clearly didn't. With some remark about the niceties of life being wanting, she marched out of the hall in the wake of Captain Clodiak. Before Wilt could say that all he needed was to get to the toilet, the acned clerk had intervened. 'Say, Mr Wilt,' he said, 'I didn't know you were a cricket player. Why, only three weeks ago you were saying you couldn't tell me what you English call a curve ball.'

'Some other time,' said Wilt, 'right now I need to get to . . . er . . . a washroom.'

'You sure you don't want—'

'Definitely,' said Wilt, 'I am perfectly all right. It's just a . . . never mind.'

He hobbled out of the hall and was presently ensconced in a cubicle fighting a battle with the box, the bandage and his trousers. Behind him, the class were discussing this latest manifestation of British Culture with a greater degree of interest than they had shown for Wilt's views on voting patterns. 'I still say he don't know anything about cricket,' said the PX clerk, only to be countered by the navigator and the engineer who were more interested in Wilt's medical condition. 'I had an uncle in Idaho had to wear a support. It's nothing unusual. Fell off a ladder when he was painting the house one spring,' said the engineer. 'Those things can be real serious.'

'I told you, Major,' said the Corporal, 'two radio transmitters, one tape recorder, no bomb.'

'Definitely?' asked Glaushof, trying to keep the disappointment out of his voice.

'Definite,' said the Corporal and was supported in this by the Major from the Demolition and Excavation Section who wanted to know whether he could order his men to move the dumpers back. As they rolled away leaving Wilt's Escort isolated in the middle of the parking lot, Glaushof tried to salvage some opportunity from the situation. After all, Colonel Urwin, the Intelligence

Officer, was away for the weekend and in his absence Glaushof could have done with a crisis.

'He had to come in here with that equipment for some reason,' he said, 'transmitting like that. Any ideas on the matter, Major?'

'Could be it's a dummy run to check if they can bring a bomb in and explode it by remote control,' said the Major, whose expertise tended to make him one-track-minded.

'Except he was transmitting, not receiving,' said the Corporal. 'They'd need signals in, not out, for a bomb. And what's with the recorder?'

'Not my department,' said the Major. 'Explosively, it's clean. I'll go file my report.'

Glaushof took the plunge. 'With me,' he said. 'You file it with me and no one else. We've got to shroud this.'

'We've done that once already with the safety trucks and quite unnecessarily.'

'Sure,' said Glaushof, 'but we still gotta find out what this is all about. I'm in charge of security and I don't like it, some Limey bastard coming in with all this equipment. Either it's a dummy run like you said, or it's something else.'

'It's got to be something else,' said the Corporal, 'obviously. With the equipment he's using, you could tape lice fucking twenty miles away it's that sensitive.'

'So his wife's getting evidence for a divorce,' said the Major.

'Must be goddam desperate for it,' said the Corporal, 'using two transmitters and a recorder. And that stuff's not general issue. I never seen a civilian using homers that sophisticated.'

'Homers?' said Glaushof, who had been preoccupied by the concept of lice fucking. 'How do you mean, homers?'

'Like they're direction indicators. Signals go out and two guys pick it up on their sets and they've got where he is precise.'

'Jesus!' said Glaushof. 'You mean the Russkies could

have sent this guy Wilt in as an agent so they can pin-point right where we are?'

'They're doing that already infra-red by satellite. They don't need some guy coming in waving a radio flag,' said the Corporal. 'Not unless they want to lose him.'

'Lose him? What would they want to do that for?'

'I don't know,' continued the Corporal. 'You're Security, I'm just Technical and why anybody wants to do things isn't my province. All I do know is I wouldn't send any agent of mine any place I didn't want him caught with those signals spelling out he was coming. Like putting a fucking mouse in a room with a cat and it can't stop fucking squeaking.'

But Glaushof was not to be deterred. 'The fact of the matter is this Wilt came in with unauthorized spy equipment and he isn't going out.'

'So they're going to know he's here from those signals,' said the Corporal.

Glaushof glared at him. The man's common sense had become intensely irritating. Here was his opportunity to hit back. 'You don't mean to tell me those radios are still operational?' he shouted.

'Sure,' said the Corporal. 'You tell me and the Major here to check the car for bombs. You didn't say nothing about screwing his transmission equipment. Bombs, you said.'

'Correct,' said the Major. 'That's what you did say. Bombs.'

'I know I said bombs,' yelled Glaushof, 'you think I need telling?' He stopped and turned his attention lividly on the car. If the radios were still working, presumably the enemy already knew they'd been discovered, in which case . . . His mind raced on, following lines which led to catastrophe. He had to make a momentous decision, and now. Glaushof did. 'Right, we're going in,' he said, 'and you're going out.'

Five minutes later, in spite of his protests that he wasn't driving any fucking car thirty miles with fucking spooks following his fucking progress, not unless he had a fucking escort, the Corporal drove out of the base. The tape in the recorder had been removed and replaced with a new one, but in all other respects there was nothing to indicate that the car had been tampered with. Glaushof's instructions had been quite explicit. 'You drive right back and dump it outside his house,' he had told the Corporal. 'You've got the Major here with you to bring you back and if there's any problems, he'll take care of them. Those bastards want to know where their boy is they can start looking at home. They're going to have trouble finding him here.'

'Ain't going to have no trouble finding me,' said the Corporal, who knew never to argue with a senior officer. He should have stuck to dumb insolence.

For a moment, Glaushof watched as the two vehicles disappeared across the bleak night landscape. He had never liked it but now it had taken on an even more sinister aspect. It was across those flatlands that the wind blew from Russia non-stop from the Urals. In Glaushof's mind, it was an infected wind which, having blown around the domes and turrets of the Kremlin, threatened the very future of the world. And now somewhere out there someone was listening. Glaushof turned away. He was going to find out who those sinister listeners were.


## Chapter fourteen


'I got the whole place wrapped up, sir, and he's still inside,' said Lieutenant Harah when Glaushof finally reached Lecture Hall 9. Glaushof didn't need telling. He had had enough trouble himself getting through the cordon the Lieutenant had thrown up around the hall and in other circumstances would have expressed himself irritably on the Lieutenant's thoroughness. But the situation was too serious for recrimination, and besides he respected his second-in-command's expertise. As head of the APPS, the Anti Perimeter Penetration Squad, Lieutenant Harah had been through training at Fort Knox, in Panama and had seen action at Greenham Common disguised as a British bobby where he had qualified for a Purple Heart after being bitten in the leg by a mother of four, an experience which had left him with a useful bias against women. Glaushof appreciated his misogyny. At least one man in Baconheath could be relied on not to lay Mona Glaushof and Harah wasn't going to play footsy with any CND women if and when they tried breaking into Baconheath.

On the other hand, he seemed to have gone too far this time. Quite apart from the six hit-squad men in gas masks by the glass fronted door to the lecture hall and a number of others crouching under the windows round the side a small group of women were standing with their heads up against the wall of the next building.

'What are those?' Glaushof asked. He had a nasty suspicion he recognized Mrs Ofrey's Scottish knitwear.

'Suspected women,' said Lieutenant Harah.

'What do you mean "suspected women"?' demanded Glaushof. 'Either they're women or they aren't.'

'They came out dressed as women, sir,' said the Lieutenant, 'doesn't mean to say they are. Could be the terrorist dressed as one. You want me to check them out?'

'No,' said Glaushof, wishing to hell he had given the order to storm the building before he had put in an appearance himself. It wasn't going to look too good spread-eagling the wife of the Chief Administrative Officer against a wall with a gun at her head, and to have her checked out sexually by Lieutenant Harah would really foul things up. On the other hand even Mrs Ofrey could hardly complain about being rescued from a possible hostage situation.

'You sure there's no way he could have got out?'

'Absolute,' said the Lieutenant. 'I got marksmen on the next block in case he makes the roof and the utilities tunnels are sealed. All we got to do is toss a canister of Agent Incapacitating in there and there's going to be no trouble.'

Glaushof glanced nervously at the row of women and doubted it. There was going to be trouble and maybe it would be better if that trouble could be seen to be serious. 'I'll get those women under cover and then you go in,' he said. 'And no shooting unless he fires first. I want this guy taken for interrogation. You got that?'

'Absolute, sir,' said the Lieutenant. 'He gets a whiff of AI he wouldn't find a trigger to pull if he wanted to.'

'Okay. Give me five minutes and then go,' said Glaushof and crossed to Mrs Ofrey.

'If you ladies will just step this way,' he said, and dismissing the men who were holding them hurried the little group round the corner and into the lobby of another lecture hall. Mrs Ofrey was clearly annoyed.

'What do you mean—' she began but Glaushof raised a hand. 'If you'll just let me explain,' he said, 'I realize you have been inconvenienced but we have an infiltration situation on our hands and we couldn't afford the possibility of you being held hostage.' He paused and was glad to see that even Mrs Ofrey had taken the message. 'How absolutely dreadful,' she murmured.

It was Captain Clodiak's reaction that surprised him. 'Infiltration situation? We just had the usual class no problem,' she said, 'I didn't see anybody new. Are you saying there's somebody in there we don't know about?'

Glaushof hesitated. He had hoped to keep the question of Wilt's identity as a secret agent to himself and not have news of it spreading round the base like wildfire. He certainly didn't want it getting out until he had completed his interrogation and had all the information he needed to prove that the Intelligence Section, and in particular that bland bastard Colonel Urwin, hadn't screened a foreign employee properly. That way the Colonel would take a fall and they could hardly avoid promoting Glaushof. Let Intelligence get wind of what was going on and the plan might backfire.

Glaushof fell back on the 'Eyes off' routine.

'I don't think it advisable at this moment in time to elucidate the matter further. This is a top-security matter. Any leak could severely prejudice the defensive capabilities of Strategic Air Command in Europe. I must insist on a total information blackout.'

For a moment the pronouncement had the effect he had wanted. Even Mrs Ofrey looked satisfactorily stunned. Then Captain Clodiak broke the silence. 'I don't get it,' she said. 'There's us and this Wilt guy in there, nobody else. Right?' Glaushof said nothing. 'So you bring up the stormtroopers and have us pinned against the wall as soon as we walk out and now you tell us it's an infiltration situation. I don't believe you, Major, I just don't believe you. The only infiltration I know of is what that bastard sexist lieutenant did up my ass and I intend to formalize a complaint again Lieutenant Harah and you can pull as many phoney agents out of your pinhead imagination as you like, you still aren't going to stop me.'

Glaushof gulped. He could see he'd been right to describe the Captain as a feisty woman and entirely wrong to have allowed Lieutenant Harah to act on his own. He'd also been fairly wrong in his estimation of the Lieutenant's antipathy for women though even Glaushof had to admit that Captain Clodiak was a remarkably attractive woman. In an attempt to save the situation he tried a sympathetic smile. It came out lopsided. 'I'm sure Lieutenant Harah had no intention of—' he began.

'So what's with the hand?' snapped the Captain. 'You think I don't know intentions when I feel them? Is that what you think?'

'Perhaps he was doing a weapon check,' said Glaushof, who knew now he would have to do something really astonishing to regain control of the situation. He was saved by the sound of breaking glass. Lieutenant Harah had waited exactly five minutes before taking action.

It had taken Wilt rather more than five minutes to unravel the bandage and slide it down his trouser leg and reassemble the box in a position where it would afford him some measure of protection from the spasmodic antics of his penis. In the end he had succeeded and had just tied the entire contraption together rather uncomfortably when there was a knock on the door.

'You okay, Mr Wilt?' asked the engineer.

'Yes, thank you,' said Wilt as politely as his irritation allowed. It was always the same with nice idiots. The sods offered to help in precisely the wrong way. All Wilt wanted now was to get the hell out of the base without any further embarassment. But the engineer didn't understand the situation. 'I was just telling Pete how I had an uncle in Idaho had the same support problem,' said the engineer through the door.

'Really?' said Wilt, feigning interest while actually struggling to pull his zip up. A thread of bandage had evidently got caught in the thing. Wilt tried pulling it down.

'Yea. He went around for years with this bulky thing on until my Auntie Annie heard of this surgeon in Kansas City and she took my Uncle Rolf down there and of course he didn't want to go but he never did regret it. I can give you his name if you like.'

'Fuck,' said Wilt. A stitch on the bottom of his zip sounded as though it had torn.

'Did you say something, Mr Wilt?' asked the engineer.

'No,' said Wilt.

There was a moment's silence while the engineer evidently considered his next move and Wilt tried holding the bottom of the zip to his trousers while wrenching the tag at the same time. 'As I see it, and you've got to understand I'm not a medical man myself I'm an engineer so I know about structural failure, there's muscle deterioration in the lower—'

'Listen,' said Wilt. 'Right now where I've got a structural failure is in the zip on my trousers. Something's got caught in it and it's stuck.'

'Which side?' asked the engineer.

'Which side is what?' demanded Wilt.

'The . . . er . . . thing that's stuck in it?'

Wilt peered down at the zip. In the confines of the toilet it was difficult to see which side anything was. 'How the hell would I know?'

'You pulling it up or down?' continued the engineer.

'Up,' said Wilt.

'Sometimes helps to pull it down first.'

'It's already bloody down,' said Wilt allowing his irritation to get the better of him. 'I wouldn't be trying to pull the fucking thing up if it wasn't down, would I?'

'I guess not,' said the engineer with a degree of bland patience that was even more irritating than his desire to be helpful. 'Just the same if it isn't right down it could be the thing . . .' He paused. 'Mr Wilt, just what is it you've got in the zip?'

Inside the toilet Wilt stared dementedly at a notice which not only instructed him to wash his hands but seemed to suppose he needed telling how to. 'Count to ten,' he muttered to himself and was surprised to find that the zip had freed itself. He'd also been freed from the unwanted helpfulness of the engineer. A crash of breaking glass had evidently disturbed the man's blandness. 'Jesus, what's going on?' he yelled.

It was not a question Wilt could answer. And by the sound of things outside he didn't want to. Somewhere a door burst open and running feet in the corridor were interspersed with muffled orders to freeze. Inside the toilet Wilt froze. Accustomed as he had recently become to the hazards seemingly inherent in going to the lavatory anywhere outside his own house, the experience of being locked in a cubicle with a hit squad of Anti Perimeter Penetration men bursting into the building was new to him.

It was fairly new to the engineer. As the canisters of Agent Incapacitating hit the floor and masked men armed with automatic weapons broke through the door he lost all interest in the problems of Wilt's zip and headed back into the lecture hall only to collide with the navigator and the PX clerk who were dashing the other way. In the confusion that followed Agent Incapacitating lived up to its name. The PX clerk tried to disentangle himself from the engineer who was doing his best to avoid him and the navigator embraced them both under the illusion he was moving in the other direction.

As they fell to the ground Lieutenant Harah loomed over them large and quite extraordinarily sinister in his gas mask.

'Which of you is Wilt?' he yelled. His voice, distorted both by the mask and by the effects of the gas on their nervous systems, reached them slowly. Not even the voluble engineer was able to help him. 'Take them all out,' he ordered and the three men were dragged from the building gurgling sentences that sounded as if a portable recorder with faulty batteries was being played under water.

In his cubicle Wilt listened to the awful noises with growing apprehension. Breaking glass, strangely muffled shouts and the clump of boots had played no part in his previous visits to the airbase and he couldn't for the life of him imagine what they portended. Whatever it was he'd had enough trouble for one evening without wishing to invite any more. It seemed safest to stay where he was and wait until whatever was happening had stopped. Wilt switched off the light and sat down on the seat.

Outside, Lieutenant Harah's men reported thickly that the hall was clear. In spite of the eddies of gas the Lieutenant could see that. Peering through the eyepiece of his gas mask he surveyed the empty seats with a sense of anti-climax. He had rather hoped the infiltrator would put up a show of resistance, and the ease with which the bastard had been taken had disappointed him. On the other hand he could also see that it had been a mistake to bring in the assault dogs without equipping them with gas masks. Agent Incapacitating evidently affected them too. One of them was slithering about the floor snarling in slow motion while another, in an attempt to scratch its right ear, was waving a hindfoot about in a most disturbing manner.

'Okay, that's it,' he said and marched out to question his three prisoners. Like the assault dogs they had been totally incapacitated and he had no idea which was the foreign agent he was supposed to be detaining. They were all dressed in civilian clothes and in no state to say who or what they were. Lieutenant Harah reported to Glaushof. 'I think you better check them out, sir. I don't know which son of a bitch is which.'

'Wilt,' said Glaushof, glaring at the gas mask, 'his name is Wilt. He's a foreign employee. Shouldn't be any difficulty recognizing the bastard.'

'All Limeys look the same to me,' said the Lieutenant, and was promptly rewarded with a chop across his throat and a knee in his groin by Captain Clodiak who had just recognized her sexist assailant through his gas mask. As the Lieutenant doubled up she grabbed his arm and Glaushof was surprised to see how easily his second-in-command was swept off his feet by a woman.

'Remarkable,' he said. 'It's a genuine privilege to witness—'

'Cut the crap,' said Captain Clodiak, dusting her hands and looking as though she would like to demonstrate her expertise in karate on another man. 'That creep said a sexist remark and you said Wilt. Am I right?' Glaushof looked puzzled. He hadn't recognized 'son of a bitch' as being sexist and he didn't want to discuss Wilt in front of the other women. On the other hand he didn't have any idea what Wilt looked like and someone had to identify him. 'Maybe we'd better step outside to discuss this, Captain,' he said and went out the door.

Captain Clodiak followed him warily. 'What do we have to discuss?' she asked.

'Like Wilt,' said Glaushof.

'You're crazy. I heard you just now. Wilt an agent?'

'Incontrovertible,' said Glaushof, pulling brevity.

'How so?' said Clodiak, responding in kind.

'Infiltrated the perimeter with enough radio transmitting equipment hidden in his car to signal our position to Moscow or the moon. I mean it, Captain. What's more it's not civilian equipment you can buy in a store. It's official,' said Glaushof and was relieved to notice the disbelief fade from her face. 'And right now, I'm going to need help identifying him.'

They went round the corner and were confronted by the sight of three men lying face down on the ground in front of Lecture Hall 9 guarded by two incapacitated assault dogs and the APP team.

'Okay, men, the Captain here is going to identify him,' said Glaushof and prodded the PX clerk with his foot. 'Turn over, you.' The clerk tried to turn over but succeeded only in crawling sideways on top of the engineer, who promptly went into convulsions. Glaushof looked at the two contorted figures with disgust before having his attention distracted even more disturbingly by an assault dog that had urinated on his shoe without lifting its leg.

'Get that filthy beast off me,' he shouted and was joined in his protests by the engineer who objected just as strongly though less comprehensibly to the apparent attempts the PX clerk was making to bugger him. By the time the dog had been removed, a process that required the efforts of three men on the end of its chain, and some sort of order was restored on the ground Captain Clodiak's expression had changed again. 'I thought you said you wanted Wilt identified,' she said. 'Well, he's not here.'

'Not here? You mean . . .' Glaushof looked suspiciously at the broken door of the lecture hall.

'They're the men the Lieutenant told us to grab,' said one of the hit-squad. 'There wasn't anyone else in the hall I saw.'

'There's gotta be,' yelled Glaushof. 'Where's Harah?'

'In there where you—'

'I know where he is. Just get him and fast.'

'Yessir,' said the man and disappeared.

'You seem to have got yourself a problem,' said Captain Clodiak.

Glaushof tried to shrug it off. 'He can't have broken through the cordon and even if he has he's going to burn on the fence or get himself arrested at the gate,' he said. 'I'm not worried.'

All the same he found himself glancing round at the familiar dull buildings and the roadways between them with a new sense of suspicion as though somehow they had changed character and had become accomplices to the absent Wilt. With an insight that was alarmingly strange to him he realized how much Baconheath meant to him; it was home, his own little fortress in a foreign land with its comfortable jet noises linking him to his own hometown, Eiderburg, Michigan, and the abattoir down the road where the hogs were killed. As a boy he had woken to the sound of their squeals and an F111 screaming for take-off had the same comforting effect on him. But more than anything else Baconheath with its perimeter fence and guarded gates had been America for him, his own country, powerful, independent and freed from danger by his constant vigilance and the sheer enormity of its arsenal. Squatting there behind the wire and isolated by the flat reaches of the Fens from the old crumbling villages and market towns with their idle, inefficient shopkeepers and their dirty pubs where strange people drank warm, unhygienic beer, Baconheath had been an oasis of brisk efficiency and modernity, and proof that the great US of A was still the New World and would remain so.

But now Glaushof's vision had shifted and for a moment he felt somehow disassociated from the place. These buildings were hiding this Wilt from him and until he found the bastard Baconheath would be infected. Glaushof forced himself out of this nightmare and was confronted by another. Lieutenant Harah came round the corner. He was clearly still paying for his sexist attitude to Captain Clodiak and had to be supported by two APPS men. Glaushof had almost been prepared for that. The garbled noises the Lieutenant was making were something else again and could hardly be explained by a kick in the groin.

'It's the AI, sir,' one of the men explained, 'I guess he must have loosed off a canister in the lobby.'

'Loosed off a canister? In the lobby?' Glaushof squawked, appalled at the terrible consequences to his career such a lunatic action seemed certain to provoke. 'Not with those women—'

'Affirmative,' ejaculated Lieutenant Harah without warning. Glaushof turned on him.

'What do you mean, affirmative?'

'Absolute,' Harah's voice hit a new high. And stuck there. 'Absolute absolute absolute absolute . . .'

'Gag that bastard,' shouted Glaushof and shot round the corner of the building to see what he could do to rescue the situation. It was beyond hope. For whatever insane reason Lieutenant Harah, perhaps in an attempt to defend himself against a second strike from Captain Clodiak, had wrenched the pin from a gas grenade before realizing that his gas mask had come off in his fall. Gazing through the glass doors at the bizarre scenes in the lobby, Glaushof was no longer worried about Mrs Ofrey's interference. Draped over the back of a chair with her hair touching the floor and happily obscuring her face, the wife of the Chief Administrative Executive resembled nothing so much as a large and incontinent highland ewe which had been put rather prematurely through a Fair Isle knitting machine. The rest of the class were in no better shape. The astro-navigation officer lay on her back, evidently re-enacting a peculiarly passive sexual experience, while several other students of British Culture and Institutions looked as though they were extras in some film depicting the end of the world. Once again Glaushof experienced the ghastly sensation of being at odds with his environment and it was only by calling up reserves of approximate sanity that he took control of himself.

'Get them out of there,' he shouted, 'and call the medics. We got a maniac on the loose.'

'Got something,' said Captain Clodiak. 'That Lieutenant Harah's going to have a lot to answer for. I can't see General Ofrey being too pleased with a dead wife. He'll just have to play three-handed bridge with the Commander.'

But Glaushof had had enough of the Captain's objective standpoint. 'You're responsible for this,' he said with a new menace in his voice. 'You talk about questions you're going to have to answer some yourself. Like you deliberately assaulted Lieutenant Harah in the execution of his duty and—'

'Like the execution of his duty includes getting his hand up my . . .' interrupted the Captain furiously and then stopped and stared. 'Oh my God,' she said and Glaushof, who had been preparing for another demonstration of karate, followed her gaze.

In the broken doorway of Lecture Hall 9 a hapless figure was trying to stand up. As they watched, it failed.


# Chapter fifteen


Fifteen miles away Wilt's Escort beeped its erratic way towards Ipford. Since no one had thought to provide the Corporal with adequate directions and he had distrusted Glaushof's assurances that he would be well protected by the Major and the men in the truck behind him, he had taken his own precautions before and after leaving the base. He had provided himself with a heavy automatic and had computed a route which would cause maximum confusion to anyone trying to cross-reference his position on their receivers.

He had achieved his object. In short, he had travelled twenty quite extraordinarily complicated miles in no time at all. Half an hour after leaving Baconheath he was still only five miles from the base. After that he had shot off towards Ipford and had spent twenty minutes pretending to change a tyre in a tunnel under the motorway before emerging on a minor road which ran for several miles very conveniently next to a line of high-tension electricity pylons. Two more tunnels and fifteen miles on a road that wound along below the bank of a dyked river, and Inspector Hodge and the men in the other listening van were desperately transmitting messages to one another in an attempt to make out where the hell he had got to. More awkwardly still, they couldn't be entirely sure where they were either.

The Major shared their dilemma. He hadn't expected the Corporal to take evasive action or to drive – when he wasn't lurking in tunnels – at excessive speed along winding roads that had presumably been designed for single-file horse traffic and had been dangerous even then. But the Major didn't care. If the Corporal wanted to take off like a scalded cat that was his problem. 'He wants an armed escort he better stay with us,' he told his driver as they skidded round a muddy ninety-degree bend and nearly landed in a deep water-filled drain. 'I'm not ending my life in a ditch so slow down for Chrissake.'

'So how do we keep up with him?' asked the driver, who had been thoroughly enjoying himself.

'We don't. If he's going any place outside hell its Ipford. I've got the address here. Take the motorway first chance you get and we'll wait for him where he's supposed to be going.'

'Yes sir,' said the driver reluctantly and switched back to the main road at the next turn-off.

Sergeant Runk would have done the same had he been given the chance but the Corporal's tactics had confirmed all Inspector Hodge's wildest dreams. 'He's trying to lose us,' he shouted shortly after the Corporal left the airbase and began to dice with death. 'That must mean he's carrying dope.'

'That or he's practising for the Monte Carlo Rally,' said Runk.

Hodge wasn't amused. 'Rubbish. The little bastard goes into Baconheath, spends an hour and a half and comes out doing eighty along mud roads no one in their right minds would do forty on in daylight and backtrack five times the way he's done – he must have something he values in that car.'

'Can't be his life, and that's for certain,' said Runk who was struggling to keep his seat. 'Why don't we just call up a patrol car and pull him for speeding? That way we can have him searched for whatever he's carrying.'

'Good idea,' said Hodge and had been about to send out instructions when the Corporal had taken radio refuge in the motorway tunnel and they'd lost him for twenty minutes. Hodge had spent the time blaming Runk for failing to have an accurate fix on his last position and calling for help from the second van. The Corporal's subsequent route near the power lines and below the river bank had made matters still more awkward. By then the Inspector had no idea what to do, but his conviction that he was dealing with a master-criminal had been confirmed beyond doubt.

'He's obviously passed the stuff on to a third party and if we go for a search he'll plead innocence,' he muttered.

Even Runk had to agree that all the evidence pointed that way. 'He also happens to know his car's been wired for sound,' he said. 'The route he's following he's got to know. So where do we go from here?'

Hodge hesitated. For a moment he considered applying for a warrant and conducting so thorough a search of the Wilts' house that even the minutest trace of heroin or Embalming Fluid would come to light. But if it didn't . . . 'There's always the tape recorder,' he said finally. 'He may have missed that in which case we'll get the conversations he had with the pick-up artist.'

Sergeant Runk doubted it. 'If you ask me,' he said, 'the

only way you're going to get solid evidence on this bugger is by sending Forensic in to do a search with vacuum-cleaners that'd suck an elephant through a drain pipe. He may be as canny as they come but those lab blokes know their onions. I reckon that's the sane way of going about it.'

But Hodge wasn't to be persuaded. He had no intention of handing the case over to someone else when it was patently obvious he was on the right track. 'We'll see what's on that tape first,' he said as they headed back towards Ipford. 'We'll give him an hour to get to sleep and then you can move in and get it.'

'And have the rest of the bloody day off,' said Runk. 'You may be one of Nature's insomniacs but if I don't get my eight hours I won't be fit for—'

'I am not an insomniac,' snapped the Inspector. They drove on in silence broken only by the bleeps coming from Wilt's car. They were louder now. Ten minutes later the van was parked at the bottom of Perry Road and Wilt's car was announcing its presence from Oakhurst Avenue.

'You've got to hand it to the little sod,' said Hodge. 'I mean you'd never dream to look at him he could drive like that. Just shows you can never tell.'

An hour later Sergeant Runk stumbled out of his van and walked up Perry Road. 'It's not there,' he said when he got back.

'Not there? It's bloody well got to be,' said the Inspector, 'it's still coming over loud and clear.'

'That's as may be,' said Runk. 'For all I care the little shit's tucked up in bed with the fucking transmitters but what I do know is that it's not outside his house.'

'What about the garage?' Runk snorted.

'The garage? Have you ever had a dekko in that garage? It's a ruddy furniture depository, that garage is. Stuffed to the roof with junk when I saw it and if you're telling me he's spent the last two days shifting it all out into the back garden so as he could get his car in there . . .'

'We'll soon see about that,' said Hodge and presently the van was driving slowly past 45 Oakhurst Avenue and the Sergeant had been proved right.

'What did I tell you?' he said. 'I said he hadn't put it in the garage.'

'What you didn't say was he'd parked the thing there,' said Hodge, pointing through the windscreen at the mud-stained Escort which the Corporal, who hadn't been prepared to waste time checking house numbers in the middle of the night, had left outside Number 65.

'Well, I'm buggered,' said Runk. 'Why'd he want to do a thing like that?'

'We'll see if that tape has anything to tell us,' said the Inspector. 'You hop out here and we'll go on round the corner.'

But for once Sergeant Runk wasn't to be budged. 'If you want that bloody tape you go and get it,' he said. 'A bloke like this Wilt doesn't leave his car down the road without a good reason and I'm not learning too bleeding late what that reason is, and that's final.'

In the end it was Hodge who approached the car warily and had just started to grope under the front seat when Mrs Willoughby's Great Dane gave tongue inside the house.

'What did I tell you?' said Runk as the Inspector clambered in beside him puffing frantically. 'I knew there was a trap there somewhere but you wouldn't listen.'

Inspector Hodge was too preoccupied to listen to him even now. In his mind's ear he could still hear the baying of that dreadful dog and the sound of its terrible paws on the front door of the Willoughby's house.

He was still shaken by the experience when they arrived back at the station. 'I'll get him, I'll get him,' he muttered as he made his way wearily up the steps. But the threat lacked substance. He had been outwitted yet again and for the first time he appreciated Sergeant

Runk's need for sleep. Perhaps after a few hours his mind would come up with a new plan.

In Wilt's case the need for sleep was paramount too. The effects of Agent Incapacitating on a body already weakened by the administration of Dr Kores' sexual cordial had reduced him to a state in which he hardly knew who he was and was quite incapable of answering questions. He vaguely remembered escaping from a cubicle, or rather of being locked in one, but for the rest his mind was a jumble of images, the sum total of which made no sense at all. Men with masks, guns, being dragged, thrown into a jeep, driven, more dragging, lights in a bare room and a man shouting dementedly at him, all formed kaleidoscopic patterns which constantly rearranged themselves in his mind and made no sense at all. They just happened or were happening or even, because the man shouting at him still seemed somehow remote, had happened to him in some previous existence and one he would prefer not to relive. And even when Wilt tried to explain that things, whatever they were, were not what they seemed, the shouting man wasn't prepared to listen.

It was hardly surprising. The strange noises Wilt was in fact making hardly came into the category of utterances and certainly weren't explanations.

'Scrambled,' said the doctor Glaushof had summoned to try and inject some sense into Wilt's communications system. 'That's what you get with AI Two. You'll be lucky if he ever talks sense again.'

'AI Two? We used standard issue Agent Incapacitating,' said Glaushof. 'Nobody's been throwing AI Two around. That's reserved for Soviet suicide squads.'

'Sure,' said the doctor, 'I'm just telling you what I diagnose. You'd better check the canisters out.'

'I'll check that lunatic Harah out too,' said Glaushof and hurried from the room. When he returned Wilt had assumed a foetal position and was fast asleep.

'AI Two,' Glaushof admitted lugubriously. 'What do we do now?'

'I've done what I can,' said the doctor, dispensing with two hypodermics. 'Loaded him with enough Antidote AI to keep him out of the official brain-death category . . .'

'Brain-death category? But I've got to interrogate the bastard. I can't have him cabbaging on me. He's some sort of infiltrating fucking agent and I got to find out where he's from.'

'Major Glaushof,' said the doctor wearily, 'it is now like zero three hundred hours and there's eight women, three men, one lieutenant and this . . .' he pointed at Wilt, 'and all of them suffering from nerve-gas toxicity and you think I can save any of them from chemically induced psychosis I'll do it but I'm not putting a suspected terrorist wearing a scrotal guard at the head of my list of priorities. If you want to interrogate him you'll have to wait. And pray. Oh yes, and if he doesn't come out of coma in eight hours let me know, maybe we can use him for spare-part surgery.'

'Hold it there, doctor,' he said. 'One word out of any of these people about there being—'

'Gassed?' said the doctor incredulously. 'I don't think you realize what you've done, Major. They're not going to remember a thing.'

'There being an agent here,' shouted Glaushof. 'Of course they've been gassed. Lieutenant Harah did that.'

'If you say so,' said the doctor. 'My business is physical welfare not base security and I guess you'll be able to explain Mrs Ofrey's condition to the General. Just don't call on me to say she and seven other women are naturally psychotic.'

Glaushof considered the implications of this request and found them decidedly awkward. On the other hand there was always Lieutenant Harah . . . 'Tell me, doc,' he said, 'just how sick is Harah?'

'About as sick as a man who's been kicked in the groin and inhaled AI Two can be,' said the doctor. 'And that's not taking his mental condition beforehand into account either. He should have been wearing one of these.' He held up the box.

Glaushof looked at it speculatively and then glanced at Wilt. 'What would a terrorist want with one of those things?' he asked.

'Could be he expected what Lieutenant Harah got,' said the doctor, and left the room.

Glaushof followed him into the next office and sent for Captain Clodiak. 'Take a seat, Captain,' he said. 'Now I want a breakdown of exactly what happened in there tonight.'

'What happened in there? You think I know? There's this maniac Harah . . .'

Glaushof held up a hand. 'I think you should know that Lieutenant Harah is an extremely sick man right now.'

'What's with the now?' said Clodiak. 'He always was. Sick in the head.'

'It's not his head I'm thinking about.'

Captain Clodiak chewed gum. 'So he's got balls where his brain should be. Do I care?'

'I'd advise you to,' said Glaushof. 'Assaulting a junior officer carries a very heavy penalty.'

'Yeah, well the same goes for sexually assaulting a senior one.'

'Could be,' said Glaushof, 'but I think you're going to have a hard time proving it.'

'Are you telling me I'm a liar?' demanded the Captain.

'No. Definitely not. I believe you but what I'm asking is, will anyone else?'

'I've got witnesses.'

'Had,' said Glaushof. 'From what the doctors tell me they're not going to be very reliable. In fact I'd go so far as to say they don't even come into the category of witnesses any longer. Agent Incapacitating does things to the memory. I think you ought to know that. And Lieutenant Harah's injuries have been medically documented. I don't think you're going to be in a position to dispute them. Doesn't mean you have to, but I'd advise you to co-operate with this department.'

Captain Clodiak studied his face. It wasn't a pleasant face but there was no disputing the fact that her situation wasn't one which allowed her too many options. 'What do you want me to do?' she asked.

'I want to hear what this Wilt said and all. In his lectures. Did he give any indications he was a communist?'

'Not that I knew,' said the Captain. 'I'd have reported it if he had.'

'So what did he say?'

'Mostly talked about things like parliament and voting patterns and how people in England see things.'

'See things?' said Glaushof, trying to think why an attractive woman like Ms Clodiak would want to go to lectures he'd have paid money to avoid. 'What sort of things?'

'Religion and marriage and . . . just things.'

At the end of an hour, Glaushof had learnt nothing.


## Chapter sixteen

Eva sat in the kitchen and looked at the clock again. It was five o'clock in the morning and she had been up since two indulging herself in the luxury of a great many emotions. Her first reaction when going to bed had been one of annoyance. 'He's been to the pub again and got drunk,' she had thought. 'Well, he won't get any sympathy from me if he has a hangover.' Then she had lain awake getting angrier by the minute until one o'clock when worry had taken over. It wasn't like Henry to stay out that late. Perhaps something had happened to him. She went over various possibilities, ranging from car crashes to his getting arrested for being drunk and disorderly, and finally worked herself up to the point where she knew that something terrible had been done to him at the prison. After all he was teaching that dreadful murderer

McCullum and when he'd come home on Monday night he'd been looking very peculiar. Of course he'd been drinking but all the same she remembered saying . . . No, that hadn't been Monday night because she'd been asleep when he got back. It must have been Tuesday morning. Yes, that was it. She'd said he looked peculiar and come to think of it what she really thought was that he had looked scared. And he'd said he'd left the car in a car park and when he'd come home in the evening he'd kept looking out the front window in the strangest way. He'd had an accident with the car too and while at the time she had just put that down to his usual absent-mindedness now that she came to think about it . . . At that point Eva had turned the light on and got out of bed. Something terrible had been going on and she hadn't even known it.

Which brought her round to anger again. Henry should have told her but he never did tell her really important things. He thought she was too stupid and perhaps she wasn't very clever when it came to arguing about books and saying the right things at parties but at least she was practical and nobody could say that the quads weren't getting a good education.

So the night passed. Eva sat in the kitchen and made cups of tea and worried and was angry and then blamed herself and wondered who to telephone and then decided it was best not to call anyone because they'd only be cross at being woken in the middle of the night and anyway there might be a perfectly natural explanation like the car had broken down or he'd gone to the Braintrees for a drink and had had to stay there because of the police and the breathalyser which would have been the sensible thing to do and so perhaps she ought to go back to bed and get some sleep . . . And always beside this bustle of conflicting thoughts and feelings there was the sense of guilt and the knowledge that she had been stupid to have listened to Mavis or to have gone anywhere near Dr Kores. Anyway, what did Mavis know about sex? She'd never really said what went on between her and Patrick in bed – it wasn't one of those things Eva would have dreamt of asking and even if she had Mavis wouldn't have told her – and all she'd ever heard was that Patrick was having affairs with other women. There might be good reasons for that too. Perhaps Mavis was frigid or wanted to be too dominant or masculine or wasn't very clean or something. Whatever the reason it was quite wrong of her to give Patrick those horrid steroid things or hormones and turn him into a sleepy fat person – well, you could hardly call him a man any longer could you? – who sat in front of the telly every night and couldn't get on with his work properly. Besides, Henry wasn't a bad husband. It was just that he was absent-minded and was always thinking about something or other that had no connection at all with what he was supposed to be doing. Like the time he'd been peeling the potatoes for Sunday lunch and he'd suddenly said the Vicar made Polonius sound like a bloody genius and there's no reason to say that because they hadn't been to church for two Sundays running and she'd wanted to know who Polonius was and he wasn't anyone at all, just some character in a play.

No, you couldn't expect Henry to be practical and she didn't. And of course they'd had their tiffs and disagreements, particularly about the quads. Why couldn't he see they were special? Well, he did, but not in the right way, and calling them 'clones' wasn't helpful. Eva could think of other things he'd said that weren't nice either. And then there was that dreadful business the other night with the cake icer. Goodness only knew what effect that had had on the girls' ideas about men. And that really was the trouble with Henry, he didn't know what romantic meant. Eva got up from the kitchen table and was presently calming her nerves by cleaning out the pantry. She was interrupted at six-thirty by Emmeline in her pyjamas.

'What are you doing?' she asked so unnecessarily that Eva rose to the bait.

'It's perfectly obvious,' she snapped. 'There's no need to ask stupid questions.'

'It wasn't obvious to Einstein,' said Emmeline, using the

well-tried technique of luring Eva into a topic about which she knew nothing but which she had to approve.

'What wasn't?'

'That the shortest distance between two points is a straight line.'

'Well it is, isn't it?' said Eva, moving a tin of Epicure marmalade from the shelf with pilchards and tuna fish on it to the jam section where it looked out of place.

'Of course it isn't. Everyone knows that. It's a curve. Where's Daddy?'

'I don't see how ... What do you mean "Where's Daddy?" ' said Eva, completely thrown by this leap from the inconceivable to the immediate.

'I was asking where he is,' said Emmeline. 'He's not in, is he?'

'No, he isn't,' said Eva, torn now between an inclination to give vent to her irritation and the need to keep calm. 'He's out.'

'Where's he gone?' asked Emmeline.

'He hasn't gone anywhere,' said Eva and moved the marmalade back to the pilchard shelf. Tins didn't look right among the jam-jars. 'He spent the night at the Braintrees.'

'I suppose he got drunk again,' said Emmeline. 'Do you think he's an alcoholic?'

Eva clutched a coffee jar dangerously. 'Don't you dare talk about your father like that!' she snapped. 'Of course he has a drink when he comes home at night. Nearly everyone does. It's quite normal and I won't have you saying things about your father.'

'You say things about him,' said Emmeline, 'I heard you call him—'

'Never mind what I say,' said Eva. 'That's quite different.'

'It isn't different,' Emmeline persisted, 'not when you say he's an alcoholic and anyway I was only asking a question and you're always telling us to—'

'Go up to your room at once,' said Eva. 'You're not speaking to me in that fashion. I won't have it.'

182

Emmeline retreated and Eva slumped down at the kitchen table again. It was really too trying of Henry not to have instilled some sense of respect in the quads. It was always left to her to be the disciplinarian. He should have more authority. She went back into the larder and saw to it that the packets and jars and tins did exactly what she wanted. By the time she had finished she felt a little better. Finally she chased the quads into dressing quickly.

'We'll have to catch the bus this morning,' she announced when they came in to breakfast. 'Daddy has the car and—'

'He hasn't,' said Penelope, 'Mrs Willoughby has.'

Eva, who had been pouring tea, spilt it. 'What did you say?'

Penelope looked smug. 'Mrs Willoughby has the car.'

'Mrs Willoughby? Yes, I know I've spilt some tea, Samantha. What do you mean, Penny? She can't have.'

'She has,' said Penelope looking smugger still. 'The milkman told me.'

'The milkman? He must have been mistaken,' said Eva.

'He isn't. He's scared stiff of the Hound of Oakhurst Avenue and he only delivers at the gate and that's where our car is. I went and saw it.'

'And was your father there?'

'No, it was empty.'

Eva put the teapot down unsteadily and tried to think what this meant. If Henry wasn't in the car . . .

'Perhaps Daddy's been eaten by the Hound,' suggested Josephine.

'The Hound doesn't eat people. It just tears their throats out and leaves their bodies on the waste ground at the bottom of the garden,' said Emmeline.

'It doesn't. It only barks. It's quite nice if you give it lamb chops and things,' said Samantha, unintentionally dragging Eva's attention away from the frightful possibility that Henry might in his drunken state have mistaken the house and ended up mauled to death by a Great Dane. And then again with Dr Kores' potion still coursing through his veins . . .

Penelope put the idea into words. 'He's more likely to have been eaten by Mrs Willoughby,' she said. 'Mr Gamer says she's sex-mad. I heard him tell Mrs Gamer that when she said she wanted it.'

'Wanted what?' demanded Eva, too stunned by this latest revelation to be concerned about the chops missing from the deep-freeze. She could deal with that matter later.

'The usual thing,' said Penelope with a look of distaste. 'She's always going on about it and Mr Gamer said she was getting just like Mrs Willoughby after Mr Willoughby died on the job and he wasn't going the same way.'

'That's not true,' said Eva in spite of herself.

'It is too,' said Penelope. 'Sammy heard him, didn't you?'

Samantha nodded.

'He was in the garage playing with himself like Paul in 3B does and we could hear ever so easily,' she said. 'And he's got lots of *Playboys* in there and books and she came in and said . . .'

'I don't want to hear,' said Eva, finally dragging her attention away from this fascinating topic. 'It's time to get your things on. I'll go and fetch the car . . .' She stopped. It was clearly one thing to say she was going to fetch the car from a neighbour's front garden, but just as clearly there were snags. If Henry was in Mrs Willoughby's house she'd never be able to live the scandal down. All the same something had to be done and it was a scandal enough already for the neighbours to see the Escort there. With the same determination with which Eva always dealt with embarrassing situations she put on her coat and marched out of the front door. Presently she was sitting in the Escort trying to start it. As usual when she was in a hurry the starter motor churned over and nothing happened. To be exact, something did but not what she had hoped. The front door opened and the Great Dane loped out followed by Mrs Willoughby in a dressing-gown. It was, in Eva's opinion, just the sort of dressing-gown a sex-mad widow would wear. Eva wound down the window to explain that she was just collecting the car and promptly wound it up again. Whatever Samantha's finer feelings might persuade her about the dog, Eva mistrusted it.

'I'm just going to take the girls to school,' she said by way of rather inadequate explanation.

Outside the Great Dane barked and Mrs Willoughby mouthed something that Eva couldn't hear. She wound the window down two inches. 'I said I'm just going to . . .' she began.

Ten minutes later, after an exceedingly acrimonious exchange in which Mrs Willoughby had challenged Eva's right to park in other people's drives and Eva had only been prevented by the presence of the Hound from demanding the right to search the house for her Henry and had been forced to confine herself to a moral critique of the dressing-gown, she drove the quads furiously to school. Only when they had left was Eva thrown back on her own worries. If Henry hadn't left the car at that awful woman's − and she really couldn't see him braving the Great Dane unless he'd been blind drunk and then he wouldn't have held much interest for Mrs Willoughby − someone else must have. Eva drove to the Braintrees and came away even more worried. Betty was sure Peter had said he hadn't seen Henry nearly all week. It was the same at the Tech. Wilt's office was empty and Mrs Bristol was adamant that he hadn't been in since Wednesday. Which left only the prison.

With a terrible sense of foreboding Eva used the phone in Wilt's office. By the time she put it down again panic had set in. Henry not at the prison since Monday? But he taught that murderer every Friday . . . He didn't. He never had. And he wasn't going to teach him on Mondays either now because Mac wasn't a burden on the state, as you might say. But he had given McCullum lessons on Friday. Oh no, he hadn't. Prisoners in that category couldn't have cosy little chats every night of the week, now could they? Yes, he was quite sure. Mr Wilt never came to the prison on Fridays.

Sitting alone in the office, Eva's reactions swung from panic to anger and back again. Henry had been deceiving her. He'd lied. Mavis was right, he had had another woman all the time. But he couldn't have. She'd have known. He couldn't keep a thing like that to himself. He wasn't practical or cunning enough. There'd have been something to tell her like hairs on his coat or lipstick or powder or something. And why? But before she could consider that question Mrs Bristol had poked her head round the door to ask if she'd like a cup of coffee. Eva braced herself to face reality. No one was going to have the satisfaction of seeing her break down.

'No thank you,' she said, 'it's very kind of you but I must be off.' And without allowing Mrs Bristol the opportunity to ask anything more Eva marched out and walked down the stairs with an air of deliberate fortitude. It had almost cracked by the time she had reached the car but she hung on until she had driven back to Oakhurst Avenue. Even then, with all the evidence of treachery around her in the shape of Henry's raincoat and the shoes he'd put out to polish and hadn't and his briefcase in the hall, she refused to give way to self-pity. Something was wrong. Something that proved Henry hadn't walked out on her. If only she could think.

It had something to do with the car. Henry would never have left it in Mrs Willoughby's drive. No, that wasn't it. It was . . . She dropped the car keys on the kitchen table and recognized their importance. They'd been in the car when she'd gone to fetch it and among them on the ring was the key to 45 Oakhurst Avenue. Henry had left her without any warning and without leaving a message but he had left the key to the house? Eva didn't believe it. Not for one moment. In that case her instinct had been right and something dreadful had happened to him. Eva put the kettle on and tried to think what to do.

'Listen, Ted,' said Flint. 'You play it the way you want. If you scratch my back I'll scratch yours. No problems. All I'm saying is—'

'If I scratch your back,' said Lingon, 'I won't have a fucking back to be scratched. Not one you'd want to scratch anyway, even if you could find it under some bloody motorway. Now would you mind just getting out of here?'

Inspector Flint settled himself in a chair and looked round the tiny office in the corner of the scruffy garage. Apart from a filing cabinet, the usual nudey calendar, a telephone and the desk, the only thing it contained of any interest to him was Mr Lingon. And in Flint's view Mr Lingon was a thing, a rather nasty thing, a squat, seedy and corrupt thing. 'Business good?' he asked with as little interest as possible. Outside the glass cubicle a mechanic was hosing down a Lingon Coach which claimed to be de luxe.

Mr Lingon grunted and lit a cigarette from the stub of his last one. 'It was till you turned up,' he said. 'Now do me a favour and leave me alone. I don't know what you're on about.'

'Smack,' said Flint.

'Smack? What's that supposed to mean?'

Flint ignored the question. 'How many years did you do last time?' he enquired.

'Oh Jesus,' said Lingon. 'I've been inside. Years ago. But you sods never let up, do you? Not you. A little bit of breaking and entering, someone gets done over two miles away. You name it, who do you come and see? Who's on record? Ted Lingon. Go and put the pressure on him. That's all you buggers can ever think of. No imagination.'

Flint shifted his attention from the mechanic and looked at Mr Lingon. 'Who needs imagination?' he said. 'A nice signed statement, witnessed and everything clean and above-board and no trade. Much better than imagination. Stands up in court.'

'Statement? What statement?' Mr Lingon was looking uneasy now.

'Don't you want to know who from first?'

'All right. Who?'

'Clive Swannell.'

'That old poove? You've got to be joking. He wouldn't—' He stopped suddenly. 'You're trying it on.'

Flint smiled confidently. 'How about the Rocker then?'

Lingon stubbed his cigarette out and said nothing.

'I've got it down in black and white. From the Rocker too. Adds up, doesn't it? Want me to go on?'

'I don't know what you're talking about, Inspector,' said Lingon. 'And now if you don't mind . . .'

'Next on the list,' said Flint, savouring the pressure, 'there's a nice little piece down Chingford called Annie Mosgrave. Fond of Pakis, she is. And Chinese threesomes. Sort of cosmopolitan, isn't she? But she writes a nice clean hand and she doesn't want some bloke with a meat cleaver coming round one night.'

'You're fucking lying. That's what you're doing,' said Lingon, shifting in his seat and fumbling with the cigarette packet.

Flint shrugged. 'Of course I am. I mean I would be. Stupid old copper like me's bound to lie. Specially when he's got signed statements locked away. And don't think I'm going to do you the favour of locking you away too, Teddie boy. No, I don't like drug buggers. Not one little bit.' He leant forward and smiled. 'No, I'm just going to attend the inquest. Your inquest, Teddie dear. I might even try to identify you. Difficult of course. It will be, won't it? No feet, no hands, teeth all wrenched out . . . that is if there is a head and they haven't burnt it after they've done the rest of what was you over. And they do take their time over it. Nasty really. Remember Chris down in Thurrock. Must have been a terrible way to die, bleeding like that. Tore his—'

'Shut up,' shouted Lingon, now ashen and shaking.

Flint got up. 'For now,' he said. 'But only for now. You don't want to do business: that's fine with me. I'll walk out of here and you won't be seeing me again. No, it'll be some bloke you don't even know comes in. Wants to hire a coach to take a party to Buxton. Money on the table, no hassle and the next fucking thing you know is you'll be wishing it had been me instead of one of Mac's mates with a pair of secateurs.'

'Mac's dead,' said Lingon almost in a whisper.

'So they tell me,' said Flint. 'But Roddie Eaton's still out and about and running things. Funny bloke, Roddie. Likes hurting people, according to my sources, specially when they've got enough knowledge to put him away for life and he can't be certain they won't talk.'

'That's not me,' said Lingon. 'I'm no squealer.'

'Want to bet on it? You'll be screaming your rotten little heart out before they've even begun,' said Flint and opened the door.

But Lingon signalled him back. 'I need guarantees,' he said. 'I got to have them.'

Flint shook his head. 'I told you. I'm a stupid old copper. I'm not selling the Queen's pardon. If you want to come and see me and tell me all about it, I'll be there. Till one o'clock.' He looked at his watch. 'You've got exactly one hour twelve minutes. After that you'd better shut up shop and buy yourself a shotgun. And it won't do you any good picking up that phone because I'll know. And the same if you leave here to use a call-box. And by five past one Roddie will know too.'

Flint walked out past the coach. The rotten little bastard would come. He was sure of that and everything was fitting nicely, or nastily, into place. And Hodge was screwed too. It was all very satisfactory and only went to prove what he had always said, that there was nothing like years of experience. It helped to have a son in prison for drug smuggling too, but Inspector Flint had no intention of mentioning his sources of information to the Superintendent when he made his report.

# Chapter seventeen

'An infiltrating agent?' boomed the Airforce General commanding Baconheath. 'Why wasn't I informed immediately?'

'Yes sir, that's a good question, sir,' said Glaushof.

'It is not, Major, it's a lousy question. It isn't even a question I should have to ask. I shouldn't have to ask any questions. In fact I'm not here to ask questions. I run a tight ship and I expect my men to answer their own questions.'

'And that's the way I took it, sir,' said Glaushof.

'Took what?'

'Took the situation, sir, faced with an infiltrating agent. I said to myself—'

'I am not interested in what you said to yourself, Major. I am only interested in results,' shouted the General. 'And I want to know what results you've achieved. By my count the results you've achieved amount to the gassing of ten Airforce personnel or their dependants.'

'Eleven, sir,' said Glaushof.

'Eleven? That's even worse.'

'Twelve with the agent Wilt, sir.'

'Then how come you just told me eleven?' demanded the General, toying with the model of a B52.

'Lieutenant Harah, sir, was gassed in the course of the action, sir, and I am proud to report that without his courage in the face of determined resistance by the enemy we could have encountered heavy casualties and possibly a hostage situation. Sir.'

General Belmonte put the B52 down and reached for a bottle of Scotch before remembering he was supposed to be in command of the situation. 'Nobody told me about a resistance situation,' he said rather more amicably.

'No, sir. It didn't seem advisable to issue a press release in the light of current opinion, sir,' said Glaushof. Having managed to avoid the General's questions he was prepared to apply more direct pressure. If there was one thing the Commander hated it was any mention of publicity. Glaushof mentioned it. 'As I see it, sir, the publicity—'

'Jesus, Glaushof,' shouted the General, 'how many times have I got to remind you there is to be no publicity? That is Directive Number One and comes from the highest authority. No publicity, dammit. You think we can defend the Free World against the enemy if we have publicity? I want that clearly understood. No publicity for Chrissake.'

'Understood, General,' said Glaushof. 'Which is why I've ordered a security blackout, a total no-traffic command to all information services. I mean if it got out we'd had an infiltration problem . . .'

He paused to allow the General to get his strength back for a further assault on publicity. It came in waves. When the bombardment had finished Glaushof produced his real target. 'If you'll permit me to say so, sir, I think we're going to be faced with an informational problem on the Intelligence side.'

'You do, do you? Well, let me tell you something, Major, and this is an order, a top priority directive order, that there is to a security blackout, a total no-traffic command to all information services. That is my order, you understand.'

'Yes, sir,' said Glaushof, 'I'll institute it immediately to the Intelligence Command. I mean if we had a leak to the press there . . .'

'Major Glaushof, that is an order I have given you. I want it instituted pre-immediate to all services.'

'Including Intelligence, sir?'

'Of course including Intelligence,' bawled the General. 'Our Intelligence services are the best in the world and I'm not jeopardizing standards of excellence by exposing them to media harassment. Is that clear?'

'Yessir,' said Glaushof and promptly left the office to order an armed guard to be placed on Intelligence HQ and to instruct all personnel to initiate a total no-traffic command. Since no one knew at all precisely what a no-traffic command was the various interpretations put on it ranged from a ban on all vehicles entering or leaving civilian quarters to a full alert on the airfield, the latter having been intermittently in force throughout the night thanks to wafts of Agent Incapacitating Two sounding off the toxic-weapon-detection sensors. By mid-morning the diverse rumours circulating were so manifestly at odds with one another that Glaushof felt safe enough to bawl his wife out over Lieutenant Harah's sexual insubordination before catching up on his sleep. He wanted to be in good shape to interrogate Wilt.

But when, two hours later, he arrived at the guarded room in the hospital Wilt was evidently in no mood to answer questions. 'Why don't you just go away and let me get some sleep?' he said blearily and turned on his side.

Glaushof glared at his back.

'Give him another shot,' he told the doctor.

'Give him another shot of what?'

'Whatever you gave him last night.'

'I wasn't on duty last night,' said the doctor. 'And anyhow who are you to tell me what to give him?'

Glaushof turned his attention away from Wilt's back and glared instead at the doctor. 'I'm Glaushof. Major Glaushof, doctor, just in case you haven't heard of me. And I'm ordering you to give this commie bastard something that'll jerk him out of that bed so I can question him.'

The doctor shrugged. 'If you say so, Major,' he said and studied Wilt's chart. 'What would you recommend?'

'Me?' said Glaushof. 'How the hell would I know? I'm not a goddam doctor.'

'So happens I am,' said the doctor, 'and I'm telling you I am not administering any further medication to this patient right now. The guy's been exposed to a toxic agent—'

He got no further. With a nasty grunt Glaushof shoved him through the doorway into the corridor. 'Now you just listen to me,' he snarled, 'I don't want to hear no crap about medical ethics. What we've got in there is a dangerous enemy agent and he doesn't even come into the category of a patient. Do you read me?'

'Sure,' said the doctor nervously. 'Sure, I read you. Loud and clear. So now will you take your hands off me?'

Glaushof let go of his coat. 'You just get something'll make the bastard talk and fast,' he said. 'We've got a security problem on our hands.'

'I'll say we have,' said the doctor and hurried away from it. Twenty minutes later a thoroughly confused Wilt was bundled out of the hospital building under a blanket and driven at high speed to Glaushof's office where he was placed on a chair. Glaushof had switched on the tape recorder. 'Okay, now you're going to tell us,' he said.

'Tell you what?' asked Wilt.

'Who sent you?' said Glaushof.

Wilt considered the question. As far as he could tell it didn't have much bearing on what was happening to him except that it had nothing whatsoever to do with reality. 'Sent me?' he said. 'Is that what you said?'

'That's what I said.'

'I thought it was,' said Wilt and relapsed into a meditative silence.

'So?' said Glaushof.

'So what?' asked Wilt, in an attempt to restore his morale slightly by combining insult with enquiry.

'So who sent you?'

Wilt sought inspiration in a portrait of President Eisenhower behind Glaushof's head and found a void. 'Sent me?' he said, and regretted it. Glaushof's expression contrasted unpleasantly with that of the late President. 'Nobody sent me.'

'Listen,' said Glaushof, 'this far you've had it easy. Doesn't mean it's going to stay that way. It could get very nasty. Now, are you going to talk or not?'

'I'm perfectly prepared to talk,' said Wilt, 'though I must say your definition of easy isn't mine. I mean being gassed and—'

'You want to hear my definition of nasty?' asked Glaushof.

'No,' said Wilt hastily, 'certainly not.'

'So talk.'

Wilt swallowed. 'Any particular subject you're interested in?' he enquired.

'Like who your contacts are,' said Glaushof.

'Contacts?' said Wilt.

'Who you're working for. And I don't want to hear any crap about teaching at the Fenland College Of Arts and Technology. I want to know who set this operation up.'

'Yes,' said Wilt, once more entering a mental maze and losing himself. 'Now when you say "this operation" I wonder if you'd mind . . .' He stopped. Glaushof was staring at him even more awfully than before. 'I mean I don't know what you're talking about.'

'You don't, huh?'

'I'm afraid not. I mean if I did—'

Glaushof shook a finger under Wilt's nose. 'A guy could die in here and nobody would know,' he said. 'If you want to go that way you've only to say so.'

'I don't,' said Wilt, trying to focus on the finger as a means of avoiding the prospect of his going any way. 'If you'd just ask me some questions I could answer . . .'

Glaushof backed off. 'Let's start with where you got the transmitters,' he said.

'Transmitters?' said Wilt. 'Did you say transmitters? What transmitters?'

'The ones in your car.'

'The ones in my car?' said Wilt. 'Are you sure?'

Glaushof gripped the edge of the desk behind him and thought wistfully about killing people. 'You think you can come in here, into United States territory and—'

'England,' said Wilt stolidly. 'To be precise the United Kingdom of England, Scotland—'

'Jesus,' said Glaushof, 'You little commie bastard, you have the nerve to talk about the Royal Family . . .'

'My own country,' said Wilt, finding strength in the assuredness that he was British. It was something he had never really thought much about before. 'And for your information, I am not a communist. Possibly a bastard, though I like to think otherwise. You have to ask my mother about that and she's been dead ten years. But definitely not a communist.'

'So what's with the radio transmitters in your car?'

'You said that before and I've no idea what you're talking about. Are you sure you're not mistaking me for someone else.'

'You're named Wilt, aren't you?' shouted Glaushof.

'Yes.'

'And you drive a beat-up Ford, registration plates HPR 791N, right?'

Wilt nodded. 'I suppose you could put it like that,' he said. 'Though frankly my wife—'

'You saying your wife put those transmitters in your car?'

'Good Lord no. She hasn't a clue about things like that. Anyway, what on earth would she want to do that for?'

'That's what you're here to tell me, boy,' said Glaushof. 'You ain't leaving till you do, you better believe it.'

Wilt looked at him and shook his head. 'I must say I find that difficult,' he muttered. 'I come here to give a lecture on British Culture, such as it is, and the next thing I know I'm in the middle of some sort of raid and there's gas all over the place and I wake up in a bed with doctors sticking needles into me and . . .'

He stopped. Glaushof had taken a revolver out of the desk drawer and was loading it. Wilt watched him apprehensively. 'Excuse me,' he said, 'but I'd be grateful if you'd put that . . . er . . . thing away. I don't know what you've got in mind but I can assure you I am not the person you should be talking to.'

'No? So who should that be, your controller?'

'Controller?' said Wilt.

'Controller,' said Glaushof.

'That's what I thought you said, though to be perfectly honest I still don't see that it helps very much. I don't even know what a controller is.'

'Then you better start inventing one. Like the guy in Moscow who tells you what to do.'

'Look,' said Wilt, desperately trying to get back to some sort of reality which didn't include controllers in Moscow who told him what to do, 'there's obviously been some terrible mistake.'

'Yeah, and you made it coming in here with that equipment. I'm going to give you one last chance,' said Glaushof, looking along the barrel of the gun with a significance Wilt found deeply alarming. 'Either you spell it out like it is or . . .'

'Quite,' said Wilt. 'Point taken, to use a ghastly expression. What do you want me to tell you?'

'The whole deal. How you were recruited, who you contact and where, what information you've given . . .'

Wilt stared miserably out the window as the list rolled on. He had never supposed the world to be a particularly sensible place and airbases were particularly nonsensical, but to be taken for a Soviet spy by a lunatic American who played with revolvers was to enter a new realm of insanity. Perhaps that's what had happened. He'd gone clean out of his tiny. No, he hadn't. The gun was proof of some kind of reality, one that was taken for granted by millions of people all over the world but which had somehow never come anywhere near Oakhurst Avenue or the Tech or Ipford. In a sense his own little world with its fundamental beliefs in education and books and, for want of a better word, sensibility, was the unreal one, a dream which no one could ever hope to live in for long. Or at all, if this madman with his cliché talk of guys dying in here and nobody knowing had his way. Wilt turned back and made one last attempt to regain the world he knew.

'All right,' he said, 'if you want the facts I'll give them to you but only with men from MI5 present. As a British subject I demand that right.'

Glaushof snorted. 'Your rights ended the moment you passed that guardhouse,' he said. 'You're telling me what you know. I'm not playing footsy with a lot of suspect faggots from British Intelligence. No way. Now talk.'

'If it's all the same to you I think it would be better written down,' said Wilt, playing for time and trying frantically to think what he could possibly confess. 'I mean, all I need is a pen and some sheets of paper.'

For a moment Glaushof hesitated before deciding that there was something to be said for a confession written out in Wilt's own hand. That way no one could say he'd beaten it out of the little bastard. 'Okay,' he said. 'You can use the table.'

Three hours later Wilt had finished and six pages were covered with his neat and practically illegible hand-writing. Glaushof took them and tried to read. 'What you trying to do? Didn't anybody ever teach you to write properly?'

Wilt shook his head wearily. 'If you can't read, take it to someone who can. I've had it,' he said and put his head on his arms on the table. Glaushof looked at his white face and had to agree. He wasn't feeling too good himself. But at least Colonel Urwin and the idiots in Intelligence were going to feel worse. With a fresh surge of energy he went into the office next door, made photocopies of the pages and was presently marching past the guards outside communications. 'I want transcripts made of these,' he told the head of the typists' pool. 'And absolute security.' Then he sat down and waited.

## Chapter eighteen

'A warrant? A search warrant for 45 Oakhurst Avenue? You want to apply for a search warrant?' said the Super-intendent.

'Yes, sir,' said Inspector Hodge, wondering why it was that what seemed like a perfectly reasonable request to him should need querying quite so repetitively. 'All the evidence indicates the Wilts to be carriers.'

'I'm not sure the magistrate is going to agree,' said the Superintendent. 'Circumstantial evidence is all it amounts to.'

'Nothing circumstantial about Wilt going out to that airbase and giving us the run-around, and I wouldn't say her going to that herb farm was circumstantial either. It's all there in my report.'

'Yes,' said the Superintendent, managing to imbue the word with doubt. 'What's not there is one shred of hard evidence.'

'That's why we need the search, sir,' said Hodge. 'There've got to be traces of the stuff in the house. Stands to reason.'

'If he's what you say he is,' said the Superintendent.

'Look,' said Hodge, 'he knew he was being tailed when he went out to Baconheath. He had to know. Drives around in circles for half an hour when he comes out and gives us the slip—'

'And that's another thing,' interrupted the Superintendent, 'your bugging the blighter's car without authorization. I consider that highly reprehensible. I want that understood clearly right now. Anyway, he may have been drunk.'

'Drunk?' said Hodge, finding it difficult to make the transition between unauthorized bugging being reprehensible, which in his opinion it wasn't, and Wilt being drunk.

'When he came out of Baconheath. Didn't know whether he was coming or going and went round in circles. Those Yanks drink rye. Sickly muck but it goes down so easily you don't notice.'

Inspector Hodge considered the suggestion and rejected it. 'I don't see how a drunk could drive that fast, not on those roads without killing himself. And choosing a route that'd take him out of radio contact.'

The Superintendent studied the report again. It didn't make comfortable reading. On the other hand there was something in what Hodge had said. 'If he wasn't pissed why leave the car outside someone else's house?' he asked but Hodge had already concocted an answer to that one.

'Shows how clever the little bastard is,' he said. 'Not giving anything away, that bloke. He knows we're onto him and he needs an explanation for all that run-around he's given us so he plays pissed.'

'If he's that bloody clever you're not going to find anything in his house and that's for sure,' said the Superintendent and shook his head. 'No, he'd never have the stuff on his own doorstep. He'd have it stored somewhere miles away.'

'He's still got to move it,' said Hodge, 'and that means the car. Look, sir, Wilt's the one who goes to the airbase, he collects the stuff there and on the way home he hands it over to a third party who distributes it. That explains why he took such pains to lose us. There was a whole twenty minutes when we weren't picking up any signals. That could have been when he was offloading.'

'Could have been,' said the Superintendent, impressed in spite of himself. 'Still, that only goes to prove my point. You go for a search warrant for his house you're going to end up with egg all over your face. More important, so am I. So that's out. You'll have to think of some other way.'

Hodge returned to his office and took it out on Sergeant Runk. 'The way they carry on it's a bloody wonder we ever nick any bugger. And you had to go and sign for those fucking transmitters . . .'

'You don't think they give them out without being signed for,' said Runk.

'You didn't have to land me in the shit by putting "Authorized by Superintendent Wilkinson for covert surveillance." He loved that.'

'Well, wasn't it? I mean I thought you'd got permission . . .'

'Oh no, you didn't. We pulled that stroke in the middle of the night and he'd been home since five. And now we've got to retrieve the bloody things. That's something you can do tonight.'

And having, as he hoped, ensured that the Sergeant would spend the day regretting his indiscretion, the Inspector got up and stared out of the window for inspiration. If he couldn't get a search warrant ... He was still pondering the question when his attention was distracted by a car parked down below. It looked hideously familiar.

The Wilts' Escort. What the hell was it doing outside the police station?

Eva sat in Flint's office and held back the tears. 'I didn't know who else to come to,' she said. 'I've been to the Tech and phoned the prison and Mrs Braintree hasn't seen him and he usually goes there if he's ... well, if he wants a change. But he hasn't been there or the hospital or anywhere else I can think of and I know you don't like him or anything but you are a policeman and you have been ... helpful in the past. And you do know Henry.' She stopped and looked appealingly at the Inspector.

It wasn't a look that held much appeal for Flint and he certainly didn't like the notion that he knew Wilt. He'd tried to understand the blighter, but even at his most optimistic he'd never supposed for one moment that he'd got anywhere near fathoming the horrible depths of Wilt's extraordinary character. The sod came into the category of an enigma made all the more impossible to understand by his choice of Eva as a wife. It was a relationship Flint had always preferred not to think about, but here she was sitting foursquare on a chair in his office telling him, evidently without the slightest regard for his feelings, even as though it were some sort of compliment, that he knew her Henry. 'Has he ever gone off like this before?' he asked, with the private thought that in Wilt's shoes he'd have been off like a flash – before the wedding.

'No, never,' said Eva, 'that's what's so worrying. I

know you think he's . . . peculiar, but he's really been a good husband.'

'I'm sure he has,' said Flint for want of anything more reassuring to say. 'You don't think he's suffering from amnesia.'

'Amnesia?'

'Loss of memory,' said Flint. 'It hits people who've been under strain. Has anything been happening lately that might have caused him to flip . . . to have a nervous breakdown?'

'I can't think of anything in particular,' said Eva, determined to keep any mention of Dr Kores and that dreadful tonic out of the conversation. 'Of course the children get on his nerves sometimes and there was that horrible business at the Tech the other day with that girl'dying. Henry was ever so upset. And he's been teaching at the prison . . .' She stopped again as she remembered what had been really worrying her. 'He's been teaching a dreadful man called McCullum on Monday evenings and Fridays. That's what he told me anyway, only when I phoned the prison they said he never had.'

'Had what?' asked Flint.

'Never been there on Fridays,' said Eva, tears welling up in her eyes at this proof that Henry, her Henry, had lied to her.

'But he went out every Friday and that's where he told you he was going?'

Eva nodded dumbly and for a moment Flint almost felt sorry for her. A fat middle-aged woman with four bloody tear-away kids who turned the house into a blooming bearpit and she hadn't known what Wilt was up to? Talk about being as thick as two short planks. Well, it was about time she learnt. 'Look, Mrs Wilt, I know this isn't easy to . . .' he began but to his amazement Eva was there before him.

'I know what you're going to say,' she interrupted, 'but it isn't true. If it had been another woman why did he leave the car in Mrs Willoughby's?'

'Leave the car in Mrs Willoughby's? Who's Mrs Willoughby?'

'She lives at Number 65, and that's where the car was this morning. I had to go and get it. Why would he want to do that?'

It was on the tip of Flint's tongue to say that's what he'd have done in Wilt's place, dump the car down the road and run like hell, when something else occurred to him.

'You wait here,' he said and left the room. In the corridor he hesitated for a moment and tried to think who to ask. He certainly wasn't approaching Hodge but there was always Sergeant Runk. And Yates could find out for him. He turned into the open-plan office where the Sergeant was sitting at a typewriter.

'Got an enquiry for you, Yates,' he said. 'Have a word with your mate Runk and find out where they tailed Wilt last night. I've got his missus in my office. And don't let him know I'm interested, understand? Just a casual enquiry on your part.' He sat on the edge of the desk while Yates was gone five minutes.

'Right balls-up,' said the Sergeant when he returned. 'They followed the little bugger out to Baconheath airbase with a radio tail. He's in there an hour and a half and comes out driving like a maniac. Runkie reckons Wilt knew they were on to him, the way he drove. Anyway they lost him, and when they did find the car it was outside some house down the road from the Wilts' with a fucking big dog trying to tear the front door down to get at Hodge. That's about the strength of it.'

Flint nodded, and kept his excitement to himself. He'd already done enough to make Hodge look the fucking idiot he was; he'd broken the Bull and Clive Swannell and that little shit Lingon, signed statements and all; and all the time Hodge had been harrying Wilt. So why drop him in it any further?

Why not? The deeper the bugger sank the less he'd be likely to surface. And not only Hodge but Wilt too. The bastard had been the original cause of all Flint's misfortunes and to be able to drag him through the mire together with Hodge was justice at its most perfect. Besides, Flint still had to make the catch with Lingon, so a diversion was just what he needed. And if ever there was a diversion ready to hand it was sitting in his office in the shape of Mrs Eva Wilt. The only problem was how to point her in Hodge's direction without anyone learning what he had done. It was a risk he had to take. He'd better check first, though. Flint went to a phone and looked up the Baconheath number.

'Inspector Hodge speaking,' he said, slurring the name so that it might well have been Squash or Hedge, 'I'm calling from Ipford Police Station in connection with a Mr Wilt ... A Mr Henry Wilt of 45 Oakhurst Avenue, Ipford. I understand he visited you last night.' He waited while someone said he'd check.

It took a long time and another American came on the line. 'You enquiring about someone called Wilt?' he asked.

'That's correct,' said Flint.

'And you say you're police?'

'Yes,' said Flint, noting the hesitancy in the questioner with intense interest.

'If you'll give me your name and the number to call I'll get back to you,' said the American. Flint put the phone down quietly. He'd learnt what he needed and he wasn't having any Yank check his credentials.

He went back to his office and sat down with a calculated sigh. 'I'm afraid you're not going to like what I'm going to tell you, Mrs Wilt,' he said.

Eva didn't. She left the police station white-faced with fury. Not only had Henry lied to her but he'd been cheating her for months and she hadn't had an inkling.

Behind her Flint sat on in his office staring almost ecstatically at a wall-map of Ipford. Henry Wilt, Henry Bloody Wilt, was going to get his comeuppance this time. And he was out there somewhere, somewhere in one of those little streets, holed up with a dolly bird who must have money or he would be back at his job at the Tech.

No, he wouldn't. Not with Eva in pursuit. No wonder

the bugger had left the car down the road. If he'd any sense he'd have left town by now. The bloody woman would murder him. Flint smiled at the thought. Now that *would* be poetic justice, no mistake.

'It's more than my life's worth. I mean I'd do it, I'd happily do it but what if it gets out?' said Mr Gamer.

'It won't,' said Hodge, 'I can give you a solemn assurance on that. You won't even know they're there.'

Mr Gamer looked mournfully round the restaurant. He usually had sandwiches and a cup of coffee for lunch and he wasn't sure how well Boneless Chicken Curry washed down with a bottle of Blue Nun was going to agree with him. Still, the Inspector was paying and he could always get some Solvol on the way back to the shop. 'It's not just me either, it's the wife. If you knew what that woman has been through these last twelve months you wouldn't believe me. You really wouldn't.'

'I would,' said Hodge. If it was anything like what he'd been through in the last four days, Mrs Gamer must be a woman with an iron constitution.

'It's even worse in the school holidays,' Mr Gamer continued. 'Those fucking girls . . . I don't usually swear but there's a point where you've got to . . . I mean you can't begin to know how awful they are.' He stopped and looked closely into Hodge's face. 'One of these days they're going to kill someone,' he whispered. 'They bloody near did for me on Tuesday. I'd have been as dead as a dodo if I hadn't been wearing rubber-soled shoes. Stole my statue from the garden and when I went round to get it . . .'

Hodge listened sympathetically. 'Criminal,' he said. 'You should have reported it to us straight away. Even now if you made a formal complaint . . .'

'You think I'd dare? Never. If it meant having them all carted off to prison straightaway I might but it doesn't work like that. They'd come home from court and . . . it doesn't bear thinking about. Take that poor sod down the road, Councillor Birkenshaw. He had his name up in lights on a french letter with a foreskin on it. Floated right down the street it did and than they went and accused him of showing his privates to them. He had a horrible time trying to prove he hadn't. And look where he is. In hospital. No, it's not worth the risk.'

'I can see what you mean,' said Hodge. 'But this way they wouldn't ever find out. All we need is your permission to—'

'I blame the bloody mother,' Mr Gamer went on, encouraged by the Blue Nun and the Inspector's apparent sympathy. 'If she didn't encourage the little bitches to be like boys and take an interest in mechanical things it'd help. But no, they've got to be inventors and geniuses. Mind you, it takes some sort of genius to do what they did to Dickens' lawnmower. Brand new, it was, and God knows what exactly they did to it. Supercharged it with a camping-gas cylinder and altered the gear ratio too so it went like the clappers. And it's not as though he's a well man. Anyway, he started the bloody thing up and before he could stop it was off down the lawn at about eighty and mowing their new carpet in the lounge. Smashed the piano too, come to think of it. They had to call the fire brigade to put it out.'

'Why didn't he sue the parents?' asked Hodge, fascinated in spite of himself.

Mr Gamer sighed. 'You don't understand,' he said. 'You have to live through it to understand. You don't think they admit what they've done? Of course they don't. And who's going to believe old Dickens when he says four ruddy girls that age could change the sprocket on the driveshaft and superglue the clutch? No one. Mind if I help myself.'

Hodge poured another glass. Clearly Mr Gamer was a broken man. 'All right,' he said. 'Now supposing you know nothing about it. Just suppose a man from the Gas Board comes to check the meter—'

'And that's another thing,' said Mr Gamer almost dementedly, 'gas. The bill! Four hundred and fifty fucking pounds for a summer quarter! You don't believe me, do you? I didn't believe it either. Had that meter changed and checked and it still came to the same. I still don't know how they did it. Must have been while we were on holiday. If only I could find out!'

'Look,' said Hodge, 'you let my man install the equipment and you've a very good chance of getting rid of the Wilts for ever. And I mean that. For ever.'

Mr Gamer gazed into his glass and considered this glorious prospect. 'For ever?'

'For ever.'

'Done,' said Mr Gamer.

Later that afternoon Sergeant Runk, feeling distinctly uncomfortable in a Gas Board uniform, and with Mrs Gamer asking pitifully what could possibly be wrong with the chimney because they'd had it lined when the central heating was put in, was up in the roof space. By the time he left he had managed to feed microphones through a gap in the bricks so that they lay hidden among the insulating chips above the Wilts' bedrooms. 45 Oakhurst Avenue had been wired for sound.

# Chapter nineteen

'I think we've got one hell of a problem, sir,' said the Corporal. 'Major Glaushof ordered me to ditch the car back at the Wilt guy's house and I did. All I can say is those transmitters weren't civilian. I had a good look at them and they were hi-tech British.'

Colonel Urwin, Senior Intelligence Officer USAF Baconheath, pondered the problem by looking coolly at a sporting print on the wall. It wasn't a very good one but its depiction of a fox in the far distance, being chased by a motley crowd of thin, fat, pale, or red-faced Englishmen on horseback, always served to remind him that it was as well not to underestimate the British. Better still, it paid to seem to be one of them. To that end he played golf with an ancient set of clubs and spent his idler moments tracing his family tree in the archives of various universities and the graveyards of Lincolnshire churches. In short, he kept an almost subterranean profile and was proud of the fact that he had on several occasions been taken for a master from one of the better public schools. It was a rôle that suited him exactly and fitted in with his professional creed that discretion was the better part of valour.

'British?' he said thoughtfully. 'That could mean anything or nothing. And you say Major Glaushof has put down a security clamp?'

'General Belmonte's orders, sir.'

The Colonel said nothing. In his opinion the Base Commander's IQ was only slightly higher than that of the egregious Glaushof. Anyone who could call four no trumps without a diamond in his hand had to be a cretin. 'So the situation is that Glaushof has this man Wilt in custody and is presumably torturing him and no one is supposed to know he's here. The operative word being "supposed". Obviously whoever sent him knows he never returned to Ipford.'

'Yes, sir,' said the Corporal. 'And the Major's been trying to get a message on line to Washington.'

'See it's coded garbage,' said the Colonel, 'and get a copy to me.'

'Yes, sir,' said the Corporal and disappeared.

Colonel Urwin looked across at his deputy. 'Seems we could have a hornet's nest,' he said. 'What do you make of it?'

Captain Fortune shrugged. 'Could be any number of options,' he said. 'I don't like the sound of that hardware.'

'Kamikaze,' said the Colonel. 'No one would come in transmitting.'

'Libyans or Khomeini might.'

Colonel Urwin shook his head. 'No way. When they hit they don't signal their punches. They'd come in loaded with explosives first time. So who's scoring?'

'The Brits?'

'That's my line of thinking,' said the Colonel, and wandered across to take a closer look at the sporting print. 'The only question is who are they hunting, Mr Henry Wilt or us?'

'I've checked our records and there's nothing on Wilt. CND in the sixties, otherwise non-political.'

'University?'

'Yes,' said the Captain.

'Which one?'

The Captain consulted the computer file. 'Cambridge. Majored in English.'

'Otherwise, nothing?'

'Nothing we know of. British Intelligence would know.'

'And we're not asking,' said the Colonel, coming to a decision. 'If Glaushof wants to play Lone Ranger with the General's consent he's welcome to the fan-shit. We stay clear and come up with the real answer when it's needed.'

'I still don't like that hardware in the car,' said the Captain.

'And I don't like Glaushof,' said the Colonel. 'I have an idea the Ofreys don't either. Let him dig his own grave.' He paused. 'Is there anyone with any intelligence who knows what really happened, apart from that Corporal?'

'Captain Clodiak filed a complaint against Harah for sexual harassment. And she's on the list of students attending Wilt's lectures.'

'Right, we'll start digging back into this fiasco there,' said the Colonel.

'Let's get back to this Radek,' said Glaushof, 'I want to know who he is.'

'I've told you, a Czech writer and he's been dead since God knows when so there is no way I could have met him,' said Wilt.

'If you're lying you will. Shortly,' said Glaushof. Having read the transcripts of Wilt's confession that he had been recruited by a KGB agent called Yuri Orlov and had a contact man called Karl Radek, Glaushof was now determined to find out exactly what information Wilt had passed to the Russians. Understandably it was proving decidedly harder than getting Wilt to admit he was an agent. Twice Glaushof had used the threat of instant death, but without any useful result. Wilt had asked for time to think and had then come up with H-bombs. 'H-bombs? You've been telling this bastard Radek we've got H-bombs stashed here?'

'Yes,' said Wilt.

'They know that already.'

'That's what Radek said. He said they wanted more than that.'

'So what did you give him, the BBs?'

'BBs?' said Wilt. 'You mean airguns?'

'Binary bombs.'

'Never heard of them.'

'Safest nerve-gas bombs in the world,' said Glaushof proudly. 'We could kill every living fucking thing from Moscow to Peking with BBs and they wouldn't even know a thing.'

'Really?' said Wilt. 'I must say I find your definition of safe peculiar. What are the dangerous ones capable of?'

'Shit,' said Glaushof, wishing he was somewhere under-developed like El Salvador and could use more forceful methods. 'You don't talk you're going to regret you ever met me.'

Wilt studied the Major critically. With each unfulfilled threat he was gaining more confidence but it still seemed inadvisable to point out that he already regretted meeting the bloody man. Best to keep things cool. 'I'm only telling you what you want to know,' he said.

'And you didn't give them any other information?'

'I don't know any. Ask the students in my class. They'll tell you I wouldn't know a bomb from a banana.'

'So you say,' muttered Glaushof. He'd already questioned the students and, in the case of Mrs Ofrey, had learnt more about her opinion of him than about Wilt. And Captain Clodiak hadn't been helpful either. The only evidence she'd been able to produce that Wilt was a communist had been his insistence that the National Health Service was a good thing. And so by degrees of inconsequentiality they had come full circle back to this KGB man Radek whom Wilt had claimed was his contact and now said was a Czech writer and dead at that. And with each hour Glaushof's chances of promoting himself were slipping away. There had to be some way of getting the information he needed. He was just wondering if there wasn't some truth drug he could use when he caught sight of the scrotal guard on his desk. 'How come you were wearing this?' he asked.

Wilt looked at the cricket box bitterly. The events of the previous evening seemed strangely distant in these new and more frightening circumstances but there had been a moment when he had supposed the box to be in some way responsible for his predicament. If it hadn't come undone, he wouldn't have been in the loo and . . .

'I was having trouble with a hernia,' he said. It seemed a safe explanation.

It wasn't. Glaushof's mind had turned grossly to sex.

Eva's was already there. Ever since she had left Flint she had been obsessed with it. Henry, her Henry, had left her for another woman and an American airbase slut at that. And there could be no doubt about it. Inspector Flint hadn't told her in any nasty way. He'd simply said that Henry had been out to Baconheath. He didn't have to say any more. Henry had been going out every Friday night telling her he was going to the prison and all the time . . . No, she wasn't going to give way. With a sense of terrible purpose Eva drove to Canton Street. Mavis had been right after all and Mavis had known how to deal with Patrick's infidelities. Best of all, as secretary of Mothers Against The Bomb she hated the Americans at Baconheath. Mavis would know what to do.

Mavis did. But first she had to have her gloat. 'You wouldn't listen to me, Eva,' she said. 'I've always said there was something seedy and deceitful about Henry but you would have it that he was a good, faithful husband. Though after what he tried to do to me the other morning I don't see how . . .'

'I'm sorry,' said Eva, 'but I thought that was my fault for going to Dr Kores and giving him that . . . Oh dear, you don't think that's what's made him do this?'

'No, I don't,' said Mavis, 'not for one moment. If he's been deceiving you for six months with this woman, Dr Kores' herbal mixture had nothing to do with it. Of course he'll try to use that as an excuse when it comes to the divorce.'

'But I don't want a divorce,' said Eva, 'I just want to lay my hands on that woman.'

'In that case, if you're going to be a sexual helot—'

'A what?' said Eva, appalled at the word.

'Slave, dear,' said Mavis, recognizing her mistake, 'a serf, a skivvy who's just there to do the cooking and cleaning.'

Eva subsided. All she wanted to be was a good wife and mother and bring the girls up to take their rightful place in the technological world. At the top. 'But I don't even know the beastly woman's name,' she said, getting back to practicalities.

Mavis applied her mind to the problem. 'Bill Paisley might know,' she said finally. 'He's been teaching out there and he's at the Open University with Patrick. I'll give him a ring.'

Eva sat on in the kitchen, sunk in apparent lethargy. But underneath she was tensing herself for the confrontation. No matter what Mavis said no one was going to take Henry away from her. The quads were going to have a father and a proper home and the best education Wilt's salary could provide, never mind what people said or how much her own pride was hurt. Pride was a sin and anyway Henry would pay for it.

She was going over in her mind what she would say to him when Mavis returned triumphantly. 'Bill Paisley knows all about it,' she said. 'Apparently Henry has been teaching a class of women British Culture and it doesn't take much imagination to see what's happened.' She looked at a scrap of paper. 'The Development of British Culture and Institutions, Lecture Hall 9. And the person to contact is the Education Officer. He's given me the number to call. If you want me to, I'll do it for you.'

Eva nodded gratefully. 'I'd only lose my temper and get agitated,' she said, 'and you're so good at organizing things.'

Mavis went back to the hall. For the next ten minutes Eva could hear her talking with increasing vehemence. Then the phone was slammed down.

'The nerve of the man,' Mavis said, storming back into the kitchen pale-faced with anger. 'First they wouldn't put me through to him and it was only when I said I was from the Library Service and wanted to speak to the Education Officer about the free supply of books that I got to him. And then it was "No comment, ma'am. I'm sorry but no comment." '

'But you did ask about Henry?' said Eva who couldn't see what the Library Service or the free supply of books could possibly have to do with her problem.

'Of course I did,' snapped Mavis. 'I said Mr Wilt had suggested I contact him about the Library Service supplying books on English Culture and that's when he clammed up.' She paused thoughtfully. 'You know I could almost swear he sounded scared.'

'Scared? Why should he be scared?'

'I don't know. It was when I mentioned the name "Wilt",' said Mavis. 'But we're going to drive out there now and find out.'

Captain Clodiak sat in Colonel Urwin's office. Unlike the other buildings at Baconheath which had been inherited from the RAF or which resembled prefabricated and sub-economic housing estates, Intelligence Headquarters was strangely at odds with the military nature of the base. It was in fact a large red-brick mansion built at the turn of the century by a retired mining engineer with a taste for theatrical Tudor, and eye to the value of black fen soil and a dislike for the icy winds that blew from Siberia. As a consequence the house had a mock baronial hall, oak-panelled walls and a highly efficient central-heating system and accorded perfectly with Colonel Urwin's sense of irony. It also set him apart from the rest of the base and lent weight to his conviction that military men were dangerous idiots and incapable of speaking E. B. White's English. What was needed was intelligence, brains as well as brawn. Captain Clodiak seemed endowed with both. Colonel Urwin listened to her account of Wilt's capture with very close interest. It was forcing him to reassess the situation. 'So you're saying that he definitely seemed uneasy right through the lecture?' he said.

'No question,' said Clodiak. 'He kept squirming behind the lecturn like he was in pain. And his lecture was all over the place. Incoherent. Usually he takes off on tangents but he comes back to the main theme. This time he rambled and then this bandage came down his leg and he went to pieces.'

The Colonel looked across at Captain Fortune. 'Do we know anything about the need for bandages?'

'I've checked with the medics and they don't know. The guy came in gassed and no other sign of injuries.'

'Let's go back from there to previous behaviour. Anything unusual?' Captain Clodiak shook her head.

'Nothing I noticed. He's hetero, got nice manners, doesn't make passes, he's probably got some hang-ups, like he's a depressive. Nothing I'd class as unusual in an Englishman.'

'And yet he was definitely uneasy? And there's no question about the bandage?'

'None,' said Clodiak.

'Thank you for your help,' said the Colonel. 'If anything else comes to mind come back to us.' And having seen her out into the passage he turned to look at the sporting print for inspiration. 'It begins to sound as though someone's been leaning on him,' he said finally.

'You can bet your life Glaushof has,' said Fortune. 'A guy who confesses that easy has to have had some treatment.'

'What's he confessed to? Nothing. Absolute zero.'

'He's admitted being recruited by this Orlov and having a contact man in a Karl Radek. I wouldn't say that was nothing.'

'The one being a dissident who's doing time in Siberia,' said Urwin, 'and Karl Radek was a Czech writer who died in a Gulag in 1940. Not the easiest man to contact.'

'They could be cover names.'

'Could be. Just. I'd choose something less obviously phoney myself. And why Russians? If they're from the Embassy . . . yes, I suppose so. Except that he met quote Orlov unquote in the bus station in Ipford which is outside Soviet embassy staff permitted radius. And where does he meet friend Radek? Every Wednesday afternoon by the bowling green on Midway Park. Every Wednesday same place same time? Out of the question. Our friends from the KGB may play dumb occasionally but not that dumb. Glaushof's been dealt the hand he asked for and that doesn't happen by accident.'

'Leaves Glaushof up shit creek,' said Fortune.

But Colonel Urwin wasn't satisfied. 'Leaves us all there if we don't take care,' he said. 'Let's go through the options again. Wilt's a genuine Russian probe? Out for the reasons given. Someone running a check on our security? Could be some goon in Washington came up with the idea. They've got Shi'ite suicide squads on the brain. Why use an Englishman? They don't tell him his car's being used to make the test more effective. If so why's he panicking during the lecture? That's what I get back to, his behaviour in that lecture hall. That's where I really begin to pick up the scent. Go from there to this "confession" which only an illiterate like Glaushof would believe and the state of Denmark really is beginning to stink to high heaven. And Glaushof's handling it? Not any more Ed. I'm pulling rank.'

'How? He's got a security blanket from the General.'

'That's where I'm pulling rank,' said the Colonel. 'Old B52 may think he commands this base but I'm going to have to disillusion the old warrior. About a great many things.' He pressed a button on the phone. 'Get me Central Intelligence,' he said.

## Chapter twenty

'Orders are no one in,' said the guard on the gate, 'I'm sorry but that's how it is.'

'Look,' said Mavis, 'all we've come to do is speak to the officer in charge of Education. His name is Bluejohn and—'

'Still applies, no one in.'

Mavis took a deep breath and tried to keep calm. 'In that case I'd like to speak to him here,' she said. 'If we can't come in, perhaps he'd be good enough to come out.'

'I can check,' said the guard and went into the gatehouse.

'It's no use,' said Eva, looking at the barrier and the high barbed-wire fence. Behind the barrier a series of drums filled with concrete had been laid out on the roadway to form a zigzag through which vehicles could only wind their way very slowly. 'They're not going to tell us anything.'

'And I want to know why,' said Mavis.

'It might help if you weren't wearing that Mothers Against The Bomb badge,' said Eva.

Mavis took it off reluctantly. 'It's utterly disgusting,' she said. 'This is supposed to be a free country and—'

She was interrupted by the appearance of a lieutenant. He stood in the doorway of the gatehouse and looked at them for a moment before walking over. 'I'm sorry ladies,' he said, 'but we're running a security exercise. It's only temporary so if you come back tomorrow maybe . . .'

'Tomorrow is no good,' said Mavis. 'We want to see Mr Bluejohn today. Now if you'll be good enough to telephone him or give him a message, we'd be most obliged.'

'Sure, I can do that,' said the Lieutenant. 'What do you want me to say?'

'Just that Mrs Wilt is here and would like to make some enquiries about her husband, Mr Henry Wilt. He's been teaching a class here on British Culture.'

'Oh him, Mr Wilt? I've heard of him from Captain Clodiak,' said the Lieutenant, expansively. 'She's been attending his course and she says he's real good. No problem, I'll check with the EO.'

'What did I tell you?' said Mavis as he went back into the guardhouse. '*She* says he's real good. I wonder what your Henry's being so good at now.'

Eva hardly heard. Any lingering doubt that Henry had been deceiving her had gone and she was staring through the wire at the drab houses and prefabricated buildings with the feeling that she was looking ahead into the drabness and barren years of her future life. Henry had run off with some woman, perhaps this same Captain Clodiak, and she was going to be left to bring up the quads on her own and be poor and known as a . . . a one-parent family? But there was no family without a father and where was she going to get the money to keep the girls at school? She'd have to go on Social Security and queue up with all those other women . . . She wouldn't. She'd go out to work. She'd do anything to make up for . . . The images in her mind, images of emptiness and of her own fortitude, were interrupted by the return of the Lieutenant.

His manner had changed. 'I'm sorry,' he said abruptly, 'there's been a mistake. I've got to tell you that. Now if you'll move off. We've got this security exercise on.'

'Mistake? What mistake?' said Mavis, reacting to his brusqueness with all her own pent-up hatred. 'You said Mrs Wilt's husband . . .'

'I didn't say anything,' said the Lieutenant and, turning on his heel, ordered the barrier to be lifted to allow a truck to come through.

'Well!' said Mavis furiously. 'Of all the nerve! I've never heard such a bare-faced lie in my life. You heard what he said just a moment ago and now—'

But Eva was moving forward with a new determination. Henry was in the camp. She knew that now. She'd seen the look on the Lieutenant's face, the changed look, the blankness that had been in such contrast to his previous manner, and she'd known. Without thinking she moved into the drabness of life without Henry, into the desert beyond the barrier. She was going to find him and have it out with him. A figure got in her way and tried to stop her. There was a flurry of arms and he fell. Three more men, only figures in her mind, and she was being held and dragged back. Fron somewhere seemingly distant she heard Mavis shout, 'Go limp. Go limp.' Eva went limp and the next moment she was lying on the ground with two men beside her and a third dragging on an arm.

Three minutes later, covered with dust and with the heels of her shoes scuffed and her tights torn, she was dragged beneath the barrier and dumped on the road. And during that time she had uttered no sound other than to pant with exertion. She sat there for a moment and then got to her knees and looked back into the camp with an intensity that was more dangerous in its implications than her brief battle with the guards.

'Lady, you got no right to come in here. You're just asking for trouble,' said the Lieutenant. Eva said nothing. She helped herself up from the kneeling position and walked back to the car.

'Eva dear, are you all right?' asked Mavis.

Eva nodded. 'Just take me home,' she said. For once Mavis had nothing to say. Eva's strength of purpose needed no words.

Wilt's did. With time running out on him, Glaushof had resorted to a new form of interrogation. Unable to use more forceful methods he had decided on what he considered to be the subtle approach. Since it involved the collaboration of Mrs Glaushof clad in garments

Glaushof and possibly even Lieutenant Harah had found so alluring – jackboots, suspender belts and teatless bras figured high in Glaushof's compendium of erotica – Wilt, who had been hustled yet again into a car and driven to the Glaushof's house, found himself suddenly lying on a heart-shaped bed clad in the hospital gown and confronted by an apparition in black, red and several shades of pink. The boots were black, the suspender belt and panties were red and the bra was black fringed with pink. The rest of Mrs Glaushof was, thanks to her frequent use of a sun lamp, mostly brown and definitely drunk. Ever since Glausie, as she had once called him, had bawled her out for sharing her mixed charms with those of Lieutenant Harah she had been hitting the Scotch. She had also hit a bottle of Chanel No 5 or had lathered herself with the stuff. Wilt couldn't decide which. And didn't want to. It was enough to be cloistered (the word seemed singularly inappropriate in the circumstances) in a room with an alcoholic prostitute who told him to call her Mona.

'What?' said Wilt.

'Mona, baby,' said Mrs Glaushof, breathing whisky into his face and fondling his cheek.

'I am not your baby,' said Wilt.

'Oh, but you are, honey. You're just what momma needed.'

'And you're not my mother,' said Wilt, wishing the hell the woman was. She'd have been dead ten years. Mrs Glaushof's hand strayed down his body. 'Shit,' said Wilt. That damned poison was beginning to work again.

'That's better, baby,' Mrs Glaushof whispered as Wilt stiffened. 'You and me's going to have the best of times.'

'You and I,' said Wilt, frantically trying to find some relief in correct syntax, 'and you may consider – ouch!'

'Is baby going to be good to momma now?' asked Mrs Glaushof, sliding her tongue between his lips. Wilt tried to focus on her eyes and found it impossible. He also found it impossible to reply without unclenching his teeth and Mrs Glaushof's reptilian tongue, tasting as it did of alcohol and tobacco, was so busily exploring his gums that any move that might allow it to go any further seemed inadvisable. For one insane moment it crossed his mind to bite the filthy thing but considering what she had in her hand the consequences didn't bear thinking about. Instead he tried to concentrate on less tangible things. What the hell was he doing lying on a quilted bed with a sex-mad woman clutching his balls when only half an hour ago a homicidal maniac had been threatening to plaster his brains on the ceiling with a .38 unless he talked about binary bombs? It didn't make even the vaguest sense but before he could arrive at any sane conclusion Mrs Glaushof had relinquished her probe.

'Baby's steaming me up,' she moaned and promptly bit his neck.

'That's as maybe,' said Wilt, making a mental note to brush his teeth as soon as possible. 'The fact of the matter is that I . . .'

Mrs Glaushof pinched his cheeks. 'Rosebud,' she whimpered.

'Wosebud?' said Wilt with difficulty.

'Your mouth's like a wosebud,' said Mrs Glaushof, digging her nails still further into his cheeks, 'a lovely wosebud.'

'It doethn't tathte like one,' said Wilt and instantly regretted it. Mrs Glaushof had hoisted herself up him and he was facing a nipple fringed with pink lace.

'Suck momma,' said Mrs Glaushof.

'Thod off,' said Wilt. Further comment was stifled by the nipple and Mrs Glaushof's breast which was worming around on his face. As Mrs Glaushof pressed down on him Wilt fought for breath.

In the bathroom next door Glaushof was having the same problem. Staring through the two-way mirror he'd installed to watch Mrs Glaushof putting on the regalia of his fantasies while he bathed, he had begun to regret his new tactics. Subtle they weren't. The bloody woman had clearly gone clean over the top. Glaushof's own patriotism had led him to suppose that his wife would do her duty by cosying up to a Russian spy, but he hadn't expected her to screw the bastard. What was even worse was that she was so obviously enjoying the process.

Glaushof wasn't. Gritting his teeth he stared lividly through the mirror and tried not to think about Lieutenant Harah. It didn't help. In the end, driven by the thought that the Lieutenant had lain on that same bed while Mona gave him the works he was now witnessing, Glaushof charged out of the bathroom. 'For Chrissake,' he yelled from the landing, 'I told you to soften the son of a bitch up, not turn him on.'

'So what's wrong?' said Mrs Glaushof, in the process of changing nipples. 'You think I don't know what I'm doing?'

'I'm buggered if I do,' squawked Wilt, taking the opportunity to get some air. Mrs Glaushof scrambled off him and headed for the door.

'No, I don't,' said Glaushof, 'I think you're—'

'Screw off,' screamed Mrs Glaushof. 'This guy's got a hard-on for me.'

'I can see that,' said Glaushof morosely, 'and if you think that's softening him up you're fucking crazy.'

Mrs Glaushof divested herself of a boot. 'Crazy, am I?' she bawled and hurled the boot at his head with surprising accuracy. 'So what's an old man like you know about crazy? You couldn't get it up if I didn't wear fucking Nazi jackboots.' The second boot hurtled through the door. 'I got to dress up like I'm fucking Hitler in drag before you're anywhere near a man and that ain't saying much. Like this guy's got a prick like the Washington Monument compared to yours.'

'Listen,' shouted Glaushof, 'lay off my prick. That's a commie agent you got in there. He's dangerous!'

'I'll say,' said Mrs Glaushof now liberating herself from the bra. 'Is he ever.'

'No, I'm not,' said Wilt, lurching away from the bed. Mrs Glaushof staggered out of the suspender belt.

'I'm telling you you could get yourself deep in trouble,' Glaushof called. He'd taken refuge from any further missiles round the corner.

'Deep in it is,' Mrs Glaushof shouted back and slammed the door and locked it. Before Wilt could move she had tossed the key out of the window and was heading for him. 'Red Square here I come.'

'I'm not Red Square. I don't know why everyone keeps thinking—' Wilt began, but Mrs Glaushof wasn't into thought. With an agility that took him by complete surprise she threw him back on to the bed and knelt over him.

'Choo choo, baby,' she moaned and this time there was no mistaking her meaning. Faced with this horrible prospect Wilt lived up to Glaushof's warning that he was a dangerous man and sank his teeth into her thigh. In the bathroom Glaushof almost cheered.

'Countermand my orders? Countermand my orders? You're telling me to countermand my orders?' said General Belmonte dropping several decibels in his disbelief. 'We have an enemy agent infiltration situation with possible bombing implications and you're telling me to countermand my orders?'

'Asking, General,' said the Colonel gently. 'I am simply saying that the political consequences could be disastrous.'

'Having my base blown apart by a fucking fanatic is disastrous too and I'm not standing for it,' said the General. 'No, sir, I am not having a body count of thousands of innocent American service personnel and their dependants on my conscience. Major Glaushof's handling of the situation has been absolutely correct. No one knows we've got this bastard and he can beat the shit out of him for all I care. I am not—'

'Correction, sir,' interrupted the Colonel, 'a number of people know we're holding this man. The British police called in enquiring about him. And a woman claiming to be his wife has already had to be ejected at the main gate. Now if you want the media to get hold—'

'The media?' bellowed the General. 'Don't mention that fucking word in my presence. I have given Glaushof a Directive Number One, Toppest Priority, there's to be no media intervention and I am not countermanding that order.'

'I am not suggesting you do. What I am saying is that the way Glaushof is handling the situation we could find ourselves in the middle of a media onslaught that would get world coverage.'

'Shit,' said the General, cringing at the prospect. In his mind's eye he could already see the television cameras mounted on trucks outside the base. There might even be women. He pulled his mind back from this vision of hell. 'What's wrong with the way Glaushof's handling it?'

'Too heavy,' said the Colonel. 'The security clampdown's drawing attention to the fact that we do have a problem. That's one. We should cool it all off by acting normal. Two is we are presently holding a British subject and if you've given the Major permission to beat the shit out of him I imagine that's just what—'

'I didn't give him permission to do anything like that, I gave him . . . well, I guess I said he could interrogate him and . . .' He paused and tried the comradely approach. 'Hell, Joe, Glaushof may be a shitass but he has got him to confess he's a commie agent. You've got to hand it to him.'

'That confession's a dummy. I've checked it out and had negative affirmation,' said the Colonel, lapsing into the General's jargon to soften the blow.

'Negative affirmation,' said the General, evidently impressed. 'That's serious. I had no idea.'

'Exactly, sir. That's why I'm asking for an immediate de-escalation of the security directive intelligencewise. I also want this man Wilt handed over to my authority for proper questioning.'

General Belmonte considered the request almost rationally. 'If he isn't Moscow-based, what is he?'

'That's what Central Intelligence intend to find out,' said the Colonel.

Ten minutes later Colonel Urwin left the Airbase Control Centre well satisfied. The General had ordered a

222

security stand-down and Glaushof had been relieved of his custody right to the prisoner.

Theoretically.

In practice getting Wilt out of the Glaushof's house proved rather more awkward. Having visited the Security building and learnt that Wilt had been taken off, still apparently unharmed, to be interrogated at Glaushof's house, the Colonel had driven there with two Sergeants only to realize that 'unharmed' no longer applied. Ghastly noises were emanating from upstairs.

'Sounds like someone's having themselves a whole heap of fun,' said one of the Sergeants as Mrs Glaushof threatened to castrate some horny bastard just as soon as she stopped bleeding to death and why didn't some other cocksucker open the fucking door so she could get out. In the background Glaushof could be heard telling her plaintively to keep her cool, he'd get the door undone, she didn't have to shoot the lock off and would she stop loading that fucking revolver.

Mrs Glaushof replied she didn't intend shooting the fucking lock off, she had other fucking objects in fucking mind, like him and that fucking commie agent who'd bit her and they weren't going to live to tell the tale, not once she'd got that magazine fucking loaded and why didn't shells go in the way they were fucking supposed to? For an instant Wilt's face appeared at the window, only to vanish as a bedside lamp complete with a huge lampshade smashed through the glass and hung upside-down from its cord.

Colonel Urwin studied the thing with horror. Mrs Glaushof's language was foul enough but the shade, covered with a collage of sado-masochistic images cut from magazines, pictures of kittens in baskets and puppy dogs, not to mention several crimson hearts and flowers, was aesthetically so disgusting that it almost unnerved him.

The action had the opposite effect on Glaushof. Less concerned about the likelihood of his drunken wife murdering a Russian spy with a .38 she had been trying to load with what he hoped was 9 mm. ammunition than with the prospect of having his entire house torn apart and its peculiar contents revealed to the neighbours he left the comparative safety of the bathroom and charged the bedroom door. His timing was bad. Having foiled any hope Wilt might have held of escaping by the window Mrs Glaushof had finally loaded the revolver and pulled the trigger. The shot passed through the door, Glaushof's shoulder, and one of the tubes in the hamster's complicated plastic burrow on the staircase wall before embedding in the tufted carpet.

'Jesus Christ,' screamed Glaushof, 'you meant it! You really meant it.'

'What's that?' said Mrs Glaushof, almost as surprised by the consequences of simply pulling the trigger, though definitely less concerned. 'What you say?'

'Oh God,' moaned Glaushof, now slumped to the floor.

'You think I can't shoot the fucking lock off?' Mrs Glaushof enquired. 'You think that? You think I can't?'

'No,' yelled Glaushof. 'No, I don't think that. Jesus, I'm dying.'

'Hypochondriac,' Mrs Glaushof shouted back, evidently paying off an old domestic score. 'Stand back, I'm coming out.'

'For fuck's sake,' squealed Glaushof, eyeing the hole she'd already made in the door near one of the hinges, 'don't aim at the lock.'

'Why not?' Mrs Glaushof demanded.

It wasn't a question Glaushof was prepared to answer. In one final attempt to escape the consequences of her next fusillade he rolled sideways and hit the stairs. By the time he'd crashed to the bottom even Mrs Glaushof was concerned.

'Are you OK, Glausie?' she asked and simultaneously pulled the trigger. As the second shot punched a hole in a Liberace-style bean bag, Wilt acted. In the knowledge that her next shot might possibly do to him what it had already done to Glaushof and the bag, he picked up a pink furbelowed stool and slammed it down on her head.

'Macho man,' grunted Mrs Glaushof, inappropriate to the end, and slid to the floor. For a moment Wilt hesitated. If Glaushof were still alive, and by the sound of breaking glass downstairs it seemed as though he was, there was no point in trying to break the door down. Wilt crossed to the window.

'Freeze!' shouted a man down below. Wilt froze. He was staring down at five uniformed men crouched behind handguns. And this time there was no question what they were aiming at.


## Chapter twenty-one


'Logic dictates,' said Mr Gosdyke, 'that we should look at this problem rationally. Now I know that's difficult but until we have definite proof that your husband is being held at Baconheath against his will there really isn't any legal action we can take. You do see that?'

Eva gazed into the solicitor's face and saw only that she was wasting time. It had been Mavis' idea that she should consult Mr Gosdyke before she did anything hasty. Eva knew what 'hasty' meant. It meant being afraid of taking real risks and doing something effective.

'After all,' Mavis had said, as they drove back, 'you may be able to apply for a court order or habeas corpus or something. It's best to find out.'

But she didn't need to find out. She'd known all along that Mr Gosdyke wouldn't believe her and would talk about proof and logic. As if life was logical. Eva didn't even know what the word meant, except that it always produced in her mind the image of a railway line with a train running along it with no way of getting off it and going across fields and open countryside like a horse. And anyway when you did reach a station you still had to walk to wherever you really wanted to go. That wasn't the way life worked or people behaved when things were really desperate. It wasn't even the way the Law worked with people being sent to prison when they were old and absent-minded like Mrs Reeman who had walked out of the supermarket without paying for a jar of pickled onions and she never ate pickles. Eva knew that because she'd helped with Meals on Wheels and the old lady had said she never touched vinegar. No, the real reason had been that she'd had a pekinese called Pickles and he'd died a month before. But the Law hadn't seen that, any more than Mr Gosdyke could understand that she already had the proof that Henry was in the airbase because he hadn't been there when the officer's manner had changed so suddenly.

'So there's nothing you can do?' she said and got up.

'Not unless we can obtain proof that your husband really is being held against . . .' But Eva was already through the door and had cut out the sounds of those ineffectual words. She went down the stairs and out into the street and found Mavis waiting for her in the Mombasa Coffee House.

'Well, did he have any advice?' asked Mavis.

'No,' said Eva, 'he just said there was nothing he could do without proof.'

'Perhaps Henry'll telephone you tonight. Now that he knows you've been out there and they must have told him . . .'

Eva shook her head. 'Why should they have told him?'

'Look, Eva, I've been thinking,' said Mavis, 'Henry's been deceiving you for six months. Now I know what you're going to say but you can't get away from it.'

'He hasn't been deceiving me the way you mean,' said Eva. 'I know that.'

Mavis sighed. It was so difficult to make Eva understand that men were all the same, even a sexually subnormal one

226

like Wilt. 'He's been going out to Baconheath every Friday evening and all that time he's been telling you he's got this prison job. You've got to admit that, haven't you?'

'I suppose so,' said Eva, and ordered tea. She wasn't in the mood for anything foreign like coffee. Americans drank coffee.

'The question you have to ask yourself is why didn't he tell you where he was going?'

'Because he didn't want me to know,' said Eva.

'And why didn't he want you to know?'

Eva said nothing.

'Because he was doing something you wouldn't like. And we all know what men don't think their wives would like to know, don't we?'

'I know Henry,' said Eva.

'Of course you do but we none of us know what even those closest to us are really like.'

'You knew all about Patrick's chasing other women,' said Eva, fighting back. 'You were always going on about his being unfaithful. That's why you got those steroid pills from that beastly Dr Kores and now all he does is sit in front of the telly.'

'Yes,' said Mavis, cursing herself for ever mentioning the fact. 'All right, but you said Henry was undersexed. Anyway that only goes to prove my point. I don't know what Dr Kores put in the mixture she gave you . . .'

'Flies,' said Eva.

'Flies?'

'Spanish flies. That's what Henry called them. He said they could have killed him.'

'But they didn't,' said Mavis. 'What I'm trying to get across is that the reason he wasn't performing adequately may have been—'

'He's not a dog, you know,' said Eva.

'What's that got to do with it?'

'Performing. You talk as though he were something in a circus.'

'You know perfectly well what I meant.'

They were interrupted by the arrival of the tea. 'All I'm saying,' Mavis continued when the waitress had left, 'is that what you took for Henry's being undersexed—'

'I said he wasn't very active. That's what I said,' said Eva.

Mavis stirred her coffee and tried to keep calm. 'He may not have wanted you, dear,' she said finally, 'because for the last six months he has been spending every Friday night in bed with some American servicewoman at that airbase. That's what I've been trying to tell you.'

'If that had been the case,' said Eva, bridling, 'I don't see how he could have come home at ten thirty, not if he was teaching as well. He never left the house until nearly seven and it takes at least three-quarters of an hour to drive out there. Two three-quarters make . . .'

'One and a half hours,' snapped Mavis. 'That doesn't prove anything. He could have had a class of one.'

'Of one?'

'One person, Eva dear.'

'They're not allowed to have only one person in a class,' said Eva. 'Not at the Tech. If they don't have ten . . .'

'Well, Baconheath may be different,' said Mavis, 'and anyway they fiddle these things. My bet is that Henry's teaching consisted of taking off his clothes and—'

'Which just shows how much you know about him,' interrupted Eva. 'Henry taking his clothes off in front of another woman! That'll be the day. He's too shy.'

'Shy?' said Mavis, and was about to say that he hadn't been so shy with her the other morning. But the dangerous look had come back on to Eva's face and she thought better of it. It was still there ten minutes later when they went out to car park to fetch the quads from school.

'Okay, let's take it from there,' said Colonel Urwin. 'You say you didn't shoot Major Glaushof.'

'Of course I didn't,' said Wilt. 'What would I do a thing like that for? She was trying to blow the lock off the door.'

'That's not the version I've got here,' said the Colonel,

referring to a file on the desk in front of him, 'according to which you attempted to rape Mrs Glaushof orally and when she refused to co-operate you bit her leg. Major Glaushof tried to intervene by breaking the door down and you shot him through it.'

'Rape her orally?' said Wilt, 'What the hell does that mean?'

'I prefer not to think,' said the Colonel with a shudder.

'Listen,' said Wilt, 'if anyone was being raped orally I was. I don't know if you've ever been in close proximity to that woman's muff but I have and I can tell you the only way out was to bite the bitch.'

Colonel Urwin tried to erase this awful image. His security classification rated him 'highly heterosexual' but there were limits and Mrs Glaushof's muff was unquestionably off them. 'That doesn't exactly gel with your statement that she was attempting to escape from the room by blowing the lock off with a .38, does it? Would you mind explaining what she was doing that for?'

'I told you she was trying . . . well, I've told you what she was trying to do and as a way out I bit her. That's when she got mad and went for the gun.'

'It still doesn't explain why the door was locked and she had to blow the lock. Are you saying Major Glaushof had locked you in?'

'She'd thrown the fucking key out of the window,' said Wilt wearily, 'and if you don't believe me go and look for the thing outside.'

'Because she found you so sexually desirable she wanted to rape you . . . orally?' said the Colonel.

'Because she was drunk.'

Colonel Urwin got up and consulted the sporting print for inspiration. It wasn't easy to find. About the only thing that rang true was that Glaushof's ghastly wife had been drunk. 'What I still don't understand is why you were there in the first place.'

'You think I do?' said Wilt. 'I came out here on Friday night to give a lecture and the next thing I know I've been gassed, injected, dressed up like something that's going to be operated on, driven all over the place with a fucking blanket over my head and asked insane questions about radio transformers in my car—'

'Transmitters,' said the Colonel.

'Whatever,' said Wilt. 'And told if I don't confess to being a Russian spy or a fanatical raving Shi'ite Muslim I'm going to have my brains plaster all over the ceiling. And that's just for starters. After that I'm in a horrible bedroom with a woman dressed up like a prostitute who hurls keys out of the window and shoves her dugs in my mouth and then threatens to suffocate me with her cunt. And you're asking me for an explanation?' He sank back in his chair and sighed hopelessly.

'That still doesn't—'

'Oh, for God's sake,' said Wilt. 'If you want insanity explained go and ask that homicidal maniac Major. I've had a bellyful.'

The Colonel got up and went out the door. 'What do you make of him?' he asked Captain Fortune who had been sitting with a technician recording the interview.

'I've got to say he convinces me,' said Fortune. 'That Mona Glaushof would screw a fucking skunk if there weren't nothing better to hand.'

'I'll say,' said the technician. 'She's been humping Lieutenant Harah like he's a human vibrator. The guy's been taking mega-vitamins to keep up.'

'Dear God,' said the Colonel, 'and Glaushof's in charge of security. What's he doing letting Mona Messalina loose on this one for?'

'Got a two-way mirror in the bathroom,' said the Captain. 'Could be he gets his thrills through it.'

'A two-way mirror in the bathroom? The bastard's got to be sick watching his wife screwing a guy he thinks is a Russian agent.'

'Maybe he thought the Russkies have got a different technique. Something he could learn,' said the technician.

'I want a check run on that key outside the house,' said the Colonel and went out into the passage.

'Well?' he asked.

'Nothing fits,' said the Captain. 'That Corporal in Electronics is no fool. He's certain the equipment he saw in the car was British classified. Definitely non-Russian. No record of it ever being used by anyone else.'

'Are you suggesting he was under surveillance by British Security?'

'It's a possibility.'

'It would be if he hadn't demanded MI5 attendance the moment Glaushof started putting the heat on,' said Urwin. 'Have you ever heard of a Moscow agent calling for British Intelligence when he's been blown? I haven't.'

'So we go back to your theory that the Brits were running an exercise on base security systems. About the only thing that adds up.'

'Nothing adds up for me. If it had been a routine check they'd have come to his rescue by now. And why has he clammed? No point in sweating it out. Against that we've got those transmitters and the fact that Clodiak says he was nervous and agitated all through the lecture. That indicates he's no expert and I don't believe he ever knew his car was tagged. Where's the sense?'

'You want me to question him?' asked the Captain.

'No, I'll go on. Just keep the tape running. We're going to need some help in this.'

He went back into his office and found Wilt lying on the couch fast asleep. 'Just a few more questions, Mr Wilt,' he said. Wilt stared blearily up at him and sat up.

'What questions?'

The Colonel took a bottle from a cupboard. 'Care for a Scotch?'

'I'd care to go home,' said Wilt.

# Chapter twenty-two

In Ipford Police Station Inspector Flint was savouring his triumph. 'It's all there, sir,' he told the Superintendent, indicating a pile of folders on the desk. 'And it's local. Swannell made the contact on a skiing trip to Switzerland. Nice clean place, Switzerland, and of course he says he was the one who was approached by this Italian. Threatened him, he says, and of course our Clive's a nervous bloke as you know.'

'Could have fooled me,' said the Superintendent. 'We nearly did the bugger for attempted murder three years ago. Got away because the bloke he scarred wouldn't press charges.'

'I was being ironical, sir,' said Flint. 'Just saying his story for him.'

'Go on. How did it work?'

'Simple really,' continued Flint, 'nothing too complicated. First they had to have a courier who didn't know what he was doing. So they put the frighteners on Ted Lingon. Threaten him with a nitric acid facial if he doesn't co-operate with his coach tours to the continent. Or so he claims. Anyway he's got a regular run to the Black Forest with overnight stops. The stuff's loaded aboard at Heidelberg without the driver knowing, comes through to Ostend and the night ferry to Dover and halfway across one of the crew dumps the muck over the side. Always on the night run so no one sees. Picked up by a friend of Annie Mosgrave's who happens to be in his floating gin palace nearby and . . .'

'Hang on a minute,' said the Superintendent. 'How the hell would anyone find a package of heroin in mid-Channel at night?'

'The same way Hodge has been keeping tabs on Wilt. The muck's in a bloody great suitcase with buoyancy and a radio signal that comes on the moment it hits the water.

Bloke beams in on it, hauls it aboard and brings it round to a marker buoy in the Estuary and leaves it there for a frogman to pick up when the gin palace is back in the marina.'

'Seems a risky way of going about things,' said the Superintendent, 'I wouldn't trust tides and currents with that amount of money involved.'

'Oh, they did enough practice runs to feel safe and tying it to the chain of the marker buoy made that part easy,' said Flint. 'And after that it was split three ways with the Hong Kong Charlies handling the London end and Roddie Eaton fixing this area and Edinburgh.'

The Superintendent studied his fingernails and considered the implications of Flint's discoveries. On the whole they seemed entirely satisfactory, but he had a nasty feeling that the Inspector's methods might not look too good in court. In fact it was best not to dwell on them. Defending counsel could be relied on to spell them out in detail to the jury. Threats to prisoners in gaol, murder charges that were never brought . . . On the other hand if Flint had succeeded, that idiot Hodge would be scuppered. That was worth a great many risks.

'Are you quite certain Swannell and the rest haven't been spinning you a yarn?' he asked. 'I mean I'm not doubting you or anything but if we go ahead now and they retract those statements in court, which they will do—'

'I'm not relying on their statements,' said Flint. 'There's hard evidence. I think when the search warrants are issued we'll find enough heroin and Embalming Fluid on their premises and clothing to satisfy Forensic. They've got to have spilt some when they were splitting the packages, haven't they?'

The Superintendent didn't answer. There were some things he preferred not to know and Flint's actions were too dubious for comfort. Still if the Inspector had broken a drug ring the Chief Constable and the Home Secretary would be well satisfied, and with crime organized the way it was nowadays there was no point in being too scrupulous. 'All right,' he said finally. 'I'll apply for the warrants.'

'Thank you, sir,' said Flint and turned to go. But the Superintendent stopped him.

'About Inspector Hodge,' he said. 'I take it he's been following a different line of investigation.'

'American airbases,' said Flint. 'He's got it into his head that's where the stuff's been coming in.'

'In that case we'd better call him off.'

But Flint had other plans in mind. 'If I might make a suggestion, sir,' he said, 'the fact that the Drug Squad is pointing in the wrong direction has its advantages. I mean Hodge has drawn attention away from our investigations and it would be a pity to put up a warning signal until we've made our arrests. In fact it might help to encourage him a bit.'

The Superintendent looked at him doubtfully. The last thing the head of the Drug Squad needed was encouraging. He was demented enough already. On the other hand . . .

'And how exactly is he to be encouraged?' he asked.

'I suppose you could say the Chief Constable was looking for an early arrest,' said Flint. 'It's the truth after all.'

'I suppose there's that to it,' said the Superintendent wearily. 'All right, but you'd better be right with your own cases.'

'I will be, sir,' said Flint and left the room. He went down to the car pool where Sergeant Yates was waiting.

'The warrants are all settled,' he said. 'Have you got the stuff?'

Sergeant Yates nodded and indicated a plastic packet on the back seat. 'Couldn't get a lot,' he said, 'Runkie reckoned we'd no right to it. I had to tell him it was needed for a lab check.'

'Which it will be,' said Flint. 'And it's all the same batch?'

'It's that all right.'

234

'No problem then,' said Flint as they drove out, 'we'll look at Lingon's coach first and then Swannell's boat and the back garden and leave enough for Forensic to pick up.'

'What about Roddie Eaton?'

Flint took a pair of cotton gloves from his pocket. 'I thought we'd leave these in his dustbin,' he said. 'We'll used them on the coach first. No need to bother going to Annie's. There will be something there anyway, and besides, the rest of them will try to get lighter sentences by pointing the finger at her. All we need is three of them as guilty as sin and facing twenty years and they'll drop everyone else in the shit with them.'

'Bloody awful way of going about police work,' said Yates after a pause. 'Planting evidence and all.'

'Oh, I don't know,' said Flint. 'We know they're traffickers, they know it, and all we're doing is giving them a bit of their own medicine. Homeopathic, I call it.'

That wasn't the way Inspector Hodge would have described his work. His obsessive interest in the Wilts' extraordinary domestic activities had been alarmingly aggravated by the noises coming from the listening devices installed in the roof space. The quads were to blame. Driven up to their rooms by Eva who wanted them out of the way so that she could think what to do about Henry, they had taken revenge by playing long-playing records of Heavy Metal at one hundred watts per channel. From where Hodge and Runk sat in the van it sounded as though 45 Oakhurst Avenue was being blown apart by an endless series of rythmic explosions.

'What the fuck's wrong with those bugs?' Hodge squealed, dragging the earphones from his head.

'Nothing,' shouted the operator. 'They're highly sensitive . . .'

'So am I,' yelled Hodge, stubbing his little finger into his ear in an attempt to get his hearing back, 'and something's definitely wrong.'

'They're just picking up one hell of a lot of inter-ference. Could be any number of things produce that effect.'

'Like a fifty-megaton rock concert,' said Runk. 'Bloody woman must be stone deaf.'

'Like hell,' said Hodge. 'This is deliberate. They must have scanned the place and spotted they were being bugged. And turn that damned thing off. I can't hear myself think.'

'Never known anyone who could,' said Runk. 'Think-ing doesn't make a sound. It's an—'

'Shut up,' yelled Hodge, who didn't need a lecture on the workings of the brain. For the next twenty minutes he sat in comparative silence trying to figure out his next move. At every stage of his campaign he had been out-manoeuvred and all because he hadn't been given the authority and back-up he needed. And now the Superin-tendent had sent a message demanding an immediate arrest. Hodge had countered with a request for a search warrant and had been answered with a vague remark that the matter would be considered. Which meant, of course, that he'd never get that warrant. He was on the point of returning to the station and demanding the right to raid the house when Sergeant Runk interrupted his train of thought.

'That jam session's stopped,' he said. 'Coming through nice and quiet.'

Hodge grabbed the earphones and listened. Apart from a rattling sound he couldn't identify (but which came in fact from Emmeline's hamster Percival getting some exercise in her wheel) the house in Oakhurst Avenue was silent. Odd. The place hadn't ever been silent before when the Wilts were at home. 'The car still outside?' he asked the technician.

The man turned to the car monitor. 'Nothing coming through,' he muttered and swung the aerial. 'They must have been using that din to dismantle the transmitters.'

Behind him Inspector Hodge verged on apoplexy.

'Jesus, you moron,' he yelled, 'you mean you haven't been checking that fucking car all this time?'

'What do you think I am? A bleeding octopus with ears?' the radio man shouted back. 'First I have to cope with all those stupid bugs you laced the house with and at the same time I've got two direction indicators to listen in to. And what's more I'm not a moron.'

But before Hodge could get into a real fight Sergeant Runk had intervened. 'I'm getting a faint signal from the car,' he said. 'Must be ten miles away.'

'Where?' yelled Hodge.

'East, as before,' said Runk. 'They're heading back to Baconheath.'

'Then get after them,' Hodge shouted, 'this time the shit isn't going to get back home before I've nabbed him. I'll seal that fucking base off if it's the last thing I do.'

Oblivious of the ill-feeling building up behind her Eva drove steadily towards the airbase. She had no conscious plan, only the determination to force the truth, and Wilt, out of somebody even if that meant setting fire to the car or lying naked in the roadway outside the gates. Anything to gain publicity. And for once Mavis had agreed with her and been helpful too. She had organized a group of Mothers Against The Bomb, some of whom were in fact grandmothers, had hired a coach and had telephoned all the London papers and BBC and Fenland Television to ensure maximum coverage for the demonstration.

'It gives us an opportunity to focus the world's attention on the seductive nature of capitalist military-industrial world domination,' she had said, leaving Eva with only the vaguest idea what she meant but with the distinct feeling that Wilt was the 'It' at the beginning of the sentence. Not that Eva cared what anyone said; it was what they did that counted. And Mavis's demonstration would help divert attention away from her own efforts to get into the camp. Or, if she failed to do that, she would see to it that the name Henry Wilt reached the millions of viewers who watched the news that night.

'Now I want you all to behave nicely,' she told the quads as they drove up to the camp gates. 'Just do what Mummy tells you and everything is going to be all right.'

'It isn't going to be all right if Daddy's been staying with an American lady,' said Josephine.

'Fucking,' said Penelope, 'not staying with.'

Eva braked sharply. 'Who said that?' she demanded, turning a livid face on the quads in the back seat.

'Mavis Motty did,' said Penelope. 'She's always going on about fucking.'

Eva took a deep breath. There were times when the quads' language, so carefully nurtured towards mature self-expression at the School for the Mentally Gifted, seemed appallingly inappropriate. And this was one of those times. 'I don't care what Mavis said,' she declared, 'and anyway it isn't like that. Your father has simply been stupid again. We don't know what's happened to him. That's why we've come here. Now you behave yourselves and—'

'If we don't know what's happened to him how do you know he's been stupid?' asked Samantha, who had always been hot on logic.

'Shut up,' said Eva and started the car again.

Behind her the quads silently assumed the guise of four nice little girls. It was misleading. As usual they had prepared themselves for the expedition with alarming ingenuity. Emmeline had armed herself with several hatpins that had once belonged to Grandma Wilt; Penelope had filled two bicycle pumps with ammonia and sealed the ends with chewing-gum; Samantha had broken into all their piggy banks and had then bought every tin of pepper she could from a perplexed greengrocer; while Josephine had taken several of Eva's largest and most pointed Sabatier knives from the magnet board in the kitchen. In short the quads were happily looking forward to disabling as many airbase guards as they could and were only afraid that the affair would pass off peacefully. In the event their fears were almost realized.

As they stopped at the gatehouse and were approached by a sentry there were none of those signs of preparedness that had been so obvious the day before. In an effort to maintain that everything was normal and in a 'No Panic Situation' Colonel Urwin had ordered the removal of the concrete blocks in the roadway and had instilled a fresh sense of politeness in the officer in charge of entry to civilian quarters. A large Englishwoman with permed hair and a carload of small girls didn't seem to pose any threat to USAAF security.

'If you'll just pull over there I'll call up the Education Office for you,' he told Eva who had decided not to mention Captain Clodiak this time. Eva drove past the barrier and parked. This was proving much easier than she had expected. In fact for a moment she doubted her judgement. Perhaps Henry wasn't there after all and she had made some terrible mistake. The notion didn't last long. Once again the Wilts' Escort had signalled its presence and Eva was just telling the quads that everything was going to be all right when the Lieutenant appeared from the guardhouse with two armed sentries. 'Pardon me, ma'am,' he said, 'but I'd be glad if you'd step over to the office.'

'What for?' asked Eva.

'Just a routine matter.'

For a moment Eva gazed blankly up at his face and tried to think. She had steeled herself for a confrontation and words like 'stepping over to the office' and 'a routine matter' were somehow threateningly bland. All the same she opened the door and got out.

'And the children too,' said the Lieutenant. 'Everybody out of there.'

'Don't you touch my daughters,' said Eva, now thoroughly alarmed. It was obvious she had been tricked into the base. But this was the opportunity the quads had been waiting for. As the Lieutenant reached for the door handle Penelope poked the end of the bicycle pump through the window and Josephine pointed a carving knife. It was Eva's action that saved him from the knife. She wrenched at his arm and at the same time the ammonia hit him. As the stuff wafted up from his soaked jacket and the two sentries hurled themselves on Eva, the Lieutenant gasped for air and dashed for the guard-house vaguely aware of the sound of girlish laughter behind him. It sounded demonic to him. Half suffocated he stumbled into the office and pressed the Alert button.

'It rather sounds as if we have another problem,' said Colonel Urwin as sirens wailed over the base.

'Don't include me,' said Wilt. 'I've got problems of my own like trying to explain to my wife what the hell's been happening to me the last God knows how many days.'

But the Colonel was on the phone to the guardhouse. For a moment he listened and then turned to Wilt. 'Your wife a fat woman with four daughters?'

'You could put it like that, I suppose,' said Wilt, 'though frankly I'd leave the "fat" bit out if you meet her. Why?'

'Because that's what just hit the main gate,' said the Colonel and went back to the phone. 'Hold everything . . . What do you mean you can't? She's not . . . Jesus . . . Okay, okay. And cut those fucking sirens.' There was a pause and the Colonel held the phone away from his ear and stared at Wilt. Eva's shouted demands were clearly audible now that the sirens had stopped.

'Give me back my husband,' she yelled, 'and take your filthy paws off me . . . If you go anywhere near those children . . .' The Colonel put the phone down.

'Very determined woman, is Eva,' said Wilt by way of explanation.

'So I've gathered,' said the Colonel, 'and what I want to know is what she's doing here.'

'By the sounds of things, looking for me.'

'Only you told us she didn't know you were here. So how come she's out there fighting mad and . . .' He stopped. Captain Fortune had entered the room.

240

'I think you ought to know the General's on the line,' he announced. 'Wants to know what's going on.'

'And he thinks *I* know?' said the Colonel.

'Well, someone has to.'

'Like him,' said the Colonel, indicating Wilt, 'and he's not saying.'

'Only because I haven't a clue,' said Wilt with increasing confidence, 'and without wishing to be unnecessarily didactic I'd say no one in the whole wide world knows what the hell's going on anywhere. Half the world's population is starving and the overfed half have a fucking death-wish, and—'

'Oh for Chrissake,' said the Colonel, and came to a sudden decision. 'We're taking this bastard out. Now.'

But Wilt was on his feet. He had watched too many American movies not to have ambivalent feelings about being 'taken out'. 'Oh no you're not,' he said backing up against the wall. 'And you can cut the bastard abuse too. I didn't do anything to start this fucking madhouse and I've got my family to think about.'

Colonel Urwin looked at the sporting print hopelessly. He'd been right to suspect the British of having hidden depths he would never understand. No wonder the French spoke of 'perfidious Albion'. The bastards would always behave in ways one least expected. In the meantime he had to produce some explanation that would satisfy the General. 'Just say we've got a purely domestic problem on our hands,' he told the Captain, 'and rout Glaushof out. Base security is his baby.'

But before the Captain could leave the room Wilt had reacted again. 'You let that maniac anywhere near my kids and someone's going to get hurt,' he shouted, 'I'm not having them gassed like I was.'

'In that case you better exercise some parental control yourself,' said the Colonel grimly, and headed for the door.

# Chapter twenty-three

By the time they reached the parking lot by the gates it
was clear that the situation had deteriorated. In an
entirely unnecessary effort to rescue their mother from
the sentries – Eva had already felled one of the men with
a knee-jerk to the groin she had learnt at a Rape Resistance Evening Class – the quads had abandoned the Wilts'
car and, by dusting the second sentry with pepper, had
put him out of action. After that they had occupied the
gatehouse itself and were now holding the Lieutenant
hostage inside. Since he had torn off his uniform to
escape the ammonia fumes and the quads had armed
themselves with his revolver and that of the sentry writhing on the ground outside, they had been able to isolate
the guardhouse even more effectively by threatening the
driver of an oil tanker which had made the mistake of
arriving at the barrier and forcing him to offload several
hundred gallons of fuel oil on to the roadway before
driving tentatively into the base.

Even Eva had been appalled at the result. As the stuff
swilled across the tarmac Lieutenant Harah had driven
up rather too hurriedly in a jeep and had tried to brake.
The jeep was now enmeshed in the perimeter fence and
Lieutenant Harah, having crawled from it, was calling for
reinforcements. 'We have a real penetration situation
here,' he bawled into his walkie-talkie. 'A bunch of leftist
terrorists have taken over the guardhouse.'

'They're not terrorists, they're just little girls,' Eva
shouted from inside, only to have her words drowned by
the Alert siren which Samantha had activated.

Outside in the roadway Mavis Mottram's busload of
Mothers Against The Bomb had gathered in a line and
had handcuffed themselves together before padlocking
the ends of the line to the fence on either side of the
gateway and were dancing something approximate to the

can-can and chanting 'End the arms race, save the human' in full view of three TV cameras and a dozen photographers. Above their heads an enormous and remarkable balloon, shaped and veined like an erect penis, swung slowly in the breeze exposing the rather confusing messages, 'Wombs Not Tombs' and 'Screw Cruise Not Us' painted on opposite sides. As Wilt and Colonel Urwin watched, the balloon, evidently force-fed by a hydrogen cylinder, shed its few human pretensions in the shape of an enormous plastic foreskin and turned itself into a gigantic rocket.

'This is going to kill old B52,' muttered the Colonel who had until then been enjoying the spectacle of Lieutenant Harah covered in oil and trying to get to his feet. 'And I can't see the President liking it too much either. That fucking phallus has got to hit prime time with all those cameras.'

A fire truck shot round the corner past them and in a jeep behind it came Major Glaushof, his right arm in a sling and his face the colour of putty.

'Jesus,' said Captain Fortune, 'if that fire truck hits the oil we're going to have a body count of thirty of the Mothers.'

But the truck had stopped and men were deploying hoses. Behind them and the human chain Inspector Hodge and Sergeant Runk had driven up and were staring wildly about them. In front the women still kicked up their legs and chanted, the firemen had begun to spray foam on to the oil and Lieutenant Harah, and Glaushof was gesticulating with one hand to a troop of Anti Perimeter Penetration Squad men who had formed up as near the Mothers Against The Bomb as they could get and were preparing to discharge canisters of Agent Incapacitating at them.

'For fuck's sake hold it,' yelled Glaushof but his words were drowned out by the Alert Siren. As the canisters dropped into the roadway at the feet of the human chain Colonel Urwin shut his eyes. He knew now that Glaushof was a doomed man, but his own career was in jeopardy. 'We've got to get those fucking kids out of there before the cameras start playing on them,' he bawled at Captain Fortune. 'Go in and get them.'

The Captain looked at the foam, the oil and the drifting gas. Already a number of MABs had dropped to the ground and Samantha had added to the hazards of approaching the guardhouse by accidentally-on-purpose firing a revolver through one of the windows, an action which had drawn answering fire from Glaushof's APP Squad.

'You think I'm risking my life . . .' the Captain began but it was Wilt who took the initiative. Wading through the oil and foam he made it to the guardhouse and presently four small girls and a large woman came out with him. Hodge didn't see them. Like the cameramen his attention was elsewhere, but unlike them he was no longer interested in the disaster taking place at the gates. A canister of AI had persuaded him to leave the scene as quickly as possible. It had also made it difficult to drive. As the police van backed into the bus and then shot forward and ricocheted off a cameraman's car before sliding off the road and onto its side, he had a moment of understanding. Inspector Flint hadn't been such an old fool after all. Anyone who tangled with the Wilt family had to come off worst.

Colonel Urwin shared his feelings. 'We're going to get you out of here in a chopper,' he told Wilt as more women slumped across the gateway.

'And what about my car?' said Wilt. 'If you think I'm leaving . . .'

But his protest was shouted down by the quads. And Eva.

'We want to go up in a helicopter,' they squealed in unison.

'Just take me away from all this,' said Eva.

Ten minutes later Wilt looked down from a thousand

244

feet at the pattern of runways and roads, buildings and bunkers and at the tiny group of women being carried from the gate to waiting ambulances. For the first time he felt some sympathy for Mavis Mottram. For all her faults she had been right to pit herself against the banal enormity of the airbase. The place had all the characteristics of a potential extermination camp. True, nobody was being herded into gas chambers and there was no smoke rising from crematoria. But the blind obedience to orders was there, instilled in Glaushof and even in Colonel Urwin. Everyone in fact, except Mavis Mottram and the human chain of women at the gate. The others would all obey orders if the time came and the real holocaust would begin. And this time there would be no liberators, no successive generations to erect memorials to the dead or learn lessons from past horrors. There would be only silence. The wind and the sea the only voices left. And it was the same in Russia and the occupied countries of Eastern Europe. Worse. There Mavis Mottram was already silenced, confined to a prison or a psychiatric ward because she was idiosyncratically sane. No TV cameras or photographers depicted the new death camps. And twenty million Russians had died to make their country safe from genocide, only to have Stalin's successors too afraid of their own people to allow them to discuss the alternatives to building more machines to wipe life off the face of the earth.

It was all insane, childish and bestial. But above all it was banal. As banal as the Tech and Dr Mayfield's empire-building and the Principal's concern to keep his own job and avoid unfavourable publicity, never mind what the staff thought or the students would have preferred to learn. Which was what he was going back to. In fact nothing had changed. Eva would go on with her wild enthusiasms; the quads might even grow up to be civilized human beings. Wilt rather doubted it. Civilized human beings were a myth, legendary creatures who existed only in writers' imaginations, their foibles and faults expurgated and their occasional self-sacrifices magnified. With the quads that was impossible. The best that could be hoped was that they would remain as independent and uncomfortably non-conforming as they were now. And at least they were enjoying the flight.

Five miles outside the base the helicopter set down beside an empty road.

'You can drop off here,' said the Colonel, 'I'll try and get a car out to you.'

'But we want to go all the way home by helicopter,' shouted Samantha above the roar of the rotors, and was joined by Penelope who insisted she wanted to parachute onto Oakhurst Avenue. It was too much for Eva. Grabbing the quads in turn she bundled them out onto the beaten grass and jumped down beside them. Wilt followed. For a moment the air around him was thick with the downblast and then the helicopter had lifted off and was swinging away. By the time it had disappeared Eva had found her voice.

'Now look what you've been and done,' she said. Wilt stared round at the empty landscape. After the interrogation he had been through he was in no mood for Eva's whingeing.

'Let's start walking,' he said. 'Nobody's coming out to pick us up and we'd better find a bus stop.'

He climbed the bank onto the road and set off along it. In the distance there was a sudden flash and a small ball of flame. Major Glaushof had fired a tracer round into Mavis Mottram's inflated penis. The fireball and the little mushroom cloud of smoke above it would be on the evening TV news in full colour. Perhaps something had been achieved after all.

# Chapter twenty-four

It was the end of term at the Tech and the staff were seated in the auditorium, as evidently bored as the students they themselves had previously lectured there. Now it was the Principal's turn. He had spent ten excruciating minutes doing his best to disguise his true feelings for Mr Spirey of the Building Department who was finally retiring, and another twenty trying to explain why financial cuts had ended any hope of rebuilding the engineering block at the very time when the College had been granted the staggering sum of a quarter of a million pounds by an anonymous donor for the purchase of textbooks. In the front row Wilt sat poker-faced among the other Heads of Departments and feigned indifference. Only he and the Principal knew the source of the donation and neither of them could ever tell. The Official Secrets Act had seen to that. The money was the price of Wilt's silence. The deal had been negotiated by two nervous officials from the United States Embassy and in the presence of two rather more menacing individuals ostensibly from the legal division of the Home Office. Not that Wilt had been worried by their attitude. Throughout the discussion he had basked in the sense of his own innocence and even Eva had been overawed and then impressed by the offer of a new car. But Wilt had turned that down. It was enough to know that the Principal, while never understanding why, would always be unhappily aware that the Fenland College of Arts and Technology was once again indebted to a man he would have liked to fire. Now he was lumbered with Wilt until he retired himself.

Only the quads had been difficult to silence. They had enjoyed pumping ammonia over the Lieutenant and disabling sentries with pepper too much not to want to make their exploits known.

'We were only rescuing Daddy from that sexy woman,' said Samantha when Eva rather unwisely asked them to promise never to talk about what had happened.

'And you'll have to rescue your Mother and me from Dartmoor if you don't keep your damned traps shut,' Wilt had snapped. 'And you know what that means.'

'What?' asked Emmeline, who seemed to be looking forward to the prospect of a prison break.

'It means you'll be taken into care by horrible foster parents and not as a bloody group either. You'll be split up and you won't be allowed to visit one another and . . .' Wilt had launched into a positively Dickensian description of foster homes and horrors of child abuse. By the time he'd finished the quads were cowed and Eva had been in tears. Which was the first time that had happened and was another minor triumph. It wouldn't last, of course, but by the time they spilled the beans the immediate dangers would be over and nobody would believe them anyway.

But the argument had aroused Eva's suspicions again. 'I still want to know why you lied to me all those months about teaching at the prison,' she said as they undressed that night.

Wilt had an answer for that one too. 'You heard what those men from MI5 said about the Official Secrets Act.'

'MI5?' said Eva. 'They were from the Home Office. What's MI5 got to do with it?'

'Home Office, my foot, Military Intelligence,' said Wilt. 'And if you choose to send the quads to the most expensive school for pseudo-prodigies and expect us not to starve . . .'

The argument had rumbled on into the night but Eva hadn't needed much convincing. The officials from the Embassy had impressed her too much with their apologies and there had been no talk of women. Besides, she had her Henry home again and it was obviously best to forget that anything had happened at Baconheath.

And so Wilt sat on beside Dr Board with a slight sense of accomplishment. If he was fated to fall foul of other people's stupidity and misunderstanding he had the satisfaction of knowing that he was no one's victim. Or only temporarily. In the end he beat them and circumstances. It was better than being a successful bore like Dr Mayfield – or worse still, a resentful failure.

'Wonders never cease,' said Dr Board when the Principal finally sat down and they began to file out of the auditorium, 'a quarter of a million in actual textbooks? It must be a unique event in British education. Millionaires who give donations usually provide better buildings for worse students. This one seems to be a genius.'

Wilt said nothing. Perhaps having some common sense was a form of genius.

At Ipford Police Station ex-Inspector Hodge, now merely Sergeant Hodge, sat at a computer terminal in Traffic Control and tried to confine his thoughts to problems connected with flow-patterns and off-peak parking systems. It wasn't easy. He still hadn't recovered from the effects of Agent Incapacitating or, worse still, from the enquiry into his actions the Superintendent had started and the Chief Constable had headed.

And Sergeant Runk hadn't been exactly helpful. 'Inspector Hodge gave me to understand the Superintendent had authorized the bugging of Mr Wilt's car,' he said in evidence. 'I was acting on his orders. It was the same with their house.'

'Their house? You mean to say their house was bugged too?'

'Yes, sir. It still is for all I know,' said Runk, 'we had the collaboration of the neighbours, Mr Gamer and his wife.'

'Dear God,' muttered the Chief Constable, 'if this ever gets to the gutter press . . .'

'I don't think it will, sir,' said Runk, 'Mr Gamer has moved out and his missus has put the house up for sale.'

'Then get those bloody devices out of there before someone has the place surveyed,' snarled the Chief Constable before dealing with Hodge. By the time he had finished the Inspector was on the verge of a breakdown himself and had been demoted to Sergeant in the Traffic Section with the threat of being transferred to the police dog training school as a target if he put his foot wrong just once again.

To add insult to injury he had seen Flint promoted to Head of the Drug Squad.

'The chap seems to have a natural talent for that kind of work,' said the Chief Constable. 'He's done a remarkable job.'

The Superintendent had his reservations but he kept them to himself. 'I think it runs in the family,' he said judiciously.

And for a fortnight during the trial Flint's name had appeared almost daily in the *Ipford Chronicle* and even in some of the national dailies. The police canteen too had buzzed with his praises. Flint the Drug Buster. Almost Flint the Terror of the Courtroom. In spite of all the efforts the defence counsel had made, with every justification, to question the legality of his methods, Flint had countered with facts and figures, times, dates, places and with exhibits, all of which were authentic. He had stepped down from the witness box still retaining the image of the old-fashioned copper with his integrity actually enhanced by the innuendoes. It was enough for the public to look from him to the row of sleazy defendants in the dock to see where the interests of justice lay. Certainly the Judge and jury had been convinced. The accused had gone down with sentences that ranged from nine years to twelve and Flint had gone up to Superintendent.

But Flint's achievement led beyond the courtroom to areas where discretion still prevailed.

'She brought the stuff back from her cousins in California?' spluttered Lord Lynchknowle when the Chief Constable visited him. 'I don't believe a word of it. Downright lie.'

'Afraid not, old chap. Absolutely definite. Smuggled the muck back in a bottle of duty-free whisky.'

'Good God. I thought she'd got it at that rotten Tech. Never did agree with her going there. All her mother's fault.' He paused and stared vacuously out across the rolling meadows. 'What did you say the stuff was called?'

'Embalming Fluid,' said the Chief Constable, 'Or Angel Dust. They usually smoke it.'

'Don't see how you can smoke embalming fluid,' said Lord Lynchknowle. 'Mind you, there's no understanding women, is there?'

'None at all,' said the Chief Constable and with the assurance that the coroner's verdict would be one of accidental death he left to deal with other women whose behaviour was beyond his comprehension.

In fact it was at Baconheath that the results of Hodge's obsession with the Wilt family were being felt most keenly. Outside the airbase Mavis Mottram's group of Mothers Against The Bomb had been joined by women from all over the country and had turned into a much bigger demonstration. A camp of makeshift huts and tents was strung out along the perimeter fence, and relations between the Americans and the Fenland Constabulary had not been improved by scenes on TV of middle-aged and largely respectable British women being gassed and dragged in handcuffs to camouflaged ambulances.

To make matters even more awkward Mavis' tactics of blockading the civilian quarters had led to several violent incidents between US women who wanted to escape the boredom of the base to go souvenir-hunting in Ipford and Norwich and MABs who refused to let them out or, more infuriatingly, allowed them to leave only to stop them going back. These fracas were seen on TV with a regularity that had brought the Home Secretary and the Secretary of State for Defence into conflict, each insisting that the other was responsible for maintaining law and order.

Only Patrick Mottram had benefited. In Mavis' absence he had come off Dr Kores' hormones and had resumed his normal habits with Open University students.

Inside the airbase, too, everything had changed. General Belmonte, still suffering from the effect of seeing a giant penis circumcise itself and then turn into a rocket and explode, had been retired to a home for demented veterans in Arizona where he was kept comfortably sedated and could sit in the sun dreaming of happy days when his B52 had blasted the empty jungle in Vietnam. Colonel Urwin had returned to Washington and a cat-run garden in which he grew scented narcissi to perfection and employed his considerable intelligence to the problem of improving Anglo-American relations.

It was Glaushof who had suffered the most. He had been flown to the most isolated and radioactive testing ground in Nevada and consigned to duties in which his own personal security was in constant danger and his sole responsibility. And sole was the word. Mona Glaushof with Lieutenant Harah in tow had hit Reno for a divorce and was living comfortably in Texas on the alimony. It was a change from the dank Fenlands and the sun never ceased to shine.

It shone too on Eva and 45 Oakhurst Avenue as she bustled about the house and wondered what to have for supper. It was nice to have Henry home and somehow more assertive than he had been before. 'Perhaps,' she thought as she Hoovered the stairs, 'we ought to get away by ourselves for a week or two this summer.' And her thoughts turned to the Costa Brava.

*

But it was a problem Wilt had already solved. Sitting in The Pig In A Poke with Peter Braintree he ordered two more pints.

'After all I've been through this term I'm not having my summer made hellish in some foul camp site by the quads,' he said cheerfully. 'I've made other arrangements. There's an adventure school in Wales where they do rock-climbing and pony-trekking. They can work their energy off on that and the instructors. I've rented a cottage in Dorset and I'm going down there to read *Jude The Obscure* again.'

'Seems a bit of a gloomy book to take on holiday,' said Braintree.

'Salutary,' said Wilt, 'a nice reminder that the world's always been a crazy place and that we don't have such a bad time of it teaching at the Tech. Besides, it's an antidote to the notion that intellectual aspirations get you anywhere.'

'Talking about aspirations,' said Braintree, 'what on earth are you going to do with the thirty thousand quid this lunatic philanthropist has allotted your department for textbooks?'

Wilt smiled into his pint of best bitter. 'Lunatic philanthropists' was just about right for the Americans with their airbases and nuclear weapons, and the educated idiots in the State Department who assumed that even the most ineffectual liberal do-gooder must be a homicidal Stalinist and a member of the KGB – and who then shelled out billions of dollars trying to undo the damage they'd done.

'Well, for one thing I'm going to donate two hundred copies of *Lord of the Flies* to Inspector Flint,' he said finally.

'To Flint? Why him of all people? What's he want with the damned things?'

'He's the one who told Eva I was out at . . .' Wilt stopped. There was no point in breaking the Official Secrets Act. 'It's a prize,' he went on, 'for the first copper

253

to arrest the Phantom Flasher. It seems an appropriate title.'

'I daresay it does,' said Braintree. 'Still, two hundred copies is a bit disproportionate. I can't imagine even the most literate policeman wanting to read two hundred copies of the same book.'

'He can always hand them out to the poor sods at the airbase. Must be hell trying to cope with Mavis Mottram. Not that I disagree with her views but the bloody woman is definitely demented.'

'Still leaves you with a hell of a lot of new books to buy,' said Braintree. 'I mean, it's all right for me because the English Department needs books but I shouldn't have thought Communication and—'

'Don't use those words. I'm going back to Liberal Studies and to hell with all that bloody jargon. And if Mayfield and the rest of the social-economic structure merchants don't like it, they can lump it. I'm having it my way from now on.'

'You sound very confident,' said Braintree.

'Yes,' said Wilt with a smile.

And he was.

Carl Hiaasen
Special limited edition
**Skin Tight/Native Tongue**  £4.99
*Two bestsellers for the price of one!*

A double dose of satire from Florida's finest – and funniest – crime writer

The Sunshine State's very own Carl Hiaasen is the modern master of the comic crime thriller. Straight from the murky waters of the Florida badlands, here's a manic double bill of Hiaasen at his zany and original best. First, *Skin Tight* – a wonderful indictment of the American obsession with beauty and success. (Not to mention barracudas.) To follow, *Native Tongue* – a brilliant rollercoaster farce at the expense of the Island theme park industry. (Abandon your sanity at the gateway to the Amazing Kingdom of Thrills.)

But be careful! As humorist P.J. O'Rourke puts it: 'Reading Carl Hiaasen will do as much damage to the Florida tourist industry as an actual visit to Florida itself . . .'

'Reading him is violently pleasurable – a bit like being on a terrifyingly good rollercoaster' *Daily Mail*

'Hiaasen is seriously funny, and highly recommended' *Irish Times*

All Pan books are available at your local bookshop or newsagent, or can be ordered direct from the publisher. Indicate the number of copies required and fill in the form below.

Send to:    Pan C. S. Dept
                Macmillan Distribution Ltd
                Houndmills Basingstoke RG21 2XS
or phone:   0256 29242, quoting title, author and Credit Card number.

Please enclose a remittance* to the value of the cover price plus: £1.00 for the first book plus 50p per copy for each additional book ordered.

*Payment may be made in sterling by UK personal cheque, postal order, sterling draft or international money order, made payable to Pan Books Ltd.

Alternatively by Barclaycard/Access/Amex/Diners

Card No. ☐☐☐☐☐☐☐☐☐☐☐☐☐☐☐☐☐☐☐

Expiry Date ☐☐☐☐☐☐

———————————————————————————

Signature:

Applicable only in the UK and BFPO addresses

*While every effort is made to keep prices low, it is sometimes necessary to increase prices at short notice. Pan Books reserve the right to show on covers and charge new retail prices which may differ from those advertised in the text or elsewhere.*

NAME AND ADDRESS IN BLOCK LETTERS PLEASE:

..........................................................................................................

Name _____

Address_____

_____

_____

_____

6/92